LEGALIST

TOR BOOKS BY L. E. MODESITT, JR.

THE GRAND ILLUSION
Isolate
Councilor
Contrarian
Legalist

THE SAGA OF RECLUCE
The Magic of Recluce
The Towers of the Sunset
The Magic Engineer
The Order War
The Death of Chaos
Fall of Angels
The Chaos Balance
The White Order
Colors of Chaos
Magi'i of Cyador
Scion of Cyador
Wellspring of Chaos
Ordermaster
Natural Ordermage
Mage-Guard of Hamor
Arms-Commander
Cyador's Heirs
Heritage of Cyador
Recluce Tales
The Mongrel Mage
Outcasts of Order
The Mage-Fire War

Fairhaven Rising
From the Forest
Overcaptain
Sub-Majer's Challenge

THE COREAN CHRONICLES
Legacies
Darknesses
Scepters
Alector's Choice
Cadmian's Choice
Soarer's Choice
The Lord-Protector's Daughter
Lady-Protector

THE IMAGER PORTFOLIO
Imager
Imager's Challenge
Imager's Intrigue
Scholar
Princeps
Imager's Battalion
Antiagon Fire
Rex Regis
Madness in Solidar
Treachery's Tools
Assassin's Price
Endgames

THE SPELLSONG CYCLE
The Soprano Sorceress
The Spellsong War
Darksong Rising
The Shadow Sorceress
Shadowsinger

THE ECOLITAN MATTER
Empire & Ecolitan (comprising *The Ecolitan Operation* and *The Ecologic Secession*)
Ecolitan Prime (comprising *The Ecologic Envoy* and *The Ecolitan Enigma*)

THE GHOST BOOKS
Of Tangible Ghosts
The Ghost of the Revelator
Ghost of the White Nights

OTHER NOVELS
The Forever Hero (comprising *Dawn for a Distant Earth*, *The Silent Warrior*, and *In Endless Twilight*)
Timegods' World (comprising *Timediver's Dawn* and *The Timegod*)
The Hammer of Darkness
The Green Progression
The Parafaith War
Adiamante
Gravity Dreams
The Octagonal Raven
Archform: Beauty
The Ethos Effect
Flash
The Eternity Artifact
The Elysium Commission
Viewpoints Critical
Haze
Empress of Eternity
The One-Eyed Man
Solar Express
Quantum Shadows

LEGALIST

L.E. MODESITT JR.

TOR
TOR PUBLISHING GROUP
NEW YORK

This is a work of fiction. All of the characters, organizations, and events portrayed in this novel are either products of the author's imagination or are used fictitiously.

LEGALIST

Copyright © 2025 by Modesitt Family Revocable Living Trust

All rights reserved.

A Tor Book
Published by Tom Doherty Associates / Tor Publishing Group
120 Broadway
New York, NY 10271

www.torpublishinggroup.com

Tor® is a registered trademark of Macmillan Publishing Group, LLC.

EU Representative: Macmillan Publishers Ireland Ltd, 1st Floor,
The Liffey Trust Centre, 117–126 Sheriff Street Upper, Dublin 1, DO1 YC43

The Library of Congress Cataloging-in-Publication Data is available upon request.

ISBN 978-1-250-38575-8 (hardcover)
ISBN 978-1-250-38576-5 (ebook)

The publisher of this book does not authorize the use or reproduction of any part of this book in any manner for the purpose of training artificial intelligence technologies or systems. The publisher of this book expressly reserves this book from the Text and Data Mining exception in accordance with Article 4(3) of the European Union Digital Single Market Directive 2019/790.

Our books may be purchased in bulk for specialty retail/wholesale, literacy, corporate/premium, educational, and subscription box use. Please contact MacmillanSpecialMarkets@macmillan.com.

First Edition: 2025

Printed in the United States of America

10 9 8 7 6 5 4 3 2 1

In Memoriam
To my father, the consummate legalist

MAIN CHARACTERS

Laureous Imperador
Laureous II Heir to the Imperador
Delehya Youngest child and daughter of Laureous, from his second wife
Gunnar Solatiem First Marshal
Haeltyn Kaahl High Justicer

Prudhyr Fraenk Imperial Administrator of Agriculture
Taeryl Laergaan Imperial Administrator of Commerce
Tybaalt Salaazar Imperial Administrator of the Treasury
Engar Tyresis Imperial Administrator of Waterways
Carsius Zaenn Imperial Administrator of Natural Resources

Iustaan Detruro Premier, and Councilor from Enke
Luaro Maatrak Floor Leader, and Councilor from Ondeliew
Dominic Ysella Councilor from Aloor, Chairman of Waterways Committee

Chaarls Aashen Councilor from Sudaen, Agriculture Committee
Alaaxi Baertyl Councilor from Veerlyn, Military Affairs Committee
Paolo Caanard Councilor from Point Larmat, Chairman of Foreign Affairs Committee
Astyn Coerl Councilor from Tryar, Waterways Committee
Haamlyn Commodus Councilor from Kathaar, Commerce Committee
Symeon Daenyld Councilor from Neewyrk, Chairman of Military Affairs Committee
Gaastyn Ditaero Councilor from Endor, Waterways Committee
Alaan Escalante Councilor from Silverhills, Military Affairs Committee
Dannyl Grieg Councilor from Whulte, Waterways Committee
Sammal Haafel Councilor from Nuile, Agriculture Committee
Aksyl Haarst Councilor from Suvion, Commerce Committee

MAIN CHARACTERS

Oskaar Klempt   Councilor from Vhooryn, Chairman of Commerce Committee
Aldyn Kraagyn   Councilor from Encora, Justiciary Committee
Eduardo Maalkyn   Councilor from Hyarh, Commerce Committee
Haans Maessyn   Councilor from Uldwyrk, Waterways Committee
Stefan Nortaak   Councilor from Oersynt, Waterways Committee
Voltar Paastyn   Councilor from Zeiryn, Waterways Committee
Georg Raathan   Councilor from Gaarlak, Chairman of Agriculture Committee
Graandeyl Raendyr   Councilor from Obaan, Commerce Committee
Ahslem Staeryt   Councilor from Machtarn, Chairman of Justiciary Committee
Stron Thaalyr   Councilor from Eshbruk, Chairman of Natural Resources Committee

Lyaard Khaard   Senior Clerk for Ysella
Paatyr Jaasn   Junior Clerk for Ysella

LEGALIST

PROLOGUE

Machtarn—34 Springfirst 812

DOMINIC Mikail Ysella stepped from the rented coach and surveyed the Council Hall, a modestly imposing gray stone building, with an accompanying building holding stables, the two being the only structures for more than a hundred yards in any direction on Council Avenue. Unsurprising, given that it had only been recently completed. Close to a mille to the north, beyond the Way of Gold, stood the gates to the Imperador's Palace. Ysella's left hand momentarily dropped to the grip of the short truncheon at his waist, concealed largely by his bluish-gray suit coat. He glanced back over his shoulder to the south, toward the bulk of the city and the harbor beyond, then shook his head. Machtarn might be the capital of the Imperium of Guldor, but it wasn't that much larger than Aloor, or Aloor as it had once been, and was certainly less cosmopolitan than old Aloor—before the Imperador Laureous leveled half of it.

Ysella looked to the coachman. "I might be a while."

"I'll be here, Ritter."

Ysella managed not to offer an amused smile at the title that had come with his election to the Council, a title already held by his older brothers, solely because they inherited or would inherit sufficient lands. He walked to the arches framing the entrance to the Council Hall, where two guards in pale green uniforms stood.

"Sir?" inquired one, politely.

"I'm the new councilor-elect from Aloor."

The other guard gestured and, when a youth in a gold and red uniform appeared, said, "Escort the councilor-elect to the Premier's office." The guard then turned back. "All new councilors get their pins and credentials there."

"Thank you." Ysella followed the messenger from the entry foyer down a wide hallway to a green marble archway, beyond which was an anteroom with several desks. Behind each desk sat a clerk in a forest-green military tunic. The messenger guided Ysella to an older clerk at the leftmost desk.

"Sir, do you have your election warrant?"

"I do." Ysella extracted the long leather wallet from his inside jacket pocket, removed the warrant, and presented it.

The clerk scanned it, then looked up, frowning. "Ritter Ysella . . . from the former . . ."

"The former ruler of Aloor? Yes, he was my grandsire. I'm the first generation allowed to run for public office."

The clerk nodded, checking through several folders before opening one and studying it. "Premier Detruro indicated he wanted to meet with you. If you'd let me confirm that he's free, sir."

"Of course."

As the clerk stood and made his way to the closed door in the middle of the rear wall, Dominic surveyed the chamber. The white walls bore few marks of use, although areas above the brass sconces of the wall lamps looked slightly duller, likely from repeated removal of the soot from the burning oil.

In moments, the clerk reappeared. "The Premier will see you, sir. Go right in. I'll have your credentials and pin by the time you return."

"Thank you." Ysella made his way to the half-open door and stepped into the study, closing the door.

"I'm pleased to meet you, Ritter Ysella," Iustaan Detruro declared as he stood.

At that moment, Ysella realized how tall the muscular but balding premier actually was, more than two heads taller than Ysella, who was a touch above average height.

Detruro gestured to the chair in front of the ornately carved goldenwood desk, then seated himself.

Ysella sat and waited, smiling pleasantly as he met Detruro's eyes, trying to get a sense of the Premier, since, unlike some, he could only discern feelings through careful observation.

"I've wondered what you'd be like."

"I suspect I'm not much different from any other councilor who's an unmarried third son," replied Ysella.

"I understand you're a legalist. That's not exactly usual in a family with lineage such as yours."

"I had no interest in subsisting on familial alms."

Detruro's laugh was warm, amused, and doubtless practiced. "You look younger than most councilors."

"I doubtless am." *Given that you're barely twenty-six.*

"You're not wearing a gladius."

"I understood that blades longer than a belt knife aren't allowed in the Council building." Ysella didn't mention his dislike of dueling, still occasionally practiced among landors.

"Wise and considerate of you to have discovered that. Have you found lodgings?"

"Not yet. I'm staying with Councilor Aashen. He's a distant cousin. By relationship, although Sudaen isn't that close to Aloor."

"Chaarls should prove helpful, but I'd suggest you stay away from the Citadel area. It's cheaper, but rather rough. There are some smaller suitable dwellings close to Camelia Avenue near Imperial University."

"Imperial University?" Ysella was unaware that Machtarn held such an institution.

"It's only been open the last three years. The Imperador felt a university was necessary after the Trinitarians closed down their college."

"I hadn't heard that." As he spoke, Ysella managed not to wince. While Aloor was a good four hundred milles from Machtarn, everyone in Aloor, at least those in every landed family, had heard about how Laureous exiled all of the scholars at the Trinitarian Seminary to Neewyrk in the far northeast of Guldor. Although rumors abounded, no one knew exactly why, and for some reason, no one had mentioned the new Imperial University. Possibly because few in Aloor dared to criticize the Imperador, and fewer still wanted to praise him.

"I understand you have some background dealing with water law."

Rather than explain in detail, Ysella nodded, adding, "Some background, but not so much as an older and experienced legalist in such matters."

"I'd thought to assign you to the Waterways Committee."

Ysella understood that as well. Young men from landed families who were councilors all knew something about land, agriculture, and the grain exchanges, as well as labor, from dealing with the susceptibles, and other less endowed persons, who did most of the manual labor on estates.

"The chairman of the Waterways Committee is Councilor Sheem, and when you can, you should introduce yourself. The new Council will be sworn in next Duadi. I look forward to working with you." Detruro stood abruptly. "The clerks will have your office assignment and provide you with your keys and everything you need."

Ysella didn't quite scramble to his feet. "Thank you, Premier Detruro." He inclined his head politely before turning and leaving the office.

1

Machtarn—20 Fallend 819

AT a third after second bell of the morning, Ysella stepped through the main door into his second-floor office in the Council Hall, actually two offices. The space on the right contained his two clerks, and a bench where visitors could sit. His equally small personal office on the left held a desk, a file chest, a narrow bookcase, and three chairs, accessed by a door in the middle of the wall between the two spaces. A single window behind his desk was the principal source of light, but his personal office also had a separate door to the main corridor, which had proved useful once in a great while.

"Good morning," offered Ysella to the senior clerk, Lyaard Khaard.

"The same to you, Ritter. Paatyr went down to get the morning *Tribune*. He should be back any moment. You received only a few letters this morning."

"Complaints or petitions, I imagine." *Since anything personal gets delivered to the house.*

"And a message from Premier Detruro," added Khaard.

"Another announcement to all councilors."

"It didn't look like those, sir."

"I can always hope." Ysella smiled, ruefully, before entering his office, where he immediately took off his overcoat and hung it on the wall peg. He crossed the room to open the interior window shutters. Although there wasn't any frost on the glass, he felt the chill. By Yearend there would be frost, and the Council Hall would be almost uninhabitable, not that it wasn't close to that already, despite the small wall stove and the heavy blue-gray woolen suit that he wore.

He turned to his desk, picked up the letter knife—a miniature replica of an Alooran gladius—and opened the envelope from Detruro. He extracted the note card and read it, still standing.

Dominic—

I'd appreciate it if you'd stop by my office around third bell this morning.

The note was signed with a flowery "I" accompanied by the seal of the Premier.

Ysella had no doubt what was on Detruro's mind, what with all the "discussion" in the Waterways Committee about which districts should receive priority in the appropriations legislation. Because the Council would be called to order at fourth bell, Ysella intended to be on time, since his relations with Detruro had been little more than polite from the first, no matter what Ysella did to be friendly.

As Ysella laid the note on the desk, Paatyr Jaasn, the junior clerk, knocked on the half-open door. "Would you like to see the *Tribune* immediately, sir?"

"I think that means I need to," said Ysella dryly, stepping away from the desk and taking the newssheet. "Thank you. If you'd close the door."

"Yes, sir."

After seating himself behind his desk, Ysella began to read the lead story above the fold.

WAR LOOMING?

"Nothing more than a senile war hound!" That was how Atacama's Grande Duce Almaetar described Imperador Laureous after the Atacaman three-deck galleon *Victorya Grande* opened fire on the Guldoran frigate *Paelart* for entering Atacaman waters offshore from Port Lenfer in the Gulf of Nordum on Duadi, the second of Fallend.

While the *Paelart* suffered only minor damage, her cannon crippled the Atacaman vessel, forcing it to return to Port Lenfer . . .

Given the almost uncritical support of Laureous previously evidenced by the newssheet, Ysella doubted that the damage to the *Paelart* was minor.

. . . the Grande Duce has been increasingly strident in his denunciations of Guldoran efforts to rein in the depredations of so-called privateers sailing out of small isles in the Cataran Delta . . .

Guldoran First Marshal Gunnar Solatiem has vowed to deploy naval marines to deal with the privateers if the Grande Duce refuses to remove them, despite Atacaman claims that no such privateers exist and that such attacks would require Atacama to defend its lands and honor . . .

Ysella shook his head, then read through the rest of the newssheet.

The only other article of interest reported that Commodore Daargaen, the head of naval procurement, charged Jaahn Escalante with refusal to abide by the price of tin agreed to contractually. Escalante claimed that "unavoidable circumstances," as spelled out in the contract, required him to increase prices to the Navy. Ysella had certainly heard of the Escalante family, given that Alaan Escalante was the current councilor from Silverhills. However, Alaan had never mentioned family or relations in their brief conversions, and the fact that the *Tribune* didn't mention Alaan suggested that any relationship wasn't close.

Even so, it could get sticky, particularly since Alaan serves on the Military Affairs Committee.

Ysella felt slight surprise that he hadn't been contacted by Reimer Daarkyn, the *Tribune* newshawk assigned to cover Council committees, including the Waterways Committee.

But he'll likely show up today . . . and certainly no later than tomorrow. With a wry smile, Ysella set aside the newssheet and slit open the first of the three envelopes on his desk, extracted the letter, checking the signature and seal—that of Cyraen Presswyrth, a familial acquaintance from Khuld. Then he began to read.

Councilor Ysella—

As you may recall, last spring you met with landowners from Khuld and Daal. At that time, you indicated that you'd look into obtaining funding to deepen the channel in the upper reaches of the Khulor River to return it to its previous depths. Recent reports from Machtarn suggest that the funds presently in the Waterways appropriations would be insufficient to accomplish more than a few milles of deepening.

The inability to transport agricultural goods and produce effectively by water is already creating considerable hardship on all those dependent on river transport, something that could be counted on in the times of your grandsire.

In other words, you're not delivering the way your grandsire did when he was king of Aloor.

When Ysella finished the first letter, he opened and read the next two. All three were similar and came from the heads of landed families with ties to his own family, which was why they'd written.

They have no idea what it took to get the funding that I managed. But then, Ysella also knew that they didn't care. All they knew was that he hadn't gotten them all they wanted and felt they needed.

He stood, picked up the three letters, and carried them into the anteroom. "Lyaard, if you'd draft replies to these, politely saying that I fully understand the difficulties that they face, that the Waterways Committee obtained as much funding as was possible under the strictures set forth by the Imperador, and that I'll be looking for every opportunity to add funds in the future to deepen the upper reaches of the Khulor River."

"Yes, sir."

"While you're handling that, I'm going to meet with the Premier."

From where he sat at the other desk, Jaasn rolled his eyes.

"I know," replied Ysella, "I'm *so* fortunate."

Khaard failed to conceal an amused smile.

Ysella left his office on the upper level, one of the more distant offices from the Council floor, despite his position as chairman of the Waterways Committee, and made his way down to Detruro's office.

There, one of the newer clerks said, "You can go in. He's expecting you, sir."

"Thank you."

Ysella closed the inner office door behind himself.

"Dominic," Detruro began warmly, but without rising from behind his desk, "so good of you to come by early." He gestured to the chairs.

Ysella took the chair to his right. "I'm at your service, Premier. Might this have something to do with the worsening situation in the Gulf?"

"That's going to be a problem, but this is more immediate and far less . . . profound." Detruro cocked his head slightly, then said, "I've heard that the discussions in the Waterways Committee were, shall I put it, rather warm."

"We did report out the Waterways appropriation with the provisions you suggested." *More or less demanded*. But Ysella saw no point in putting it that way.

"Those provisions were what the Imperador required, as well as additional funding for harbor improvements at Port Reale, particularly with the buildup of the Atacaman fleet at Port Lenfer."

"We included those." Ysella waited.

Finally, Detruro spoke again, his voice smooth, his face almost immobile. "The vote was five to two in favor, I understand."

"That's correct. Councilor Grieg and Councilor Ditaero could not accept the funding limitations for river and canal works in their districts. Both declared they'd oppose the entire appropriation measure unless they got what they needed. Grieg insisted on more funds for the River Patrol—"

"That's understandable. On the other side of the Rio Doro is Atacama. I've talked to Grieg about surplus funds for that. I'm more concerned about Ditaero. Endor's a port city, but the Imperador is less concerned there, especially with the problems the local commercers gave his grandsire. Giving in to a crafter like Ditaero also won't sit well with half the landors and some commercers. Nor are there enough marks in this year's remaining funds to meet his . . ."

"Requirements?"

"Demands, in fact."

Ysella frowned. That suggested that Detruro had already indirectly felt out Ditaero. "There are only eight councilors firmly allied with the crafters."

"They're not the problem. The eighteen business and commerce councilors are. They've decided to vote together, with the crafters, to force greater funding for ports besides Port Reale."

Ysella understood the numbers. The landed councilors only held twenty-four out of the fifty Council seats. "And if we can get one of the crafters to support the appropriations . . . you can break the tie."

Detruro nodded, a mere acknowledgment.

"Is there anyone else among the crafters? Or . . ."

"Ditaero's the most vulnerable."

"What, if anything, can I promise him?"

"I understand that he might be happier on the Natural Resources Committee, since logging is, shall I say, of great importance to him."

"Elections are two years away," Ysella pointed out, "unless the Imperador dissolves the present Council . . . or unless you have something else in mind."

"That's the best I can do, Dominic. I hope you can persuade Ditaero. Neither the Imperador nor the Heir are that pleased with the Waterways section of the appropriations." Detruro's eyes flicked toward the office door, if but for an instant.

"We kept the total to a touch more than you requested." *Which is better than most other committee chairmen managed.*

"If every committee came in a bit higher, we'd exceed the available revenues. You know we don't have support for an increase in land tariffs or year-end taxes."

Ysella did know that, because most of the landors' worth was tied up in land, as was the Imperador's. Since the Imperador paid land tariffs—if at half the rate of landholders—neither the landors nor the Imperador favored higher tariffs, and the commercers and small shopholders threatened to refuse paying higher year-end taxes unless land tariffs were increased.

"Without higher government revenues," Detruro continued, "we would have to issue Imperial Treasury bonds. The Imperador refuses to do that, and if he did allow it, none of the banques will buy bonds at any rate the Treasury can afford . . . according to Treasury Administrator Salaazar."

So, we may have to cut appropriations. Salaazar claims the Imperador is furious with the banques, threatening to shut them down."

"Wouldn't that be . . . difficult?"

"Impossible, in practice. Even High Justicer Kaahl would rule against something like that, but Laureous is getting less and less reasonable, as we all know."

"What does the Heir think?"

"When he does think, he understands that would make matters worse." Detruro's eyes went to the door, again momentarily, before he smiled. "That's all I wanted to tell you."

Ysella discounted the smile, given the coolness in the Premier's eyes. "I'll do what I can."

"I'm sure you will," replied Detruro, the smile fading from his lips as he stood.

In return, Ysella also stood, inclined his head politely, then turned and left the office, closing the door, wondering at the implied inconsistencies in what Salaazar had said to Detruro. *Or were they accurate statements that reflected the Imperador's occasional irrationality when facts didn't accord with his wishes?*

Ysella made his way back to the second level, where he knocked on the door to Ditaero's office, and stepped inside.

Both clerks looked up. "Sir?"

"Is the councilor available?"

"Let me see, sir," said the older clerk, who stood and then slipped into the councilor's personal office, before returning quickly. "You can go on in, sir."

Ysella nodded to the clerk, then stepped into the inner office, where he cheerfully said, "Good morning, Gaastyn."

"You're here about the appropriations, aren't you, Dominic?" Before Ysella could say more, Ditaero went on. "I can't do it. Without more repairs to the levees, we can't use the river year-round, and that means the loggers and the millworkers don't get paid."

"I understand, but there'll be more funding next year."

"Those men and their families will go hungry this year."

"I don't like it any more than you do. I have the same problem. Growers in the upper reaches of the river can't get goods and produce to Sudaen. They're laying off workers. Opposing the entire appropriation won't get them any more funding, and it won't make the Premier or the Imperador inclined to be supportive in the future. The Premier mentioned that you might prefer to be on the Natural Resources Committee." Ysella knew what Ditaero thought about that but wanted to tell Detruro he'd mentioned it.

"I can't do it. I told you that from the beginning. That doesn't include the problems with the piers. If I support the appropriation and then end up on the Natural Resources Committee, everyone will say I sold out. You've done the best you can. I'd like to support you, but if I don't publicly oppose the appropriation the newssheets in Endor and Aaken will have my name in headlines as agreeing to screw the commercers in Endor and the loggers and riverfolk in Aaken and Jaykarh."

"Always the newssheets," said Ysella sardonically.

"Especially the frigging *Tribune,* but the *Endor Star* isn't any better."

"All the appropriations may have to be cut."

"I heard something about that from Haans Maessyn." Ditaero snorted. "The Imperador can build more ships that sit in the harbors most of the time, and get damaged when they don't, but we can't pay for things that are productive?"

"The Imperador worries that Grande Duce Almaetar will attack Port Reale."

"With what? Most of his army is in the west, near Cuipremaan, fifteen hundred milles west of Porte Reale."

"You and I know that," said Ysella. "But the Imperador's never forgotten the Atacaman raid of Zeiryn."

"That was ten years ago." Ditaero shook his head. "Anyway, you can convey my regrets to the Premier . . . and to our beloved floor leader, if you feel it necessary."

"You've never cared for Luaro, but he's pleasant enough."

"Sponges are pleasant enough, too, except they soak up whatever the commerce types pour on them. I'll see you on the floor."

"Until then . . . but think about what I said."

"I will. I doubt I'll change my position, though."

From Ditaero's office, Ysella returned to his own, where he found Reimer Daarkyn waiting on the bench just inside the door.

The graying newshawk immediately stood. "Councilor—"

"I can only give you a little time." Ysella gestured, then walked to his personal office, noticing that, as always, Daarkyn carefully closed the door and waited for Ysella to sit before seating himself.

"You have tin mines in your district," said Daarkyn conversationally. "What do you make of Jaahn Escalante's attempt to get more marks from the Navy? Do you know him personally?"

"I've never met him. The first time I heard about this was when I read the *Tribune* this morning."

"What do you make of it?"

"Do you want a quote from me?" Ysella kept his voice light.

"It might be helpful."

"Unless there are extraordinary circumstances involved that I'm unaware of, Sr. Escalante's apparent refusal to honor the price is unwise and unlikely to be accepted by the Navy. Commodore Daargaen will, of course, be the one to decide that, based on all the facts."

Daarkyn nodded, jotting a few notes on the folded sheet of paper, then asked, "Have you talked to Councilor Escalante—his cousin—about this?"

"No. I've had to deal with other matters."

"Do you think that Councilor Escalante's position on the Military Affairs Committee will affect the commodore's decision?"

"Since I don't know the commodore and haven't talked to the councilor, I don't know. Also, Councilor Escalante is only one of the members of the committee, and he's not the chairman." Ysella smiled pleasantly, then asked, "What else are you pursuing this morning, Reimer?"

"Nothing much."

Ysella laughed. "Meaning that you'd rather not say."

"Well . . . there are rumors that we'll be seeing more of the Imperador's daughter, who apparently isn't as discreet as her sire."

"How can she not be discreet?" asked Ysella. "I'm sure she's chaperoned day and night." *Unlike her sire and brother.*

"Women, even the youngest, have their ways. I'd rather not say more."

"Perhaps we'll see her at the Imperador's Yearend Ball." Sensing that the newshawk wasn't about to say more, not without more haggling and time, Ysella stood.

"Thank you, Councilor," declared Daarkyn.

Once the newsie left, Khaard looked into Ysella's personal office.

"He wanted to know my thoughts about the tin contract." Ysella paused. "I know you don't care much for Daarkyn, but, as I've said before, it's better that I've granted him access than having him shadow me whenever I leave the Council Hall and pester me when I'm worried about other matters." Besides, Ysella often learned more than he revealed, and there was little point in antagonizing the newssheets.

Because of the time he'd spent with Daarkyn, Ysella had to hurry down to the first level and then to the Council chamber, where he took his place behind his desk, the last one at the left end of the front row, since he was the most junior of the committee chairmen.

At fourth bell, as the chime calling the Council to order sounded, Ysella glanced around the chamber, where all fifty councilors appeared to be present. At the adjoining desk sat Ahslem Staeryt, the councilor from Machtarn and chairman of the Justiciary Committee.

"Get on with it," muttered Staeryt as Floor Leader Maatrak moved to the lectern in the center of the dais.

Maatrak rapped the gavel, then declared, "The matter before the Council is the passage of the combined appropriations bill. Each committee chairman has one-sixth of a bell to make a statement about that committee's proposed appropriations, beginning with the honorable chairman of the Agriculture Committee."

Ysella took a deep breath. A sixth of a bell for each of the seven chairmen—that meant a full bell before he, as the last chairman, had to summarize Waterways appropriations . . . and then there would be amendments and votes on the amendments and then another vote on each section.

The tall, blondish, and burly Georg Raathan strode to the lectern, replacing Maatrak, smiled broadly, then began in a booming voice, "As always, we could have done with more funding, but the funds available will allow greater grain storage in a number of locations . . ."

Ysella listened, suspecting he'd learn little new.

After Raathan spoke for the Agriculture section, the chairmen of the Commerce, Foreign Affairs, Justiciary, Military Affairs, and Natural Resources Committees each spoke.

Finally, it was Ysella's turn. When he reached the lectern, he smiled wryly. "Following such distinguished chairmen is a dubious pleasure. So I'll simply state the facts."

He cleared his throat, then went on, "Here in Guldor, both the Imperador and sometimes even the Council take our internal waterways for granted. But if the river channels and river piers and docks aren't dredged and otherwise maintained adequately, growers at the head of the Khulor River, the Lakaan River, the Eshbruk River, the Karh River, the Rio Doro, and especially the Rio Azulete cannot use those waterways. Over time, fewer crops and produce will reach the cities, and food prices will rise. More people will be hungry. The same is true of other goods. The Waterways Committee has abided by the recommendations of the Imperador, but the results of that accommodation will cost us all in years to come. Each year that maintenance is neglected, the costs to Guldor will increase. Every one of your districts will suffer more each year that such maintenance is insufficient. No amount of rhetoric will change that. I would prefer more funding, and only support the present Waterways appropriation because there appears to be no alternative."

After a pause, Ysella concluded. "There's little else I can say." Then he turned. "I yield any time remaining to the floor leader."

Maatrak, clearly surprised at the shortness of Ysella's remarks, struggled to extract his considerable bulk from his chair and return to the dais. When he took his place at the lectern, he immediately said, "The Council will now vote on those amendments to the Agriculture section registered with the floor clerk." After placing a stack of papers on the lectern, he lifted the first one and read, "An amendment to cancel funding for grain depots and to shift the funding to increased port facilities in Ondeliew and Sudaen. Councilor Aashen will speak to the amendment."

Ysella tightened his lips. The amendment was clearly Maatrak's, given that he was essentially the head of the commerce councilors, as well as floor leader, and represented Ondeliew.

Aashen rose from his desk in the chamber, stepped up on the dais, and took the lectern. "One of the reasons for funding grain depots is because Guldor lacks port facilities at Sudaen capable of loading grain ships effectively. Likewise, Ondeliew has similar difficulties with facilities for metals, particularly iron and copper . . ."

As Aashen spoke, Staeryt turned to Ysella. "You wouldn't allow that in committee, I take it?"

Ysella shook his head. "It's a backdoor way of reducing agriculture funding to funnel funds to support commercer industry." No matter how Ysella voted on the amendment, if his vote got out, most voters in Aloor would be unhappy one way or the other. While votes were secret, the more astute observers of the Council could often deduce votes.

When Aashen finished, Maatrak took the lectern and declared, "Councilors will mark their cards and submit them to the tally clerk."

Ysella took out a blank card from those held upright in the wide slot at the corner of the desk, marked the negative box, then walked to the vote box, waited his turn, and dropped the card in the box. After the clerk crossed off his name, Ysella returned to his desk to wait the third of a bell before the vote closed.

"You think we can finish all this by tomorrow afternoon?" asked Staeryt.

"We should. There are only fifty amendments registered. The real question is whether what passes will be accepted by the Imperador."

"The only question there is how unreasonable he'll be," murmured Staeryt.

Two-thirds of a bell later, the clerk turned the tally sheet over to Maatrak, who walked to the lectern and declared, "Twenty-eight councilors having voted in the negative, twenty-two in favor, the amendment is rejected."

"Interesting. Not all the commercers voted for it," said Staeryt quietly.

"Some don't want anything going to landor districts." Ysella didn't say more because Maatrak began to introduce the vote on the second amendment to the Agriculture appropriation.

The Council session lasted until fourth bell of the afternoon, when Maatrak recessed the Council until fourth bell on Tridi morning. For all of the amendments offered, only two had been adopted, neither of which measurably changed the total appropriation, but then, the Council hadn't yet debated the most controversial areas—military and waterways spending.

After leaving the Council chamber, Ysella returned to his office, made some changes to the letters Khaard had drafted, then donned his winter riding jacket, collected his worn leather case, and walked to the Council stables, a separate building to the north of the Council Hall. There, he saddled his chestnut, led him out of the stable, mounted, and rode south to Imperial Boulevard. The stone-paved road led from the harbor to the Palace of the Imperador, with only a few scattered buildings flanking the boulevard south of Council Avenue until a half mille north of Imperial University. Still, there were more now than when he'd first been elected.

After riding a block east on Camelia Avenue, Ysella turned north onto the cul-de-sac that was Averra Place—he still wondered from where the name had come—and rode past four two-story dwellings to the fifth, equally modest. Ysella believed in reducing fire hazards as much as possible, and so all the exterior walls were stone, and the roof of slate. He guided the chestnut up the lane to the smaller rear building, also stone, that held a stable sufficient for four mounts and a chaise, an arms/exercise room, as well as a few rooms for the couple who served him. Caastyn Cruart, a stipended Imperial Army squad leader, served as part valet, groom, and general aide, and his wife Gerdina was the maid and cook.

By the time Ysella neared the stable, Caastyn had the stable door open.

"Good afternoon, sir."

"The same to you, Caastyn. How is everything here?"

"All's well. I checked at the post centre. There were two letters and an envelope delivered by messenger. They're on your study desk. How was your day?"

"Long. Six straight bells of votes on appropriations amendments." Ysella reined up and dismounted, retrieving his case in the process. "Jaster, here, had his usual long and boring wait. I'm not so sure that the Council stables aren't warmer than my office."

"They might be." Caastyn chuckled. "Have you decided when you'll be leaving for Aloor?"

"Not to the day. After the Imperador's Yearend Ball, but when depends on the weather." Ysella patted the chestnut's shoulder, said "Good fellow," then handed the reins to Caastyn.

"You still thinking of taking the post coach?"

"That's the fastest way."

"Still long and uncomfortable. Better you than me, sir." Caastyn smiled, then turned and led the chestnut into the stable.

Ysella entered the house through the door on the side porch that opened into the parlor, then crossed the main hall to the study on the other side, where he set his case on the desk, before making his way to the kitchen door, peering in, and asking, "What might be for dinner, Gerdina?"

"Creamed basil fowl with noodles and green beans, sir," replied Gerdina, not looking away from the wood-burning stove that shared the chimney with the parlor fireplace.

"That sounds good."

"I wouldn't be cooking it, Ritter, if it weren't."

Ysella chuckled, then withdrew to the study. After settling behind the dark walnut desk, he opened the first of the two letters, from his mother, given the handwriting on the envelope, and began to read.

Dear Dominic—

Your father and I are so looking forward to seeing you. We know you have to stay in Machtarn until after the Yearend Ball, as one of the unstated requirements of being a councilor, but we all miss you, especially at Yearend.

Haekaan is taking over more of the daily management of the lands, and the same is true for Taeryn with what Raemyna will receive, since he was fortunate in his marriage . . .

Did he have any choice, given that our familial lands couldn't be divided any further?

More than a few of the eligible young ladies have made indirect inquiries about how long you'll be staying . . .

Ysella smiled, an expression amused and rueful. *I wasn't interested in most of them before, and the ones I liked weren't acceptable to you and Father. Why would that change now? Because I now have a title and some independent income?* He continued to read.

We don't know what you hear in Machtarn, but I thought you ought to know that your uncle Nathanyal died last week. He never was the same after that bout with the red pox last year...

Ysella nodded. The red pox had struck the south and west of Guldor harder than the more northern districts. In fact, Premier Detruro's wife had been one of the victims, although, since both sons were old enough to be on their own, the Premier hadn't had to worry about them.

... Your cousin Haarkyl wasn't expecting it, and will probably have difficulty coming up with the marks for the various expenses, including the seal tax. He and Saera will be moving into the big house on the grounds in the next few weeks, although Saera isn't thrilled. The place is more than a bit run-down and needs work, but Haarkyl feels that it's up to him to keep up familial appearances...

It always was.

... especially since his youngest daughter shows signs of being an empath. At least, that's not so much of a drawback for a girl, especially if she could marry someone like you, who can't be persuaded against his will. She could also act as the holding empath. That could be quite a savings for a small holding, which would likely be the best she could do. I hope she'll keep that prettiness. That might be enough to attract a halfway suitable husband...

When Ysella finished reading this mother's letter, which mentioned a few other deaths and two disappearances, among other news that was half gossip, he set it aside and opened the envelope delivered by messenger, from Sullynd & Smarkaan. He smiled as he read the opening lines.

Ritter Ysella—
Your offer for the building at the east end of Harbor Way has been accepted. Full payment to us must be completed before Year-end...

"Excellent!" Ysella read the details, then stood, walked to the file chests on the low stand, opened the second one, and slipped the letter into the proper file, each file referring to a different property in Machtarn, all of which he'd acquired since becoming a councilor.

He returned to his desk to open the remaining envelope, one showing a Machtarn address with which he was unfamiliar, and one the usual size for an invitation. He extracted the card and began to read.

> *Ritter and Ritten Alaan Escalante*
> *Request the honor of Your Presence*
> *For Dinner*
> *Furdi, the Twenty-eighth of Fallend,*
> *Sixth Bell of the Afternoon.*

Ysella frowned. Although Alaan was a good ten years older than Ysella, he'd only been elected to the Council in the last election. While friendly and cheerful in the Council Hall, Alaan had never made overtures to Ysella, and had politely declined the two invitations to dinner that Ysella had tendered.

A belated response to your earlier invitations? Or a way to introduce you to someone? Or something to do with Alaan's possible relationship with Jaahn Escalante . . . or something else entirely?

He wrote the date into the small journal he kept in the study, but was still puzzling over the invitation when Gerdina rang the dinner bell.

Leaving the invitation on the desk, Ysella stood and walked to the dining room, where both Cruarts stood waiting. He smiled and gestured to the table, knowing that his family would be horrified to see him eating with those they regarded as servants. Then the three seated themselves.

Ysella nodded to Gerdina.

She lowered her head and spoke quietly, but clearly, "Almighty Trinity of Love, Power, and Mercy, we thank you for the life we lead, the shelter we have, and those we love. We humbly ask you to bless the companionship we share and the food we will partake, in the name of the Three in One."

Once Gerdina finished, Ysella took a sip of the wine, Silverhills white, then a small morsel of the creamed fowl, knowing that neither of the Cruarts would eat or drink until he did, no matter what he said.

After several bites, Ysella asked, "Did you hear anything interesting at the post centre . . . or elsewhere?"

"Couldn't say that I heard much different, sir," replied Caastyn. "Folks worry about the winter. Price of firewood's gone up a lot."

"I hadn't thought about firewood," mused Ysella. "I knew good timber for shipbuilding was getting scarce. What about coal?" The tin mines near Aloor used coal to smelt tin, but it could certainly heat a fireplace or a stove.

"There isn't any near Machtarn, not so far as I know."

"Then we'd best lay in more wood," replied Ysella.

"I was going to mention that, sir."

"Go ahead. Wouldn't want you two to run short while I'm gone. Go over what you might need, and we can talk about that tomorrow evening."

"We'll be doing that, sir."

"Good. How is your daughter faring?"

"Been a bit of a rough patch with the babe, like we told you, but Raf's new position with the harbor authority is working out," replied Gerdina. "They finished up the cottage behind his folks' place in Southtown. We won't see them as much . . ."

Ysella nodded, listening while he ate, and thinking about the fact that he needed to do exercises and spar with Caastyn after dinner.

2

ON Tridi morning, Ysella stepped into the Council chamber little more than a sixth before fourth bell, immediately smelling the woodsmoke that invariably escaped from the large wall stove that contributed minimal heat. He saw that most councilors were already at or near their desks, including all the committee chairs except Georg Raathan. But then, Raathan had already introduced the Agriculture appropriations and would have time before he needed to vote.

Ysella looked to the dais, where, on the right side, Detruro and Maatrak spoke quietly, with their intent stiffness suggesting a definite tension.

"Detruro doesn't look pleased," murmured Staeryt. "One of the clerks said that an Imperial messenger visited the Premier."

"Demanding funding for more warships, no doubt."

Staeryt chuckled. "How could you possibly know that?"

"Because I have such close contacts with the Palace empaths," replied Ysella in a low but sarcastic tone.

"You've never worried about empaths. Why?"

"They've never bothered me." Ysella's words were true in both meanings, but he avoided directly mentioning his impermeability to empathetic manipulation.

"You're fortunate. That might change as you gain more seniority, especially if you're summoned to the Palace."

"This Imperador will never summon me. You know that."

"I almost feel sorry for any empath who works at the Palace." Staeryt paused, then added, "Only almost."

Ysella smiled faintly.

Floor Leader Maatrak moved to the lectern in the center of the dais. "The Council will continue its consideration of the combined appropriations bill with Military Affairs. Before Chairman Daenyld introduces that section, I must remind the Council that the Imperador has made it clear that he will reject any appropriations measure that does not include funding for three additional first-rate ships of the line. While I oppose those ships, it is my duty to inform the Council of the Imperador's position." Maatrak then stepped back, nodding to Symeon Daenyld.

The bearded Daenyld strode toward the lectern, his thinning chin-length red hair moving slightly with each step. Once there, he surveyed the chamber for several long moments before speaking. "I appreciate the honorable floor leader's reminder of the Imperador's concerns. The committee also shares those concerns. We have, however, recommended funds to build six frigates, rather than three first-rate ships of the line, in accord with the assessments Fleet Marshal Haarwyk provided last year. Those frigates can be built more quickly and will give the fleets greater flexibility in dealing with both pirates and with possible Atacaman . . . overreach . . ."

Ysella turned his eyes to Detruro, whose frown grew more pronounced with each word that Daenyld uttered.

Daenyld closed by saying, "I have pledged my loyalty to the Imperador, but the greatest loyalty to him is to save him and all Guldor from his own folly."

"Loyalty or not, I hope he's got good personal guards," murmured Staeryt from his desk beside Ysella.

"He's supposedly close to the Heir," replied Ysella.

"The Heir agrees with his father about the first-rate ships," said Staeryt. "He went to Neewyrk to inspect the construction of the last one. So Daenyld's taking on both father and son, and that's foolhardy."

But voicing that to Daenyld was useless, Ysella knew.

Maatrak returned to the lectern and announced, "The vote is upon the amendment to restore funding for three first-rate ships of the line, and to delete funding for six frigates. Councilor Baertyl will speak to the amendment."

Baertyl stepped onto the dais and moved to the lectern. "The Imperador has requested the amendment in order to build more heavily armed warships to deal with future Atacaman hostilities." Then he stepped away from the lectern.

Ysella's jaw dropped. In his years in the Council, he'd never heard such a perfunctory endorsement, and that meant that no member of the Military Affairs Committee supported the amendment.

Maatrak returned to the lectern, and the chime announced the beginning of the third of a bell allowed for voting.

Ysella removed a blank card from the slot in his desk, marked it in opposition to the amendment, followed Staeryt to the vote box, dropped the card in the box, and returned to his desk to wait until the vote closed.

The wait was almost silent, as if none of the councilors wanted to say anything, knowing that any remark against the amendment might get back to the Palace.

Less than two-thirds of a bell later, Maatrak walked to the lectern, looked at the tally sheet, and declared, "Thirty-seven councilors having voted in the negative, six in favor, and with seven abstentions, the amendment is rejected." Barely pausing, he announced, "The second amendment is to transfer fifty thousand marks from the building budget for Port Reale to the building budget for the Naval Yard at Neewyrk. Councilor Daenyld will speak to the amendment."

Daenyld immediately took the lectern. "The amendment is to rectify an imbalance in maintenance and building funds from last year's appropriations that should have been included in the proposal before the Council. It's supported unanimously by the committee . . ."

Even with the endorsement of the Military Affairs Committee, the amendment wasn't approved by anywhere close to unanimity, but by a vote of thirty-one to nineteen.

Ysella suspected that most of the craft-leaning councilors voted against it, just to show that they could and would vote as a bloc.

More than three bells passed, with some eight amendments to the Natural Resources appropriations offered, seven of which failed, before Ysella had to take the lectern to speak to the Waterways appropriations.

"After a great deal of effort, the Waterways Committee has presented appropriations that meet"—*almost*—"the guidelines presented by the Imperador. We could not meet all the needs within those parameters, but had to prioritize based on the urgency and the projected results of meeting those needs . . ." When Ysella finished, he nodded and returned to his desk.

Maatrak returned to the lectern. "The first amendment is to supply additional funds for pier and levee repairs to the Karh River from Jaykarh to Aaken and additional port facilities in Endor. The leadership opposes this amendment because its inclusion will increase appropriations beyond the limits of anticipated revenues. Councilor Ditaero will speak to the amendment."

Ditaero immediately took the lectern, speaking intently and firmly, his forehead wrinkled in concentration. "This amendment will not appreciably increase total appropriations, but it will make a significant difference to the working people of the northeast. The funding in the existing appropriations language will only cover half of the necessary repairs to the levees and piers along the Karh River. Crafters, loggers, timbermen, and others depend on the river. Commerce in Endor relies on the port, and it was hit harder by storms in the last three years than any other port in all Guldor, yet would receive less funding. Without full repairs some may no longer have jobs. In addition, without those repairs, it may not be possible to obtain the amount of timber necessary to build the frigates funded in the Military Affairs appropriations . . ."

For all of Ditaero's intensity, his amendment was defeated, if closely, twenty-six votes opposed, and twenty-four in favor.

Another bell and two amendments later and the approval of the Waterways section, Maatrak announced, "The vote is on the passage of the annual appropriations for the coming year."

As the chime sounded, Ysella reached for another blank voting card.

"What do you think?" asked Staeryt, his voice low.

"The vote will be close, and no matter how it turns out, neither the Imperador nor the Heir will be pleased."

"I can't say I disagree with you on that."

A third of a bell later, Detruro walked to the lectern holding the tally sheet. "Twenty-six voting for the Appropriations Act, twenty-four against, the Council has approved the measure. The Council is recessed until further notice, or until Unadi, the twenty-fifth of Fallend, whichever occurs first."

With that, Detruro raised the gavel and tapped the wooden plate on one corner of the lectern.

Ysella waited for several moments before he rose, looking around for Alaan Escalante, but the older councilor had been one of the first to leave. So Ysella waited to let the remainder of the more impatient councilors leave the floor. He wasn't in any hurry, especially since he suspected that the Council would be back in session well before the twenty-fifth.

As he turned toward the door, he saw and heard Maatrak addressing Daenyld.

"Symeon . . . weren't you a little hard on the Imperador?"

"Not so hard as I could have been. You know that as well as I do. We need three more oversized first-rate warships like a smith needs three anvils."

"I share your views, but excessive rhetoric is not especially productive."

"If the Imperador were ten years younger . . . and if . . ." Daenyld broke off his words as Detruro walked toward the two of them.

"Because of your stand against the Imperador's amendment," said Detruro, "we may be here until well after Yearend."

"So be it," replied Daenyld. "The Imperador can only reject an appropriation twice."

Detruro shook his head. "That's a custom, not a law."

"Besides . . . would the Imperador like certain . . . irregularities to become public?"

"He'd likely regard that as a threat. So would the Heir. I'd leave well enough alone, Symeon, but you'll do as you will . . . and always have." Detruro turned abruptly, as if he'd just recognized that Ysella was there.

"Dominic, thank you for the way you handled the Waterways issues. I appreciated your discretion."

Then Detruro turned and walked from the chamber, not looking anywhere near Daenyld.

"Iustaan has always appreciated discretion, especially where he's concerned," declared Daenyld cynically before following the Premier.

Ysella turned to Maatrak, asking quietly, "Irregularities?"

"Dirty laundry in the Palace, might involve the Imperial family in unpleasant personal ways, but I won't be the one to air it, and neither should you." Maatrak offered a crooked smile, then gestured toward the chamber door.

Ysella nodded politely, then preceded Maatrak. Once out in the main corridor, he turned right, toward the staircase leading to the second level. Before he reached the stairs, he saw a councilor moving toward him, then recognized Aashen.

"Dominic . . . do you have a moment?"

"Of course." Ysella moved to the side of the corridor where Aashen stood.

"Do you have any idea why Symeon insisted on including funding for the six frigates?"

"You have to admit that he's right," said Ysella.

"Of course he's right, but why would he risk the Imperador's anger?"

"I don't know. It's clear he had more in mind than merely good policy." Ysella paused, smiled sardonically, and added, "Unless he hoped to provoke the Imperador into a rage and give him heart failure."

"Laureous may be losing his mind, but he's a tough old bastard. He even limits the Heir's spending, which has to gall young Laureous. He didn't mourn when he lost his first wife and then the first Heir. He also doesn't carry grudges, because people who anger him too much don't live long enough for grudges to be carried."

Ysella nodded, well aware of the Imperador's anger, then said, "Maatrak made a comment about irregularities and dirty laundry in the Palace."

Aashen laughed softly. "Both father and son have had love children, but they've chosen young women who won't complain and provided well for them. The only legitimate child who's not married is Delehya. She's only seventeen or eighteen. We might see her at the Imperador's Yearend Ball this year, but I don't see a girl that young being a problem, despite a rumor or two. If there's a problem, it's likely to be with procurement, improper payments, or someone bribing an Imperial functionary—and Laureous has been death on that sort of thing. So I'd say that's unlikely."

"I thought as much, but you've been in Machtarn longer. Like you, I don't understand Daenyld's blind insistence on the frigates."

"The Imperador won't accept it. That means we'll be in session until Yearend . . . at the very least."

"My thought as well," said Ysella. "And before I forget, I wanted to tell you again how much I enjoyed the dinner last week."

"Even with Alabard's rant about the need for a strong Imperador?"

Ysella chuckled. "As one of the old sages said, we don't get to choose our family, only our friends. I'm glad you and Bhettina are both."

"Thank you."

After leaving Aashen, Ysella walked up the stairs to the second level.

"Any more letters?" he asked as he stepped into the clerks' section of the office.

"Just a message from Councilor Escalante," replied Khaard.

Doubtless in response to my message. "Thank you."

After stepping into his office, Ysella immediately opened the envelope on his desk.

Escalante's note was brief.

Dominic—
We're so glad you can join us for dinner on the twenty-eighth.
We're both looking forward to it.

The reply didn't shed any light on why Ysella had been invited, but the most likely possibilities were that the Escalantes needed a suitable male to fill out the table or that Alaan wanted something from Ysella, possibly in regard to his relative's difficulties with the Navy.

Setting the letter on the desk, he walked to the north-facing window and looked out, not that he could see the Imperial Palace, and wished that he could leave for Aloor. The appropriations for the coming year were the last necessary legislative business for the Council, and in late fall few constituents—or others—wrote or wanted to influence matters before the Council, simply because there was little they could affect.

He shook his head, still wondering what in the world had possessed Daenyld to insist on increasing the numbers of frigates and to oppose the Imperador's amendment.

3

EVEN though the Council wasn't scheduled to meet on Furdi, Ysella entered his office early, well before third bell, suspecting that the day would be anything but uneventful.

"Anything from the Premier?" he asked.

"No, sir," replied Jaasn. "The *Tribune*'s on your desk. Do you think the Imperador's angry enough to dissolve the Council?"

"He'll be angry, but if he dissolves this one, elections might give him a Council less to his liking. Also, the Establishment Act forbids spending that isn't approved by the Council." *Not that Laureous hasn't disregarded it before, but never on the entire annual appropriations.*

"Some of the other clerks think he might dismiss the Premier," replied Jaasn.

Khaard shook his head. "That would leave the floor leader as acting premier, and you might as well call him a commercer."

While Ysella agreed with his senior clerk, he only said, "The Imperador has a working relationship with the Premier. Hardly close, but working. In turn, the Premier has a working relationship with the floor leader." *If barely working at times.* "I'm hopeful that matters can be worked out." *Hopeful, but not terribly optimistic.*

With a pleasant smile, he turned. Once in his personal office, Ysella's first act was to take off his overcoat and hang it up. After drawing the inner window shutters back, he picked up the newssheet and settled behind his desk. The headline of the lead story was predictable—COUNCIL CHALLENGES IMPERADOR.

Then he began to read.

> Yesterday, the Imperial Council of Guldor passed the annual appropriations for the forthcoming year. Total funding was close to what the Imperador requested, but the measure contains several provisions earlier opposed by the Palace, particularly a denial of three first-rate ships of the line . . .

The story also suggested that Daenyld's "bookkeeping" transfer of fifty thousand marks from Port Reale to the Neewyrk Naval Yard might not set well with the Palace, but stated that no one in the Palace had anything to say about the appropriations.

Not publicly, in any event.

The other interesting article was a brief mention that Fleet Marshal Haarwyk was found ill in his office at the Palace and was undergoing treatment by the Imperador's physicians.

The very officer who recommended frigates over first-rate ships of the line.

Ysella shook his head. Haarwyk's chances of recovery didn't look good, even though the Fleet Marshal had submitted the effectiveness assessments a year ago in response to an inquiry from the Military Affairs Committee and hadn't commented at all recently.

That raised another question. If Haarwyk's "illness" was linked to the appropriations measure, how had the Imperador found out about Daenyld's floor mention of the assessment so quickly? That mention was the first public statement in more than a year, although someone on the Military Affairs Committee might have informed the Palace about committee deliberations. Or possibly a newshawk from the *Tribune* could have relayed the floor statement to a contact at the Palace and asked for a comment. *Quite possibly Daarkyn.*

Ysella was still thinking over the possibilities when Jaasn knocked on his half-open door.

"A message from the Premier's office, sir." The junior clerk entered and handed over the sealed envelope.

"Thank you," said Ysella, waiting until Jaasn had left.

Then Ysella slit open the envelope from the Premier.

Inside was a white card.

Councilor Symeon Daenyld was killed early yesterday evening as he was returning to his house. The assailants are currently unknown.

Either the Imperador or the Heir had to be behind it. At the same time, Ysella knew that would never come out.

At the bottom of the card, in a different hand, was another sentence.

All committee chairmen are requested to meet in the Premier's conference room at fifth bell today.

Ysella recognized the second hand—that of Detruro.

He stood, leaving the card on the desk, and walked back to the anteroom, where he told the two clerks about Daenyld's murder.

"It had to be someone from the Palace," Jaasn declared instantly.

"Even if the Imperador was behind it," replied Khaard, "he'd make sure no one from the Palace was involved."

"Everyone will still know who was behind it," said Jaasn.

"What will the Premier do, sir?" asked Khaard.

"He's called a meeting of the committee chairs. Beyond that . . . it's too early to say."

"The Imperador must be really upset," volunteered Jaasn. "First, the Fleet Marshal and now Councilor Daenyld."

"It's possible that the Imperador had nothing to do with either," said Ysella dryly. "Possible, but highly improbable."

After Ysella returned to his desk, he kept mulling over Haarwyk's reputed illness, thinking how the Imperador had no need to deal with the Fleet Marshal, since all Haarwyk had done was offer an assessment—a year ago, no less!

Was Laureous losing his mental sharpness or being excessively vindictive? Or was Haarwyk coincidentally ill at an inconvenient time? Or was the Heir involved?

Right now, there's no way to tell. But Ysella knew that the most prudent assumption was that the Imperador was being vindictive, especially since that vindictiveness had increased in the last year or so.

At a sixth before fifth bell, Ysella walked into the Premier's office, where the junior clerk gestured to the conference room door.

After entering the chamber, Ysella wasn't totally surprised that he wasn't the first. Both Georg Raathan and Oskaar Klempt stood to one side of the table.

"I thought you might be here early," said Raathan jovially.

"One of our few similarities," replied Ysella, glancing up at the fair-haired and much taller councilor. "Did either of you note the newssheet story about Fleet Marshal Haarwyk?"

"We were just discussing that," replied Klempt. "Haarwyk's illness doesn't seem coincidental, but if the Imperador wanted to send a message, Symeon's death was more than sufficient."

"Unless Haarwyk's 'illness' was a message to senior naval officers," suggested Raathan.

"That kind of message could keep officers from telling the Imperador what he should know," said Ysella. "That's worrisome."

"Much of the Imperador's recent behavior has been worrisome," countered Klempt, stopping as the conference room door opened and Staeryt and Stron Thaalyr entered, followed by Paolo Caanard.

Several moments passed before the Premier entered, gestured to the table, and sat at the head. The others quickly seated themselves.

Ysella momentarily frowned when he realized that Maatrak, even though floor leader, wasn't present, and that all those present were of landor background.

"You all know about Symeon," began Detruro. "Does anyone not know about Fleet Marshal Haarwyk?"

"Have you heard anything about the Fleet Marshal's condition?" asked Klempt.

"I have not, but the Palace wouldn't rush to inform me or the Council."

"What about your sources?" asked Caanard.

"I've heard nothing from them so far." Detruro paused, slightly. "I'm very concerned about the Imperador's recent actions. I warned Symeon, but I had no idea that Laureous would respond so viciously. Even the Heir, I understand, is having difficulty in calming his father. Laureous feels that everyone wants to remove him."

"Most people still don't see that side of him," Klempt pointed out. "He's kept Guldor ordered and prosperous."

"They don't see because the Council has worked to minimize the effect of his temper," added Staeryt. "Sometimes, the Heir has helped, but less so recently."

"Much less so," said Caanard. "From what I've heard—"

"Exactly," replied Detruro, cutting off Caanard. "If we can't maintain that balance, Guldor could go the way of Teknold."

Ysella wondered if Teknold had really been that great, even with its strange machines. And what good had the machines done? Susceptibles were less expensive and more reliable, especially for jobs like picking fruits and gathering vegetables.

"How, exactly, do you plan to maintain that balance, Iustaan?" asked Kempt.

"That's why I called you together. Unless you have any better ideas, we'll have to accept what the Imperador requests, for now, but young Laureous is even less . . . flexible than his sire, and who knows how much more intractable he might become as Imperador."

"You're not suggesting . . ." began Raathan.

"Almighty, no! Guldor needs an Imperador, especially after the example of Teknold, but the Council needs more power to keep things in balance. What I would like each of you to do over the winter recess is to think about ways that we might achieve a better balance without any more bloodshed and disguised assassinations."

"Scarcely disguised," said Thaalyr disgustedly.

"How do you propose to reduce the Imperador's power?" asked Staeryt.

"That's why you're here," replied Detruro. "Revolts and rebellions are dangerous. We need a way to make a gradual change. We need to make it before the Heir becomes Imperador, and it has to be perceived as benefitting everyone while not humiliating the position of the Imperador."

What Detruro really meant, Ysella suspected, was that such a change had to be one that left the landors in control of the Council. Ysella also knew that all the other councilors in the room accepted that, almost without thinking, although no one was about to mention it.

"That's why I wanted to give you all some time to consider the matter," replied Detruro. "Do you have any other questions?"

"When do you think we'll find out about the marshal?" asked Klempt.

Ysella stifled a wince, then saw Caanard's face freeze for an instant.

"I have no idea," declared Detruro pleasantly. "The Palace has not been especially accommodating . . . as I mentioned."

"As usual," murmured Thaalyr, his voice just loud enough to be heard by everyone at the table.

Detruro stood. "Please plan to be in your offices for the next few days. I have no idea when the Imperador will deign to respond to the appropriations measure."

Ysella rose from the table with the others, but let them take the lead in following Detruro from the conference room. Once he was in the main corridor, the only two councilors waiting for him were Raathan and Staeryt.

"You were rather quiet, Dominic," said Raathan. "What do you think?"

"I don't like it, but the Premier's right. We have to find a quiet but effective way to rein in the Imperador, whoever he may be." Ysella looked to Staeryt. "Is there any change we could make to the Establishment Act that might accomplish that end?"

"That's not the problem. Getting the Imperador to sign it would be, and, at the moment, that seems unlikely. Remember, he signed the act only to preclude the possibility of secession by the northeast districts, after the fall of Aloor."

Ysella had heard that from childhood, and that Laureous had almost exhausted his treasury between the consolidation of the northeast and the short war against Aloor. "You're the best legalist in the Council. If you can look into it and draft some wording changes that sound modest, but would have the desired effect, perhaps the rest of us can find a way, over the next year, to obtain the Imperador's consent."

"I have to say I don't see that coming," replied Staeryt.

"Neither do I, but if the chance arises . . . and we're not ready . . ."

"Your point is well taken, Dominic. As the Premier said, we do have some time." After a definite frown, Staeryt turned in the direction of his first-floor office.

"Do you have any idea how you'll get any agreement from the Imperador or the Heir?" asked Raathan quietly.

"None whatsoever," Ysella said cheerfully, "but as Ahslem said, we do have some time."

With an amused expression, Raathan shook his head, then said, "I suppose stranger things have happened. I'll see you later."

As Raathan headed toward his office, Ysella walked to the staircase.

After he returned to his office and thought over what had happened in the conference room, he had to smile at how Detruro had accomplished two goals—getting the committee chairmen to accept what Laureous had essentially demanded and planting the idea that the Council needed to consider a significant reform in how Guldor was currently governed.

But whether that reform can be accomplished without destroying Guldor is another question, especially since most landors would rather have a despot for Imperador than any form of populist government. And Laureous would likely consider it treason.

4

JUST past third bell, Ysella left the Council building and made his way to the stables. After saddling Jaster and leading him out, he rode through a misty fog down Imperial Boulevard and to the Banque of Machtarn, just off First Harbor Way.

There, under the scrutiny of a guard, he tied the chestnut to a hitching post and entered the banque, his leather case in hand, ignoring the teller's window and walking to the desk of a clerk to the left.

The clerk looked at Ysella, taking in the pin on the lapel of his suit coat. "Councilor Ysella, what can we do for you, sir?"

"I need to withdraw marks from my account in the form of a certified draft to another party."

"You'll have to see Sr. Lamaant for that, sir." The clerk stood. "This way, if you would."

Then he led the way to the desk of an older and graying man, a clerk Ysella hadn't met before. "Sr. Lamaant, the councilor needs a certified draft." Then the younger clerk eased away.

Ysella took the chair in front of the desk.

"How much do you require, Councilor?"

"Four hundred fifteen marks, payable to Sullynd & Smarkaan."

"The property legalists?"

Ysella nodded.

"You understand I'll have to check your account balance, sir."

"Of course." Ysella managed a pleasant tone, despite being slightly irritated, but then he'd never encountered Lamaant before, and he couldn't complain that the clerk didn't know him.

"I'll be right back, sir."

Lamaant returned in less than half a sixth, looking slightly disconcerted, but managing a very warm smile. "You certainly have funds more than adequate for such a withdrawal, Councilor Ysella. I must apologize, but I usually work in the commerce section, and Sr. Fiorte's wife died unexpectedly, and the other senior disbursing clerk was at his daughter's wedding in Obaan." The clerk opened a leather-bound folder, dipped his quill, and began to write, very carefully.

"I can see where you wouldn't be as familiar with those needing disbursing services."

"Unfortunately, Ritter." Lamaant finished filling out the draft, then stood, holding the folder. "It will be only a moment, while I get the manager's signature and seals."

Less than a sixth later, Ysella left the banque with the draft in his case, mounted the chestnut, and rode four blocks to the east, where he tied his mount, looking to the doorman in front of the gray stone building.

"I trust he'll be safe here for a sixth or so."

"That he will be, Councilor."

"Thank you."

The copperplate sign beside the door through which Ysella entered the building read SULLYND & SMARKAAN. Inside was an anteroom, with a clerk at a desk.

"Councilor Ysella," declared the clerk, "Sr. Sullynd said to show you in whenever you arrived. Let me tell him that you're here."

"Thank you." *He's likely more interested in the banque draft than me.*

In moments, the clerk returned and escorted Ysella into the oak-paneled office featuring a corner wall stove, resulting in the warmest chamber in which Ysella had been all day.

Haasl Sullynd stood, smiling broadly, as Ysella stepped into the office. "You're always punctual, if not early, and a pleasure to deal with, Councilor."

"I thought it might be best not to wait until it was too close to Yearend." Ysella stepped forward, set the case on the desk, and opened it, extracting the draft and extending it to Sullynd.

The property legalist took the draft, checked it, then laid it on the desk and gestured to the chairs before seating himself behind the desk.

Ysella took one of the chairs in front of the desk.

"Since you're so early, we'll be able to have the deed recorded and to you by next Duadi, certainly no later than Tridi."

"I appreciate that."

"Might I ask what plans you might have for the property? And the tenant?"

"That will depend on the tenant and how other matters turn out. In the next few months, likely nothing, so long as the tenant pays his rent. I'd like the same arrangement with you for handling the rent payments, since there are times . . ."

"When you cannot be in Machtarn. We understand, and it won't be a problem," Sullynd said. "The same fee will apply, of course."

"Of course."

"That we can easily do, since we were handling it for the previous owner." The property legalist paused. "There is one thing. You already own the adjoining parcels... This purchase gives you the largest parcel of land on Second Harbor Way."

"That was the idea." *And it's the only land high enough that neither tides nor storms are likely to create that much damage.* Ysella smiled pleasantly.

"Are you thinking of other acquisitions?"

"I won't be looking until Winterend at the earliest, but if you have anything similar, you could let me know then."

Sullynd nodded, then cleared his throat. "I read in the newssheet that Councilor Daenyld was killed. I also heard that he supported measures not in favor with the Imperador."

"Both are true. I have no way of knowing whether the two events are connected."

"You're one of the more experienced councilors, Ritter. What do you think?"

"No one seems to know anything about Councilor Daenyld's murder. That suggests his death was carefully planned and carried out on the orders of someone influential and powerful."

"You're being unusually cautious," declared Sullynd wryly.

"I do know that the Imperador has become... less predictable in his acts in the last year. This is an obvious concern to the Council. My position, as you well know, is less than favored by the Palace, despite the fact that I've never opposed the Imperador." *Not publicly.*

"Do you think Guldor even needs an Imperador?"

Ysella laughed softly. "Given the makeup of the Council, Guldor needs an Imperador, just one with a little less power. There needs to be more of a balance of power between the Council and the Imperador."

Sullynd frowned. "How would you do that?"

"By allowing a large majority of the Council to override the Imperador." With a wry smile, Ysella added, "Not that the Imperador would presently approve of such a change."

"For a councilor, you don't seem to approve totally of that august body."

"I'm not in favor of either the Imperador or the Council having absolute power, but I'm one of seven committee chairmen, and the most junior. And, as you know, one without inherited marks."

"There are more than a few councilors with less than you, despite appearances." Sullynd leaned back slightly in his chair. "You have the sense to understand your position. Too many younger sons of landor families don't." After a pause, he went on. "I'll let you know as soon as the deed's recorded."

Ysella stood, understanding that the conversation was over, and that he had to end it. "I appreciate your helpfulness. Thank you."

Sullynd rose, not quite ponderously. "We're always here. I'll keep an eye out for other possibilities."

After a polite nod, Ysella turned and left the office.

On his ride to his house, he considered what Sullynd had said about whether Guldor even needed an Imperador. If that was a view held by many commercers, Detruro would have to be more careful.

Ysella shook his head. *To think we might need the Imperador to keep the commercers and crafters in check.*

5

ON Quindi morning, Ysella turned his mount over to one of the Council's stableboys and was leaving the stables when Georg Raathan approached.

"Good morning, Georg."

Raathan glanced up at the gathering grayish-green clouds. "I'd wager on snow or cold rain by afternoon." After a slight hesitation, he went on, "Yesterday, you seemed certain there might be a way to get the Imperador to relinquish power."

"There's always a way. That's not the question. It's whether the price is worth paying, for either side. Right now, all I have is a vague hope that it's possible."

"Might I ask if you have a reasonable basis for that hope?"

"Reasonable?" asked Ysella, with the hint of a laugh. "At present, no. But if the Imperador continues to abuse power—"

"What if the Heir takes the throne in the meantime?"

"That could make it easier. Then the Council can make the point that while the great Laureous was reasonable, his successor is not." Ysella turned toward the Council Hall, and the two began to walk.

"Laureous hasn't been reasonable for years, but people still want to believe he once was."

"Maybe his empaths help with that."

"Hardly," replied Raathan. "He doesn't like empaths. He thinks they should stay on the lands keeping susceptibles in line. He'd rather rely on the Palace Guard and the Army."

"Most of the Army is posted along the Rio Doro or in the north dealing with possible Argenti smugglers and raiders. Many senior Navy officers aren't happy with the way Laureous disregarded their recommendations. I can see that, in the right circumstances, various military leaders would be amenable to some . . . limitations . . . on the Imperador especially if the Council made clear that he retained a limited power of legislative rejection."

"So that two-thirds or three-quarters of the Council could override a rejection?"

"Something like that," agreed Ysella.

"The Council would like that, but would the Imperador ever accept such a limitation?"

"Not right now, but it might be possible in the future, especially if councilors spoke quietly about the matter in the interim."

"You're talking about a quiet revolution, Dominic."

Ysella shook his head. "A quiet *reform*. No one wants a revolution. If we can get a quiet reform, with structural limits on both the Imperador and the masses, we can avoid a future revolution. The last thing we need is crafters and commercers pushing to remove the Imperador or make him a figurehead. We certainly don't want to go the way of Teknold."

Raathan nodded slowly, stopping short of the guards at the doors to the Council Hall. "It's something to think about."

"It is." Ysella gestured toward the doors, following Raathan into the Council Hall, then made his way to the staircase and his office.

When he entered, Khaard immediately said, "No messages so far, sir, but you have a few letters."

"Have you learned anything from the other clerks?"

"Everyone believes the Imperador is behind Councilor Daenyld's death, but none of them have heard about any proof."

"As if it's necessary," commented Jaasn.

"Lack of proof makes action difficult," replied Ysella. *At least, direct action.*

Once in his office, after removing his overcoat and opening the inner shutters, Ysella settled behind his desk and began to read the newssheet.

The *Tribune* story was comparatively brief.

> Councilor Symeon Daenyld was found dead outside his Machtarn home early Duadi evening. According to Daenyld's houseman, the councilor died after being shot by several crossbow quarrels . . . Machtarn city patrollers have been unable to identify or locate the attackers . . .
>
> According to sources at the Palace, the Imperador deplores the incident, declaring that such violence has no place in Machtarn.
>
> Daenyld was in his third term and served as the Chairman of the Military Affairs Committee. He is survived by three sons and one daughter . . .

That's it? Ysella's lips curled into a wry smile, knowing that, had he been in Daenyld's place, the newssheet story would have been briefer, given that he was a less distinguished councilor, an unwed third son with no offspring, a few thousand marks, and only two modest houses and several harbor properties.

He read through the rest of the newssheet, but found nothing else about the Council or Daenyld. Nor were there any stories about possible hostilities between Guldor and Atacama in the Gulf of Nordum.

Ysella turned to the letters. Four were from landholders requesting greater funding to pay for deepening the upper reaches of the Khulor River, and one demanding that Ysella do something about the senile idiot in the Palace. When Ysella examined the envelope, he realized the letter was effectively anonymous, because the signature was unintelligible and the address on a street he'd never heard of, and he knew every street in Aloor. *Quite well.*

Even so, that letter had to come from someone of at least modest means, because posting a letter from Aloor to Machtarn cost a good fraction of the daily wage of a laborer or susceptible.

As Ysella thought about the oddity of such a letter, Khaard knocked on the half-open door to the inner office. "Sir . . . an urgent message from the Premier."

"Doubtless declaring when the Council will convene to deal with the Imperador's rejection of the appropriations." Ysella walked to the door, where he took the envelope.

"Could it be anything else, sir?"

"It could be, but it's unlikely." Ysella used the miniature-sword letter knife to slit open the envelope, then extracted the white card, read it, and showed it to Khaard.

> *The Council will resume its session at fifth bell. All councilors should be present for a possible series of votes.*

"Is that to amend the appropriations measure?" asked Khaard.

"Most likely, but we'll see."

After Ysella returned to his desk, he drafted notes for his clerks to use in writing responses to the first four letters and turned them over to Khaard, then forced himself to wait. At a third before fifth bell, he made his way to the Council chamber, where he stood beside his desk.

Staeryt arrived within a few moments. "Have you heard anything?"

"Ahslem . . . you know our honorable premier prefers to avoid living reminders of less honorable times in the history of the Imperium of Gold."

"You've known that for years. Why have you sought reelection? Not that I haven't asked you that before."

"My response remains the same." Ysella offered a sarcastic grin. "My present position is preferable to the other feasible alternatives. Besides,

I can occasionally accomplish something of worth, which would be far more difficult in Aloor."

Both turned as Detruro appeared and walked to the dais, where Maatrak waited. The two conversed briefly before Detruro walked to the lectern and the chime sounded once.

"The Council will be in order," declared the Premier, who waited for the remaining councilors to take their places. Finally, he said, "As I suggested when the Council voted, the Imperador rejected the appropriations as passed. He only wrote five words on the first page. Those words are: 'Do what I told you!' There was no other guidance. I have also learned that Fleet Marshal Haarwyk died of his illness, despite the valiant efforts of the Imperador's physicians and even the ministrations of the Imperador's daughter . . ."

The Imperador's daughter? What does she have to do with the Fleet Marshal? She's only seventeen or eighteen . . . or was that what Daarkyn was alluding to? With that thought, Ysella missed Detruro's next few words.

". . . if we refuse to pass the appropriations in accord with the Imperador's wishes, according to law, he cannot spend anything beyond salaries and obligations already incurred. In his present state of mind, he will ignore the law. Also, if we refuse to pass appropriations as he demands, he'll certainly dismiss me. Whether he will also dissolve the Council and call for new elections, I do not know. It's certainly a possibility."

"You're saying we have no choice," exclaimed Klempt from his desk.

Detruro rapped the gravel twice, loudly. "You're out of order, Councilor. However, for purposes of discussion, regular order will be suspended." After a pause, Detruro went on. "In response to your words, Councilor, at present, our choices are limited."

"So let him dissolve the Council," said Maessyn. "That won't get him his first-rate ships of the line."

"You're correct," replied Detruro. "It is true that, if no appropriations are agreed upon, the banques cannot honor any government drafts. Nor would they, since there are no procedures in place for such. Payment in gold will be required, which is impractical and often impossible. The Imperador's personal wealth will keep the Palace from being unduly inconvenienced for several months, but all the rest of Guldor will suffer."

"What if we adjourn without acting?" asked someone from the back of the chamber.

"The Imperador could recall us, but he'd more likely call new elections."

"You're the Premier. What do you suggest?" asked another voice Ysella didn't recognize.

"For now, I suggest we pass the appropriations as the Imperador demanded." Detruro paused, then added, "For now."

After a long moment of silence, Detruro declared, "The Council will resume proceedings under regular order. There being no other matters before the Council, the matter under consideration is a motion to amend the rejected appropriations to substitute three first-rate ships of the line for the six frigates previously authorized."

"A point of order!" called out Maatrak. "Councilors are allowed to speak for or against any amendment proposed to a previously passed bill."

"The honorable councilor from Ondeliew is recognized to speak to the proposed amendment for no more than one sixth." Detruro stepped back from the lectern but did not leave the dais.

Maatrak advanced to the lectern and immediately began. "As most of you know, I have opposed the building of unnecessarily large warships. If that were the only issue here, I'd vote for the amendment. Grudgingly, I admit. But the larger issue is that we have an Imperador who no longer possesses the analytical and sharp mind he once did, but who thinks that he still does. In addition, the Heir has rather close ties to the Haamyt Brothers . . ."

Ysella looked to Staeryt and asked in a murmur, "The ones building the first-rate ships?"

Staeryt nodded.

". . . and if we do not draw a line here and now," Maatrak concluded, "we will continue to receive vindictive messages and worse . . ."

"He's right about drawing the line," said Staeryt quietly, "but now's not the time. The rest of Guldor doesn't yet know how senile Laureous has become. Or how much worse the Heir will be."

"True," replied Ysella, "and it's going to be hard on everyone while they learn."

Detruro returned to the lectern. "Are there any other councilors to speak to the amendment?" He waited . . . and waited, then said, "The vote is on the amendment to the appropriations measure. Councilors have a third in which to vote."

Ysella reached for a blank voting card, filled it out, casting his vote for the amendment, and made his way to the voting box, where he deposited it before returning to his desk. Then he turned to Staeryt. "We'll see how many follow your advice and the lead of the Premier."

"The amendment will pass. A majority of councilors would prefer not to follow Daenyld's example."

"Not when it's too soon to do any good," interjected Caanard from his desk to the right of Staeryt.

And possibly fatal. But Ysella merely nodded, thinking about what he could do.

Slightly less than two-thirds of a bell passed before Detruro took the tally sheet from the clerk and announced, "Twenty-seven councilors having voted in the affirmative, nine opposed, and thirteen abstaining, the amendment is passed. The vote is now on the amended appropriations. Councilors have a third in which to vote."

Two-thirds of a bell later, Detruro announced the vote on the revised appropriations—twenty-seven in favor, twenty-two abstaining.

So the Heir can tell his father that no councilor opposed final passage. Ysella's lips twisted into a cynical smile.

Then Detruro announced, "The Council stands in recess until Unadi, the twenty-fifth." Then he rapped the gavel and left the lectern.

"Just like that?" asked Caanard.

"He might be trying to keep other councilors from being the Imperador's next victim, Paolo," said Staeryt.

"What about him?" asked Aashen from behind Ysella.

"Even the Heir isn't that stupid," answered Staeryt. "Killing the Premier after he delivered what the Imperador demanded wouldn't sit well with anyone."

Ysella nodded as he stood. He hoped Detruro's assessment of the situation—and of the Imperador's mind—was correct. *But then, anything else would have been worse.*

By the time he reached his office and stepped inside, he wasn't totally surprised to see Reimer Daarkyn rise from the bench beside the door. Without a word, he gestured for the newshawk to accompany him into his private office.

Reimer closed the door, seated himself, and asked, "How did Detruro manage that?"

"Manage what?" replied Ysella. "He passed the appropriations, as necessary."

"Why didn't the twenty-two vote no, instead of abstaining?" Daarkyn leaned forward slightly.

Rather than give the obvious answer, and risk being misquoted, Ysella asked, "Why do you think they did?"

Daarkyn smiled sardonically. "You tell me."

"I'll leave it for you to figure out."

"Do you really think the Imperador won't know what they meant?" The newshawk raised both eyebrows.

"They didn't oppose him, and the Council passed the amended appropriations he demanded."

"So the Council gave him what he wanted, but told him he was wrong?"

"I'm not about to guess what the Imperador will think. He insisted on certain appropriations. He got what he asked for."

Daarkyn's left boot tapped the worn wooden floor several times. "And he won't be able to find out who voted which way."

Ysella waited, then asked, "What else do you know, besides what was in the newssheets, about Councilor Daenyld's murder?"

"That's largely what I know." Daarkyn added, "I've been trying to reach Councilor Escalante, but he won't see me, and he should."

"What about the Premier?" Ysella suspected he knew the answer.

"He never sees me. They both want to hide things." Daarkyn's boot again registered his impatience.

"That's their decision, not yours or mine."

"Do you know what Councilor Escalante is hiding?"

"I don't know if he's hiding something or if he's not. With everything going on, I haven't spoken to him recently. I've been more involved with my own committee."

"How did the appropriations for waterways work out for your district?" Daarkyn straightened in the chair.

"All the districts needing waterways improvements received some funding. There weren't sufficient funds to fully meet all the needs."

"Do you think the Imperador was being unreasonable in insisting on building large warships?"

"That was his decision, and, as Imperador, he has the final say."

Daarkyn shook his head. "Can't you say anything that says something?"

"If we don't work within the government, we destroy the purpose of government. I'd rather not do that."

"Then you'd have the Imperador lead Guldor to ruin?"

"I didn't say anything of the sort," replied Ysella in an amused tone of voice. "Do you think the Imperador is leading Guldor to ruin?"

"You should have been a newshawk, Councilor." Daarkyn offered a cynical smile.

"I think not, Reimer. You're far better at it than I'd ever be."

"What happens next?"

"I assume the Imperador will accept the appropriations. The Council did as he recommended. There's no logical reason for him not to accept the final version."

"Can I quote you on that?"

"Of course."

"Thank you."

After Daarkyn left, Ysella wondered about his words, but they'd been a calculated risk, suggesting that the Imperador would be illogical if not irrational if he rejected the appropriations after getting what he demanded.

He had no doubt that his words would appear in the *Tribune*.

6

WHILE Ysella had a number of doubts about the existence of the Almighty, and certainly about the deity's beneficence, voicing such was unwise, especially for a councilor, as was neglecting services more than occasionally. So, on Quindi evening, he walked eight long blocks to the Trinitarian chapel, a simple oblong structure with gray stone walls and a slate roof, just off Camelia Avenue east of Imperial University. The side windows were essentially long rectangles with a triangle at top and bottom, thus making them extended hexagons comprised of individual triangular glass panes.

Once he entered, he slipped into his small section of a pew, toward the rear and away from the center of the nave, by choice, since, as he had explained to Presider Haelsyn, his duties as a councilor from Aloor often necessitated his absence. While he waited, he listened to the harpsichord, the most recent musical instrument to grace the chapel. Ysella still had his doubts about the harpsichord, partial as he was to violins and violas, but he had to admit its superiority in providing background melodies or accompanying singers.

Shortly, the painfully thin Presider Haelsyn, wearing a plain green cassock, stepped forward to the center of the sanctuary, a simple raised platform with a lectern on each side. The stone wall behind the sanctuary held three golden orbs forming an arc, representing the Almighty Trinity of Love, Power, and Mercy.

With the appearance of the presider, the harpsichord died away, and in that moment of silence, everyone rose.

The presider's tenor voice barely reached Ysella, but the words were familiar enough. "Let us offer thanks to the Almighty for the days that have been and for those to come, through his love, power, and mercy."

"Thanks be to the Almighty, for his love, power, and mercy," replied the congregation in unison, although Ysella merely mouthed the words.

The presider lowered his hands, and the congregation seated itself.

Then the choir, in pews to each side in front of the sanctuary, began the anthem.

> "*Praised be our Creator, our Definer, and Endower,*
> *Almighty enduring truth whose love, mercy, and power . . .*"

Following the anthem, the presider began the Acknowledgment.

"Our days are but fleeting threads in the fabric of time, our rocks of solidity but grains of sand, washed hither and thither by the storms of fate and chance. This we acknowledge. Our vaunted knowledge is but a single candle flickering in the darkness of the Great Night. This we acknowledge . . ."

Following the Acknowledgment, the presider moved to the lectern on the right and began his homily. "As we come to the end of the year, after we take stock of what we have, do we give thanks for what we have or do we compare that to what our neighbors and acquaintances have? Do we look forward to the coming year with dread or hopefulness? Do we praise those we value, or do we complain about what they have not done for us . . ."

As Presider Haelsyn continued with his homily, Ysella thought of Laureous, who never seemed happy with anything, except possibly conquering or crushing anyone or anything that affronted him.

Even he can't conquer the infirmities of age . . . and death.

That wasn't the question, Ysella knew, but rather how much damage Laureous could do to Guldor before he died and whether Detruro and the Council could rein him in before he destroyed the Imperium he had built.

As Ysella stood to leave the chapel after the service, he knew he had to do his exercises and spar at least a bit with Caastyn. *Preparing and staying ready for what you don't ever want to do again.*

7

ON Findi morning, Ysella rose a bit later, as usual on enddays. He had the house to himself, as well, given that Findi was a day off for both Caastyn and Gerdina, another reason why he'd needed to spar after services on Quindi. So he made himself a large mug of café and ate one of the sugar-spiced croissants Gerdina always left for him.

As he sat at the breakfast room table, he sipped the café, then picked up the morning edition of *The Machtarn Tribune*, turning his attention to the lead article.

> On a swift midday vote yesterday, the Imperial Council acceded to the Imperador's demand for funding three first-rate ships of the line, with twenty-seven councilors approving the revised appropriations, and twenty-two abstaining. After the untimely deaths of Councilor Symeon Daenyld, the Chairman of the Military Affairs Committee, and Fleet Marshal Elias Haarwyk, the abstentions were likely a symbolic vote of protest against the Imperador's insistence on the costly first-rate warships.
>
> The only councilor willing to comment was Dominic Ysella (Aloor), who said, "The Council did as he recommended. There's no logical reason for him not to accept the final version."
>
> In fact, the Palace announced late yesterday that the Imperador approved the appropriations, although the measure was "barely acceptable." The Imperador was said to be considering "other options," but the Palace gave no indication of what those options might be. The most likely acts would be for the Imperador to dismiss the Premier or call for new elections . . .

Ysella finished reading the article, which explained why there wouldn't be any funding difficulties in the near future and hinted that the Council wasn't about to test the Imperador's patience anytime soon. That hardly surprised him, since Laureous could definitely shut down the newssheet at a moment's notice. *Unlike the banques.*

After he finished his café and cleaned up after himself, he donned a winter riding jacket and walked outside. After studying the high but thick, green-tinged gray clouds, he decided that rain was unlikely anytime soon. He then entered the stable and saddled Jaster, then led the gelding out, closing the stable doors before mounting. He took a quick look at Caastyn and Gerdina's quarters, but the shutters were closed, and only a thin wisp of smoke rose from the chimney, suggesting that they'd gone to spend the day with their daughter Krynn and her husband Raf.

Even if you do get married, you'll never see your family unless you travel to Aloor . . . or your wife will never see her relatives if she lives here with you. Unless, of course, you wed someone from Machtarn, and that wouldn't set well in Aloor.

Then he leaned forward and patted the gelding on the shoulder. "We might as well take another look at what we bought." He rode the gelding down the drive to Averra Place. At the end of Averra, he turned Jaster west on Camelia Avenue, then south on Imperial Boulevard. On the ride to Second Harbor Way, he saw only a few carts, two coaches, and a handful of men on foot, trudging toward the harbor, most likely returning to their ships.

When he reached Second Harbor Way, he turned the gelding east. At the end of two blocks, he reined up and surveyed the north side of the street. Each of the five adjacent small parcels of land he now owned held a shop of some sort, a hatter, a shoemaker, a woolen-draper, a greengrocer, and a stationer. Each shop paid rent. In time, if the number of ships using the harbor increased, Ysella might realize a healthy gain, but if not, the rents added up, and that didn't include those from the building he also owned on the end of First Harbor Way.

"Good day, Ritter!" The greeting came from Jens Kaalad, the stationer, who was opening the store, because people, especially those families where both parents worked, did their shopping on Findi morning.

"The same to you, Jens." Ysella eased the chestnut toward the stationer, then reined up. "How are you doing?"

"Well enough, sir. Not so well as I'd like." Kaalad shrugged. "Been a hard year. Not as bad as last year, though. Glad to see that the Council didn't get into a battle with the Imperador."

"Right now, that wouldn't have served anyone."

Kaalad looked up to Ysella. "Sir . . . ?"

"You're worried, from your expression. About what, if I might ask?"

"You're a councilor, Ritter. How long do you think the Imperador's going to last?"

"I have no idea. You're worried about the Heir?"

"My cousin . . . his son worked in the kitchen at the Palace . . . he was saying that young Laureous is worse than his sire, what with his snitches and who they know . . . and the Heir's always saying nasty things about his sister . . ."

While Ysella had heard about the changes in the Heir, he hadn't heard about snitches, and that was worrying. "I take it that the young man doesn't work at the Palace now."

"He left a week's wages behind so he didn't have to explain."

"Does he have another job?"

Kaalad grinned. "He's a cook at Haryiat's. The pay is about the same, and we're all happier."

"That's good."

"You'll not be changing the rent, will you?"

Ysella shook his head. "Not now. We'll see next year."

"Fair's fair, sir. We appreciate it, Ritter."

"How do the others"—Ysella gestured to the other shops west of Kaalad's—"feel about the Heir?"

"Saakyt said that you can't pickle a rotten Heir."

Ysella nodded. That sounded like the greengrocer.

"No one else wants to say anything. They're afraid of the Heir's snitches."

"How long has that been going on?"

"Maybe a year . . . mostly since the Imperador got so ill last spring." Kaalad stopped speaking and half turned as a man opened the door to the draper's shop.

"Good morning, Braax!" called Ysella cheerfully.

The draper looked up, surprised, then answered, "And to you, Ritter. If you'll be excusing me, sir?"

Ysella laughed warmly. "Get your shop ready. I won't keep you."

"Thank you, sir." Braax almost scurried back into his shop.

Kaalad shook his head, then said, "I won't be keeping you, sir."

"More like I shouldn't be keeping you. I hope you have a good morning. It looks like it won't rain, at least not until much later." Ysella nodded, watched while Kaalad entered his shop, then turned the chestnut back west toward the cross street he could take to get on First Harbor Way.

He doubted that he'd see much at the other building, which was mostly a warehouse, although it also held a felter's shop and a saddlery. The warehouse, however, was the most profitable, given that warehouse space halfway close to the harbor was hard to come by with the increases in shipping in the last few years.

The Heir's snitches?

He shook his head.

8

SINCE the Council would be in session on Unadi, although it might be pro forma, Ysella made certain that he arrived at the Council Hall early. While the rain was light, it was cold and fell steadily for the entire ride to the Council Hall. Ysella's oilskin kept him mostly dry, except for his trousers below the knees. As he suspected, the ostlers and stableboys had their hands full, and he unsaddled and took care of the gelding before making his way to the Council Hall.

"Any word from the Premier . . . or anyone else?" asked Ysella as he entered his office, immediately shedding the oilskin.

"No, sir," replied Khaard. "A few letters. That's all."

"Is the rain getting heavier, sir?" asked Jaasn.

"Not heavier, but it is getting colder, with some icy drops mixed in."

"Freezing rain or maybe snow . . . they're both bad," muttered the junior clerk.

"If the Imperador actually signed the appropriations, the way the newssheet reported," said Ysella, "then the Premier will adjourn the Council until sometime in Winterend."

"What do you think, sir?" asked Khaard.

"It's likely, but these days, anything could happen." *And that's an understatement.*

When Ysella entered his personal office, he hung up the oilskin, but left the inner window shutters closed, instead lighting the wall lamp. Then he picked up the *Tribune* and began to read, starting with the lead article, which reported that Guldoran frigates, using improved cannon, had sunk three sloops manned by Atacaman pirates. The newssheet refrained from pointing out that the operation would have been difficult for a first-rate ship of the line in the shallower waters off the Cataran Delta.

Ysella wondered exactly how one could improve the cannon itself, but suspected that meant improved propellants and compression fuse-lighting. He suspected that, in a few days, the Grande Duce would retaliate. He also worried about reports of heavy rain in Aloor and the areas farther south, since too much rain would wash out recently planted wheat-corn, even if that was his brothers' problem and no longer his worry.

When he finished the newssheet, he turned his attention to the letters, opening and reading each in turn, jotting down quick notes for the clerks. Several letters outlined waterway problems on the upper part of the Khulor River, as if he could do anything until after the Council resumed work in the new year. Three others implored him to raise tariffs on imported Sargassan swampgrass rice.

Two of the remaining letters, neither terribly well written, each with a carefully blurred signature and a different but improbable address in Aloor, insisted that the Council needed to rein in the Imperador before he destroyed Guldor. Three similar anonymous letters regarding reining in the Imperador were written in a good hand, with proper grammar, suggesting that at least some landors were behind the correspondence.

Sometime after Ysella turned the letters and notes over to Khaard, Jaasn knocked on the half-open door, then entered with an envelope. "From the Premier, sir."

"Telling us when we'll meet . . . or not, no doubt," said Ysella as he stood and took the envelope.

"Yes, sir," agreed Jaasn before withdrawing.

The simple message stated that the Council would convene at fifth bell, and Ysella had the feeling he wouldn't care for what the Premier had to say.

Given that, and the anonymous letters, Ysella arrived in the Council chamber a sixth early, looking around for Aashen, whom he found standing at the rear of the chamber talking with Aldyn Kraagyn.

Both looked up, but Aashen spoke first. "You look like you have something on your mind, Dominic."

"I do. Over the past week I've received essentially anonymous letters." Ysella explained briefly.

"You're curious if either of us has?" asked Kraagyn.

"Exactly."

Aashen frowned. "I can't say that I have."

"I have to confess," said Kraagyn, with a wry half smile, "that I've gotten two recently. They sound like those you received, but one was posted in Paelart, the other in Encora."

"Paelart's not that far from Aloor," mused Aashen.

"But Sudaen's not that much farther," Ysella pointed out. "It might be interesting to find out if others have gotten such missives."

"I can ask around," volunteered Kraagyn.

Aashen only nodded.

Given Aashen's traditional outlook, that didn't surprise Ysella, but he didn't say anything because he saw Maatrak walking toward the lectern as the chime rang out and he had to hurry to get to his desk and seat himself.

Maatrak stepped behind the lectern, rapped the gavel, and declared, "The Council will be in order. The Premier has a few words." Then he stepped aside.

Detruro moved to the lectern, pausing until all councilors had taken their places. "As reported in the newssheets, the Imperador signed and approved the amended appropriations. He also sent the Council a letter whose contents I will not read. Currently, Council clerks are writing out a copy for each councilor. Those will be available to all councilors within the next two bells. The Imperador's letter is not considered to be privileged or confidential . . ."

That's as much as telling us to show it to anyone we wish.

". . . Unless any councilor has a motion to the contrary, I will be adjourning the Council until further notice or until Tridi, the ninth of Winterend, 820, whichever occurs first." Detruro paused, then asked, "Do I hear any motion?" After surveying the chamber, he concluded, "Hearing no objection, the Council is hereby adjourned."

For several moments, the chamber was silent. Then Staeryt turned to Ysella. "I can't wait to see what the Imperador wrote, especially after how the *Tribune* quoted you. It's interesting that Iustaan didn't want to read it, though."

"That's to give us a chance to read it before the newshawks descend on us," suggested Caanard from beside Staeryt. "It's likely got derogatory language about the Council."

"If not worse," suggested Ysella.

"Do you think we'll actually get a full winter recess?" asked Staeryt.

"That's up to the Imperador," replied Caanard. "I can't see the Premier calling us back in session, except at the Imperador's demands. Iustaan has got his hands full and then some."

"Oh?" asked Ysella. "What besides Laureous?"

"Isn't that enough?" replied Staeryt.

"It is, but I get the feeling he's worried about more than the Imperador."

Even though Ysella was certainly no empath, he sensed that Caanard knew more than he wanted to say. "Don't most of us have worries beyond the Council?"

"You've got fewer than most, Dominic," declared Staeryt. "You've got a good house, a secure seat in the Council, and, from what I can tell, no wife or other excessive expenses."

"Not having a wife might be a greater worry than having one," said Caanard, smiling broadly.

"That's a worry I wouldn't mind undertaking," replied Ysella. "If I could find the right woman."

"I don't see you looking all that hard," countered Caanard.

"I will be going to Aloor after Yearend."

"You've gone there at least twice a year for six years, and come back empty-handed every time," pressed Caanard, grinning. "Maybe you should take a better look around at the Imperador's Yearend Ball . . . if you're attending, after all this."

"I wouldn't miss the chance to add to the Imperador's expenses," replied Ysella. There was always the chance he might learn something useful, since he had learned about the first property he'd bought at the ball.

"Also," added Staeryt, "the Imperador keeps track of which councilors avoid the ball. Sometimes, their districts get less than favorable treatment from Imperial functionaries."

"You don't have to remind us, Ahslem," said Caanard.

"It might be better if the Council had a Yearend Ball," mused Ysella, "except we can't afford it."

"The Imperador wouldn't stand for it," replied Staeryt.

Ysella glanced around, realizing that the three of them were the only ones in the chamber, except Maatrak, who turned a chill glance in their direction. "I suppose we need to get back to our offices to discover how the Imperador has chastised us."

"I can wait for that," declared Caanard dryly as he turned toward the chamber door.

Ysella and Staeryt followed, and in little more than a sixth Ysella was in his own office.

"Sir?" asked Khaard.

"Not a total disaster, Lyaard. The Imperador approved the appropriations, reluctantly, and sent the Council a message that the Premier refrained from reading. We'll each get a copy."

"It could have been much worse, couldn't it, sir?"

"I've learned that things could always be worse, but that doesn't make something bad any better. We'll have to see." Ysella managed a cheerful smile, then headed for his personal office to sign—or correct—the replies the two clerks had written.

Less than a bell later, Jaasn brought him an envelope. "From the Premier, sir."

"Thank you. That has to be the copy of whatever the Imperador sent." Once Jaasn left, Ysella opened the envelope and read the single sheet within.

Premier Detruro—
  The appropriations measure finally enacted with such reluctance by the Council is barely acceptable and does not serve well the needs

of the Imperium, whose defense against warlike neighbors must remain strong. Strength is not served by second-rate or third-rate warships, something of which we should not have to remind the Council, but by the predominance of power, represented by first-rate warships. Nor should we have to remind the less than honorable councilors that they are members of the Imperial Council and that they act on behalf of the Imperador and all Guldor and not in their own personal and often selfish interests.

We must emphasize that any further transgressions by the Council will not be treated so forgivingly.

At the bottom of the sheet were written the words "The original document was signed and sealed by the Imperador."

Ysella saw why Detruro didn't want the newshawks to get the document immediately, although there would be some reference to it in the morning newssheet.

He put the copy in his case, donned his oilskin, turned down the wick in the oil lamp and blew it out, then walked into the outer office. "Close up, and go home. I'll see you in the morning, but unless something urgent comes up, we'll be working short bells until I leave for Aloor." He didn't have to say that the two would be working shorter bells during the entire winter recess because that was a given.

"Thank you, sir."

"Until tomorrow." Ysella walked out wearing the oilskin, although the rain had stopped; it was easier than carrying it, and it also broke the wind.

9

SURPRISINGLY to Ysella, both Duadi and Tridi passed uneventfully, and he managed to fit in two sessions of sparring with Caastyn. While the clouds and rain departed, both days and nights grew noticeably colder, enough so that, had there been clouds, what fell from them would have been snow. On Furdi, Ysella's day at the Council Hall happened much like the previous two, and he and the clerks again closed the office early.

After riding home, Ysella went to his study and checked the address of the Escalantes, then wrote a reply to his mother's letter, briefly describing what waterway improvements he'd managed to get for Aloor and that the Council had deferred to the Imperador on funding naval warships. While it was unlikely his parents would repeat his words, there was no sense in being other than politely factual.

When he finished the letter, he changed to a slightly more formal suit for dinner, a darker gray-blue than he wore during the day, and spent some time with his personal account ledgers.

At half before sixth bell, he led Jaster out of the stable, mounted, and made the comparatively short ride to the Escalante house, a two-story dwelling like Ysella's, but half again as big. It sat on a slight rise on Cuipregilt Avenue, which paralleled Camelia Avenue one block to the south.

As Ysella rode up the drive, Alaan Escalante came out to the side porch. "You can tie your mount inside the stable. Everyone else has a carriage."

"Thank you. Jaster will appreciate that." For all of Alaan Escalante's courtesy, Ysella would have been surprised if the other councilor had not offered shelter for Jaster. After tying the gelding inside the stable, Ysella walked to the side porch—Alaan had remained standing there—and the two entered the front parlor from the side door.

Once inside, Alaan gestured to the dark-haired woman attired in a pale maroon dress and jacket, seated on one side of a settee. "I don't believe you've met my wife Amaelya."

Ysella inclined his head. "I haven't had that pleasure."

Alaan turned slightly toward a man who immediately stood. He had blond hair and a short-cut blond beard and appeared close to the same age as Alaan.

"And Ritter Antonan Roddek and his wife Lurreta, and Lurreta's younger sister Mystera. They're family friends from Silverhills."

None of the women wore headscarves, not even draped over their shoulders, strongly suggesting that they were houseguests and hadn't left the dwelling recently.

"I'm pleased to meet you all." Ysella noted that the dark-haired Mystera looked to be in her mid-twenties and had a pleasant countenance . . . and was likely one of the reasons he'd been invited.

"I see you rode," said Amaelya. "In this weather?"

"It's easier on me, and on the horse, and since I'm not married, it's also simpler."

"Are you ready for some refreshment?" asked Alaan. "I can offer red or white wine. Silverhills, either way."

Ysella smiled. "Could you serve anything else? Red, please."

"I could," replied Alaan, smiling in return, "but why serve less than the best?"

"You're fortunate it's from your district."

"Indeed." Alaan nodded to the serving woman, then said, "Sammal and Haanara should be here shortly."

For a moment, Ysella wondered, then realized that Alaan was referring to Councilor Haafel and his wife Haanara. He also understood where he was supposed to be and took the empty straight-backed armchair next to the settee where Mystera sat.

"What brings you to Machtarn?" Ysella asked the young woman.

She shifted her weight on the settee, turning but slightly to reply. "Ritter Roddek had business here. Lurreta wanted to do some shopping and thought I might enjoy it as well. There wasn't much to do in Silverhills, and I've never been to Machtarn."

"How long have you been here?"

"Just a week."

"What do you think of the city—and the shopping—so far?"

"I thought it might be more impressive."

You should have seen it six years ago. "The Imperador has been rather cautious in spending marks on the city." *Except on the Palace.*

"It's not very colorful. All the buildings seem to be gray stone."

"It's more inviting in seasons other than late fall or winter. We see a great deal of rain in Fallend."

"Ritter Roddek didn't mention that." Mystera glanced toward her sister, then back to Ysella, her eyes not quite meeting his.

"I imagine your family thought it would be useful for you to see Machtarn." *And to be seen.*

"They did mention that." Mystera's tone held a touch of resignation.

"Families often have agendas for younger sons or daughters."

"Is that why you're a councilor?" she asked with the hint of a smile.

"In a way," Ysella admitted.

"In a way?" asked Mystera.

"It provides more independence." *From family, at least.*

Before Mystera could reply, Alaan Escalante stood and walked to the front-hall doorway. "Here come Sammal and Haanara."

Once the councilor from Nuile and his wife entered and were introduced, followed by another sixth of pleasant talk, the group repaired to the dining room.

Ysella found himself seated between Amaelya and Haanara and across from Sammal.

From the head of the table, Alaan said, "In the name of the Almighty and his love, power, and mercy, we thank you for what we are about to receive and for the company we are so grateful to share, in the name of the Three in One."

That blessing was one of the shortest that Ysella recalled ever hearing, except for his father's.

The serving woman immediately began to place bowls before the diners, a fowl consommé with flecks of herbs, paired with Silverhills white wine.

After everyone had taken at least a spoonful of soup, Amaelya turned to Ysella and said, "I'm so glad you could come, Dominic. I've heard so much about you lately. Alaan's been most impressed at how you've accomplished so much so quietly. What might be your secret?"

"I don't know that there's any secret. I try to be fair and make sure that my district never gets more than its deserved share." Ysella took another spoonful of soup, which was hot and delicately flavored.

"I can see how that would undercut any argument that you're being unfair, but how is that perceived in your district?" asked Haanara.

"Since my district got little in the past, so far no one's complaining . . . at least not too much."

Haanara smiled.

Amaelya asked, "Do people in Aloor bring up the fact that you're not married?"

Although Mystera immediately looked toward Ysella, he replied, "I have the feeling that's the least of their concerns."

"You've never thought of marrying?" asked Haanara.

Ysella offered an amused smile. "Certainly, I've thought of it, but when I was younger, I had little but myself to offer, and I was . . . reluctant to wed under the available circumstances."

Marrying a landor daughter would have required a standard of living not supported by his income as a legalist, and that would have meant being dependent on his father or, in time, his older brothers. Marrying anyone not from a landor background would have alienated his family.

Alaan nodded understandingly, as did Amaelya.

"And now?" asked Lurreta. "You're a Ritter in your own right, and the income of a councilor is not a pittance."

"You also have a handsome dwelling," added Amaelya.

"Acquiring and furnishing it was only possible because I was not married. Now . . ." Ysella shrugged. He didn't feel the need to mention that his income from his properties exceeded his income as a councilor, even if it had taken years of financial care to save up the marks to buy the properties.

"In addition to being a councilor," added Alaan, "Dominic is also a distinguished legalist in water and waterways law. That's why he's chairman of the Waterways Committee."

Not wanting to remain the subject of conversation, Ysella replied, "Both Sammal and Alaan have distinguished themselves. Alaan, in particular, has had a rather difficult time these past few weeks."

"More like impossible," declared Sammal. "The Council asked for recommendations from the Fleet Marshal, and when the Military Affairs Committee followed those recommendations, the committee chairman and the Fleet Marshal both ended up dead." He looked to Alaan. "Aren't you the most senior member of the committee now?"

"I believe Alaaxi Baertyl and I have the same seniority," replied Alaan, "but since the Premier will decide the next chairman, there's little point in speculating."

Sammal cleared his throat, then asked, "Ritter Roddek, might I ask what brings you to Machtarn at this dismal time of year?"

"Various business matters, those that make no sense to travel for individually. Eventually, they get to be naggingly numerous. Now that all the harvests are in, I thought I might as well deal with them all, and Lurreta might see if the shopping here was better than in Silverhills."

"Is it, Ritten?" Sammal asked Lurreta.

"There are a few things we seldom find in Silverhills."

"Perhaps, in time," interjected Ysella dryly, "Machtarn will gain what Aloor once had."

Sammal grinned, if briefly, while Lurreta looked momentarily stunned. Mystera appeared confused.

At that moment, Amaelya nodded slightly, and the serving woman began to collect the soup bowls.

"Aloor wasn't much of a threat a century ago," said Ysella. "The real threat is so often excessive use of power, especially used willfully."

"Why do you think that would be true now?" asked Alaan thoughtfully.

Ysella, having waited until everyone had been served, took a look at his plate, which held a lightly breaded whitefish, accompanied by a small ramekin of a white remoulade, along with cheese-laced potatoes, and mixed sweet peppers.

"You didn't answer my question, Dominic," said Alaan lightly.

"I was enjoying looking at dinner," replied Ysella. "Excessive use of power is always a danger because it tends to alienate or destroy friends and allies, and forces enemies to build up arms out of fear and concern."

"You don't believe in using power?" asked Antonan Roddek.

"I believe in power, just not excessive power. That was part of the problem in Aloor. The king ignored the landors' council, impoverished the crafters, and abused the susceptibles. When Laureous attacked, few saw much benefit in supporting him."

"The Imperador might not appreciate that parallel," replied Antonan.

"I don't believe I made any comparison," said Ysella pleasantly.

"No, you didn't, but—"

"I think we should leave it at that, Ritter Roddek," interrupted Sammal smoothly. "We've all seen power abused; it's unpleasant and often unnecessary."

"All too often unnecessary," agreed Haanara.

Ysella caught the smallest of nods from Amaelya, and then as Alaan saw his wife, a quick frown from him. This time, Mystera glanced from Sammal to Roddek, with an expression that might have been incomprehension or bafflement that Roddek didn't reply.

Ysella also could see that Roddek wasn't entirely pleased, but he waited.

Finally, Roddek said, "Well, you all have had more experience in dealing with power, but I think we need a strong Imperador."

"If I might change the subject," said Ysella, after having taken a bite of the fish, "what kind of fish is this? It's quite good."

"I have no idea," admitted Amaelya cheerfully. "Maranara chose it and said we'd enjoy it."

"It is excellent," added Lurreta. "We don't get good fish in Silverhills. So it's definitely a treat."

While Ritter Roddek's words, tone, and expression all agreed with his wife, Ysella saw that Mystera did not care for the fish.

The conversation during the remainder of the main course and dessert—a lemon cake—centered more on the weather and what might improve Machtarn, both in terms of shopping and housing. Ysella said comparatively little.

After dessert, followed by brandy, Sammal rose. "This has been a marvelous dinner, Alaan and Amaelya. We do thank you, but we're not so young as the rest of you."

"We're so glad you could come," Amaelya replied warmly.

"We wouldn't have missed it for anything," added Haanara.

Once the Haafels departed, Amaelya said, "There are a few things I'd like to talk over with Lurreta and Mystera. We'll be in my study."

The three women had no sooner left the dining room than Alaan said quietly, "Ritter Roddek would like a word with you in the parlor, if you don't mind, Dominic. I'll be back in a bit."

Ysella was hardly surprised, but led the way to the parlor, followed by Roddek.

The older landor took one of the armchairs, and Ysella took one facing him.

"Because of your experience in water law, I hoped you could provide me with some counsel, Dominic."

"I'll do the best I can."

Roddek cleared his throat. "It's not widely known, but I have an interest in the Silverhills winery, and the winery has encountered a difficult situation."

Ysella nodded and waited.

"Unlike much of southern Guldor, Silverhills is a bit drier and higher, and the soil and weather make it excellent for vineyards. That also means we sometimes need to divert water for irrigation. Unhappily, there is a tannery downstream of the main section of the vineyards. They claim they have documented senior water rights, and we're taking too much from the stream. They've threatened legal action. We've always used water from the stream, from long before there was a tannery there . . ."

Ysella listened while Roddek explained in depth, and more depth.

When the older man finished, he looked to Ysella. "What are your thoughts?"

"I have a few questions. First, have you been irrigating every year since the fall of Aloor? And second, have you filed a declaration of appropriation to document your rights?"

"A declaration of appropriation? Why would we need that? We've used the stream for years. It runs right through the vineyards."

Ysella managed not to wince. "Let me explain. Silverhills was part of Aloor. Water law in Aloor was based on the riparian law, where the property owner controls the rights to use water flowing through his land.

Water law in Guldor is based on prior appropriation, where the first beneficial use of water is the most senior right. Either way, you'd seem to have the rights. But . . . to assure those rights, after the conquest of Aloor, landowners needed to file a declaration of appropriation with the Imperial Administrator of Agriculture or risk losing those rights. Because you didn't file, the tannery is claiming you lost the rights. However, since the winery exercised those rights, it's clear that you never abandoned or relinquished them. To clarify the situation, hopefully without additional legal action, you can still file the declaration, *but* often the agricultural administrator has imposed a fine for failure to file in a timely manner. It's possible that the tannery will contest the filing, but past legal actions would support your rights."

"No one told me anything about that," protested Roddek.

"The requirement was imposed in 773, two years after the fall of Aloor. It's been in effect ever since."

"Why didn't anyone know?"

"Perhaps they did, but never did anything because no one said anything. I would file the declaration as soon as possible, using a water legalist in Silverhills, just to forestall action to limit your rights by the tannery."

"Couldn't the Waterways Committee pass a law?"

"They did. That's why landowners in Aloor didn't immediately lose their rights."

"So I have to file this . . . declaration to retain something that the winery already had, but might lose?"

"If you don't, sooner or later, the questions of who owns what rights will end up before the Justiciary. That would be more expensive, and you might lose some of those water rights, on the grounds that you effectively relinquished control."

"Can't you do that for me?"

Ysella shook his head. "I don't have all the legal and other information. Also, it has to be filed in Silverhills, preferably quietly." *If I filed it, it would likely encourage the tannery to drag out legal proceedings.*

"More bother," snorted Roddek. "I'm not upset with you, Dominic. I just don't understand why Arturo or his father didn't take care of this."

"I hate to say this, but maybe they didn't get around to it, and then figured that it didn't matter. That happens more often than it should."

Roddek shook his head. "I appreciate your clarifying the situation." He looked to his right, then said, "We're done here, Alaan. Dominic's been very helpful. The rest is unhappily up to me and to . . . Arturo."

Ysella had the feeling that Roddek had wanted to use a few more-than-derogatory terms in referring to Arturo, who was likely a relative.

Roddek stood and walked toward the hallway. "I need a few moments."

"Take your time," replied Escalante as he entered the parlor.

Ysella started to stand, but the older councilor gestured for him to keep his seat, then took the armchair Roddek had vacated. "It seems we're both seeking your advice. I assume you saw the newssheet story about my cousin Jaahn."

"I read the article. I wondered if there was a relationship."

"When the matter came up, my initial reaction was to tell Symeon, since he was chair of the Military Affairs Committee, and I knew he'd oppose favorable treatment for anyone. Then Symeon was killed, and that left me and Alaaxi as the senior members of the committee. Iustaan has already appointed me chair, although he didn't want to make it public so soon after Symeon's death."

"And your cousin and your family are exerting pressure?"

"Of course. Doesn't family always get involved?"

Where landor families are involved, invariably. "They try, at times."

"I'd welcome your thoughts on the matter."

"Would your family want you to commit suicide?" asked Ysella. "I mean, if you pressured the Navy not to go after your cousin so that he can extort more from the Navy—and that's the way the newssheets will print it—how exactly will the Imperador react when he's already furious with the committee?"

"You think the newssheets really would?"

"They've asked me about it, and one newshawk asked why you wouldn't talk to him."

"That had to be Reimer Daarkyn." Escalante shook his head. "I'm not sure Jaahn would care that much about my fate, but there's the rest of the family."

"Right now, with the Imperador the way he is, nothing can be done about that contract, even if there is some sort of price-increase language."

"That's unfair, and we both know that, Dominic."

"Unless and until the Council changes the Establishment Act and the Imperador agrees, these sorts of things will continue."

"That will never happen."

"Never say 'never.'" Ysella laughed softly. "Always say 'almost never.' It's much safer."

"I suppose you're right."

"My oldest brother said I'd never be a councilor. I wagered with him. It cost him two hundred marks." And those two hundred marks had given Ysella a start toward saving enough to start buying undervalued properties in Machtarn.

"Remind me not to wager against you." Escalante stood.

So did Ysella.

"Thank you for talking to Antonan. I didn't realize some of what you told him. Besides, I knew he'd listen more to you."

While Ysella wasn't close to being an empath, he'd suspected that Escalante might have been listening. "Sometimes, it's useful to enlist authority, even when you know they'll say something similar to what you would have."

"Especially when they've known you for a long time," replied Escalante dryly. "I won't keep you longer. You've been thoughtful and helpful."

"Good fortune with the committee and the Imperador."

"I'll need it." Escalante turned. "I'll get a lantern and walk you out to the stable."

"Thank you."

After walking to the stable and mounting Jaster, as Ysella rode back toward his own house, he pondered why he'd initially been invited. Most likely to fill out the table and allow the Escalantes to say that they'd introduced Mystera to one of the most eligible bachelors in Machtarn. The invitation had been sent before Ritter and Ritten Roddek had arrived, and Ysella strongly doubted that Roddek would have written in detail about his water-rights problem. *Although he might have asked if Alaan knew anyone conversant in water law.*

That all fit, but whether it was totally correct, Ysella doubted he'd ever know.

10

ALTHOUGH Ysella half expected a further outburst from the Palace, the next five days were uneventful, which allowed him to take possession of his latest property and make preparations for his forthcoming journey to Aloor.

On Furdi morning of the last week of the year, however, as he ate breakfast and sipped his café, he wondered what awaited him in Aloor.

After breakfast, Ysella left the house and headed toward the stable under high dark gray clouds and a chill, if light, wind. In the distance to the northeast, he actually saw sunlight, suggesting that the clouds might clear. In turn, that raised the possibility that he wouldn't have to have Caastyn drive the chaise through snow to the Imperador's Yearend Ball . . . as had happened the previous year.

When Ysella reached the Council stables, he saw that only a few councilors had bothered to show up, or at least not early. He let one of the ostlers stable Jaster, then made his way to his office.

"Good morning, Lyaard, Paatyr. It'll be another short day today, so you can both get an early start on the Yearend holiday, and remember, you also have Unadi off."

"You're still leaving on Duadi, sir?" asked the senior clerk.

"Unless it snows heavily." Ysella paused. "Is there anything . . . ?"

"Several messages and some letters. The *Tribune* came early, and it's on your desk."

"Thank you. I'll take a look and hope there aren't any problems that can't wait." There usually weren't so late in the year, but given the Imperador's actions, Ysella wasn't assuming that past patterns would hold.

First, after doffing his heavy winter riding coat and hanging it up, he picked up the newssheet, immediately taking in the lead story.

> Yesterday, First Marshal Solatiem announced that during the fourth week of Fallend, naval marines from three Guldoran frigates and two shallow-draft sloops attacked a series of islands off the Cataran Delta northwest of Port Lenfer and burned ten small vessels, killing scores of pirates, and capturing the rest. He also promised that the Navy would "continue until we've removed all the pirates."

The Grande Duce of Atacama protested the invasion of Atacaman territory and declared that the "Guldoran predators will pay more dearly than they can imagine..."

The rest of the article summarized the history of intermittent attacks and counterattacks that had begun with the Atacaman raid on Zeiryn ten years earlier, but did not provide any update on the damage to the *Paelart*.

Was it so badly damaged that no one can say... or does the Imperador not want any mention of partial Atacaman success?

Ysella's other concern, not that he could do anything about it, was the Imperador's reaction to the newssheet's not quite pointed reference to the success of frigates and smaller ships in dealing with the Atacaman pirates. That was the newssheet's immediate problem, not the Council's, but the more the Imperador pressured the newssheet, the harder it became to find out even general information.

He set aside the newssheet and picked up the first message, from Alaan Escalante, then opened it and began to read.

> *Dominic—*
> *I must apologize for my tardiness in thanking you for your tactful handing of the water law matter with Ritter Roddek. I suspect he also conferred with other legalists, because he made a comment about your knowing the law well before he left yesterday. He's likely going to have either very cold or very warm conversations with certain relations.*

Ysella nodded. Alaan hadn't wanted to write until he was certain of Roddek's reaction to the advice, but then, in Alaan's position, Ysella would have waited as well.

> *Your other suggestions were most helpful, particularly given the apparent escalation of hostilities in the Gulf of Nordum.*
> *If we don't see you at the ball, we both wish you a safe and uneventful trip to Aloor.*

Ysella slipped the note into his leather case, since it would go into a file in his study at home. He looked to the next envelope, from the Premier, which held a copy of a notice to all councilors announcing the appointment of Alaan Escalante as chairman of the Military Affairs Committee. Ysella definitely didn't envy Escalante's having to attend the Yearend Ball immediately after the controversy over first-rate ships of the line. But then, the ball was seldom enjoyable for councilors, necessary as attendance was.

He turned to the first letter in the short stack in his in-box, opening and reading it.

> *Councilor Ysella—*
> *We have received word that the appropriations measure approved by the Imperador does not contain funding adequate to remediate fully the shallowing of the upper reaches of the Khulor River in order to return it to its previous depths.*
> *We had hoped that, with your understanding of the needs of those along the river and your expertise in waterways, you would have been able to obtain the necessary funding. In this regard, I would like to request that when you return to Aloor in Winterfirst you meet with those of us who will suffer from that lack of funding . . .*

The rest of the letter presented in great and unnecessary detail all the reasons why and to what extent the landholders of Aloor, Khuld, Daal, Nuile, and Sudaen would be disadvantaged and suffer financial privation because of the failure of the Council to appropriate the requisite funds to remediate the shallowing of the upper reaches of the river.

The signature was that of Cyraen Presswyrth, on behalf of the affected landholders.

Ysella shook his head. *Almost fifty years after the fall of Aloor, some of them are acting as if nothing has changed.*

Because he knew that he needed to cool down before thinking about a response, he set the letter aside and picked up the next one. Unfortunately, it was on the same subject . . . as were the following four . . . and all were postmarked with the same date—as if they all wanted to make sure he met with them or perhaps to emphasize their point.

The seventh letter contained yet another "anonymous" message demanding that he—and the Council—stop bending over backward to accommodate an increasingly mad and senile Imperador.

The eighth letter wanted to know if the Imperial Waterways administrator had any plans for rebuilding the abandoned tin-mining docks on the north branch of the Khulor River. That didn't make much sense to Ysella, given that the mines had been abandoned long before the fall of Aloor and the north branch had silted up so much that even small flatboats had trouble during the spring runoff.

Setting aside the last letter, Ysella took out paper and pen and began to write notes for the reply to the Presswyrth letter agreeing to a meeting.

When he finished, he carried the letters and notes out to Khaard. "Draft responses to these five based on the notes. File the anonymous letter with the others, and draft a response to the last one saying that I haven't heard of any plans to replace the old docks, and that it would appear unlikely at this time because the north branch is no longer navigable . . ."

Once Ysella finished his instructions, he said, "I'm going to see if Councilor Caanard is available. I'll be back after that to review and sign the letters."

"Yes, sir."

Ysella walked from the office, hoping Caanard was in and, as chair of the Foreign Affairs Committee, might have some insight on various matters. He made his way down to the first level and almost to the end of the corridor, where he entered Caanard's office.

"Is the councilor in?"

Even before the sole clerk in the outer office could reply, Caanard stepped out of the personal office. "I thought I heard a familiar voice. Come on in."

After following Caanard, Ysella closed the door and took the chair across the desk from the older councilor. "I was wondering if you'd heard anything more about matters with Atacama than appeared in this morning's newssheet."

"A bit more, but nothing of substance."

"Is it likely we'll lose the First Marshal over his mentioning frigates and sloops?"

"These days, one can never say definitively, but I'd judge not. The good Marshal Solatiem only mentioned them and did not extol their comparative worth." Caanard chuckled.

"Have you heard anything from any of the scattered kingdoms of the Teknold Confederacy?"

"Seeing as either Guldor or Atacama could wipe out what they call fleets without any difficulty, none of them will take sides. The Polidorans couldn't care less." Caanard's tone suggested that he didn't much care, either.

"With all the difficulty with Atacama, will we see any envoys at the ball?"

"From the Confederacy and the Polidoran Comity, and, of course, from Argental. That's Ramon Hekkaad. Have you met him?"

"Only briefly."

"He's been posted here for a little less than two years. Very bright and has interesting observations. He will make jokes about what we call winter. There's no envoy from Atacama, but we haven't had one since Zeiryn."

"I've already gotten letters protesting the appropriations. What about you?" asked Ysella.

"A score already, but my district is only a day away by post, two at most. You'll likely get more."

"I'll be gone before some of them arrive . . . or they may accost me when I get to Aloor."

"I've noticed one thing about you, Dominic. I hope I don't offend you, but I've wondered. You always say 'Aloor.' You never say 'home.'"

Ysella laughed softly. "I have a hard time with that."

Caanard nodded. "We all have our peculiarities. I always talk about our house, whether it's the one in Point Larmat or the one here. I picked that up from Patrice." He paused. "I hope you'll ask her to dance at least once."

Ysella smiled. "I can do that." He understood that Caanard didn't want to say more about envoys, politics, or the Imperador, and he stood to leave. "I'll see you at the ball."

"Until then," replied Caanard.

Ysella walked back to his office, where he read over the responses that Khaard and Jaasn had prepared. He signed most, but added postscripts to two before returning them to the clerks. Then he looked at the committee schedule, which showed no hearings or meetings until after the first two weeks of Winterend, when the Council resumed its normal schedule.

After leaving the Council Hall at half past second bell, Ysella reached his house just after third bell and reined up outside the stable. Jaster gave a snort, and released a small white cloud.

As Ysella dismounted, Caastyn appeared. "You're early. Any problems?"

"No more than usual. I would like to spar now," said Ysella. "That is, after I take care of Jaster. Would that be inconvenient, rather than later?"

"No, sir. There's nothing pressing."

"You're sure?"

Caastyn grinned. "I might have a better chance with you earlier. I'll get the blades and jackets ready."

Once Ysella finished with Jaster and settled the gelding into his stall, he went to the house and shed his winter riding jacket and his suit jacket, then walked back to the arms and exercise room next to the stable. There he donned the padded and selectively armored jacket, while Caastyn pulled on one similar. Then the two squared off.

"You first, tonight," Ysella declared.

Caastyn raised his blade, feinted, then back-cut, but Ysella anticipated and parried the cut, but had to jump back as he beat down Caastyn's blade.

Caastyn recovered and attacked low, but Ysella slid the other's blade away from his body, ignored the apparent opening that had to be a trap, then angled his own blade toward Caastyn's knee, but Caastyn blocked the slash and countered.

Ysella backed off and circled to the left, feinted, then came in on a low thrust.

Caastyn slipped the blade, and Ysella had to back off before Caastyn could strike.

After a third of a bell's worth of attacks, counterattacks, feints, false feints, blocks, and parries, Ysella was breathing harder than he would have liked and sweating heavily. He stepped back and said, "I think that's enough."

"You were getting sloppy at the end," said Caastyn.

"I know. That's why I called an end." Ysella grinned. "I don't want any severe bruises before going to the Yearend Ball tomorrow night."

"You don't think you'll need arms at the ball, do you?" asked Caastyn, clearly jesting.

"Only for dancing," replied Ysella, "but there's always the possibility of brigands on the drive back from the Palace. You'll have the small crossbows in place, I trust?"

"I will, and a spear, just in case."

"I'll have to leave my gladius with you in the chaise, as usual."

"You always bring it when you ride in the chaise, but not when you ride alone."

"It's too much of a temptation and an invitation when I'm alone, and Jaster can get me away from using a blade. In the chaise, and not on my hip, it's only a defensive weapon."

"For a councilor, I suppose, that's for the best. For someone who never wants to use a blade, you put in a lot of effort making sure you can."

"There's always the possibility that I could be wrong, and it becomes necessary," said Ysella with a wry smile, blotting his forehead with the back of his sleeve. "I'll see you at dinner."

He headed into the house to cool down and wash up.

11

ON Findi evening, the last evening of the year 819, Caastyn and Ysella left the house at a third after sixth bell, the last bell of day, with Caastyn driving the chaise. Under his heavy and warm black overcoat, Ysella wore deep blue formalwear, edged in dark gray, with a matching cravat. The Imperador's Yearend Ball began officially at the first bell of evening, but given all the coaches and carriages, driving the more than two milles to the Palace would take close to a bell, not considering possible delays at the gates and the entry to the Palace.

While highwaymen usually didn't appear within Machtarn, Caastyn had both small crossbows already cocked in their brackets on the dashboard below the short spear, and he wore the gladius he'd used as an army squad leader. Ysella's gladius was in its scabbard behind his boots on the chaise floor.

They didn't encounter other carriages until they neared the Palace gates, where they halted behind a silver-trimmed carriage with a pair of footmen on the rear stand. As the large carriage moved through the gates, Caastyn eased the chaise forward to where the guards waited.

"Sir?" asked the Palace guard.

Ysella leaned forward and tendered the invitation.

The guard read it, returned it, and said, "Welcome to the Palace, sir," then added to Caastyn, "After you drop off the Ritter at the entrance, chaises go to the left, carriages to the right. There are hitching rails and warming stoves in both places." The guard's voice already sounded hoarse.

"Thank you," replied Ysella.

Once Caastyn had the chaise moving up the stone road toward the Palace, he suggested, "You might look for some eligible ladies this year. Not that you will, sir, but you're not getting any younger."

"There aren't that many."

"The *Tribune* said the Imperador's youngest daughter was coming out at the Yearend Ball."

"No matter how attractive she is, that's one young lady to avoid."

"If you wed her . . ."

"Relationships mean nothing to the Imperador or the Heir. Remember, he's the second Heir. His older brother had a hunting accident after he suggested that it was time for Laureous to step down, and the death of his youngest son has never been adequately explained." Ysella suspected that the first Heir had done more than talk, but no one he knew had said anything.

"It could be he's mellowed."

"He'd have to melt, and I don't see that happening." Ysella laughed cynically.

"Stranger things have happened, sir."

"True, but not usually for the better."

When the chaise neared the formal entrance to the Palace, Caastyn again slowed the chaise to wait for the carriages ahead to discharge their occupants before he could come to a halt.

Ysella turned to Caastyn. "I'll likely send for you around third evening bell."

"Don't leave early for me, sir . . . not if you find the lady you think you won't."

"I'll keep that in mind, but I don't want Gerdina worrying about you."

"She'd have my head, sir, if I kept you from the right young lady."

"I'll see you around third bell," Ysella repeated dryly before carefully stepping from the chaise. He followed the couple ahead up the marble steps to the polished bronze doors, past the guards and into the entry rotunda, where an attendant in the darker red of Imperial service staff asked his name and took his overcoat.

From there Ysella made his way to the ballroom, where he was announced by a functionary with a booming voice that was still lost in the hubbub of conversation.

Ysella smiled and glanced to the north side of the ballroom at the dais and throne for the Imperador, and the lesser throne for the Imperadora. He found a sideboard, asked for and received a glass of Silverhills red, then slowly made his way across the ballroom looking from small group to small group, while the musicians played occasional music, waiting until the Imperador—or the Heir—appeared to signal that the dancing could begin.

While Ysella immediately saw several older councilors, he decided against joining them. When he turned he found Alaaxi Baertyl moving toward him, accompanied by his wife Junae, whose almost filmy headscarf, now worn over her shoulders, matched perfectly the teal of her dress.

"You're easy to pick out, Dominic," declared Alaaxi, "in the deep blue."

"As are you, Alaaxi, especially given your lovely wife." Ysella lifted his wineglass slightly in greeting.

"You're far too charitable, Dominic," replied Junae warmly, "but I appreciate the flattery."

"It's not flattery," replied Ysella, with a smile, because Junae was indeed attractive, although she was at least a decade older than Ysella, with striking silver-white hair, a flawless complexion, and clear blue eyes.

"You're kind."

"I'm afraid that's an opinion not held by some," Ysella replied, holding the glass from which he'd drink little. "As you know, I'm known for being less diplomatic than I might be."

"You always say that, Dominic, but you're known for your tact."

"Only by those who don't know me that well."

"A question, Dominic, before we're interrupted," said Alaaxi, easing closer. "Why do you think the Premier picked Alaan Escalante over me?"

"I honestly don't know." *I suspect, but don't absolutely know.*

"What are your feelings about it?"

"My feelings have little impact on Iustaan. I suspect one reason might be the problem with the tin contracts between Alaan's cousin Jaahn and the Navy."

"What does that have to do with it?" asked Alaaxi sharply.

"The appointment makes it impossible for Alaan to intercede on Jaahn and his family's behalf, because, if he does, the *Tribune* will print it and the Imperador will know immediately." All of which was true, but likely not the reason why Detruro chose Escalante over Baertyl.

Alaaxi frowned.

Junae glanced at Ysella with a trace of a sad smile. "You explain so well, Dominic. I always appreciate your thoughtfulness."

"I don't know that I'm always correct, but I do my best, Junae."

"Councilor Ysella," intruded another voice, "if I might have a moment?"

"Excuse me," said Ysella politely before turning to a stocky, but not heavyset, dark-haired man, in white formalwear, with the red and gold bands on the jacket cuffs that designated Imperial functionaries. A middle-aged woman also in white with hair too black to be entirely natural accompanied the Imperial Waterways administrator. "Sr. Tyresis, a pleasure to see you once more."

"Oh," said Tyresis, "might I introduce Sra. Kaechar. She's on the Imperador's staff."

"You might." Ysella inclined his head to Kaechar. "My pleasure."

Attractive as the middle-aged woman was, Ysella had no doubt she was a strong empath, given the emotional pressure of friendliness and charm she doubtless projected, feelings that he'd never been able to sense. Her presence meant Tyresis had both requests and questions and wanted to determine Ysella's truthfulness. Unfortunately, she might also discover Ysella's immunity to empaths, unless Ysella was very, very careful in reading her face.

"I understand that you were most instrumental," began Tyresis, "in keeping the Waterways appropriation very close to the Imperador's recommendation."

"Your recommendation, I believe," replied Ysella.

"The Imperador was kind enough to consider my recommendation, although the final version was his."

"It always is," returned Ysella.

"How is it that you manage to meet the recommendations, or at least come far closer than other committee chairmen?"

"I understand that the Imperador is most particular and that it's best to understand that it's unwise to cross him." Ysella offered a smile he hoped was understanding.

"Most prudent. Would that others were more prudent."

"In general," replied Ysella cautiously, "from what I've seen, most councilors tend to be prudent, and all are very devoted to keeping Guldor strong and healthy."

"Different councilors likely have differing definitions of what is meant by strong and healthy."

Ysella managed a chuckle. "All men have slightly different understandings of quite a few words."

Sra. Kaechar nodded politely.

Abruptly, Tyresis asked, "You're one of the few councilors who's not married, aren't you?"

For a moment, the question disconcerted Ysella, but he said, "So far as I know, the only ones I'm certain aren't married are me and the Premier. He was widowed by the red pox."

"On another matter . . . Did you ever meet the late Fleet Marshal?"

"I wouldn't have known him if he were standing next to you," replied Ysella, not in the slightest disconcerted by the second question, given how much he'd wondered about Haarwyk.

"Did he ever meet with Symeon Daenyld?"

"I have no idea. I know that Councilor Daenyld requested information, as part of his duties as chair of the Military Affairs Committee."

Tyresis nodded. "Thank you, Councilor. I appreciate your forthrightness."

Ysella nodded to the empath. "A pleasure to meet you, Sra. Kaechar."

Kaechar merely nodded in return before the two turned and moved away.

Ysella took the slightest sip of the Silverhills red, his first, in fact, and glanced around the ballroom.

At that moment, a fanfare Ysella immediately recognized as "The Triumph of the Imperador" sounded through the ballroom. Conversations came to an immediate halt as the Imperador and Imperadora entered the ballroom and made their way to the throne dais. The Heir and his wife the Princesa followed. Last came a statuesque redhead in a dark green gown, with a headscarf of the same shade across her shoulders, escorted by a senior naval officer, a commander. She had to be Delehya, although she was never referred to as a princesa, only as Lady Delehya, because she was the only child of the Imperador's second wife, and thus not in the line of succession.

Even at a distance, Ysella could see that she was exceedingly attractive. With an amused smile, he shook his head.

As soon as the Imperador seated himself on his throne, he gestured, and the musical ensemble began to play—music suitable to a courteille. In moments, the center of the ballroom filled with dancers, while those individuals who wanted to continue conversing moved closer to the walls and the various sideboards.

To his left, past several senior naval officers and their wives, Ysella caught sight of a stocky man in a silver uniform accompanied by a woman in a formal tunic and trousers of the same color and shade, with no trace of a headscarf. With a smile, Ysella made his way to the older couple who could only have been Ramon and Leona Hekkaad—the Argenti envoy to Guldor and his wife. Both were pale-skinned like all Argenti, possibly the result of thousands of years of living on a vast expanse of forest and alpine meadows close to a mille and a half higher than most of Guldor. Icy peaks rose another two milles above their habitable area, mountains that formed the northern border of Guldor and the southern border of Argental, a land that remained largely mysterious to most in Guldor, certainly to Ysella.

"Good evening, Ramon, Leona. How are you on this chilly evening?"

"Quite comfortable, Councilor," replied Leona. "Your chilly weather is springlike for me. Not so much for Ramon, as you know."

Ysella did, having heard at the previous Yearend Ball the envoy's tale of barely surviving a silverstorm as a child, an event he claimed left him feeling chilled for the rest of his life, and something Ramon's grown children found strange, if not bewildering.

"I'm glad to see you here, Ritter," said Ramon, looking squarely and forthrightly at Ysella. "Apparently, being a committee chairman is more dangerous than I realized."

"If one doesn't heed the Imperador's recommendations, it can be. You're fortunate in Argental not to be subject to the power of a single individual."

"There is that," replied the envoy, taking a sip of white wine, glancing sideways toward his wife for but a moment. "But the Assembly never reaches decisions quickly."

"Is it rancorous?"

"Yes, but that rancor is largely verbal. We've observed what happens in other lands."

"Speaking of other lands, have you heard anything interesting about the Grande Duce?"

Ramon laughed, but not loudly. "Hardly. The Grande Duce sent our envoy back to Cimaguile with a message that no replacement was welcome. I found out yesterday."

"If I might ask, what was the rationale? Or was any announced?"

"Our envoy declined to comment negatively on the Imperador of Guldor and said that envoys were there to listen and convey information, not to comment on rulers."

"That sounds eminently reasonable to me."

"Rulers, even assemblies, often have a different view of what might be reasonable," said Ramon, but there was a hint of a smile at the corner of his lips and in his eyes.

"That's true of councilors as well," replied Ysella. "We just don't have as much power."

"You didn't escort anyone to this ball or the last," observed Leona.

"I've never married, but if you have an unmarried sister . . ." Ysella said suggestively as he waggled his eyebrows flirtatiously.

"Alas, Councilor, I only have brothers."

"Just my fortune," replied Ysella mournfully, before flashing a quick grin.

Leona smiled in return.

Ramon shook his head, then said, "We mustn't keep you, but it was good to see you again."

As the Argenti envoy eased away, Ysella turned to see Lady Delehya leave the dais with an older naval officer, apparently to dance, and he wondered if that was a way of indicating that Delehya would be dancing . . . or if the Imperador was choosing her dance partners.

Ysella shook his head and turned, then saw Alaan Escalante, standing with two other councilors and their wives, beckon to him. When Ysella neared the group, he recognized the two councilors as Stron Thaalyr and Georg Raathan. He also saw that the three wives were in a slightly separate group.

"I saw you talking with some Imperial functionary earlier," declared Thaalyr.

"Sr. Tyresis, the Waterways Administrator."

"Government business, at the ball?" asked Georg Raathan genially. "How novel."

"Someone looking at us might get that impression as well," replied Ysella.

Escalante smiled. "Four Council committee chairs, and all landors. That might suggest something to the conspiracy-minded."

"Conspiracies at a ball, though?" asked Thaalyr.

"A good place to meet, actually," declared Ysella humorously. "We can all protest we never wanted to be here—"

"But Khacya did," interjected Raathan. "I don't know about your wives."

Thaalyr and Escalante exchanged wry smiles.

"Exactly," said Raathan.

"Dominic doesn't have that particular worry," commented Alaan Escalante.

"Not yet, anyway," added Raathan.

Amaelya Escalante turned and said with an amused smile, "Blaming the women, as usual."

Ysella kept his laugh to himself and slipped away as the other two women joined Amaelya and their husbands. After leaving the group, he handed his still nearly full wineglass to a Palace attendant collecting glasses with a tray.

Ysella moved along the area between those dancing and those conversing until he saw the Premier talking with Sammal Haafel and Haanara. He moved closer.

"Good evening, Dominic." Detruro's voice was pleasant, but not inviting.

"The same to you."

"You ought to have a lady with you, Dominic," declared Sammal, "even if you didn't seem that interested in the young thing at Alaan's the other night."

"She wasn't Dominic's type," said Haanara. "I could see that from the beginning. He was kind and polite, and she wasn't attracted in the slightest."

"You hear anything interesting this evening?" asked Sammal unabashedly.

"I did." Ysella turned slightly to include Detruro. "For what it's worth, I was talking with Ramon Hekkaad, the Argenti envoy . . ."

"Oh?" asked Sammal.

"You may have heard, but . . ." Ysella explained about the expulsion of the Argenti envoy to Atacama.

"No . . . I hadn't heard that," admitted Detruro. "It's good to know. Thank you."

"I saw the Imperador's daughter dancing . . ." ventured Ysella.

"The Imperador will likely choose with whom she dances," said Detruro, "although it's said she has a mind of her own, which may explain a few rumors."

"Rumors?" asked Sammal.

"Scurrilous gossip, not worth repeating," said Detruro coldly.

"Quite good-looking," said Haanara quickly. "She must get the looks from her mother."

"If the official portraits are remotely close to accurate," replied Detruro, "Laureous was rather handsome as a young man."

"Couldn't tell it now," murmured Haanara.

"None of us here look as good as we once did, except for Dominic," declared Sammal, "and his time will come, just like everyone else's."

Ysella caught the slight stiffening in Detruro's posture and said, "Sometimes, I feel like it's already come."

"You're still young," insisted Haanara.

"Only comparatively." Ysella nodded to Detruro. "I won't keep you. I thought you should know."

He eased away, wondering at Detruro's cutting off talk of the rumors when he saw one of the Imperador's functionaries in white moving toward him. As she approached, he realized it was Sra. Kaechar and inclined his head politely.

"The Imperador would like to see you, Councilor. If you'd accompany me?"

"Of course." Ysella couldn't help but wonder what he'd done to interest the Imperador, concerned that at present any attention from anywhere in the Palace was worrisome, especially after his words about the appropriations had appeared in the *Tribune*.

Kaechar led the way along the edge of the dancing area toward the dais.

Ysella saw Ahslem Staeryt, who was dancing with his wife, look in his direction and half stumble. *He knows something, and it's not good.*

"Your Highness, Councilor Ysella," said Kaechar evenly, inclining her head and stepping back, leaving Ysella looking up at the Imperador, a gaunt-faced and rail-thin figure, with short-cut and sparse silver hair, wearing a gold military-style jacket and trousers.

"At least you've done something besides squat on your family lands," said Laureous.

"Yes, Your Highness."

"And you actually followed my recommendations."

"I read them carefully, sir."

"One of the few who did, apparently." Laureous coughed several times, cleared his throat, then went on. "With your background, I assume you dance at least adequately."

"Yes, Your Highness."

"Excellent. In a dance or so, I'd like you to dance one dance with my daughter Delehya. That way, she can't say I've limited her partners to ineligible men or those without stature. You can wait at the side of the dais." The Imperador's sardonic laugh was hoarse and rattling.

Ysella inclined his head respectfully, then moved away slightly.

The Imperador turned to the red-haired Imperadora and murmured something Ysella didn't catch. The Imperadora replied, and Ysella thought she said "slight improvement."

Before he moved away, Ysella did catch a few of Laureous's words in reply. ". . . only other royal blood in Guldor . . ." He managed not to wince, but was grateful that he'd managed not to anger the Imperador.

"A pleasure to see you here, Councilor Ysella," said a husky man in white formalwear with an overlarge midsection standing near the end of the dais.

Belatedly, Ysella recognized Taeryl Laergaan, the Imperial Administrator of Commerce. "While it's been some time since we last met, I'm glad to see that you're looking well, Administrator Laergaan." As he spoke, Ysella kept one eye on the dance floor, not wanting to be caught flat-footed when the music paused and Lady Delehya returned to change partners.

"The same to you, Councilor. I see that you've continued to increase your holdings in the harbor area."

"Slightly," replied Ysella, wondering why Laergaan was taking an interest in Ysella's modest properties. "Land and buildings tend to be more permanent than a councilor's seat."

Laergaan laughed, a low rumble. "Well said . . . and too true."

The man to whom Laergaan had been previously talking stepped forward slightly. "We haven't met. Carsius Zaenn."

"He's the new Natural Resources Administrator," explained Laergaan.

"I'd like a moment with you," said Zaenn, "but I see that will have to wait."

Ysella realized that the music had paused, and that a tall man he didn't recognize was escorting Delehya back to the dais.

From Ysella's left, Kaechar said, "If you would, Counselor Ysella."

As the older and taller man stepped aside, Ysella moved forward and inclined his head. "Lady Delehya, Councilor Dominic Mikail Ysella, at your service."

"The pretender to the throne of Aloor?" Delehya's voice was only slightly sultry and held a hint of amusement as she looked at him assessingly, her eyes almost even with Ysella's.

"The same family, Lady, but the pretender would be my father or, in time, my eldest brother. I'm a third son, and just a councilor and a legalist." As the music began, which Ysella recognized as a waltz, he asked, "Would you care to dance?"

"Do we have any choice, Dominic?"

"Not according to your father, but I still would ask."

"I thank you for that." She slipped into his arms.

Ysella was careful to maintain proper positioning as he guided her across the marble floor.

"You know," she said within moments, "you're the youngest man with whom I've danced, and the best dancer."

As she spoke, Ysella smiled, taking in her almost studied indifference. "There might be a slight truth to both, but . . . but only slightly, as we both know, if for different reasons, especially since you're more persuasive than just through your words or obvious femininity." While that was a guess, it wasn't much of one.

Delehya stiffened, slightly, and only for a moment. "More persuasive? Different reasons? I don't know you at all."

"You know what I mean. You also know that we both come from a regal line and that neither of us can nor will rule. We'll only succeed through other means."

"Is that an indirect attempt at proposing or opening the door to negotiations?" Delehya's tone was not only humorous, but teasing.

"I'm not, attractive as you are. That wouldn't be a good idea for either of us. It might work if I were premier and wealthy, but I'm neither. I'm not the one who could give you anything close to what you desire," he said quietly, "except a pleasant dance and friendship. Besides, you're looking for as much independence as possible."

She managed the hint of a shrug without affecting her dancing. After several long moments, she said, "You're different."

"So are you. I doubt your father knows how different." Ysella paused. "You liked Marshal Haarwyk, didn't you?"

"He was a good man. I learned a great deal from him in the last year or so . . . and not in the way some of the scandalsheets imply."

Scandalsheets? About the rumors Maatrak and Detruro won't discuss? "I didn't know him, but I had the impression that he was most honorable."

"Too honest and too good. Perhaps learning from good men is dangerous."

"Oh?" asked Ysella.

"If you care in the slightest, that's a problem."

In your family, it could be deadly. "You're rather cynical for a lady so young."

"Wouldn't you . . ." Delehya broke off her words and laughed softly, then saying, "But you are, aren't you, behind that practiced charm? And that's why you're not married?"

"Partly, if in a different way."

Delehya smiled, almost guilelessly. "I think I'll tell my father you're nice, but not much more."

"And I'll tell everyone that you're beautiful, intelligent, and charming—and that I could never live up to what you need."

She frowned. "You mean all of that, don't you?"

"Why wouldn't I? It's true. Besides, if all that I say is true, then I never have to worry about telling lies."

"You're dangerous in a different way, Dominic."

So are you, Delehya. "As a councilor, I have little choice."

Before long, the music ended, and Ysella escorted Delehya back toward the dais, where she said softly, "I understand. Thank you, and not just for the dance."

The man waiting for the next dance with Delehya was Iustaan Detruro. After Ysella's momentary surprise, he nodded to Detruro and stepped aside, thinking that the Imperador was obviously trying to have men theoretically eligible meet Delehya under open and controlled circumstances.

Good fortune with that. From his brief encounter with Delehya, Ysella had no doubt that in any battle of wills between the Imperador and his daughter, Delehya was likely to prevail, which left Laureous with the option of removing her or limiting the damage, neither of which was likely to work out well. In addition, Laureous clearly wanted Delehya married and out of the Palace before it became known—particularly widely known—that she might be an empath, both for the Imperador's sake and Delehya's. An empath that close to the throne represented too many kinds of danger.

Without looking hurried, Ysella moved away from the Imperador and his family and made his way to a sideboard, where he asked for and received a wineglass of Silverhills red. After several sips, he set the glass down, barely touched, on the corner of another sideboard and headed toward a group of councilors and their wives, but decided against joining them when he saw Junae Baertyl watching the dancers from the edge of the open area off the dance floor. Then he looked to where Alaaxi Baertyl spoke intently to Chaarls Aashen, whose wife Bhettina was nowhere to be seen, and walked over to Junae.

"I saw you dancing with Lady Delehya," said Junae. "You made a good couple on the floor. You dance better than she does."

Ysella caught a hint of wistfulness. "I should. I'm fifteen years older."

"You're still young, Dominic."

"Since Alaaxi seems otherwise occupied, would you like to dance?"

"I would, if you wouldn't mind . . ."

"How could I mind?" Ysella extended a hand, then led her out. The music was for a slower courteille.

For a time, they danced, before Junae said, "You were kind to Alaaxi."

"He's a good man." *Honest, but not as bright as he might be.*

"Where do you think everything is going, Dominic?"

"I'm hoping that the Premier can work matters out with the Imperador."

"Is that possible?"

"I don't know. I'll help as I can."

"The Premier doesn't care that much for you."

"Does that make any difference? We need to rein in whoever is Imperador. Not too much, or we'll end up like the Grand Democracy of Teknold, or at best, the squabbling Assembly of Argental."

"You don't trust the people that much, do you?"

"I don't trust anyone or any government that doesn't have limits. People always want more than they deserve or should have." Ysella laughed quietly. "I know. With my family history, I probably shouldn't comment."

"Maybe that's why you should." Junae's voice was soft.

"Most people don't think that way."

"What did you think of Lady Delehya? Or . . . what did she think of you? Wasn't that why you were asked to dance with her?"

Ysella shook his head. "I was asked as a relatively safe gesture, so that Laureous could show how open and generous he was, even to the grandson of the last king of Aloor." He smiled wryly. "Both the Lady Delehya and I understood that."

"More likely she understood that after dancing with you."

"I may have added to her understanding. She's anything but naïve."

"How could she be? She's survived in that family."

As the music stopped. Ysella led Junae back to where he had met her. Alaaxi and Chaarls were still engaged, and neither looked toward Ysella and Junae.

"Thank you, Dominic."

"It was my pleasure." And it had been. Ysella inclined his head in considerably more than a perfunctory manner before turning away.

For the next bell or so, he wandered from group to group, chatting briefly before moving on, making sure he saw and was seen by most of the councilors present, as well as by a few Imperial Administrators. He spent a few passing and polite moments with Natural Resources Administrator Zaenn, careful to offer nothing but pleasantries.

Then he found the group where Paolo and Patrice Caanard chatted with Oskaar Klempt and Aldyn Kraagyn and their wives.

"If you wouldn't mind, Paolo," said Ysella, "I'd like to ask Patrice to dance."

"I accept," declared Patrice before her husband could respond, although his laugh was one of amusement.

As Ysella led Patrice away from the group, she said warmly, if with a hint of teasing, "I thought you'd never come."

"All good things in their time," he quipped back, taking her hand and easing them into the flow of the courteille.

"I read what you said in the newssheet. That was brave."

Not so brave, just calculated to seem so. "Not so brave as it seemed. Having me killed for saying that would have reflected badly upon the Imperador."

"With Laureous the way he is now, it was brave."

Ysella wasn't about to argue, not with a woman who was pleasant, intelligent, and wanted to dance with him. "Do you still like coming to the Yearend Ball?"

"It's not liking. It's more a macabre fascination, wondering when it all will come crashing down."

"You think so?"

"It will before long once the Heir becomes Imperador. He's far worse. Did you know that he had his wife's maid flogged to death because she wasn't deferential enough."

"How did you find that out?"

"A neighbor's cook knows the late maid's mother." Patrice paused. "Things might have been different if Aloor had been stronger."

Ysella shook his head sadly. "No. It would have been worse. Trust me."

Patrice shivered slightly. "Really?"

"I'm afraid so."

"You're destroying my illusions, Dominic." She smiled.

"Not again. I did that at the last ball."

"This time was worse. I could almost picture you on a throne."

"Not as the third son." *And not with my brothers.* "Are you going to Point Larmat for Winterfirst?"

"Where else? It's almost as bad as Machtarn." Patrice shivered.

"I think you've mentioned that. Even damper, and not any warmer."

"Aloor has to be warmer."

"It is, but it gets a great deal of cold rain, and it's small."

"I wouldn't have thought that."

"The real capital of the kingdom of Aloor was Sudaen."

"I can see that."

As the music stopped, Ysella began to escort Patrice back to her husband.

"Thank you, sweet prince." Patrice grinned. "You are a prince by blood, aren't you."

"More like a prince-pretender."

"That will do."

Once Ysella left the group, he went to look for Ahslem Staeryt, which took a while, but when he finally located Staeryt, he drew him aside.

"What is it, Dominic?"

"You looked stunned when you saw me with one of the Imperador's functionaries. Why?"

"Lorya Kaechar is one of the Imperador's strongest empaths."

While Ysella was well aware of that, he asked, "How did you know that?"

"Because empaths can't testify in open court, even as witnesses, without another empath watching and monitoring them. Kaechar often performs that function, where Imperial interests are involved."

"That never came up in any legal case I handled."

"Dominic, water law is all about documentation, precedent, records, and numbers. Who said what to whom has almost no bearing on anything."

Ysella hadn't considered that aspect of water law, but Staeryt was right, and Ysella realized that he hadn't thought it through, partly because almost all empaths were women, and few women owned land or water rights. "What else do you know about her?"

"The Imperador trusts her more than most empaths, but since he regards empaths as a necessary evil, I'm not sure how deep that trust might be." Staeryt paused. "Did you see that Iustaan danced twice with Lady Delehya?"

"I didn't. I can't say that I was looking."

"You danced with her. What's she like?"

"She is well-mannered, well-spoken, and quite aware of the charade without ever saying so. She also dances well."

"You don't have any interest?"

"I have a strong interest in self-preservation, Ahslem. The Imperador isn't about to let me any closer to Lady Delehya than when I was dancing . . . if that." Ysella smiled cynically. "Besides, there's no way I could keep her in the fashion to which she's accustomed." *Not without becoming a Palace lapdog or caged bird.*

Staeryt nodded slowly. "I hadn't thought about that. Even the Premier isn't that well-off, although I understand he does have significant lands near Enke." He raised his eyebrows inquiringly.

Ysella chose to answer the unasked question. "I have a small house in a nice area in Aloor. It has a good view of the park where the palace used to stand. Scarcely suitable for Lady Delehya."

"Just by her presence, she's going to make matters interesting."

"She already has," Ysella pointed out dryly, thinking about the newssheet story about Fleet Marshal Haarwyk's death. "Even if we don't know all the details." He smiled, then added, "I think I've greeted and mingled enough. I likely won't see you until the Council reconvenes. Survive Winterfirst as well as you can."

"You're leaving now?"

"I've done the necessary. No one will miss me. Good evening, Ahslem."

As Ysella suspected, no one else nodded to him as he made his way from the ballroom to the rotunda, where he reclaimed his heavy overcoat. From there, he asked a page to notify Caastyn, then stood inside the shimmering bronze door, waiting for the chaise.

The page returned first. "Your chaise is on the way, sir."

"Thank you."

After a bit, Ysella stepped outside the doors, but almost a sixth passed before Caastyn arrived, and Ysella walked swiftly down the steps and climbed into the chaise.

"I hope your evening wasn't that cold," Ysella said.

"Not too bad, sir. I stayed near the warming stove. They had hot cider for us. Seemed a little better than last year, but that could be that it didn't snow this year." Caastyn eased the chaise away from the Palace.

"Did you check the crossbows?"

"Yes, sir. You think . . ."

"It's unlikely, but you never know. Anyone out with a buggy or a chaise won't have that many marks or much jewelry, and anyone with marks and jewelry will be in a sturdy carriage with armed guards. Still . . . there might be a brigand desperate enough or foolhardy enough to gamble on attacking someone on Yearend, thinking they might not be careful. If anyone is out, they'll be half a mille southwest of the Palace gates. It's dark, and there are only a few buildings that far north on Imperial Boulevard. Farther south there are more people and a bit more light."

Caastyn nodded.

Ysella watched as the chaise traveled down the stone drive to the Palace gates and then turned west on the Way of Gold, before heading south on Imperial Boulevard.

Before that long, Caastyn said, "Feeling something like an empie, sir. Seems like it's in front."

"Better tie the reins now."

"Yes, sir. You sure you can handle this?" As he spoke, Caastyn looped the reins around the knob rising from the dashboard, while Ysella carefully eased one of the crossbows from its bracket, looking into the darkness, almost wishing he were an empath rather than a resistant, or possibly an isolate. He could feel the empath, and that alone indicated an attack. He could only guess at what she projected, most likely fear and coercion, not that fear would have much impact on Caastyn, but fighting off sensual coercion was harder.

"We'll see," replied Ysella. He thought the empath was ahead on the east side of the boulevard, but he couldn't determine the distance, because a strong empath could project from farther away.

"Halt the buggy!" demanded a voice out of the darkness ahead, high enough that Ysella knew the speaker was mounted.

Despite the constant pressure on the leads, the chaise horse slowed gradually. Ysella looked sideways, where Caastyn struggled to resist the empath's projected feelings.

Ysella said nothing, merely waited as the brigand rode closer until he could make out the outline of the rider against the slightly lighter night sky. As soon as he was certain, he loosed the quarrel.

"Ugghh!"

As the brigand slumped in the saddle, Ysella felt the power of the empath's emotions drain away, most likely because she had taken in the emotional jolt from the wounded brigand.

Caastyn recovered the leads and urged the horse forward at a healthy trot, while Ysella set aside the first crossbow and lifted the second, but no one else appeared or followed the chaise down Imperial Boulevard.

After a short time, Caastyn said, "Doesn't sound like anyone's following, sir. Seems stupid to attack with only the two of them."

"There might have been a third who decided it wasn't worth the risk. To them, it wouldn't have seemed like that much of a risk. A chaise usually only carries two, and coming from the Palace, they'd have figured that it would be a couple with the man driving."

"If you ever wed, sir, you'll need a good carriage and guards, I think."

"Also," Ysella admitted, "before I get too much older. This could easily have gone very badly." It also illustrated something else—that no one was patrolling Imperial Boulevard for a good mille south of the Way of

Gold. The Imperador most likely saw no need to use his guards, and the city didn't want to pay for patrollers where few lived. He would have also wagered that, whether the brigand lived or died, there'd be no mention of the attack in the newssheets.

The rest of the drive back to the house was quiet with no sight of other riders or carriages. Still . . . Ysella didn't lower his guard until he and Caastyn had the horse and chaise safely inside the stable.

After helping Caastyn and locking up the house, Ysella made his way upstairs to his bedchamber, thinking over the events of the evening.

What exactly did Laureous have in mind for Delehya? For what other reasons had Ysella been chosen to dance with her? And why had Laureous sent Lorya Kaechar to accompany Tyresis and to ask questions to which the Imperador already had the answers?

To create the impression of allowing Delehya a choice of suitors and a husband? Or trying to dispel the rumors about her and Haarwyk? Or something more and less obvious?

Ysella knew there had to be more there. He also knew he was too tired and too distracted to think clearly. Perhaps in the morning.

12

AT fourth bell of the afternoon on the ninth of Winterfirst, Ysella stepped out of the post coach in front of the town hall in Aloor, some seven long blocks from his house. He glanced back to the northeast at the stone-paved street that turned into the paved post road extending northeast all the way to Machtarn. Despite the wind, not nearly so cold as in Machtarn, there were no clouds in the pale green sky.

"Councilor Ysella, sir!" cheerfully called a voice to his left.

Ysella turned to see a young man in the driver's seat of a small closed carriage across the street. After a moment, he recognized his oldest brother's son. "Cliven!"

"Yes, sir! I'm to drive you to your place, and wait for you, and then take you to Grandsire's for dinner."

"How did you get here so soon?" asked Ysella as he lifted the single half-trunk he'd brought with him and carried it to the carriage.

"Erskaan was watching for the post coach to cross the river bridge."

Ysella set the trunk in the boot, turned, and as he climbed into the carriage asked, "How are your mother and father doing?"

"The rains washed out some of the winter wheat-corn. Father hasn't said much, but I can tell he's worried." Cliven eased the carriage forward and east from the town hall. At the next corner, he turned north, finally turning west on Second Street after two blocks.

Not quite a third of a bell passed before Cliven slowed and halted in front of the narrow two-story house that had survived the Guldoran "restructuring" of Aloor. It had taken Ysella two years to restore it and the modest carriage house after he bought it—the longest two years of his life, because he'd still been living with his parents and struggling as a legalist.

After Ysella exited the carriage, he looked up to Cliven. "I'd like to wash up, but I'll be as quick as I can."

"Take your time, sir. I don't mind waiting."

Ysella smiled as he lifted the half-trunk from the carriage boot, knowing that Cliven would find driving his uncle around far easier than the chores on the land would have been. Most people didn't consider how tiring supervising susceptibles could be, even with the help of an empath as experienced and reliable as Kyranna had proved to be.

Ysella didn't quite make it to the front door before it opened and a gray-haired woman stood there.

"It's about time you got here, Councilor."

"I thought you weren't working anymore, Perri," replied Ysella.

"Getting this small place cleaned up isn't that much work. Besides, less trouble for me to do it a few times a year than try and explain to one of the young ones."

"I do appreciate it."

"You go and get yourself cleaned up, sir. There's warm water in the pitcher by the basin. Don't want your father blaming me for making you late for dinner."

"We could always blame Cliven," replied Ysella with a grin.

"Sir, don't you be thinking that. He's got enough to worry about."

Especially his father. Not that Ysella's brother Haekaan was cruel, but sometimes he could be thoughtlessly overdemanding, and Jaeralyn was too traditional a wife to protest overtly, although Ysella suspected that she often managed to soften Haekaan behind closed doors.

"I'll hurry," Ysella promised.

In moments, he had the half-trunk up in his bedchamber—spotlessly clean and with the faintest scent of cloves and orange. The inner shutters were half open, affording a view of the park where the former palace and outbuildings had once stood.

He stripped off his travel-worn garb, washed up, and used the warm water he'd saved to shave off his travel beard. Then he dressed, in his usual deep blue woolen trousers and jacket, several shades darker than Alooran blue, with a cream cotton shirt, and the red cravat favored by many councilors.

He headed down the stairs less than two-thirds of a bell after entering the house.

Perri stood by the door. "By the Almighty, you look like a councilor now."

"Don't wait up for me," he said. "I might be back in two bells or not until close to fourth bell."

"I'll turn in when it feels right, Ritter."

Even after six years, it still felt odd when Perri used his title, given how long she'd been a family retainer. He grinned. "I'm sure you will, no matter what I say."

"Ritter Cliven'll be waiting, and so will Ritten Kaelyn."

"You're right about that." Ysella walked swiftly from the house to young Cliven and the carriage.

"That was swift."

"I don't want to keep everyone waiting."

"Father'll be late, and Uncle Taeryn won't be there. Aunt Raemyna's baby came early, just yesterday."

"I didn't know she was expecting."

"They didn't want to tell anyone outside of Aloor, after . . . everything."

That, Ysella understood, given that after her firstborn, a daughter, Raemyna had suffered three miscarriages. "The baby?"

"He's healthy."

So far . . . and Taeryn has a son, which will be fine . . . if he lives. "Have they chosen a name?" asked Ysella as he climbed into the coach.

"Not that I've heard."

Ysella nodded as he closed the coach door. After all Taeryn and Raemyna had been through in the last few days, he would have been surprised if they had come to dinner, especially since the coach trip from the lands that Taeryn managed and that Raemyna would inherit took more than a bell.

The drive from Ysella's townhome to his father's lands took less than two-thirds of a bell. It was close to sixth bell when young Cliven, his name the same as that of his grandfather, turned off the back road that eventually led to Nuile and up the drive to the hillside residence. It had once been the residence of the eldest heir to the throne of Aloor, which Ysella's father had retained, but with only a fraction of the original lands. The other princely residence—south of Aloor—had gone to Ysella's recently deceased uncle Nathanyal.

The well-maintained stone drive led to an expansive two-story redstone mansion, flanked to the north by the stables, a large barn, and a long bunkhouse for the estate workers, with a small separate cottage for Kyranna. The south side once held extensive tiered flower gardens, but those had been turned into more practical vegetable gardens well before Ysella had been born. Beyond the gardens stood the small chapel used for services by the family and holding workers.

Young Cliven brought the carriage to a halt in front of the main entrance. "Tell Father and Grandfather I'll be there as soon as I finish with the horses and carriage."

"I will, and thank you for the ride," said Ysella as he got out of the carriage.

"You're welcome, sir. We already set out the tack for your mare."

"I appreciate that . . . very much." Ysella turned and made his way up the marble walk to the heavy bronze-bound entry doors.

As he approached, a young woman in Alooran-blue livery opened one of the doors. "Good evening, Councilor."

"The same to you. You're new, aren't you?"

"Yes, sir. Since Fallfirst. I'm Maadlyn."

"I'm pleased to meet you, Maadlyn. How do you like it here?"

"It's so much better than Nuile."

Ysella knew that wasn't saying much. "I'm glad you like it."

"Everyone's in the main parlor, sir."

"Thank you."

Ysella walked through the circular receiving hall, flanked by modest studies on each side, and into the wide center hall that stretched straight back to the covered veranda, used primarily in late spring, summer, and early fall. From there he turned left through a generous archway into the large parlor.

His parents sat in the large blue armchairs that bore a slight resemblance to small thrones, while Haekaan and Jaeralyn sat in smaller armchairs to one side.

"Dominic! You don't look a day older!" exclaimed Ysella's mother, Kaelyn, turning slightly in her chair.

"He does," said his father not quite gruffly, "but you'd never admit it."

"And you'd have all of us burned to ashes before we even lived, Cliven Dumaar Ysella," replied Kaelyn warmly and with a smile.

Ysella smiled, even as he thought that could so easily have happened had his grandsire not surrendered before Guldoran troopers entered Aloor. "After this last Council session, I do feel older, but so does most of the Council."

"Being a councilor's still easier than running the lands," declared Haekaan dryly.

"Physically, yes," replied Ysella, taking the vacant armchair clearly left to him.

He'd barely seated himself before Maadlyn reappeared, carrying a tray with a single wineglass.

Red Silverhills, without a doubt. "Thank you." Ysella glanced around, noting that everyone had a glass, but he suspected Erskaan and Ennika's wine was watered, although both looked to be close to full-grown.

"How was the post coach?" asked Jaeralyn.

"Rough, as usual, but we didn't run into rain or snow."

"How long will you be in Aloor?" asked the senior Cliven, almost diffidently.

"The usual. I'll have to leave at the end of Winterfirst."

"The newssheet here said several eligible councilors and others danced with the Princesa Delehya and you were one of them. Is that so?" asked Jaeralyn.

"Well . . . first off, she's not a princesa, only a lady. The Imperador asked me to dance with her, and I did. She's attractive and intelligent, and very aware of everything around her. She dances well, and we had a short and pleasant conversation."

"You actually met with the Imperador?" asked Erskaan.

"Did he know who your family is?" asked Haekaan.

"He was quite well aware of our ancestry. He mentioned it to the Imperadora. Asking me to dance with Delehya was a gesture. An important gesture, but a gesture nonetheless. She danced twice with the Premier. Since he's widowed and fairly well-off, I understand, if she has to wed for political reasons, he'd be more likely."

"He's old," scoffed Ennika. "You're better-looking."

"Lady Delehya would be a far better political ally than a wife," replied Ysella dryly.

Both Haekaan and the senior Cliven frowned.

"Aren't you ever going to get married, Uncle Dominic?" asked Ennika.

"Possibly when I'm old and gray." Before there was another question, Ysella asked, "How is Raemyna doing? Young Cliven told me on the way out from town."

"Better than Taeryn, in some ways," replied Kaelyn. "She's got her family close. Taeryn's determined she shouldn't try to have another, no matter what."

"Rylessa's in good health, and she's a bright little girl," added Jaeralyn.

Ysella couldn't help noting that neither his father nor his brother replied to the women's observation.

At that moment, young Cliven hurried into the parlor.

"Your wine's on the table there," said Jaeralyn quietly.

"You missed Uncle Dominic telling us about when he danced with the Imperador's daughter," said Ennika.

"Is she pretty?" asked young Cliven.

"Very," said Ysella. "But she's definitely not my type."

"What is your type?" asked Jaeralyn, teasingly. "Is there a type you'd find appealing?"

"I imagine so. I haven't found her yet."

"Have you really looked?" asked Ennika.

Jaeralyn looked hard at her daughter.

"I'm sorry, Uncle Dominic. That was unpardonable."

"I accept the apology, but to be fair, it's a good question, and I probably haven't."

"I think that's enough probing of your uncle's private life," said Kaelyn, rising from her chair. "He needs to eat, and it wouldn't hurt the rest of us, either."

Because the dining room table could seat thirty people, if not more, and often had, Ysella knew, the eight sat around the upper end, with Ysella's father at the head, and his mother to his right, with Ysella to the left.

Once everyone was seated, Kaelyn nodded to her husband.

The senior Cliven cleared his throat, then said, "May the Almighty bless this food and those under this roof, in the name of the Three in One."

Kaelyn announced, "It's a simple dinner tonight because we didn't know exactly when Dominic would arrive."

Ysella let himself smile. Simple, for his mother, meant only one meat or fowl dish, but at least two kinds of potatoes, two vegetables, hot rolls, plus the appropriate condiments and sauces, and some sort of sweet dessert. The meat dish turned out to be breaded and sautéed veal served with a wine reduction, with both fried and cheesed potatoes, pole beans, and boiled spiced turnips.

"Have you done anything more to your house in Machtarn?" asked Kaelyn once everyone was served and had a chance at a few mouthfuls.

"Not since I was last here. I did buy another bit of harbor property."

"It likely cost you more than ten hectares here," said Haekaan.

"Probably," replied Ysella, "but the rents don't depend on the weather, and Machtarn is growing."

"You're not turning into a commercer, are you?" pressed Haekaan, mock-seriously. "You still won't carry a gladius."

"Not yet, and councilors can't." Besides, Ysella still remembered a certain duel.

After more light conversation, Ysella's father said, "I know that, as committee chairman, you have to balance the needs of the other members of the committee and other councilors, but . . . a number of friends are concerned . . ."

"That I didn't do enough?"

"Some have hinted that," said the elder Cliven.

"Aloor got almost no funding for waterways until I became chair. If I'd funneled a disproportionate amount into Aloor, I'd no longer be chair." *In fact, I might not be alive, given what happened to Daenyld.*

"I'll pass that along." The elder Cliven paused, then asked, "How serious is the fighting with Atacama? Do you think they'll attack Zeiryn again, or Encora?"

"I doubt it, but I don't know. The problem appears more to be small pirate ships attacking merchanters or smaller harbors. The First Marshal's reported success in wiping out the ships and pirate bases on some of the islands in the Gulf. They'll never get them all, not for years, with all the islands . . ."

By the end of the dinner and the honey-cheese dumplings, Ysella had been questioned thoroughly and eaten more than he should have. *But that's not so bad once in a while.* He wouldn't be eating with the family often, not with a ride of between half and two-thirds of a bell each way. That was fine with him.

Before he was about to leave, his father said, "If you have a little time," and gestured for Ysella to follow him into his study. The older man didn't sit down, but turned and asked, "Is it as bad in Machtarn as the newssheets say?"

"I don't know what the newssheets here say, but it's not good. Sometimes, it seems as though the Imperador is bright enough, but he goes into rages whenever things don't go his way. I'm fairly certain he had Councilor Daenyld murdered and Fleet Marshal Haarwyk poisoned."

"How was he with you? Honestly?"

"We didn't talk about anything except a brief mention that I followed his recommendations in the Waterways appropriations and my dancing with Delehya. He definitely made it clear, if indirectly, that dancing with Delehya was a gesture. I made it clear that I understood. She is very attractive, and we could be friends, at a distance, but she's the Imperador's daughter and used to far more than I'll ever be able to provide."

"Speaking of that . . ."

"Don't worry. I've been careful, and I could live on the rents from my properties alone, if I had to." Ysella smiled. "Even if I married."

"That's good. I worried . . ."

"You don't have to." *Not for that reason.*

"Are you ever coming back to Aloor . . . permanently?"

"I don't know. I still find being a councilor interesting. I seem to be good at it. Better than managing lands, probably."

"There aren't any good water legalists in Aloor since you left."

"I'll keep that in mind when the next election is called."

The older man pursed his lips, then finally said, "We worry about you being so visible in Machtarn."

"I worry, too, sometimes. But managing a holding is dangerous as well, if in a different way. Besides, I'm better suited to being a legalist and a councilor. Who could look out for Aloor better in the Council?" *Even if some of your acquaintances complain that I haven't done enough.*

"What do you think about the Heir?"

"Unless we can find a way to curb the power of the Imperador, the Heir will be worse." Ysella didn't hide the bleakness he felt.

"You'd better find a way. The Premier doesn't seem able to do so."

"He's working on it." *Just not urgently enough.*

The elder Ysella shook his head. "I won't keep you. Your mother asked me to remind you of dinner on Findi afternoon."

"I'll be here."

"We'll see you then."

After leaving his father, Ysella walked out to the stables, thinking that the dinner had been pleasant, which wasn't always the case and why he worried about dinner on Findi. *But you can always hope.*

He was still thinking over the pitfalls of family dinners as he rode back to his house in town on his chestnut mare—kept at the estate while he was in Machtarn.

13

ON Furdi morning, after Ysella finished his breakfast of ham strips, one fried egg, and a maize muffin, he stood and turned to Perri. "Thank you."

"My pleasure, sir."

Ysella handed her an envelope containing mark notes. "This should be enough for food and other things to keep the house going. Let me know before you run short."

"I can do that, sir. What time will you be wanting dinner?"

"Perri . . . you don't have to fix anything for me."

"Ritten Kaelyn sent me here to make sure you ate right and didn't have to worry about little things. I won't be disappointing her." Perri offered an amused smile. "Besides, I like being here. Less to worry about."

Ysella almost shook his head, saying instead, "Sixth bell tonight, then, but please make it a light meal."

"Yes, sir."

From Perri's enigmatic smile, Ysella knew the meal wouldn't be that light.

After he left the breakfast room, so small that it only held a table for four, chairs, and a high narrow chest, Ysella donned his winter overcoat over his suit coat and left the house, walking toward the center of the older part of Aloor.

He first stopped at the almost ancient redstone building that held the Banque of Aloor, entering through the ironbound golden oak doors that hadn't changed since he was a boy.

The single guard smiled and said, "Welcome back, Councilor."

"You're still here, Daakyn? You were talking about going to Daal."

"I went there and looked, and Selorys came here and looked, and we decided that Aloor was better for us. She's working as a seamstress for Powys. We got married at the first of Fallend. Sr. Ghawyn's looking for another guard so I can become a junior ledger clerk. I told you I was studying nights with Sr. Kuartyn."

"Congratulations!"

"We're living in the stable quarters at my folks', right now, but we figure we'll have the cottage finished by Springend."

"It sounds like you're doing well."

"Yes, sir."

Ysella smiled and walked to the teller's cage. "Good morning, Jaime. I need to make a deposit."

"Another draft on the Banque of Machtarn, sir?"

"Exactly."

"Might be near two weeks before it clears."

"That's fine. I won't be needing it before then." In fact, Ysella wouldn't be needing it at all. The marks he deposited were a quiet way of letting the banque know he was invested in Aloor. It also didn't hurt to have his funds in more than one banque.

Once Ysella had the deposit receipt, he went to one of the desks at the side. "Is Sr. Mauryn available?"

"He should be, Councilor, but let me see."

In moments, Ysella sat before the ancient but well-polished chestnut desk, across from the head of the banque. Haalas Mauryn was ten years younger than Ysella's father, and the banque had been in his family for at least four generations. Ysella had no idea how they'd managed it through the times following the fall of Aloor.

"What should I know about what's happening in Machtarn, Dominic?"

"It's not much different from last summer, except that the Imperador has become more prone to rage if he feels someone hasn't done what he wants. When he's enraged, he acts more impulsively than in his former quietly calculating manner. Unprovoked, he's much the same as he always was."

"The story about the Yearend Ball suggests he's going to use his young daughter to some end." Mauryn leaned back, if slightly, and brushed a wisp of white hair off his forehead.

"More like he wants her married off quickly to someone who can control her and keep her in the style to which she's accustomed. I could be wrong, but I don't think that will work out well."

"Oh? How do you know?" The banker leaned forward.

"I only danced once with her, but she looks like her mother and takes after her father, and she's very intelligent."

"You're not interested?"

"That would be disaster for me, and for Aloor, especially since the Imperador wouldn't allow it."

"What about the Premier? How long can he keep the Council in line?"

"As long as the Imperador supports him, and he doesn't provoke the Imperador."

Mauryn nodded, unsurprised. "Some of the landors hoped for more help with dredging the Khulor River."

"The Imperador laid down some stringent requirements. I had to work within them. I did get more than in previous years. Did you hear about Councilor Daenyld?"

"The newssheet said he was murdered."

"Right after he opposed the Imperador on the military appropriations."

"Ah . . ."

"If landors here want another councilor, it will be years before they'll have one who's the chair of the Waterways Committee."

Mauryn nodded, thoughtfully. "Gives a man thought."

"You might pass that along."

"I might."

"Anything else?"

"There is something. It's not likely to be popular."

Ysella waited.

"The usury law. It sets the maximum interest rate so low that we can't loan marks for anything very risky." Mauryn paused. "That's not it, exactly. It's that with the rate so low, we'd be foolish to make some loans. They might benefit the town or the district, but with margins so tight, we have to stick to what's safest."

"I'm not on that committee, but I'd be happy to look into it."

"Fair enough."

After another third of a bell, Ysella left the banque and walked to the town hall, where he confirmed his reservation for the assembly hall on the coming Unadi for his open meeting.

Then he headed toward a building well back from the main street, a single-story yellow brick structure that had seen better days. The signboard above the door held a single word—CHRONICLE.

The door squeaked as Ysella entered and looked around the large dim room before his eyes landed on one familiar face.

The other face belonged to Eraak Staavn, who offered a smile both cynical and tired as he caught sight of Ysella. He stood from behind a small desk half-covered in sheets of paper and walked to meet Ysella. "You didn't waste much time getting here."

"You wouldn't like it if I shared the news before seeing you," returned Ysella cheerfully. "First, I've confirmed the open meeting at the town hall on Unadi at fourth bell. I'd appreciate a brief mention in tomorrow's newssheet."

"You wrote earlier. The story's ready. You always have that meeting, so I don't need to update it much."

"What else do you want to know?"

"Why couldn't you get more funding for the river?"

"Because Aloor needs a live chairman of the Waterways Committee." Ysella repeated what he'd told Mauryn. In response to a question about Delehya, he also repeated what he'd said to the banker.

"What about the fighting in the Gulf of Nordum?"

Ysella was happy to tell Staavn what he knew, as well as provide details about the final appropriations and other matters apparently not yet known in Aloor but printed in *The Machtarn Tribune*. Almost a bell passed before he said, "That's about all."

Staavn laughed. "All you feel free to tell me."

"And won't get us both in trouble."

"What's a little trouble for a councilor?"

"Ask Symeon Daenyld," replied Ysella lightly.

"You're too serious, Councilor."

"If I weren't, you wouldn't listen," countered Ysella with a smile.

"Well . . . you're better than Fader was. Have to give you that."

That's not saying much. But Ysella wasn't about to say so, knowing Staavn was trying to get more. "I do my best to keep you informed. I got here late yesterday afternoon." With a pleasant smile, Ysella left the building, but not before arranging for the newssheet to be delivered to his house for the next month, which cost extra, but was well worth it.

His next stop was at Hydaar & Fhaen, Legalists, where the older clerk ushered him into the office of Luvaal Fhaen, the junior partner.

Fhaen immediately stood as Ysella entered. "Councilor."

"Dominic, please." Ysella settled into one of the chairs across the desk from Fhaen. "What's happened that I should know about? Especially items my family wouldn't tell me."

Fhaen squared himself in his chair. "The inheritance levy will hit your cousin Haarkyl pretty hard. Nathanyal didn't have much set aside, and Saera isn't known for her frugality."

And with both Haarkyl and Saera wanting to keep up appearances . . . Ysella nodded.

"Is that partly why you became a legalist?" asked Fhaen. "You've never said much."

"With two older brothers, I knew everyone was stretched thin, and managing a holding never appealed to me. Anything else?"

"Jaahn Escalante's son Lohan is trying to buy the old Ahnkaar tin mine from Mylls Ahnkaar and Ritten Wythcomb . . . claims he wants to help out the heirs after Thenyt's death. Both of them murdered. They haven't found who did it."

"Do you know any more?"

Fhaen shook his head.

"Sounds like the Escalantes might be taking advantage of a family already hard up . . . and they're trying to get the Navy to pay for that."

"Young Escalante claims not." Fhaen's tone was ironic. "I'm also hearing that more than a few holdings lost some of their winter wheat-corn to the late rains."

"And that might make paying land tariffs hard?"

"That was implied, but not said." Fhaen paused, then said, "You know some of the older landors will complain about not enough funds for deepening the river?"

Ysella replied as he had before, and the conversation moved into his answering some of Fhaen's questions about Machtarn and the Council for another third or so.

Once Ysella left Fhaen's office, he made his way to various shops, talking to clerks and proprietors. By midday, he was getting hoarse, as well as thirsty and hungry, and he made his way to the patrol station a block from the town hall.

Ysella didn't recognize the patroller at the desk, but said, "I'm Councilor Ysella. I'm looking for Lieutenant Ghavan. Is he anywhere around?"

"He might be somewhere. Why do you want to know?"

"I wanted to talk to him, if he's free."

"About what?"

"Whether he wants you to know is up to him."

"You a legalist, or something?"

"Yes, I'm a legalist, and something else." Ysella smiled politely.

"Never heard of you."

"I was born and raised here, but I've been in Machtarn for the last few months."

"When I see Ghavan, I'll tell him you were looking for him."

Ysella managed not to wince, but then saw Ghavan walk out from the corridor to the rear of the patrol station.

"Dominic! When did you get back?" The lieutenant smiled broadly.

"Last night. I wondered if you'd like to get something to eat with me."

"I can manage that. It'll have to be short, though. Corners all right?"

"That's fine."

As soon as the two were outside walking across the street to a tavern on the corner opposite the patrol station, Ysella asked, "Mateus, who's the patroller on the front desk?"

"Dawes Kaarpn. Why?" Ghavan's voice immediately turned concerned.

"Once we're settled at Corners, before we get down to what I came to tell you, I'd like to recount how I was greeted."

"I can guess, but I'd like to hear the details."

The building holding Corners had been there as long as Ysella could remember, and the inside oiled-oak walls were so ancient they looked almost black in the dim light. Ysella let Ghavan lead the way to a corner table, where the lieutenant took the chair that allowed him to watch the front door.

A narrow-faced older serving woman appeared and looked to Ghavan. "The usual?"

"That'll do."

The server looked to Ysella, frowning for a moment before nodding. "You're the councilor, aren't you, Ritter Ysella's youngest?"

"Guilty as charged," replied Ysella. "I'll have the potato-fowl hash, with the special sauce, and a small lager."

"Be a few moments, sirs." The server headed toward the kitchen behind the bar.

"Now . . . what were you going to tell me?" asked Ghavan.

Ysella related word for word the exchange with Kaarpn.

"I'm not surprised."

"It sounds like I'm not the first."

"Not at all."

"Then why is he on desk duty?"

"He's married to the captain's daughter, and the captain insisted."

Ysella nodded. "Any chance of putting him on night tavern duty?"

"I did. He got roughed up pretty bad, and not by souses. He picked on a miner. One who was sober. That's why he's on the desk."

"What about having him write up records?"

"You haven't seen his pawprints."

"My condolences," said Ysella. "Before we get to the news, how are Denesya and the boys?"

"They're all healthy . . . now. Rhelyn had a touch of the red pox, but he's fine. None of the rest of us did, thank the Almighty."

"That's good. Now . . . what do you want to know about Machtarn or the Council?"

"Anything you think I should know."

"Funds for waterways are scarce. Could lead to squabbles or worse about who gets priority for using the river wharves downstream from the shallows . . ." Ysella went on to summarize other matters he thought might be most of interest to Ghavan. By then, their orders arrived, and Ysella took a healthy swallow of the lager.

"I think I'd rather deal with Kaarpn and the captain than the Council," declared Ghavan.

"Matters quiet here?"

"Pretty much. Well . . . except for the Wythcomb murders."

"I heard about them, but no one could tell me much."

"Thenyt and his son disappeared near the end of Fallfirst. Two weeks ago, their bodies turned up in the old tailings pond when the heavy rains washed out part of the berm and drained a good part of the pond. Too much of a mess to tell much except their heads were bashed in."

"What about the mine?"

"I'd heard one of Jaahn Escalante's boys was interested in buying it. Interesting, because Thenyt Wythcomb didn't want to sell, said there was still good ore there. Mylls Ahnkaar wanted to sell, and he still does."

"Who's the heir?"

"No heir, except Khael Wythcomb's widow. They'd been married less than a year. No children yet."

Ysella hadn't known Khael had married, but he didn't say so.

By the time both had finished eating, Ysella felt he had a better idea of what was and wasn't happening in Aloor. He walked back to the front of the patrol station with Ghavan, where he said, with an amused smile, "Give my best to Patroller Kaarpn."

"I will, but he won't appreciate it."

"And you take care of yourself and Denesya."

"I'll do my best."

Ysella turned from the patrol station and headed west. He had more than a few others to visit before he headed back to the house.

14

AFTER breakfast on Quindi morning, before he set out, Ysella checked the porch basket beside the front door and was pleased to see the *Chronicle* had been delivered, as arranged. While it only published on Duadi and Quindi, the newssheet would still help him catch up and stay abreast of local events, particularly those outside the landor ambit—and possibly major happenings in Machtarn, if with a delay.

He took the newssheet to the small study off the narrow front hall and began to look for the story Staavn had promised, finding it, short as it was, on the bottom of the front page.

> Aloor's councilor, Ritter Dominic Ysella, has returned from Machtarn and will be holding an open meeting at the Aloor town hall next Unadi, the thirteenth of Winterfirst at fourth bell of the afternoon. The councilor will inform attendees of recent acts by the Imperial Council and will answer questions about the impact on Aloor . . .

He turned his attention to other articles. He winced at the one stating that the annual appropriations passed by the Council didn't provide adequate funding for navigational improvements for the upper Khulor River, "despite the efforts of the Waterways Committee chairman, Dominic Ysella, the councilor from Aloor."

One short article quoted the First Marshal regarding how raids against the Gulf pirates were proceeding "according to plan." Ysella suspected they weren't going as well as the marshal would have liked.

Another article covered the recently discovered deaths of Thenyt and Khael Wythcomb. The deaths were especially suspicious, given the Imperial Navy's decision to force the Escalante family to supply tin at the lowest possible contracted price, and the interest of Lohan Escalante in purchasing the Ahnkaar tin mine, undoubtedly on behalf of familial interests.

When Ysella finished reading, he told Perri he was leaving and not to fix a full dinner, but a cold supper, since he'd be going straight to services from his meetings.

"You're sure about that, Ritter?"

"Very sure. It's part of being a councilor."

"If you say so, Ritter."

Ysella laughed softly, knowing that was Perri's way of implying she disagreed, then said, "You might be right, but I do know, if I don't meet and greet when I'm here, people will forget who their councilor is."

Perri didn't speak, but offered an amused smile.

After leaving the house, Ysella headed for the Aloor Grain Exchange, effectively composed of four grain factors and their clerks. Three factors dealt individually with the various large landor holdings, while one dealt with smaller and the tenant growers. All four united in negotiating prices on grain coming from Aloor and going to the southern grain exchange in Sudaen, which handled grain from across the central southeast of Guldor, either for export or transshipment to the central coast or the northeast coast of Guldor. At times, the four resorted to dealing with the central grain exchange in Point Larmat, both in seeking better prices and to exert Aloor's independence.

On Furdi, Ysella had stopped by to see Rhend Jarrell, the factor handling grain from the Ysella lands, but it had been late in the day and Jarrell had left and Ysella didn't wish to miss the grain factor again. Ysella reached the exchange before third bell and found the graying Jarrell looking over ledgers.

"Councilor, I heard you were looking for me." Jarrell gestured to one of the battered chairs in front of his desk.

"I was and still am. Do you have some time to talk?" Ysella took the nearest chair.

"I do. Right now, there's not much trading or shipping going on. Nothing much in the futures market, either. It'll all pick up in a month or so. What's on your mind? You're not going to get into the family grain business, are you?"

"Almighty, no. I just want to hear your thoughts on two things. First, how what the Council has done has affected you and other factors and, second, the possibilities of grain shortages."

Jarrell frowned.

"Start with your problems with the Council." From what Ysella had heard and seen, factors and other well-off commercer types always had problems with the Council.

"Where should I start?" The factor smiled sourly.

Ysella offered a cheerful smile in return. "Anywhere you want."

"Then, I'd have to start with the Council. It seldom places any priority on the business and factoring side of agriculture. As if grain and produce sold themselves." He gave a cynical smile. "That might have something to do with most of the councilors being landors and assuming that everyone else in the Council knows how grains get marketed and sold."

"Less than half the councilors are landors now, and there will be fewer with every election, I suspect," replied Ysella. "But your point remains accurate. What are the most important measures that the Council has neglected?"

"First off, remove, or at least increase, the limit on the interest rates paid on loans for property, buildings, and machinery."

Ysella frowned, thinking about what Haalas Mauryn had said. "Wouldn't that impoverish everyone?"

Jarrell shook his head. "Too many marks are going into loans for buying land because it's the safest investment and because it doesn't cost that much to hold it. We looked at building a large flour mill and a mill with water-powered looms, but we couldn't raise enough marks because the maximum rate of return was three parts on a hundred. That's far too low for the risk."

"Can such a mill be built?"

"There's already a mill like that in Teknold." Jarrell smiled. "I've got the plans."

"What rate would make sense?"

Jarrell shrugged.

"No councilor will support eliminating the maximum rate," Ysella pointed out.

"Five or six parts on a hundred at a minimum. That's my best guess."

"What else?"

"Remove the export tariffs, especially on grains. All they do is keep growers from producing more. Instead, you could impose a tax on the resale of grains by the exchanges. You could set the rate so the total revenues were roughly the same, but in time the revenues would increase . . ."

Ysella continued to listen until Jarrell finished with his list of issues and proposals, then asked, "What are your thoughts on grain shortages? I'm not talking about prices, placing marks on futures, or any of that, but I do know that futures prices give an indication of what growers and buyers think might happen."

"You know about all the rains. Well, wheat-corn futures for early summer are up. Maize-corn prices are a bit down."

"How do they compare to the summer of 815?" That was the last time of hard fall rains, as Ysella recalled.

"Right now, they look close," admitted Jarrell. "Why are you so interested?"

"Because bad years mean landors who haven't been careful get in trouble, and so do small growers. Higher prices mean more people hungry or dying."

"That's always the case."

Ysella nodded. *But it'll be worse with an increasingly arrogant and senile Imperador or a more arrogant Heir.*

Jarrell frowned. "You think the Imperador might not handle it well?"

"The Heir would be more of a problem."

"I've heard rumors about him. More than rumors, in fact. How will knowing about harvests help you and the Council?"

"We might be able to inform some of the Imperial administrators and Palace aides." *Not that Laureous will listen, but it will allow word to get out that he didn't.* "That might help. I don't want to go through what we did with the appropriations again next year." That was certainly true, because as a committee chairman, Ysella could become a target, like Daenyld. "I just want to hear what you think is most likely for grains, pork, and beef."

"In general terms, only . . ."

Ysella settled in to listen intently.

When he left the exchange nearly a bell later, he had the feeling that Jarrell presented too optimistic a view, particularly about the impact of his proposed "reforms," but he was still glad he'd talked to the grain factor.

From the grain exchange he took a long walk to the northeast corner of Aloor, the section containing most of the smiths and other crafters, where he headed for the shop of Thaern Waaltar, the tinsmith frequented by his father and brothers.

When he stepped into the shop, a youth, likely an apprentice, looked up from a small workbench.

"Sir, one moment. I'll get the master."

Ysella didn't have a chance to respond before Waaltar appeared. For an instant, the tinsmith looked puzzled before saying, "I didn't expect you here, Ritter Ysella."

"I didn't expect it either, Thaern, but I don't know anyone with more knowledge about tin than you. If you wouldn't mind sharing some of that knowledge—not about your techniques, but about tin . . ."

"I don't know what I can tell you that's special, but I can tell you what I know."

"It may not be special to you, or other tinsmiths, but there are some things I need to know because of possible problems that might come before the Council this year."

Waaltar motioned toward an open doorway. "Best we go there."

Ysella led the way to the small room, lit only by a small window covered by an iron grate. On the wall shelves on one side were various items, mainly pewter plates, bowls, platters, and pitchers of various sizes, possibly as examples for customers, or for quick sale. The only furniture was a small table.

"What would you like to know, Councilor?"

"Do you have any idea about how much tin ore might remain in the Ahnkaar mine?"

"From what I've heard, there's plenty of ore. That's not the problem. It's deep enough that the tunnels keep taking on water, and it takes so much more time and effort to remove the water that no one would buy the tin at what it cost." Waaltar paused. "Might I ask why you're so interested, sir?"

"It's a matter that might come before the Council. You may have heard that a Ritter Escalante from Silverhills attempted to overcharge the Navy for tin. In addition, his son Lohan has tried to purchase the old Ahnkaar tin mine. I recently learned that both Thenyt and Khael Wythcomb were murdered after Thenyt refused the offer to sell. I worry that something's going on, and questions might come before the Council when we meet in Winterend. I don't want to be blindsided. I figured you'd be one of the few who might know more than what's in the newssheets."

Waaltar nodded slowly. "Thought it might be something like that."

"What else can you tell me?"

"Aelyn Wythcomb's the only one who might know more, far as I could tell."

"You've met her?"

Waaltar nodded. "Just before they stopped working the mine, Thenyt stockpiled tin. He'd sell it to me and local crafters who needed small amounts. Said it was the least he could do so as we'd not be at the mercy of the metal factors. She's been doing it since . . . Thenyt and Khael . . . disappeared."

"Is she at the old place on the hill northeast of the mine?"

"Was the last time I got tin, three weeks back."

"Have you heard about anyone else expressing interest in the mine?"

The tinsmith shook his head. After a moment, he added, "Thenyt did say that if anyone could find a better way to pump out the water, the tin was there. You think young Escalante has a way?"

"I have no idea," Ysella admitted. "I appreciate the information and taking the time to talk with me." He looked across the shelves. "What's the best piece here?"

Waaltar smiled. "You don't have to buy anything."

"No, but I'd like to. The best?"

"The small pitcher here." Thaern pointed. "It's silver. No lead at all."

"How much?"

"Well . . . ?"

"For anyone you didn't know," pressed Ysella.

"Four marks."

Ysella took out his wallet and handed over five marks. "I like the pitcher, and I appreciated the information." He paused. "You're probably very busy, but on Unadi, I'll be holding a meeting at the town hall. Fourth bell of the afternoon. If you or any friends have any questions about the Council or what's happened in Machtarn, I'll do my best to answer them."

Waaltar took some clean rags from a corner of the shelves, wrapped the pitcher in them, and then slipped it into a small burlap bag that he handed to Ysella. "You really didn't have to, sir."

"I took your time, and, besides, I like the pitcher."

"I appreciate it, sir. It's been a slow fall."

"Take care."

"Thank you, sir."

While the pitcher was too large for cream or sauces, and too small for beverages, he could have carried it easily on his coming calls, but decided it was better to detour back to the house and drop it off before meeting anyone else.

When he entered the house, Perri appeared in moments.

"I thought you wouldn't be back until late, sir."

"I ended up buying something, and didn't want to carry it around for the rest of the day." He removed the pitcher from the bag and displayed it.

Perri studied it. "It's pretty . . ."

"It's the wrong size for most things, but I liked it."

"The bag might be more useful."

"Use the bag and rags as you see fit. I need to get back to work." Catching her dubious look, he added, "Meeting and talking to people is work."

When he left the house, the wind had shifted and blew from the southeast. While it should have felt warmer, it felt colder, possibly because of the dampness.

He headed into the wind and toward the shops south of the center of town. For the next four bells, he made his way from shop to shop.

After finishing that round of visits, Ysella made his way to the Trinitarian chapel two blocks southwest of the town hall. He arrived a sixth before services began, taking a seat in his reserved and small section of the pew. The chapel had been rebuilt five years after Laureous had leveled the previous chapel, because, according to rumor, the presider had called the Imperador a "barbarian from the east." Neither the presider nor the chapel had survived.

A few already seated parishioners looked in Ysella's direction, nodded, and returned to their murmured conversations or merely waited. The harpsichordist continued playing hymnal melodies that Ysella doubted he'd soon forget, given that all harpsichordists played the same pre-service holy repertoire.

Not soon enough for Ysella, the not-quite-corpulent Presider Maabak placed himself in the center of the sanctuary directly in front of the redstone wall holding the same three golden orbs of Love, Power, and Mercy that graced every Trinitarian chapel.

Ysella rose with the rest of the congregation as the presider began the service. "Let us offer thanks to the Almighty for the days that have been and for those to come, through his love, power, and mercy . . ."

Ysella followed the service almost by rote, not having to exercise much thought, wondering what Maabak might offer for his homily.

In time, the presider moved to the lectern and began. "As we begin a new year, it is time to consider what we have learned in the past year and how to employ the wisdom that comes from the Almighty to make the coming year more fruitful, not in seeking personal prosperity, but in doing good where we can and avoiding evil . . ."

By the end of the homily, Ysella was more than ready to avoid not only evil, but also the evils of repetition in different phrases and keys.

He hoped to quietly avoid Maabak, but the presider made his way to Ysella before he could leave the chapel without giving the impression of fleeing.

"It's so good to see you here for services, Councilor."

"I do what I can, Presider Maabak. I only returned late on Tridi afternoon."

"Will we be seeing more of you?"

"Without a doubt . . . until I have to resume my duties in Machtarn."

"We all appreciate your being here," replied Maabak. "I was concerned about your spiritual well-being because I hadn't heard anything from Machtarn since Presider Nattyn retired, but Presider Haelsyn finally wrote me that you've also been dutiful in attending his chapel."

As if I could afford to be otherwise. "He's quite diligent."

"As he should be. I won't keep you. Have a good endday."

"Thank you." As Ysella left the chapel, he noted, not for the first time, that no other congregant sought out Maabak.

He walked back to his house, where Perri greeted him in the small front hall.

"You got a few letters and messages in the basket. I put them on your desk. I'll have some meats and cheese, along with apple slices, in less than a sixth."

"Thank you. That sounds perfect."

"Would you like lager or wine?"

"Lager this evening, please."

Perri headed back to the kitchen, while Ysella took off his overcoat and hung it on one of the wall pegs in the hall, then washed up.

Almost exactly a sixth later, Perri rang the small silver bell, and Ysella made his way down to the dining room, where his meal and lager awaited him, somewhat more than he'd anticipated, but since he'd eaten nothing since breakfast, that was probably for the best, and Perri had known that would be likely. In time, Perri removed his now-empty plate, but he still sipped the lager in his beaker.

Perri reappeared in the dining room. "Everything's cleaned up, Ritter. I'll be leaving some pastries for your breakfast, and I'll be back on Unadi morning."

Ysella stood. "Thank you. I do appreciate it, Perri."

"It's better for me, too." The serving woman smiled.

"Have a good endday."

"You, too."

After seeing Perri out, Ysella went back to the study, carrying his beaker, and lit the oil lamp over the desk. He began reading the first message, from his eldest cousin, Haarkyl.

Dominic—

It's good to see you survived the carnage in Machtarn.

If you have a bell free, it would be good if you stopped by the holding and we had refreshments around noon next Tridi. If that doesn't work, feel free to suggest a time . . .

Ysella shook his head. He wasn't about to respond to that message before talking to his parents. Haarkyl always had something in mind, and not always for the best for anyone but Haarkyl. He set that message aside, and opened the next.

Councilor Ysella—

We would very much appreciate the opportunity to meet with you before you return to Machtarn. We understand that you have many people clamoring for your attention, but we believe we have some factual information that will be of use to you as Chairman of the

Waterways Committee in determining future funding for waterways projects...

The signature line held two names—Pietro Sulymar and Gherard Brandt, who jointly owned wharves and warehouses on the Khulor River southwest of Aloor.

...if you would name a date, time, and place, we would be more than pleased to come to Aloor...

Ysella set that message aside as well, although he knew he'd have to meet with the two. *And they know you need as much hard information as you can muster.*

He opened the third message, one from Cyraen Presswyrth requesting that Ysella set aside a few moments to meet with Rugaar Maartyn about possible future waterways improvements. Ysella smiled wryly at one phrase—"Sr. Maartyn's uncle, Aldyn Kraagyn, recommended that he consult with you." Which likely meant that Maartyn's father had leaned on Kraagyn, the councilor from Encora, and Kraagyn had said something to the effect that young Rugaar needed to talk to someone on the Waterways Committee.

Ysella paused his perusal of messages to write out a quick reply to Presswyrth agreeing to meet with Maartyn, if Maartyn came to Aloor and provided advance notice. At the same time, he wondered why Presswyrth hadn't asked for the meeting for himself and others that he'd previously requested.

The last message was much simpler. It just said, "Glad to see you're being effective in Machtarn. Hope you can stop by some time." The signature was that of Legrand Quaentyn, the legalist for whom Ysella had read water law and under whom he had worked for several years.

That I can certainly do.

Then he turned to the letters.

The first two pleaded for improved waterways feeding into the Khulor River, largely impractical from what Ysella had researched, but he smiled as he opened and read the third letter.

Dominic—

We're glad you escaped Machtarn largely unscathed, and we'd like to see you before you get inundated with supplicants and worse before the next Council session begins.

Both Gineen and I are hoping you'd join us for a simple dinner next Quindi night after services here at the holding. We'll assume you're coming unless you demur . . .

The signature was that of Bruuk Fettryk, who'd read law alongside Ysella and then opened a general practice in Aloor. Early in the previous year, he most unexpectedly inherited a holding south of Aloor, an occurrence that had happily shocked Fettryk and his wife. There was also a map sketched below the signature.

Still smiling, Ysella penned the dinner into his datebook, then leaned back in his chair, thinking.

Now that he'd made the rounds, and reminded everyone that he had returned and inquired about health and concerns, he could spend the remainder of the month dealing with the matters that couldn't be addressed by meeting and greeting, not that he wouldn't have to meet with too many more people until he returned to Machtarn.

And that doesn't include family. He took a deep breath, followed by a sip of lager.

15

FINDI morning Ysella slept slightly later than usual, though not as late as he would have preferred, and woke to find the usual damp winter chill pervading the house. The patchy fog outside lent an air of gloom to the still-early morning as he padded downstairs barefoot and resurrected the fire in the wall stove, before going to the kitchen, where he had some of the apple strudel Perri had left along with some slices of salted beef from the cooler and a beaker of lager.

After washing up, shaving, and dressing, he settled behind the study desk and began to write replies to the various letters and messages, because, if he didn't get them to the post centre or to one of the freelance messengers before fifth bell, they wouldn't get out until Unadi morning.

He didn't get to the post centre until right before fifth bell, but a messenger still waited for deliveries, glad to take Ysella's messages and marks. By the time he walked back to his house, the fog had dissipated with the colder wind out of the north-northeast.

For the rest of the morning and early afternoon, he jotted down notes for his meeting on Unadi, then dug out the maps he'd used when he'd been a practicing water legalist and looked over the most detailed map of the area around the Ahnkaar mine. While there weren't any large streams nearby, the amount of water mentioned by Waaltar implied some sort of subterranean stream or aquifer.

A third after first afternoon bell, he put away the maps and papers and walked out to the stable, where he groomed and saddled the chestnut mare.

As he led the mare out of the stable, Saunder Hapmaan stepped down from the rear stoop of the adjoining house, slightly larger than Ysella's. "Back in town for Winterfirst, Councilor?"

"That I am. How was your fall?"

"Too wet if you ask me. Good for the apothecary, though." Hapmaan shivered, not surprisingly since he only wore a jacket and not an overcoat.

"Physicians needing lots of medicines?" asked Ysella conversationally.

"Nurses and midwives, too," added Hapmaan.

"You running short of anything?"

Hapmaan laughed loudly. "You always ask that."

"It's a way for me to find out where there might be problems."

"We've mostly got what we need. Time's where we're short. More fevers and consumption this fall. There's been a call for white willow bark, but it takes time to prepare the bark. Same's true for most useful herbs or plants."

"Your son still working for you?"

"He is and doing well. He and Dhacya have the quarters above the shop." Before Ysella could pose another question, Hapmaan asked, "Will the Atacaman pirates get us into a war?"

"That's up to the Grande Duce and the Imperador."

Hapmaan shivered again. "Getting colder. Feels like winter's here to stay. I'll talk to you later." The apothecary turned and retreated into his house.

Ysella glanced up, noted the smoke emerging from two of his neighbor's chimneys, then mounted and rode down the drive, guiding the mare toward the north road that led to the holding.

A few people on the street looked or nodded as he rode past, but he didn't see anyone he recognized in the town proper. Once he was on the north road, he kept an eye out for other riders, but only saw a few wagons or riders.

He didn't stop at the front entrance to the main house but continued to the stables, where a middle-aged man with a short salt-and-pepper beard opened the stable door as Ysella dismounted.

"Good afternoon, Councilor."

"The same to you, Jhomas. You think it might snow later?"

"No, sir. Might get a hard freeze, though. Seems colder for this early in winter."

"You'd be one to know that."

"Yes, sir. You want me to unsaddle the mare?"

"No, thank you, but I'd appreciate it if you'd make sure she has water and a bit of grain."

"Yes, sir."

Once he cared for the mare, Ysella walked to the main house, glancing to the north, where a thin trail of smoke issued from the small empath's cottage. He shook his head, thinking about Kyranna, and the lonely lives empaths led, mainly on estates, because they weren't trusted in the cities, except in the pleasure trade, or as freelance trackers. On estates, they weren't part of the family, yet were superior to the workers, who were largely susceptibles. *And even the best of them are disliked by the susceptibles and feared by the landowners, except for the handful who are resistant to empaths.*

Once in the house, he took off his overcoat before making his way to the parlor, where he found his mother, Jaeralyn, and Ennika talking and sipping wine.

Maadlyn immediately appeared. "Would you like some wine, sir?"

"Red, please."

The serving girl nodded and hurried off.

"You might as well join us," said Kaelyn. "Your father wanted a little time with your brothers and the boys."

"What went wrong . . . or not as well as it should have?" asked Ysella dryly.

Jaeralyn offered an amused smile. "How could you possibly think that?"

Ennika grinned broadly.

"Pasture gates, broken fence railings, spoiled feed, roof leaks that didn't get noticed, lanes with weak edges . . . ?"

"You've covered most of them, dear," replied Kaelyn tartly.

"It's not something you forget," said Ysella pleasantly before turning to take the wineglass from the tray Maadlyn held and murmuring, "Thank you."

"What have you been doing the past few days?" asked Jaeralyn.

"Meeting people, trying to find out the problems that worry them."

"The newssheet had a story about your open meeting," ventured Ennika.

"Where everyone complains and wants everything we have to pay for," said Kaelyn.

"Well . . . they're occasionally right," admitted Ysella. "The Imperador has a hard time understanding that excess first-rate ships of the line don't do much to maintain waterways or harbors or post roads."

"You said that comparatively diplomatically, dear. How would you assess his abilities these days?"

"As less than they were or should be, and unfortunately superior to those of his Heir."

"And yet the Council does nothing," said Kaelyn.

"So far," replied Ysella.

"Premier Detruro lost his backbone when he lost his wife, I fear," declared Kaelyn. "But the Detruros have always been saved by their women."

"Or, they created that impression," replied Ysella, "in order to mitigate the reaction that would have fallen on them."

"That's worse," murmured Ennika.

"True enough, child," said Kaelyn, "but best you keep such thoughts to yourself and only to women you trust. Too many women, especially landor women, betray other women for momentary favor or position."

"The same is true of landor men," Ysella pointed out.

"How could that possibly be?" Kaelyn's tone was acidly scornful.

From the parlor archway, Ysella's father said sarcastically, "Because they learned from their wives and mothers."

"Did you have a useful meeting?" asked Kaelyn sweetly.

"As useful as possible," replied the elder Cliven, taking his usual armchair.

"Useful is good."

Jaeralyn maintained a pleasant expression, one that appeared almost frozen for a time.

Ysella could scarcely fail to notice that almost a sixth of a bell passed before Haekaan and Taeryn entered the parlor, and longer before the younger Cliven and Erskaan arrived. Almost silently, Maadlyn served wine to each as they appeared.

"How is Raemyna?" Ysella asked Taeryn once the recent arrivals were settled.

"She's much better. Kharl is a strong and greedy little pig. It helps Raemyna that he's got a wet nurse for the night."

"Her milk would be better," said Kaelyn, "but she's fortunate she can nurse at all."

After all she's been through, she's fortunate to be alive. That was definitely a thought Ysella wasn't about to share.

"What have you been digging at, Dominic?" asked the elder Cliven.

"Tin. Not literally, but I'd like to find out more about the Ahnkaar mine. I talked to Thaern Waaltar . . ." Ysella summarized what the tinsmith told him, then added, "I'd never heard anything about Khael Wythcomb, let alone that he was married."

"That was something no one wanted to talk about. Rather disgusting, really," said Kaelyn. "But since you asked . . ."

Ysella nodded for her to continue.

"You know that the Wythcombs really aren't landors. All that land . . . well, most of it's worn out and too rocky and subject to flooding in heavy rains, but all the rain runs off. The only thing valuable is, or was, the tin under it. No real landor wanted a daughter marrying into such a family." Kaelyn paused. "You might remember the Braathwells?"

"Only by name," said Ysella.

"That's not surprising. No one wanted to talk about them. Owyn Braathwell married Alyandra Scalante—the Scalantes of Silverhills. She didn't have much choice. Rhycard Scalante had five daughters. Alyandra was the youngest. She had a dowry, but with five daughters it wasn't much. Owyn drank, and he wagered, too much and too often. In less than two years, he went through Alyandra's dowry and all the marks he'd raised by mortgaging his lands, which weren't the best to begin with . . ."

Ysella had a good idea where the tale of woe was headed, but continued to listen.

"... of course, he got Alyandra with child. He was furious that she delivered a girl and not a boy who might have had a chance at marrying the daughter of a well-off landor, unlikely as that was. Just before the Banque of Aloor arrived to foreclose on his lands and holding, he killed Alyandra. He was still raving about how her demands for finery led him to gamble when Rhycard Scalante put a crossbow bolt through him. The Scalantes raised Aelyn, except Rhycard's wife died when Aelyn was twelve, and there weren't any marks left for her, and he married her off to Khael Wythcomb—not long before it came out that Thenyt Wythcomb and Mylls Ahnkaar were losing marks on the mine and needed to close it. To make matters worse, Rhycard died less than a month after the wedding. He was good-hearted, but left something to be desired as a holder. His younger brother was a councilor, but he died young."

"Quite a story," said Ysella.

"Every bit's true," said the elder Cliven.

"I never heard that," declared Jaeralyn.

"Neither did I," added Haekaan.

Taeryn only nodded sadly.

"What happened to the Braathwell lands?" asked young Cliven.

"Neighboring landors bought parcels. I think Raemyna's parents have some," said Kaelyn, quickly adding, "Not the lands she'll inherit, though. Hers are a bit better, especially after all Taeryn's done."

"How's cousin Haarkyl doing?" asked Ysella. "He invited me to come by next week."

"He'll either want to persuade you that he should get marks from me," said the elder Cliven coolly, "or he'll want you to help him out, one way or another, with the Council."

"I suppose I should go, if for appearance's sake."

"Only for appearance's sake," interjected Kaelyn. Then she stood. "It's time for dinner."

Ysella found himself again on his father's left, across from his mother, with Jaeralyn beside him, but this time, Kaelyn looked to him and said, "If you would, Dominic..."

Ysella thought, then said, "In these times of confusion and consternation, may the Almighty bless this food and those who partake of it, so that it might strengthen our bodies for the work we must accomplish and guide our minds to do what is best, in the name of the Three in One."

"Very nice," murmured Jaeralyn.

"Thank you," replied Ysella quietly before watching as Maadlyn began to serve, beginning with his father, each plate containing slices of lamb with a mint sauce, curry-fried rice, boiled new potatoes, butter-baked squash, and pickled peppers.

As soon as everyone was served and the elder Cliven began to eat, Kaelyn said, "I thought we'd invite over the Paarkyls next Findi. You never met Evalynn. She's really quite attractive and far too intelligent for the remaining eligible landors anywhere nearby." Then she looked directly at Ysella. "You will be here?"

Ysella knew it wasn't a question. Besides, he'd never met the young woman, and having refreshments and dinner couldn't be that bad, could it? Except, with his family around, anything was possible. "I'll be here."

"Excellent. It's already arranged."

The faintest hint of a smile crossed Jaeralyn's lips, but only momentarily.

"The lamb is excellent," Ysella said, nodding to his mother. "How did the sheep handle all the rain?"

"We had to keep them in the higher pastures longer than we would have liked," replied Haekaan, "but we didn't get any rain rot. Also had to move them more often."

"And the cattle?"

"We cut back the herd some," said the elder Cliven. "We sold earlier than most and got better prices, but it'll still hurt some this coming year."

Ysella nodded. He recalled moving cattle when the ground was too wet.

The rest of dinner conversation dealt mainly with matters involving the holding, partly because Ysella asked questions to keep talk away from his personal and professional life and from details about the Council and other councilors, since so many councilors came from landor families and word tended to get around.

He left as early as was polite, after reassuring his mother, twice, that he would be present for dinner the next Findi.

16

AFTER breakfast on Unadi morning, Ysella wrote several more letters, including a short note to Raemyna wishing her and Kharl the best and telling her that he missed her at the family dinner and that he hoped to see her before too long.

Before leaving the house, he checked the mail and message basket and found a single letter from Rugaar Maartyn proposing he call on Ysella on Tridi morning, the fifteenth of Winterfirst, between third and fourth bell, since Maartyn had already planned to be in Aloor then.

Very much in a hurry. Ysella shook his head and wrote a quick note in return agreeing to third bell.

Then he stepped outside, noting the high greenish-gray clouds, and the bite to the cold air, both of which suggested the possibility of cold rain or light snow. He walked to the post centre and handed over the letters and the coins necessary to dispatch them, after which he made his way to Legrand Quaentyn's house.

The older legalist opened the front door himself. His white hair was thinner than when Ysella had visited the previous summer, and his face was gaunter, but the welcoming smile was as warm as ever.

"Dominic! It's always so good to see you. Do come in . . . if you have the time."

"This morning I have plenty of time. Later today, not so much."

Quaentyn stepped back and motioned for Ysella to enter, then said, "I read that you're having another one of those open meetings. It's too bad more landors don't attend."

"It is what it is." *Most of the landors wouldn't lower themselves to attending a meeting where commercers, tradesmen, and crafters were present.*

Because the parlor off the modest entry hall was quite warm, and the billets of wood in the wall stove burned steadily, Ysella shed his overcoat quickly before taking the chair offered by Quaentyn, while the older man reseated himself in the armchair closest to the stove.

"From what little of Machtarn that gets printed in the *Chronicle,* you seem to have managed to be successful as Waterways Committee chairman without making yourself a target."

"Only in Machtarn, I fear. I've had quite a few letters from landors here complaining that I didn't do enough for Aloor in the latest appropriations."

"You expected anything different?"

Ysella chuckled. "Not really. I hoped, but the landors who survived here, including my own family, still haven't forgotten how privileged their predecessors were when Aloor was a sovereign land. Some of the waterways elsewhere need more immediate attention, and, of course, the Imperador has his priorities."

"He always has. I get the impression from the newssheets that he's as arrogant as ever and more impatient."

"I'm afraid there's a great deal of truth in the newssheet reports." Ysella paused. "How are you doing?" *Particularly since Deyrdra died.*

"Well enough. Both Hayley and Maergot look in on me daily, if not more often. I've got enough laid by that it'll outlast me."

"You look to be in good health."

"Not so good as last time you were here, but I've got a few years in me."

"Is there anything I missed here that I should know?"

"Not that much, except there's been talk that Captain Chaaltyn's been siphoning off marks from the patrol accounts."

"I hadn't heard that, but he's got his daughter's husband on the payroll, and few of the other patrollers are happy about it."

"That figures." Quaentyn coughed, then said, "Cyraen Presswyrth had something to do with Chaaltyn becoming patrol captain."

"Presswyrth's from Khuld."

"But he has lands and water rights southwest of Aloor, some of them from the foreclosure sales of the Braathwell lands."

Ysella smiled wryly. In landor-dominated towns, everything was tied to everything else, one way or another.

"Why the smile?"

"Because the Braathwell foreclosure ties into another problem I've been looking into." Ysella summarized the connection to the Ahnkaar tin mine.

"I knew about the mine from Thenyt's will, but I hadn't heard about the Escalantes' interest in buying it."

From there the conversation turned into reminiscences about some of the water-law cases they'd handled together. More than a bell passed before Ysella bid Quaentyn good day, and headed toward the town hall.

Once there, he began a search through recent changes in registered water rights and land holdings. For the first bell or so, he found nothing. Two-thirds of a bell after that, he discovered that Rugaar Maartyn bought fifty hectares bordering and to the west of the Ahnkaar mine lands, with "any associated or yet to be discovered water rights."

To the west? That's uphill and almost completely sand and boulders except for the top of the ridge.

Ysella had a good idea what Maartyn knew or suspected about the land, but he also wondered where Maartyn obtained the funds. If his uncle was Aldyn Kraagyn, he had to be a young man, although his father might be the older brother who held the family lands. Or perhaps Rugaar was acting for the family to avoid attention. Over the next bell, Ysella found nothing else of interest.

A third before fourth bell, Ysella entered the meeting hall to make sure of the lectern's position in the middle of the dais. As he'd requested, the long table had been moved back against the wall, and the lectern was in place.

Although no one was yet in the hall, he left quickly—he didn't want to be cornered and have to break away—and made his way to the clerk's office, empty except for the clerk, Lyam Dattaur.

"Thank you, Lyam. The hall's just the way I requested."

"You're welcome, Councilor. You think there'll be as many as last summer?"

"I don't know. We'll have to see. Is there anything I should know?"

"Not much. We had a hard freeze two weeks back, and the building drains backed up. Got pretty rank in here until it thawed and they got them cleaned out." Dattaur grinned. "Read that some eligible councilors danced with the Imperador's daughter. Were you one of them?"

"Only one courtesy dance. That was just right," replied Ysella.

Before long, the bells in the town hall tower chimed, and Ysella stepped into the meeting hall and walked to the center of the dais, where he surveyed the fifty to sixty men in various groups. There were no women, unsurprisingly, since only male property owners, men in certain professions, or who owned their own shops, could vote. Ysella thought two disparate and well-attired groups were likely landors. The group farthest back, almost in a corner, looked to be workingmen, a group he hadn't seen at previous meetings. Then again, they also might own warehouses.

Once the conversations died away, Ysella announced, "Welcome to the meeting. I'm Councilor Dominic Ysella. Since I'm also chairman of the Council's Waterways Committee, I'll begin by explaining what projects in and around Aloor will be funded and to what extent . . ."

When he finished, he said, "If any of you have questions about waterways, please ask them now. After I've answered waterways questions, I'll try to answer questions on other Council actions."

From the roughly dressed group in the back of the chamber came the first question. "Why didn't the Council fund all the deepening of the Khulor River headwaters?"

"Two reasons. First, the marks available for all projects are limited because Imperial revenues were lower this past year. Second, the Imperador rejected appropriations in excess of his recommendations. Because Aloor's needs were greater, we received considerably more than many districts, but not as much as necessary to complete dredging . . ." As he spoke he kept his eyes on the group.

The moment Ysella finished, someone called out, "We're always shorted."

"Do you want me to recommend that the Imperador increase land tariffs, year-end taxes, or fees to pay for more?"

"They're already too high," someone else retorted.

"The way matters are now," said Ysella, almost at the top of his voice, "we may be able to fund most of the remainder next year."

"That won't help this year!"

"I know that. You know that. The Imperador knows that, but there are only so many marks, and every district has needs of some sort."

"You're supposed to get more."

"I have," replied Ysella loudly and cheerfully, looking directly at the questioner. "If you want to check what's been done while I've been chair of the Waterways Committee, Aloor has gotten more funds for waterways than it ever has. But I can't obtain marks that aren't in the Treasury."

For the next bell, Ysella did his best to answer waterways questions. Then came the other questions.

"Is the Imperador failing?"

"His intelligence appears unchanged. His patience is considerably diminished."

"Will the First Marshal intervene to stop the Navy from forcing Ritter Escalante to sell tin at a loss?"

"I have no idea. I'm not aware of whether Ritter Escalante will make or lose money on the contract, but allowing those who supply goods to increase prices over what they bid means that the Imperial government will have to pay more and have fewer funds for other procurements or will have to increase tariffs and taxes."

"Are you being considered to marry the Imperador's daughter."

"No."

"Is the Council considering an attempt to amend the Establishment Act?"

"I'm not aware of any such attempt, but under the act, the Council can always recommend changes . . ."

Another two-thirds of a bell passed before Ysella said, "Since there are no more questions, the meeting is over."

As he turned to leave the dais, Eraak Staavn appeared. Ysella had glimpsed him earlier, talking to some of those at the meeting. "Councilor?"

"Yes?" replied Ysella politely.

"Do you think the deaths of Thenyt and Khael Wythcomb are linked to Jaahn Escalante's problems with the tin contract?"

Ysella shook his head. "I don't know." As he answered, he saw the few remaining men look at Staavn and immediately leave the chamber.

"What about Lohan Escalante's attempt to buy the Ahnkaar mine?"

"I heard that Ritter Escalante's son made an offer. I've never met either Escalante—"

"What about Councilor Escalante? I assume you know him."

"I know most councilors, some better than others."

"And Alaan Escalante?"

"I've been to his house once. I've invited him to mine. He declined because of other engagements."

"Did he talk to you about the tin contract?"

"I asked him about it. He said he had little contact with that part of the family."

"He's been appointed chairman of the Military Affairs Committee. Do you think he'll use that position to favor his cousin?"

"Not unless he wants to commit suicide."

Staavn frowned. "How can you be so sure?"

"Symeon Daenyld opposed the Imperador. Symeon is dead."

Staavn's frown deepened. "You sound quite convinced."

"The Imperador wrote a letter to the Council. It's privileged; so I can't divulge its exact content, but the gist was that the Council wasn't to oppose his recommendations. The language was quite strong."

Staavn gave a low whistle, then asked, "Do you know a Rugaar Maartyn?"

"I've heard the name. I've never met him. I believe he's related to Councilor Aldyn Kraagyn."

"From Encora?"

Ysella nodded, then asked, "What has Maartyn done? You wouldn't be asking out of idle curiosity."

"He's bought land around Aloor, and no one seems to know much about him."

"You think he's somehow tied to Lohan Escalante?"

"The thought had occurred to me," said Staavn dryly. "It obviously occurred to you?"

"Only after you told me about his land purchases. Two purchases, or one purchase and an attempted purchase, by outsiders no one has heard of don't seem coincidental."

"Do you know anyone connected to the owners of the Ahnkaar mine?"

"I've heard the names, but I've never met any of them. It doesn't sound healthy to get involved."

"That's what I like about you, Dominic. You're almost skeptical enough to be a newshawk."

"I think I prefer being a water legalist and a councilor."

Staavn shook his head, then said, "Thank you."

Ysella watched him go before leaving the chamber to tell Lyam that the meeting was over.

17

AFTER dressing on Duadi, Ysella claimed the *Chronicle* from the front porch basket and carried it to breakfast, where he sipped café while he read, occasionally taking a bite of croissant or of his single fried egg.

> Councilor Dominic Ysella began his semi-annual open meeting with a brief summary of actions taken by the Imperial Council affecting Aloor. He admitted that not all the deepening of the upper reaches of the Khulor River could be funded. He also said that all Guldoran waterways projects were underfunded because the Imperial government lacked adequate revenues...

Staavn's article cited a few more specifics about other questions Ysella had answered, but did not mention the Imperador's daughter. After that, the remainder seemed almost peripheral to what Ysella had said.

> The councilor did not address one of the reasons for that shortfall, which may be that the Imperador is more interested in building unnecessary first-rate ships of the line, which are too costly to hazard in battle and too large to patrol the shallow waters holding Gulf islands that shelter Atacaman pirates...
>
> In response to questions, the councilor declined to speculate on whether the recent reports about Imperial tin contracts or the recent murders of Thenyt and Khael Wythcomb were linked to recent purchases or attempted purchases of large sections of land near the recently closed Ahnkaar tin mines. Councilor Ysella was clear in stating that he neither knew nor had met the purported purchasers...

Ysella returned to finishing his breakfast, thinking that he definitely needed to refresh his recollection of certain aspects of water law.

Especially before you see Staavn again or meet with Rugaar Maartyn.

He finished breakfast and was headed for his study when he glimpsed a messenger leaving the front porch. He retrieved the single message envelope from the basket, which bore the return address of:

G.B.
South River Docks

G.B.? Ysella frowned as he reentered the house and closed the front door. Then he nodded. It had to be a reply from Gherard Brandt. Once he was in his study, he slit open the envelope and read the message.

Councilor Ysella—
Pietro Sulymar and I very much appreciate your willingness to meet with us at your house at fourth morning bell on Quindi, 17 Winterfirst.
We look forward to seeing you then.

The rather floridly ornate signature was that of Gherard Brandt, with a violet wax seal.

Ysella wondered what "information" would be of interest to him as chairman of the Waterways Committee, but suspected it would be something he already knew, or something he didn't, but which was irrelevant, just to begin gaining support for something they already had in mind.

He set the message aside and turned his thoughts to the possible water-rights questions that might be involved with Rugaar Maartyn's land purchase, as well as what might lie behind the disagreement over selling the mine between Aelyn Wythcomb and Mylls Ahnkaar.

18

Just after third bell on Tridi morning, Ysella answered the door to find a blue-eyed, black-haired young man standing there with an open warm smile.

"Thank you for meeting with me, Councilor," offered Rugaar Maartyn in a pleasing baritone voice.

Ysella distrusted him on sight, but replied, "Come in. We'll meet in my study." He stepped back, letting Maartyn enter, then motioned toward the open study door. Following Maartyn, he gestured to the chair before taking his own seat.

For a moment, Ysella studied the younger man, then said, "Ritter Presswyrth indicated that you had some interest in waterways, but wasn't terribly specific."

"Not so much waterways, but water law. I understand that, besides being the chairman of the Council's Waterways Committee, you're an excellent water legalist, and you're the only member of the Council with experience in both aspects of water law. I mean, in both practicing water law and making it."

"Water law was my practice, but there are certainly other good water legalists, and the laws haven't changed since they were conformed to a prior appropriation standard all across Guldor under the Establishment Act."

"I wondered about that." Maartyn paused. "I'm also curious about any difference between subsurface and surface rights, for example, if an aquifer is the source of a stream, how do the stream rights affect the aquifer or the other way around?"

"Generally speaking, rights are rights, and holders aren't restricted in beneficial uses unless such usage causes harm to another rights holder."

"What if the other rights holder isn't currently using his rights?" asked Maartyn not quite casually.

"That varies by circumstances, but temporary abstinence from use doesn't forfeit registered or usage-created rights. Even a longer abstinence doesn't necessarily result in forfeiture."

Maartyn nodded, then asked, "If rights holders draw from the same aquifer, does one kind of use hold priority over another?"

"The older right, under prior appropriation, has to be met first, but the holder can only take water that's proven to meet beneficial-use criteria."

"Are there any exceptions?"

"The Imperador or the Council can preempt or restrict water rights in the public interest, but that requires a finding of need and a specific edict by the Imperador or an act of the Council."

"What might qualify as a need under law?"

"Those are determined on a case-by-case basis. I could see restricting use if an upstream user made the water unusable for all downstream users, but that's only hypothetical."

"Case-by-case," mused Maartyn. "Could someone petition the Council?"

"Not unless they'd first approached the Waterways administrator or the Natural Resources administrator, depending on the location of the waters, and been rejected."

"Thank you very much for making all that clear. I do appreciate it, Councilor. My uncle said that you were the right person for me to talk to."

"Your uncle? Councilor Kraagyn?"

Rugaar smiled. "No, my other uncle, Merkall Klein. He's from Khasaar."

Ysella managed to keep from nodding. The Kleins had the reputation of being one of wealthiest families west of the hills running down the middle of the south of Guldor. Many landors in Aloor, Nuile, and Daal harbored suspicions that the family quietly backed Laureous after the Crossbow Plot to unseat Ysella's great-grandfather failed, although no evidence implicating the Kleins ever came to light. "You're fortunate to have distinguished uncles on both sides, then."

Maartyn chuckled. "Fortunate . . . and challenging."

"Is there anything else?"

"No, sir."

Ysella stood. "I hope I've been helpful."

Maartyn quickly came to his feet. "More than helpful."

After Maartyn left, Ysella considered their comparatively brief conversation. While the younger man never mentioned the Ahnkaar mine, Ysella had no doubt that Maartyn's concerns about some aspect of water rights involved the mine and wanted to explore some way to affect those rights.

Since the Ahnkaar mine used water, if only to remove it, Mylls Ahnkaar and Aelyn Wythcomb's rights were senior to any rights Maartyn gained by purchase of the adjoining land. That also confirmed, in Ysella's mind, that Rugaar Maartyn was either working with Lohan Escalante or had another interest in the mine.

Which means you ought to look into the matter further.

At the same time, Ysella wondered why he still hadn't heard from Presswyrth about a meeting over future deepening of the upper reaches of the Khulor River.

Ysella went to the stable and saddled the mare, and headed south out of Aloor toward the family lands now held by his cousin Haarkyl. While the sky held high gray clouds, and the air was cold and damp, there was almost no wind. Close to a bell later, he turned off the road and rode up the weathered, barely maintained stone drive to the redstone main house, similar in layout to Ysella's father's mansion, but less than two-thirds the size, with fewer outbuildings. No smoke rose from the separate cottage reserved for an empath, although he had no idea whether Haarkyl had an empath, besides his youngest daughter, Caethya, who was seven.

When Ysella neared the front entry, half a bell before noon, he was debating whether to ride to the stables when Saera hurried out.

"Dominic! Ride around to the stables! Haarkyl will meet you there." Saera gave a wave and a nod before hurrying back into the house.

As Saera had promised, Haarkyl stood beside the open stable door when Ysella reined up.

"I apologize for arriving a little early," said Ysella. "My morning meeting wasn't quite as long as I thought, and the ride out went more quickly than I recalled." He dismounted and led the mare into the stable, following Haarkyl.

"You're fortunate. Two weeks ago, with all the rain, you might not have made it at all. From what we heard, we got twice as much as your father did. We usually do. In a dry year, that's for the best. Unfortunately, this has been a very *wet* year."

"Both Haekaan and Taeryn remarked on that," replied Ysella.

Haarkyl opened the door to a clean stall. "Are you going to unsaddle her?"

"I thought I would."

"Then come to the house when you're done. I've got something I'd like to finish."

"That's no problem. I didn't mean to disrupt your day."

Haarkyl laughed. "I'm the one who invited you. I'll see you in a bit." He turned and walked swiftly from the stable.

Ysella unsaddled the mare, then found a brush and comb and spent a little more time on the mare's coat before walking to the rear of the house.

When he neared the door, a red-haired girl who couldn't have been more than ten opened it and announced, "I'm to take you to the parlor, sir."

"Thank you." Ysella thought. Saera had red hair. "You wouldn't be Sarana, would you?"

"Yes, sir. Mother said she'll join us shortly."

When the two reached the parlor, which appeared little different than when he'd seen it two years earlier, although several pieces of furniture had been replaced, and the room was neater and cleaner, he took a seat in an armchair, while Sarana sat on a stool nearby.

"You're the oldest girl, aren't you?"

"The older daughter, sir. Kyl is older, but he's a boy, and Caethya is seven."

"How do you like living here?"

"I like it. I have my own room now. So does Caethya, and that's very good."

If Caethya was an empath, as Ysella had heard, that was indeed for the best.

After almost a third of a bell, Saera appeared, quickly followed by Haarkyl. Saera motioned to her daughter, and Sarana left the parlor.

"We're so glad you could come, Dominic," declared Saera warmly. "We haven't seen you in what, almost two years?" She took an armchair across from Ysella.

"Something like that," Ysella agreed. "Longer than that at the old house on the other section."

"I thought it might be easier for you to get here." Haarkyl seated himself. "On a good day, the old house is almost a bell farther from Aloor. You're still at the house in town, aren't you?"

"Two modest dwellings are all I can afford."

"I don't see how you manage even that," said Haarkyl.

"It's simple," replied Ysella. "I didn't get married. Now that I can afford to, I scarcely have the time to look."

"Do you want some suggestions?" Saera grinned wickedly. "I have a few cousins."

"Spare him," said Haarkyl. "Let him get into trouble on his own."

"Like you did?"

Haarkyl shook his head.

"How are you settling in?" asked Ysella.

"We've still got a lot of Father's stuff to sort through," said Haarkyl. "He kept almost every paper he ever got."

"As well as every broken scrap," added Saera. "We've managed to sell some of the metal to various smiths."

"Every mark helps, I imagine," replied Ysella.

"As the youngest son, you'd know." Haarkyl's voice was even.

While Ysella discerned a touch of bitterness, he only said, "A hard year?"

"Harder than I want to go into. We've had to let some of the workers go, even some susceptibles, and that meant, with the rains, we lost some of the crops. We're also looking for an empath."

Ysella wasn't about to press the matter. "Your daughter Sarana is sweet and well-mannered. She seems quite bright."

Saera smiled broadly. "Thank you. She's already getting to be quite a help."

"What about Kyl and Caethya?" asked Ysella.

"Kyl's been a help with almost everything," said Haarkyl quickly.

"Caethya," added Saera, "is actually good with the livestock . . . when she's not tired."

Ysella hadn't considered that possibility, and wondered if other empaths could sway animals with emotion. *Or is it too much effort with little return compared to directing susceptibles?*

As Ysella thought about those trade-offs, Haarkyl asked, "How are things with the Council?"

Ysella provided a summary of the situation with the Council and the Imperador and finished by explaining about the limitations on waterway funds for Aloor.

Haarkyl nodded. "The *Chronicle* took a bit of a swipe at you on that."

"They decide not to reelect me, and they'll get less in the future."

"If that happened . . . how are you fixed?"

"I'll go back to being a water legalist. I've been careful, so it shouldn't be a problem." He offered an amused smile. "I'd still be a Ritter."

Sarana appeared in the archway. "Latraana says that refreshments are ready."

"Then we should enjoy them," declared Saera, standing as she spoke.

Ysella followed Haarkyl and Saera to the dining room, where three places were set at one end of the long, polished oak table.

"Lager for you, I believe," said Saera, gesturing to one of the places on the side.

"Yes, thank you."

Within moments, all three had drinks—ale for Haarkyl and Saera and lager for Ysella—and the serving woman, presumably Latraana, had placed two platters on the table filled with various small items, including sausage slices with melted cheese; toast squares topped with a pickled tomato slice, thin white cheese, and basil strips; fried spiced crayfish balls; and late-melon slices.

"This looks delicious," said Ysella, hungry after the morning meeting and the ride from Aloor.

"All from the holding," explained Saera.

"With some skillful preparation," added Haarkyl.

"I can see that," replied Ysella.

After the three served themselves, Saera asked, "How are Raemyna and the baby doing?"

"On Findi, Taeryn said they were doing well. He also said that she wasn't going to have any more children. I sensed that he's afraid of what another child might do to her . . ."

"Wise man," said Saera, "unlike some we've seen . . ."

From there on, the conversation was all about family and the lands, except there was no further mention of Caethya.

Almost two bells passed before Ysella saddled the mare and started down the drive on the ride back to Aloor and his house, questioning why he'd been invited. Certainly, neither had asked for anything or hinted at it, except possibly for the mention of letting some workers go, and the hint that they hadn't been able to hold an empath. That wasn't a surprise, given what Haarkyl had said and what Ysella's mother had written. Ysella had the feeling that Nathanyal had not handled the holding well, and that Haarkyl and Saera were struggling.

He shook his head as he guided the mare onto the road back to Aloor.

19

QUINDI'S *Chronicle* provided little new information except for the article mentioning further successful naval attacks on Atacaman pirates in the Gulf of Nordum, and Ysella had to wonder how long it might be before the Grande Duce retaliated.

After breakfast, he went to his study until fourth bell, when he answered the door and admitted Pietro Sulymar and Gherard Brandt. Sulymar was pale and sandy-haired, which suggested Atacaman or Argenti ancestry somewhere in his background, while Brandt was definitely from darker-skinned landor heritage.

Once the two were seated in the study, Ysella asked, "What might be this information that might be of use to me?"

"Have you heard of the recent work of Professor Gastaan Ritchen at Ondeliew College?" asked Brandt.

"I can't say that I have," Ysella admitted.

"With the help of several accomplished metalsmiths, he has developed a device—something he calls an engine—that burns coal to turn water into pressured steam. That steam powers a piston that turns a shaft. The shaft can be attached to either a wheel or a water screw."

Ysella frowned. "To what end?"

"There are several possible ends," said Sulymar patiently, in an almost patronizing tone. "This steam engine, as Professor Ritchen calls it, could power cloth mills or wagons, or ships so that they wouldn't be as dependent on the wind."

"They might be able to replace mules or oxen in plowing fields," added Brandt. "Some of the coal miners think it could be used to pump water from the mines from greater depths than hand pumps."

"I can see where that might be useful," said Ysella, thinking about the Ahnkaar mine, "but elaborate metalsmithing is expensive, far more so than labor or horses or oxen. That cost would seem to limit the use of this . . . engine."

"For now, but devices improve over time," said Sulymar enthusiastically.

"Some do, and some don't," countered Ysella. "Even if this . . . engine improves, I'm at a loss to see how this applies to me or to the Waterways Committee."

"With this engine, boats could go upstream more easily, and waterways could handle more cargoes," Brandt pointed out.

"That would benefit everyone," said Ysella, "but if this engine is so good, why aren't we seeing it?"

"There's only been a small one built," replied Sulymar. "We wanted you to know about it."

"Are you suggesting that the Council fund the building of a larger one?" asked Ysella.

"That would be helpful," said Brandt, "but we're not asking right now. We thought it would be useful for Council committee chairmen to know about the engine. In the future, the engine might also be useful for naval warships."

In short, you're preparing the ground for a later request for Treasury funds. "I do appreciate your letting me know about the possibilities for this engine. Any future funding requests might be received more favorably if the professor could show success in an existing application, such as pumping water from mines, or propelling a boat upstream with useful cargo."

Brandt nodded. "We can see the wisdom in that, and others have made similar suggestions. We won't take any more of your time, but we did wish to make you aware of the steam engine and its possibilities."

Ysella stood. "I appreciate your doing so. I look forward to hearing about practical applications."

Brandt and Sulymar both stood.

"We'll keep you informed, Councilor."

After seeing the two to the door, Ysella returned to his study, walking back and forth beside the desk, thinking about both the visit . . . and the steam engine. His first instinct had been that the pair were laying the groundwork to obtain Council funds. But if the engine could do all that they implied, why did they need Council funds?

Almost immediately, he thought of Haarkyl, unable to harvest what the lands had produced because he didn't have the marks to pay the workers needed for the harvesting. The steam engine might well do things muscle power couldn't do, but building *anything* took coins up front, and an untested machine was too much of a risk for individuals or even banques.

Not when the banques won't buy government paper.

Then there was the other problem—that a disproportionate share of wealth in Guldor lay with landors and their land, and with the expenses of feeding and paying workers—even the low wages for susceptibles—most landors didn't have a hoard of marks. *You might have more free marks than Haarkyl.*

That thought bothered Ysella, true as it might be. He also wondered if Rugaar Maartyn or Lohan Escalante knew about the steam engine, or something like it, because, if they did...

Perhaps you should pay a visit to Aelyn Wythcomb.

After another third of a bell of self-debate, he walked to the kitchen. "Perri, I'll be leaving shortly to meet with someone. You know I'm eating with the Fettryks tonight after services."

"No reason for me to go anywhere, Ritter." She smiled. "I'll see you in the morning."

"I just wanted you to know."

"I appreciate that."

Close to half a bell later, he reined up at the top of the low crest of the road. To his left, the slightly rutted road led down to the Ahnkaar mine, almost a mille away. The mine buildings looked intact, and a heavy timber gate sealed off the tunnel into the hillside. Below the mine entrance and to the north lay the tailings pond, and slightly farther north a break in the scrub vegetation likely signified a creek or stream.

Ysella looked to his right, where a narrow lane curved up a gentle slope. At the top was the Wythcomb house, a long single-story dwelling with two wings that formed a V. After a moment, Ysella urged the mare forward onto the lane. As he neared the house, he saw that all the windows on the right side were shuttered, as if that entire wing had been closed. The doors to the modest stable were also closed, as was the door to the small building beside the stable.

Is anyone living here?

Since the tinsmith had said Aelyn Wythcomb was still there, Ysella rode up to the ironbound front door, dismounted, tied the mare to the worn bronze hitching post, and walked to the front door, where he used the heavy bronze knocker. Then he waited.

After a time, the peephole in the door opened, and a voice asked, "What do you want?"

"I'm Councilor Dominic Ysella, and I'm here to see Ritten Aelyn Wythcomb."

"I'll tell her." The peephole closed.

More time passed before the peephole opened again, then closed. Moments later, a stocky middle-aged woman in gray livery opened the door.

"Ritten Wythcomb will see you, Councilor." The woman stepped back and opened the door wider.

Ysella entered and followed her through a square entry foyer into a hallway on the left, then into a parlor not much larger than the one in his house in Aloor. A woman as tall as he was, wearing dark mourning green, stood beside an armchair upholstered in gray velvet, the fabric showing a certain amount of age. She could have been anywhere from five to ten years younger than Ysella, and her figure was neither slender nor muscular. Her short, chin-length black hair set off intent gray eyes as she said, "Good day, Councilor. What brings you out here?"

"You, after a fashion."

Aelyn gestured to the armchair facing hers, and seated herself. "In what fashion?"

Ysella seated himself in the gray armchair, which creaked faintly under his weight. "In regard to the Ahnkaar/Wythcomb tin mine."

"You want to buy it, or are you here to persuade me to agree to sell to someone Ritter Ahnkaar prefers?" Aelyn's lips curled slightly as she finished.

"I don't think you should sell it at all. At least, not anytime in the near future."

"Then why are you here? Certainly not to court or console the recent widow."

Ysella saw a trace of a bitter smile, or perhaps a hint of cynical amusement. "Neither. I am sorry about your losses, but I wanted to talk to you and to inform you about certain matters."

"Thank you. Start with the information, if you would." Aelyn's eyes centered on Ysella, seemingly comfortably.

"Some of this you obviously know. Other parts I doubt you do." Ysella began with Jaahn Escalante's attempt to "renegotiate" his naval tin contract, then mentioned Lohan Escalante's rumored attempt to buy the mine.

"It's not a rumor." Aelyn paused, then said firmly, "He and Mylls were close to physically forcing me to sign."

Ysella winced, although he sensed that Aelyn Wythcomb wasn't the type to be forced.

"Go on," said Aelyn.

Ysella described Rugaar Maartyn's purchase of the land uphill from the mine and his subsequent visit and questions about water law.

"Why did you check the legal records?"

"Because I'm skeptical of intertwined coincidences."

"Is there more?"

"As a matter of fact, there is." He leaned forward, elbows on knees, and told her about the brief morning meeting with Sulymar and Brandt, adding, "This professor has already built a small steam engine. That would indicate that it's practical—"

"You're suggesting this engine might be effective enough to pump water out of the mine?" For an instant, her eyes flicked toward the window and the mine.

"Not immediately, but I have observed that once word of any improvement gets out, others flock to copy and improve it. I wouldn't be surprised if someone will have a working steam pump within the next few years."

"A pump, not the engine for ships?"

"There are far more marks to be made quickly in mining, and a few pumps could make a great difference, particularly in your mine."

"Are you involved in the steam engine venture?" Again, her lips curled, if almost imperceptibly.

"Not in the slightest. I believe those supporting it came to me in the hopes of getting Council funds in the future."

"What about Sr. Maartyn?"

"I suspect that he wants the Council to grant him certain water rights. I was not encouraging."

"I appreciate your coming out here and providing this information. I must ask why you bothered." Aelyn leaned forward slightly, her voice showing curiosity.

"Because I didn't want anyone to take advantage of your not knowing those facts."

"Why? You've never met me, and I only know you and your family by name."

"I suppose because I've seen too much unfairness."

"Are you really that noble?"

"Basic fairness isn't being noble. It's what everyone deserves, not that they often get it."

"True enough." She paused once more. "I understand that you've never married. Do you have something against women?"

Ysella thought he saw a glint in her eye. "Not in the slightest."

"But you're not married at your age. You're not unattractive, and you come from a distinguished family, and the Imperador allowed you to dance with his daughter."

"More like ordered."

"Politics, then."

Ysella debated for a moment, then said, "I'm the youngest of three sons, and there wasn't any land for me. I wasn't attracted to any eligible woman who had sufficient land to support a family. So I became a legalist, and that led to becoming a councilor."

"From what I heard from my great-aunt, councilors aren't paid that much. At least, my great-uncle wasn't. Still, many women would wed a councilor."

"So it's said, but interest in a title seldom seems to go with perception and intelligence, let alone the possibility of mutual attraction."

The hint of a frown crossed Aelyn Wythcomb's brow; then she laughed quietly. "Spoken like a legalist."

Ysella shook his head. "I know. I'm terribly pedantic."

"But honest and neither crude nor cruel." She paused. "With your family background, doesn't it feel strange for you to be a councilor under the Imperador?"

"I can't change the past. None of us can. We have to do the best we can now. Being a water legalist in Aloor was about as far as I thought I'd ever get. When the chance to run for councilor came up, I gambled, and it worked out."

"I doubt you gambled. Thenyt said he'd never seen anyone work as hard as you did to get such a thankless position."

"That was kind of him."

"Kind? From him? I think not." She straightened in her chair. "I will say that you've been kind to ride out here and let me know what you have."

"I only thought it fair." *Especially since life hasn't been especially fair to you.*

"Who suggested you come?"

"No one. It was my decision. I'd thought about it since last week, but this morning I decided to come."

Aelyn Wythcomb stood. "I won't keep you, but I do appreciate your taking the time to come out here. It's not a short ride."

Ysella stood as well. "If you have any questions about water rights or law, I'll be here in Aloor until the end of the month. My house is on Second Street, number 420."

"No office here in Aloor?"

"I'm afraid not, Ritten."

"I'll see you out." She led the way from the parlor to the front door, opening it and standing back.

Ysella stopped before departing, looked into her intent gray eyes, then inclined his head. "Do take care, Ritten."

"Thank you, again."

Ysella thought he discerned a hint of warmth in her voice. "I'll repeat myself. If you have any questions—"

"I won't hesitate," she declared firmly.

"Good," he replied with a smile, turning toward the mare.

By the time Ysella mounted, the door was closed, and the house once more appeared deserted.

As he rode down the lane, he couldn't help feeling there was a great deal more to Aelyn Wythcomb than met the eye, and quite a bit was already visible. *But she's in mourning, and she definitely isn't a woman to be rushed or pushed.* At the same time, he was glad he'd decided to meet her and tell what she didn't know. At the very least, if she did decide to sell, she'd be in a better negotiating position.

But he still wondered about her interest in him. Most women he'd met wouldn't have asked why he wasn't married. *But then, a never-married man your age is a bit unusual, especially one from a landor background.*

Since he had some time before going to services, rather than return to the house, he rode to the town hall and made his way inside, looking for Lyam Dattaur, who was in his office.

"Afternoon, Councilor. What brings you here?"

"I was thinking about looking at the unpaid land tariffs. Since we're in the new year . . ."

"They're open to legalists, property owners, and councilors. Seeing as you're all three, you can look."

The councilors to whom Dattaur referred were actually district councilors, but Ysella saw no point in making a correction.

The clerk stood and extracted a key ring from somewhere. Ysella followed Dattaur down the narrow hall to the second doorway, where the clerk unlocked a small chamber holding several file chests on a stand, then lit the wall lamp.

"I updated the entries yesterday. More unpaid than last year, but not so bad as 812, when some holders lost lands."

"I'd hope not," replied Ysella, given that the economic troubles of that year contributed to his winning the Council seat and similar troubles might contribute to his losing it.

"I'll leave you. Snuff the lamp and let me know before you leave the building."

"I will."

Once Dattaur left, Ysella went to work, searching for any possible tariff liens on the Ahnkaar mine, as well as any on family properties. After a bell, he was convinced that there were none. Not finding any was a relief, although that didn't preclude unregistered banque mortgages or other obligatory debts.

He snuffed the lamp and returned to Dattaur's office. "Thank you."

"Find what you were looking for?"

"No . . . and that's good."

Dattaur grinned. "Worried, were you?"

"More like concerned . . . about a friend who'd never tell me." That was true in a way, because none of those concerned would have admitted being unable to pay land tariffs, but none were friends, but family and someone he'd only just met.

From the town hall, Ysella rode the comparatively short distance to the *Chronicle* building, where he found Eraak Staavn.

"What news do you have for me?" asked the newshawk, straightening slightly in his chair.

"Not much, except to say that after your comments in Duadi's edition, I had a very interesting visitor. Have you ever heard of Rugaar Maartyn?" Ysella settled onto the stool in front of Staavn's narrow, paper-piled desk.

"The name sounds familiar," replied Staavn offhandedly, his eyes avoiding Ysella's.

"I think that means you have and don't want to admit it," said Ysella. "In any event, he doesn't live in Aloor. He's a relative of another councilor and was referred to me. He wanted information on water rights and water law."

"Why you?" Staavn leaned forward.

"I thought you might be able to answer that question, since your story mentioned land purchases. Land purchases almost invariably involve water rights."

The newshawk smiled crookedly. "You'll likely find out, if you haven't already. Maartyn bought the land south and uphill of the Ahnkaar mine. I got the impression that he's either working with or against Lohan Escalante in trying to acquire the mine."

"I heard that Khael Wythcomb's widow has no interest in selling. How accurate do you think that is?"

"I wouldn't know," replied Staavn. "I went out to the Wythcomb place. She wouldn't see me."

"Widow in mourning, perhaps?"

"Word is that she stood off Mylls Ahnkaar when he pressed her to sell."

"Was Ahnkaar the one to tell you?"

"Not in so many words, but . . ." The newshawk's lips curled. "What's your interest?"

"The naval tin contract. That could affect the Council, especially since Alaan Escalante is now chairman of the Council's Military Affairs Committee."

"What else do you think?"

"Right now, I don't know."

"You sure about that?"

"I really don't *know,* and I'm not in a position to guess."

"You're a frigging bastard, Dominic," said Staavn flatly, but not angrily, leaning back in his chair, if only slightly.

"What else about Rugaar Maartyn?" Ysella shifted his weight on the uncomfortable stool.

"He's tied to the Klein family, and I get the feeling they want to buy into Aloor in some way. Maartyn's purchase might be the first of many."

"That's not good," Ysella pointed out. "Particularly for townspeople here. Might not hurt to mention in your story that the Kleins are known for buying cheap and then jacking up prices."

"What source would confirm that?"

"A legalist in Machtarn who wishes to remain anonymous, possibly. I'll deny it and file a suit for defamation if you quote me directly."

Staavn chuckled. "I said you were a bastard. For something that general, a respected but anonymous source will do."

"Especially since most people already know that, even if they need to be reminded."

"Do you have any more of that 'not much news' sowshit?"

Ysella shook his head. "Not much happens in Machtarn during Winterfirst, except the Imperador laying the foundation for marrying off his headstrong and quite intelligent daughter as soon as he feasibly can. Preferably to a man able to keep her in check."

"I'll save that for when there's an announcement," said Staavn dryly.

"If I do come up with more news before I return to Machtarn, I'll let you know."

"Much appreciated."

Ysella could almost feel Staavn's eyes on him as he left the building.

Once he untied and mounted the mare, he rode down several streets before turning toward the Trinitarian chapel. When he finally arrived, it was still a third before fifth bell, but he dismounted and tied the mare to the hitching rail closest to the side door before entering and making his way to his seat in the back. He was early enough that the chapel was silent for a time before the harpsichordist began to play.

The service progressed like any other service over which Maabak presided, with a comparatively brief, if prosaic, homily about the need for what Maabak called "routine kindness" in daily life, the idea that kindness shouldn't be something done only occasionally or specially, but an ongoing part of daily life. The homily made Ysella question whether he gave himself too much self-approval for visiting Aelyn Wythcomb.

But you know you needed to do it, even if it was partly to make you feel better.

It didn't help that he'd been intrigued by her, and that she certainly wasn't a weeping widow, so to speak.

After services, Ysella managed to escape before encountering Presider Maabak, and soon rode south on the road to Daal toward the Fettryk holding.

Almost two-thirds of a bell passed before Ysella rode between the redstone posts flanking the gravel and clay drive leading to the house, surrounded by two barns and several sheds. According to what Fettryk had written months earlier, the lands bequeathed by Fettryk's great-uncle weren't extensive, perhaps comparable in size to those managed by Taeryn and Raemyna, but close to a tenth part was rich bottomland, far more productive per hectare than many of the higher lands held by Ysella's father or those deeded prospectively to Raemyna.

Even before Ysella neared the one-story dwelling, perhaps half the size of Aelyn Wythcomb's house, Bruuk Fettryk stood waiting on the covered side porch, then led Ysella to the barn containing stalls.

"You're a bit early, but you often are."

Ysella laughed. "I don't want to be late, and I leave extra time for delays. If there aren't any . . . well . . . then I'm early."

"That's harder on you," returned Fettryk, "but more considerate of us."

Once the two stalled the mare, they walked back to the house, which, although modest for a holding, seemed to be in good condition.

"This is all well-kept," said Ysella. "Are you still a practicing legalist?"

"Absolutely. Gineen's more than capable of running the holding. That way, we're not quite so much at the mercy of the weather, and the grain and livestock markets. The house in town is now more of an office." Bruuk opened the side door and led the way to the parlor.

Ysella immediately recognized some, but not all, of the furniture, as Gineen hurried into the parlor, a wide smile on her face, her eyes bright.

"We're so glad you could come, Dominic."

"I was going to drop in on you two, but your invitation came before I could make arrangements."

"As I recall," said Gineen, "it's either Silverhills red or lager."

"Either. I'll leave it up to you."

She returned almost before Ysella and Bruuk had seated themselves, with three glasses holding Silverhills red. She tendered one to Ysella and the second to her husband before taking an armchair herself, one of three in a rough semicircle. "It's really not a family dinner—only the three of us. We already fed the children."

"How are they doing?" asked Ysella.

"They miss some of their friends, but on the whole the change has been good for them. They've been a help in getting us settled."

"Will I ever get the whole story of how you two became Ritter and Ritten?" asked Ysella. "All you ever said was the lands were bequeathed by an uncle you never knew you had."

"I suppose it can't hurt, and you're known to keep confidences." Bruuk looked to Gineen.

She nodded.

"You already know," began Bruuk, "that my father's lands have to go to my brother."

"I'm familiar with that situation," replied Ysella dryly, letting himself sink into the armchair.

Bruuk grinned. "I know." After a moment, he asked, "Do you recall any landor holding these lands when we were growing up?"

"No. I can't say that I do. I wondered, but assumed that whoever managed the lands did it on behalf of a landor who had greater holdings elsewhere."

"Not exactly," replied Bruuk, pausing to take a sip of his wine. "The landowner actually lived here and managed the lands, quite well, in fact, at least until the year or so before his death. He was my grandfather's brother, Kaastar, and he had no heirs, male or female. I never knew that he existed until the legalists contacted me."

Ysella glanced to Gineen, who again nodded, then asked, "Why all the secrecy, and why did the lands come to you, rather than to your father?"

"Because my grandfather refused to acknowledge his brother, and refused to pass his lands on to my father unless he also rejected Grandfather's brother, who was, of course, Father's uncle. My father and my brother refused to accept Kaastar, and they never told me. You may recall that my brother's almost ten years older than I am. When my granduncle died, the terms of his will stipulated that the lands should come to me. My father contested the will, but it was too well drawn and documented. So . . ." Bruuk shrugged.

"Drafted by Legrand?" asked Ysella.

"Who else," replied Bruuk with a chuckle. "Legrand never let me know until Kaastar died."

That figures. Legrand's always been ethical and professional. "Why was he rejected and never acknowledged?" asked Ysella. "If you don't mind?"

"Let's say that he didn't like women . . . and had an intimate male friend, who died a year or so before he did."

"And no one would acknowledge your granduncle as landor and Ritter." Ysella understood that, because same-sex cohabitation and carnal knowledge had been prohibited under the laws of old Aloor and were barely tolerated in Guldor. "The lands went to you because they had to go to a male blood relative, if possible, and you were the one most removed from those who rejected him?"

"Exactly," replied Bruuk, leaning back into his chair.

Ysella shook his head. "How did your family react?"

"Father won't talk about it. I'm welcome there, but he won't come here. Shahan accepts it, because he never expected more, although I think he's a little miffed that I have lands before he does. We've asked him and Karola for dinner. They always regret."

Ysella looked to Gineen.

Her smile was one of grim amusement. "That's their problem. They rejected Granduncle Kaastar. So he rejected them. Kaastar must have figured that Bruuk would be at least grateful."

Bruuk took another sip of wine before replying. "Which I am. I do wish I'd known him. From what we found here, he had excellent taste, and he managed the lands well. He was partial to cattle, and we've added a small flock of sheep."

"And expanded the kitchen garden," added Gineen, with a quick grin. "I always wanted a larger garden."

"What about you, Dominic?" asked Bruuk, his voice casual. "I read that some folks complained that you didn't get enough waterways funds."

Ysella explained as quickly as he could, then asked, "Have you ever encountered a Rugaar Maartyn?"

Bruuk frowned in thought. "Not really. He stopped by the house . . . well, the office, since it was after we moved the family and most things here. He was looking for a property legalist. Why?"

Ysella explained the tin-mine situation, including his brief visit with Aelyn Wythcomb.

"That sounds a bit sticky," suggested Gineen. "But it was kind of you to let her know. I've only encountered her a few times. She was always pleasant, if a little distant. From what I heard, she didn't have much choice about marrying Khael Wythcomb . . . and then to lose her grandfather—he was really her father for most of her life—and with Khael and his father murdered so soon after they were married . . ." She shook her head.

"There's likely more there," said Ysella. "If anything new comes to your attention, I'd appreciate your letting me know."

"We can do that," said Bruuk. "Oh, did I tell you that I ran into your cousin Haarkyl at the grain exchange a while back?"

"No, you didn't."

"I thought I mentioned it in my letter last month. He didn't look very happy for a man who inherited a holding."

"He probably wasn't. I visited him on Tridi. I think Uncle Nathanyal let a lot of things slip in the last year or so, maybe before that."

"It's getting late," said Gineen. "Perhaps we should move to the dining room, and we can tell you more about the holding." She stood.

So did Bruuk and Ysella.

Ysella had a strong feeling that the rest of the evening would be about reminisces and the holding, or about legalistic efforts, but he also knew he'd enjoy the conversation and the company, without having to worry about every word.

20

BECAUSE Ysella stayed later than he anticipated talking to Bruuk and Gineen, he had a slow ride home in the dark, and slept late on Findi morning. He woke to lazy snowflakes drifting out of greenish-gray clouds, but the clouds vanished by noon, as did the light covering of snow.

By second afternoon bell, he rode north on the road to the family holding. As before, he saw a few wagons, two other riders, and two carriages, but only from a distance. After he reached the main house, he rode straight to the stable, where he unsaddled and stalled the mare before going to the main house. He shed his overcoat and gloves in the rear entry foyer, and hung the overcoat on a wall peg.

Since no one was yet in the parlor, he made his way to his mother's study.

Kaelyn looked up from her desk with a pleasant smile, slipping the pen she held into its holder. "Good. You're here early. The Paarkyls should be here shortly. I told them third bell."

"What should I know about the young lady?"

"Evalynn? She's really quite attractive and far too intelligent for most of the remaining eligible landors anywhere nearby."

"I believe you mentioned those traits last Findi." *Word for word.* "What *else*?"

"As I recall, she's rather petite and demure. She has clear skin and a pleasant speaking voice. She dresses well."

Doesn't every landor young lady looking for a husband? Ysella merely nodded.

"I believe she has some lands that would go with her hand, an older holding with a modest dwelling." Kaelyn's tone definitely sounded approving.

"Lands aren't a principal concern for me."

"Lands, dear, should always be a concern. They're the foundation of prosperity."

Only when one owns them and not the other way around. "Is there anything else you can tell me about Evalynn Paarkyl?"

"Nothing that I can think of at the moment, dear."

More like nothing else you wish to tell me. "Thank you. I need a moment with Father."

"Oh?"

"I had refreshments with Haarkyl on Tridi."

"He will want to know about that, I'm sure. Best you tell him before company arrives."

"I'd thought to." Ysella smiled warmly and left the study.

He didn't find his father in his study, but in the adjoining library, seated next to the fireplace filled with two large chunks of firewood, recently added, since they were only beginning to catch fire.

"I saw Haarkyl on Tridi."

The elder Cliven lowered the ledger he'd been studying. "Did he ask for marks?"

"No." *Even if he did indicate they were facing difficulties.* "He did say that they'd had to sort through a lot of papers, because Uncle Nathanyal kept every scrap of paper he ever got."

"I wouldn't be surprised if they didn't have to deal with a lot of broken tools and the like."

"Saera mentioned that they'd sold some scrap to metalsmiths."

"At least they had sense enough to do that. Anything else?"

"Not really. They've cleaned up the place quite a bit from the way it was."

"Hardly a surprise. Nathanyal couldn't be bothered to clean and didn't want anyone but family in the house after Chaarlyn died. Saera had her hands full with the relic of a house where Nathanyal insisted they live."

"You didn't ever mention that."

"No point in it. Nothing was going to change Nathanyal's mind. Anything else?"

"Have you heard the name Rugaar Maartyn?"

"Should I?"

"No, but it might be wise to listen for it now. Cyraen Presswyrth referred him to me. He's a nephew of Councilor Aldyn Kraagyn and a nephew of Merkall Klein. *Those* Kleins. He's bought land near the Ahnkaar mine, and he asked questions about water law. He's got something devious in mind dealing with water rights . . . and possibly the Council. I thought you should know."

"I appreciate that. Anyone referred by Presswyrth and related to the Kleins needs to be watched. Why did he seek you out?"

"Ostensibly for my experience as a water legalist, but more probably to make my acquaintance so he can request something from the Waterways Committee."

"Whatever it turns out to be, don't do it, unless you know the situation inside and out."

"That was my inclination."

"Stick with it." The elder Cliven lifted the ledger in his lap slightly.

Ysella sensed the impatience, but said, "I have one other question. I understand that Ritten Wythcomb's great-uncle was a councilor . . ."

"Oh . . . that was Maelcar Scalante. I haven't heard his name in years. He died suddenly in office years ago. His widow and son stayed in Machtarn. She was from somewhere near there and had lands and funds of her own."

"Thank you. I won't keep you," said Ysella.

"I appreciate the information, Dominic."

"My pleasure, sir." And it was, in a way, reflected Ysella as made his way to the parlor.

Maadlyn appeared before he could take a seat. "Could I get you something to drink, sir?"

"Not now. When company arrives and you get their drinks, I'd like a Silverhills red."

"Yes, sir."

Ysella took one of the side armchairs, but before long Ennika appeared.

"You're here early, Uncle Dominic."

"I've never liked being late, Ennika."

"I don't, either, and I don't like it when things happen I can't control, and then I'm late."

Ysella's smile held amusement. "That makes two of us, but sometimes it happens that way."

"Happens what way?" asked Jaeralyn as she and Haekaan entered the parlor, followed by young Cliven and Erskaan.

"When being late is beyond one's control."

"That's the least of things to worry about," declared Haekaan. "Nothing compared to the weather, or a drop in grain prices. Or if the rain washes rank algae into a seep in the field."

"Or the red flux strikes out of nowhere," added Erskaan.

"Enough," said Jaeralyn firmly but quietly.

Ysella heard voices coming from the entry foyer and stood. So did Haekaan, young Cliven, and Erskaan.

Kaelyn escorted three individuals into the parlor. "Most of you know each other, except for the young lady, who is Evalynn, accompanied by her parents, Ritter Naartyn Paarkyl and Ritten Lynnal Paarkyl. The dark-haired gentleman in the dark blue jacket is our youngest son and councilor, Dominic."

From what Ysella saw as the Paarkyls stood in the archway into the parlor, his mother had described Evalynn accurately—except for one thing. Compared to the others in her family, or everyone in Ysella's family, Evalynn's skin color was at best several shades lighter, suggesting Atacaman or Argenti background somewhere, but Ysella immediately said, "I'm pleased to meet you. I haven't had the pleasure, unless it occurred when I was very, very, young."

Naartyn Paarkyl smiled. "As I recall, you were four at the time."

"It's good to see you all again," declared Jaeralyn.

"And, as usual," came the voice of the elder Cliven from behind the Paarkyls, "I'm a touch behind."

In moments, everyone was seated, with Evalynn in the armchair closest to Ysella, and Maadlyn began to take wine requests.

Evalynn asked for Silverhills white, then said to Ysella, "Mother never mentioned that you were a councilor. She said that you'd done exceptionally well."

"For the youngest son, at least," replied Ysella.

"How did you become a councilor?" Evalynn turned more in her chair toward Ysella.

"I started out as a legalist, a water legalist, in fact. When the previous councilor died just before elections were called, I used the petition option to require the district councilors to put me on the ballot against their choice. Then I visited every house in Aloor and as many holdings as I could get to. I won by less than a hundred votes. No one wanted to go against me in the last election."

"You actually talked to all those people? I mean crafters and all?"

"Any property or shop owner can vote. Their votes count as much as do landors'."

"You're anything but a crafter."

"True," replied Ysella, "and I'd do poorly at most crafts." He paused as Maadlyn handed Evalynn a glass of Silverhills white and one of Silverhills red to him. "Much as I appreciate good crafting."

"Appreciating excellence in crafting is one thing. Actually doing it is another, don't you think?" A touch of distain infused her words, and her eyes shifted to Jaeralyn momentarily.

"Absolutely," replied Ysella cheerfully. "Appreciating is so much easier than doing."

For a long moment, Evalynn was silent. Finally, she asked, "Do you like being a councilor, or do you find it tedious at times?"

"I don't exactly love being a councilor, and at times it's definitely tedious.

Even so, I've discovered that I can make a useful contribution, and I like working at something meaningful."

"But doesn't the Imperador make all the important decisions?"

"He makes the few major decisions, but the Council makes most of the decisions that impact people."

Evalynn's frown conveyed incomprehension.

Ysella suppressed a sigh. "Take Waterways, for example. The Imperador recommends a level of expenditures, but the Council decides how many of those marks go to which districts for what projects."

"Oh . . . I didn't know that."

Ysella had the feeling that the evening would be long and, as Evalynn herself had put it, very tedious.

21

ON Unadi, Ysella awoke again to light snow flurries. After breakfast, since he had no engagements, pressing or otherwise, he decided to draft possible legislation to lift the ceiling imposed on interest rates, or what of it he could without the precise statutory references. That took most of the day, and he was far from finished when he set aside his pen.

Duadi morning dawned sunny, if cold for Aloor.

As he sipped his café at the breakfast table, Ysella began to read the *Chronicle.*

> Last Tridi, Atacaman pirates attacked the *Provident,* a supply ship bound for Port Reale, looting the vessel, and then setting it afire . . . less than half the crew escaped in a dinghy . . .
>
> Newly appointed Imperial Fleet Marshal Raul Dhaantyn declared, "If the Grande Duce will not put a stop to such depredations, then we will."

Ysella frowned. *I thought that's what we were already doing.*

The rest of the newssheet contained local events, including a barn fire on a smallholding, an unidentified man found dead in the alley behind Corners on Findi night, and a finding by the district justicer that one Mykar Juul was guilty of grand theft, and sentenced to exile.

Most likely, he'll be dropped off on an isle off Medarck or Sargasso.

After breakfast, Ysella again checked the mail and message basket, retrieved three envelopes, and carried them to his study, looking at the return addresses—none from Aloor.

The first was another letter from Phillipe Chellwyn, a landor from west of Sudaen, who'd written Ysella at least four times in the past year. Ysella debated setting it aside, then read it anyway, since not replying would make matters worse.

> *Councilor Ysella—*
>
> *While you are to be congratulated for obtaining more funding for improvements along the Khulor River, that funding is less than necessary to meet existing needs, let alone what will be required in the years to come . . .*

The one consolation Ysella could take was that Chellwyn didn't live in the Aloor district. The downside was that doubtless some of his landor acquaintances did. That was exactly the reason Ysella spent so much time visiting and listening to property owners who weren't landors and crafters with shops.

The second letter came from Antonin Desaar, a landor near Daal, who expressed similar sentiments, if far more politely and indirectly.

The third letter was signed by Cyraen Presswyrth.

Councilor Ysella—

My deepest thanks for your taking the time to meet with Sr. Maartyn, and doing so as quickly as you did.

I appreciate your thoughtfulness in spending time with him and in explaining the intricacies of water law and the degrees of appropriation priorities and how they're established . . .

Ysella frowned. Presswyrth had to know that much about water law, at least in general terms, and he'd never been so solicitous before. Then Ysella smiled. Most likely Presswyrth had tried to explain, and Maartyn ignored his advice. *Could it be that Presswyrth is in debt in some fashion to Merkall Klein . . . or someone else in the Klein family, and your explanation reinforced his position and credibility with them?*

Best of all, the rest of the letter didn't deal with the Waterways appropriation, although Ysella wondered why, unless Presswyrth's much earlier letter suggesting a meeting had been to prepare the way for Maartyn.

Ysella settled into the chair behind his desk, thinking about how he'd need to reply to each of the letters. Then he began to write.

Close to a bell later, he finished the carefully worded letter to Phillipe Chellwyn, which he'd put off until last, and turned to reading through what he'd drafted on Unadi. At that moment, he heard a pounding on the front door, followed by Perri's steps.

Although Ysella couldn't make out the words, he clearly heard the anger in the man's voice. He was on his feet before Perri appeared in the study doorway.

"There's a Ritter Ahnkaar to see you, sir. He seems upset."

And I know why. Ysella smiled sourly. "Just withdraw to the back of the house, Perri. I'll see him."

Ysella checked the truncheon at his belt, hoping he wouldn't need it, but well aware that anger made men not only violent, but also stupid. He walked to the door, opening it wide so that his movements wouldn't be hampered, then said to the tall, burly man standing there, "Ritter Ahnkaar?"

"That's me. What right do you have to mess with my property?"

"I don't have anything to do with your property."

"Liar. That mine is my property."

"Ritter . . . why don't you come in? You don't have to stand out here in the cold and shout." Ysella's hand closed around the truncheon's grip.

Ahnkaar lunged for Ysella, who, rather than retreating, stepped forward and slammed the truncheon where it would immobilize Ahnkaar.

The older man doubled over, and Ysella's knee came up and struck the underside of Ahnkaar's jaw, snapping his head back.

Ysella was amazed that the gray-haired Ahnkaar still stood, if staggering some. The older man started to reach for his belt knife.

"Don't!" snapped Ysella, the force of his voice stopping Ahnkaar.

Before Ahnkaar could do anything more, Ysella said, "Killing a councilor is a death sentence, and after what you tried I could legally kill you. You'd also lose the mine."

"I'd still like to . . ." muttered Ahnkaar.

"Why? I'm the one who's trying to save you and Ritten Wythcomb."

"So you can profit?"

"No. So the Escalantes and Kleins don't get a foothold in Aloor. So you can mine more tin in another few years."

"With a seasprite's story about a magic engine that can pump out the mine? Nothing can pump all that water."

"If nothing can pump that water, then why do at least two different men want to buy the mine, and why did one buy the adjoining land? I don't see the Kleins or Escalantes buying worthless properties."

"Why do you care?" Ahnkaar's voice held both anger and puzzlement.

"I don't like the way they're sneaking around Aloor, and I have the feeling we don't know the worst." Ysella stepped back, truncheon still in hand. "Would you like to come in and talk about it?"

"We can talk right here," growled Ahnkaar.

"Because Lohan Escalante's father is trying to avoid delivering on a naval tin contract, and I've been trying to find out what's behind it, especially after I heard about the attempt to buy the mine and the murder of Thenyt and Khael Wythcomb. When I found out that someone's built a small steam engine that could be used to pump water from a mine, I thought they might be trying to buy your mine cheaply before someone builds a bigger version of the steam engine."

"So why didn't you come to me first?"

"I thought about Aelyn Wythcomb first because my family knew Thenyt and, frankly, because it appeared someone was trying to pressure her to sell." *And because you might have been behind Thenyt and Khael's deaths.*

"Likely story."

"I don't know anyone in this mess. I didn't know about the attempt to buy the mine until I returned from Machtarn less than two weeks ago. I found out about the steam engine or pump last Quindi, and since I knew where the Wythcomb house was, I went there because I didn't want either of you blindsided."

For several moments, Mylls Ahnkaar didn't speak. Finally, he said, "That's all well and good, but what am I supposed to do until this . . . steam . . . device works? If it even works. I don't have that many marks left."

"At the least, you could use the information about the steam engine to bargain for a better price from Lohan Escalante if the Escalantes want it so badly," replied Ysella. "Or you might try selling part of your interest to Rhend Jarrell. He might be interested and has a few spare marks. He also knows something about machines, although I have no idea if he knows about the steam engine."

Ahnkaar frowned. "It doesn't matter. Aelyn Wythcomb owns more than half, and she won't sell. Without her consent . . ."

"For any further mining to take place it would require a petition to the Imperial Justiciary, and it would likely be denied because she's the majority holder," Ysella finished.

"You a legalist?"

"Yes. My practice was water law." Ysella wondered how Ahnkaar didn't know that if he'd talked to Aelyn Wythcomb. *But then Ahnkaar doesn't seem like the thinking type, or the type to give anyone a chance to explain when he's angry.*

"Was?"

"I'm the councilor from Aloor and have been for more than six years. It's hard to practice law of any kind in Aloor when you're spending most of the year in Machtarn."

"Fine. Stay out of this."

"I'm not interested in buying, selling, or interfering in the Ahnkaar mine. I will provide legal advice to Aelyn Wythcomb if she requests it or if other legal information comes to light that I think she should know." Ysella looked coldly at Ahnkaar, adding, "And I will get *more* involved if anything happens to her."

Ahnkaar didn't meet Ysella's eyes. "Legalists!" He turned, stalked back to the hitching post, untied his mount, mounted, and rode off.

Ysella didn't move until Ahnkaar was well down the street. As he stepped back and closed the door, he saw Perri standing there, holding a heavy iron skillet. "I see I had reinforcements."

"You didn't need them. You've never needed them. I heard what you did in Sudaen. Your folks kept it real quiet." Perri shook her head. "Not like Ritter Ahnkaar. Folks said he killed a miner years back. He got away with it, too."

That didn't surprise Ysella, but he smiled sardonically as he thought about Ahnkaar's parting word. *Complaining about legalists, when one likely saved his neck?*

Ysella returned the truncheon to its belt holder, and walked back to his study.

After perhaps a sixth of pacing and thinking, he sat down at the desk and began to write, then reread what he'd written.

Ritten Wythcomb—

I thought you would like to know that Ritter Mylls Ahnkaar paid me a visit earlier today. He was somewhat agitated, but seemed slightly less so when he departed.

I told him the same facts that I told you. I also informed him that I have no interest in buying or selling the Ahnkaar mine, but that I do have a professional interest in seeing that whatever you and Ritter Ahnkaar decide, whether you agree or not, is handled fairly under the law.

If you have any other questions, you can write or call upon me, at your convenience.

He signed and sealed the envelope, then donned his overcoat for the walk to the post centre to post all four letters. There would be plenty of time later to revise and work on his legislative proposals. He also wished he could have written more to Aelyn Wythcomb, especially after his evening with Evalynn Paarkyl, but that would have to wait.

22

AFTER breakfast on Tridi, Ysella walked to the patrol station, and once inside, stopped at the duty desk, where he asked politely, "Is Lieutenant Ghavan in, Patroller Kaarpn?"

"He's in his office, second door over there."

"Thank you."

The patroller nodded.

As Ysella turned toward Ghavan's half-open door, he found himself surprised at Kaarpn's response, a far cry from their first encounter.

The lieutenant motioned Ysella in before he could knock, then asked, "What did you do to Mylls Ahnkaar? He came in here yesterday morning and demanded we lock you up for assault, but when Kaarpn asked for the details, Ahnkaar said to forget it, that Kaarpn was useless."

Ysella took the single chair across the desk from Ghavan. "Ahnkaar tried to pound in my front door, and then attacked me. I defended myself. He didn't like it."

"I thought it might be like that. So did Kaarpn."

"Kaarpn was a lot more friendly this time."

"Ahnkaar comes in complaining a lot, demands that Kaarpn, or whoever's on the desk, do something to someone who's annoyed him. It's never enough to warrant a charge, but it takes up time." Ghavan paused, looking Ysella up and down. "Ahnkaar's a head taller than you, and he wouldn't say how you assaulted him."

"He lunged at me and got a truncheon where it usually stops someone cold, then took a knee to his chin. He was a little shaky after that, but not for long."

"Where did you learn that?"

"From a former Imperial squad leader I ran into in Machtarn. I practiced a lot."

"As a Ritter, you could carry a gladius," ventured Ghavan. "I can't believe you weren't trained in blade skills."

"I was, but a gladius is unnecessary temptation." *For both brigands and me.*

"If I might ask, what did you do to get Ahnkaar so riled up?"

"I recommended to Ritten Aelyn Wythcomb that she not sell the mine at present."

"You think Ahnkaar was involved in the murders?"

"You'd know better than I would. He obviously gets worked up easily, but you said both their heads were bashed in. If he attacked one of them, it would seem likely that the other could have gotten away or would have more wounds than a broken skull. How did they disappear?"

"According to Ritten Wythcomb, the two of them walked down to check the mine about midmorning. They usually did that daily, if at different times. Sometimes she went, sometimes not. She waited for the tinsmith to come for some tin, and then took the wagon to town. When she got back, they hadn't returned. She unloaded the wagon, and drove down to the mine. The mine was locked up, with no sign of either of them. The serving woman said that they'd never come back to the house. Ritten Wythcomb drove back to town and reported here. She was worried, because her husband and his father wouldn't ever have walked away. I came out with another patroller, but it started to rain, heavy-like, and if there were any tracks anywhere, we couldn't find them."

"So she was largely in sight of people away from the mine, and they saw the two walk away," said Ysella. "Why didn't anyone look in the tailings pond?"

"You can't see deeper than a few digits in that water, and it's four or five yards deep in places, or it was before the rain broke through the dam on the north side. The top of the dam was rough-paved with slag from the mine. Without all that rain, it might have been years before anyone found the bodies . . . if they lasted that long."

"What about Mylls Ahnkaar?"

"He went to Nuile early that morning. Didn't get back until after sunset. People with him all the time as well. He could have planned it, but there was no way he could have done it himself."

Ysella shook his head. "Do you think you'll ever know?"

"I'd wager on Ahnkaar, but proving it . . . that's another thing."

"What about the Escalantes or the Kleins?"

Ghavan shrugged. "No one's ever pinned anything on either family. That tin contract with the Navy might be the first time they get stopped."

"All they'll lose there is a few marks," said Ysella sarcastically.

"Be nice to be able to think like that."

"Wouldn't it," agreed Ysella. "Is there anything else going on?"

"Not anything as odd as the mine situation. Except that there was another dead man behind Corners this morning. No one knew who he was, either. Nothing in his wallet or pockets. Cleaned out."

"Older man?" asked Ysella.

"About your age. Might have been a former army or navy ranker. That's about it."

While Ysella was tempted to link the dead man to the Wythcomb murders, such a linkage made no sense, because the murders occurred weeks ago, but that was Ghavan's problem.

From the patrol station, Ysella made his way to the office of Hydaar & Fhaen, where he waited for a third of a bell before Luvaal Fhaen's client departed. Ysella noted that the door to the personal office of the senior partner, Haasyn Hydaar, remained closed.

As soon as Ysella entered and shut the door, Fhaen gestured to the chairs and said, "The word is that you've gotten involved with Aelyn Wythcomb."

"If involved means providing information that might affect the value of the mine, talking to her for less than half a bell, and sending her a letter telling her that I shared the same information with Mylls Ahnkaar." Ysella settled into the chair directly across the desk from the legalist.

"That wasn't quite the way Mylls put it to Haasyn yesterday afternoon." Fhaen's lips twisted sardonically. "At least, at first."

"He tried to get the patrol on me as well. He failed to mention that he assaulted me first. I won't press you on what he claimed about me, since he's a client of your partner."

"He's not my client, thank the Almighty, but I appreciate the courtesy. Might I ask what got him so upset with you?"

"Although I could claim privilege, I won't. I met with Ritten Wythcomb briefly last Findi." Ysella summarized what he said, then added, "After I repulsed Ahnkaar's assault, I gave him the same information. I also sent a letter to the Ritten informing her that I'd told Ahnkaar what I'd told her."

"Couldn't tell that you're a legalist . . . except for the truncheon, that is."

"I got to carrying it in Machtarn. I never thought I'd need it here."

"Most people here know who you are . . . or your family."

Except certain patrollers. "Which is why Mylls Ahnkaar had no trouble finding and pounding on my door, though I'd never met him." Ysella paused. "What can you tell me about Aelyn Wythcomb, besides being Khael Wythcomb's widow and heir?"

"Not much. She's from a landor family out of Silverhills, Scalante family, I think. Same family as the councilor from Silverhills some years back. Her grandparents raised her after her parents both died. Haasyn might know more. He's been the legalist for the Ahnkaar family, but neither of us has had any contact with the Wythcombs."

"Has the name Rugaar Maartyn ever come up to you?"

Fhaen shook his head. "I can't say it has. Why?"

"He stopped by to see me, ostensibly about water law, but there was something more behind the visit. So I did a little checking, and he recently bought property adjoining the Ahnkaar mine. His uncle is also Merkall Klein."

"Those Kleins?" A sour expression followed the words.

Ysella nodded.

"Very interesting. I appreciate the information. Haasyn will also find it interesting."

"Anything I should know that you can tell me?"

"Not right now."

"Then I won't impose any longer." Ysella stood.

So did Fhaen. "No imposition. You're welcome anytime."

After leaving Fhaen's office, Ysella walked to Legrand Quaentyn's house, hoping the older legalist might be able to help.

Once again, Quaentyn opened the front door, and his smile was warm as ever. "Dominic! I didn't think I'd see you quite so soon again."

"I'd like some of your recollections and expertise."

Quaentyn stepped back and opened the door wide. "Do come in. You have all the expertise you need, but my recollections—those I remember—are at your disposal." He led the way to the parlor, warm enough, although the wall stove held mostly red coals, and sat down.

Ysella took the chair nearest Quaentyn. "We talked about water rights and the Ahnkaar tin mine last time. What else can you tell me about the Wythcombs, especially about Aelyn?"

The older legalist frowned. "Well . . . they weren't really landors, at least in the minds of most landors, but they had enough land that no one wanted to gainsay that. When Thenyt married Tressa, there was more than a little talk, because she was a cousin of sorts to Mylls Ahnkaar, even if she lived in Nuile. Deyrdra always said that Tressa was a stern old biddy. She kept Thenyt in line. I think Ellyann died young because dealing with Mylls wore her out. They only had Myltan. He and his father barely speak. Possibly that's why he went in the Navy. I heard that he got command of a frigate last year. He and his wife have a house in Port Reale."

"And Aelyn Wythcomb?"

"Are you interested in her?"

"Interested enough to know more, anyway."

"Her grandparents married her off. She had a small dowry, and it paid off Thenyt's mine debts, but the price for that was that both Thenyt's and Khael's wills named her as sole heir."

"Thenyt and Tressa didn't have any other children?"

"None that survived."

"How did . . . you were Thenyt's legalist?"

Quaentyn nodded.

"Let me guess," said Ysella. "You were the only one in town he trusted? Even though you were a water legalist?"

"Something like that."

"Aelyn?" prompted Ysella.

"You are interested," mused Quaentyn.

"I don't know enough to be interested."

"Well . . . she has a mind of her own. She was the one who insisted on the wills. Not her grandparents. She pointed out that, if anything happened to Khael, without such a direct legal expression, she'd be saddled with a conservatorship that might easily disenfranchise her and leave her unable to support any children."

"Was she right?"

"It was possible, if unlikely. I was only asked if that could happen. I said it could."

"What do you think of her?"

"Like many intelligent women, she's tried to make the best of the situation in which she found herself. With a surname of Braathwell, she didn't have many options."

Ysella frowned. "Who knows about the wills?"

"The probate findings are open to any legalist."

"I'd have to say that someone with a suspicious mind . . ."

Quaentyn nodded, but added, "Both Thenyt and Khael were quite outspoken about not selling the mine."

"You think someone killed them, thinking she'd be easier to persuade?"

"Just my feelings, Dominic."

"I've seldom known your feelings to be wrong."

Quaentyn offered a quietly amused laugh. "As I recall, I felt you'd never win that first election for councilor."

"You were supportive, but a shade dubious."

"Not only about your chances, but also about how you'd fare when you discovered how little power a councilor has."

"There are ways." Ysella smiled, if briefly, then asked, "You think the Kleins are involved in the murder? Or the Escalantes?"

"I'd be surprised if the Kleins weren't, but not all the Escalantes. Just Jaahn and his family. Alaan isn't bright or devious enough for that, and he knows it, thank the Almighty."

That's likely why his family put him up for councilor.

"What are you going to do about Aelyn Wythcomb, Dominic?"

"I don't know. I don't want to rush in. That would mark me as an opportunist. Perhaps write her another seemingly innocuous letter . . ."

"If I were you, I'd mention her name here and there."

"So people know I'm concerned."

Quaentyn nodded. "It might help her situation if people knew you're concerned. You do have a bit of power, and some might back off. I can mention your concern quietly to a few people, if you'd like."

"If you would, I'd appreciate it."

Quaentyn grinned.

"Not a word beyond concern."

The older legalist laughed quietly.

"You know me too well."

"Well enough. Is there anything else?"

"Not right now. If there is, I know where to find you." Ysella stood. "And thank you."

When he stepped out of the house, a cold, damp wind rushed past him, reinforcing the fact that even in Aloor, winter could be bitter.

23

Between working on legislative initiatives and continuing to visit shops and knocking on doors, Ysella found that Furdi and Quindi passed quickly. A third or so after second bell on Findi, he rode along the north road to his parents' holding, thinking about Aelyn Wythcomb and how he should write his next letter to her.

But it's far too soon for that.

While he'd wondered about Aelyn's question about his unmarried state—entirely unexpected—she'd made it seem like honest curiosity, and once he'd explained, she'd not said more. Then again, in her position, even if she were attracted to him, she couldn't afford any more indication than he'd seen. *Perhaps she's curious, or she could be like you, wanting to know more, and knowing that her acceptable options are as limited as yours are.*

As a single man, and especially as a councilor, if Ysella showed an overt interest in a recently widowed woman, especially one widowed by murder, so soon after her husband's death . . .

He shook his head. The reaction would be terrible . . . for both of them. *And you're assuming she's at least passingly interested.*

As he continued to ride north, the wind remained steady—and bitter. By the time he reached the holding and had the mare in her stall, even the stable felt warm.

Young Cliven walked from the stable to the house beside him. "When are you going back to Machtarn, sir?"

"Most likely on the thirty-fifth. That will allow a margin for bad weather and some time to prepare for the next Council session."

"Do you think the Imperador will declare war on Atacama?"

"There's no reason for him to do that. We're only attacking pirates."

Ysella was glad to enter the main house, although the rear entry foyer didn't feel much warmer than the stable. After hanging his heavy riding jacket on a wall peg, he made his way past the kitchen, where Sorya, the cook, and her assistant were busy preparing dinner, and to his mother's study.

"As usual, you're early," declared Kaelyn, gesturing to one of the chairs. "We can talk."

Ysella had no doubt about the subject, one of the reasons he'd come to the study before dinner. He seated himself and smiled pleasantly, as if he had no idea what she'd say.

"Dear, Lynnal Paarkyl sent me a lovely note. Evalynn found you most entertaining and very polite, and very informed about what happens in Machtarn."

Those have to be her mother's words. "I did my best."

"When are you planning to call on her?"

"Sometime after Father is crowned king of a reconstructed land of Aloor."

"You won't ever find a better match, Dominic. At your age you may not find one at all."

"I'm thirty-three. The Premier is at least ten years older than I am, and he's likely under consideration to marry the Imperador's daughter."

"*That* will never happen. Never. He's made a career out of pleasing that awful Laureous."

"You think Laureous would allow his daughter to wed anyone who hadn't pleased him?"

"Well . . . he hasn't been known for his taste." Kaelyn frowned, then added, "Evalynn is sweet. She's attractive, and she's moderately intelligent. Why won't you consider her?"

"She wants a traditional landor husband. I'm not. I never will be. She'd be miserable in Machtarn, and I'd be miserable here trying to eke out a living as a marginal landor. On top of that, there's no real attraction between the two of us."

"And you can do better in Machtarn?"

"So far, I am."

"What am I going to tell Lynnal?"

"How about the truth? That I'm ill-suited to her lovely and intelligent daughter, and that I have the sense not to make both of us miserable."

"I can't put it that bluntly."

"Then tell her, for better or worse, the only sort of living I can make is as a councilor and legalist in Machtarn and that would mean removing Evalynn from her family. I'm sure you can find a way to convey that it wouldn't be a good match for reasons you didn't know when you arranged for us to meet."

"Such as your using physical violence on Mylls Ahnkaar, not that he didn't deserve it. Couldn't you have dispatched him with a gladius?"

Ysella was only slightly surprised that word had reached his mother. "You know how I feel about blades and duels."

"Really, dear. You do make matters difficult for yourself."

"That's why it's best that I remain mostly in Machtarn. The difficulties there are more suited to my abilities." Ysella stood, since they'd both said all that needed to be said.

"You might want to see your father before dinner."

Since that was a strong suggestion, if not a maternal order, Ysella said, "I'll do so now."

The elder Cliven was not in the library, but in his study, seated at the desk. "Best if you close the door."

Ysella did so, but did not seat himself.

"I heard Mylls Ahnkaar tried to charge you with assault. How did you let that happen?"

"He pounded on my door and attacked me."

"Did you provoke him?"

"Hardly. Last week I told you about Rugaar Maartyn. That seemed odd enough that I checked recent land sales in the district, and I got the feeling that both Maartyn and Lohan Escalante were interested in the Ahnkaar mine. So I told Aelyn Wythcomb. Before I got in touch with Ahnkaar, he was pounding on my door. After I stopped him, I told him everything I told Ritten Wythcomb. He still left muttering about legalists."

"How did you get to her?" asked the elder Cliven. "I heard she's not seeing anyone."

"I went to her front door and knocked. I said I was the councilor from Aloor and needed to talk to her. I briefed her on what I found out. She thanked me and showed me out. I was there barely a third."

"Did you tell her what to do?"

"Only that she shouldn't be in a hurry to sell the mine, but the choice was hers." Ysella didn't mention the steam pump since he'd rather the family found out about it from others.

"You make it sound straightforward."

"Parts are, and parts aren't. What I told the Ritten and Mylls Ahnkaar was straightforward. What's going on with land and water rights might not be. I don't know enough to say. Rugaar Maartyn is also linked to Cyraen Presswyrth, who might have ties with Merkall Klein."

"Always the frigging Kleins. Your great-grandfather should have executed Kalleyn Klein when he had the chance." The elder Cliven slowly shook his head. "Just avoid Mylls. He'll take care of himself before long."

"He's irritated most of the district patrollers, I've heard."

"That's just the beginning." The elder Cliven forced a smile. "I'll see you in a bit."

Ysella left the study and walked toward the parlor. In the hallway outside the archway into the parlor, he encountered Jaeralyn.

"I heard you cut Mylls Ahnkaar down to size," she said with a smile.

"Does the entire town know about it?"

"By now . . . possibly. Did you really talk to Aelyn Wythcomb?"

Ysella didn't know whether to groan or sigh. He did neither. "Just about water rights and the fact that several people might want to buy the mine."

"They say she's very good-looking."

"She's in mourning."

"That's not an answer," said Jaeralyn with the slightest hint of teasing.

"She's good-looking. She's also very intelligent, and asked some very incisive questions before politely thanking me, and showing me out the door."

"Formal mourning only lasts a month," added Jaeralyn. "I ran into Gineen in town the other day."

"Can we leave it at that?" asked Ysella quietly.

"Only if you'll promise to write Aelyn after a month's up."

"Why . . ."

"You'd be good for each other. And no, I won't tell anyone else. Including anyone in the family." Then Jaeralyn turned toward the kitchen.

For several moments, Ysella just stood there.

Women . . . and Aloor can be a very small place.

He moved into the parlor and took a seat.

Before long, Ennika joined him, moving a stool beside his chair. "Uncle Dominic?"

"Yes?" Ysella turned to her.

"Can I come visit you in Machtarn when I'm older?"

"That depends," he replied cautiously.

"On what?"

"How old you are. Until you're an adult, you'd need your parents' permission, and someone to accompany you. Once you're an adult, that depends on whether you have the funds to pay for the trip." He looked up as Kaelyn, Jaeralyn, Haekaan, young Cliven, and Erskaan all entered the parlor and took seats.

"Taeryn and Raemyna won't be coming," declared Kaelyn. "Taeryn doesn't want her or young Kharl traveling in this weather."

"I can't say I blame him," replied Ysella.

"That's something you won't have to worry about," said Kaelyn sweetly.

"Certainly not in the immediate future," Ysella agreed cheerfully. He noted that Jaeralyn merely nodded, then asked, "Did I smell roast lamb?"

"You did indeed," said Ysella's father as he entered the parlor, "with roasted potatoes, and green stuff, and fresh hot rolls."

At the words "green stuff," Ysella smiled. When his father wanted to tease Kaelyn, that phrase for vegetables often came up, even if the vegetables happened to be yellow summer squash.

"You probably shouldn't stay too long tonight," added the elder Cliven. "There are clouds on the horizon to the north." He pursed his lips as if he might say more, then stopped as Maadlyn handed him a glass of Silverhills red.

Before long, everyone had a beverage, and Haekaan asked Ysella, "What old acquaintances have you been visiting?"

"Legrand Quaentyn . . . you know he's widowed now? And Luvaal Fhaen. I had dinner with Bruuk and Gineen Fettryk last Quindi night after services . . ."

From Haekaan's question, Ysella could tell that the dinner conversations would be friendly and without controversy or anything that could possibly be unpleasant.

24

ON Tridi morning, which dawned sunny, if cold for Aloor, Ysella set out on the part of his duties that he dreaded—visiting all the remaining legalist offices in Aloor, and talking with at least one legalist in each.

His first stop was at the offices of Gaadwarn & Thaayr, located on the main street, a block from the town hall.

When he walked in, the elderly clerk, Newal Ghray, looked up from his desk on the right side of the anteroom and asked, "Who would you be wanting to see this morning, Councilor?"

"Is either of the partners in?"

"Sr. Thaayr is, sir. I'll tell him you're here."

In moments, Ghray ushered Ysella into the walnut-paneled office of Corvaan Thaayr, who stood as Ysella entered.

"I wondered when you'd show up." Thaayr gestured to the chairs and reseated himself.

Ysella took the chair. "I've been a bit tied up with waterways and water rights . . . and then there's always family."

"That happens," said Thaayr. "Lyam Dattaur said you'd been going through some of the property and tariff records." The legalist raised his eyebrows.

Ysella nodded. "A few things came up after I got here."

"I understand Mylls Ahnkaar didn't take to your explaining water rights to the widow Wythcomb."

Ysella managed a smile. "Not exactly. I discovered that several parties might be interested in purchasing the mine. I felt she might not know of that interest. I also later explained that to Ritter Ahnkaar. Ritten Wythcomb thanked me politely and showed me to the door. When Ahnkaar showed up at my house, he tried to assault me, then had the nerve to try to claim I'd assaulted him. I had a witness. When the duty patroller questioned Ahnkaar, he backed off."

Thaayr nodded. "That's more in accord with what I've heard about Ahnkaar." He paused. "I didn't know you were acquainted with the widow."

"I'd never met or seen her before introducing myself. Her name came up in the course of another matter involving the Council."

"Oh?"

"The tin contract with the Navy that Jaahn Escalante doesn't want to honor. I'd rather not go into details."

"I'm not pressing."

"As always, I want to know if you have concerns that might affect the Council."

"From what I've heard, you did about as much as you could on the waterways funding. You'll press for more, I trust?"

"Until the needs here are completely met."

Thaayr paused briefly before saying, slowly and very deliberately, "There is another issue. It doesn't involve your committee, but it's getting to be a problem for several of our clients, and probably for the Banque of Aloor as well."

"The usury limit?"

"Exactly. You heard about it?"

"Several others have mentioned it. No one has before."

"That's because it wasn't a problem before. The cap was high enough. Now, it's not. The other problem with this is that, if the Council doesn't raise the limit, you're going to see more and more marks in the hands of families like the Kleins."

"In a general way . . . I suppose that makes sense."

"Let me explain. Suppose . . . just suppose that Merkall Klein lends marks to someone to build something, like a sawmill or maybe a new river port. Under the law, he can't charge interest of more than three parts on a hundred. So he doesn't. Instead, he makes an agreement that gives him special rights or lower rates. That means everyone else pays more."

"That's not supposition, is it?" asked Ysella.

"Let's say that I've heard rumors. If . . . if those rumors are accurate, it also means whoever is in Klein's favor gets more of an advantage, and the Kleins profit more."

Ysella managed not to sigh. "I'm not on that committee, but I'll look into the possibilities and see what I can do."

Another third of a bell passed before Ysella left the building and made his way to a much smaller office a block off the main street, where a small sign beside the door read DAFFYD SHAELDN, LEGALIST.

He opened the door and stepped inside.

The young legalist sitting behind a desk to the right looked up. "You know I don't have much to say to you."

"You've said that in the past." *I'm from a landor family, and because I am, you think I can't ever support anything for the good of those who aren't landors.* "But you could still offer suggestions." *Ones that might have a chance of being considered.*

"I have. Votes for women. More legal protections for susceptibles. Fewer marks for unnecessary ships . . ." The blond, sandy-haired legalist, who was clearly of Argenti or Atacaman background, shook his head. "Nothing ever comes of them."

"Actually, the Council attempted to cut back on unnecessary ships. It cost the Military Affairs Committee chairman his life."

"What a pity . . ." Shaeldn's words held no sympathy.

"We'll continue with that effort, pity or not. What else?"

"Better housing for the poor. The poorhouses are overcrowded and a disgrace."

"The poorhouses—"

"I know. Your usual answer is that the poorhouses are the responsibility of the district, not the Council. But the district does as little as possible. Couldn't you at least set some sort of minimum standard for them, and possibly a requirement for providing a certain number of beds based on a district's population? Right now, some poor families will walk to where there are beds and food. That means that towns don't want to provide space and beds, but if there was a standard . . . then the towns wouldn't be trying to provide as little as possible in order to keep the poor away."

Ysella had to admit that Shaeldn had a point. "That bears some thought."

"From you, it's a first step."

"You have considered that the Imperador limits the amount of funds available to the Council?"

"The Council ought to be limiting the funds available to the Imperador," replied the young legalist.

"Some of us are working on that," said Ysella.

"That would be a first."

"I'll see you later." Ysella smiled politely, turned, and left the small office. Shaeldn didn't offer a last comment.

The third office Ysella visited was that of Gherhaard & Haastun, Property Legalists, where the reception clerk was a gray-haired woman—and the wife of Ghermaan Gherhaard.

"Good morning, Councilor," she said cheerfully.

"The same to you, Sra. Gherhaard." Ysella remained standing, but turned to face her.

"At the moment, I'm the only one here. I assume you're not looking for property, seeing as you have a lovely house already."

"As you know, I do try to discover what concerns the people of Aloor have in the hope that possibly the Council can address those concerns or become aware of them."

"Would you like a prioritized list?" she asked with a hint of amusement in her voice.

"It couldn't hurt," he replied, "especially if the Council actually had the authority to accomplish those items."

"What about abolishing or lowering the Imperial seal tax on property transfers?"

"Councilor Staeryt got an amendment to the Seal Tax Act passed in the last session, which would have reduced the seal tax to one mark for property transfers from parents to children on holdings of less than forty hectares. The Imperador rejected it. He said it would reduce Imperial revenues too much, and he couldn't justify a tax reduction for smallholders and not for landors."

"You're always so informative, Councilor." She glanced past him toward the door, but no one entered.

"You asked."

"Why is there so much the Council cannot do?"

"You know as well as I do, Sra. Gherhaard. The Council is restricted by the Establishment Act." *And given that, without it, the Imperador could legally return to rule by decree . . . although that might well fragment Guldor.*

"Have you considered a Reestablishment Act?"

"Putting something like that into law would require the consent of the Imperador or a revolution, if not both."

"You don't strike me as a revolutionary, Councilor."

"That's because revolutions never end up where the revolutionaries thought they would. Too many people get killed, often the revolutionaries." Ysella shifted his weight from one foot to the other.

"But if the Imperador isn't the kind to give up power willingly, how will you change things?"

"The least costly way would be to persuade the Imperador to change his mind."

"I doubt that the Heir would appreciate that in the slightest." Her lips curled momentarily.

"You have a good point. But then, you always do." Ysella paused. "I was reviewing property titles and tariff records the other day. I noticed that there were several land sales to mostly unfamiliar names, except for one belonging to a young relative of Merkall Klein."

"Very few longtime landors from Aloor have the funds for purchasing large tracts of land, or so it would seem."

"And outsiders are willing to pay more?"

"We haven't seen any great rise in prices so far." Her voice became more matter-of-fact.

That's worse. But then, no one in my family has the funds to acquire significantly more land. "I appreciate the information. Is there any other information I can provide?"

"I can't think of anything, Councilor."

"Then I'll bid you good day." Ysella nodded, then departed.

By midafternoon, he'd visited the remaining three legalists on his mental list, where he largely listened and learned little and nothing that surprised him. Then, he headed for Paddock, the tavern in Aloor most frequented by the more affluent non-landor residents.

Only a handful of tables in the tavern were occupied, as Ysella suspected, given that it was midafternoon in the middle of the week. He only took three steps into the tavern before Jaime Drenkal approached him. Some five years younger than Ysella and the son of Paddock's owner, Drenkal alternated the daily management of the tavern with his father.

"You look thirsty, Dominic. How about a lager?"

"I'd like that, Jaime, but I'll pay for it."

"You always do," Drenkal said with a momentary grin. "That's why I always offer." He gestured to the serving girl, then led Ysella to a corner table in the rear. After the two seated themselves, Drenkal said, "You've been back three weeks, and it's the first I've seen you. Usually, you show up sooner."

"I had to look into some things that are likely to affect the Council, and they got more involved than I'd anticipated, as did some family matters."

"Oh . . . you mean with your cousin Haarkyl having to take over the holding? I also heard that your brother's wife had a hard time with her child." Drenkal's voice became more solicitous.

"Both, but both Raemyna and Kharl seem to be doing much better now." Ysella took a healthy swallow from the beaker the serving girl had set before him.

"Can you talk about the Council matters?"

"Some." Ysella gave a brief outline of Jaahn Escalante's tin contract and Lohan's attempt to buy the Ahnkaar mine. He did not mention Aelyn Wythcomb or Rugaar Maartyn, directly or indirectly. He took another swallow of lager.

"I suppose it was too bad about Thenyt and Khael, but . . ." Drenkal shrugged, his eyes straying toward the door.

"But?"

"Seemed to me that Khael was more interested in spending nights at Corners or here, especially for a man married less than a year. Not at all like his father. Thenyt grumped about Tressa being a stern biddy, but he never came here without her. Wasn't the same after she died. Red flux, you know."

"I didn't know. She died when I was in Machtarn." Ysella set down the beaker after another swallow. "You've still got the best lager in town. And I was thirsty."

"That's because we brew it." Drenkal smiled. "You're always thirsty when you come here. You still talking to folks?"

"Always. How else would I find out what bothers people or what they want from the Council."

"Mostly to be left alone, I'd say."

"Unless they want the seal tax reduced, or landors along the Kuhlor River who want the channel deepened." Ysella smiled cynically.

"They got the land cheaper because there wasn't a waterway they could use. Now they want our tariffs and taxes used to make a waterway where there wasn't so they can sell their land to outsiders for more."

"Sra. Gherhaard said there were more outsiders buying lands around Aloor. Have you seen any?"

"I've seen some well-dressed fellows I didn't know who never asked the price of anything."

"And you and your father know almost everyone in Aloor." *Who can afford to come here.*

"Those who want, and can pay, for a good meal and the best ale and lager." Drenkal offered an amused smile.

"What haven't I heard that I should? Especially any angry or worried mutterings."

"I don't know as things are that bad. Not yet, anyway. More than a few folks weren't happy about the Imperador demanding more expensive warships that never get used. Some of Dad's poorer relatives are pissed about the seal tax. They say it takes marks from folks at a time when they have the least and when they've lost someone."

Ysella listened, occasionally asking questions for another third, slowly sipping the remainder of the lager. Finally, he said, "Thank you. I appreciate your thoughts."

"Dad says I'm wasting my time talking to you. He says the Council's worse than useless, and things will never change."

Ysella laughed softly. "My great-grandfather thought like your father, but things *always* change. Otherwise, my father would be ruling Aloor from a palace that no longer exists, instead of worrying about the weather and the market prices of grains and livestock."

"I don't think I'll tell him that."

Ysella eased back his chair. "The lager still half a mark?"

"A mark these days. The best costs more."

"It always does." Ysella stood, then left two mark notes on the table. "So does good information. Give my best to your father, even if he thinks I've wasted your time."

Drenkal grinned. "I tell him you're a reliable paying customer. That's something he can't argue."

"Until later."

Once outside the tavern, Ysella turned his overcoat collar up to shield against the wind and headed home.

25

By the time Ysella left the—thankfully—uneventful family dinner on Findi, he felt more than ready to return to Machtarn. He'd visited every shop and crafter, as well as at least one person in every legalist office in Aloor. He hadn't learned much new or relevant in the past week. So, on Unadi morning he arranged for space on the post coach back to Machtarn on Tridi, then sent a message to his parents saying that certain Council business had come up requiring his presence in Machtarn.

He also sent a very brief letter to Aelyn Wythcomb, saying the same thing, giving her his address in Machtarn in case any water-rights issues involving the mine came up. On Duadi, he arranged for Perri to close the house and for young Cliven to return his mare, and Perri, to his family's holding on Furdi.

On Tridi morning, he left the house early, knowing it was a long walk with his half-trunk, but didn't want to impose on anyone unless necessary.

All six seats on the coach were taken, and Ysella found himself seated beside a man several years younger whose attire suggested some form of merchanting. Once the driver's assistant closed the coach doors, and the post coach began to move, Ysella said to his seatmate, "I'm Dominic Ysella."

"Bheryl Wydham. I overheard that you're the councilor from Aloor."

"At least until the next election. Might I ask what you do?"

"I work for Duffay & Lybraan, glaziers for manufactories. We make the glass carboys and smaller vessels used to contain oil of vitriol, in its various formulations, as well as other vitriolic liquids. We also arrange for filling the vessels and delivering them. I visit apothecaries, manufactories, naval yards, and the like to ascertain their needs and arrange for purchases."

Ysella had heard of oil of vitriol, but almost nothing of its uses.

"Is this something recent?"

"The oil has been around for centuries, but until a few years ago, it was difficult to make, except in small batches. The use of lead chambers makes it far more available."

"What is it used for?"

"Mostly to help other processes . . ." What Wydham said after that made little sense to Ysella, except that the very corrosiveness of oil of vitriol was at the heart of its usefulness.

As Wydham continued to talk, Ysella couldn't help thinking that, rather suddenly, matters were changing around him quickly, what with glass carboys of vitriolic substances and the possibilities of steam pumps and steam engines.

Abruptly, Wydham broke off his explanation and said, "I'm sorry, but I do get overly enthusiastic. There are so many possibilities now."

Looking at the younger man, in a way, Ysella felt far older, despite the relatively few years between them. After several long moments, he asked, "How will these possibilities change life?"

"One of the changes might be to restore the fertility to worn-out lands. Combining oil of vitriol with phosphate rock in the right proportions can create a substitute for manure or replace it in places where sufficient manure is not available. It's useful in making other vitriols as well, and dilute versions can clean certain metals . . ."

For the next bell, Ysella listened. Then he said, "Since you've been so kind, might I ask a favor of you? Is there anything within the power of the Council that might prove helpful to manufactories such as the one you work for?"

"I haven't thought about it, but one of our problems is getting carboys and containers to places without waterways. Even the best roads are often unsuited to heavy wagons. Better roads would help. Right now, there's no way we can afford to deliver carboys to Aloor or Nuile. I suppose it doesn't matter, since no one in either town needs significant quantities of oil of vitriol, but Sr. Lybraan wanted to make sure."

"Most places that will benefit from the possibilities you talked about will be ports or on navigable rivers or waterways?"

"For now, from what I've seen," replied Wydham.

"What about Machtarn?"

"Excellent location! Wide river and a good port. You'll see. The Imperador was farsighted in choosing it for his capital." Wydham yawned. "Please excuse me."

"Will you be taking the post coach all the way to Machtarn?"

Wydham shook his head. "I'll be getting off at Point Larmat. I'll take a coastal packet from there back to Devult."

"What do you think about steam from coal-fired furnaces powering pumps or engines?"

The younger man cocked his head. "I shouldn't say much."

"So more than a few people are working out how to make it work?"

"You might say that, sir," replied Wydham with an amused smile.

"If your business is successful in getting it to work, a good use would be pumping water out of mines."

"Really?" Wydham stifled another yawn.

"Really. That's one reason mines are closed, not because they don't have ore or coal."

"I thank you for that information, sir. Now, if you will excuse me, it's been a long two weeks." Wydham pulled his short-billed cap down over his dark-rimmed eyes.

In moments, or so it seemed to Ysella, the younger man was half asleep.

How could you be so unaware of all that? Ysella shook his head. The answer was unhappily simple. Aloor was no longer the center of anything, and changes happened where there were more people and faster ways to travel. *Although a steam engine could possibly speed travel upstream.*

There was also the likelihood that those working on such devices weren't talking, just as Sr. Wydham hadn't wanted to say more. *Unless, like the professor from Ondeliew College, they need marks to build their engines or devices.*

26

YSELLA finally arrived in Machtarn on Furdi, the fourth of Winterend, in late afternoon. The journey had taken two days longer than he'd planned, as a result of heavy rains southwest of Point Larmat. He took a hire-coach from the coach station to his house, where he stepped out into the cold still air, far more frigid than in Aloor even under a cloudless sky.

Caastyn rushed down the drive as Ysella took the half-trunk from the coach boot, then turned and paid the driver.

"You're back a bit sooner than you planned, sir," said Caastyn, lifting the half-trunk one-handedly.

"I finished everything I could. It's a good thing I left early. The weather was terrible."

Caastyn gestured to the calf-high dirty snow flanking the stone drive. "Snowed right after you left, and it didn't stop till last week. Not much at one time, but it adds up." He turned toward the house.

Ysella walked beside Caastyn. "How are you and Gerdina doing?"

"It's been quiet. You've got some letters and a few messages waiting for you."

"Has there been anything important in the newssheets about the Council or the Imperador?"

"Not much. A few mentions of attacks on the Gulf pirates, mostly by the latest Fleet Marshal."

"Fleet Marshal Dhaantyn?"

"He's the one. Do you think we'll end up in a war against Atacama?"

"I hope not. As you've told me, everyone loses in war. The winner is the land that loses the least." Ysella smiled sardonically.

"Too many people who want war never really fought and suffered in one. The ones who fought and came out unscathed too often believe they survived through skill. Skill isn't enough. It takes both skill and good fortune."

"That's true of more than war," replied Ysella. *Except the consequences of misfortune aren't usually as fatal as in war.*

Caastyn laughed harshly and briefly.

Once he entered the house Ysella took the half-trunk from Caastyn and lugged it up to his small dressing chamber, where, somehow, Gerdina had already carried up two pitchers of warm water. He washed and shaved off the short scraggly beard he'd grown on the trip. Then he pulled on a pair of older trousers, a shirt, and an old vest before heading down to the kitchen.

"Thank you for the warm water, Gerdina. I do appreciate it."

"My pleasure, sir."

Ysella turned and walked to the study, where he lit the lamp before looking at his desk, and the short stack of letters and messages. *More than a few.*

The first thing he did was sort them out by those whose names or addresses he recognized. Then he opened the first, from Alaan Escalante, whose message was short.

Dominic—

If you get back before Quindi, the fifth of Winterend, I'd appreciate your joining me for refreshments on Findi the sixth at third bell of the afternoon.

He must be worried about something concerning Military Affairs... and his cousin's tin contract.

While it was too late in the afternoon to send a reply, he could and would write an acceptance first thing in the morning.

The second envelope he opened came from Iustaan Detruro, which surprised Ysella, since Detruro had never sent a message or a letter to Ysella's house.

I'll be in my office all mornings except Findis until the Council convenes. I'd very much like to meet as soon as practicable for you.

Ysella couldn't help wondering what had occurred during his absence. If the Imperador had died or was expected to, it couldn't have been kept from the newssheets. That applied to the Heir as well, and a declaration of war certainly couldn't be kept secret—but a great deal might not make the newssheets and might be worse than a little troublesome.

After setting aside Detruro's letter, he turned to the one from Aldyn Kraagyn.

Dominic—

I recently discovered that you graciously agreed to meet with my nephew, Rugaar Maartyn. I'd like to thank you for that kindness.

At the same time, I must emphasize that I had no knowledge of his meeting with you until after the fact, nor did I know that young Rugaar may have made arrangements in a way that suggested I had an interest in whatever he had in mind . . .

I have no such interest, and I defer to your judgment in this . . .

Kraagyn's letter strongly suggested that he was anything but happy with what Maartyn had in mind and wanted to make that clear. This strengthened Ysella's skepticism about whatever Maartyn and Lohan Escalante were attempting, as well as his concerns about what Merkall Klein intended to pursue in Aloor.

Haans Maessyn wrote the next letter. It was dated two weeks earlier and posted in Uldwyrk, but had a return address in Machtarn.

I know you're in Aloor, but I don't have an address for you there. Once we're both back in Machtarn, I'd like to stop by your house and talk before the Council reconvenes, if that's possible. I'll be returning to Machtarn by ship, arriving the last few days of Winterfirst . . .

Ysella quirked his lips as he considered that ships were likely more comfortable and often faster than the post coach, at least with favorable winds. In winter, winds tended to blow out of the northeast, which would have sped Maessyn's voyage. He wondered what Maessyn didn't want to discuss in the Council building.

From Maessyn's missive he turned to the one from Ondeliew, from Gherard Brandt, thanking Ysella for meeting with Brandt and Sulymar and begging Ysella's indulgence as the two kept him informed of Professor Gastaan Ritchen's progress. That was fine with Ysella, although he suspected the glaziers in Devult would have a working engine before the professor.

But you never know . . . about so many things.

The last letter was from Haasl Sullynd.

Councilor Ysella—

As per your instructions, we have for possible sale two harbor parcels you might be interested in considering.

We also have received an offer for all of your properties on Second Harbor Way. Although we informed the prospective purchaser that you were unlikely to entertain any offer, as property legalists we are obliged to convey the offer.

We would appreciate seeing you at your convenience to discuss these matters once you return to Machtarn . . .

Ysella shook his head.

He could answer those most pressing after dinner and the others as practical, since he definitely wanted to meet with Iustaan Detruro in the morning.

27

AT breakfast on Quindi morning, as Ysella ate and sipped his café, he read every article in *The Machtarn Tribune,* then reread the small article on the front page.

> Two Guldoran frigates engaged and sank the Atacaman three-deck galleon *Victorya Grande* after it fired at two Guldoran cutters returning from operations against pirates in the Gulf of Nordum. Two months ago, the *Victorya Grande* inflicted heavy damage on the Guldoran frigate *Paelart* while the *Paelart* was returning to Port Reale.

There were no comments from the Palace or the Navy or from the Grande Duce, which Ysella found strange.

Since he had written replies to all letters and messages after dinner on Furdi evening, once he finished breakfast, he donned a winter riding jacket and headed for the stable, where Caastyn had already groomed and saddled Jaster.

"Thank you for arranging for the *Tribune* to be delivered here. It's a bit more costly, but it's getting so I need to know what happened before I arrive at the Council."

"Does seem that way, sir." Caastyn grinned. "For us, too."

"I do appreciate it. I have a number of people to visit, but whether they'll all be available is another question. So I have no idea when I'll be back."

"We aren't going anywhere, sir."

Ysella led the gelding from the stable and mounted, then rode down the drive to Averra Place and onto Camelia Avenue to the post centre. He posted the letters and arranged for immediate delivery of his acceptance to Alaan Escalante, as well as a message to Haans Maessyn, suggesting that Maessyn stop by the house first thing on Unadi morning. Then he remounted Jaster, and rode north to the Council stables. After turning Jaster over to the duty ostler, he made his way directly to the Premier's office.

The clerks ushered him into Detruro's private office, and Detruro gestured to the chairs before the desk. "I appreciate your coming, Dominic."

"I returned to Machtarn late yesterday. Since you've never contacted me at home, I assume something out of the ordinary has occurred."

"Not yet, but there are certain potential difficulties. The Imperador suffered through a bout of a common flux. He seems to have recovered, mostly, but he's weaker. He refuses to appoint the Heir as his regent, which is a sign of his continuing mental acuity, but I worry how long that acuity will last with his declining physical strength."

"And the Heir?"

"With the current powers of the Imperador under the Establishment Act, the Heir will destroy Guldor, possibly within a few years."

"Unfortunately, I'd have to agree with you," admitted Ysella.

"Given that, what would you suggest as a feasible course of action for the Council?"

"We need a change to the Establishment Act that Laureous will accept, or could be persuaded to accept. A Reestablishment Act, if you will, although I wouldn't call it that. There's a danger in drafting anything, because Laureous might well call it treason."

"These days, he's likely to call anything he doesn't like treason. If you were drafting such an act, how far would you go in limiting the powers of the Imperador?"

For a moment, Ysella was stunned. Much as he'd thought about such limitations, he hadn't expected such a question. After a silence that seemed to last for a full sixth of a bell, he replied, "I thought Ahslem Staeryt was working on that."

"He considered it, after you suggested it, but felt that he wasn't the right person. Since you obviously have . . ."

Ysella decided not to mention that he'd only considered it after Detruro's suggestion. "I'd retain the Imperador's power to block legislation, but allow a greater majority vote of the Council to override that veto. I'd allow the Council to appoint the heads of the administrative offices . . ." As well as he could, Ysella sketched out the parameters of a legally limited Imperium, then waited.

Detruro nodded. "You've thought this out. I suspected you might have. If you wouldn't mind, could you write that out in a more detailed and legislative fashion? By yourself, without using your clerks?"

"Why me?"

"Because there's no one else with the legal skills and the ability to draft such a proposal and to keep it totally quiet. Too many people watch me. The other committee chairmen respect you. Not all of them *like* you, but they respect you. And . . . no one would suspect I'd turn to you."

Ysella had a strong feeling the last point weighed heavily. "While I've thought about this for a time, drafting an act or a new charter for Guldor won't be something I can dash off."

"I know. What comes out of your committee is always precise and well-drafted, and not because of the staff legalist. That's why I wanted to meet with you as soon as practicable." Detruro paused. "You understand that this has to be just between the two of us?"

"If we're to be successful," replied Ysella dryly, "it can't be any other way."

"Exactly."

"On another question . . . how close are we to war with Atacama?"

"There won't be a declaration of war unless Grande Duce Almaetar attacks Guldoran lands with Atacaman forces."

"Do you think the skirmishes will remain confined to the Gulf islands?"

"First Marshal Solatiem has no plans to attack anywhere else."

Ysella understood.

"How did those in Aloor react to the Waterways appropriation?" asked Detruro.

"Some of the older landors complained. I pointed out that removing me would guarantee that they'd get less for years to come."

Detruro chuckled. "Good for you."

"What about complaints from Enke?" asked Ysella.

"No one important has complained."

"Even about your dancing with the Imperador's daughter?"

Detruro smiled wryly. "You danced with her. What do you think?"

"She's beautiful, very intelligent, extremely strong-willed, and accustomed to a level of luxury I could never aspire to." *Nor would I want to, with what it would entail.* "She could make a man extraordinarily happy or miserable, if not both."

The Premier laughed, softly. "I could not agree more."

"Have you heard anything more about her?"

"The Imperador hasn't mentioned Lady Delehya in our few meetings. I'm not about to ask."

Ysella had the feeling that Detruro wasn't entirely forthcoming, but did not press, although he wondered why the Imperador didn't try to dispel the rumors about Delehya. *Except addressing them in any way would confirm them.* "Have you heard more about the tin contract between the Navy and Jaahn Escalante?"

"Escalante has agreed to honor his commitment. He's not happy. I understand that he got no support from Alaan Escalante, possibly because someone advised Alaan that to support Jaahn would be unwise. I understand you were that someone." Detruro offered an amused smile. "I talked to Alaan shortly after you did. He told me that you had advised him—strongly—against supporting his cousin. Your involvement made my task much easier." After a slight hesitation, he asked, "Do you have any questions?"

"Not at the moment."

"Then, when you have a proposal we can go over, let me know." Detruro stood.

So did Ysella. "I will."

"I appreciate your taking this on. Best of fortune."

Ysella nodded, then turned and left.

From the Premier's office, Ysella made his way up to his own, where he found his clerks at their desks. Both looked up in surprise.

"Sir!" declared Khaard. "We didn't expect you until next week."

"I came early to deal with some matters." Which was true, but Ysella certainly hadn't expected Detruro's request, although it was as much order as request. "Since I was here, I thought I might as well catch up on whatever mail there happens to be. Bring it into my office."

All in all, there were only thirty-seven letters, most of them posted in the last week—but knowledgeable people didn't expect councilors to be in Machtarn until the beginning of Winterend. By next week, Ysella knew there would be more.

Still, it took him close to two bells to read through the letters and jot down notes for Khaard and Jaasn to follow in drafting responses. Although most of the letters were about waterways, three were about raising the usury interest rate cap, and none of those were from anyone who'd mentioned the problem in Aloor.

After Ysella left his office, and as he walked back to the stables, he realized there was another reason why Detruro wanted him to draft the proposed act. *That Aloor wouldn't be in the slightest unhappy to see the Imperador's powers limited.*

He smiled wryly.

From the stable he rode Jaster back down Imperial Boulevard to the offices of Sullynd & Smarkaan, some four blocks east of Imperial Boulevard on First Harbor Way. After tying the gelding under the eyes of the building doorman, Ysella entered and announced himself to the clerk.

"Yes, sir. Sr. Sullynd said you would be here at some time. He's conferring with Sr. Smarkaan, but I'll tell him that you're here."

Ysella had to wait less than a sixth before Haasl Sullynd left Smarkaan's office and ushered Ysella into the warm oak-paneled office.

As he sat down in the chair across the desk from the property legalist, Ysella said, "I just returned to Machtarn yesterday. What's the offer on the properties?"

Sullynd pursed his lips. "It's not so much the offer, although it would provide you with a gain of almost three parts in ten on your initial investment. It's that Sr. Gustov Torryl made it. He . . . doesn't expect a refusal."

"From your expression, I take it that those who refuse Sr. Torryl often have . . . difficulties?"

"Ah . . . that might be one way of putting it."

"Perhaps you could arrange a meeting with Sr. Torryl so that he can explain why he would like these properties."

"Sr. Torryl does not meet with anyone. His legalist transacts all his . . . business."

"I see. Who is his legalist?"

"Sollem Faarn."

The name meant nothing to Ysella. "Well . . . perhaps you could arrange a meeting with his legalist so that he can explain. Preferably on Tridi, or later in the week, late in the afternoon, since I'll be tied up with Council matters earlier in the day. Or I could contact him, if you could direct me."

"It might be best if we replied to Sr. Faarn, and you meet him here," said Sullynd quickly.

"Even so," replied Ysella, "before we meet, I'd like to know where his office is. Practicing legalists are required to have a physical address, you may recall."

"Sr. Faarn has such, but no one ever finds him there."

The more Ysella heard, the less he liked it. "I'd still like the address. What can you tell me about Sr. Faarn?"

"Very little. He read law with Sr. Sammel Varsach more than ten years ago. Legalist Varsach was elderly. He left active practice years ago and died last year. Faarn is a general legalist, and, so far as we know, has never had any significant claims against his practice."

He wouldn't, not if his clients are like Torryl.

"Are you considering Sr. Torryl's offer?"

"Not until after I meet with either Torryl or Faarn. By the way, do you happen to know where Sr. Torryl's place of business might be?"

"Very few, if any, know that. I'm not one of them."

Ysella stood. "Let me know, and find Faarn's address for me. I'll wait."

"I'll see what I can do, Ritter."

Almost a sixth later, Sullynd returned with an envelope that he handed to Ysella.

"Thank you." Ysella's smile was polite, but little more. He turned and left the office, knowing that he needed to do some research.

Once outside and mounted, he considered the possibilities, wondering if he should talk to any of the shopkeepers on his properties. Then he shook his head. *The fewer who know about this right now, the better.*

With that thought, he turned the gelding back toward Imperial Boulevard. When he reached the house, he dismounted and led Jaster into the stable, where he unsaddled and groomed him, still thinking over how to handle the situation with Sr. Torryl or his legalist. He'd barely finished stalling Jaster when Caastyn and Gerdina entered the stable.

"You're back early," said Caastyn.

"I finished what I needed to do today. Have either of you ever heard of Gustov Torryl?"

"What I've heard isn't good, sir," replied Caastyn. "Commercer of sorts, and folks who cross him have misfortunes not of their own making. Raf said it's best to stay away from him."

"What does your daughter think?"

"Krynn said he was evil," declared Gerdina. "One of the seamstress's girls told him she wasn't interested. They found her naked body between the piers the next morning."

"And no one did anything?"

"No one cares much about poor girls," stated Gerdina quietly.

"That type doesn't care much for poor boys, either," added Caastyn.

Ysella looked to Caastyn. "Is there any way you or Raf could find out more about him? Fairly soon. Especially without letting anyone know you're interested?"

"There are a few people who might know."

"It also might be wise to close and clamp the outside shutters in the evening."

Caastyn raised his eyebrows. "What did you do to offend him?"

"Nothing . . . yet, but he wants to buy something I'm not inclined to sell. Once you deal with people like that, it never ends."

Caastyn nodded slowly, while Gerdina looked at her husband and frowned.

"I'd like to know more," added Ysella, "definitely before I meet with his legalist."

"We'll see what we can find out, sir," said Caastyn. "Gerdina might have better fortune than Raf or me."

"Also, anything you can find about his legalist, Sollem Faarn. But keep it as quiet."

"We have our ways," added Gerdina quietly, before saying, "Dinner at the usual time?"

"That would be good. I'll be working in my study."

28

ON Findi, at half after second afternoon bell, Ysella began the ride to Alaan Escalante's house on Cuipregilt Avenue, studying the streets and side lanes off Imperial Boulevard with more care than usual. When he rode up the drive, Alaan Escalante came out to the side porch and motioned toward the stable, as he had before.

By the time Ysella tied Jaster inside the stable, Escalante joined Ysella, and the two walked back to the house and to the parlor, where the wall stove held both glowing coals and several pieces of wood recently added.

"Amaelya won't be joining us," said Escalante, "she's still in Silverhills. Red wine, I presume?"

"Of course."

The older councilor turned to the serving woman, standing in the archway. "Two reds."

She nodded and turned away.

Escalante gestured toward the armchairs, and by the time the two were seated the server had returned with two wineglasses. Escalante waited a moment, then lifted his glass to Ysella. "Thank you for coming on short notice. Your earlier advice was most helpful, and made what could have been a difficult situation much easier." He took a sip of the wine and then set the glass on the side table beside his chair.

"I'm glad I was of assistance," returned Ysella, following Escalante's example and taking a sip of wine.

"I hope I can rely on you again. Amaelya and I went to Silverhills after the Imperador's Ball, and I returned last week. Amaelya won't rejoin me until it's warmer here. I can't say I blame her. The day after I got back, First Marshal Solatiem and Fleet Marshal Dhaantyn called on me . . . here."

Ysella frowned. "That's unusual, even if you're now chairman of the Military Affairs Committee. Might I ask why they came to see you and not Iustaan?"

"Ostensibly, they came to inform me that the Imperador will insist on funding yet another first-rate ship of the line in the coming year . . . and to tell me that they need more frigates and cutters, not another first-rate ship. I pointed out that the last chairman who tried to thwart the Imperador did not fare especially well. I also asked if anyone had ever found out about the crossbow bolts that killed Daenyld."

"What did they say about that?" Ysella glanced toward the archway into the hall, not that he expected anyone to be there.

"The crossbow bolts were forged by the armorer used by the Palace Guard."

"Someone hushed that up. But why would they tell you? They'd deny it if you said anything publicly."

"They worry that the Imperador's judgment has become erratic, and the Heir is declining to intercede. More important, neither the Navy nor the Army is particularly sanguine about the Heir assuming the throne with all the powers of his father. Apparently, he's stepped up efforts to cultivate officers within the Palace Guard . . ." Escalante allowed the sentence to trail off as he gave Ysella a meaningful look.

Ysella barely managed to keep his jaw in place. "You do know what they're implying?"

"Guldor needs change. That was obvious, but why are they coming to me, and not Iustaan?"

"Because, if it leaks out, they'll deny it, and you'll follow Symeon," replied Ysella.

"That's what I thought." Escalante frowned, looking at the wall stove momentarily. "I still could be in trouble if they leak it. Especially if the Imperador dies, and the Heir finds out. So what do I do?"

"Exactly what you've done. Do nothing more, and don't tell anyone else, not even Amaelya. I'll talk to Iustaan, and that way there's no direct link between you and him, at least for a few days. You're to avoid all private meetings with him for now. That way, if the Imperador or one of his aides questions you, you can honestly say you haven't met with the Premier in over a month and that you've never said anything to him or to the newssheets. If you keep it to that, even an empath would find that you're telling the truth."

"That's thin, Dominic."

"I know, but it's the best I can do right now. I need to think this through." *Because, all of a sudden, there's a great deal more urgency to completing Detruro's government-reform proposal . . . and greater risk, particularly if the Heir discovers what we're working on.*

"I can see that," said Escalante, pursing his lips worriedly.

"On another less fraught subject, I have a question for you. Do you know why your cousin Jaahn's son Lohan is trying to buy property in Aloor?"

"He is?"

Ysella nodded.

"I have no idea. I didn't know he was."

"Have you had any contact with Merkall Klein?"

"Almighty, no." Escalante gave a tight headshake. "He's poison. You know that. Why do you ask?"

"Some people connected to him are rather interested in water rights and property in Aloor, at the same time as Lohan Escalante. I wondered if you knew."

"I avoid the Kleins as much as I possibly can."

"That's good advice for anyone," said Ysella. "One last question. All of a sudden, I've gotten a number of letters and inquiries about raising the usury rate cap. I wondered if this is an interest just in Aloor, or is it something you've heard?"

"The Silverhills Banque has been pressing me on that for several months. I thought it was a problem only for them. What do you think?"

"It's getting to be a problem in a number of districts, and it'll be interesting to see if other councilors report similar interest. It might be worth listening for. Did you find out anything else noteworthy while you were back home?"

For almost another bell, Ysella asked most of the questions, nursing his wine with care.

At perhaps a sixth after fourth bell, Ysella left Escalante and rode back to his own house, noting as he dismounted outside the stable that Caastyn and Gerdina appeared to be gone, probably visiting their daughter and her husband, as they often did on Findi.

After stalling Jaster, Ysella returned to the house and settled behind his desk, thinking for a while before beginning to write points for the draft legislation he needed to present to Detruro, hopefully before matters got out of hand. Once he had the major issues on paper, he turned to the first point—restricting the powers of the Imperador, in a way that gave the Imperador limited real authority but allowed a significant majority of the Council to override him.

Two bells later, when Caastyn knocked on the open study door, Ysella was still writing out basic points and subpoints dealing with restructuring the Council. He hadn't yet gotten to outlining how to structure the various Imperial administrative departments.

"Ritter, we're back."

"Did you have a good visit with Krynn and Raf?"

"We always do."

"Does either of them know anything about Sr. Torryl?"

"No one has ever seen him, only his legalist."

"I thought Krynn said that a girl who turned him down ended up dead in the harbor."

"The legalist said that Sr. Torryl wanted to meet her. She refused. She was found dead. Two other girls also vanished and were never found." Caastyn paused, then said, "Raf also said there's no one alive who's made an enemy of Sr. Torryl."

"Then, I'd better not make an enemy of him. Does anyone know where he lives?"

Caastyn shrugged. "No one seems to know."

"What about his legalist?"

"Legalist Faarn has an office in the small building beside the port authority . . ."

Ysella refrained from nodding; that confirmed the address Sullynd had provided.

". . . and there are always two clerks and an armed guard there. They receive and send documents. Legalist Faarn is seldom, if ever, there, but when he is, he arrives in a coach with a pair of guards. He never stays long, either."

Ysella frowned. A legalist with a coach and guards? "Thank you. I appreciate it. Very much."

After Caastyn left, Ysella forced his mind back to the rough outline of what would have to be a total reorganization of the government of Guldor, disguised as a few minor changes. *If you can even find a way to accomplish it.*

The last thing he needed was to deal with someone like Torryl, or his legalist, while he tried to draft something to change the entire power structure of Guldor in a way that didn't seem as radical as it needed to be.

29

AFTER washing up and shaving on Unadi morning, Ysella began to dress, then extracted a hardened leather vest from his armoire, one covered with silk on the front and padded with silk on the back, and donned it under his shirt. In summer, it would have been uncomfortably warm, but in midwinter that was hardly a problem.

He ate breakfast quickly, then went to his study to work on legislative language while he waited to see if Haans Maessyn showed up, since he hadn't gotten a response from Maessyn.

At half before third bell, Maessyn arrived, and Gerdina showed him into the study.

"I appreciate you seeing me here, Dominic." Maessyn settled into the straight-backed chair as if it were upholstered.

"What is it that can't be talked about in the Council Hall?"

"Something I thought you should know about before the Council resumes."

"Something within the Council?" asked Ysella.

"Something that's likely to affect the entire Council. You know that Luaro Maatrak and Iustaan Detruro don't exactly see eye to eye?" said Maessyn cynically.

"That's not exactly a secret. Maatrak's essentially a merchant type, a commercer if you will, and Detruro is a landor through and through. But Grieg and Coerl are crafters, and so are others, to a great extent."

"Exactly," said Maessyn. "Even if I'm more of a crafter, I've made no secret that I prefer Luaro's view and approach. So do quite a few others."

"Maatrak's going to call a vote to replace the Premier?"

Maessyn shook his head. "Sometime in the coming session, he's going to call a vote allowing councilors to state whether they primarily support landor principles, commercer principles, or crafter principles."

"What if a councilor doesn't want to make a statement?"

Maessyn offered an enigmatic smile, leaning forward slightly.

"You mean Maatrak's rounded up enough commercers with marks to publicize councilors who don't make a choice?"

"He hopes it won't come to that. We think those who vote for a councilor ought to know where every councilor stands in terms of basic principles."

"I don't have a problem with that," said Ysella. "So long as such statements are voluntary. The Establishment Act is silent on councilors professing views on government, except for forbidding personal slander. I worry such groupings might splinter the Council."

"The Council is already splintered. It might be better to have the differences in the open."

"Political parties, like the ones that brought down Teknold?"

"The parties didn't bring down Teknold," said Maessyn. "Their failure did."

"Do you have any idea how to keep that from happening?" asked Ysella. "Or does Maatrak?"

"We haven't talked about that," said Maessyn.

"It might be worth considering before you bring it up in the Council." Before Maessyn could say more, Ysella went on. "Some sort of break between landors, commercers, and crafters has to come sooner or later. Detruro knows that."

"What does he intend to do about it? Talk is cheap."

"That's true. It's also much less expensive than lives and blood."

"Do you have an answer?"

"For everyone's sake, especially yours and Maatrak's, I'd talk quietly about it, and bring up differences in outlooks. Say we may need a more formalized structure to work out differences, but don't press the matter too hard now, given the instability of the Imperador."

"Isn't that just saying not to do anything?"

Ysella shook his head. "I'm saying to work for it slowly. I've written out some thoughts on it."

"You have?" Maessyn's voice held considerable surprise. "But you've said very little."

"Haven't I tried to work out every councilor's needs on the Waterways Committee? Have I used my position to force through excessive funding for Aloor?"

"No. We all think you've been fair . . . or as fair as the Imperador allowed. But what does that have to do with parties?"

"If we're going to change things, we need a system that facilitates working things out. Adopting different names based on different outlooks won't solve anything. It's likely to make things worse, if that's all Maatrak does."

Maessyn frowned.

Ysella waited, watching Maessyn's face work through the implications. Finally, Maessyn said, "You might have something there."

"So do you and Maatrak," replied Ysella, "but we don't want to make things worse, not now."

"Why do you think that?"

"I worry about the Heir. If the Council seems splintered and dysfunctional, and the Imperador dies, that would give young Laureous the perfect excuse to disband the Council, whereas if the Council reforms itself in an orderly fashion that might give us more power and the Imperador less."

"I'll have to think about that."

Please do. "Talk it over with Maatrak. I'd be happy to speak with him as well."

"You will keep this between us, Dominic?"

"I won't be telling anyone, except Maatrak if he comes to see me." The last thing Ysella wanted was an untidy fracture along "party" lines, or even rumors of such.

"Thank you. You've always kept your word. I won't keep you longer."

Ysella escorted him to the door and returned to his study, shaking his head, and wondering how he could incorporate political parties into his charter in a way that wouldn't lead to what happened to the Grand Democracy of Teknold. Yet given what Maessyn had told him, he doubted that the Council would approve any continuation of a system that continued obvious landor domination, but anything that obviously precluded that domination would be opposed by the landor councilors.

He jotted down a few thoughts, then donned his winter riding jacket. He found Caastyn in the stable, saddling Jaster.

"Do you need anything else, sir?"

"Not now. I'm heading to the Council Hall, but I'll be returning, possibly before midday. I'd like you to be prepared to accompany me on some scouting. I'm worried about the legalist working for Gustov Torryl."

"That's not good. Should we carry crossbows and cranequins?"

"I hope we don't need them, but it might be better to be prepared."

"Yes, sir."

Ysella took the gelding's reins and led him out to the drive, where he mounted, then started out. The ride to the Council Hall was cold, given that Ysella headed into a brisk wind out of the north. At the Council stables, he was glad to dismount and turn the gelding over to the duty ostler.

"Don't unsaddle him," Ysella told the ostler. "I'll be back in a bell or so."

"Yes, sir."

Once inside the Council Hall and at his desk, Ysella drafted a warrant of inspection—for records rather than for waterways properties—then took the copy to Khaard. "I'd like this written out under the committee letterhead and made ready for me to sign and have sealed as quickly as possible."

The senior clerk read through it, frowning.

"I believe some illegal property transfers are taking place in the harbor and nearby, but without inspecting the records it will be impossible to determine. It's something I'd like to ascertain before the Council convenes, while I have time to deal with it personally."

While Khaard and Jaasn worked to complete the warrant of inspection, Ysella walked down to Detruro's office. Fortunately, the Premier was in and available.

Ysella closed the door.

"Problems, already?" asked Detruro.

"Yes, but not with your project. Yesterday, Alaan Escalante had me over for refreshments. Several days ago, First Marshal Solatiem and Fleet Marshal Dhaantyn called on him . . ." Ysella recounted what Escalante said, then waited for Detruro's reaction.

"I can't say I'm surprised. They both know how cautious Alaan is. They might not have expected him to be circumspect enough, and I doubt they would have expected him to talk to you. It's helpful to know that's the way they feel, but the fact that they were so indirect in letting me know also suggests how wary they are."

"Of the Imperador or the Heir? Or both?"

"The Heir. Laureous couldn't care less who they talk to so long as they stay loyal. The Heir worries about every meeting where he's not present."

"What do you want me to do?"

"Nothing, except to let Alaan know that you passed on what he told you. I won't talk to him about it. Not now. Later, we'll see." Detruro smiled pleasantly. "Is that all, Dominic?"

"For the moment. I thought you should know as soon as possible."

"I appreciate that."

Ysella stood. "I won't keep you."

After leaving Detruro, Ysella returned to his own office, where he read through the score or so of letters that arrived since Quindi, writing notes to the clerks. Several complained about the Waterways appropriations, and two were about the usury interest cap. A cartage business complained about the narrowness of the post roads and their unsuitability for heavy wagons. Another expounded on the unfairness of the seal tax for small properties, while yet another wanted to know why women who owned property couldn't vote.

Ysella wondered if she worked for or knew Legalist Shaeldn.

A bell later, Ysella left his office, carrying his leather case, containing blank sheets of paper, a black crayon, a pen, and a portable inkwell. From the Council stables he rode back south along Imperial Boulevard.

When Ysella reached the Machtarn District Hall, he tied Jaster to one of the hitching rails closest to the patroller on duty by the doors, then said, "I'm Councilor Dominic Ysella, here on Imperial Council business."

The young patroller grinned. "Go ahead. I'm just here to keep order."

Ysella smiled in return. "We have similar jobs, in a way." He entered the building and stopped at the desk. "Property tax and registration records."

"Halfway back on the left, sir."

The clerk at the desk before a closed and ironbound door looked up. "Sir?"

Ysella smiled politely. "I'm here to inspect certain harbor property records."

"No one can do that without the approval of the records administrator or his deputy."

"I understand that. I'm Imperial Councilor Dominic Ysella. I'm chairman of the Council Waterways Committee, and I have a committee warrant to inspect the records of properties adjoining and near the harbor. I'm also a water legalist registered with the district."

"I'll still have to get the deputy records administrator, sir."

"That's fine. I'll wait."

The clerk returned shortly with a balding thin-faced man who looked incapable of ever smiling and said, "Councilor, this is Deputy Records Administrator Huldruk." The clerk immediately stepped away.

Huldruk didn't quite meet Ysella's eyes as he said, "Clerk Ruustyn wasn't exactly clear why you're here."

Ysella repeated what he'd said before, adding, "I'm wearing a councilor's pin. Here are my card and credentials, and here is the inspection warrant."

"This is most unusual . . ."

Ysella sighed politely. "If the committee didn't suspect something unusual was going on, I wouldn't be here."

"You can't remove anything from the files."

"That's the last thing I'd ever want to do," declared Ysella. "I will be taking notes, however, and I'll be happy to show Clerk Ruustyn my case when I leave."

"Ah . . . that won't be necessary. I'll send one of my aides down with a lamp."

"Excellent. This might be very short . . . or it might take several bells."

Huldruk departed.

Ysella waited almost a sixth before a very young man arrived with a lamp.

"Wyllum Wisstah, sir. You're the councilor looking at the records. I might be able to help."

"Good. I'd like to begin with the records of the properties along both Harbor Ways."

"Yes, sir."

Ysella soon realized that, even with Wisstah's help, his search wouldn't be quick. Before long he found a piece of harbor property located next to the port authority building, but the owner wasn't Sollem Faarn, but the "Gustov Torryl Trust." After two bells, Ysella located and noted a score of properties owned by the Torryl Trust, for which, not totally to Ysella's surprise, the trustee was one Sollem Faarn. Two of those properties adjoined Ysella's on Second Harbor Way, and if Faarn or the Torryl Trust obtained them, the Trust would hold a significant section of Second Harbor Way east of Imperial Boulevard.

The only property in the name of Sollem Faarn was a residence on Pleasant Lane.

Abruptly, Ysella laughed, if harshly, and continued to search for another half bell before deciding that he'd located enough of the "Torryl Trust" properties.

Then he turned to Wisstah. "Are trusts holding properties required to be registered?"

"Uh . . . yes, sir. Those are in a different section."

"I need to check one trust."

"Yes, sir." Wisstah looked puzzled, but Ysella didn't explain. He followed the young clerk to that section, where he read the entries carefully—and discovered that the registration of the Torryl Trust contained the note that Sr. Gustov Torryl died on 13 Springfirst 812 and that the trust passed to the trustee, one Sollem Faarn, which was perfectly legal, assuming that Gustov Torryl ever existed. Even if he had, Faarn might be guilty of concealing Torryl's death, although Ysella suspected Faarn had been careful to avoid outright lies.

Either way, the circumstances suggested the villain was none other than Sollem Faarn. *At least for the last seven years.*

That still left the question of what to do about Faarn.

There was something about trusts . . . something he was missing. He stepped back from the file chest and turned to Wisstah. "Thank you. That will do for now."

The two walked quietly back to the main corridor.

Once outside the heavy door to the records, Ysella stopped at the clerk's desk. "Thank you, Clerk Ruustyn. I appreciate your assistance. The committee may need more information in the future. It may not. That will depend on others, but I did want to thank you."

Then he opened his case. "As you can see . . . just my notes."

Ruustyn looked to Wisstah, who nodded, then replied, "Thank you, sir."

Ysella turned to the younger clerk. "Thank you, Wyllum. You made my search much easier and quicker."

"My pleasure, sir."

When Ysella left the district hall, he nodded to the patroller, the same one who had seen him enter the hall. "Thank you for keeping an eye on my mount. I appreciate it."

"He was good company, sir. Didn't talk too much."

Ysella smiled, then untied Jaster, mounted, and turned the gelding north on Imperial Boulevard for the short ride back to his house.

Caastyn appeared as Ysella led Jaster into the stable. "How soon do you want to leave?"

"Not long, but I want to see if there are any letters or messages. Between a sixth and a third, I'd judge."

"I'll be ready. Do we need anything else?"

"Not today. We're just looking."

After stalling Jaster so he could have water and a little fodder, Ysella went to his study.

There was only a single message on his desk, from Sullynd & Smarkaan.

Legalist Faarn will meet with you at our offices at fourth bell on Tridi afternoon, 9 Winterend.

If this is not convenient, please let us know today.

Ysella set the message on the desk, then nodded. Tridi was what he'd asked for, if less convenient, but he needed the time to get better prepared. Then he walked back to the stable.

"Where are we headed, sir?"

"Number 321, Pleasant Lane, off Cuipregilt Avenue, some five blocks east of Imperial Boulevard. It's the dwelling of Legalist Sollem Faarn, who handles all the legal affairs of Gustov Torryl."

"That's about where all the mansions start," replied Caastyn. "What about Torryl's mansion? If his legalist has that big a dwelling, how large is his?"

"He doesn't seem to have one. Or if he does, I couldn't find any record of it." For the moment Ysella wasn't about to mention Torryl's purported death.

"Maybe he doesn't live in Machtarn, and this legalist really handles everything?"

"I have some thoughts along that line." Ysella led Jaster from his stall out onto the drive, where he mounted.

Then the two headed east. They rode past Alaan Escalante's house before getting to Pleasant Lane, which angled to the southeast off of Cuipregilt Avenue. The first dwellings on the lane were markedly larger than the Escalante house, and by two blocks farther southeast, most were definitely mansions.

At first glance, Sollem Faarn's gray stone mansion appeared similar to the others, although the outbuilding that clearly held a stable also had larger living quarters, possibly to house the guards that accompanied him. As Ysella rode closer to the house, what initially surprised him was the lack of a wall around the grounds, unlike many of the other large dwellings. Then he realized that all the gardens were low, and there were no trees anywhere close to the main house or the outbuilding. The pale blue shutters looked thicker than most Ysella had seen, suggesting that they might be iron-backed.

"It's built like a fortress, if not obviously," he said to Caastyn.

"Pretty much."

"I imagine his carriage is more like an armored coach as well."

"Looks like he worries people might come after him, but if he's Torryl's legalist, that makes sense."

"He might be more than that. We'll have to see." What Ysella saw confirmed what he suspected after looking at the property records. "Is anyone watching us?"

"Not that I can tell."

"Well, it won't matter. We won't be coming back here." *One way or another.*

"You found what you wanted to know?" asked Caastyn.

"Enough for now. We'll head back. I've got Council work to do."

"The Council's not in session yet, is it?"

"No, but I won't have time to deal with everything when it is."

Caastyn laughed. "I'm glad I'm not in your boots."

"As far as I'm concerned, it's still better than worrying about a holding." Ysella smiled wryly. "I'm meeting with Faarn on Tridi afternoon at the property legalists', and I'd like you to come with me. Since he'll doubtless have guards, having you might be best for me."

"I'll be ready."

"You always are." Ysella looked at the cold and empty lane ahead. "We'll turn left at the next corner." Then he looked back, momentarily, at Faarn's mansion, where the only signs of life were the trails of whitish smoke rising from the chimneys.

Once Ysella returned to the house and took care of Jaster, he went to his study. He paced back and forth, trying to remember what it was about trusts. He'd almost never dealt with trusts in practice as a water legalist, except for a few for underage children. Trusts weren't that frequent in Guldor, nor had they been in old Aloor.

He turned to the shelves on one side of the study, looking through the titles of the legal treatises, one after another, until he found the pertinent volume. Relatively thin, it dealt primarily with structuring trusts for various circumstances, but he found one line that might be useful in dealing with Faarn.

> Under the Imperial legal code, trusts established or used in a fashion to hide the true ownership of assets or to avoid legal prosecution or liability are considered fraudulent and are classed as grand theft if so proven . . .

Did the continued use of property transfers to the Torryl Trust prove an intention to hide true ownership? It was certainly to mislead those selling to him, thinking that they were selling to the notorious Gustov Torryl and that they had no other feasible choice. That was certainly deceptive, but did that, in itself, make the trust fraudulent or prove an illegal purpose? It was certainly designed to intimidate.

But Ysella wasn't about to trust his legal skills on that, not without some formidable allies. He also needed to write out four very clean and complete copies of the notes he'd taken at the district hall and prepare a letter to Legrand Quaentyn.

30

ON Duadi morning, Ysella left the house early with four sets of notes detailing all the properties held by the Torryl Trust—or at least all those Ysella had found. First, he rode to the post centre, where he dispatched the letter of instruction to Legrand Quaentyn, along with the documentation, in case matters did not go as planned.

From there he made his way to the Council Hall, reaching his office moments after Khaard had unlocked it and was lighting the wall stove.

"You're here early, sir."

"I need to meet some councilors." Ysella took off his riding jacket and hung it in his personal office, then returned to the front office, carrying his leather case. "I'd like you to make a copy of something as soon as you're finished getting the office ready. It might be needed for evidence later." Ysella took out one set of papers and handed them to the senior clerk. "After you finish making the copy, put the original in the locked file chest and the copy in an envelope on my desk."

"Yes, sir."

"I'm going to try to see Councilor Staeryt and the Premier, if they're in their offices. I have no idea how long that might take, but I will need the copy as soon as possible."

Khaard nodded. "I'll take care of it, sir."

"Thank you."

Ysella walked down to the main level. Since Staeryt was the councilor from Machtarn, there was a good chance he'd be in, although the Council wasn't scheduled to convene until Tridi.

When Ysella reached Staeryt's office, the one clerk present looked up in surprise. "Yes, sir?"

Because the clerk clearly didn't recognize him, Ysella said, "Dominic Ysella, to see Councilor Staeryt."

"Yes, sir." The clerk hurried into the side office, returning immediately. "Go right in, sir."

Case in hand, Ysella entered the private office, closing the door as he did.

Staeryt rose briefly from the behind his desk, gestured to the chairs in front of the desk, and reseated himself. "You look rather determined."

"Unfortunately," replied Ysella as he sat down. "Does the name Gustov Torryl mean anything to you?"

"The elusive king of thieves? I've heard of him. I've never met or seen him, though."

"That's hardly surprising. His name came up, and I did a little legal research." Ysella explained what he found in the district property records, but not his own involvement.

"That would explain why the patrollers can't catch him. You think that Faarn is using Torryl's name to threaten people into selling property?"

"I'm fairly certain, but I also ran across a legal reference to trusts used to disguise the true owner as fraudulent and a felony."

Staeryt frowned, then nodded. "Now that you mention it . . . that's definitely in the legal code. I can't recall anyone being charged. I imagine that's because most trusts are for underage children or incapacitated adults."

"The problem in Machtarn is that people who haven't followed 'Torryl's' wishes have disappeared or died. A dead man can't have committed those crimes, and the only person who would know is Faarn."

"What do you have in mind?"

"Getting the Imperial district legalist to incarcerate and try him on multiple counts of using a fraudulent trust. Any real evidence of the other crimes has long since vanished."

Staeryt offered an amused smile. "So why are you talking to me?"

"To give you a copy of the evidence so I can tell the district legalist that a number of well-placed Imperial officials know about the fraudulent trust. I'm also letting the Premier know, as well as sending a copy to a legalist well away from Machtarn."

"You're skeptical of the Imperial district legalist?"

"I suspect quite a few people have been skeptical of Faarn, but no one has wanted to deal with him. How high that willful ignorance goes, I don't know, but I'd rather be prepared than not." Ysella opened his case and handed one set of the documents to Staeryt.

"Better you than me," said the older councilor as he accepted the documents.

"I appreciate it, Ahslem. I'd appreciate it if you wouldn't tell anyone . . . unless something happens to me."

"I'll keep them safe and hope I won't need to use them. The Premier won't be happy about this, you know."

"I know, but he can't afford being accused of covering up something like this, and it's much better for everyone for me to deal with the district legalist." Ysella stood. "Thank you."

"Keep me informed, if you would."

"I certainly will."

From Staeryt's office, Ysella walked the short distance to the Premier's office, where he waited for almost a sixth before the Administrator of Agriculture left.

"I hope you weren't waiting too long, Dominic," offered Detruro with his usual warm smile, which meant nothing.

"Not that long."

"How are you coming on that project?"

"It's coming, but I'm here on another more immediate but less vital matter." Ysella handed Detruro a copy of the documents and then went on to explain about the dead Gustov Torryl and the very alive Legalist Faarn.

Like Staeryt, Detruro frowned. "That sounds more like a matter for Ahslem Staeryt."

"I've already met with him, but I'm not asking for your direct assistance, or his. I'm asking that you keep a copy of the evidence before I meet with the Imperial district legalist to bring the matter to his attention."

Detruro's frown deepened. "You're not suggesting that he's covering this up?"

"More like he'd rather not deal with it. I'm convinced that Faarn has been behind a number of associated crimes blamed on the very much dead Gustov Torryl, but there's neither enough evidence nor anyone who's survived willing to testify against Faarn. The evidence of the fraudulent trust, however . . ."

Detruro nodded. "I understand. You want the district legalist in a position where he has to charge Faarn and take him into custody and where he knows that there's little option."

"That was my thought."

Detruro chuckled. "In a way, you've justified my choice of you for the reestablishment charter. Who else would think of fraudulent trusts as a way to put away someone like Faarn? It fits, in a way. You try to charge someone like that with murder or theft, and no one would believe it, but charging him with legal chicanery with documented proof . . ."

"There are enough counts for him to be exiled, which doesn't seem as harsh as execution, but which removes him from Guldor."

"If the district legalist chooses to act."

"That's why I'm here."

Detruro sighed. "You can tell District Legalist Smootn—I think he's still in that position—that I'd hate to bring his name up to the Imperador for refusing to act, because some legalist has been able to hide behind his profession."

"Thank you. I trust it won't be necessary."

"It very well may be, Dominic." Then Detruro smiled, not pleasantly, adding, "But if it is, it will add to the pressure we can apply to the Imperador later."

Ysella could see that.

Detruro stood. "Best of fortune with the district legalist."

Ysella came to his feet. "Thank you. I'll keep you informed."

"I look forward to hearing how it all turns out."

In short, try not to involve me, and let me know when it's all over.

After leaving the Premier's office, Ysella returned to his own office, read through the recent mail, and made his notes for the two clerks while Khaard finished copying the document. Ysella then placed the newly copied version in his leather case and walked to the Council stables.

From there he rode south toward the center of Machtarn under increasingly cloudy skies, with a cold wind at his back until he reined up outside the district justiciary building across from the district hall.

As he dismounted, Ysella looked to the young patroller posted by the doors. "I'm Councilor Ysella, and I need to meet with the district legalist. Is it all right if I leave my horse here? I shouldn't be too long."

"That will be fine, sir. Not much happens here."

"Thank you."

Ysella entered the building and found the anteroom serving the district legalist and approached the middle-aged and graying clerk.

"I'm Imperial Councilor Dominic Ysella here to see Imperial District Legalist Smootn."

"I'm sorry . . . I missed your name," said the clerk tiredly.

"Dominic Ysella. Imperial Councilor. Chairman of the Waterways Committee."

"He's in a meeting, Councilor."

"I'll wait."

"It may be a little while."

"At present, I have some time."

Almost half a bell passed before a thin, almost gaunt man walked through a side door in the antechamber. He paused as he took in Ysella, who immediately stood as he saw the clerk trying to get the older man's attention.

"Imperial Councilor Dominic Ysella, here to see you, District Legalist Smootn. I'm chairman of the Waterways Committee."

Smootn looked momentarily confused. "I'm sorry. Did we have an appointment?"

"We did not. The matter came up rather suddenly, and the Council didn't wish to have you surprised."

"I have another appointment before long, Councilor . . ."

"Ysella. It won't take long for me to fill you in on the matter."

Smootn gestured, almost reluctantly, to the closed door to one side of and behind the clerk's desk, and Ysella followed the district legalist into an office, closing the door.

"What is this matter, may I ask?" asked Smootn as he seated himself, his eyes not quite meeting Ysella's.

"I assume you've heard about the exploits and crimes of Gustov Torryl?"

"Hasn't everyone? But no one seems able to find him," declared Smootn.

"That might be because he's been dead for years, and his purported legalist appears to be behind the crimes." Ysella explained the situation as he removed the last set of documents from his case and handed them to Smootn. When he finished describing Sollem Faarn's pattern of actions, he concluded, "While there are years of crimes concealed by this fiction, we both know that attempting to unravel them would take years, if not longer. It might cost more lives without resolving anything. Charges and convictions on multiple counts of using a fraudulent trust would result in a finding of guilt and a sentence of exile."

"Just on this documentation? How do I know you didn't make this up?"

"It's all in the records across the street. I'm also a registered legalist here in Machtarn, and I'm not about to falsify documents. These are abridged copies of the originals. Both the chairman of the Council Justiciary Committee and the Premier have copies as well. We would all prefer to have this handled quietly. So should you, especially since Faarn's actions have gone undetected for years. That might not reflect well on the Imperial Justiciary. On the other hand, capturing and securing the man behind a long series of unsolved disappearances . . ."

Ysella could almost see the calculations behind Smootn's eyes. Finally, he said, "You know that it won't look good for us to do an armed approach to Legalist Faarn's dwelling. It could be . . . difficult. In any event, preparations will take some time, because I'll need to marshal enough patrollers."

Ysella nodded at the tacit confirmation that Smootn was well aware of the dangers involved with Faarn. "I thought as much. I'm meeting with Legalist Faarn tomorrow. He conveyed that his client, Gustov Torryl, is interested in property I own—"

"Tomorrow . . . that's not possible."

"I never thought it would be. I'll agree to look at the proposed documents of sale at my property legalists' office next week. When that date is set, which it should be by tomorrow, I'll let you know. That should make it much easier for you." Ysella paused. "That is, of course, if Faarn doesn't find out. I think the Premier would find that very unsatisfactory."

Smootn swallowed. "We will be very careful. I will not mention the name of the corrupt legalist."

"That might be for the best." As Ysella spoke, he had an uneasy feeling about Smootn, and sensed that he needed to be more careful. "I'll let you know in the next day or so."

"Sooner would be better," declared the district legalist.

"He's the one who sets the time and date," replied Ysella, standing.

He could sense Smootn's eyes on his back as he left the legalist's private office.

Once outside, he rode back to the house, where he found Caastyn cleaning out the stable.

"You're back early," said Caastyn.

"Come tomorrow, that will change. After you finish, I need to talk to you. I'll be in my study."

Ysella unsaddled and groomed Jaster, then walked back to his study. He was still considering possible options for dealing with the district legalist and Faarn when Caastyn arrived and took the chair across the desk.

"I think I've gotten myself in a dangerous position, Caastyn. I met with the Imperial District Legalist for Machtarn this morning to make him aware of the fact that Legalist Faarn is using a fraudulent trust as a way of hiding his own crimes. While District Legalist Smootn has agreed to bring charges against Faarn, I got the feeling that he already knew about Faarn and that, despite his agreement, he'll delay arresting Faarn, giving Faarn a chance to leave Guldor or to remove me. Either way, before long Faarn's likely to know I'm after him."

"Raf's always felt that the patrollers weren't allowed to look into some things." Caastyn paused. "What do you need from me?"

"We'll need to keep the house shuttered at night on the ground level, and I'll need you to accompany me at times for a few days."

"That might not stop an assassin, sir."

"They'll be a little less likely to attack two riders than one, and two pairs of eyes can see more than one."

"Why do you think Faarn won't just kill you and keep doing it?"

"I distributed evidence of his actions to the Premier and others, and they know I went to the district legalist. No matter what, there will be enough information to expose Faarn. He'll know that. At the least, he'll have to flee or go into hiding. My guess is that he'll also want to strike at me before he leaves Machtarn. I'm meeting with him tomorrow, but he may not find out by then."

"Is meeting with him a good idea?"

"No . . . but I can always hope that he'll flee immediately or attack me where I have a chance to defend myself. I don't think that will happen, though. He's the kind who attacks where and when he can't be seen."

"You don't think he'll leave?" asked Caastyn.

"I doubt it. He'll be angry, and he'll want to strike back, preferably when he thinks I won't expect it."

"Then I'd better make sure we're prepared. Is there anything else, sir?"

"Not right now."

"I'll see what I can do." Caastyn stood and left the study.

Once alone, Ysella looked at the papers on one side of the desk. After a few moments, he picked up a single sheet, read it, and set it aside, before dipping his pen in the inkwell and returning to drafting the proposed government and Council "reestablishment" legal structure for Detruro. *And you haven't the faintest idea how to work in political parties that don't yet exist.*

31

ON Tridi morning, after an uneasy sleep, Ysella again donned the silk-leather vest, a white shirt, a pale blue cravat, and a simple dark blue suit. Over breakfast, he read the *Tribune* and found nothing alarming, then adjourned to his study and spent a bell working on the draft reorganization legislation, still wondering how he could come up with a Council structure to facilitate compromise. Then he headed to the stable, where Caastyn waited with both mounts.

"Have you seen anyone skulking around this morning?" asked Ysella, half-seriously, although he doubted word of his actions had yet reached Faarn.

"Not anywhere nearby, but I wouldn't be that close. I'd wait somewhere along Imperial Boulevard."

"So you're suggesting we take a more roundabout way?"

"It can't hurt."

Ysella laughed. "We'll head east and then follow Jacquez north to Council Avenue. It's more direct, but a little slower."

"It's also more open, with fewer places for attackers to hide," Caastyn pointed out.

"I'll come back that way, then." Ysella eased Jaster forward.

"Good idea," said the older man as he rode up beside Ysella as they headed down the drive.

The two reined up outside the doors to the Council stables just before third bell, where Ysella turned and said, "You don't need to stay. I doubt anyone will wait all day for me, but I'll leave early and be back at the house around third bell so we can get to the property legalists' offices before fourth bell."

"You sure about that?"

"I doubt that Legalist Faarn or his men know what I look like. They'll need the meeting to make sure who I am before they attack. They've been careful that way."

Caastyn winced.

"What am I supposed to do? Let this disgrace to the profession get away and continue his ways? Let the likely corrupt district legalist continue in office?"

"Isn't there another way?"

"The evidence has been there for years. Others have to know, but no one has done anything."

"As usual," muttered Caastyn.

Ysella agreed, but merely nodded as he left Caastyn and rode into the stables.

After turning Jaster over to one of the ostlers, Ysella made his way to his office, where he quickly went through the few letters that had arrived since Duadi, making notes for the replies. Just before noon, he walked into the Council chamber and took his seat beside Staeryt.

"How are matters going with the Imperial district legalist?" asked the older councilor.

"Not well, I fear. I have the suspicion that the questionable legalist may have corrupted the legal system of Machtarn."

"That's hardly surprising," replied Staeryt. "What do you intend to do?"

"Find out how bad the situation is. Your committee may have to investigate." *Which wouldn't be all that bad if it creates more pressure on the Imperador and the Heir.*

"Try not to make that necessary, Dominic. The Council needs you, and so does Detruro, although he'll never admit it."

The sound of the chime saved Ysella from replying, and Luaro Maatrak took the lectern and announced, "The Council is now in session."

Immediately, Detruro followed Maatrak to the lectern. "There is no official business scheduled for today. I would like to remind all committee chairmen that hearing schedules for the remainder of Winterend are due in the Premier's office by noon on Quindi. The current policy for scheduling changes remains in effect . . ."

Ysella nodded. The often-repeated words ran through his mind. *Except for special circumstances and approved by the Premier, changes must be made a week or more in advance.*

After the announcements, Maatrak recessed the Council, subject to the order of the Premier.

Ysella returned to his office and signed or corrected the responses drafted by his clerks, then left the office and rode home by the slower and more open way. Once there, he went back to work on his reform legislation.

After another bell, a thought occurred to him. It had been over a month since the death of Khael Wythcomb, and he could certainly write an ostensibly innocuous letter to Aelyn Wythcomb. His second thought was that such a letter had to be written most carefully. *Most carefully.*

He decided he was too pressed to write that kind of careful letter at the moment and went back to the simpler, or more direct, task of aligning Imperial administrators under the Council.

At third bell, Ysella set aside his drafting, again, and readied himself for the ride to meet with the property legalists and Sollem Faarn, a meeting which he dreaded. Nevertheless, he donned his riding jacket and walked out to where Caastyn held the mounts ready. Ysella noted his leather crossbow case behind Jaster's saddle. Caastyn had his crossbow out, with a wrist sling.

"After seeing the legalist's dwelling," said Caastyn, "I thought hunting gear might be more appropriate."

"I hope that won't be necessary, but better prepared and unnecessary than necessary and unprepared." Ysella mounted; then both headed down the drive.

For all of their careful study of the streets and side streets, neither saw anything to give them pause. Then again, a good assassin would leave no obvious traces.

As the two neared the building holding the offices of Sullynd & Smarkaan, Ysella studied everyone on the street or near the building more carefully, not that there were many out and about in the winter chill.

Caastyn remained mounted while Ysella dismounted and tied Jaster to the hitching post closest to the building entrance. As Ysella entered and closed the door, Caastyn rode away from the building.

No sooner was Ysella inside than Haasl Sullynd appeared, smiling nervously. "You're early, Ritter, but you can wait for Legalist Faarn in the settlement room." He turned and escorted Ysella to a small chamber illuminated by two high and narrow windows, and holding little more than a circular table surrounded by four chairs. "It shouldn't be long. He is always punctual."

"Have you dealt with him before?"

"Not personally. Sr. Smarkaan has once before, several years ago. Now . . . if you will excuse me." Sullynd didn't quite flee, but his rapid withdrawal bothered Ysella as he took off his riding jacket and laid it across the back of one of the chairs.

He waited almost a third of a bell.

Ysella stood as Faarn entered the office, not out of respect, but because sitting put him at a disadvantage in more ways than one.

The legalist was a nondescriptly pleasant-looking figure slightly taller than Ysella with thinning brown hair, a squarish chin, and intent watery-green eyes. He wore a black suit, with a white shirt and black cravat, and his eyes surveyed Ysella quickly but intently. "You don't wear a gladius."

"Wearing one invites temptation," replied Ysella.

"Oh, that's right. Landors have a code of sorts about not attacking an unarmed man. Such nobility can be a disadvantage, don't you think?"

"One man's disadvantage might be another's advantage."

"Have you considered Sr. Torryl's offer?"

"I find I'm having difficulty understanding why a man I've never met and whom I've never heard of is so suddenly anxious to obtain my properties."

"Times are changing in Machtarn, as you obviously know. He's being most generous, and he wouldn't have to be that kind. You'd come away with a handsome profit, without the bother of collecting undependable rents."

"So far, they've been very dependable," said Ysella.

"That could change very quickly. That can happen here in Machtarn. An unforeseen illness. A fire . . . who knows?" Faarn's warm smile didn't cover the chill beneath the words. "Another advantage: You wouldn't be seen as leveraging your position as chairman of the Waterways Committee after you got all those funds for improving the docks and port facilities here in Machtarn. Those things do get out, you know."

"Especially if someone wishes for them to come out. A number of my properties were purchased well before the Waterways Committee funded improvements."

"But if you sold those properties before the forthcoming improvements are funded, no one could fault you . . . whereas . . . if you sold them later . . ."

"You have a point," agreed Ysella, "but there's no law against a councilor buying property that he anticipates will increase in value over time."

"Laws and popular acceptance do not always agree," said Faarn.

"Tell me. I've heard it said that anyone who refuses to sell or to acquiesce in other matters to Sr. Torryl tends to face extreme difficulties."

"Sr. Torryl doesn't take refusal lightly. That's true . . . but with an eminently reasonable councilor such as you, I don't see why some sort of . . . accommodation could not be reached. Perhaps an increase in the offer of one part in twenty."

"One part in ten might be better."

"I doubt Sr. Torryl would go much beyond one part in fifteen."

"Possibly one part in fourteen."

Faarn frowned, then nodded. "That might be possible."

"I'd have to see such an agreement in writing."

"We can have that by tomorrow afternoon."

"It would have to be on Unadi or Duadi, and after third afternoon bell," replied Ysella. "I have certain Council duties."

"Then on Unadi afternoon, at fourth bell. I will see you here, then." With that, Faarn turned and left the settlement room.

Faarn's abrupt departure froze Ysella, if only momentarily, and he quickly donned his riding jacket and gloves and stepped out of the settlement room, stopping as Sullynd turned to him.

"That was quick," said the property legalist, a puzzled expression on his face. "Usually talks take longer. He said fourth bell on Unadi. Is that correct?"

"I believe so, but we'll see on Unadi." Ysella smiled politely, then departed the building. Once outside, he looked to the west at a dark coach headed in the general direction of Faarn's office. Ysella immediately untied the gelding and mounted.

Caastyn rode toward him, then reined up. "Two guards and the driver. So far as I could tell, no others. One of the guards had a crossbow."

"We'll ride after the coach, slowly, to see where he's headed."

The two followed at a distance, crossing Imperial Boulevard and heading toward the port authority building, but Ysella reined up once he saw the coach halted outside the legalist's office. "He might drive that way on Unadi, and he might not." Then he turned Jaster back east, and the two men rode to Imperial Boulevard, where they turned north, heading back to the house.

"What happened?" asked Caastyn. "Was that the legalist in black? He looked satisfied, in a strange way."

"Did he see you?"

"I doubt it."

"Good. We're supposed to meet on Unadi. I get the feeling that meeting isn't likely. If it turns out that way, I lose the chance to get him exiled, and then I'll have an enemy for life."

Ysella couldn't help thinking that selling the properties would have been the easiest and least dangerous path, but he didn't like the thought of further enabling Faarn. He had to admit that, except for the trust, most of the evidence of Faarn's criminality was anecdotal and circumstantial.

"You think he'll try to leave Machtarn?"

"I don't know. If he's smart, he might. But he's also as cold as a white cougar in the silver heights, and just as deadly, and he doesn't want to give up his power and wealth."

"Both ill-gotten. Looks like I'm going to be riding with you for the next week or so."

"You always complain that your life lacks the excitement it once had."

"You would remind me." But Caastyn smiled.

32

FURDI morning, Ysella woke early, thinking he needed to write Aelyn Wythcomb. As he dressed, he put on the silk-leather armor vest, hoping that he wouldn't need it. He looked at the gladius and scabbard that hung at one end of the armoire, then shook his head. Before sitting at the table for breakfast, Ysella went to find Caastyn, who was in the stable.

"You look like you've got something in mind, sir." Caastyn offered a bemused smile.

"I'm sure you have a good idea what it is. We're going to visit the Imperial district legalist first thing after I finish breakfast. That way, I have a better chance of informing him about the time of the meeting with Faarn."

"Also less chance of running into Faarn's guards," replied Caastyn. "It'd be better if there were no chance."

"You're right, but what if Faarn doesn't do anything before the meeting and then shows up, and patrollers under the district legalist don't because I haven't told him? Then I've lost any chance of a comparatively quiet resolution to the mess." *And also gotten a black eye, if not worse, with the Imperial Justiciary, Ahslem Staeryt, and the Premier.*

"You haven't left yourself much of a way out. That's because others didn't want to do the hard work. So *we* have to." Caastyn shook his head. "After I got my stipend, I thought I was done cleaning up Imperial messes."

"You don't have to go."

"I don't like it, but I'm not about to let that bastard get away. That girl in the harbor was a friend of Krynn's."

"I didn't know..."

"Neither did I. Gerdina told me last night."

Everything gets more complicated.

Before Ysella could think of something appropriate to say, Caastyn added, "I'll have everything ready for you."

"Thank you."

"It's one of those things that have to be done." Caastyn smiled crookedly. "Too bad we're the ones who have to do it."

As Ysella made his way back to the kitchen, he wondered why he'd thought his plan was simple and workable. Except... it *was* workable, the only problem being that Faarn might not be the only casualty. *It might have been better to kill him with a truncheon in the settlement room and claim self-defense.*

He ate sparingly and quickly, drinking a single mug of café, and then donned his winter riding jacket and gloves and headed back to the stable. Predictably, Caastyn had the mounts ready, as well as the crossbows, although Ysella's was in the case behind his saddle.

Once the two mounted and headed out, Caastyn said, "You're trying to meet with him before Faarn gets to him?"

"There's a good chance. I didn't set the meeting time until after the district legalist likely left his office yesterday, and Faarn strikes me as very deliberate."

Caastyn nodded, then said, "Once you're inside the building, I'm going to make myself less obvious, where I can cover the front."

"Whatever you think best. You've had far more experience." *Considering I've had none.* "I'll try to make it as quick as possible."

"Makes sense" was all Caastyn said.

As Ysella rode south on Imperial Boulevard, he couldn't help thinking about another provision that needed to be included with his reforms—that the Justiciary should be independent from either the Council or the Imperator, but that justicers and high legalists had to be able to be removed by the Council through some acceptable means. How High Justicer Kaahl would view that was another question, although Kaahl seemed to interpret the laws as written, not as Laureous often wanted.

The closer Ysella got to the justiciary building, the more intently he studied the horses, carriages, and wagons on Imperial Boulevard and the side streets, but he saw no one who looked suspicious. Even the square beside the justiciary building was almost empty when Ysella reined up. Before he dismounted, he took another quick look around, but still didn't see anyone nearby. He dismounted, tied Jaster to the hitching post closest to the steps up the main door, and said to the duty patroller, "I won't be long."

"Don't break your neck, sir," returned the patroller. "I'm not going anywhere."

Ysella smiled and hurried inside, making his way to the office of the Imperial district legalist.

The same clerk that Ysella had encountered before looked up. "Councilor, Legalist Smootn isn't here yet. He shouldn't be long, though."

"Is he in the building? Or hasn't he come in yet?"

"He always comes here first, sir."

"Thank you. I'll be back in a bit." With those words, Ysella returned to the building entrance and stood outside, studying the street in both directions. He didn't see Caastyn, which was likely for the best, nor did he see any obviously armed men, only the slow movement of wagons intermittently appearing and lumbering toward the harbor.

A sixth passed, although it felt like an entire bell, before a carriage came to a halt before the entrance, and Legalist Smootn stepped out and walked toward the building entrance.

Ysella stepped down, positioning himself so that the legalist couldn't avoid him. "Legalist Smootn, the meeting is set up for fourth afternoon bell on Unadi."

Smootn recoiled as if the words had actually struck him.

"Remember? I'm Councilor Ysella."

"You're a fool, Councilor. Let it go." Smootn moved to one side.

Ysella moved as well, blocking him. "You can't. Not if you want to remain district legalist for long."

"Let me pass. I'll have nothing—"

"TAKE COVER! MOVE!" boomed Caastyn's voice from somewhere.

Hammer-like blows slammed into Ysella's body, but he managed to lurch back toward the comparative shelter of the building entry, at the same time seeing Legalist Smootn crumpled on the stone steps, with at least one crossbow quarrel through his back.

Numbness instantly radiated from the side of Ysella's skull, and a vise squeezed his chest tighter and tighter. Helplessly, he felt himself sliding down the side of the entryway.

Then there was only reddish darkness . . . and nothing.

33

Voices from everywhere assaulted Ysella. He couldn't make out the words, couldn't see. He felt he was falling . . . or being carried. Waves of heat and cold washed across him. He couldn't move. A vest of pain pressed his chest on all sides, and the left side of his skull burned with a fiery tingling.

The voices faded, and hot darkness swallowed him again.

The next time he woke, someone said words he still couldn't understand. There was a mug at his lips. Something in his mouth. The liquid was almost as hot as the side of his head, and some of it dribbled across his chin and neck.

When he woke again, he could see enough in the dim light to realize he was in his own bedroom.

"Are you awake, sir?" asked a voice. Ysella belatedly recognized it as Gerdina's.

". . . think so . . ." he managed to get out, if hoarsely.

"You should try to drink a bit, if you can."

Ysella nodded, barely.

Gerdina held the mug to his lips, and he took a small swallow of lager, then a second.

"Enough . . . right now." As Gerdina removed the mug, he realized his hands and arms were restrained and that his body was propped up at a slight angle. He noticed that Caastyn wasn't there. "Caastyn . . . is he . . . ?"

"Caastyn's fine, Ritter. He wasn't too happy with the patrollers at first, except for the young one supposed to guard the building. Your horse is fine, too, and your papers are on your desk. You're going to need some time to heal."

"How long . . . what day . . . ?"

"It's Unadi, midmorning."

"Unadi . . . that can't . . ."

"You've got broken or fractured ribs, and the quarrels had frog poison on them. How it got into that gash in your skull, Caastyn doesn't know. You almost died. You would have been dead without that leather-and-silk body armor." Gerdina stood and set the mug on the bedside table. "I'm going to unstrap you. You got pretty restless once you started to recover from the poison."

"Poison?" Ysella said stupidly.

"There was frog poison on the quarrels," Gerdina repeated patiently. "Some of it got into that gash on the side of your head. Couldn't have been much, or you'd have died."

Ysella tried to shift his weight slightly, and lances of pain shot through his chest and ribs.

"The doctor said you need to sit up as much as you can and sleep with your body straight but propped up. He said that would help the pain."

"How bad . . . ?"

"From what he could tell, your ribs didn't splinter, but if you're not careful . . ."

"Or if I get shot again, they could." Ysella remained perfectly still while Gerdina undid the straps.

As Gerdina finished, she said, "Krynn told me to thank you. Maree was her friend."

"I didn't do anything, except find some papers and get shot. Whatever else happened, Caastyn did."

Gerdina smiled, a cool expression. "Without you, he wouldn't have known who the killer really was, but he can tell you the rest when he gets back. He's doing some shopping. And he is *fine*. He's worried about you, a great deal. He'll be glad that you're finally in your right mind."

Ysella looked at the single armchair in the corner. "I suppose I should sit up, or try."

Almost as soon as Ysella sat on the edge of the bed, he began to cough, and more pains lanced through his ribs and chest.

"The doctor said that would happen when you first sat up."

"Did he say how long before the ribs heal?"

"At least a month, and no riding. Now, let's get you to the chair."

Ysella moved slowly, but with every step he felt some pain. Once seated, and after some coughing, he felt a touch better.

"I've got some hot fowl soup," said Gerdina. "I'll bring some up."

Ysella wasn't all that fond of fowl soup, but he also wasn't about to argue. Besides, he needed something to regain at least a little strength.

The fowl soup helped . . . some.

Just before noon, Caastyn stepped into the bedroom. "Good to see that you're halfway up."

"It took two of us to get me from the bed to here," replied Ysella. "I also had some of Gerdina's fowl soup. It helped." He paused. "She said there was frog poison on the quarrels."

"That, or something just as bad." Caastyn lifted the newssheet he carried. "Quindi morning's *Tribune*. I thought you might like to know what's come out so far."

Ysella took the newssheet, feeling a certain weakness in his arms, and began to read.

DISTRICT LEGALIST KILLED; COUNCILOR SEVERELY WOUNDED

Yesterday morning, two men with army crossbows shot and killed Machtarn District Legalist Wyllum Smootn and severely wounded Imperial Councilor Dominic Ysella. The two attackers were wounded by a district patroller and by Councilor Ysella's bodyguard, but succumbed to their injuries. The attack was reputedly ordered by Legalist Sollem Faarn, whom the councilor and the district legalist had been investigating for legal fraud and possible associated murders.

Faarn fled his house before he could be arrested. His whereabouts are unknown at this time.

Authorities have been suspicious of Faarn for years, given his legal associations with Gustov Torryl, now deceased, and a number of unsolved murders and disappearances. According to Acting District Legalist Foerst, no hard evidence was ever unearthed implicating Faarn until the recent investigation by District Legalist Smootn and Councilor Ysella.

Authorities have already begun to search Faarn's elegant and capacious residence, and early discoveries "tend to confirm Faarn's criminal activities," declared the acting district legalist. Faarn's wife and children are reported to have been living most of the time near Devult . . .

Councilor Ysella was struck in the chest by two poisoned crossbow bolts, and it is not yet known whether the unmarried councilor will survive . . .

Ysella lowered the newssheet and let Caastyn take it. "Bodyguard? You're more than that."

"Trying to explain more would have confused everyone." Caastyn snorted.

"Has there been any more in the newssheets?"

Caastyn shook his head. "There's nothing else to sell newssheets. No more killings, no more sign of the missing legalist. No one cares about fraudulent trusts."

"I would have been more concerned about Faarn's whereabouts, except that Gerdina suggested I didn't have to worry."

"Let's just say that Raf and I knew he'd be getting ready to leave

Machtarn. Best that everyone thinks he got away and is on the run. No one will miss the other two thugs, either. With no bodies, there's no way to blame anyone. No one's looking, anyway." Caastyn grinned. "And all Guldor knows that you were the one who discovered his crimes, and almost died for it."

"Me and Smootn," said Ysella sardonically.

"Smootn paid for being bought off. It's better for everyone, and his family, that he died doing his duty."

"You thought Faarn's thugs would be there, didn't you?"

"Thought it was more likely than not. I don't think they were there for you, though. They were trying to get Smootn. You happened to be in the wrong place at the right time."

"I should have listened to you," Ysella admitted.

"We all learn by making mistakes. I'm a bit older. So I've learned more."

"That's a very polite way of saying that I should listen more. I'll do my best in the future."

"I hope so. I might not be around next time."

Ysella almost laughed, except his ribs hurt too much.

34

By Tridi morning, Ysella was able to get cleaned up, shave, and dress himself, if with some help from Caastyn, and use the stairs—very slowly. The numbness on the side of his head had vanished, but the gash still hurt and seemed slow to heal.

As he sipped café and ate breakfast, slowly, he began to read the *Tribune*. His eyes jumped to the story near the bottom of the front page.

> **FIRE GUTS MANSION OF VANISHED LEGALIST**
> Late Duadi evening, a fire broke out in the Pleasant Lane mansion of Legalist Sollem Faarn, wanted in connection with the killing of Imperial District Legalist Wyllum Smootn and the wounding of Councilor Dominic Ysella . . .
>
> Machtarn fire authorities reported that the fire began in a basement storeroom when barrels of an unknown flammable substance ignited. The fire was so intense that the entire structure was destroyed except for stone and masonry . . .

Ysella knew with certainty Faarn must have had connections who didn't want to be exposed, and the fire was a very easy way to destroy all evidence. The only question was who those connections might be. *As if they'll ever come to light now.*

Compared to that article, there was little else of interest in the newssheet, and he proceeded with breakfast, after which he went to his study. He settled behind his desk, with appropriately located pillows to keep him from inadvertent sudden movements as he worked, slowly, trying to think more carefully before writing down legislative language for the government-restructuring proposal.

At a little past fourth bell, Gerdina answered the door and brought him two messages. The first was from Alaan Escalante.

Dominic—
Amaelya and I were stunned to hear that you'd been attacked and severely wounded for bringing to light a criminal enterprise that has victimized many in Machtarn for years.

If there's anything I can do, please don't hesitate to ask.
We both wish you an easy and speedy recovery and look forward to the time when we can again enjoy your company.

Ysella half smiled at Escalante's inclusion of his wife, given that she was still in Silverhills and would be for several more weeks—and there was no way that she could have gotten a letter to her husband quickly enough to know how she felt.

The second was from Ahslem Staeryt and was similar to the message from Escalante, except that Staeryt had also written that he had not realized that Ysella's investigation was as dangerous as it turned out to be and that the Justiciary Committee would be looking into possible revisions in the Imperium's legal code.

He set the messages aside, knowing he didn't have to reply immediately. Slightly before noon, he heard a knock on the front door.

Gerdina answered and then entered the study. "It's Premier Detruro."

"Have him come in."

"He shouldn't stay long."

"He won't. He never does."

In moments, Iustaan Detruro strode into the study, stopping short of the desk, surveying Ysella, and then nodding almost approvingly. "You're looking much better than I thought you might, Dominic."

"If it had only been fractured ribs, I'd be in better shape. Some of the quarrels Faarn's men used were smeared with frog poison—that's why the head gash has been slow to heal. And, no, I don't know how the poison got to my scalp."

"Quarrels and frog poison? It's a wonder you survived. Most people die from the smallest amounts." Detruro shook his head, but remained standing. "You know that you upset Staeryt a great deal? When no one knew if you'd make it, he was worried to death he'd have to follow up on your work."

And you'd have a hard time getting someone else to write what the Imperador might consider a rather treasonous document. "He doesn't have to worry now. The acting district legalist seems to have matters well in hand."

"Except that no one's found any trace of Legalist Faarn. After that intense fire last night, I doubt they will," continued Detruro smoothly. "Anyone who could keep a dead brigand's reputation alive for almost a decade shouldn't have any problem hiding out, but it wouldn't be in Machtarn. Faarn has likely already left Machtarn, but I'm certain that Legalist Foerst knows far more than we ever will. Foerst indicated that no marks or banque drafts were found in the house, or his office, but that a number of valuable items remained in the house, many of which were destroyed by the fire. That supports the view that Faarn fled with whatever of value that he could easily take."

"But?" asked Ysella.

"He seemed the type to plan ahead," said Detruro.

"I can answer that," replied Ysella. "I didn't give him much choice. I'd arranged to have Imperial District Legalist Smootn arrest and charge him—" Ysella had to think for a moment. "—Unadi afternoon."

Detruro offered the warm smile he often used. "You did accomplish your goal, but couldn't you have gotten there without almost getting killed?"

"Most likely I could have, if Legalist Smootn hadn't been paid by Faarn."

"You knew that?"

"No. Not until Faarn's thugs used crossbows on us. He and I were the only ones who knew what was planned or when."

"Hmmm . . ." Detruro paused. "Then are you going to do anything to correct the newssheet?"

"What would be the point, except to upset Smootn's widow? I assume he was married."

"He was. I don't know more than that."

Ysella wasn't going to press the point, though he could tell Detruro didn't fully agree with him. "I'm close to finishing the initial draft of the proposal you asked me to write." *Except for what to do about possible political parties.*

"With everything you've been through, Dominic, there's no hurry."

Ysella smiled faintly. "Writing will be far easier for me than anything else over the next few weeks. Also, I've been thinking. For this to work, there will have to be a number of corresponding changes in government structure."

"The Imperador might accept seemingly minor changes, but beyond that . . ."

"You can always have me scale it back, once I finish the first version."

"Do what you can. It will be better than anyone else can do." Detruro paused. "Don't hurry or worry about when you come back to the Council."

"I'm not about to reinjure myself." *But I also can't see myself sitting here for the next month.*

"Just be careful." Detruro's smile was actually solicitous. "I won't take any more of your time. I'll have a messenger deliver announcements and the like here until you can start coming to the Council Hall."

"I appreciate that."

"Until later, then." Detruro turned and left the study.

Ysella heard him close the front door as he left. While Detruro was concerned, Ysella wondered what Detruro might be hiding . . . and whether he ever felt anything all that deeply.

But then, couldn't people say that about you as well? Ysella smiled ironically, then returned his attention to the papers on the desk.

Well before dinner, Ysella set aside his pen and let thoughts run through his mind, when he wasn't half dozing, which was about as close to napping as possible in the sitting position that minimized his aches and pains.

Caastyn arrived to announce dinner and to provide Ysella with any help, but Ysella slowly made his way to the dining room table, where he did allow Caastyn to help him sit comfortably.

After Caastyn said the blessing, Ysella noticed that Gerdina had sliced the fowl breast on his plate into thin strips and covered it with a glaze and that the potatoes were mashed. "This looks excellent . . . and easy to eat. Thank you."

Gerdina offered a knowing smile.

"You look like you're feeling better," offered Caastyn.

"Considering the way I felt on Unadi, anything would be an improvement, but I am feeling better, until I don't move carefully."

"That'll last for a while," Caastyn cautioned.

"Once I get a bit better, you'll have to take me to and from the Council in the chaise. I don't see myself mounting and dismounting for a while."

"You shouldn't be going anywhere for a time," said Gerdina.

Ysella smiled. "I did say 'once I get better,' but I'm not going to hurry." He looked to Caastyn. "I take it that the silk and leather armor is unusable now."

"That's fair to say, sir."

"While I'm laid up, could you make arrangements for another set? As you did before."

"I'll take care of that, tomorrow." Caastyn smiled. "I'll see if I can get it for less. Haardt can always boast that his armor saved a councilor."

The three ate in silence for a time. Then Caastyn spoke quietly. "I don't mean to pry, sir, but you talked some when you weren't yourself. Most was about drafting legislation, but you kept mentioning someone called Eileen. I don't recall anyone in your family with that name."

Ysella's smile was amused but wry. "Aelyn, actually. Aelyn Wythcomb. She's a widow in Aloor. I'd advised her on water law when I was there. I was going to write her a letter after I dealt with the late Imperial district legalist."

"An older widow?" asked Gerdina.

"Hardly. She's younger than I am."

Gerdina lifted her eyebrows. "Is she looking for someone to help raise her children?"

"She was only married a short time." Ysella explained briefly about the Ahnkaar mine and how he got involved.

"Sounds to me like you're interested in her," declared Gerdina, "especially if you were thinking about her when you were almost dying."

Caastyn tried, unsuccessfully, to stifle a smile.

"I am. I waited to write her again until she was past the customary time for mourning. Aloor is a very traditional place. Everyone in town would likely know if she received a letter from Machtarn, since they already know that I advised her on her legal situation."

"Especially with your family background," said Caastyn.

"So what's stopping you now?" asked Gerdina.

"Outside of fractured ribs and frog poison, you mean?" quipped Ysella.

"Seems to me, sir," said Caastyn pleasantly, "that this lady is the first one I've ever seen you take the slightest interest in . . ."

Ysella chuckled. "I'll write her tomorrow."

35

By noon on Tridi, the twenty-first of Winterend, Ysella was more than ready to go back to working at his office at the Council Hall, no matter how much getting there and back hurt.

The physician, Phillipe Engaryn, had made two calls, each with repeated cautions against riding and running into objects for the next three weeks. Ysella's clerks, Lyaard Khaard and Paatyr Jaasn, had also sent a letter of concern and wishing him well and a speedy recovery, and also telling him that there was nothing urgent needing his attention.

In the meantime, he'd written a letter to Aelyn Wythcomb, apologizing for not writing earlier as a result of unforeseen events, and telling her that he very much enjoyed meeting her, despite the circumstances, and that he would appreciate the chance to write her. He also wrote that he'd like to call on her in the future, although when that time might be would depend on the schedule of the Council. The second letter was to his parents, with a minimal description of the events that led to his being wounded, his injuries, and an assurance that he was indeed healing.

Ysella had Caastyn post his letters. Caastyn said not a word about the letter to Ritten Aelyn Wythcomb, although Ysella caught sight of a quickly smothered smile.

Despite Detruro's promises, the first official Council announcements and other papers Ysella received had arrived almost a week later. Ysella had noted the appointment of Staanus Wrystaan as Symeon Daenyld's replacement as councilor from Neewyrk.

Most important, Ysella had finished the first draft of the proposed governmental reforms, including a section where he limited political parties to the three existing views and in which no party could hold a majority of councilors. He entitled the draft "A Governance Charter for the Imperium of Guldor," a title far too cumbersome, for all its accuracy.

He also had no doubt that everyone would find fault with it. *But we need to start somewhere.*

The papers that Detruro finally sent to Ysella largely dealt with hearing schedules. None mentioned the Imperador. Equally concerning was the lack of information about him, or his daughter, in *The Machtarn Tribune*. The *Tribune* reported how Jaahn Escalante delivered the promised tin to the Navy at the original stipulated price, with an insinuation that Councilor Alaan Escalante had been selected to chair the Military Affairs Committee to create an obvious conflict of interest if Councilor Escalante intervened in the matter.

By Duadi morning, with an eye to resuming his Council duties in person, Ysella began to organize his papers—with a completely separate folder for the government-reorganization legislative proposal—as well as revise his earlier schedule for Waterways Committee hearings.

All that took several bells.

At dinner on Tridi, after the blessing, Ysella looked to Caastyn. "Tomorrow—"

"I'll be driving you to the Council, no doubt," replied Caastyn. "I saw how you organized all those papers."

"It's been two weeks."

"You must have really hurt, sir. Otherwise, you'd have been after me days ago."

"Well . . . I can walk well enough now, if I'm careful. I'll work shorter days for a while."

"How much shorter?" asked Caastyn, if with an amused smile.

"Several bells, to begin with. After that, we'll see." Before Caastyn could pose another question, Ysella asked, "Do you know how Haardt is coming with that replacement armor?"

"He thought next week, but armor won't save you again if you don't let those ribs heal."

"I'm well aware of that," replied Ysella dryly. *Especially every morning lately.*

"You're a stubborn man, sir," said Gerdina, "but I'd appreciate it if you weren't stubbornly stupid."

"Does that mean you think a short day at the Council Hall might be acceptable, but a long one would be stubbornly stupid?"

"More like anything but a short day would be stubbornly stupid, sir," replied Gerdina, "but I just cook and clean."

"And quite a few other necessary aids lately." Ysella looked to Caastyn. "Tomorrow, I'll try leaving here at third bell and having you pick me up at second afternoon bell."

"You sure you're up to that, sir?"

"If I'm not, I'm quite certain you both will let me know, in some fashion that's not too hard on my already battered body and pride."

Caastyn chuckled. "Fair enough, Ritter."

36

WHEN Ysella carefully eased his way out of the chaise at the front entrance to the Council Hall on Furdi, cold and windy, Caastyn immediately said, "Second bell, sir?"

Ysella grinned, knowing the words weren't a question. "I'll be here."

"Very good, sir."

Ysella walked carefully toward the door, holding his case of papers.

"Good to see you back, Councilor," said the duty guard, opening the door for him, something guards usually did not do.

"Thank you. It's good to be back."

While Ysella passed several staffers in the corridor and on the steps to the second floor, he didn't see any councilors.

When he stepped into the office, both his clerks immediately stood.

Khaard was the first to recover. "Sir!"

"No, I'm not fully healed, but I'm to the point where I can do short days and still recuperate."

"We're glad you're back," declared the senior clerk. "We worried about you."

"I did appreciate the letter. Thank you," said Ysella.

"Ah . . . was it as bad as the newssheets said?" asked Jaasn.

"Actually . . . it was worse. For a short time, the doctor didn't think I'd live . . . because of the frog poison, not the fractured ribs. Now . . . where do we stand?"

"We decided to draft responses to all the letters from constituents," declared Khaard. "That way, you can sign the ones you approve and, for the others, tell us the changes you want so you won't have to write out notes to us. We didn't open any messages or letters from other councilors or those that looked personal."

"Thank you. I appreciate that. I'm doing better, but it'll be several weeks more before I'm back to full health. What else?"

"That newshawk Daarkyn keeps stopping by and inquiring about your health." Khaard frowned. "It's almost as though he was hoping for the worst."

Ysella had to agree with the senior clerk. "If I'm not with someone, I'll talk to him. Anything else?"

"The Council will convene as usual, but only for various announcements and routine business."

Ysella nodded. "While I go through the unopened letters and messages, I'd like you to draft a message to the Premier telling him I'm back in my office and asking when it would be convenient for us to meet. Then we'll see about the replies you two wrote."

"Yes, sir."

Ysella walked slowly and deliberately into his office, took off his heavy winter overcoat and hung it up, wincing as he did, then seated himself behind his desk, and lifted the first unopened letter—clearly from the Imperador—opened and read it.

> *Councilor Ysella—*
> *We were deeply concerned to hear about the attack on you, but are pleased that you are recovering. Too few councilors can claim to be as effective as you have proved to be, and we wish you the best and a rapid recovery.*

The seal and signature were that of Laureous, and he might have signed it himself.

At least he made an effort . . . or someone in the Palace did.

The second letter had an ornate seal on the envelope that Ysella did not recognize, and he opened it carefully so as not to damage that seal. He smiled as he looked at the signature, that of Ramon Hekkaad—the Argenti envoy to Guldor—and read the short note.

> *Leona and I were stunned to learn that you had been the target of assassins, but most relieved to discover that you are on the way to recovery. Who would have thought that a polite legalist and councilor would have brought to light and destroyed a long-standing criminal enterprise? In retrospect, it's obvious that, at times, at least, blood will tell.*
> *We plan to have you for dinner once you're more recovered. In the meantime, please take care. Guldor needs councilors like you.*

The outside address on the next official-looking envelope simply read "Machtarn District Council." While Ysella suspected who the sender might be, he had to read the letter to confirm his suspicion.

> *Councilor Ysella—*
> *Those of us in the entire Machtarn Justiciary and all Machtarn*

patrollers would like to offer our deepest gratitude for your selfless efforts to uncover and remove the scourge of the long-standing fraud and violence perpetrated by former legalist Sollem Faarn.

And all Machtarn patrollers? Those words suggested that the patrollers were indeed pleased that the spectre of Gustov Torryl could be removed from their worries.

You have our best wishes for a full and quick recovery and return to your duties as councilor . . .

The signature was that of District Legalist Luurynt Foerst, suggesting that Foerst had indeed replaced Smootn, which couldn't help but be for the best.
And there might be a bit of buried gratitude from Foerst as well.
The next envelope bore the name of Councilor Alaaxi Baertyl, although Ysella immediately saw that he wasn't the writer.

Dominic—
 Both Alaaxi and I were devastated to hear of the assassination attempt on you. We're so relieved neither we nor the Council will be losing you, particularly now. Your advice and concern have always been welcome and most useful and will be more so in the months and years to come.
 Please take care, and don't overdo matters in your recovery.

The signature was that of Junae.
There were also short notes wishing him well from Luaro Maatrak, Haans Maessyn, Chaarls Aashen, Paolo Caanard, Georg Raathan, and Sammal Haafel.
By the time Ysella had read through all the personal messages and mail, Khaard had the message to the Premier ready for signature and dispatch. After that, Ysella started through the replies that the clerks had drafted for his signature, the majority of which were acceptable, if sometimes requiring a postscript in Ysella's hand. Then he went through those that needed rewriting, followed by his notes on the replies to the personal letters.
While he finished what he could do by a third past fifth bell, Ysella could see that the two clerks wouldn't finish until late in the day, if not until sometime on Quindi morning.
He decided to give himself plenty of time to get to the Council chamber and left his office a good third before noon, using the bannister on

the staircase down to the first level, something he'd never had to consider before. He arrived in the chamber and took his seat with less than a sixth to spare.

Staeryt settled beside Ysella moments later. "Dominic, I didn't expect you back quite so soon."

"If it hadn't been for the frigging frog poison, I could have been here sooner."

"Most people don't survive frog poison."

"So I have heard. I only got a small incidental amount."

"Small incidental amounts have been known to be fatal. And only fractured ribs?"

"I was wearing body armor," Ysella admitted. "It didn't survive."

"So you suspected a certain amount of danger?"

"Dealing with any criminal entails danger. But assassins hired by a legalist was a bit much." The last sentence was a definite lie. Ysella just hadn't expected them outside the district justiciary building.

"How did he get away with it for so long?" asked Staeryt.

"He was very clever." Ysella paused, then said, "Here comes Maatrak."

Staeryt opened his mouth as if to ask more, but stopped as the chime sounded.

Maatrak used the gavel once and declared, "The Council is in session." Then he stepped back and let Detruro take the lectern.

The Premier looked at Ysella, as if to make sure he was present, then said, "Before we begin the official items on the agenda, I'd like to welcome back Councilor Dominic Ysella, who, as many of you may know, is still recovering from fractured ribs and poisoning resulting from an attack incurred while investigating a long-standing Machtarn criminal organization. His efforts were key in that matter. Welcome back, Councilor."

After a brief pause, Detruro went on. "Not all the committee chairmen have turned in committee schedules. I understand hearing dates will change, and that more will be scheduled, but I would very much appreciate having those schedules, tentative as they may be . . ."

A third later, Detruro recessed the Council, then stepped off the dais, and walked over to Ysella's desk. "I'll come to your office in about a bell. That way you won't have to walk down to my office."

"Thank you. I do appreciate it."

Detruro smiled, then turned and left the chamber.

"You never answered my question, Dominic," said Staeryt. "How was Legalist Faarn so clever?"

"By making people believe Gustov Torryl was still alive and ensuring all the disappearances and deaths were attributed him. He presented himself as Torryl's legalist, knowing that people assume that legalists are intermediaries."

"I still don't see how—"

"Neither did I, until the friend of someone I know vanished and turned up dead in the harbor. So I decided to look at property records. You know where that ended. I think everyone thought the trust was to keep people from finding out Torryl's location. It was, but not in the way anyone thought." Ysella got to his feet, cautiously deliberate, and began the walk back to his own office. On the way he stopped by the main committee staff office and reserved the room shared by the Waterways Committee for fifth morning bell the next day.

Once back in his office, he drafted a message to the members of the Waterways Committee, notifying them of a meeting on Quindi in order to discuss scheduling, then gave the letter and the proposed committee hearing schedule to Khaard to make copies and dispatch both to the Waterways Committee members.

After that, he signed the revised letters that Khaard and Jaasn had rewritten, occasionally adding a note. When he finished, he put the papers containing the government-reform charter in a separate large envelope and set it on the corner of the desk.

Detruro arrived less than a bell later, closing the door to Ysella's office as he entered. "You're looking much better than when I saw you last week."

"I'm feeling much better, unless I forget and move suddenly." Ysella smiled wryly. "I also won't be staying late until I'm more fully recovered."

"A very good idea."

"I got a letter from the Imperador wishing me a speedy recovery. Did you have anything to do with it?"

"Not directly. I've only seen him twice in the last month, and he wasn't in the mood to listen. I mentioned the attack on you to several others at the Palace. One of them may have suggested that the Imperador send a letter."

"How is the Imperador?"

"About the same as he's been recently. I made a quiet and indirect inquiry about the crossbow quarrels that were used on you and the Imperial district legalist."

"Any particular reason?"

"I found it rather more than coincidental that two councilors and an Imperial legalist were all shot by crossbows—and that those who used the crossbows were so accurate. The quarrels all looked to be the same as those used by the Palace Guard."

"You think the Heir was involved?" asked Ysella.

"More someone following his instructions in a way that can't be traced," replied Detruro.

"I wonder if the quarrels used on Daenyld were poisoned," said Ysella.

"I asked. The quarrels were saved, but they were cleaned of blood . . . and anything else."

"You think someone asked Faarn for a favor in Daenyld's case?"

"The Heir or someone acting for him had to know Legalist Faarn. After the initial investigation of Faarn's mansion, the Imperial High Legalist's people took over—immediately before the fire." Detruro shrugged. "There's obviously no proof, although there are those in the Palace who avoid the Heir more than before."

"Another reason for your . . . project."

Detruro nodded. "How are you coming on the draft?"

"There's a complete copy for you." Ysella made a small gesture toward the envelope. "There's nothing there or in the text to indicate the source, except, of course, my hand."

"How do you feel about it?"

Ysella smiled cynically. "It will do what I think you want. It may not be what you or anyone else really wants, but I couldn't think of any other way that would be workable over time, not after what happened to Teknold. After you read it, I'll be happy to make changes or corrections, but I'd like to hear your rationale for any changes, so I can make the changes in accord with what you have in mind."

Detruro nodded. "You're still a legalist at heart, Dominic."

"There are worse things to be—such as a legalist without a heart or conscience."

"Like the missing Legalist Faarn, you mean?"

"Among others," replied Ysella lightly.

Detruro picked up the envelope. "It's not light."

"You told me to be thorough."

"So I did. I look forward to reading it." Detruro stood and inclined his head. "Thank you. I do appreciate this, especially after what you've been through. It may be a little while before I get back to you."

"There's one other thing, Iustaan," said Ysella.

"Oh . . . ?"

"I'll likely be introducing a bill to raise the limit on usury. The banques and lenders in my district feel that they can't loan to many applicants under the current maximum rate."

"The Imperador won't sign such a bill, you know."

"I didn't think he would, but if he opposes or rejects it, that might help with getting the charter accepted. If not, at least those in my district will know I tried."

"I'll think about it."

Ysella did not stand, but nodded in return. Thinking was likely all Detruro would do.

After the Premier left, Ysella thought about the letter he'd received from the Imperador, wondering whom Detruro might have talked to with enough influence to suggest sending the letter. Certainly, the Heir had that influence, or the First Marshal, and Lorya Kaechar, the empath who'd essentially interviewed him at the Yearend Ball. *Possibly Delehya.* But would she have been involved in Detruro's normal meetings with the Imperador? Either way, there was more there than Detruro was saying.

Since it was nearing second bell, Ysella signed a few more letters, then carefully donned his winter overcoat, and stepped out of his personal office.

"I'll see you tomorrow. As I said earlier, my days will be shorter for a while."

"Yes, sir," replied Khaard. "Please be careful."

"I will."

When Ysella reached the main entrance, a sixth before second bell, Caastyn was waiting with the chaise. Ysella didn't fail to catch Caastyn's momentary expression of relief, but only said, "It's before second bell, and I'm here."

"As you said, sir." Caastyn grinned.

37

A LIGHT snow drifted from dark green-gray clouds on Quindi morning when Ysella eased himself out of the chaise in front of the Council Hall. After saying "Second bell" to Caastyn, he walked inside to his office, again using the bannister on his way up to the second level.

"Is there anything urgent I should know?" he asked as he entered the office.

"No, sir," replied Khaard. "There aren't any messages from the Premier, and not many letters. There is a message from Councilor Ditaero. They're on your desk. There's no Council session today."

"Thank you."

Once Ysella shed his overcoat and seated himself behind his desk, he read the message.

> Councilor Ditaero will be unable to attend the Waterways Committee meeting because he is still en route from Endor. We expect him to arrive by Unadi.

The message was signed by Arturo Gaanslyr, Senior Clerk.

Ysella could understand Ditaero's travel problems, given that Endor was fifteen hundred milles northeast of Machtarn and sea travel was the only feasible transportation. In winter, unfortunately, bad weather caused far more delays. For that reason, many councilors from the far southwest or far northeast simply didn't try to go to their home districts over the winter recess.

He quickly read through the letters, slit open, but still in their envelopes, and wrote quick notes on each for his clerks. Then he organized his notes for the coming committee meeting, and at a sixth before fifth bell, he walked to the largest of the three committee rooms, shared by the Waterways Committee, the Natural Resources Committee, and the Agriculture Committee.

Haans Maessyn and Stefan Nortaak were already there, standing beside the raised dais holding a long, curved desk with seven places. Ysella nodded to them and took the center seat on the desk.

Maessyn smiled and said, "You don't look all that bad for someone who wasn't supposed to live."

"The doctor told me, if someone survives frog poison for two days, they'll usually recover."

Within moments, Astyn Coerl, Dannyl Grieg, and Voltar Paastyn arrived. Since all the committee members except Ditaero were present, Ysella tapped the gavel and said, "The committee will come to order." He paused, then asked, "Are there are questions or suggestions for the hearing schedule?"

Immediately, Grieg said, "There's a hearing scheduled for late Springfirst that says Military Requirements. What will that include?"

"Port facilities at Point Larmat, Port Reale, and Machtarn, although I understand that the proposals for Machtarn are more to assure that wharves and docks can handle military vessels."

"How much of the Waterways budget will that require?" asked Grieg.

"I have no idea," replied Ysella. "We don't have detailed information from the Navy yet."

"The Navy requirements last year meant we didn't have enough funding for inland waterways," said Grieg.

"As you know," replied Ysella, "that's been an ongoing problem."

"If we'd spent more on Navy facilities in Port Reale years ago," interjected Paastyn, "Atacama wouldn't have been able to do so much damage to Zeiryn."

"From what I'm discovering," added Coerl, "we never have adequate funding. That's because the taxes and tariffs are inadequate for both waterways and the Navy."

Ysella smiled wryly. Coerl needed to learn more about the committee and what it did, but that was understandable. He'd been appointed after Yearend to replace Meerl Saant, who had died late in Fallend.

For the next half bell, Ysella let the committee members talk—complain mostly—before he finally said, "I think you've covered the problems in enough detail. Do any of you have another aspect of waterways that you feel needs a specific hearing?"

Nortaak immediately declared, "We need hearings on levees. We're losing crops all the time in the area between Oersynt and Gaarlak because the levees there aren't high enough."

"Duly noted," declared Ysella. "Anyone else?"

"What about waterworthiness and size standards for flatboats?" asked Grieg. "We lost the use of the canal to the Rio Doro for two weeks because an oversized flatboat got jammed in the canal."

"That's come up before, but if you can line up more witnesses, I can put it on the schedule near the last days of Springend."

"I'll let you know, sir."

It was close to first bell of the afternoon before Ysella ended the meeting and left the committee room.

As he neared the door of Oskaar Klempt's office, he slowed, then abruptly entered. If Klempt happened to be free, Ysella could bring up the usury-cap issue. That might be a quicker way to get action, given that Klempt was chairman of the Commerce Committee, which dealt with Treasury and banque matters.

"Councilor Ysella?" asked the older-looking clerk.

"I'd like to see Councilor Klempt briefly."

"Let me see, sir."

In moments, the clerk returned. "Go right in, sir."

As soon as Ysella closed the door, the round-faced Klempt stood and gestured to the chairs in front of the desk. "How are you coming with those ribs, Dominic?"

"Slowly," admitted Ysella.

Klempt reseated himself and asked, "What's on your mind?"

"The usury limitation. I haven't heard much about it in years, but when I returned to Aloor in Winterfirst, quite a few people mentioned it as a problem. Several said it made it hard for newer enterprises to get funding."

"It's a growing problem," admitted Klempt. "Not only in Aloor, but here in Machtarn and in my district as well."

"It's within the power of the Council to raise the cap, isn't it?" asked Ysella, knowing that he'd posed a clearly rhetorical question.

"It is, but the Administrator of the Treasury is opposed to any increase."

"What about the Administrator of Commerce?"

"Administrator Laergaan understands the problem. He claims he's tried to persuade Treasury Administrator Salaazar of the need to lift the maximum allowable rate, but Salaazar remains adamantly opposed."

"You have your doubts?"

"As recent events have demonstrated, opposing the Imperador or the Heir, or functionaries who have their ear, carries a certain risk."

"Salaazar's from Oersynt, isn't he?"

"He is."

"How did he get to be Treasury Administrator, then?"

"It's said the Imperador didn't trust anyone from the banques in Machtarn or nearby. I don't know how true that is."

Given the Imperador's mistrust of anyone who disagreed with him, Ysella suspected there was some truth in what Klempt said. "I've drafted legislation to raise the usury limit. What would happen if I introduced it?" Ysella's tone was gently ironic.

"I could manage to give it a hearing. I doubt it would go further unless the Palace changes its mind." Klempt paused, adding, "It might be for the best if a committee chairman of another committee pressed for the hearing."

Ysella understood. The entire committee was likely aware of the problem, but could not afford to show an interest in pushing for a higher rate. The committee, however, could allow a hearing, claiming political pressure made a hearing necessary. "I might do that. At least, it would show that the Council is aware of the problem."

"We can hope, Dominic. Is there anything else?"

Ysella shook his head. "Not at present." He stood carefully. "Thank you."

"My pleasure."

After leaving Klempt's office, Ysella made his way back to his office, only to find Reimer Daarkyn waiting beside the bench by the office door.

Ysella repressed a sigh. "I can give you a little time, Reimer, but, right now, my time in the office is limited. The physician says I need to be careful."

"I'd appreciate that, Councilor."

Ysella gestured for the newshawk to accompany him to his personal office.

Daarkyn closed the door before he took a seat. He waited for Ysella to settle himself behind the desk before he said, "All the reports said that you were hit by two crossbow bolts smeared with frog poison and those fractured your ribs. How are you still alive?"

"I don't remember much, but the doctor told me my bulky winter clothes and coat kept, or mainly kept, the bolts from breaking much of the skin, although a small amount of frog poison must have gotten to me, because I have no recollection of almost three days."

"Why were you investigating Legalist Faarn in the first place? It wouldn't seem to have much to do with waterways." Daarkyn tapped the floor with the toe of his boot.

"It didn't. I kept hearing about Gustov Torryl buying property, and yet no one ever met Torryl. They always met with his legalist. I decided to look into the matter and discovered all the property supposedly bought by Torryl was held by the Gustov Torryl Trust. The trustee and actual owner, however, was Sollem Faarn—and buried in the records was a notation that Torryl had died years ago. I spoke briefly with Imperial District Legalist Smootn and provided him with that information, because dealing with such is his job, not mine. I was headed to meet with him again and saw him outside the district justiciary building. That was when we were attacked. I didn't find out that he died for days."

"The newssheet story mentioned a bodyguard."

"That's incorrect. He works for me in a number of capacities, as groom, maintaining the house, watching over it when I'm in Aloor, occasionally driving me. I asked him to accompany me that morning because I thought it was possible I might be accosted. I never thought someone would send assassins."

"But your man killed the assassins. He had to have other skills."

"I believe that my man *and* the duty patroller wounded the assassins, who died of those wounds."

"You *believe*?"

"As I told you, and as the physician could certainly confirm, from a few moments after I was hit, I was unable to see or sense anything. The newssheet reported that both my man and the patroller wounded the attackers. My man confirmed it to me."

"Why did Faarn's men go after District Legalist Smootn?"

"I don't know. I presume that Faarn wanted to remove us both before Smootn ordered patrollers to arrest Faarn. From all appearances, Faarn delayed matters enough to escape."

"All appearances?"

Ysella's sigh was unfeigned. "No one has sighted Faarn. No body has been found. All easily carried valuables and marks were missing from Faarn's house, at least according to the newssheet for which you work—but, of course, the ensuing fire made confirming that difficult. Even his family was already elsewhere. That looks like an escape to me."

"Don't you worry that he's loose? That he still might come after you?"

"From all I've gathered, Faarn was a legal schemer. He used others for violence. Without them and with limited finances he's much less of a danger. If he left or leaves Guldor and changes his name, he's unlikely ever to be caught. If he were to remain here, his safety would always be in doubt."

"Hmmm . . . that is a good point. But still . . . why you? Why did you feel it necessary to get involved in something so removed from what you do as a councilor?"

"You might recall that I spent years as a legalist, and everything around Torryl and Faarn didn't smell right. So I pursued it . . . and was fortunate to survive."

"You were fortunate. Now . . ."

Ysella held up a hand. "My doctor has been most insistent that I keep my time in the office short until I've healed more, and I do have a few matters to attend to before I leave for the day. If you run across anything else, I'll be here." Ysella wasn't giving anything away because he knew Daarkyn would be back . . . and back.

Daarkyn stood. "Of course. I hope you're in better condition the next time I see you."

"That makes two of us, Reimer."

Once the newshawk left, Ysella went to work reading and signing or correcting the letters in the small stack on his desk so that the clerks could post them after he left, rather than wait until Unadi.

With effort, and a little good luck, and no more interruptions, he hoped he could get through most of them before it was time to meet Caastyn.

He knew there was no way he was attending services and listening to Presider Haelsyn until he felt much, much better.

38

ON Findi morning, Ysella looked outside at the stiff winds and swirling snowflakes and decided to stay inside, although he did use part of the day working on changes to the Waterways Committee schedule for spring and then drafting a final version for his clerks to copy on Unadi, one copy of which would go to the Premier. He also revised his draft proposal to increase the allowable rate on usury, not that it was likely to go beyond a hearing.

He wondered if he'd get any reply from Aelyn Wythcomb, but tried not to think too hard about that. Even after the time he'd spent with Reimer Daarkyn on Quindi, he didn't see any follow-up story in the *Tribune*. That concerned him as well, since he didn't trust the newshawk. But then, he didn't fully trust any newshawks.

On Unadi, the skies dawned clear, with the wind stronger and colder, and Ysella was shivering by the time he got out of the chaise outside the Council Hall. His ribs also ached more because of the shivering, although both subsided by the time he reached his office.

He immediately put Jaasn to work copying the committee hearing schedule and the short note to each councilor on the committee, and had Khaard make copies of the usury proposal.

Then he read the incoming letters on his desk, some of which came from the same people who had pressed for additional waterways funds in and around Aloor, and who politely insisted that he get more for Aloor in the next year's appropriations. In addition, five anonymous letters demanded that the Council rein in the excesses of the Imperador. Another letter, from Oersynt, wanted to know when he intended to step down as chairman of the Waterways Committee to allow other councilors to get adequate funds for their districts.

After dealing with correspondence, Ysella headed for the Council chamber for the noon session, which lasted less than a sixth and consisted of announcements by Maatrak.

Ysella waited for most of the other councilors to leave the chamber. He was about to follow them when Sammal Haafel approached, smiling. "It's good to see you back, Dominic. Staeryt told me you tracked down Sollem Faarn by checking property records. What made you think of that?"

"I did that sort of work before I became a councilor. Once a water legalist, always a water legalist, I suppose."

"Sometimes it's obvious, but only in hindsight. Good for you." Haafel chuckled. "You'd better watch out on another front. One of the *Tribune* stories mentioned you were unmarried. A comparatively young, good-looking single councilor who's also survived assassins—that's like honey for bears."

"I haven't noticed any onslaught," replied Ysella, chuckling. "I danced with the Imperador's daughter at the Yearend Ball, and she didn't send me a get-well note." *Unless she was the one behind the Imperador's letter.*

"That's not surprising." Haafel lowered his voice. "She's said to be interested elsewhere."

"Elsewhere?" Then Ysella guessed, keeping his voice low. "Not the Premier?"

"So I've heard, but it's not firm."

Detruro might, just might, be able to keep her from destroying herself... and himself. "I won't say a word." *Especially not to Iustaan.*

"For now, it's likely best. I understand she's a delightfully mixed blessing and curse."

"I only danced with her once. We talked briefly. Her current interest might be better suited."

"I won't keep you, Dominic. I wanted to say how glad I am you're recovering."

"Thank you. I appreciate it." Ysella stood carefully, as the spaces between councilors' seats and desks were narrow.

Once Ysella exited the chamber, Alaan Escalante joined him.

Ysella immediately said, "I passed on what I said I would the day after we spoke. You can understand why I haven't been able to talk to you until now. Even walking is painful. Iustaan told me he appreciated your discretion and that the information was helpful. He also said he wouldn't be talking to either of us about that subject for a time." Before Ysella finished speaking, he could see relief from Escalante.

"Thank you. I appreciate it." Escalante paused. "How are you doing . . . really?"

"My chest and ribs are sore, and any sudden movement definitely reminds me that I shouldn't. Is Amaelya back from Silverhills yet?"

"She'll be here sometime next week. I did write her about you. I got a letter back on Quindi. She hopes you'll heal quickly."

"So do I. Give her my best when you can."

"I will. And thank you." Escalante eased away.

Ysella took his time climbing the stairs. Once back in his office, he went to work on where he could fit in the possible hearings other Waterways Committee members requested.

Slightly before first afternoon bell, Iustaan Detruro appeared in Ysella's office, marching in and closing the door almost before Ysella recognized the Premier.

"I've read through your 'charter' twice. It's quite good. I penned in a few small changes, but, all in all, you've done an outstanding job. That's only the first step, unhappily." Detruro sat in the chair directly in front of Ysella's desk, placing a large envelope on the desk.

"The second being to convince the Imperial High Command that the changes are necessary to preserve Guldor and their positions from the Heir before he becomes Imperador?"

"Something along that line. Do you have any thoughts?"

"You might point out that the death of one councilor and one fleet marshal, as well as that of a district legalist indirectly linked to the Heir, and the near death of another councilor would be nothing compared to an unchecked Imperador . . . and that without a better balance of power, Guldor will fragment."

"That's a good start, for those who can think," replied Detruro. "What about the others?"

"Without a strong navy we'll be subject to continual attacks from Atacama, and not just from pirates. Only a unified Guldor can support that navy. There's also the problem of northern border incursions by Argenti smugglers if there's no unified government, as well as more brigands within Guldor. Without a stable government, banques will cut back on lending."

"You make good points, Dominic. You always do."

"One other thing," added Ysella. "Until recently, Laureous has only been whimsical upon occasion. Do senior military officers wish to trust their future to a ruler who appears to be more willful and whose whims cannot be checked, except by force, when force means civil war? Or assassinations? You might mention the similarities of the crossbow quarrels . . . and the use of frog poison. Oh . . . and undisclosed sudden deaths from illnesses, particularly in the Palace."

"That's a better point." The Premier stood. "How are you coming?"

"A little less sore every day, except if I move suddenly or bump something."

"That's good. Keep being careful." With a smile, Detruro turned and departed, leaving the door open.

Almost immediately, Khaard appeared with a stack of letters, which he set on the desk. "We sent out the committee schedules to the committee members and the one to the Premier. These are the corrected responses to letters and some of the ones you made notes on this morning." He put a smaller stack of papers on the corner of the desk. "Those are the copies of the proposed usury legislation."

"Good. Has Reimer Daarkyn been around?"

"Not so far, sir."

"That's for the best."

After Khaard departed, Ysella slid the stack of responses to where he could easily read them. With a little good fortune, he might finish signing and/or correcting them before he had to leave for the day.

39

ON Duadi morning, as he sipped café and ate his breakfast, Ysella perused the morning *Tribune*. On the back page, in the editorial and comment section, he came across a comment entitled "Smoke . . . or More?" and immediately began to read.

> Nearly three weeks ago two men used crossbows to kill Machtarn District Legalist Wyllum Smootn and severely wound Imperial Councilor Dominic Ysella. The attackers died at the scene but were later confirmed to have worked for Legalist Sollem Faarn. Over the past decade, Faarn had taken control of a sizable number of properties through a trust linked to the criminal Gustov Torryl, who died years ago.
>
> Recent evidence shows that the killers used exactly the same type of crossbow bolts as the ones used in the fatal attack on Councilor Symeon Daenyld, an attack that occurred after Daenyld opposed the Imperador's insistence on building more first-rate ships of the line.
>
> Four days after the attack on the District Legalist and Councilor Ysella, Faarn's mansion burned to the ground while under Imperial custody, leaving nothing but masonry and ashes. Faarn is still missing. Councilor Ysella was poisoned as well as shot and understandably has no memory of the days he was unconscious.
>
> There's definitely smoke here, but who set the fire . . . and why?

Ysella nodded slowly. *You'll be hearing more from Daarkyn, sooner or later.* He wasn't looking forward to it particularly.

Later, in the chaise riding to the Council Hall under high greenish-gray clouds in a cold brisk wind, Ysella asked Caastyn, "Did you read that article in the *Tribune,* the one about smoke and no fire?"

"I did. Both those attackers died within a sixth. The patroller tried to find out who sent them, but neither one said anything. They were already dying and couldn't speak." Caastyn paused. "Why do you think the newssheet printed that?"

"Likely because someone feels there was some connection between the Palace and Faarn, but can't find any hard evidence."

"There probably is," said Caastyn. "Someone had to be paying the Heir's snitches."

"And the Heir wouldn't want it traced to the Palace," mused Ysella. "Quite a few others wouldn't either, if for differing reasons."

"Do you think the Palace will shut down the *Tribune* for running the article?"

"I don't know, but they'd be wise not to."

"Wise not to?" asked Caastyn.

"The story or commentary never mentions the Palace, and there's only one implication that involves the Imperador. If the Palace shuts down the newssheet, that's almost an admission that the Palace is involved, and not a single individual."

"Hadn't thought about that. Makes sense, though."

After Caastyn halted the chaise outside the Council Hall, Ysella got out, then said, "Second bell."

"Yes, sir." Caastyn smiled, then drove away.

Ysella headed inside, aware that his ribs didn't hurt quite as much.

The remainder of the morning and early afternoon were routine, although Ysella received a letter from Gherard Brandt, stating that Professor Gastaan Ritchen of Ondeliew College was close to completing a larger steam device suitable for pumping water or for propelling a wagon or watercraft. The letter did not ask for Waterways Committee funding, although Ysella wondered when Brandt would make such a request.

After first afternoon bell, Khaard looked into Ysella's personal office and said, "Councilor Baertyl would like a few moments."

"Have him come in."

In moments, Baertyl entered and closed the door.

Ysella gestured to the chairs. "What brings you here, Alaaxi?"

"Something's going on, and Alaan's not saying anything. We had a committee meeting this morning, and he postponed the already-scheduled hearings on the Navy's request for funding the construction of more frigates and smaller ships."

"Did he say why?"

"He said that hearings would be counterproductive, whatever that means, and create problems that the Council didn't need."

Ysella repressed a sigh, softly cleared his throat, and said, "Do you recall the letter that the Imperador sent the Council after he reluctantly signed the appropriations for this year?"

"Not exactly. I recall he wasn't happy."

"He wasn't happy because the late Fleet Marshal Haarwyk and the late chairman of the Military Affairs Committee dared to suggest that more frigates and fewer first-rate ships of the line were needed. You do recall what happened to them?"

"Of course," replied Baertyl impatiently.

"Well . . . if the first hearings scheduled by the committee deal with frigates, or if any of the early hearings do, exactly what message does that send to the Imperador?"

"But we're talking about construction a year from now. We need those frigates, and we need to plan."

"Don't you think it might be wiser to let the Imperador cool down before scheduling hearings on something he doesn't want immediately after the Council convenes?" Ysella smiled patiently. "If you push Alaan on this, don't you think he might wonder if you were trying to get the Imperador mad at him? And that you were scheming to become chairman? Wouldn't holding those hearings make life very unpleasant for the new Fleet Marshal?"

"But . . . I was thinking about the best way to deal with the Atacaman pirates."

"I'm sure you were, but angering the Imperador won't get the Navy more frigates, and it might cost the Council a great deal more."

Baertyl's brow furled into a frown. "I guess I didn't look at it that way."

"So long as you didn't insist vigorously, there shouldn't be any harm done. You might tell Alaan that you were thinking so far ahead that you didn't consider the immediate impact."

"Hmmm . . . I can do that."

After Baertyl left the office, Ysella started to take a deep breath, and his ribs instantly indicated that was unwise.

How did he ever get elected? Except Ysella knew. Too many people, especially those from older landor families, often viewed councilors as lackeys for the Imperador, and saw the position of councilor as somewhere that a not-too-bright younger son couldn't do too much damage. *Until they do.*

Ysella returned to the more mundane aspects of his office and, as second bell approached, was ready to leave for the day.

Caastyn was waiting when Ysella walked out of the Council Hall and made his way to the chaise.

"You look a shade weary, sir," said Caastyn as Ysella carefully climbed into the chaise.

"This time, it's more weariness of thought, not so much the ribs."

"If it will help, you've got two letters from Aloor waiting for you." The hint of a smile appeared on Caastyn's face.

"That could be good or not so good."

"One looked like your mother's hand." Caastyn urged the chaise horse forward.

"Like I said, good or not so good."

"The other hand I didn't recognize, but it was more elegant." Caastyn hesitated, then added, "Also good or not so good, I suppose."

Elegant and from Aloor? Aelyn Wythcomb? But if so, it was likely only a polite reply to his letter explaining why he hadn't written sooner. *Still . . .* "I'll have to see. Any problems around the house?"

"No, sir. Sandlaar delivered and stacked the firewood. Good thing, too. We're running low. It's been colder than usual this late in winter."

Ysella realized he hadn't noticed, but then, he'd had a few other considerations.

After the two returned to the house, Ysella walked to his study, forcing himself not to hurry, took off his overcoat, and draped it on one of the chairs in front of the desk, before lighting the lamp overlooking the desk.

Then he sat behind the desk and picked up the two envelopes, instantly recognizing his mother's hand on one. The other envelope held a postbox number at the Aloor post centre.

After debating, momentarily, he opened the letter from his mother and began to read.

Dominic—

We read about the assassins' attack on you in the Chronicle, *so it was quite a relief to get your letter and to learn that you were getting better. Knowing you, you're likely not as well as you insist in your letter, but your hand looks steady, and that's a good sign. That awful newshawk rode out here the other day to try to find out more about what happened from us. Your father refused to speak to him. I told him that you'd written and were recovering, but that you'd not written anything different from what was in the newssheet. He was disappointed, and that was fine with me.*

I never thought that your being a councilor was such a dangerous occupation. Tedious and boring, perhaps, but not dangerous, but after what you said on your last visit and what happened to you, it's clear my assumptions were overly optimistic.

The weather here has been colder than usual, and if it remains so, your father and Haekaan may have to make some changes to the planting schedule . . .

The remainder of the letter dealt with occurrences on the lands and various family matters, including a few lines about Raemyna finally being close to recovered and Kharl being very healthy. When Ysella finished reading it, he replaced the sheets in the envelope, but left it on one side of the desk because he intended to reply before matters at the Council became more hectic, which would happen before long.

Then he carefully opened the second envelope, his eyes going to the signature—that of Aelyn Wythcomb. He swallowed and began to read.

> *Councilor Ysella—*
>
> *I deeply appreciate your kind correspondence and your efforts to keep me well informed about the legal and economic implications of recent events, particularly in regard to my interests in the Ahnkaar mine.*
>
> *Your kindness in personally making sure that I was so informed has not gone unnoticed, nor is it unappreciated. I am also grateful for your tact in not imposing on me in any fashion while I was in mourning, something others have failed to understand.*
>
> *Given your diligence and kindness, I was stunned and horrified to read about the assassination attempt on you. I was also impressed that you only mentioned that event indirectly in your letter explaining your delay in writing me, a letter I appreciated greatly, given my continuing concerns about your well-being.*
>
> *In consulting an old and trusted family legalist, I came to learn that you have his highest regard, a regard he seldom bestows, not that I was surprised after all you have done on my behalf.*
>
> *Should other instances occur where I could find your counsel valuable, I trust you will not find it amiss if I write you.*
>
> *Gratefully yours,*
> *Aelyn Wythcomb*

Ysella couldn't help smiling—broadly. Then he reread the letter, before setting it to one side.

While he waited for dinner, Ysella wrote a short reply to his mother's rather lengthy epistle and started on a reply to Aelyn. He rejected three attempts before Caastyn appeared in the study doorway.

"Dinner is ready, sir." Caastyn's eyes lingered on the letter lying on one side of the desk before he turned and headed back to the dining room.

With an amused smile, Ysella replaced the pen in its holder and stood.

Once he was seated at the dinner table and after Gerdina gave the blessing, Ysella looked to Caastyn and said, "Yes, the other letter was from Aelyn Wythcomb, and I will be writing her back."

"About time you found someone," said Gerdina warmly.

"We're hardly to that point," Ysella pointed out.

"It's a beginning," replied Gerdina.

"True," admitted Ysella. *And you do hope it leads somewhere.* He looked at the veal cutlets and the rice with raisins and spices, then cut a slice of the veal.

After dinner, he returned to the study and wrote a fourth attempt at a reply to Aelyn.

Ritten Wythcomb—
Thank you for your recent letter. I cannot say how much I appreciated your words, particularly since I did not wish to impose on you in any fashion, given all that has befallen you. Yet I did want to let you know that I was recovering well from the assassins' attack.

In response to your closing words, there is no way I would find it amiss if you choose to continue writing me, whether about legal or other matters, and would hope that you would allow me that same privilege in return, a privilege I would not only appreciate, but honor and cherish. I will warn you that, should you agree, my letters will be at greater length than this, but such prolixity requires your consent.

With warmest wishes

Ysella finally signed and sealed the letter, wondering if he was being too cautious, but deciding that, with Aelyn, caution had been rewarded.

40

BY Furdi morning, Ysella's chest and ribs only ached, unless he moved suddenly or lifted something moderately heavy. He thought about riding to the Council Hall, but realized that riding wouldn't be the problem, but mounting and dismounting certainly would be.

Another week, and then we'll see.

He was glad that the morning felt less winter-like as he rode north in the chaise on Imperial Boulevard toward the Council Hall.

As usual, letters awaited Ysella, nothing out of the ordinary, and just before fourth bell, Ysella walked down to the committee room for the Waterways Committee meeting, where he would go over the hearings scheduled over the next month.

The first councilor he saw was Gaastyn Ditaero, who had finally arrived in Machtarn and who was talking to Haans Maessyn.

"Good morning!" said Maessyn cheerfully. "You're walking better."

"I should be, after three weeks," replied Ysella, before turning to Ditaero and saying, "It's good to see you made it back to Machtarn."

"There were matters that took more time, and the voyage back was much slower than usual. Winter, you know?"

"I understand." While Ysella wondered what "matters" had delayed Ditaero, he smiled, stepped onto the dais, and took the center position at the long, curved desk.

In less than a sixth, the other four committee members arrived and took their places, the last being Voltar Paastyn.

Ysella rapped the gavel. "The committee will come to order. Next Duadi's hearing will deal with the standardization of terms commonly used by ports, docks, wharves, and other facilities handling waterborne cargoes. Are there any comments or questions?" Ysella looked first to Haans Maessyn.

"I've already gotten complaints about the hearing. Some of the bigger shippers saying that it's the first step to the Imperador controlling all commerce."

"I'm a little confused by why they'd say that," replied Ysella, who was not at all confused. "The purpose is to establish definitions so that everyone is talking about the same thing. Some ports call the time that off-loaded cargo sits on a dock without incurring a fee 'free time.' Others call it 'off-loaded allowance time.' Either way, that's different from goods stored on a pier or wharf, being neither actively off-loaded nor loaded, but simply waiting to be shipped, for which a wharfage charge is incurred." Ysella paused, then asked, "Might there be some advantage to using different terms for the same thing, and charging different rates?"

Voltar Paastyn grinned, possibly because Zeiryn was also a port city.

Maessyn smiled ruefully, then said, "I had to ask, you know?"

Ysella knew. Maessyn had been head of the Stevedores Guild and had an uneasy relationship with the commerce shipping interests in Uldwyrk. "One of the reasons for this hearing is that we have reports of various ports charging different rates based on the shipper or the recipient, rather than on the weight and type of off-loaded cargoes. The Council needs to set stricter legal guidelines so that it's clear that rates should be based on the weight and/or cubage of the goods or other bases that are consistent. But we can't set those guidelines without standard terms to which they apply . . ."

When Ysella finished, Stefan Nortaak asked, "What about foreign ships? Shouldn't they pay more?"

"Not for basic port services, unless the ship is from an outlaw nation. That's the current law. Certain tariffs, taxes, and fees on off-loaded cargoes are assessed differently for Guldoran ships than they are for foreign vessels, but those are under the direct control of the Imperial Treasurer." To change that was another aspect of Ysella's proposed charter.

Close to two bells passed before Ysella ended the meeting.

Since it was only a third before the Council convened, Ysella walked to the Council chamber and took his seat.

Before that long, Ahslem Staeryt appeared and joined Ysella.

"What are you working on in your committee?" asked Ysella.

"We're continuing on what the Imperador requested last summer."

"The update on the legal rights of susceptible individuals and the protections afforded them under Imperial law?"

"Exactly. It's been a tedious and time-consuming process. I'd like to report a bill out to the full Council before the midsummer recess. That's going to take some doing."

Ysella nodded. "I can see that. What's the biggest problem?"

"The biggest problem is the one we won't address," said Staeryt sardonically.

"You mean . . . the legal definition of a susceptible individual?"

"Exactly. The current definition basically states that a susceptible is a mature individual incapable of resisting all levels of commands, even where those commands could lead to severe bodily harm or death. Almost everyone is susceptible to the most powerful of empaths. That's why the law states 'all levels.' No one has yet come up with a better definition . . . or one more workable that isn't three paragraphs of seemingly conflicting legalese."

"So what's the next-largest issue?"

"The definitions of reasonable care, shelter, and necessities."

Ysella shook his head. "I'm glad I only have to worry about ports and waterways."

"I imagine you've got a few issues not amenable to reason."

"There are a few, but they don't impinge as significantly on people's lives."

"What else can we do, Dominic? Without legal protections, susceptibles would be at the total mercy of the merciless. In Atacama . . . well, you know what that's like. They can order a susceptible to work himself to death, and there's nothing to prohibit it. Here we have standards. They may not be as good as they could be, but we're working to make them better." Staeryt lowered his voice. "Some of the councilors from the southwest aren't exactly helpful, either."

"Aldyn Kraagyn?"

"Among others." Staeryt looked up as Maatrak walked to the lectern and stood there, waiting for the chime to ring.

After it did, Maatrak rapped the gavel. "The Council will be in order. The first order of business is consideration of a reassignment of unspent appropriations from the Agriculture Administration to the Natural Resources Administration for the purpose of road construction north of Storz to enable the development of natural resources . . ."

"Making it easy for the commercer types to dig another coal mine," murmured Staeryt.

In the end, a bell later, the measure passed, twenty-nine votes in favor, twenty opposed, and Detruro recessed the chamber subject to the call of the Premier.

Ysella again let the chamber clear before he stood, only to see Paolo Caanard walking toward him.

"You're looking much better, Dominic. Patrice told me to tell you that you'll still have to dance with her at the next Yearend Ball."

"How are you two doing?"

Caanard smiled amusedly. "Better than you, I think. I understand your committee is looking into standardizing terms and procedures at all Imperial ports."

"That's no secret. Is there something going on at Point Larmat that I should know about?"

Caanard glanced around. "Navy ships port there, often. Sometimes, they tie up the piers for weeks. They take the best berths, and they don't pay wharfage. This doesn't happen only at Point Larmat. Then the port administrator gets reprimanded because port revenues are down. What's the chance of getting a change in the law so that, say, if a naval vessel takes commercial pier space for some extended period, possibly more than a week, the Navy has to pay wharfage?"

"As I recall, the regulations allow the port administrator to note the loss of revenue."

"They do, but the Waterways Administrator only goes by the numbers."

"We'll have to give that some thought."

"I thought you'd like to know."

"I appreciate it," said Ysella. "Do you have anything interesting coming up in your committee?"

"We're looking at discriminatory tariffs by some of the countries in the Teknold Confederacy. It won't do any good, but the Heir wants some numbers. We can give him numbers, but their accuracy is questionable."

"Like too many things," replied Ysella cynically.

After leaving Caanard, Ysella returned to his office, where he reviewed and signed or corrected the responses drafted by his clerks, then donned his overcoat and left the office just before second bell.

Caastyn waited with the chaise outside the main entrance, talking to one of the building guards.

As Ysella approached, the guard stepped back.

"Good afternoon, sir."

"Thank you." Ysella smiled. "It's better than most." Then climbed into the chaise.

Once Caastyn headed west on Council Avenue, Ysella asked, "Did you learn anything interesting from the guard?"

"He and the other guards wanted to know if you'd done something the Imperador didn't like. I told him you'd done something that a legalist working for thugs and other criminals didn't like. He said that wasn't much different from the Heir."

"How many people feel that way, do you think?"

"Some, mostly folks who've seen what the Heir can do. Most just don't want to be noticed by the Imperador or the Heir."

"That sounds about right." Ysella paused. "On Unadi, I'll try going to the Council Hall half a bell earlier and stay until third bell. If I'm not too tired or too sore, I'll do it all week."

"You're not looking so tired at the end of the day."

"I'm glad the Council and committee sessions are short now." Ysella paused. "Have you heard anything from Haardt?"

"I checked with him around noon. He thinks he'll have the replacement body armor by Unadi."

"Good."

After a few moments, Caastyn said, "You got another letter from Aloor. Doesn't look familiar, though."

Ysella grinned. "You mean it's not from my mother or Ritten Wythcomb?"

"Neither one," confirmed Caastyn.

Back at the house, while Caastyn took care of the horse and the chaise, Ysella walked to the study, removed his overcoat, and picked up the single letter awaiting him. He immediately recognized the hand of Legrand Quaentyn, opened the envelope, and began to read.

> After reading the newssheet reports about the attack on you and the Machtarn District Legalist, I suspect you may not need me to produce the documents you dispatched, but I'll keep them locked away until I receive further instructions from you. You have always had a certain quiet knack for getting involved in "interesting" situations, but while it's often served you well, there are downsides, and those may well become more dangerous now that you have become more well-known. I won't say more.
>
> You also made quite an impression on someone else when you were last here. Aelyn Wythcomb came by a week or so ago. While she asked about certain legalities concerning the Ahnkaar mine, she had more than a few questions about you. She especially wanted to know if you were as honest as you seemed, a question to which I could, in all truth, affirm that you were and had been in all the years I've known you . . .

Ysella nodded and smiled. Quaentyn wouldn't have mentioned Aelyn if he didn't approve of her.

That's very good to know.

He finished reading the letter and replaced it in the envelope, then went to hang up his overcoat.

41

AT breakfast on Quindi morning, Ysella's eyes immediately went to the *Tribune*.

> ... late in the evening on the eighteenth of Winterend, three pirate vessels from Atacama landed a raiding party at Encora. The raiders set fire to four grain warehouses. One warehouse exploded, and high winds sent flames through the harbor area ... Scores of buildings burned, and the number of deaths may be in the hundreds ...
>
> The Imperador has ordered the Navy to remove "the piratical scourge" from the Gulf of Nordum permanently ...

How can the Navy do more than it already is? While Ysella knew that First Marshal Solatiem could do little more, he wondered how long the marshal would last.

As he continued through the newssheet, an article almost buried on the bottom of the fourth page caught his attention.

> **CRIMINAL PROPERTY LAW—FAIR TO WHOM?**
>
> The disappearance, or possible death, of Machtarn legalist Sollem Faarn has created an uncomfortable situation for the Imperial Justiciary. The missing legalist has been loosely linked to a number of unsolved crimes and the illegal use of a shadow trust to conceal his ownership of a large number of properties in Machtarn, particularly in the harbor district. The Imperial District Legalist has issued a forfeiture order against those properties, declaring that they were obtained, and their ownership concealed, through felonious means. Such an order supersedes any interest by Faarn's wife and children, disenfranchising them.
>
> In addition, the Justiciary is required to sell those properties at auction to the highest bidder. All of the properties are rented to various enterprises and crafters, who may also be displaced when their leases expire, if not sooner ...

Ysella didn't need to read any more, although he wondered why the *Tribune* had printed such an almost prosaic story that few people would likely read. *Even after they die, people like Faarn leave an ongoing mess, not that the bastard would have cared in the slightest... and Smootn didn't help either.*

Several questions swirled through his mind as he prepared to leave the house and as Caastyn drove him to the Council Hall, including thoughts of Aelyn Wythcomb... and whether she would write... and about what, if she did.

When Caastyn reined up outside the Council Hall, he asked, "Second bell, sir?"

"Second bell, and you'll post that letter to Legrand Quaentyn?" asked Ysella as he gingerly stepped from the chaise.

"On the way back to the house, sir."

"Thank you." Ysella turned and walked toward the building entrance, smiling as he thought about Legrand's kindness in telling him about Aelyn Wythcomb.

When he reached his office and stepped inside, he looked to his senior clerk. "Lyaard, you've made all the necessary additional copies of the proposed usury bill?"

"Yes, sir. Three for the Council Clerk, and two for your files, and the submission sheet is ready, except for your signature and the Clerk's seal."

"Excellent. I can submit them to the Council Clerk before today's session."

"I'll have them on your desk shortly, sir. Is there anything else?"

"Any messages, urgent or otherwise?"

"Just one, sir." Khaard paused. "You recall that Paatyr won't be in today?"

"I didn't, but I do now. His sister's wedding... was that it?"

"Yes, sir."

"How about the letters?"

"Not too bad. The incoming ones and the corrected responses are on your desk."

"Then I'll get to them after I take care of the message."

The message was in a plain envelope, but the paper was expensive, and the return address was the Imperial Administration building. Ysella wondered if it might be from Engar Tyresis, the Imperial Waterways Administrator, but when he opened it, he discovered it was from Carsius Zaenn, the recently appointed Natural Resources Administrator.

Councilor Ysella—
   While I'd hoped to have a few uninterrupted moments with you at the Yearend Ball, by the time I could break free I was unable to

find you. Then, after the Council's winter recess, I discovered that you'd been the target of assassins.

Given all that, I was hoping that I could stop by your office before the Council meets next Furdi morning, 34 Winterend. If that is not convenient, I would appreciate knowing and your naming a time and date.

Ysella had no idea what Zaenn wanted, but he obviously wanted something, and the only way to find out was to meet him. He wrote a reply agreeing to the date, but requesting that it be between third morning bell and a third past fifth bell, then took the message to Khaard to have it dispatched immediately.

After that, Ysella dealt with the correspondence, and spent some time considering Legalist Shaeldn's point about standards for district poorhouses. He soon realized that he didn't know enough to draft something meaningful . . . and something less than that would make matters worse.

Ysella left his office at half a bell before noon to stop by the Council Clerk's office before the session to introduce his proposed bill to lift the usury cap.

The moment he entered the anteroom, the junior clerk at the front desk said, "Yes, Councilor?"

"I have a bill to introduce, with the requisite three copies. I'd like the date of introduction to be today. Is Sr. Hoogart still in charge of that?" Ysella doubted it was otherwise, but staff changes were almost always made over major recesses, and it was better to ask.

"Yes, sir, just a moment."

Several passed before the clerk returned and led Ysella back to Hoogart's desk.

Hoogart read through the submission sheet and then read the title aloud, "A bill to raise the maximum allowable interest charge to six parts on a hundred, under the provisions of the Usury Act."

"That's correct," replied Ysella.

"If you would sign the sheet, sir."

Ysella did so, then watched as Hoogart signed the acceptance, applied the seal, and then said, "The Premier will assign it to the proper committee for consideration."

"The Commerce Committee, most likely."

Hoogart replied, "Is there anything else, sir?"

"Not today, thank you."

From the Council Clerk's office, Ysella made his way to the Council chamber, where he settled behind his small desk and waited. Before long

Staeryt appeared, but he turned to Paolo Caanard, in response to a question that Ysella didn't hear.

When Oskaar Klempt arrived, Ysella stood and gestured to him.

Klempt looked up, then walked over. "You're looking better, Dominic."

"I'm feeling better, too. I introduced the bill we discussed."

"Does the Premier know?"

"He won't be surprised. I told him I would. He said that the Imperador wouldn't sign such a bill. Right now, the Imperador won't, but who's to say that he couldn't change his mind?"

"Even if he seldom does," replied Klempt sarcastically. "What are you considering next in your committee?"

"We have a hearing Duadi on standardizing harbor terminology to allow better comparison of fees. It's hard to set standards when people don't know what you may be suggesting or requiring." Ysella smiled cheerfully. "At least, all your calculations are in marks."

"There is that," replied Klempt, glancing to the dais, and then saying, "Here comes Maatrak."

The chime rang, and Ysella hoped that Maatrak and Detruro didn't have too much to say, given that no legislation was scheduled for consideration.

After various announcements and Detruro's recessing the Council until noon on Duadi, Ysella stood and went to find Aldyn Kraagyn, who had turned away from a brief exchange with Voltar Paastyn. *Possibly about the attack?*

"Aldyn . . . this morning I read about the attack on Encora . . ."

"The *Tribune* had to know about it much earlier. I found out on Tridi. Little outside Machtarn matters to those self-absorbed newshawks—unless it involves the Imperador."

"Was it as bad as the newssheet account?"

"What they wrote was mostly accurate. But who's going to take care of the widows and orphans or pay to rebuild the wharves or the shops and houses? Encora's always getting shorted. The whole southwest is. You know that, and the Imperador wants useless first-rate ships of the line that can't do squat against shallow-draft pirate craft." Kraagyn shook his head. "And the Council doesn't have the power to change things." The older councilor paused, then said, "But thank you. Unlike some, you and your family have lived through a touch of destruction." A wry smile followed. "Have you heard any more about my nephew?"

"You mean Rugaar?"

"The same. He's latched on to Merkall Klein, and you know what I think of Merkall."

"Outside of the one meeting, I haven't heard anything—except rumors that he's been interested in buying property in Aloor, along with Lohan Escalante."

"Let me know if you hear more. I'd appreciate it."

"It's been quiet, but I can certainly do that."

"Thank you." Kraagyn inclined his head. "If you'd excuse me . . ."

Ysella definitely shared Kraagyn's concerns linking Lohan Escalante and Rugaar Maartyn, as well as Maartyn's interest in water law and rights to the Kleins.

But there's not much you can do right now.

As Ysella strolled back to his office, he considered whether he should make the effort to attend services, then decided he wasn't quite recovered enough to deal with Presider Haelsyn, although he'd need to before too long.

42

FINDI was uneventful, as was Unadi. While the *Tribune* ran follow-up stories about the pirate raid on Encora, those stories added few details, except reiterations from First Marshal Solatiem that the pirates would pay for their attacks on Guldoran territory and vessels.

On Duadi morning, Caastyn and Ysella reached the Council Hall at half past second bell, and when Ysella got out of the chaise, he said, "Third afternoon bell."

"I'll be here."

Then Ysella made his way to his office, using the bannister up to the second floor as a precaution, rather than an aid.

Once there, finding no messages, he went to work dealing with constituent correspondence. Afterward he went over his notes for the Waterways Committee, then left his office for the committee hearing room, where he found Eldyn Taarln, the Waterways Committee senior clerk, who had finished setting up.

"Is Portmaster Ridgell here yet?"

"He's in the committee office, sir. I thought he could wait there."

"I'll go talk to him, and return." Ysella walked into the adjoining office.

The weathered and angular portmaster stood as Ysella approached. "Good morning, Councilor."

"Thank you for coming."

"I appreciated the invitation, especially if it'll lead to more uniformity in ports."

"This is only a first step," said Ysella, "but we need to start somewhere. Sr. Taarln will come for you in a few moments. I wanted to greet you personally."

An amused smile split Ridgell's craggy face. "Wanted to see you as well. You don't look that bad for a man who almost died."

"Almost four weeks of recovery helps," returned Ysella. "We'll see you in a bit." With that, he turned and returned to the hearing room, where he took his place behind the curved desk.

Before long, Haans Maessyn took his seat to Ysella's immediate right, followed by Voltar Paastyn to his left. The other four committee members quickly took their seats, and just before fourth bell, Portmaster Ridgell appeared and seated himself at the witness table facing the dais.

Ysella rapped the gavel and began, "The committee will come to order." He paused, then said, "I'd like to welcome Jarral Ridgell, Portmaster of Machtarn, who is here to testify about certain difficulties in implementing regulated port procedures. I believe you have an opening statement, Portmaster."

"I do, Sr. Chairman. You asked that I explain the problems all ports in Guldor face from the perspective of the port authorities. The Machtarn Port Authority controls the port, which includes all channels, docks, and wharfs. It also includes adjacent paved areas used for temporary storage of recently off-loaded cargoes and those awaiting loading. This general pattern is true of all ports in Guldor. The charges are set by each port authority but are reviewed and approved by the Commerce Administration. The charges fall into two general categories, those applied to ships and those applied to cargoes. Unfortunately, because the various ports developed independently, the way the charges are defined means that the same ship and cargoes can be charged varying port dues in different Guldoran ports.

"There is also the problem that outland shippers may only trade through one or two Guldoran ports simply because they do not wish to deal with differing procedures and requirements from each port.

"For example, the port of Neewyrk has based its port dues on the tonnage of a vessel, while Sudaen uses a combination of vessel length and breadth, and Port Reale and Machtarn use a combination of each. Likewise, the base factors for calculating demurrage charges for cargoes left on wharfs or in storage yards vary from port to port . . ."

Ysella listened intently as Ridgell completed his statement, then said, "Thank you, Portmaster. We'll begin with a question from each councilor, along with follow-up questions on that same subject." He turned to Haans Maessyn, the most senior of the councilors other than Ysella. "Do you have a question?"

"I do, Sr. Chairman." Maessyn looked to Ridgell. "You've suggested that the bases of various charges should be identical, but aren't there other factors to consider? The weather in the northeast ports is far more severe, particularly in Neewyrk . . ."

As Maessyn finished, Ysella could see Ditaero frown, possibly because weather conditions were worse in Endor, even more exposed to the fury of the Northern Ocean.

"That's a good point, Councilor, but here in Machtarn, one of the basic factors is the time required. In some cases, ports with the best weather have the highest handling charges . . ."

Ysella moderated the questions, and found some as revealing of the councilor as the subject, such as when Stefan Nortaak, the councilor from Oersynt, asked, "Why is there a difference between demurrage charges and port storage charges?"

Because Oersynt lay well north of Machtarn, almost all water traffic on the Rio Mal was by narrow, shallow-draft craft, where wharfs weren't designed for storage, something Nortaak hadn't considered even after two years on the Waterways Committee.

Ridgell answered thoughtfully and pleasantly. "Demurrage charges generally are incurred once a cargo is left on a wharf beyond the free time period, and they're higher because they take up space on a working wharf. Storage charges are for cargoes held in storage areas that don't restrict day-to-day loading and off-loading."

The hearing lasted almost until noon, when Ysella thanked Portmaster Ridgell and recessed the committee.

As the committee members began to file out, Ysella gestured for Ditaero to join him as the two walked toward the Council chamber.

"Because I've had to cut back my time at the Council a bit, Gaastyn, I haven't had much of a chance to talk with you, especially since you were considerably delayed in returning to Machtarn. That wasn't all weather, I trust?"

"I had to meet with some people who weren't immediately available."

"Something to do with what we discussed before Yearend, and the lack of influence felt by some in the northeast."

"Something like that." Ditaero didn't quite meet Ysella's eyes.

Since he wanted to keep Ditaero off-balance, Ysella asked, half guessing, "You think you might have more influence if the crafters in the northeast joined with others?"

"You landors stick together," replied Ditaero.

"I'm not criticizing," said Ysella pleasantly. "The Council has officially ignored those informal but real groupings. Matters might be more in the open with three separate groups. My only concern would be that there be only those three groups."

"How would the Premier take that? Or the Imperador?"

"I suspect that the Premier would be far more accommodating than the Imperador, which might be why no one wants to make such interests public at the moment."

"If not now, then when?" asked Ditaero.

"When the time is appropriate, which may be a little while."

"We'll all be old and gray . . . and more toothless," replied Ditaero in a tone of sardonic exasperation.

"I don't think it will be anywhere near that long. Times are changing, even if the Imperador and the Heir aren't." *Although I suspect the Imperador's daughter is.*

"Dominic, you're acting as if you know something."

"We all have our secrets, and sometimes they're not as secret as we believe."

Ditaero shook his head.

When Ysella entered the Council chamber and took his seat, Staeryt asked, "What surprise does the Premier have today, do you think?"

"If he does, it will likely be about Atacama, but that's a guess."

At noon precisely, Maatrak gaveled the Council into session, then turned the lectern over to the Premier.

"I received a message from First Marshal Solatiem early this morning," began Detruro, "with the request that I inform the Council of recent naval actions in the Gulf of Nordum. Elements of the Southern Fleet have attacked five more isles harboring pirate enclaves and have leveled all structures on those isles and removed any surviving pirates. The Southern Fleet has implemented a blockade of Port Lenfer to allow pirate removal efforts to continue unimpeded. The first-rate ships of the line *Obaanax* and *Suvionax* are reinforcing the flotillas maintaining the blockade. In addition, two flotillas from the Northern Fleet are en route to Point Larmat to free up other ships from the Southern Fleet to patrol off southwestern Guldor."

Detruro cleared his throat, then continued, "I appreciate the efforts by all committee chairmen to submit hearing schedules, but would like to remind you all that changes, additions, or deletions to those schedules should be submitted a week in advance, except, of course, due to unexpected and unavoidable absences of witnesses."

After several more procedural announcements, Detruro recessed the Council until Furdi.

Staeryt hurried out of his chair before Ysella stood, and Caanard turned to Ysella. "Sounds like the Imperador wants all of us to understand that first-rate ships have their uses."

"No one denied that," replied Ysella with an amused smile. "We disagree on the amount of first-rate ships required for those uses."

"Don't say that too loudly," said Caanard dryly.

"An excellent point." *For now.*

Ysella followed Caanard out of the Council chamber, climbing the steps to the upper level, realizing as he did that at times he only felt a dull ache. *But it's been almost four weeks.*

When Ysella returned to his office, he first read and signed, or occasionally corrected, the responses written out by Khaard and Jaasn, then turned his attention to the folder with comments from various portmasters across Guldor to see how what they wrote compared to what Ridgell had said that morning.

He hadn't gotten through a third of the comments before third bell approached and he had to leave to meet Caastyn outside the main door.

Caastyn, as usual, was waiting. Ysella immediately climbed into the chaise, wincing slightly, and within moments, the chaise rolled down Council Avenue, heading toward Imperial Boulevard.

"Has anything of interest happened outside the walls of the Council?" asked Ysella half-wryly.

"Not a thing I know of, except you got a letter from the property legalists."

"I hope it's not another shady legalist interested in buying my harbor properties." Ysella paused for several moments. "The newssheets haven't written about Faarn since his disappearance, except the auction of his properties. There was nothing about Gustov Torryl."

"There wouldn't be. The patrollers wouldn't want to admit that they were chasing a dead man, and the district legalist wouldn't want to admit that they weren't the ones to find the illegal trust. The Imperador wouldn't like newssheet articles about either, and most folks are glad Faarn and Torryl are gone."

"I wonder if Torryl ever existed," mused Ysella. "I never read anything about his death, but that happened, according to the trust deeds, before I came to Machtarn."

"If Faarn made him up, that'd be another reason that the Imperial types wouldn't want it to come out."

"True enough." The mention of the letter got Ysella to thinking about Aelyn Wythcomb, and he again wondered when he'd hear from her, and if he'd been too forward in his reply. But then, he had to remind himself that she barely could have received his letter.

"Oh, I picked up the armor from Haardt this afternoon. He thinks it's a bit stronger than what he made before, and he also thinks it might be more comfortable."

"That would be good, I'll try it on tonight."

"You're not planning . . . ?"

"Not a thing. I want to have it handy."

"You had a hearing today," said Caastyn. "How did it go?"

"Well enough, but it's going to take work to get a framework for roughly similar procedures for ports."

Caastyn chuckled. "You ended up as chairman all because you were a water legalist."

"More because too many councilors have never been near a port."

Ysella kept an eye on other wagons, riders, and carriages, but there weren't that many on the streets in late midafternoon.

Back in his study, Ysella looked at the envelope from Sullynd & Smarkaan, not exactly his favorite property legalists, then decided to open it, especially since dinner wouldn't be ready for at least a bell. He began to read.

Councilor Ysella—

You have requested that we inform you of properties of possible interest to you in the Machtarn harbor area. As you may have read, a number of properties near those you already own, formerly owned by the legalist Sollem Faarn, will be offered at public auction . . .

When Ysella finished reading, he set the letter aside, shaking his head. He'd have to decline, immediately. The last thing he needed was to be found bidding on and possibly buying any of Faarn's properties. He worried about the newssheets discovering what he owned, despite the fact that he'd bought the first of his properties years ago and chosen them because they weren't in the area directly affected by Waterways legislation.

It's not as though you own massive amounts of property.

Still, he had to admit concern, even as he took out paper and pen to write a firm regret that he'd be unable to consider buying more harbor properties.

He also needed to try on the silk-and-leather replacement body armor.

43

YSELLA was in his office well before third bell on Furdi morning, reading through the latest letters from Aloor, and waiting for the arrival of Carsius Zaenn, the Natural Resources administrator, when Khaard knocked on the half-open door.

"A message from the Premier, sir. And another one."

"Another one?"

"The seal isn't familiar, sir." The senior clerk stepped forward and extended the two messages.

"Thank you, Lyaard."

After Khaard left, Ysella opened the envelope from the Premier, which held a brief note.

> I'd appreciate your stopping by my office before fifth bell. No need to reply.

As he set the note aside, Ysella wondered what Detruro had in mind, at the same time hoping that Zaenn showed up before long. He looked at the second envelope and smiled, recognizing the ornate seal of Ramon Hekkaad—the Argenti envoy to Guldor—then opened the envelope.

> Councilor Ysella—
> Now that you're on the way to recovery, Leona and I would like to have you over for a dinner on Furdi evening, the tenth of Springfirst, at sixth bell.
> The gathering will be small, and you're welcome to bring a guest . . .

Ysella smiled, thinking that he'd like to be able to invite Aelyn Wythcomb to accompany him to the various dinners and the occasional ball. *But that's not possible . . . not now.* However, he could look to the future . . . and hope that matters between them worked out for the best.

Ysella glanced up as Khaard knocked on the half-open door. "Administrator Zaenn, sir." Then the senior clerk stepped back.

Ysella stood as Zaenn entered, trying not to wince from the sudden movement.

Khaard quietly closed the door behind the lanky administrator.

"I can see you're not yet fully recovered," declared Zaenn, standing beside the center chair, but waiting to seat himself until Ysella did.

"I'm somewhat better every day," replied Ysella, after seating himself. "Since we only met briefly at the Yearend Ball, would you mind letting me know a bit more about you?"

"There's not much to know. My family's from Kathaar, but I've been working in the Natural Resources Administration for almost ten years, the last two as deputy administrator. Before that, I spent some time with Kathaar Ironworks."

"You wouldn't be a legalist, would you?"

"Hardly. I'm more inclined to practicality."

Zaenn's vagueness made Ysella more wary. "I'm a bit confused as to why you wanted to see me."

"We both know that you really can't separate waterways from natural resources," replied Zaenn. "Water is a natural resource, and a vital one at that. Without adequate water, we can't produce iron, for example. At the same time, water needs to be carefully managed. If water levels are too low, canals can't be used. If there's too much water in mines, the ores can't be mined."

Ysella nodded and waited; he suspected he knew where Zaenn was headed.

"Water-rights law was established to protect the rights of existing users," declared the administrator with a touch of the pedant, "which is why first uses have priority, yet there are times when the first uses are marginal in value but deprive other downstream users of the possibility of far more beneficial use."

"That was one reason, if not the only one, why Guldor replaced the riparian system with first appropriation," Ysella pointed out, "in order to permit lower-priority users to purchase the rights of senior users, allowing pricing to determine the most economic use of water."

"Only if the higher-priority users will consider reasonable prices," countered Zaenn.

Ysella offered a smile he didn't feel, and didn't care if Zaenn could see that. "A user can always petition the Natural Resources Administration for a determination of more beneficial use, which you can put before the Waterways Committee for a recommendation prior to a Council vote of approval or disapproval."

"That's rather cumbersome and time-consuming."

As it was meant to be. "What exactly do you have in mind, Administrator?"

"A change in the existing law to provide the Natural Resources Administration with an administrative mechanism to rule on such cases without recourse to Council determination."

Ysella nodded slowly. "Why might this be necessary, after all these years?"

"There are more and more instances where manufacturing and mining efforts have been stalled or blocked by inordinately high valuations of water rights."

"Inordinate by whose standards?" asked Ysella.

"By those who want Guldor to prosper and progress, as well as the Imperador and the Heir, of course."

"You do have a point." *If a biased one.* Ysella decided not to drag out the conversation. "With all the expertise you have in Natural Resources, do you have a draft of what sort of legislation you think might be helpful in that regard?"

Zaenn's smile verged on the predatory as he opened his leather case. "I thought you might find a draft useful."

"Indeed," replied Ysella. "A solid draft is always a good starting point for the committee when it considers and shapes legislation."

"I can see why the Imperador says that you're most reasonable and don't go to extremes." Zaenn extracted a large but thin envelope and slid it across the desk.

Ysella eased it to the side without making any movement to pick it up. "Too many times, extremists honestly believe they're the reasonable ones. That makes it difficult for everyone. The councilors on the Waterways Committee do what we can in those circumstances." He hesitated slightly. "Is there anything else you wish to convey?"

Zaenn shook his head. "I've intruded enough, and after your injury, I'm sure you have little time to spare."

Ysella stood. "I appreciate your coming by. It was good to talk with you and get to know a little about you." *Enough to know that I'd trust a rock serpent more.*

"The same to you." Zaenn offered a polite and meaningless smile, inclined his head, then turned and departed.

Once Zaenn was well out of sight, Ysella turned toward the window, pelted intermittently by scattered raindrops. Whether Rugaar Maartyn had any connection at all with Zaenn, Ysella had no doubt that Maartyn and Lohan Escalante were part of the group characterized by the recently departed administrator as those wanting Guldor to prosper and progress. *No matter what happens to smallholders or land-poor landors.* Or to a widow like Aelyn Wythcomb.

Ysella waited a sixth before he left the office, heading for his meeting with the Premier.

When he reached Detruro's office, the clerk greeting Ysella immediately showed him in.

"Thank you for coming early," said Detruro, gesturing to the chairs.

"I would have been here earlier, but Carsius Zaenn came by to see me."

"Oh, the most recent Natural Resources Administrator. What did he want?"

"For the Waterways Committee to write him a blank cheque to invalidate any water right that gets in the way of anything some large commercial venture wants. He even had a draft bill with him. I thanked him and said the draft would be a good starting point, and he delivered a veiled threat and admonition that I shouldn't let the committee stray far from the draft."

"I've heard that he's pleasantly unpleasant," replied Detruro. "What will you do?"

"Schedule hearings close to midsummer recess. After recess, we'll modify the bill so that it superficially looks the same but limits in some way the scope and number of exemptions. I'll need to think about that." Ysella paused. "I assume that wasn't why you wanted to see me."

"No, not at all. You may recall that I danced a number of times with the Imperador's daughter."

"And you're going to marry her?"

Detruro laughed, if with a touch of the sardonic. "You don't miss much."

"To me, it seemed obvious. You're older, but not too much older, and you have a strong personality. You have lands in Enke, which isn't close to Machtarn, and neither the Imperador nor the Heir can really control her. So, she has to be married . . . or removed. Everyone would prefer the first." *Which will make the second option easier, if it turns out to be necessary. I hope you struck a hard bargain.* "Congratulations!"

"There will be an announcement reception and dinner at the Palace on the seventeenth of Springfirst. Delehya thought you'd be the perfect Council representative at the dinner."

"Old superseded royalty and a loyal Council committee chairman."

"She also says you have a good head on your shoulders, and that you quietly and indirectly suggested me."

Ysella smiled. "I did say she should look for someone who was intelligent, powerful, with lands, and whom her father respected."

"She also said you politely rejected her."

"I did. It wouldn't have worked for me or her, and her mother doesn't like me, for some reason, although I've never met her."

Detruro raised his eyebrows. "All from one dance?"

"Half a dance, really. She can be very persuasive."

"I've already learned that," said Detruro wryly. "She asked me."

"Could it really be otherwise?"

"Not really. But that could appear to present other problems."

"Appear to present?" asked Ysella.

"She is of the Imperador's blood. There's only one surviving heir, although he has two almost-grown sons."

"You think people will suggest Imperial ambitions?" *Not that they won't.* But Ysella had to ask.

"Many, most likely." Detruro quickly asked, "Now . . . is there anyone you'd like to have accompany you?"

"No. Not for the foreseeable future, anyway."

"Then you'll get an invitation shortly." The Premier shifted his weight in his chair.

"I look forward to receiving it."

"There's another thing. About your draft plan. I've thought more about the section that recognizes political parties, but mandates three parties. Do you really think that's feasible?"

"The split between crafters and commercers already exists, and neither has the same goals as we do. If we don't work out power sharing and compromise in the next few years, if not sooner, we'll have a lot of unrest later, possibly a revolt or revolution."

"Are there enough districts where there are sufficient crafters?"

"That's one of the reasons I increased the number of councilors to sixty-six. No one has to give up anything, and we'll have to work out a transition."

"What about the limit and the minimum and maximum number of seats?"

"That's so no party can dominate by itself and no party can be forced out of existence. It's a guarantee that the weakest will have a voice, but that the strongest can get a bit more."

"Will anyone accept it?"

"Compared to what we have now? That should be easier than persuading the Imperador to sign it. And it would be best to get the Imperador's agreement rather than waiting and dealing with the Heir."

"How would you propose accomplishing that?"

"I'd wait until after your wedding." Ysella smiled. "But not too long."

"And in the meantime?"

"Perhaps you and the bride should quietly meet with senior officers in the Navy and Army . . . possibly honorable administrators as well."

Detruro frowned.

"As you know, Iustaan, she's very persuasive, and I imagine she could make you more effective."

"I'd appreciate it if you'd leave it at that, Dominic."

"I have no intention of saying more to anyone. I also won't say anything about your engagement until it's made public." Ysella smiled and added, "But the two of you could be a formidable force." He paused. "Is there anything else I should know?"

"Not that I can think of." Detruro offered a cynical smile. "That could change in less than a bell, but if it does, I'll let you know."

Ysella stood. "Then I won't take any more of your time. Again, my congratulations, and convey my best to the lady."

"I will."

Ysella made his way back to his office, where he wrote out an acceptance to Ramon Hekkaad, and then dealt with constituent correspondence.

That left him a little time before the Council was due to meet, and, reluctantly, he opened the envelope Zaenn had left and began to read the draft legislation. By the end of the first page, he could tell that his assumptions were correct, and that he would have to be extremely careful in guiding how the Waterways Committee amended the proposal. When he finished reading, he replaced the sheets in the envelope and filed it in the chest holding his committee papers and drafts.

Then he headed for the Council chamber, arriving there at a sixth before noon.

"How did your hearing go?" asked Staeryt as Ysella seated himself.

"The Machtarn portmaster was quite informative, but it will be a challenge to structure even a basic legal framework."

"I'm sure you'll manage."

"That I can likely do. Whether what we craft won't have every portmaster in Guldor after the committee is another question. I get the impression they all want to keep doing things exactly as they always have, but not having a rough standard hurts all of them, whether they want to admit it or not." Ysella stopped as he saw Maatrak approaching the lectern.

The floor leader gaveled the Council to order, then announced, "The first order of business before the Council is a vote on the legislation authorizing the transfer of unspent funds from the Foreign Affairs discretionary budget to the post-roads construction budget for the purposes of maintenance and improvement. The chairman of the Foreign Affairs Committee will address the matter first, followed by the chairman of the Commerce Committee."

Paolo Caanard took the lectern. "The purpose of this bill is to assure unspent funds are used wisely. Under the Establishment Act, each administration funded as a separate entity is free to shift funds within its own budget. Funds may only be shifted to another administrative body with the concurrence of both administrators and the approval of the Council . . ."

Ysella half listened as Caanard quickly uttered the required language, and was followed by Oskaar Klempt, since post roads fell within the jurisdiction of the Commerce Committee.

When Klempt finished speaking, Maatrak called for the vote. Less than a bell later, Detruro announced the results, the bill passing by a vote of forty-six to two.

Ysella wondered who the two might have been and who was absent.

Then Maatrak announced the second fund-transfer measure of the three on the schedule. In the end, both passed, and after the third vote, Detruro recessed the Council.

Ysella rose to leave the Council chamber when Oskaar Klempt appeared.

"Dominic, I hoped you might be able to appear as an informal witness before the Commerce Committee next Tridi morning."

Ysella had to think for a moment. "About my usury-cap proposal?"

"Not so much about your specific measure, but why you felt it is necessary for the Council to address the problem."

"Why me? I can't be the only councilor who sees the problem."

"You're not. But you represent a landor district with little commercer interest there, and you think it's a big enough problem to introduce legislation."

Ysella nodded. "And by having me speak . . ."

"Exactly."

"I'll be there."

"I appreciate it, Dominic," said Klempt warmly, before turning and leaving the Council chamber.

From the other's warmth and tone of voice, Ysella could tell Klempt meant what he'd said—and that the usury interest cap was a far bigger problem in Vhooryn.

As Ysella headed back to his office, he wondered what the Imperador would do if the Council did raise the cap . . . and how that might affect Detruro's efforts.

44

QUINDI morning began quietly, allowing Ysella to deal with correspondence and work on his statement to the Commerce Committee, as well as read several more reports from Guldoran portmasters. After he read those and made notes, he had Jaasn forward the reports to the other members of the committee, beginning with Haans Maessyn.

Then Khaard brought him a large envelope. Ysella opened it and read the short cover note from Stron Thaalyr, the chairman of the Natural Resources Committee.

> *Dominic—*
> *Here's the version of the Coal Act requested by the Natural Resources Administration. I'd appreciate it if you would take a close look at it.*

What Thaalyr's note meant was that Carsius Zaenn had pressed Thaalyr to report out the bill essentially as drafted by Zaenn's staff and that there were problems with it. While Thaalyr didn't want to upset Zaenn or the Imperador, he also didn't want Ysella blindsided by what was in the legislative proposal.

Ysella shook his head and began to read. A bell later he took out paper and pen and began to draft the first amendment of three. While the proposed Coal Act wasn't scheduled for discussion until a week from the coming Duadi, he needed to register any proposed amendments at least two working days before floor action. If he wanted other members to know about his amendments, and why they should support them, he'd have to send the amendments out before then.

The more Ysella discovered about Zaenn, the less he cared for the Natural Resources Administrator.

He was still working and struggling on the amendments when, just before noon, Reimer Daarkyn, unsurprisingly, arrived at the office.

"I appreciate your seeing me," began Daarkyn once he sat in Ysella's personal office. "How are you feeling?"

"Better, except when I inadvertently twist or turn—or cough . . . or laugh. Do you have any interesting stories?"

"No one's seen any trace of Sollem Faarn. Have you heard anything?"

"I haven't heard a word."

"It's as though he vanished. Usually, someone, somewhere, knows something, but not in the case of Faarn."

"I read the piece on smoke and fire. There was a slight hint that the Palace might be involved."

Daarkyn snorted. "Slight hint?"

"It was well done. If the Palace had said much or shut down the *Tribune*, that would have suggested involvement at some level. Was there some quiet suggestion in response to the piece?"

"Why would you think that?" replied Daarkyn sardonically.

"I suppose I have a cynical streak."

"And you have no idea about Faarn?" Daarkyn tapped the floor with the toe of his boot.

"I told you my thoughts before, but since no one's heard anything since we last talked, that suggests more strongly that he's not anywhere near Machtarn."

"Or he's dead," said Daarkyn.

"So long as he can't cause any more trouble, I don't much care," replied Ysella.

"You and most of the people in the harbor area. It's rather amazing so many feared or hated someone and yet no one in the Palace, with all the snitches reputed to serve the Heir, seems to know anything about him. Do you have any thoughts on that?"

"The piece in the *Tribune* expressed the situation accurately." *If necessarily incompletely.*

"That's all?"

"What else could I say when someone else has done a masterful job?" Ysella smiled politely.

Daarkyn offered a quiet snort, then said, "On another subject . . . you were one of a handful of men who danced with Lady Delehya at the Year-end Ball. Of that handful, you're one of a smaller group who are unmarried. And you're above reproach, which might quiet the rumors about her. You're also the only one with royal blood, even if it comes from what was a small and ill-governed land."

"All of that is largely correct," replied Ysella, deciding not to completely ignore the rumors and the barb at the end of Daarkyn's statement.

"Largely? What do you think isn't correct?"

"Aloor wasn't ill-governed, although one could claim that its governance wasn't what it could have been."

Daarkyn raised his eyebrows.

Ysella waited.

"So . . . are you pursuing the Lady Delehya?"

"I most definitely am not," replied Ysella in a cheerfully amused tone. "Nor, to the best of my knowledge, is she pursuing me."

Daarkyn frowned. "Why would . . . ?"

"Think about it, Reimer. In social position, she's above every man in Guldor except her father and her half brother. Men with wealth or position might wish to gain her attention, but given the past acts of the Imperador, who would be foolish or presumptuous enough to ask her or her father directly? They might quietly make their interest known, but to actually ask?"

"Then how did you come to dance with her if you couldn't ask?"

"The Imperador requested me, as he did with every other man with whom she danced. I wouldn't put it quite that way, for your sake, not mine, if you intend to write a story. I doubt the Imperador would be displeased if you wrote that all who danced with the Lady Delehya did so with his permission."

"What's she like?"

"She's intelligent, attractive, witty, and very perceptive. She also dances well."

"And you're not pursuing her? Why not?"

"I'm interested in someone else. Whether that will work out remains to be seen. I do know that whoever marries Delehya will need to be fully attentive to all her needs and those of her family."

"You have an interesting way of putting it, Councilor."

"Practical, I'd like to think."

"So who will she marry?"

"Whoever satisfies her needs and meets the requirements of her family. Since I don't know all those needs, I'd rather not speculate."

"So you don't know?"

"As I said, Reimer, I'm not about to speculate. I've found that certain speculations aren't worth pursuing, but then, I'm not a newshawk."

"I wasn't asking for speculation," replied Daarkyn.

"What else do you want to know?"

"What else are you doing?"

"The Waterways Committee is working on standardizing the basis of port fees and services across Guldor." Ysella offered a brief summary.

"That actually sounds worthwhile. What else?"

"If you stop by on Unadi, I'll have a copy of the committee hearing schedule for the next month waiting for you if I'm not available."

"Thank you." The newshawk stood. "I'll talk to you again at some point."

Once Daarkyn left, Ysella went back over what he'd said, but he couldn't recall anything damaging Daarkyn might put in print. *Or so you hope.*

With all the digging the newshawk had done, Ysella expected that Daarkyn had discovered Ysella's harbor property and was fishing for something else so that he could bring up the possible link between Faarn and Ysella in an unfavorable or at least sensational way.

Since there wasn't anything he could do about Daarkyn, he turned his attention back to the committee hearings, deciding as he did that he needed to attend evening services. *Not that the Almighty will do anything about Daarkyn or the Imperador except complicate matters.*

At less than a sixth after third afternoon bell, Ysella walked out of the Council Hall and climbed into the chaise.

"Long day, sir?" asked Caastyn, easing the chaise onto Council Avenue heading east.

"Not especially, except for the time endured with that newshawk Daarkyn—a third of a bell that felt like three." Ysella chuckled. "I'm not looking forward to attending services, but now that I'm well enough . . ."

"You shouldn't walk to services, yet, sir," said Caastyn.

"I hate to impose more on you."

Caastyn laughed. "I'm well paid, and you're considerate. Besides, right now, you'd have trouble dealing with a cutpurse, and if you slipped on a patch of ice, that wouldn't help your ribs."

"I won't argue." Ysella resigned himself to the fact that Caastyn was right.

Once he got home, he went to his study, where he found a letter posted from Aloor, in a feminine-looking hand he didn't immediately recognize. While he doubted it was from Aelyn Wythcomb, he couldn't think who else in Aloor might have his home address.

He opened the letter and glanced at the signature—that of Jaeralyn—and hoped that she wasn't reporting bad news.

Dominic—

No, I'm not writing about bad family news, but I thought you should know that Legrand Quaentyn died on Furdi. He'd gotten a bad flux, and his lungs were weak. Both his daughters were with him. Maergot asked me to let you know because she knew her father and you were close. She and Hayley so appreciated the fact that you made time to see him and write him long after he stopped practicing.

Ysella swallowed and lowered Jaeralyn's letter. He'd known that Legrand had become more frail, but not frail enough to die from a lung flux.

After a time, he read the rest of Jaeralyn's letter, with assorted family news. He smiled faintly at one section.

> *... the other day Ennika declared that she wanted to come to Machtarn and visit you. She also said you told her I needed to come with her. Unlike some her age, she doesn't twist the truth ...*

Since he had some time before services, he wrote a reply to Jaeralyn, thanking her for letting him know about Legrand, for confirming Ennika's honesty, and for including the married names and addresses of Maergot and Hayley.

By then, it was almost time to leave for evening services, and he made his way out to the drive where Caastyn waited with the chaise.

"You all right, sir?" asked Caastyn.

"I'm all right . . . the letter was from Jaeralyn. She wanted to let me know about the death of an old friend. Legrand Quaentyn. He taught me the law, and we've kept in touch for years. I knew he was getting weaker, but he'd seemed in good health when I saw him last month. I didn't expect . . . this so soon."

"I'm sorry, sir. Sometimes . . . more times than we'd like . . . life doesn't seem fair."

For some reason, Ysella thought of Sollem Faarn, who'd gotten away with such unfairness for so long. "Sometimes, it doesn't."

Ysella climbed into the chaise and settled himself.

"I'm glad you decided not to walk to services," said Caastyn as he guided the chaise down the lane to Averra Place, past the other houses on the cul-de-sac, and turned east on Camelia Avenue.

Before that long, Caastyn brought the chaise to a halt outside the Trinitarian chapel, its gray walls and slate roof somehow reinforcing Ysella's somber mood.

When Ysella got out, Caastyn said, "I'll be back in less than a bell. If I'm not here, please don't start walking back, sir."

"I won't," replied Ysella, appreciating the concern in Caastyn's voice.

Once he entered the chapel, Ysella settled into his reserved area of the pew, at the rear and to the side, listening to the harpsichord, his thoughts going back to the times he'd worked for and with Legrand Quaentyn and recalling how much he learned.

Shortly, Presider Haelsyn, in his plain green cassock, stepped forward into the front center of the sanctuary and the harpsichord died away.

"Let us offer thanks to the Almighty for the days that have been and for those to come, through his love, power, and mercy . . ."

Ysella half followed the service, making the appropriate responses long since learned by rote until the time came for Haelsyn to deliver his homily.

"We stand at the verge of spring, yet patches of snow remain on the ground in places, and there is no certainty that the warmth bringing new growth to light will arrive by the calendar or be displaced by chill upon occasion. That is the way of life. For all that we strive to create certainty and consistency, uncertainty and inconsistency remain. The only certainty lies in the Almighty Trinity of Love, Power, and Mercy, and in our efforts to create more love in an often cruel and evil world . . ."

Ysella wondered if the efforts by the individual councilors might at least mute the potential evil of an unchecked Imperador.

He was still musing over that when he stood to leave the chapel and Presider Haelsyn approached him.

"Councilor, we're so glad to see you. We appreciate your efforts to bring justice to Machtarn, but I worried that your absence foreshadowed continued ill health or worse."

"Fractured ribs have limited my movements, Presider, but they're healing and you'll once more have to endure my less than tuneful singing."

"Your presence alone is welcome, Councilor. I trust you will not find it amiss if I sent a copy of the article about you to Presider Maabak. Since we share your presence, I felt he should know, and I have no way of telling whether the newssheets in Aloor would print anything."

"Thank you. That was very thoughtful."

Haelsyn smiled ruefully. "Presiders also need to practice what they preach. Do take care, Councilor." Then he turned.

Ysella walked slowly from the chapel and out into the chill evening to where Caastyn waited with the chaise.

"How was the service?"

"Thoughtful. The presider made a point of meeting me afterward. He expressed appreciation for what I did, but suggested I take care in the future." Ysella climbed into the chaise.

"I'd agree with him."

"I agree with both of you," replied Ysella wryly. *Whether it's possible and whether care will be enough remains to be seen.*

45

ON Findi, the last calendar day of winter, after donning the new body armor, Ysella spent some time talking to Jaster, then saddled the gelding, led him from the stable, and mounted—carefully. After that, he took a short ride. The riding presented no challenges, nor did the silk and leather armor, but mounting and dismounting felt uncomfortable, and definitely painful at times, enough so that Ysella decided he'd need to take the chaise to the Council Hall for another week.

After the time with Jaster, he returned to his study and wrote letters of condolence to Legrand's daughters, before resuming refinement of his three amendments to the proposed Coal Act. That took most of the rest of the day.

At breakfast on Unadi, Ysella looked cautiously at the *Tribune,* but found no stories bearing Daarkyn's name or influence, or any stories of import to the Council or Aloor.

Ysella and Caastyn left the house at a third past second bell, riding through a light fog that largely dissipated by the time Caastyn halted the chaise at the Council Hall.

"Third bell," said Ysella as he exited the chaise, once more carrying his leather case, containing, among other papers, the final drafts of his amendments.

"I'll be here," replied Caastyn.

Ysella grinned. "I'm sure of that. I'll try my best not to make you wait." Then he headed to the entrance.

When he entered the office, the two clerks looked up with mild surprise, and Khaard said, "You're earlier today, sir."

"I'm getting better, and working my way back to a full day." Ysella stopped in front of Khaard's desk, adding, "Before I go over the letters, Lyaard, I have three amendments to the upcoming coal bill that I'll need copied for councilors, along with a brief description of each."

Seeing the concern in the eyes of his senior clerk, as Ysella opened his case and took out the sheets of paper, he said, "The actual text is comparatively short, and the explanation of each amendment is a moderate paragraph long, but I want you and Paatyr to put everything aside to get these done and sent out. I'll also need five copies of the amendments and explanations." Besides the three that had to go to the Council Clerk, Ysella needed two, just in case. "I only got a copy of the bill last Furdi. It's something the new Natural Resources administrator is pushing at the behest of the Imperador." *Or he wants everyone to think that*, but Ysella wasn't about to say that aloud.

"If I'm not presuming too much, sir, Administrator Zaenn did not leave the best impression with Paatyr and me."

"From what little I saw, he's not likely to impress anyone, except possibly with the extent of his arrogance, but saying so outside the office will not serve any of us well. It's better to leave the impression to Sr. Zaenn himself." Ysella paused, then asked, "Do you have any questions?"

"No, sir. Not at present."

Ysella smiled wryly. "As always, if you think I've misstated something or made an error, please let me know immediately."

Khaard smiled in return. "We can do that, sir."

"Excellent." Then Ysella made his way to his own desk.

After hanging up his overcoat, he addressed the short pile of revised letters, signing each, and adding a postscript to two. Then he began to read the new letters. The first two were from landors still unhappy with what they felt was Ysella's inability to obtain more waterways funds. Another requested a lift of the usury cap. Several pointed to the need to lower or change the seal tax, and three more anonymous letters demanded that the Council rein in the excesses of the Imperador. A letter pleading for the improvement of the poorhouses was balanced by one demanding their abolition because they drained the resources of hardworking men, whether crafters, commercers, or landors.

When he finished reading the letters, he sat behind the desk, his eyes going to the window, and thinking how seldom anyone ever wrote approving what he or the Council did. Sighing, he turned his attention to the legislative calendar.

46

TRIDI morning, Ysella and Caastyn reached the Council Hall at a sixth before third bell.

"Third bell again," said Ysella as he exited the chaise, carrying his leather case for papers.

Caastyn nodded in reply.

As Ysella walked from the chaise into the building, he wondered if and when he might get a letter from Aelyn Wythcomb, then pushed the thought aside. He had no doubt his unexpressed wishes would have little or no effect, and worrying would change nothing.

Both clerks were still sorting correspondence when Ysella stepped into the outer office, but Khaard looked up. "No messages so far, sir. There are some corrected responses on your desk, and some of today's letters are ready for you to read."

"Thank you." Ysella walked into his personal office, took off his overcoat, and settled behind the desk, first addressing the corrected responses, which needed no changes and which he signed, before turning to the incoming correspondence.

Within moments, he came across a letter from Haalas Mauryn.

Councilor Ysella—

As you may recall, when we talked over your time in Aloor during Winterfirst, I mentioned the problems the banque has encountered with the interest cap set as low as it is. I know you're busy, but I would hope that you are giving the matter some attention, if you have not already.

In talking with others over the past weeks, I've also learned that a representative of an industrial concern out of Devult, Duffay & Lybraan, I believe, spent some time in Aloor while you were here. He did not visit the banque, however, and I wondered if you might have run across him or heard anything, given that you do have the proclivity to meet with a great range of individuals during Council recesses . . .

Ysella smiled faintly as he put the letter to one side—until later in the day, when he'd have a better idea of how the Commerce Committee might handle the usury matter. At least he'd be able to tell Mauryn that he'd met with the committee and introduced proposed legislation. Then he continued reading letters until it was time to leave.

Ysella reached the doors to the Commerce Committee hearing room less than a sixth before fourth morning bell, where one of the committee aides escorted him to the witness table in front of the dais.

Klempt sat in the center of the dais desk, but turned from his conversation to instruct, "Just take the seat. This is a meeting, not an official hearing. We'll begin in a few moments."

Ysella settled himself behind the table.

Klempt spoke a few words to Aksyl Haarst, on his right, then straightened and rapped the gavel. "The committee will come to order." He paused before continuing, "I invited Councilor Ysella to speak to the committee this morning for two reasons. First, despite all the complaints about the problems with the current cap on usury rates, he was the first to introduce a bill that would raise the cap. Second, his district is, shall I say, emphatically not commercer-dominated." After a moment, Klempt then said, "If you would, Councilor."

"Thank you, Sr. Chairman. When I returned to Aloor in Winterfirst, I had no thoughts about the usury cap. I make a practice of talking to as many people as possible in my district, and a wide range of people all remarked on the problems caused by the current cap . . ." Without naming individuals, Ysella mentioned various specifics, such as the textile mill that wasn't being built, and how the low rate encouraged investments in land and raised land prices.

When he finished what he'd prepared, he added, "I'd be open to questions."

Haarst immediately said, "Councilor, how many other districts do you think might be similar to yours and why?"

"I couldn't give you a number, but I know from various sources that Nuile and Daal face many of the same problems. An industrial glazing concern in Devult sent a representative to scout the southeast of Guldor for opportunities. I spent a good bell talking to him, and his assessment was that there was little commercial development in that area except in port cities."

"How familiar are you in any depth with these conditions?" asked Graandeyl Raendyr, a commercer from Obaan.

"My family has been in Aloor for generations," began Ysella, trying not to smile as he saw Klempt stifle a grin, "and I worked as a water legalist for several years before becoming a councilor. As a result, I know something about most of the properties in Aloor. Because my office was in the center of Aloor, I also keep in touch with most of those involved in commerce."

"It would seem to me that investing in land would not be the wisest course," observed Raendyr.

"It might not be, but Aloor offers few other opportunities for modest investments, and few individuals or families have the resources for large investments."

"How representative do you think a smaller district like Aloor is?" pressed Haarst.

"It's representative of other small districts," replied Ysella, getting the impression that Haarst was skeptical of increasing the usury cap.

"Do you think small districts are a good measure of whether the cap should be increased, since they don't have much commercial activity?" asked Haamlyn Commodus, from Kathaar.

"The impact on them shouldn't be ignored," Ysella responded.

The questions went on for slightly less than a bell, when Klempt rapped the gavel and said, "It appears that the questions are becoming repetitive, and I'd like to thank Councilor Ysella for sharing his information." He looked at Ysella. "Since the committee will now go into closed session, you may leave, Councilor. We appreciate your candor."

"Thank you. I appreciate being able to contribute to your findings." Ysella stood and left the hearing room. As he walked away from the committee room, he puzzled over the veiled antagonism from Haarst and Raendyr, whom he barely knew and seldom encountered.

When he returned to his own office, he looked to Khaard. "Did anything of interest arrive in my absence?"

The senior clerk smiled. "Not much, sir, unless you consider a sealed envelope delivered by a Palace messenger. It's on your desk."

"That might be of slight interest," returned Ysella with a smile. He walked to his personal office and lifted the envelope, slitting it carefully to preserve the seal. *It might make a pleasant memento . . . if you survive the coming year.*

Then he read:

*The Imperador and the Imperadora
are pleased to request your presence
at
a reception and dinner honoring
their daughter,
the Lady Delehya,
on the seventeenth of Springfirst
at half past fifth bell.*

Ysella smiled as he noted no request for a response. The Imperador's request was tantamount to an order. He replaced the heavy card in the envelope and slipped it into his leather case.

Then he seated himself behind the desk and took out paper and pen so he could write the rough draft of his response to Haalas Mauryn, updating the banker that the Commerce Committee at least discussed raising the interest cap and telling him that, for better or worse, he had introduced the first actual proposal to do so. He'd have to confine his report on the agent of the glaziers to what Sr. Wydham had confirmed. While the fact that Duffay & Lybraan might be involved with developing a steam pump might help Aelyn Wythcomb, that was Ysella's inference, and his mentioning a mere inference might well backfire on Aelyn. That was not something he wanted to chance.

Just after first afternoon bell, Khaard announced that Councilor Raathan wished to see him, and Ysella called out, "Come on in."

Raathan closed the door to Ysella's personal office, then took one of the chairs.

"You're looking serious, Georg."

"I am. I read through your amendments, then wrestled a copy of the draft Coal Act from Stron Thaalyr. I can see why you drafted those amendments, but those issues should have been handled by the committee. That bill looks like it was drafted by one of the big mines."

"It probably was," replied Ysella, relating the note from Thaalyr and also his meeting with Carsius Zaenn.

"The way that's drafted," replied Raathan, "quite a few landors will suffer, and that doesn't count the smallholders. Althan Gregius—he's a friend of my father—has extensive lands southwest of Eshbruk. Six years back, a coal wastewater impoundment failed after a heavy rain in a wet spring. All the fish in the stream and a lot of the streamside plants died, and what fish replaced them are all small trash too poisoned to eat. Several fields bordering the stream still haven't recovered. That was six years ago. Althan lost a lot that year and the next, but he's got other lands. The damage wiped out smallholders along the stream. The mine owner said he wasn't liable for weather damage."

"I didn't know about that, but a tailings pond at a tin mine in Aloor partly failed. It happened in an area too rugged for pasture, but I thought that might happen elsewhere."

"With all the new mines opening," said Raathan, "it's going to happen again. I've sent a short letter to my committee, and likely they'll all back your amendments. I wanted to thank you, and let you know."

"I appreciate it."

Raathan stood. "We're all getting tired of the Imperador's functionaries pushing this sowshit at us."

"Be helpful if we could rein them in."

"We'd be behind that, too, if you can come up with something."

Ysella chuckled. "I'll let you know."

Raathan smiled, then turned and departed.

Maybe Detruro can pull off a restructuring of government.

47

ON Furdi, when Ysella sat down at his desk in the Council Hall, he was pleasantly surprised to find a letter from Bruuk Fettryk. Although Bruuk didn't write often, Ysella knew he'd written the legalist from his house address and wondered why Bruuk had sent his letter to the Council address.

> Dominic—
> I know I'm probably a little late. I had to send this to your office because in the move from town to the holding, I somehow misplaced your home address, but I wanted you to know, in case you didn't already, that Legrand Quaentyn died about a week ago from a harsh flux.
> As we both know, he was more than a legalist. He was a scholar of the law and a fine man. I'll miss stopping by his house and talking with him. Even though he wasn't actively practicing, he never lost touch with the legal happenings in and around Aloor. You'll be amused, and I've probably mentioned it before, but he told me more than once that Aloor hadn't had a decent water legalist since you left to become a councilor...
> You also might like to know that Gineen ran into Aelyn Wythcomb the other day. Aelyn asked Gineen if she and I knew you. They had a bit of a talk. Gineen promised Aelyn that she wouldn't divulge the details, but I gather Aelyn doesn't regard you unfavorably.

Ysella smiled faintly. If Aelyn had inquired about him, if quietly, that couldn't be too bad a sign, and he doubted Gineen would have said anything unfavorable.

But you never know how people respond to information. Still ...

After reading the letter, Ysella placed it in his case to take home. He couldn't help thinking about Aelyn, although he kept telling himself it was early for a reply from her.

After several moments, he shifted his weight in his chair and read through the official letters. By the time he dealt with all of the mundane correspondence, it was almost time to go to the Council chamber. On the way, he stopped by the Council Clerk's office, where he provided the necessary copies of his amendments to the coal bill, then continued on to the Council chamber. He arrived there about a sixth before noon and took his seat beside Staeryt.

"You're not walking as stiffly," said the older councilor.

"Not every step twinges anymore," replied Ysella.

"The newssheets haven't run any stories about Faarn lately."

"Not for the last week," commented Ysella sardonically.

"What do you think happened to him? Do you think he's in Devult? The newssheets said his family was there."

"I wonder if he had a family. The newssheet was cautious, saying that they reportedly lived most of the year near Devult." Ysella glanced around, then lowered his voice and asked, "How well do you know Graandeyl Raendyr and Aksyl Haarst?"

"Passingly well, why?"

"Raendyr was somewhat snide and condescending when I met with the Commerce Committee, and Haarst wasn't much better."

"You didn't mention that."

"I'm sorry. Oskaar wanted me to tell the committee why I'd introduced a bill to raise the usury cap."

"Oh . . . was that what you two were talking about a while back?"

"It was."

Staeryt shook his head, then grinned. "That sounds more like something a commercer would do."

"What too many people don't seem to get is that the cap hurts the wealthiest the least. They still make marks, just not as many."

"You're right," agreed Staeryt, "but people don't like to hear about anything that puts more marks in the wallets of the wealthy."

"Back to my first question. Do you have any idea why Raendyr would come across so condescendingly?"

"Besides the fact that he's often like that for seemingly no reason?"

"Thank you. I wondered if he had something against water legalists or broken-down royalty."

"With him, the royalty part might get his approval, that is, if he knew any history." Staeryt glanced toward the dais.

As the chime sounded, Maatrak walked to the lectern. "The Council will be in order. The immediate business before the Council is consideration of an Act to Amend the Bankruptcy Act. I yield to the chairman of the Commerce Committee."

Oskaar Klempt took the three side steps to the dais and walked to the lectern. "The act before the Council would establish limits on the fees charged by legalists in handling matters of bankruptcy. It has come to the attention of the Council that the legal fees charged have often exceeded the total assets of the bankrupt . . ."

Ysella nodded, having seen that very thing occur in Aloor.

Klempt spoke in favor of the bill for a sixth of a bell. No one rose to oppose it, and Maatrak called for the vote.

Slightly less than a bell later, Detruro announced the results. "Forty-two voting in favor, seven against, and one abstaining, the Act to Amend the Bankruptcy Act is passed." After a brief hesitation, he went on. "There being no other matters at present, the Council is adjourned until Duadi at noon." He rapped the gavel once.

Ysella wondered which seven councilors opposed the amendment, and why, but doubted he'd ever know.

"That was relatively painless," declared Staeryt as he rose from behind his small desk.

"This time," replied Ysella.

He stood and followed Staeryt from the Council chamber.

Outside the chamber stood Georg Raathan, clearly waiting for Ysella. "Do you have a moment, Dominic?"

"As many as you need."

"I couldn't help but overhear some of what you said to Ahslem. Do you really think removing the usury cap is a good idea?"

"I'm not in favor of removing it. My bill proposes lifting it to six parts on a hundred."

"That's doubling it."

Ysella shook his head. "Most banques won't go anywhere near that, but that's a risk. Right now, people from elsewhere are coming to Aloor and buying up land, and driving up the prices in order to profit. Combine that with the seal tax, and the poor smallholders are being driven out, and more landors than I realized." *One of whom might be my cousin.* "I'd rather have the speculators make money building mills or coming up with better ways to do things."

"I'll have to think about it."

"That's all I can ask."

As Raathan walked away, Ysella half wondered how he'd become an advocate for something the commercers wanted, but worried about pressing for.

He resumed his walk back to his office, where he'd doubtless need to read and sign more letters.

By third afternoon bell, Ysella was already at the Council Hall doors, waiting for Caastyn.

When Ysella climbed into the chaise, Caastyn turned and said, "One of the few times you've been waiting for me. Long day?"

"In a way . . . in a way. Is everything all right with you?"

"Can't complain. I finally got the carpenter to reinforce the rim joists next to the stable door and straighten the studs."

"So the door doesn't slant anymore?"

"So far, anyway. We'll see."

"Anything else?"

"You got an invitation from someone . . . and a letter from Aloor. Might be the one you're looking for." Caastyn didn't hide his amusement.

"Well . . . I'll have to see."

Once Ysella returned home, he forced himself to hang up his overcoat before making his way to the study. He immediately recognized Aelyn's hand, but set aside that envelope. He didn't want to be distracted by wondering about the other, card-sized envelope, which did indeed contain an invitation, if informal.

> *Alaaxi and I hoped you could join us for dinner next Quindi—the eleventh—for a simple dinner with acquaintances from Veerlyn around fifth bell. There are no unattached ladies involved, young or otherwise, and no obligations . . .*

The note was signed by Junae.

As he set the note to the side, Ysella smiled, knowing that he'd enjoy the dinner, and Presider Haelsyn wouldn't miss him that much.

Then he looked at the envelope from Aelyn and slit it open, carefully extracting the single sheet, and began to read.

> *Councilor Ysella—*
> *Although I presently am not in need of counsel, I find your wish to continue our correspondence agreeable. I must advise you, however, that I can be less than tactful upon occasion . . .*

Ysella smiled at her polite reprimand, given that she'd only asked for permission to write for counsel and he'd used that as an opening.

> *. . . That being so, I find I must ask why you wish to exchange letters with a widow whose only assets are slightly more than half of a*

currently unproductive tin mine, an overlarge dwelling in need of repair, and a tongue, or pen, that is not always flattering, particularly to those who show little respect. I have no other significant assets and little interest in meaningless mannerisms and conversation or correspondence of equal vapidity. I am also not given to meaningless praise or compliments.

For those reasons, I would appreciate reading your words as to why you have worked so diligently, and, I am told, occasionally even effectively, in a position that appears to have but a slight impact upon our lives.

I do look forward to your response.

Anticipatorily yours,
Aelyn Wythcomb

Ysella read the letter a second time. He couldn't say that he was surprised. He also understood that Aelyn wasn't interested in any man who couldn't think or wouldn't listen. *Or one who can't explain why he sought a position most thought meaningless. But she did write "anticipatorily yours," which suggests she is interested, if warily.*

What Bruuk had written confirmed that wariness, but Ysella certainly understood that a woman who'd been forced into one marriage would not want to enter another relationship that might lead to marriage, not when she didn't have to, and not without doing some extensive checking.

He was deep in thought when Caastyn knocked on the study door and said, "Dinner is ready, sir."

"Thank you." Ysella rose and followed Caastyn to the dining room, where all three seated themselves.

Ysella saw and smelled the crusty buried-beef pie and the fresh-baked rolls and smiled.

Gerdina looked at Ysella, as if to ask, without saying so, if he would like to offer a blessing.

"I would." He cleared his throat. "Almighty Trinity of Love, Power, and Mercy, we thank you for the life we lead, the shelter we have, and those we love. Most of all, we thank you for the blessings bestowed on us by others, by their words and deeds, and often by their silent support and care in our times of need. We humbly ask you to bless the companionship we share and the food we will partake, in the name of the Three in One."

"I haven't heard that one before," said Gerdina.

"I hadn't realized some of it before," replied Ysella quietly, before serving Gerdina, Caastyn, and then himself.

"It looks like you got another letter from that Ritten in Aloor," said Caastyn, with the hint of a smile.

"From Aelyn Wythcomb," Ysella admitted. "She agreed to correspond with me only as an equal, so long as I refrained from meaningless nothings, and if I could explain to her satisfaction why I feel what I'm doing as a councilor is worthwhile. She was quite clear that she is a widow whose only material goods are half of a currently unusable tin mine and an overlarge dwelling in need of repair."

"Sounds like she'd be good for you," said Caastyn, "if you could take the honesty all the time."

"Most men can't," added Gerdina, with an amused look at her husband, "no matter what they say."

"Not all the time," replied Caastyn cheerfully.

Hearing Caastyn's tone of voice, Ysella couldn't help chuckling.

48

WHILE Ysella wrote an immediate and thoughtful response to Bruuk Fettryk, he decided not to rush himself in replying to Aelyn, which turned out for the better, as Quindi brought more correspondence, and more replies, from portmasters. Several had pointed complaints about not wanting the Council telling portmasters what to do. Ysella spent more time than he wished writing explanations that the Council was only gathering information, in an effort to discover how to make more Guldoran ports attractive, since so many Guldoran ports charged differing amounts for differently described services.

While that was a half-truth at best, he was growing tired of seemingly every portmaster insisting his system was the best. Despite all the geographic and weather differences, he had the impression that certain ports required payments for services some vessels didn't need, or for as long as they were required to pay, and excessive fees didn't encourage trade. He also had the feeling that Guldoran shipping interests essentially controlled at least three ports, because they charged foreign vessels far, far more than they did Guldoran vessels.

First thing after breakfast on Findi, Ysella headed for the stable, where he groomed Jaster, then saddled the gelding—a painful process—and mounted. He took a short ride, but after dismounting and unsaddling Jaster, he decided trying to ride to the Council Hall wasn't yet the best of ideas.

When he returned to the house, slightly after midmorning, he attempted a reply to Aelyn.

Again, it took several laborious drafts before he had something that he felt addressed her questions, without over- or understating why he became a councilor and why he remained one. But then, he'd always felt more comfortable writing about less personal matters.

He reread the letter once more.

Ritten Wythcomb—
  Your letter arrived on Furdi, and I've delayed in replying because Quindi turned out to be busier than usual at the Council Hall, and

because I wish to offer my thoughts with the same grace and candor with which you presented yours.

First, I must compliment you on your tactful reprimand of my taking the liberty of writing you when you had not asked for my counsel. I did not wish to wait for such a letter from you because that would have failed to convey my interest in learning more about you.

When I came to your dwelling in Winterfirst, my sole intent was to inform you of my discoveries. I had no other intentions. But after our brief conversation, I was taken with your obvious intelligence, wit, and strength of purpose. Since you were in mourning, and indirectly reminded me of such, my next letters were strictly about water rights and related matters. Only after what I estimated was the end of the usual mourning period did I attempt to contact you on what I hope will become a more personal basis.

You asked why I have devoted so much of my recent life to being an "occasionally" effective councilor when the Council "appears to have but a slight impact upon our lives."

That is a fair question, but what appears to be slight to those unfamiliar with the Council can be deceiving. While the Council has little power at present to restrain the powers of the Imperador, the powers he delegated to the Council under the Establishment Act do, in fact, have more than a slight impact. Otherwise, why would some in Aloor be pressing me to use my position as chairman of the Waterways Committee to allocate more funds for waterway improvement in my district? Even while obtaining more funds for Aloor, I have tried not to use what influence I have to the detriment of other districts, but did my best to work with other members of the committee to work out as fair an allocation as possible with the funds available for waterways.

The needs of a land and its people will always be greater than the funds a government can obtain without oppressing its people. Choosing how and where those funds are used is the responsibility of the Council and its councilors. At times, as we both know, the laws of Guldor are not what they should be, but the Council endeavors to make improvements. Sometimes we are successful, sometimes not, but initial unsuccessful efforts often lay the groundwork for later success.

When I was a practicing water legalist in Aloor, I could only advise people on the law and tell them their options, even when the *choices they faced were not for the best. As a councilor, I have some small ability to improve the law, not just to interpret it, and I will continue that effort so long as I am able.*

I trust this letter will at least begin to answer your questions.

With warmest wishes

Ysella took a deep breath and signed.

49

As he ate breakfast and read the *Tribune* on Duadi morning, Ysella could hardly miss the lead story.

ATACAMAN WARSHIP SINKS GULDORAN CUTTERS

Last Tridi, the Atacaman two-deck galleon *Spritefire* sank two Guldoran cutters as they returned from operations against pirate isles in the Gulf of Nordum. The *Spritefire* outraced the Guldoran warship *Suvionax* to reach the safety of Port Lenfer . . .

First Marshal Solatiem did not respond to inquiries about the comparative lack of speed of Guldoran first-rate ships of the line . . .

Ysella grimaced at the beginning of the second paragraph, because it was clear the *Tribune* would continue to press the issue of seemingly unnecessary first-rate ships of the line, until the Imperador shut down the newssheet or the *Tribune* came up with another issue. There was always the unfortunate possibility that such an issue might be Ysella's involvement with Sollem Faarn.

Since Ysella could do nothing about that, he took another sip of café and the last bites of his eggs and ham strips, then rose and finished readying himself for the day.

As Ysella left the house and walked to the waiting chaise, he hoped that, by the following Unadi, he could resume riding to the Council Hall.

Once he was in the chaise headed toward Imperial Boulevard, he said, "This afternoon the Council will be in session until at least fourth bell. I'd suggest half past fourth bell."

"Something important?" asked Caastyn.

"It's the coal bill I mentioned earlier, and I'm offering amendments."

"Will enough councilors support them?"

"The bill is so bad that they might, but the votes will tell."

Caastyn snorted.

Neither said much more on the ride, but when Ysella left the chaise, Caastyn said, "Half past fourth bell."

"If I'm not here, it shouldn't be that long." Then Ysella headed for the building doors.

On entering his office at half before third bell, he asked, "Lyaard, have there been any messages this morning?"

"No, sir. Not a one."

Ysella frowned. Were he and Raathan the only ones concerned about the coal bill? Usually, there were some messages about major pending legislation.

You're doing what you can.

Sitting at his desk, he turned his attention to letters and responses. When he finished with them, he still had a little time before leaving for the Council chamber. For another third, he studied the legislative calendar and made some notes.

Before he left, Ysella made sure he had copies of the amendments in his case, though he knew they likely wouldn't be needed.

He took his seat in the chamber a sixth before noon.

Caanard was the next committee chairman to appear, and he stopped in front of Ysella's desk. With a sardonic smile, he said, "Are you trying to get attacked again? You're not fully recovered from your last legal foray."

"Some chairmen do their job. Some don't."

"And you're trying to do Stron's job for him?"

Ysella shook his head. "Just the part that applies to water and waterways."

"Makes sense when you put it that way. I suspect the Natural Resources Administrator won't be pleased."

"Neither will the miners who don't want to clean up their messes, most likely, but they won't pay any attention unless the amendments are adopted and become law."

"They'll blame you. Aren't you the fortunate one." Caanard turned and took his seat beside Staeryt.

Unless I'm right about Zaenn bluffing about the Imperador's support. But Ysella only nodded.

"What do you think of the coal bill?" Ysella asked Staeryt.

"It's poorly written, despite Thaalyr's efforts to improve the language. It will also allow commerce types to do whatever they want—unless, of course, the Council adopts the amendments you and Raathan proposed. In that case, there's a good chance the Imperador will reject what the Council sends him."

"You're so optimistic, Ahslem," said Ysella sarcastically, if quietly.

"That's what the Imperador always does with what he doesn't like," replied Staeryt.

"True, but we only have Zaenn's word that the Imperador feels that strongly."

"I wouldn't count on the Imperador's disinterest."

Ysella refrained from replying as the floor leader strode to the lectern.

After calling the Council to order, Maatrak announced, "The matter before the Council is a proposed Act to Prescribe and Regulate the Use of Coal. The chairman of the Natural Resources Committee will speak to the bill."

Stron Thaalyr stepped to the lectern. "With the rapid growth in the number of coal mines in Guldor, the Natural Resources Administration has determined that an overall legal framework is necessary for a consistent system of mine regulation. Administrator Zaenn forwarded draft legislation, and the committee has held hearings and marked up the bill. The changes made were not substantive, but legal and procedural to ensure conformity with existing law . . ."

Ysella refrained from shaking his head at Thaalyr's weasel-worded admission that the committee had effectively accepted the administration's language. He listened as Thaalyr continued with procedural niceties.

When Thaalyr relinquished the lectern to Maatrak, the floor leader said, "Councilor Raathan will speak against the proposed act."

Raathan took the lectern, cleared his throat, and began, "The proposed act is far from what is needed to conform coal mines in Guldor to a standard that provides safety for miners and requires adequate financial resources and stability to assure proper operation of mines. To this end, I have registered two amendments to remedy the most egregious omissions from the proposed act. I will also note that the chairman of the Waterways Committee has registered three amendments to rectify the lack of standards for the handling of mining spoil and wastewater . . ."

When Raathan finished, Maatrak announced, "The chairman of the Waterways Committee will speak to his three amendments."

Ysella stood and walked to the dais. Once at the lectern, he began, "The amendments I offer are simple and basic. The first amendment clarifies that any and all coal mining spoil not be placed near rivers or streams or in any locale where rainfall would lead to drainage into rivers and streams. The second states that mine wastewater shall not be discharged into waterways and shall be retained in impoundments sufficiently strong to preclude failure. The third states that the owner of any mining facility shall be found liable for damages created by failure to follow the requirements of the Act, specifically those involving safety, mine wastes, and wastewater . . ."

When Ysella finished describing the amendments and the reasons for each, he surrendered the lectern to Maatrak.

Maatrak declared, "The first amendment offered is to preclude any mining venture that intrudes upon or under lands owned by another besides the entity operating the mine without the full written and authorized consent of the landholder. Does any councilor wish to speak against the amendment?" Maatrak scanned the floor, waited for several moments, then said, "Seeing no one wishing to speak against, the vote is on the first amendment. Councilors have one third in which to vote."

Ysella removed a blank vote card from the holder in his desk, marked it for the amendment, and then walked to the voting box and deposited it. After a third of a bell, the chime rang, and the clerks began the tally.

Less than a third later, the clerk handed the tally sheet to Maatrak, who announced, "Forty-two voting in favor, eight opposed, the amendment is adopted." He paused, then said, "The second amendment precludes the placement of coal-mining spoil near rivers or streams. Is there any councilor desiring to speak against the amendment?" Again, the floor leader paused. "Seeing none, the vote is on the amendment . . ."

The pattern was the same for the second through fifth amendments, with those in favor of each amendment between forty-one and forty-three councilors.

The vote on the proposed act, as amended, was forty councilors for the act, and nine opposed, all of whom were likely commercers, Ysella suspected, although one or two conceivably might have been crafters.

With the passage of the Coal Act, Detruro recessed the Council until noon on Furdi, and Ysella headed back to his office, surprised that it was only slightly past fourth bell.

That left him a third of a bell to go over responses prepared by Khaard and Jaasn before he left to meet Caastyn and the clerks began to close up the office for the day.

Caastyn was waiting when Ysella stepped out of the building, although it was before half past fourth bell.

"Any letters at the house?" Ysella asked when he climbed into the chaise.

"Just one." Caastyn grinned, then added, "But not from Ritten Wythcomb. It looks like your mother's hand."

"Considering most of the letters I get at the house are from her," Ysella noted with amusement, "that's a good possibility." Since Jaeralyn had written not that long ago, he did wonder what his mother had to report.

Still, once he was back at the house, after doffing his overcoat and hanging it up, he walked to his study, opened the envelope, and began to read.

Dominic—

We do hope you're recovering from those fractured ribs. I can remember when something similar happened to your father, but that was before you were born.

> *Everyone here is doing well, with one exception. One of the susceptibles stole a crossbow and shot and killed Kyranna. Obviously, she never saw it coming. I don't understand why the susceptible did it. Kyranna was never mean to any of the workers. She was forceful at times, but not cruel or mean. Haekaan took care of the wretch who killed her, but finding another reliable and good empath is going to be a problem.*
>
> *Kyranna wasn't at all like what your uncle Nathanyal asked of his empaths. He never could keep an empath for long, and I doubt Haarkyl will be able to, either. In his position, it's more that he can't afford a good empath, and a bad one is too costly in a different way.*

Ysella wondered why his mother avoided mentioning Caethya, or was it because, if she became an effective empath, she wouldn't work long for her family?

> *We've had more rain, but not enough to wash anything out, thank the Almighty, but we heard that Haarkyl wasn't so fortunate, not that he'd ever tell us. Nathanyal always used to complain about more rain. At least Haarkyl doesn't do that, but that's likely Saera's doing . . .*

Ysella finished the letter and laid it on the desk, wondering, as his mother clearly had, why any susceptible would attack Kyranna. She'd started working at the holding when he'd been around ten, and she'd always been polite. Her one daughter had also been an empath, but she'd left about the time Ysella had started his practice. He'd heard rumors, that Kyranna's daughter might have been one of those empaths who could use hate as a weapon, but they tended to be few and short-lived, which might have been why no one spoke of her.

For some reason, he thought of Delehya, who'd managed to conceal her ability, or at least to keep it from public view, even after the scurrilous rumors about her and Haarwyk. He wondered how she and Iustaan Detruro would work matters out between the two of them, especially if someone pointed out that such a marriage carried at least a distant possibility that Detruro could be Imperador.

He mulled it over until Caastyn told him dinner was ready.

50

On Furdi morning, Ysella took one sip of his breakfast café and opened the *Tribune*.

He couldn't miss the lead story.

OBAANAX LOST TO FIRESHIP ATTACK
Late in the day of Springfirst 2nd, under the cover of a light fog, the Atacaman navy sent three fireships to attack the Southern Fleet at Port Reale. Two of the fireships were diverted by Guldoran cutters. The third fireship struck the *Obaanax,* and the first-rate ship caught fire and was effectively destroyed . . .

Ysella wondered who the Imperador would blame for that disaster, but someone would pay. He had no doubt that Laureous would order the building of another first-rate ship. That would mean something more necessary for the welfare of some part of Guldor would suffer, because Ysella didn't see the Imperador doing anything to increase government revenues.

The only other story of interest was a short article noting that a brutal late-winter storm had destroyed or severely damaged port facilities at Endor, as well as flooded much of the area around the harbor.

And that will play havoc with next year's appropriations, unless we can find unused funds somewhere and reappropriate them.

After finishing breakfast and readying himself, he headed out of the house and climbed into the waiting chaise, glancing to the north, where light greenish-gray clouds seemed to be moving slowly toward Machtarn.

"Doesn't look like rain," he observed.

"The rains are usually heavier at the beginning of Springend," replied Caastyn. "Soon as I say that, though, we'll get a downpour tomorrow."

"We'll both forget you said it," said Ysella with a smile. "Just don't forget to post the letter to my mother."

"I've got it right here." Caastyn frowned. "I still can't believe a susceptible shot the holding empath."

"I've known some empaths who were so cruel that I couldn't believe they weren't killed, but Kyranna wasn't that type."

"Could be that they didn't fear her enough. I saw that in the Army. Some men don't respect anything but force."

Ysella nodded. *But with Haekaan's reaction, it might be a while before there's any trouble.*

When Caastyn brought the chaise to a halt outside the Council Hall, he asked Ysella, "Fourth bell?"

"That would be good. The Council will be in session, but there's only a bill changing certain tariffs on the schedule, and that shouldn't take long."

"I'll be here."

Ysella entered the Council Hall, but had not reached the top of the stairs to the second level when he saw Gaastyn Ditaero heading toward him. *Probably waiting for me.* Ysella stopped. "Good morning, Gaastyn. You're worried about the damage to the port at Endor, I take it?"

"Worried?" Ditaero's voice rose in pitch and volume. "I'm more than worried. That storm destroyed half the port facilities and inflicted severe damage on the rest. There's no way the port authority there can pay for all the repairs. Without funding, the port can only handle a third of what it normally does. Scores and scores of workers will be laid off or lose their jobs permanently. That doesn't count the damage to all the houses, shops, and businesses."

"That's obviously a serious problem. Have you any thoughts on how to deal with it?"

"Pass a supplemental appropriation. What else?"

"Do you have any idea how many marks it will take?"

"It could be over a hundred thousand marks."

"Where are we going to find the funds?" asked Ysella.

"Isn't that your job as chairman of the Waterways Committee?"

"We could take the waterways improvement funds for Endor and reappropriate them for the port repairs."

"That would cost jobs for the river workers. Can't you get funding elsewhere?"

"The Imperador has limited all funding to current and anticipated revenues. The Council's choices are to take funds from something else, or to request an exemption from the Imperador's limits to use the reserve funds. Right now, the Imperador may not be in the mood to authorize the use of reserve funds."

"Why not? He'd let a port that brings in marks be unable to operate for most of the ships that use it?"

"I didn't say that. The Imperador lost the *Obaanax* to the Atacamans, and we both know that the Imperador is quite fond of his first-rate ships."

"One ship he doesn't need or really use!"

"But a first-rate ship costs over fifty thousand marks, and that's only for the ship," Ysella pointed out.

"He'll get back more marks from the harbor than he'll ever get from a warship."

"We can make that point, and the Imperador might agree to free some funds, but the Premier will have to consider the matter, and, if he agrees, bring the matter up before the Council. The Council has to pass a bill requesting the use of reserve funds. Either way, the whole Council has to vote, either on that request or on authorizing reappropriating and deciding what programs or districts have to have funding cut."

"We haven't had to do that before."

"We haven't had the reserve funds frozen before."

"Can't you do something else?"

"I'll talk to the Premier about the possibilities, but I can't promise anything."

"You've always done your best, but that might not be good enough. Conditions in Endor are really bad."

"I'll do what I can, Gaastyn."

"I know," replied Ditaero, "but will the Imperador care?"

"We'll have to see."

Ditaero shook his head, then turned away.

As Ysella continued toward his office, he wondered if he should have been more encouraging. He shook his head. There was little point in getting Ditaero's hopes up, not with the way the Imperador had been behaving.

When Ysella reached his office, he stopped inside the door. "Is there anything urgent?"

"No, sir," replied Khaard.

"I'm going to see the Premier. I'll be back after that."

When Ysella reached the Premier's office, he had to wait almost a third before Taeryl Laergaan, the Imperial Administrator of Commerce, departed and Detruro motioned Ysella into his private office.

"What is it, Dominic?" Detruro did not motion for Ysella to sit, and Ysella didn't.

"You saw the newssheet story on the winter storm that hit Endor?"

"Storms are frequent there."

Detruro's flat tone warned Ysella, but there was little point in postponing the inevitable. "I was accosted by Gaastyn Ditaero. He was close to frantic. According to him, the storm was bad enough to destroy much of the port and damage the rest."

"Fleet Marshal Dhaantyn sent me a communiqué. He also noted that the damage won't measurably affect the Northern Fleet, since it operates out of Neewyrk and only occasionally ports in Endor."

"Gaastyn claims that only a third of the port is functioning. He's not in the habit of exaggerating. Leaving two-thirds of the port unusable would cost the Treasury fees, taxes, and tariffs. If we reallocate Waterways funds, that will cost jobs . . . and other tax revenues."

"How much will repairs cost?"

"According to Ditaero, over a hundred thousand marks. That's an estimate."

Detruro winced. "What did you tell him?"

"That I'd talk to you, but, one way or another, to get funds to repair the port facilities would likely take a Council vote, and that, after the loss of one of the Imperador's beloved first-rate ships, he might not be willing to authorize the use of reserve funds, even if the Council was."

"That accurately summarizes the situation. Given the extent of the damage, though, Ditaero has every right to request funds for that kind of devastation. I'll put a motion before the Council to request the Imperador allow the Council to appropriate a hundred thousand marks for rebuilding and repair, but only for port authority buildings, piers, wharfs, dock, and other basic structures and any necessary dredging."

"So that the Imperador can see that the Council isn't asking for funds for individuals or for what he'd call frills?"

"Exactly."

"Laergaan didn't look all that pleased when he left your office."

"He never is." Detruro smiled wryly. "He's worried about something you had a hand in."

"The usury cap?"

"And the fact that many councilors agree with you. Laergaan's not totally opposed to it, but Treasury Administrator Salaazar is violently opposed, and that worries Laergaan."

"Why?" asked Ysella. "If the Imperador allowed the increase, he could issue notes or bonds at a higher rate that the banques might prefer to purchase over other investments. That is, if the Imperador would allow borrowing. Except it might be more prudent to consider increasing revenues in some other fashion, but I suspect he doesn't like either option."

"The Imperador sent me a letter urging the Council to cut back on spending," said Detruro.

"We appropriated about the same as last year."

"Except the Palace spent more."

Ysella refrained from pointing out the obvious—that the Council had no control over what the Palace spent, although Laureous had been comparatively prudent until recently. The Heir was clearly less so. *Another thing that needs changing.* Ysella also wasn't about to inquire about Delehya's spending habits, but from what she'd worn to the Yearend Ball, he doubted that she inclined toward frugality.

"Is there anything else, Dominic?"

"Not at the moment."

"You look like you're more . . . comfortable. Is that the case, or are you handling it better?"

"I'm definitely better, but I still have to be cautious."

"That's good to hear." Detruro glanced past Ysella toward the door.

"I won't take any more of your time." Ysella nodded, then turned and left.

As he walked back to his office, he wondered why the Treasury Administrator was concerned about the usury cap, since the Treasury had essentially no debt. Could Salaazar be acting on behalf of land speculators who benefitted from the low rates? Or did Salaazar or his family have substantial debts? Or was there some other reason?

He snorted quietly. There were always other reasons.

By the time he was back in his office and behind his desk, there was a short stack of letters to read, and a larger stack of corrected responses to read and sign.

A good bell passed before Khaard appeared in the doorway. "Sir, Sr. Daarkyn would like a moment of your time."

While Khaard's voice remained even, Ysella had no trouble sensing the clerk's irritation, but he said, "I'll see him for a few moments."

In moments, Daarkyn sat in the chair directly facing Ysella, leaning back slightly as he began conversationally, "There are rumors that the Lady Delehya's betrothal will be announced shortly. I thought you might know something about it."

"I can't tell you more than I did the last time you asked."

"That suggests that you know something, Councilor."

Ysella had no trouble sighing loudly. "Reimer . . . if I don't know any more, then I can't tell you anything new. If I do know something that the Imperador does not wish to be divulged, then I also can't tell you anything new."

"About his daughter's possible marriage? That's a state secret?"

"Unless and until the Imperador is no longer the absolute ruler of Guldor, I'm not about to divulge anything he doesn't want divulged—assuming I know it in the first place."

Without blinking, Daarkyn asked, "Why were you asked to testify before the Commerce Committee? Usually, councilors don't actually testify."

"I didn't testify. I spoke to the Commerce Committee about why I introduced a proposal to raise the usury cap . . ." Knowing Daarkyn would press, Ysella gave a brief summary of his reasons.

"That's all?" Daarkyn's voice was openly skeptical.

"Apparently, I was one of the few landor councilors to favor an increase. I'd like to hope others follow my example."

"You're sounding more like a commercer."

"I'm not. Certain issues affect all of us, and it's foolish not to recognize them."

"You have a broader background than many landor councilors, but I'm still not certain what prompted you to investigate the late Sollem Faarn."

"Has someone found his body or some evidence he's dead? The last I heard he was presumed missing."

"Missing or dead, why did you pursue him?"

"I don't much like legalists who hurt or kill people and, on top of that, give honest legalists a bad name."

"I've wondered about why Faarn's men targeted both you and Smootn. From what I've determined, they couldn't have known you'd be there. They had to be looking for him. From their point of view, you made matters easier. But no one in the district legalist's office knew what you'd compiled. So who told Faarn? It had to be Smootn, and that meant Faarn was out to remove you both."

"That wouldn't have worked, except as revenge," replied Ysella. "I'd made copies of what I'd discovered and sent them to a number of legalists. Smootn knew that, but not whom precisely."

"You knew Smootn was working for Faarn, didn't you?"

"Not until the moment I was shot." *Not for certain.* "After that, I was in no condition to tell anyone. By then, the story already in the newssheets was that we were both targeted for revealing who and what Faarn really was." Ysella shrugged. "*That* was largely true. By the time I could have said anything, all I could have done was to make matters worse for Smootn's widow. Is that your intention?"

Surprisingly, at least to Ysella, Daarkyn shook his head. "On that narrow point, I agree with you, and it wouldn't serve me or the *Tribune* well, either. I was curious. I still think there's more to it."

"There doubtless is. A number of the property legalists had to have known for years that Gustov Torryl never appeared, but none of them ever said anything."

Daarkyn nodded. "They still won't." The newshawk stood. "Thank you for seeing me." He nodded, turned, and left.

Ysella sat quietly for several moments. He had no doubt that Daarkyn knew about his harbor properties, but couldn't quite make a connection . . . or if he could, he couldn't make it sensational enough. *Yet . . .*

Another question surfaced: Why hadn't Daarkyn asked anything about the amendments to the Coal Act? *Perhaps because he couldn't find anything remotely improper about the amendments?*

After a time, Ysella returned to work, then left the office to walk to the Council chamber, for a session that might be longer than he anticipated. The original schedule noted only the special tariff modification bill dealing with Atacaman vessels, but since seeking an exemption to release frozen reserve funds was a privileged motion, it would take precedence over the tariff bill.

Staeryt was already at his desk when Ysella seated himself. "I hear we're going to ask the Imperador for more funds to rebuild the port at Endor."

"I'm not surprised. Gaastyn told me about the damage this morning when I arrived."

"I don't know why they ever built a port," said Staeryt disparagingly. "There's almost nothing there."

"Except half the best timber in Guldor and no other effective way to transport it."

"Mere practicalities," chuckled Staeryt.

"And possibly more coal, according to Natural Resources Administrator Zaenn," said Ysella, "if those mines he wants don't divert all the water in the river."

"When will we find out if the Imperador rejected the Coal Act?" asked Staeryt.

"With all the amendments, I doubt if the clerks have finished engraving the final bill. So he won't get it before Findi at the earliest. Then Zaenn will have to read it, and the Council's amendments are buried in the procedural details. I'd say we'll have the Imperador's reaction next Duadi or Tridi. Even if they hurry, Unadi would be the earliest."

Both looked up as the chime rang and Detruro, rather than Maatrak, took the lectern. He waited for several moments before speaking.

"As some of you know, a severe winter storm struck the harbor at Endor, destroying or severely damaging two-thirds of the port . . ." Detruro summarized the extent of damage and the financial impact on local shops, businesses, and shippers, as well as the negative impact on Imperial finances. "For those reasons, the first order of business will be a vote on a request to the Imperador to allow the use of one hundred thousand marks from reserve funds for rebuilding vital port structures and facilities, and only for those purposes. Since this is a privileged motion, there will be no debate. Councilors have one third in which to vote."

Staeryt looked to Ysella. "What do you think?"

"Wouldn't you rather have more tariff and port revenues, and fewer people in the northeast starving, than another first-rate ship of the line?"

"Since you put it that way," said Staeryt sardonically as he pulled out a blank voting card.

In the end, thirty-seven councilors approved the request to the Imperador and two abstained. Ysella suspected that most of the eleven who voted against the measure were landors from inland districts, but that was only a guess.

"The next order of business," said Maatrak, from the lectern he'd taken after Detruro announced the previous vote, "is an amendment to the tariff code to raise the tariffs on all goods produced in Atacama or shipped in Atacaman vessels to one part in five of the assessed value. There are no amendments registered. Councilor Caanard will speak to the amendment."

Ysella found it interesting that Caanard was addressing the amendment, since Klempt was chairman of Commerce Committee, which suggested Klempt opposed the amendment. *But then, he's a commercer, through and through.*

Caanard took the lectern. "The Imperador requested this tariff not only to warn the Grande Duce that his tacit support of pirates using the Gulf of Nordum to attack and raid merchant vessels is unacceptable, but also to recoup the costs required to remove these pirate vessels and bases . . ."

When Caanard finished, Maatrak called for the vote.

Almost two-thirds of a bell later, Maatrak announced that the measure had passed by a vote of thirty-five in favor and fourteen opposed.

Ysella watched Klempt, whose stoic face bore little expression through the entire vote, supporting Ysella's impression of where Klempt stood on the tariff increase.

"There being no other business, the Council is recessed until noon on Duadi." Maatrak gave a perfunctory tap of the gavel.

Ysella stood, and approached Caanard. "I take it that the good chairman of the Commerce Committee is not overly enthused about tariff increases?"

"The good chairman, as you put it, feels the increased tariffs will cost Guldoran merchants dearly and will have little impact on Atacama."

"Do you think he's right?" asked Ysella.

Caanard offered a wryly amused smile. "Partly. It will hurt Guldoran importers who've been bringing in cheaper earthenware and other goods and profiting from the price difference. The Atacamans can't compete on higher-quality goods in the first place—except for some gemstones, and that's not a large market."

Ysella understood Caanard's smile. While Caanard came from a landor family, Patrice was from a well-off merchanter family and had definitely educated her husband on merchanting and trade. "So it wasn't worth fighting the Imperador on the bill?"

"Hardly."

"I thought the same, but you'd know more than I."

Caanard laughed softly, then said, "Until later."

Ysella nodded politely, then headed back to his office, knowing he'd have enough time to catch up on routine matters before leaving for the day, and preparing for dinner with Ramon and Leona Hekkaad. He still wondered why, after two years, Hekkaad decided to invite him for what sounded like an intimate dinner.

Even though Ysella left the Council Hall slightly before fourth bell, Caastyn was already waiting outside.

Ysella climbed into the chaise, commenting, "I'm sorry you have to drive me home and then out again tonight—"

Caastyn's laugh cut off Ysella's words. "Sir, men working for most families have to drive everywhere all the time. They'd love to have my position." He eased the chaise away from the Council Hall.

"Perhaps so far as driving and taking care of the horses," replied Ysella, "but I've required quite a bit beyond that."

"And you pay well," said Caastyn. "I know. I've compared. And our quarters are much better."

Ysella certainly hoped so, but he kept his reply to, "The clouds to the north are darker. Let's hope we don't get rain until after you pick me up."

"We might be fortunate. They're not moving much."

"No more letters today?" asked Ysella, not that he expected any.

"Not a one, sir."

Once Ysella was back at the house, he went over the monthly property management statement for Winterfirst that he'd received from Sullynd & Smarkaan, who deposited the rents in a separate property account at the Banque of Machtarn, but found nothing amiss.

Then he thought about what to wear to dinner. Since Hekkaad hadn't specified attire, Ysella decided what he wore was sufficient—a dark blue wool coat and trousers, with the lighter blue cravat. He did, however, wash up some before leaving the house.

On the quiet, chill ride, Ysella remained absorbed in his thoughts until Caastyn turned the chaise onto Crestview Place. The cul-de-sac off the north end of Pleasant Lane held exactly three dwellings, the third being the northernmost, a severe gray stone mansion with a semicircular drive leading up to the front entry steps as well as a side service drive.

"Imposing," said Caastyn.

"The dwelling belongs to the Argenti government and is used for official purposes, and not only for housing their envoy."

After Caastyn brought the chaise to a halt, Ysella got out. "I'd judge around second evening bell."

"I'll be here."

Ysella knew Caastyn would be early, but restricted himself to "Thank you." Then he took the steps up to the covered entry. A bronze plaque proclaimed LEGATION OF ARGENTAL on the gray stone wall beside the large single door. Ysella used the bronze knocker, and in moments a gray-haired woman in muted, black-trimmed silver livery opened the door.

"Good evening, Councilor." She stepped back. "Let me take your overcoat."

"Thank you."

After relieving himself of the heavy coat, he followed the woman to a small personal parlor, rather than a large receiving parlor or salon.

"It's good to see you!" said Ramon Hekkaad enthusiastically as he stood.

Leona smiled as well, but didn't rise from the armchair, although she said, "You hardly look like a man who almost died."

Ramon gestured to the armchair facing the pair he and his wife had taken, then seated himself.

Ysella settled into the surprisingly comfortable armchair. "This is my first social engagement since the attack."

The gray-haired woman reappeared in the doorway, and Ramon asked, "What would you like to drink?"

"White wine."

Ramon nodded to the server, who turned and departed.

"From what you've said, I get the impression that you're not an overly social person," said Leona, "or am I mistaken?"

"I'm afraid you're correct. Part of that comes from not being married, and part because I'm younger than most councilors."

"Another reason might be precisely because you *are* a councilor," suggested Ramon, "since councilors are Ritters, but often without great wealth."

Ysella nodded. "I worry that too many women see the title and expect wealth."

"You worry too much," said Leona. "You're a councilor, and were a successful legalist. You're not unattractive."

"You're kind, dear lady, but I still worry."

"You're young. Keep your eyes open."

"Is it my imagination, or is there less rigid social . . . structure in Argental?"

Both Leona and Roman laughed.

"I gather I'm mistaken," said Ysella ruefully.

Before Ysella could go on, the server returned with a tray holding three wineglasses: two holding red wine, and one with white. She served Ramon, Ysella, and then Leona.

Once the server left, Ramon lifted his glass. "With thanks for your recovery."

"My appreciation to you both," returned Ysella, then sipped his wine, finding it an excellent Silverhills white.

"I noticed that the *Tribune* mentioned your part in amending the Coal Act," said Ramon evenly.

"I merely tried to keep mining waste out of rivers and waterways," replied Ysella.

"That still makes you more visible than other councilors."

"Sometimes, that happens."

Ramon offered an amused smile.

After a moment, since he hadn't gotten a full answer, Ysella asked, "So . . . there is a firm set of social levels in Cimaguile?"

Ramon smiled. "Not in the same way as in Guldor. Very few are exceedingly rich. They take great pains never to reveal it."

"But everyone knows?" suggested Ysella.

Leona shook her head. "Outside of a few in a family, no one knows. If that much wealth were known, it would be a disgrace. Certainly, the well-off conceal some of their wealth to deal with unexpected misfortunes, but most offer some of it, quietly, to productive people who can better use it to greater effect. Or families cooperate to build something that is needed."

How can that possibly work? Ysella decided on a less confrontational reply. "Wouldn't some people waste the funds?"

"They might—once. But life in Argental isn't easy, and it was less so in the past. Wasters find life difficult."

"And laziness is a form of wasting?" asked Ysella.

"Of course," said Leona cheerfully.

"And theft as well?"

"Proven theft can result in being left in the heights," said Ramon.

Ysella shivered. From what he'd heard, even in full summer the heights were *cold*. "Then does everyone live in a house much the same size as everyone else?"

"Oh, no. Different people and different families have different needs and requirements," replied Leona. "There aren't any tiny huts or huge mansions."

"Do the wealthy convert their funds into jewels or gold, or art objects? Or merely secrete banque notes in hidden vaults?"

"Who would sell them precious stones or build those vaults without everyone eventually knowing?" asked Leona, almost teasingly.

"Art for vanity is also frowned upon," added Ramon.

"Then from what you say, I don't imagine most houses in Cimaguile are as spacious as this."

"It's not as spacious as it appears, Dominic. The legation staff live here as well." Ramon smiled broadly. "Not that we don't have most comfortable quarters."

The server reappeared in the parlor doorway.

"I see that dinner is ready," declared Ramon as he stood.

Ysella and Leona followed him into a moderately large dining room with a table similar to the one in Ysella's parents' dining room. Three places were set at one end, illuminated by two candelabra. Ramon took the end chair.

As Ysella seated himself, he noted the silver-rimmed, white porcelain dinnerware. "Everything is both beautiful and impressive."

Ramon chuckled. "I'm afraid we can't take any credit for that. It belongs to the legation, but Leona planned and helped with the dinner itself. I hope you like seafood."

Ysella smiled. "I like any food that's well-prepared."

"Then you should enjoy this."

The server filled the crystal wineglasses with white Silverhills, then returned with small white porcelain soup bowls, one for each diner, with a hint of steam lifting from each.

"Crab bisque," said Leona.

Ysella couldn't remember the last time he'd had any bisque, crab or otherwise. He waited until Ramon lifted his spoon, but took several spoonfuls before thinking to say, "This is excellent. I can't remember when I've had a bisque this good."

"It's been a while for us, as well," said Ramon.

"This was also a good time for us to have it," added Leona.

After the server cleared away the bowls, she returned with plates, each holding a cooked and seasoned lobster restuffed into its shell along with dark small mushrooms, all topped by a cream sauce and accompanied by rice pilaf and pickled green beans.

Ysella took his time, savoring the first bite, then said, "This is definitely special."

"We hoped you'd like it," said Leona.

"Since we do," added Ramon with a smile.

Ysella took several more, small bites.

After a short time, Ramon commented, "The Council seems to have had some difficulties with the Imperador."

"More so recently," replied Ysella.

"What do you think will happen after the Imperador dies?"

"That will depend on when and how," replied Ysella. "No one really wants the Heir, but few want the turmoil of a revolution. Laureous only had three sons, officially anyway. The elder was too impatient, and the youngest died mysteriously, so there's no clear alternative. Even if people would accept an Imperadora, which I don't see happening, Lady Delehya is too young."

"There are rumors that she might also be an empath," ventured Ramon.

"That makes it less likely."

"What does the Premier think?"

"He's been at the Palace more than usual, but what that means . . ." Ysella shrugged.

"If you were Premier," asked Leona, "what would you do?"

"I'm not Premier, and it's rather unlikely that I ever will be."

"But if you were?"

"In that most improbable event," said Ysella sardonically, "I'd look to find a way to limit the powers of the Imperador, balance his powers with greater power vested in the Council, and hope it would work."

"You wouldn't remove the position of Imperador?" asked Ramon.

"No. Unchecked rule by the Council would be worse than unchecked rule by the Heir."

"It's too bad you're not Premier," declared Leona.

"I'm not, and at present, Iustaan Detruro is doing a better job than I could. Premier is a thoroughly thankless position, and it would be worse if the Council had more power."

"You sound as though you wouldn't want to be Premier. Why?" asked Ramon.

"To do the job well is impossible, and to do it decently would be extraordinarily frustrating."

"You don't seem to have that high an opinion of other councilors."

"I have a high opinion of some, less of others. That's not the reason. The reason is that the perceived needs of all the councilors will always be greater than the resources and marks available. If the Premier keeps the Council from exceeding the available funds, the councilors and those they represent will be displeased. If he does not, the Imperador will be."

"You're more cynical than your age would suggest," replied Ramon wryly, then glancing to one side, "I believe Jahana is here to remove the plates and serve dessert."

"I'd like to say realistic," said Ysella.

"Is there any difference?" asked Leona.

Ysella grinned ruefully. "Probably not."

Dessert consisted of meringue shells filled with lemon curd and topped with a puff of whipped cream, light and crunchy, sweet, but not too heavy. Even so, Ysella took a small bite, then another. "This is a perfect ending."

"Perfect, yes," declared Ramon, "ending, no. Icefire comes last."

"Icefire? A cordial from Argental?"

"What else?" asked Leona.

Once the dessert plates were cleared, the server presented each diner with a cordial glass holding a clear liqueur tinged with the faintest hint of blue.

"Sip it carefully," suggested Ramon.

Ysella took the smallest sip, which initially felt like liquid ice . . . and then seared the back of his palate with fire, momentarily taking his breath away. Once he recovered, he said, "I see why it's called Icefire."

"It's traditional, especially for leave-taking. We're very glad you could come this evening because it will be some time before we'll have another opportunity."

"You're returning to Cimaguile for a time?" Ysella took a tiny sip of the Icefire.

"I got a communiqué just before your attack. I'm officially being recalled for consultations with the Assembly. We couldn't have left until now because none of the passes were open for safe travel. Those consultations may take some time."

"Until the Assembly decides whether to risk an envoy?" asked Ysella sardonically.

"The Imperador has already threatened to hold me personally responsible for brigands in the mountains, although they raid both sides of the border."

"The problem is," added Leona, "that the Guldoran troopers don't try very hard, and the Argenti border force has caught and executed far more than the Guldorans."

Ysella managed not to frown, because he'd never heard that description of the problem. "Why might that be?"

After looking to Ramon, who nodded, Leona replied, "Part of it might be because the Argenti border force uses empaths to track the brigands."

That surprised Ysella, although it certainly made sense, assuming the empaths could sense emotions at some sort of distance, but he'd never spent much time with any empaths, since he'd known he'd never run a holding. He'd never heard of empaths being used as an integral part of any military force. "I take it that it's practical."

"Argental can be very practical," added Ramon. "Art for art's sake is strongly discouraged. Excessive and nonfunctional decoration is deplored. Slavery, even of susceptibles, is prohibited because it restricts more productive use of resources, and the use of empaths as supervisors is frowned upon."

"I can't say that I've heard much about that," Ysella admitted. "But then I've learned quite a bit more about Argental tonight. When will you be leaving?"

"Shortly. I'd appreciate it if you didn't mention it for a few days. Not the dinner. Just the leaving."

"I won't."

"Before you go, I have a gift of sorts. It's something I hope you never have to employ, but with the unpredictability of your Imperador, it unfortunately might be useful." Ramon extracted from his inside jacket pocket an oversized envelope thick enough to contain at least three sheets of paper, and extended it to Ysella. "It's your personal and unconditional writ of entry to Argental. It doesn't expire, and it's only good for you and your family, should you acquire such."

For a moment, Ysella didn't know what to say, especially since he'd only heard rumors about the rare writs. He finally managed, "I'm profoundly honored, but a touch worried that you feel I might need this."

"We hope you don't, but it's the least we can do."

For what? Ysella had no idea why Ramon felt the way he did. "Thank you." He paused, knowing that it was unlikely that he'd ever see the couple again. "I take it that it's a long and arduous trip."

"Three weeks, if we don't encounter bad weather, and there's almost always bad weather in the heights."

"Let's hope you don't."

"It might be less arduous than what you face."

After the last small sips of Icefire, the three walked to the front door, where Ysella donned his overcoat, and took his leave. "Thank you. I enjoyed the dinner, and I deeply appreciate your gift, even if I never have to use it."

"Having it might give you more options," said Leona.

Ysella had the feeling the writ might well have been her idea. He smiled warmly. "Possibly." He started down the steps to where Caastyn waited with the chaise. As he climbed in and looked back, the legation door closed.

Once Caastyn had the chaise on Pleasant Lane, he asked, "How was your dinner, sir?"

"Most pleasant. I learned quite a few things about Argental."

Even before the chaise turned off Pleasant Lane, the wind picked up and the air got progressively colder. Sleet began to pelt the chaise as Caastyn turned onto Averra Place.

Ysella did his best to help Caastyn deal with the horse and the chaise so they could get both out of the sleet as quickly as possible.

As they walked to the house, Ysella said, "Thank you again."

"Won't say it was my pleasure, sir, but I was glad to do it."

"Let's hope tomorrow's warmer. Real spring has to come *sometime* soon."

Caastyn laughed.

51

ON Quindi evening, Caastyn drove Ysella to the Baertyls' house. It was one of two on Silverside Way, a cul-de-sac two blocks south of Pleasant Lane and the larger dwellings surrounding the burned-out remains of Faarn's mansion.

"Two bells, sir?" asked Caastyn as he brought the chaise to a halt in front of the pedestrian gate. The walkway led to a neat two-story gray stone house perhaps a third larger than Ysella's.

"Two and a half. I can wait inside where it's warm if dinner finishes early. Besides, Alaaxi and Junae won't mind." Some couples would, Ysella knew—the Nortaaks among them. Ysella, however, couldn't imagine the most traditional Councilor Stefan Nortaak and his very proper wife inviting Ysella to anything, judging from the two times he'd met Ritten Nortaak at the Yearend Ball.

Ysella gingerly stepped out of the chaise, then walked to the gate and let himself into the low walled garden encompassing the front of the property—excepting the paved drive leading to the carriage house and stable.

Junae opened the front door while Ysella was several yards away. "Dominic, you're still moving a bit carefully. Do your ribs still hurt?"

"Only when I'm not careful, and I try to be *very* careful these days," he finished wryly.

Junae stepped back to allow Ysella to enter the front foyer, then said, "We were very worried about you."

"I very much appreciated your note," Ysella replied as he took off his overcoat and hung it on one of the pegs beside the door.

"You deserved it and more. I'm glad you could come." She smiled warmly, adding, "Our guests are Hirahm and Nezbala Cottesdov. Hirahm has a large holding northeast of Veerlyn, possibly the largest. Alaaxi has known Hirahm from boyhood."

Given that Alaaxi was the fourth son, and from what Junae said, Hirahm had to be the eldest, Ysella suspected Hirahm wanted something. Nevertheless, he returned Junae's smile. "I appreciate knowing that."

"You always understand, Dominic."

"Not always, Junae, but you make matters clear." *Without being obvious.* "Is dinner a surprise?"

Junae laughed sweetly. "I do hope not. We should join the others." She turned, and Ysella accompanied her toward the parlor.

"White Silverhills, still?" asked Junae as Chaarese, the serving maid, appeared from somewhere.

"Absolutely."

Junae looked to Chaarese, who nodded and slipped away.

Alaaxi Baertyl stood as Ysella and Junae stepped through the square archway from the center hall to the parlor, comfortably warm from the cast-iron wall stove. Hirahm Cottesdov rose more slowly, if with a pleasant smile.

"Hirahm, Councilor Dominic Ysella."

"I'm pleased to meet you, Ritter Cottesdov, Ritten Cottesdov," said Ysella warmly. "You must be close friends with Alaaxi and Junae to have traveled so far in this weather to visit them." Ysella waited until Alaaxi and Junae started to seat themselves before taking the small armchair clearly left for him.

Hirahm Cottesdov was a few digits taller than Alaaxi and perhaps a shade taller than Ysella, with the usual dark landor skin and straight, short-cut black hair streaked with light gray. His hard brown eyes studied Ysella intently, if but for a moment. Nezbala's complexion was almost identical to her husband's, but her neck-length mahogany hair softened the angularity of her face. Her green eyes were as hard as her husband's.

Hirahm took a sip of red wine, doubtless Silverhills red, then chuckled and said, "I promised Nezbala that I'd bring her to Machtarn. The only time that makes sense is after winter and before planting. Jerom can handle most of that. I've known Alaaxi more than forty years, and you keep in touch with old friends. That is, if you don't want to lose them."

"Sometimes, despite your best efforts, you do anyway, as we all discover," said Ysella. "How are you finding Machtarn?"

Chaarese reappeared, presented Ysella with his wineglass, and left the parlor.

"It's grown a bit since the last time I was here." Hirahm glanced to his wife. "That was before we married."

Nezbala nodded.

"Alaaxi tells me that you're the chairman of the Waterways Committee," said Hirahm, after another small sip of wine.

"For the past few years."

"What happened to Chairman Aloyst?"

"He resigned for reasons of health." *Because it wouldn't have been healthy for him to remain in office after the way he'd limited waterways funding to the districts of a select few councilors had gotten out.*

"He didn't seem that old."

"He wasn't, but that was his decision. As far as I know, he didn't consult anyone over it, certainly not me." *Not after Ysella made sure certain facts became available where the newshawks could find them. That was also why Ysella made certain all committee decisions and recommendations were as fair as he could make them before they were released to the public—and the newsies.*

"Things have definitely changed," mused Hirahm. "How did you come to be a councilor so young?"

Ysella chuckled. "I'm a legalist, a water legalist. I read the laws about who could run for the Council. While the usual way to get a nomination is from the district council, a documented and attested petition is also allowed. It's extremely cumbersome and time-consuming, by design. It took me a month to get enough signatures of property owners. I didn't announce what I was doing, but I made certain everything was absolutely by the law. After I won the first election, I didn't need a petition to run again, and the other Council candidate in the second election fared even less well."

"You must be very successful in delivering for those who supported you," said Hirahm blandly.

"I'd like to think that I've been successful in doing what's best for all Aloor," replied Ysella. "Also, I've tried to be fair in assuring that the committee allocates its funds where they do the most good for all of Guldor, not just the districts of the committee members."

"I don't recall the funding for waterways as being that generous."

"It's not. That's why the committee requires documented recommendations from any district council seeking funds and why anyone can write with recommendations and comments."

"That seems to favor the most vocal."

"The committee and staff work very hard to concentrate on documented facts. If we discover false or misleading claims . . . well, let's say that it's difficult to trust future recommendations from those sources."

"Very interesting," declared Hirahm pleasantly.

"Quite," added Nezbala, not as pleasantly, before saying, "I understand you're not married. That must give you more time for your . . . duties as a councilor."

"There have been times when I wish I'd found someone." Ysella managed a grin, adding, "I'm still looking."

"You're not that old," said Hirahm.

Ysella saw Alaaxi's puzzlement over the change in conversation and added, "Now, if I'd met Junae before you did, Alaaxi . . ."

"You'd have been . . . maybe ten," countered Junae amusedly.

"Fate was against me," replied Ysella, mock-morosely.

"Fate's always against someone," said Nezbala, "at times it's against each of us, whether it's the weather or a blight or a livestock flux."

After a short conversation on fate, Junae rose and announced, "I do believe dinner is ready, and we shouldn't leave it to fate. Besides, we'd rather not eat it overcooked or cold."

Alaaxi stood. "Well said, dear."

"Dinners are far easier to handle than politics."

"We can agree on that," said Nezbala as she and her husband also stood and joined the others in moving to the dining room.

Ysella thought the dinner was excellent from the tomato-basil soup to the roasted game hens stuffed with rice, accompanied by mushrooms with gingered carrots, followed by hot apple tarts glazed with cinnamon honey, and concluding with an aged Silverhills brandy. He didn't feel in the slightest guilty about skipping services.

Best of all, the conversation avoided politics and centered mostly on reminiscing by Alaaxi and Hirahm on the good times they had growing up in Veerlyn.

When it came time for Ysella to leave, Junae accompanied him to the door.

There, Ysella turned to her. "Even though Hirahm had something else in mind, I enjoyed the evening, and the dinner was wonderful. Thank you."

"I have to thank you as well," said Junae quietly. "Alaaxi really didn't have any way to extract himself gracefully, not from someone so close to his family."

"I could see that."

"It turned out for the best. Hirahm understood soon enough that he couldn't rely on the old ways."

What Junae didn't say was that Alaaxi hadn't understood the interplay between Ritter Cottesdov and Ysella, although it was clear she had.

After a slight hesitation, she added, "You might end up changing everything . . . if you can avoid crossbows and frog poison . . . and the Heir."

"Rather large 'if's, don't you think?"

"Perhaps, but you're already one of the more powerful councilors."

"I'll do what I can."

"You always have . . . and thank you again."

Ysella inclined his head, then opened the door, where he could see that Caastyn was waiting with the chaise on the other side of the gate.

As he made his way down the stone walk, he wondered if it was at all possible that Aelyn Wythcomb might turn out to be somewhat like Junae.

You can hope.

But he also knew that hope was never enough, either in love or politics.

52

Duadi morning, after he settled at the breakfast table, Ysella opened the *Tribune* and began to read.

GULDORANS BANISHED FROM ATACAMA, LEGATION SHUTTERED

On the last day of Winterend, Grande Duce Almaetar declared that there was "no possibility" of peaceful relations with the Empire of Gold and expelled all the remaining staff of the Guldoran legation in Cuipremaan. An Atacaman army detachment escorted the nine Guldorans to the Polidoran clipper *Kossdeas* before it departed for Machtarn.

The Grande Duce also declared that all Guldorans currently living in Atacama have one month in which to leave or to renounce their Guldoran citizenship. Those failing to do either will have all their assets confiscated and will be required to do "public service" for a year, after which they will be exiled . . .

"These actions are merciful," declared the Grande Duce, "compared to the Guldoran brutality of burning peaceful villages on the Atacaman isles in the Gulf of Nordum . . ."

Ysella took a long sip of café, then a bite of a croissant with a touch of berry preserves, before he returned to finish the front-page article and continuing to read and eat.

On the next to last page, he focused on a much smaller story.

Yesterday, the Machtarn District Legalist filed criminal fraud charges against Mallyk Torrenz and Jaahn Rysten, property legalists associated with Machtarn Harbor Properties, for knowingly concealing the fraudulent nature of the Gustov Torryl Trust scheme used by the missing legalist Sollem Faarn . . .

District Legalist Foerst stated that while other property legalists may have occasionally processed sales to the Torryl Trust, "there is no evidence that they were aware of the fraudulent nature of the trust . . ."

Meaning that some of them suspected it, but Foerst couldn't prove it. Ysella wondered if Foerst would pursue the matter further, but doubted it, given the vague links between the Palace and Faarn's deceased assassins; the Palace likely wanted the matter closed. *But Daarkyn still might pursue a story.*

The fact that the newshawk hadn't asked about the Coal Act amendments still worried Ysella, since Daarkyn usually pressed on *everything*.

Ysella shook his head and folded up the newssheet, concentrating on finishing his breakfast.

In another third, he was outside, climbing into the chaise, without an overcoat, given three days of sunny weather that finally created an impression of spring which might last.

"Unless I suffer some unforeseen setback, starting next Unadi, I'll go back to riding to the Council Hall."

"Those ribs hurt more than you let on, didn't they?"

"They might have," admitted Ysella grudgingly.

"Might have?" Caastyn grinned.

Ysella shook his head, then slowly sat back to enjoy the sunlight and the absence of damp chill.

More carriages than usual lined up outside the Council Hall when Caastyn halted the chaise before the doors. "Is something going on, sir?"

"Not that I know of," said Ysella as he got out of the chaise, "but there might be an unannounced hearing before the Military Affairs Committee after what happened in Cuipremaan. That's just a guess."

"As good as any," replied Caastyn. "Fourth bell?"

"A third after, I think."

"I'll be here."

On his walk from the entrance to his office, Ysella didn't encounter any councilors in the hallways, but he saw that the committee room used by the Military Affairs Committee was already in use, early as it was.

As soon as he stepped into the office, Khaard said, "The only message is from the Premier."

"Thank you." Ysella made his way to his personal office, where he opened the message, which simply said the Premier had an important announcement to make at the beginning of the Council session.

Important announcement? That the Imperador rejected the request for reserve funds? That he's declared war on Atacama? Or something else entirely?

Ysella set the message aside. He'd find out in less than four bells. Turning his attention to the letters on his desk, he noted the third letter in the stack of incoming correspondence had an outside address of Hydaar & Fhaen, Legalists, Aloor.

Ysella frowned, knowing it almost certainly had to come from Luvaal Fhaen, although Fhaen had never written before. He began to read.

Councilor Ysella—

First of all, I'd like to offer condolences on the death of Legrand Quaentyn. He was a solid legalist and a remarkable man, and I know you were very close to him.

I also have received word that you have introduced legislation and spoken to the Council's Commerce Committee in favor of an increase in the cap on usury. All of us at the firm heartily support you on that for a reason that isn't often mentioned—that less scrupulous individuals use other indirect and unethical means to compensate lenders. This practice gives a disproportionate advantage to lenders willing to skirt the law and creates more corruption at a time when we should be striving for less.

We've also sent a similar letter to the Commerce Committee making this point, but I felt we should make you aware of our support as well as inform you of our communication with the committee.

The letter was indeed signed by Luvaal Fhaen.

Nodding, Ysella set it to one side and lifted the next envelope.

Ysella wondered if Reimer Daarkyn might show up after the story in the *Tribune*, but there were no interruptions. He finished reading all the incoming letters and making notes on each for the clerks, as well as signing some outgoing correspondence, before leaving for the Council chamber a sixth of a bell before noon.

He'd barely stepped into the Council chamber when Stron Thaalyr turned and stepped toward him. "Dominic, have you heard anything about the Coal Act?"

Ysella wondered why Thaalyr thought he might know, given that the Coal Act had been marked up, such as it had been, and reported out of Thaalyr's committee, but he replied, "I haven't heard a thing."

"The Premier sent that message . . . and I thought you might know."

"I'm guessing, and it's only a guess, that what the Premier will announce has more to do with the request for reserve funds. I could be wrong." After a brief hesitation, Ysella asked, "Have you heard anything from Administrator Zaenn?"

Thaalyr shook his head. "Nothing. That's why I'm concerned."

Since Thaalyr had done what amounted to Zaenn's bidding, Ysella didn't see why Thaalyr would be that worried, unless Thaalyr felt he might be punished for not reining in Ysella and Raathan. "We'll have to see."

"Thank you, Dominic."

"You're welcome." Ysella walked to his desk and seated himself.

As the sound of the noon bells faded, Maatrak stood at the lectern and said, "The Council will be in order. The Premier has an announcement before the first order of business."

As Maatrak stepped back, Detruro moved to the lectern. "As you all recall, there was a great deal of speculation as to whether the Imperador would agree to release reserve funds to repair the extensive damage to port facilities at Endor. The Imperador did, in fact, agree to the use of those funds, with the stipulation that their use be carefully documented and the expenditures monitored by the Waterways Administration. Questionable expenditures will be jointly reviewed by the Waterways Committee and the Waterways Administrator, and those not found to be basic to port administration or for replacing equipment and buildings destroyed by the storm will be replenished from the Waterways appropriation for the Endor district."

"How did Detruro manage that?" murmured Staeryt.

"Does it matter?" murmured Ysella in return.

Without another word, Detruro left the lectern.

Maatrak stepped forward and immediately declared, "The matter before the Council is consideration of amendments to the Child Labor Act . . ."

Ysella half listened because he knew the text of the amendments, which, among other things, changed the age at which children could be indentured or apprenticed from ten to twelve, and prohibited hard labor for any individual under the age of sixteen, amendments which shouldn't have been necessary, but had unfortunately turned out to be.

As Maatrak finished the legalese, Ysella straightened.

"Councilor Staeryt will speak to the need for the amendments," declared the floor leader.

Staeryt rose and made his way to the lectern. "Events of the last five years have revealed certain deficiencies in the Child Labor Act . . ."

Ysella mostly listened to what he already knew, and, in little more than a bell, the consolidated amendments passed, forty-eight votes for, none against.

After Maatrak recessed the Council, Ysella stood and looked for Paolo Caanard, moving to intercept him.

The older councilor smiled as he saw Ysella. "What have I done now, Dominic?"

"Nothing that I know of. I have a question, though. What do you know about brigands in the mountains along the northern border with Argental?"

"I know that the Imperador is concerned about them, but has been reluctant to shift border patrollers to deal with them."

"Is the problem getting worse because the Argenti are more effective on their side of the border, and that encourages the brigands to attack more in Guldor?"

Caanard lifted his eyebrows. "That's not widely known, and the Imperador would likely prefer that it not be."

"Because he doesn't want to shift troopers to the north because of the increasing tensions with Atacama, and he doesn't have adequate funds to hire more troopers?"

"As those of us who bother to count have learned, the government is underfunded in quite a few areas, for reasons we also know." Caanard's smile shaded toward wintry. "Why are you interested?"

"I overheard a mention of the problem, and I wasn't about to discuss it without knowing more. You seemed to be one of the few who might know."

"You didn't ask Alaan, I take it?"

"I saw you first." *And Alaan probably doesn't know.*

Caanard offered a quiet but harsh laugh.

"Has the Imperador conveyed anything to you about the recent decrees of the Grande Duce?"

"Not yet. He may not. He prefers to dictate his wishes to the Premier." Abruptly, Caanard smiled ruefully. "I'm sorry. I don't mean to be brusque, but . . ."

"The Imperador is making matters hard on everyone and then blaming them?"

"Or maintaining an icy lack of communication."

"What sort of conspiracy are you two hatching?" interjected Georg Raathan as he stepped closer.

"The usual," replied Ysella. "Trying to fix things while appearing to do nothing." He offered a mock frown. "Or is it the other way around?"

Raathan looked to Ysella. "Have you heard anything about the Coal Act?"

"Nothing. Stron Thaalyr hasn't heard, either."

"The way he's been acting, the Imperador will reject it," declared Caanard.

"He might not," replied Ysella.

"You think not? After everything else . . ."

"The Coal Act costs him nothing," Ysella interjected. "If it's not passed, the damage could cost the Treasury and all Guldor a great deal. The fact that he agreed to the funds for Endor suggests he's still weighing things."

"At the moment, anyway," replied Caanard dryly, before he turned and headed for the chamber door.

"Paolo's in a sour mood," observed Raathan.

"He's worried. Foreign affairs aren't going well."

"He's not the one who caused the problems."

"No, but I don't imagine he has any way to resolve them that agrees with what the Imperador wants, and agreeing with Laureous will make matters worse." Ysella turned to the door.

Raathan kept pace.

Once the two were in the hall, Raathan said, "Do you really think the Imperador might approve the Coal Act?"

"There's a good chance, but matters could always change."

"I worry about the Heir, Dominic."

"Who in their right mind doesn't?" Ysella kept his tone sardonic but light.

"Can the Premier do anything?"

"I have the feeling he's trying. We'll have to see."

"I hope you're right." Raathan nodded and headed for his office.

Once Ysella climbed the stairs and returned, only Jaasn was in the office, but he hastily explained, "Lyaard will be back in a little while, sir. There are a few more letters on your desk, and more responses for you to sign."

Ysella offered a resigned smile. "I'll attend to both."

The remainder of the day was uneventful, and although he had to spend some time completing his preparations for the Waterways Committee meeting on Tridi, he met Caastyn right after fourth bell. He was pleased that the skies were clear and there was only a light breeze.

"Long day, sir?" asked Caastyn once the chaise was headed west on Council Avenue.

"Not too bad, as days go. Anything new?"

"You got two letters. Gerdina heard something interesting from Krynn, though."

"Oh?"

"No one's seen much of the Heir's snitches lately. There's been talk that there might be new ones, quieter-like."

"I can't say I like the sound of that."

"Me neither, sir. That's why I thought you might want to know."

As Caastyn drove, Ysella pondered what that might mean, besides the fact that young Laureous didn't want his agents known, which suggested he was collecting his various agents and planning something—*or that his father was much closer to dying.*

Once back at the house, Ysella headed for the study and looked at the two envelopes, one from Sullynd & Smarkaan and one from Aloor. The handwriting on the letter posted in Aloor was unfamiliar and definitely not Aelyn's.

Oh, well. You could hope.

The envelope only bore the postmark and the initials "M.B." and "Aloor" on the exterior. While the initials gave Ysella a hint as to the author, he wasn't sure until he opened the envelope and began to read.

Councilor Ysella—

Hayley and I both appreciated your letters and your kind and thoughtful words about Father. Much more than that, we appreciated the letters you wrote him, and the many times you stopped to see him. He was always so cheerful after your visits.

I don't know that he told you, but he was so proud of you, and what you have already accomplished.

Father already determined that his legal treatises and books are to be split between you and Bruuk Fettryk. He made a list of which go to each of you. I know you will not be back in Aloor for some time, but Bruuk will keep your share of the books in his Aloor office until you return.

Once more, Hayley and I thank you for your years of thoughtful kindness.

Maergot Bonnstyl

The gift of the legal books and treatises surprised him. Ysella hadn't expected anything at all, but Legrand never wanted anything to go to waste, and no one else in his family was a legalist. *Kind and practical, to the end.*

After several long moments, he put down that letter and picked up the one from Sullynd & Smarkaan, slitting it open, and reading it.

Councilor Ysella—

Since you have been a favored client for many years, I thought you should be among the first to know that Sr. Allaard Smarkaan has chosen to retire from the active practice of property law. He will be replaced by Morenz Sullynd, who has been working with Haels & Goelyn for the past several years.

> *Henceforth, the firm will be known as Sullynd & Sullynd, and will continue to provide all the services you have previously used. We look forward to continuing to serve you.*
>
> *Haasl Sullynd*

Ysella nodded slowly. A while back, Sullynd had mentioned that Smarkaan previously dealt with Sollem Faarn. Had Foerst implied that an early retirement for Smarkaan was for the best, or had Smarkaan decided that himself?

Either way, it didn't much matter, and he needed to write a thank-you letter to Maergot Bonnstyl.

53

AT breakfast on Tridi morning, Ysella was unsurprised by one of the front-page stories in *The Machtarn Tribune* and barely paused in sipping his café.

ARGENTI ENVOY RECALLED

The Argenti Assembly suddenly recalled Envoy Ramon Hekkaad to Cimaguile, ostensibly for "consultations." The Assembly did not inform the Imperador of that recall until almost a week after Sr. Hekkaad left Machtarn. Premier Iustaan Detruro insisted he received word of the recall only within a few bells of the Palace. The Imperador has offered no comment on Hekkaad's departure, although sources indicate the Assembly was displeased with the Imperador's demands that Argental deal with brigands attacking on both sides of the northern border...

The second page contained a small story about the Imperador's release of reserve funds to assist in the rebuilding of the storm-damaged port facilities at Endor. There was almost no mention of the Council in the story.

Since the Imperador agreed, he'll take all the credit.

The drive to the Council Hall was cooler and breezier than it had been on Duadi, and neither Caastyn nor Ysella had much to say. Ysella's thoughts centered on the upcoming Waterways Committee meeting.

When Ysella reached his office, Khaard handed him a message. "From the Premier."

"Thank you."

Ysella walked to his desk, thankful the weather no longer required an overcoat or a riding jacket, and opened the short message.

Dominic—
I'd appreciate it if you would stop by my office before going to the floor.

Iustaan

Ysella wondered what Detruro had in mind, but there were too many possibilities, and any of them could be wrong. He returned the note to the envelope, which he slipped into the bottom desk drawer. Then he started in on the correspondence and the responses.

Following that, he reviewed the day's legislative schedule and the registered amendments, then spent a sixth or so going over the papers for the committee meeting before putting them into his leather case. As he left the office, he turned to Khaard and said, "I'm heading to the committee meeting, and I won't be back until after the Council recesses this afternoon."

The senior clerk nodded.

Ysella was the first councilor in the committee room, but Voltar Paastyn appeared while Ysella organized his papers at his place in the center of the long, curved desk on the dais.

"Good morning, Dominic."

"The same to you, Voltar."

Haans Maessyn entered next, followed by the other four committee members over the next sixth, Astyn Coerl trailing in barely before the four chimes of the bell.

Moments after that, Ysella gaveled the committee to order. "Several of you have mentioned situations where watercraft unsuited to a particular waterway have caused various problems, from death and injury to blocking the waterway. I also understand that there appears to be some legal confusion involving such occurrences. How frequent are these problems?"

Ysella waited for a response.

After a moment, Haans Maessyn spoke. "It depends on the waterway. There are certainly more boats on the Rio Azulete and the Rio Doro. There don't seem to be more on the Khulor River. We've had several incidents around Uldwyrk."

"We've had three in the last year at Endor," added Ditaero. "Two of them flatboats."

"Nothing on the Lakaan River, although that's not in my district," said Stefan Nortaak, "and I might have missed something."

"Seems like there's something every month on the Rio Doro," added Dannyl Grieg.

Ysella nodded. "So there's general agreement on the fact that there's a problem. I've looked into the legal side, and there are a few difficulties. First, while there are generally accepted procedures for boats and ships, not everyone and certainly not all mariners who aren't Guldoran, agrees on those procedures. Second, there's no part of the government specifically legally responsible for enforcing adherence to those procedures."

Maessyn frowned. "Are you suggesting the committee do nothing?"

Ysella offered an amused smile. "So far I haven't suggested anything. I'm just pointing out the background."

"The Imperador isn't about to fund enforcement patrollers for waterways," said Nortaak.

"What would they enforce?" asked Paastyn. "The Mariners Code is a set of guidelines."

"Even if we made it law," countered Nortaak, "there'd be no way to enforce it."

Although he knew the answer, Ysella asked, "Is there a better or more comprehensive set of guidelines or procedures?"

"If there is," said Maessyn, "I don't know about it, and getting pilots and masters to abide by something they've never heard of would likely make matters worse."

"Besides," interjected Gaastyn Ditaero, "we've got loggers with flatboats, and getting them to understand and comply would be impossible."

"Getting loggers to understand anything would be impossible," murmured Maessyn from where he sat beside Ysella.

"The Mariners Code isn't that hard to understand," declared Paastyn. "It provides simple directions for boats and ships."

"Then why can't we turn it into law?" asked Coerl.

"Without any enforcement mechanism," said Ditaero, "everyone could get away with breaking the law. We don't want to enact toothless laws and set a precedent for enacting something meaningless. The Council's already seen as toothless too often."

"Then why are we discussing this?" asked Grieg.

"As I recall," said Ysella, "because most of us thought there might be a problem."

Grieg looked to Ysella. "You're the legalist and the chairman. What do you suggest?"

"I'd recommend that we establish the Mariners Code as the accepted set of procedures on all waterways and onshore waters," said Ysella. "Then we make anyone who causes an accident or blocks a waterway presumptively liable for violating the code unless they can prove otherwise or that they had no other option. Let marks be the enforcement mechanism. People won't bring legal action unless there are significant losses, but we establish that there is a code to follow. If, in time, we still have a problem, then we have a stronger basis for creating some sort of enforcement system."

"I don't know . . ." began Grieg.

For almost two bells, Ysella merely moderated the comments. Then he said, "We're beginning to repeat ourselves. I move that legislation be drafted along the lines discussed, and that the committee consider that draft once it is completed and presented to the committee for approval, amendment, or rejection."

"I second the motion," Maessyn immediately said.

"All in favor?" asked Ysella.

Maessyn, Ditaero, Paastyn, and Nortaak raised their hands to agree with Ysella.

"So ordered," said Ysella evenly. "The committee stands adjourned." He rapped the gravel once.

Maessyn waited until the rest of the committee members had left before turning to Ysella. "You knew where this would end up, didn't you?"

"Is there something you'd like to change?" asked Ysella. "If you have a better idea or approach, I'd be happy to hear it."

Maessyn shook his head. "No. What you proposed makes sense. It was . . . interesting. It's a good thing you're a legalist as well as a landor." He smiled briefly. "I'll see you later."

From the committee room, Ysella walked to the Premier's office, where he had to wait until Alaan Escalante left before Detruro gestured for him to enter the personal office.

"Something new affecting the Navy?" asked Ysella as he closed the door.

"Nothing you don't already know," replied Detruro, seating himself behind the desk and gesturing to the chairs before it, then waiting until Ysella sat before saying more. "There are several things I'd like you to know, however. First, the Imperador signed the Coal Act, with the amendments. His transmittal letter was short, saying that he'd signed it, but Carsius Zaenn delivered the signed act and the transmittal. Zaenn said that the Imperador had reservations about some provisions, and that the Natural Resources Administration would be monitoring matters closely." Detruro looked to Ysella.

"I'd recommend we send copies of the act to the Agriculture Administrator and the Waterways Administrator," replied Ysella. "Some of those provisions affect them."

"I'd thought as much."

"One other thing, I had dinner with Ramon Hekkaad and his wife the other night. He hinted that he might be recalled. Then this morning . . ."

"It appears he was. And?"

"He indicated the Assembly of Argental was not pleased with Guldor's failure to deal with the brigands on Guldor's side of the border. In light of what I read this morning, I thought you should know."

Detruro raised his eyebrows.

"He only hinted," lied Ysella.

"This time, it didn't make much difference," said Detruro, "but it would be helpful to know such *hints* earlier."

"I understand."

Detruro smiled politely. "That's all I had for now."

Ysella nodded and left, making his way to the Council chamber.

He was immediately met by Aldyn Kraagyn.

"Dominic, you know I'll be offering an amendment to the tariff revision act?"

"You're proposing to raise the rates on imported swampgrass rice, it appears. I take it that you've got a few landors growing rice?"

"Not so much the number, as who they are."

"I understand," replied Ysella. "I appreciate your reminding me. Have you heard any more about Rugaar Maartyn?"

"I can't say I have. Have you?"

"Not recently. That's why I asked." Ysella smiled. "I won't keep you. You have others you need to convince."

Ysella stepped into the Council chamber a good sixth before noon, when he caught sight of the wiry white-haired figure of Staanus Wrystaan, Daenyld's replacement as councilor from Neewyrk. Since he'd only seen Wrystaan from a distance and had a little time, he walked over to greet him. "Good day. We haven't been introduced, but I'm Dominic Ysella. I was rather indisposed when you were appointed to the Council, and this is the first time I've seen you. I wanted to greet you since I didn't have the opportunity earlier."

An amused smile replaced Wrystaan's initial puzzled expression. "It's good to meet you. I read about your exploits: discovering a fraudulent trust and nearly getting killed for your diligence. Not many legalists would take such a risk."

"I'd hoped to avoid violence with that approach, but I obviously miscalculated. Might I ask if you sought to replace Symeon or if others prevailed upon your good nature?"

"In a moment of weakness, I agreed to fill the position, but reserved the right to step down at the next election, although my son would prefer to keep running the family business."

"Oh?"

"Papermaking and printing."

"That sounds more demanding than being a legalist."

"If you do it right, pulp, paper, and ink don't argue back," said Wrystaan dryly. "That also might be why I was pressed—pardon the pun—into being councilor. What about you?"

"I didn't like some of the law, but practicing legalists can seldom change the law. So I thought I'd try. I'm still trying."

Wrystaan smiled. "Effectively, I've heard." He glanced at the dais where Maatrak approached the lectern. "I won't keep you."

"It's good to meet you, semi-officially, anyway."

"The same."

As the chime rang out, Ysella took his seat.

After Maatrak called the Council to order, he turned the lectern over to Detruro.

The Premier smiled before he began. "I'm pleased to inform the Council that the Imperador has signed and approved the Coal Act as amended by the Council, and I'd like to thank Councilor Raathan and Councilor Ysella for their work in improving it. Natural Resources Administrator Zaenn has stated that he will be monitoring the implementation carefully." With that, Detruro stepped away from the lectern.

"Amazing," said Staeryt sarcastically. "The Imperador didn't reject an act that holds people halfway accountable."

"That's because the provisions don't affect him or his family," returned Caanard.

Maatrak tapped the gavel lightly. "The matter before the Council is the Comprehensive Revision of Agricultural Tariffs Act . . ."

Ysella took a deep breath. He knew there were a number of amendments registered, each of which involved an agricultural commodity of particular concern to certain landors.

"Councilor Raathan will speak to the proposed act."

Raathan stepped onto the dais and took the lectern. "At the time the Imperium was established, immediately after the amalgamation of Aloor, items on the tariff schedule of Aloor, such as it was, were simply added to the Guldoran schedule. As a result, there are often separate schedules and rates for the same items because they are described differently . . ."

Ysella sighed. It would be a long day, followed by an equally long day on Furdi, and possibly on Quindi as well.

While no one spoke against the bill, given that it was a practical necessity, Aldyn Kraagyn offered the first amendment: to increase the tariff on imported swampgrass rice.

Kraagyn reasoned that swampgrass rice was so much cheaper than rice grown in Encora that too many growers—and their workers—would suffer without the tariff.

From Ysella's point of view, the tariff would increase the cost of food for everyone, but knowing how the vote would come out, he decided not to rise in opposition. He voted against the amendment, which passed with thirty-one votes in favor and eighteen opposed.

Three bells and eleven votes on amendments later, Maatrak recessed the Council until noon on Furdi, and Ysella walked back to his office, where he spent half a bell on correspondence before leaving and heading out to where Caastyn waited with the chaise.

54

ON Furdi, Ysella's day began with a review of the draft legislation establishing a code of maneuvering priorities for waterways with the Waterways Committee legalist and ended with the legislative session lasting until two-thirds past fourth bell, with three more amendments and a vote on final passage still remaining for Council action.

Quindi morning's *Tribune* contained little of special interest to Ysella, with the possible exception of a short article stating that the Treasury was reviewing applications for new banques in Devult, Eshbruk, and Suvion.

Ysella frowned at that. Local banques didn't require an Imperial charter unless they wanted regional banque status, with the additional rights and responsibilities involved. He wondered when the Treasury would make a decision and forward the charters to the Council for approval. While Devult and Suvion were certainly large enough to support two regional banks, Ysella had his doubts about Eshbruk.

But then, Eshbruk is close to where some of those newer coal mines are being developed, and it could be that mining interests wanted a banque to cater to their needs.

When Ysella finished breakfast and readying himself, he met Caastyn in the drive under a hazy green sky. As he climbed into the chaise, he said, "Today should be the last day you'll be driving me around, but it will be a long day and night, since you'll have to wait at the Palace for me."

"Unless it rains, that shouldn't be a great trial," replied Caastyn as the chaise left the drive and started down Averra Place toward Camelia Avenue.

After a short while, Caastyn said, "You haven't said much about this affair tonight, sir."

"I was ordered not to. It's for the announcement of the engagement of the Premier to the Imperador's daughter. Please keep it to yourself until after you leave me at the Palace tonight. I'm the representative of the Council, since, obviously, the Premier won't be able to perform that function."

"You're not the floor leader," Caastyn said evenly.

"I wasn't exactly given a choice," replied Ysella. "I was told that I'd be representing the Council. Accepting was unwise, but refusing would have been more so."

Caastyn chuckled. "You do get yourself in interesting positions, sir."

"Unfortunately, that sometimes gets you in less than comfortable situations."

"It's better than unending routine. Besides, it's good to have a position with meaning."

While Ysella agreed, he had to admit, if only to himself, there was a great deal of routine and much less meaning. *But better than none.*

When Caastyn halted the chaise outside the Council Hall, Ysella noted the carriages and coaches lined up outside, then recalled from the master committee schedule that the Fleet Marshal was slated to brief the Military Affairs Committee.

"Third bell, this afternoon," said Ysella as he left the chaise, knowing it could be a bit later than that, but not much, given that Detruro also had to be at the Palace.

"Yes, sir."

Once Ysella reached his office, he discovered he had no messages. Since he didn't have a Waterways Committee meeting, he could concentrate on reading and signing or revising the replies to incoming correspondence. He finished with the correspondence by fifth bell and turned his attention to the document drafted by the Waterways Committee staff. After two-thirds of a bell, he slipped the draft into his leather case, knowing he'd be working on the draft over endday. Then he headed for the Council chamber, hoping he could find Alaan Escalante before the Council session began.

Paolo Caanard was already talking to Escalante, but Ysella eased closer, effectively insinuating himself into the conversation.

". . . do you mean to say that the Fleet Marshal refused to comment on whether the Navy will increase its presence in either Siincleer or Point Larmat? Or Machtarn, for that matter?" asked Caanard with a hint of snideness.

"He said Machtarn was best suited as a commercial port, and that the Navy was exploring other options for a fleet port between Neewyrk and Port Reale. He mentioned no other possible ports by name."

Caanard raised his eyebrows, as if in disbelief.

Ysella stepped into the momentary silence. "Did the briefing, or meeting, touch at all on the reputed problems with Argental or only on the real ones with the Grande Duce?"

"Fleet Marshal Dhaantyn deferred to the First Marshal on the Argenti question because it is not within the scope of naval operations," replied Escalante. "Marshal Solatiem said that the Imperador had valid concerns about brigands along the northern border and that mountain-trained troopers are being moved into that area, but that it would obviously take time."

In short, the Army doesn't have many and is training more. "Anything of interest you can tell us about what's happening in the Gulf of Nordum?"

"Only that operations are continuing and that the Atacaman eastern fleet is largely trapped in Port Lenfer."

"Are those your words?" asked Caanard. "Or did Dhaantyn actually say something like that?"

"Those are close to his words, as I recall."

Caanard shook his head and turned toward his desk.

"Not terribly informative, I take it?" said Ysella to Escalante.

"The Southern Fleet is making progress, but there are scores of isles in the Gulf," replied Escalante. "That's what I got out of it." He glanced in the direction of Caanard, then returned his eyes to Ysella and lowered his voice. "Paolo wants immediate results in a campaign that requires slow and methodical efforts."

"Like the Imperador," murmured Ysella.

Escalante's chuckle held bitterness.

As Maatrak rapped the gavel sharply, Ysella and Escalante moved to their desks and seated themselves.

"The matter before the Council remains the Comprehensive Revision of Agricultural Tariffs Act. The amendment before the Council is to increase the tariff on cane sugar from Sargasso by three parts in a hundred. The councilor from Jeeroh will speak to the amendment . . ."

Ysella nodded. Sugar beets didn't have as high a concentration of sugar as did cane, and grew in a cooler climate. Needless to said, the growers of Jeeroh wanted protection.

After the two brief speeches, with Maessyn opposing the amendment by claiming that only a small part of Guldor benefitted, while everyone's table would pay more, Maatrak called for the vote.

Ysella voted against the amendment, agreeing with Maessyn, and the amendment was defeated, with only twenty-three in favor and twenty-six opposed. While Maessyn's argument against the increase was the same as the one against swampgrass rice, the difference, apparently, was that sugar prices affected more people in Guldor than did the cost of rice. *Or more people who could vote.*

In the end, the revised Agricultural Tariffs Act passed by an overwhelming margin, with forty-three in favor and seven opposed. Ysella left the chamber just before third bell, stopping by his office long enough to gather his leather case before hurrying out to meet Caastyn.

The air was mild, but muggy, and he found himself sweating slightly by the time he settled into the chaise.

"Wasn't quite as short a day as you thought, was it?" asked Caastyn.

"No, but not that much longer."

"No sign of rain," said Caastyn.

"With the dampness in the air," replied Ysella, "I'd wager we'll get some tomorrow."

"Don't think I'll take that wager. Just so it doesn't rain tonight."

"Any letters at the house?"

"Not a one. Looking for a certain one from Aloor?"

Ysella laughed. "Of course." He still worried that he might have pressed Aelyn too hard. *But when letters are all you have to bridge the distance...*

As soon as they reached the house, Ysella washed up and changed into his gray-edged, deep blue formal garb with the matching cravat—the only formalwear he had.

Then he and Caastyn left the house at half before fifth bell. The reception would begin at half past fifth bell, and while there certainly wouldn't be the same number of coaches and carriages as at the Yearend Ball, driving to the Palace would still take close to a bell, considering the distance and minor delays at the gates or the entry to the Palace. As before, Caastyn had both already-cocked small crossbows in their brackets on the dashboard below the short spear and wore the gladius he'd used as an army squad leader.

The only other carriage they saw was navy blue and already proceeding up the drive through the Palace grounds as Caastyn slowed the chaise and came to a halt at the Palace gates.

Ysella leaned forward and tendered the invitation.

The guard read it, returned it, and said, "Welcome to the Palace, sir," then added to Caastyn, "After you drop off the Ritter at the entrance, go to the right."

Once Caastyn had the chaise well away from the gates headed uphill to the Palace, he said, "It's too bad you couldn't bring Ritten Wythcomb."

"I don't know that the Palace would be the best location and situation for our first social event together." *Assuming that we ever have a social event together.*

"You'd make it work, sir."

"I appreciate your confidence, but much of that depends on the Ritten."

"Doesn't it always, sir?" replied Caastyn cheerfully.

When the chaise pulled up to the main entrance, Ysella alighted and started to present his invitation. A footman stepped forward and stopped him. "No need of that, Councilor Ysella."

Ysella wondered who had informed the footman, but then Lorya Kaechar, attired in formal whites, stepped forward, smiling. Ysella had no doubt she was radiating friendliness as only an empath could.

"Welcome, Councilor."

"Thank you. You're my escort?"

"Only as far as the private salon. From there, you're on your own." She half turned, clearly expecting him to walk beside her.

Ysella did as she expected. "But you'll be at the reception, I assume."

"Where else, but you're scarcely likely to get lost there . . . or anywhere."

"To what do I owe your gracious presence?"

"Your safety. It would be incredibly embarrassing to have any misfortune occur to you or the Premier, but he's already arrived."

"And to make certain I have no malign intent against anyone, no doubt."

"With you, Councilor, how could I possibly tell? But then, you're one of the few who understands the need for the peaceful continuation of the Imperium."

"The Imperium can only continue if matters remain peaceful, and failure of the Imperium would be a disaster."

"As I said," returned Kaechar.

"But does every Imperial administrator understand that?" What Ysella really wanted to ask was whether the Heir did, but he couldn't afford that question.

"Does every councilor?" countered Kaechar, turning off the main corridor and onto a cross corridor that ended over thirty yards ahead where two Palace guards in red and gold flanked open doors framed with an arch of spring flowers. Ysella had no idea from where those flowers came, unless the Palace had a hothouse or two, which was certainly possible.

"I'd say the vast majority do, as does the Premier, but you already know that, and so does the Imperador."

"You do know, don't you, that the Imperador was somewhat surprised that the Premier requested you to represent the Council?"

"No, but I suspected he might be."

"Why did he pick you?"

"I don't know. I suspect that he picked a senior councilor who knows matters must change for both the Imperium and the position of Imperador to survive—but that such a change must be peaceful." Ysella emphasized the word "must" a bit.

"You are in an interesting position, Councilor." Kaechar stopped short of the guards and smiled politely. "Do enjoy the reception and the dinner."

"I will. Thank you, Sra. Kaechar."

"You're welcome, Councilor." She waited for Ysella to enter, then followed, but immediately moved to a position against the wall inside the left-hand door.

As Ysella entered the private salon, larger than any salon he'd ever been in, he saw a large oval table clad in white. At the center of the table, a tiered floral centerpiece rose almost two yards. Platters of all manner of dainties surrounded it. To his right stood a large sideboard where a server in red and gold supplied beverages. Golden chair rails set off the creamy white walls of the salon, while the walls above the rails held stylized golden replicas of the Imperial seal.

As Ysella had often observed in larger gatherings, there were several groups: elegantly dressed women, groups of men only, and two groups with both men and women, who wore their headscarves loosely around their shoulders. Something about the reception bothered him, and it took him several moments to realize exactly what it was.

Delehya's the daughter of the Imperador, and the Imperador's going to announce her engagement to the Imperium's Premier—and there are only perhaps fifty people here?

Ysella was still considering that thought when, on the far side of the chamber, Detruro stepped away from two uniformed naval officers and gestured for Ysella to join him. Ysella approached the Premier, scanning the figures in the salon. The two uniformed men had to be the First Marshal and the Fleet Marshal because both wore naval blues, although the dark-haired one appeared younger and was likely Fleet Marshal Dhaantyn.

Ysella also caught sight of Engar Tyresis, the Waterways Administrator, and Taeryl Laergaan, the Imperial Administrator of Commerce. Laergaan spoke to a large man in white formalwear.

Ysella had no idea who several of the others might be, although he thought he saw Carsius Zaenn in a dim corner talking with another administrator he thought might be Tybaalt Salaazar, the Administrator of the Treasury.

"You look to be in good spirits, Iustaan," said Ysella cheerfully.

"I'm slightly surprised in that regard," replied Detruro. "It does give one pause."

"Will the Lady Delehya join the reception?" asked Ysella.

Detruro shook his head. "The Imperador and his family will join us in the private dining room."

"Another intimate space like this?" asked Ysella with a tinge of sarcasm.

"Slightly smaller." Detruro gave Ysella a wry half smile.

"She can't be allowed to mingle, at least not until you're married?"

"Something along those lines."

"Has a date been set?"

"Yes, but it won't be made public for a while." Detruro lowered his voice to a murmur. "The thirty-sixth of Springend. You'll be there as well."

"Rather symbolic, in a way."

"She thought so as well." Detruro turned as a heavyset man in white formalwear several years older than the Premier approached, the same man who had been talking to Laergaan. "Sr. Poncetaryl, I'd like you to meet Councilor Ysella. Dominic, Sr. Poncetaryl is the presidente of the Banque of Machtarn."

Poncetaryl inclined his head. "I'm pleased to meet you. It's not every descendant of royalty who becomes a legalist and fights against criminal corruption."

"The only one I know," interjected Detruro lightly. "He's also chairman of the Waterways Committee and quite an expert on all facets of water law."

"You've obviously crammed a lot of experience into a very few years."

"It's possible, if that's all one does."

"That's right. You've never married, the newssheets said."

"Not so far," replied Ysella.

"And you didn't try to court Lady Delehya?" asked Poncetaryl with a touch of levity.

"I danced with her once," admitted Ysella. "We could be friends, but I'm not suited to her."

"You're not suited to her? What—"

"Everything," interjected Ysella before the banker could ask more, "especially when her father is the Imperador."

"That's one of the things I appreciate about Dominic," said Detruro. "He thinks things through." With that, the Premier guided Ysella to the pair of naval officers. "First Marshal Solatiem, Fleet Marshal Dhaantyn, I'd like you both to meet Councilor Ysella. Besides being a senior councilor, he's the chairman of the Waterways Committee."

Both officers inclined their heads.

"It's a pleasure to meet you both," returned Ysella. "The committee is working to reconcile standards at all Guldoran ports and create a statutory basis for existing waterway encounters. When the time comes, we'd like to have your recommendations. We really shouldn't dwell on that here, but I did want to let you know."

"That's very good information," replied the dark-haired Dhaantyn.

"Thank you for mentioning it. We will offer recommendations at the appropriate time."

Solatiem smiled and said, "Since this reception is about the Premier and Lady Delehya, I'd like to indulge my curiosity. I understand that you two were among the few to dance with her at the Yearend Ball."

"We were," admitted Detruro, "but the Imperador chose who danced with his daughter."

"It makes sense," said Dhaantyn. "You two are the most distinguished among men who are eligible, but you're obviously on good terms."

Before Detruro could speak again, Ysella said, "While the Lady Delehya is intelligent, beautiful, perceptive, and an excellent dancer, from the first moment I danced with her, I felt as though we didn't quite match, and that she would be a far better friend. When I saw the Premier dancing with her, I immediately realized that they were much better suited to each other."

"You've never married." Dhaantyn's words weren't quite an accusation.

"As third son, I inherited nothing. So I spent my early years as a legalist. I'm only now in a position to afford a family. Let's say I hope to be able to find the right woman."

"More like some of our young commanders, I'd say," commented Solatiem. "Nothing wrong with that."

"Not at all," agreed Dhaantyn quickly.

"I think we need to get you a glass of wine," said Detruro, easing Ysella away from the two marshals and toward the sideboard.

Ysella took a glass of a white wine, and sipped. While not Silverhills, it was definitely excellent.

"If you'll excuse me," said Detruro.

"Of course." Ysella took another sip, reflecting on Detruro's clear intent to introduce him to the two marshals. He wasn't so sure about the banker.

As he turned and made his way to the table with the dainties, Carsius Zaenn joined him.

"I understand you had quite a bit to do with the amendments to the Coal Act," said Zaenn pleasantly, but coolly.

"Only the sections dealing with water. That is my responsibility." Ysella took a small, spiced prawn from a tray, using an ivory toothpick.

"Those amendments will be costly and may keep some mines from being developed."

"Without those amendments, some waterways could be poisoned enough to ruin entire crops and kill livestock." *And that still might happen.*

"We'll be looking at those requirements closely," declared Zaenn in a pleasantly cool voice.

Ysella still recognized the threat. "I understand. Have you ever met the Lady Delehya?"

"At the Yearend Ball, as did you."

Ysella took another prawn and ate it. "She struck me as quite perceptive."

"Perhaps you should listen to her, then, as if you could."

"I won't have to. The Premier will have the benefit of her perception." Ysella smiled pleasantly, adding, "The Waterways Committee will also be looking at compliance with the law." Then he nodded and made his way to where Administrator Tyresis and his wife conversed with another couple.

"Councilor," said Tyresis. "I must say I hadn't expected you here." He half turned. "I don't believe you've met my wife, Heraana."

Ysella inclined his head to Heraana, whose shoulder-length light brown hair was carefully curled and likely equally carefully colored. "My pleasure."

"And mine," she replied. "I've heard that you do more than sit in the Council Hall."

"A few things," replied Ysella.

"Such as trying to keep Administrator Zaenn from ruining the rivers," added Tyresis, "and despoiling croplands."

"Oh . . ." said Heraana, "was Zaenn the one who called you an old woman for worrying too much?"

"I should have treated him like the venomous snake he is," replied Tyresis. "Unfortunately, there are some who nurture snakes."

"Was Zaenn the choice of the Heir rather than the Imperador?" asked Ysella.

"How did you guess," replied Tyresis sarcastically.

"Do you have any idea how the Heir feels about the Coal Act?"

"If he knew what was in it, he might be concerned, but he's less concerned about details and more about loyalty . . . and from whom he can 'borrow' marks that he'll forget to repay."

"Whereas the Imperador cares about both details and loyalty?" asked Ysella, wondering why Tyresis mentioned the Heir's seeking out marks.

"I'll leave that to your judgment," replied Tyresis, but Heraana nodded slightly.

"Might I ask how you two met?" asked Ysella, knowing he'd gotten what little he could about either the Imperador or the Heir from Tyresis.

Tyresis looked to Heraana. "You tell the story so much better."

She offered an amused smile. "My cousin and I were invited to a midsummer dinner at a lodge near Silverhills. So was Engar. We had gotten out of the carriage and were walking toward the lodge, when I saw Engar walking toward us, or rather to a point ahead of us with a long walking stick or staff. He told us to stand back because there were two snakes in the bushes beside the walkway. I asked him what kind, and he said, 'They're snakes.' I said, 'Let me see before you attack them. Most snakes around here aren't venomous. Some actually prey on the cuiprepoints.'"

Heraana shrugged. "They were redbacks, most likely getting ready to mate, and no danger at all. That's how we met."

"I still don't care much for snakes," said Tyresis.

"The only snakes that bother me," added Heraana, "are the human kind."

"I'd have to agree with you," replied Ysella.

Ysella continued to converse with the two until a bell chimed, and he followed the others to the private dining room. While it was smaller than the private salon, if not by much, the décor matched that of the salon. Ysella quickly estimated the table was set for possibly fifty diners, and that, from the place cards, couples were seated together in rough precedence, and adjusted so that there was an alternation of men and women where possible. His place was with Myra Solatiem to his left and Luciala Dhaantyn to his right.

Neatly and politely isolated.

Ysella remembered what he'd read—not that he'd ever been invited to the Palace—that everyone should find their place, then stand behind their chair as the Imperador and his family entered. As soon as the Imperador took his seat, so should everyone else. The Imperador, in a gold and silver formal military coat, stepped into the dining room first, followed by the Imperadora, then Delehya, again in green, a shade somewhat lighter than what she'd worn at the ball. Behind Delehya followed Lorya Kaechar, but only for a few steps. Kaechar positioned herself beside the door, where she could survey the entire table.

The Heir and his wife aren't included? Ysella wondered what was behind that, or was it to avoid having the entire family in the same chamber at the same time?

Even after the Imperador seated himself, there was no blessing. The slightly gray-faced Imperador raised a goblet and proclaimed, "Welcome to the Palace and for joining us in celebration of the coming wedding of our daughter, the Lady Delehya, to the most honorable Ritter Iustaan Detruro, Premier of the Imperial Council of the Imperium of Guldor."

The Imperador's voice was hoarse and difficult to hear, although Ysella was comparatively close.

"Enjoy the dinner and the company." Then Laureous inclined his head in the direction of Delehya.

Ysella glanced across the table, not recognizing the couple seated beside the Imperadora, but wondering if they might be her parents, given how much younger she was than Laureous. Beside them sat Sr. Poncetaryl and his wife, with Commerce Administrator Taeryl Laergaan and his wife next.

He turned to Myra Solatiem, an attractive dark-haired woman with the dark-honey complexion suggesting a landor background. She looked perhaps ten years younger than her husband. "We obviously haven't met formally. As the place card says, I'm Dominic Ysella."

"The councilor who was almost killed for exposing a scoundrel legalist, I presume?" Her tone was one of amusement.

"Alas, but since I'm also a legalist, I had to do something. I just didn't expect such a violent reaction."

"My husband appreciates professional ethics such as yours. He gets rather perturbed if he sees misconduct by anyone in the Navy." Myra paused, then asked, "What kind of legalist?"

"The kind of most use to the Navy, I suspect. I'm a water legalist, in addition to being a councilor, not that I actively practice now." Ysella paused as servers appeared, from seemingly everywhere, presenting each diner with a whitefish and watercress soup to start.

"Since you're chairman of the Council's Waterways Committee, your background must help a great deal."

"To some extent, but there's always something new to learn, usually when another problem arises." Ysella hesitated, then asked, "Might I inquire as to how you met the marshal?"

"By accident, of course. We never should have encountered each other. My family is from the Veerlyn area. I was the youngest of six. According to my mother, I was quite unexpected, since my youngest sibling is eight years older . . ."

From Myra's speech alone, Ysella had no doubt she came from a well-off landor background, and he was happy to listen.

". . . and to be direct about it, my arrival upset certain familial plans."

"Like long-arranged marriages and land determinations?"

Myra laughed softly, but warmly. "You would understand."

"I'm the third son, and the lands were split between my father and my uncle."

"You're also a man. I have three older brothers, and two sisters. In any event, when I was twelve, my mother took me and my oldest sister to Veerlyn to do some shopping, for fabrics and quite a few other things. We started early on Findi, as it had to be. With one thing and another, it was well past noon before we were ready to return to the holding. Something fell off the back of the carriage. Nothing important, a bottle stand, but one of the upper-class cadets at the Military Institute—they could go into town on Findi afternoons—saw it and ran after the carriage.

"He was quite nice, and he and my sister talked for a little bit. Not very long, but somehow, he got her to give her name and address. He wrote her on and off for a year or two, but she couldn't very well keep writing him after she was formally engaged. So I asked if I could. I felt sorry for him, and, I think, in a way, he didn't want to disappoint this young girl. We kept writing, and six years later he showed up at the holding. We were married two years later, and I've never regretted it."

"That's quite a story," said Ysella. "And you ended up eventually married to the highest-ranking officer in Guldor."

"After all those years of writing, I knew he'd amount to something."

"You were obviously right." Ysella quickly finished his soup before the servers returned, removed the bowls, and presented each diner with a gold-edged, white porcelain plate containing petite veal fillets in an egg-cream sauce flavored with minced shallots and tarragon, accompanied by spring beans and potatoes imperial, along with small, hot croissants.

"What about you?" asked Myra.

Ysella briefly summarized his background.

"Then you could marry now," Myra pointed out, "if you're so inclined."

"I've been inclined for several years. Your story is encouraging, though, because I've embarked on correspondence with someone in Aloor that, like you, I met totally by accident. We'll see where it leads."

"Be honest, but gently so."

Ysella chuckled. "I'm trying, but I don't want to overwhelm her, nor come across as too distant."

"If that's the way you feel, it has a good chance of working out."

I certainly hope so.

The remainder of the conversation was lighter, much of it with Luciala Dhaantyn, interspersed with dessert, which consisted of chocolate tarts amandine, with a dollop of lemon sherbet, followed by cordials.

After that, the Imperador nodded to Detruro, who stood, waiting several moments for various conversations to subside before beginning to speak.

"I'd like to thank all of you for coming tonight to share our good news and happiness. As many of you know, months ago I had no idea that such an intelligent, perceptive, and talented young woman would appear in my life so quickly and decisively. I cannot thank her enough for her belief in me, nor can I ever repay the Imperador and Imperadora for their trust in allowing me to wed their only daughter . . ."

When Detruro finished, Delehya rose and stood beside him. The Imperador and Imperadora rose, bowed slightly to the couple, then left the dining room, but Detruro guided Delehya to where Ysella stood.

"Lady Delehya, you're poised and beautiful, as always," said Ysella.

"Could I afford to be otherwise?" she asked dryly, adding, "I'm glad you came—may I call you Dominic?"

"You may, Lady."

"Delehya, in private." She smiled, impishly. "We'll doubtless see much more of you, if not for a while, but I wanted to thank you for your counsel . . . and understanding."

Ysella saw Lorya Kaechar moving from where she'd been posted by the door and said, "Thank you. I won't keep you."

"We need to follow the Imperador," said Detruro quietly.

In moments, Kaechar stood beside Ysella, even before Detruro and Delehya had left the dining room. "Will you tell me what she said?"

"Of course. She thanked me."

Kaechar frowned. "For what?"

"For telling her at the Yearend Ball that I wasn't the right person for her."

"You said that?"

"Why wouldn't I? It's true."

The empath gave a small headshake, followed by a rueful smile. "Someday, I might actually come to like you, Councilor." Then she turned and left the dining room.

Ysella sensed almost everyone looking at him, but he maintained a pleasant smile as Solatiem stepped closer to his wife and addressed Ysella. "That was . . . interesting."

"The Lady Delehya thanked me for telling her she and the Premier were better together than she and I would ever be."

"When did you ever speak to her before?"

"One dance at the Yearend Ball. That's all."

The First Marshal appeared momentarily disconcerted, but Myra Solatiem said cheerfully, "Sometimes, a dance, or a letter, is all it takes." Then she winked at Ysella.

Solatiem smiled amusedly and said, "I'm certain we'll be seeing more of you, Councilor." Then he guided his wife toward the doors.

As Ysella turned to leave the private dining room, Sr. Poncetaryl and his wife moved to intercept him.

"Councilor, you seem to be in the Imperial family's good graces," declared the banker, if with what seemed forced heartiness to Ysella.

"More in the Premier's, I suspect," returned Ysella. "We've worked together for years."

"The Lady Delehya seemed glad to see you," said Poncetaryl's wife.

"She was most gracious, but I've been told she usually is. I wouldn't know, except from others."

As the Poncetaryls departed, Ysella thought that Poncetaryl seemed more than merely surprised that Delehya had greeted Ysella, and no one else, but before he could give that much thought Engar and Heraana Tyresis joined Ysella.

Tyresis grinned. "Now, everyone will be wondering about you."

"As they should," added Heraana, "especially the snakes."

"Have a pleasant endday," said Tyresis, before the couple moved toward the doors.

"Thank you. You two as well."

By the time Ysella got to the Palace entrance, several carriages had already lined up, and he saw Sr. and Sra. Poncetaryl waiting for theirs. In the end, when Caastyn arrived, there was only one coach between the Poncetaryls' carriage and the chaise, and Ysella walked back to the chaise and climbed in.

"Just stay close to the other carriages," he told Caastyn.

"I'd thought the same. They've both got guards as footmen. No sense in not taking advantage of them."

Once the chaise was on the Way of Gold headed toward Imperial Boulevard, a respectfully close distance behind the latter of the two coaches, Caastyn asked, "How was the dinner, sir? Didn't seem like there were that many carriages."

"For the celebration of the engagement of the daughter of the Imperador, the reception and dinner were incredibly modest," said Ysella, "though most people would have found them lavish."

"Do you think circumstances . . . ?"

Ysella laughed. "I doubt that Detruro has spent an unwatched instant with Delehya. The only circumstances I can imagine are that the Imperador wants her under control and out of the Palace as soon as possible. The wedding is likely to be soon, and that will create more rumors about scandalous behavior on her part." Ysella absently wondered why the rumors about Delehya seemed to have subsided. *Or haven't you been where you'd hear them because of your injuries?*

"Almost makes you feel sorry for Lady Delehya."

"More than almost," replied Ysella. *And before the next few years are over, more than a few others will likely be sorry as well.* Why Ysella felt that way, he couldn't have said, but he felt a certainty about it.

55

WHEN Ysella arrived at the breakfast table on Findi morning, Gerdina smiled and said, "You're back on the front page of the newssheets again."

"I hope it's about attending the engagement dinner."

"Not quite," she replied.

Ysella offered a wry smile, picked up the *Tribune,* and began to read.

> With a comparatively small, if lavish, reception and dinner last night at the Imperial Palace, Imperador Laureous announced the engagement of his only daughter, the Lady Delehya, to Ritter Iustaan Emyll Detruro, Premier of the Imperial Council and Councilor from Enke...
>
> Besides the Imperador and the Imperadora, notable guests at the dinner included First Marshal Gunnar Solatiem, Fleet Marshal Raul Dhaantyn, Presidente Omar Poncetaryl of the Banque of Machtarn, Administrator of the Treasury Tybaalt Salaazar, Administrator of Commerce Taeryl Laergaan, and Councilor Dominic Ysella, as the representative of the Imperial Council...
>
> According to sources at the Palace, the total number of guests was less than fifty, less than might be expected, but the Imperador has always avoided excessively large numbers of invitees for affairs that are primarily about family...

Ysella couldn't help rereading one of the sections of the lengthy story...

> ... although Councilor Ysella was rumored to have been one of the possible suitors for the Lady Delehya, he was overheard to say that the Premier "was a better match for the Lady Delehya," perhaps not surprising given the Councilor's background and exploits...

Where did they get that information? Although Ysella had told several people that Detruro was a better match, he suspected Lorya Kaechar was the source, if indirectly, which made matters more interesting... and slightly unsettling.

When Ysella finished the story, he took several sips of café, then quickly read through the rest of the newssheet, which contained a brief story noting that the Polidoran clipper *Kossdeas* had ported in Machtarn with the nine staffers from the Guldoran legation exiled by the Grande Duce. There was also an announcement of the public auction sale of the properties formerly held by the Gustov Torryl Trust. The only other news story bearing indirectly on the Council was one noting that the price of lumber in Guldor was already increasing because of the damage to the port facilities at Endor and to sections of the river immediately to the west.

After breakfast, Ysella went to his study, his thoughts going back to the previous evening, particularly to the Imperador.

Was his ill health another reason for such a comparatively small and private dinner? And why wasn't the Heir present?

He was still thinking over those and other questions when Caastyn returned from his daily trip to the post centre.

Caastyn smiled broadly as he handed Ysella two letters, one of which had to be from Aelyn Wythcomb, with the second from Bruuk Fettryk. "It looks as though she was interested enough to reply."

"Unless it's a letter saying that she's not interested in more correspondence," replied Ysella.

"Wouldn't she just fail to write you back?"

"She's too well-mannered for that."

"Then I'll hope she's agreeing to more letters," replied Caastyn.

"That makes two of us."

After Caastyn left the study, Ysella decided to read Bruuk's letter first.

Dominic—

You've obviously been busier, or more noticed, this year. I read a favorable story in the Chronicle *about how you amended the Coal Act to protect streams and landowners from coal wastes not handled properly. Let's hope the Imperador approves it . . .*

One of the problems of distance: Laureous has already signed it and Bruuk might not know yet.

I also thought you might like to know that Jaahn Escalante bought up a chunk of property to the north of the Ahnkaar mine, and there are whispers that young Rugaar Maartyn is trying to buy more land around Aloor. From what I've heard, they're offering prices that the most well-off landors couldn't or wouldn't pay. We certainly couldn't.

Maergot Bonnstyl stopped by my office in town the other day.

Actually, she brought almost a small cart of legal books and treatises that had been her father's, along with some bookcases. She said she'd written you about half being yours. I've got your half set up in the study as well. There's no hurry. They can stay there as long as you wish. In the meantime, the combined volumes make me look like the most scholarly legalist in Aloor and for several hundred milles in any direction . . .

In addition, I thought you might like to know that Gineen ran into Aelyn Wythcomb in town again. This time, Aelyn sought out Gineen. While Gineen wouldn't offer details, I think it's fair to say that Ritten Wythcomb is interested in you. From what I've overheard and seen, she was appreciated more by Thenyt in passing than by Khael at any time . . .

If there's anything I can do for you in Aloor, let me know. For what it's worth, I wish you the best of fortune with Ritten Wythcomb.

With what Bruuk had written, Ysella was almost afraid to open the letter from Aelyn Wythcomb. Finally, he slit the envelope and extracted the sheets of paper.

At least it's not a single page.

Councilor Ysella—

Thank you for your timely and considered reply to my questions. Your words are well-chosen, yet surprisingly direct, and in accord with my inquiries about you. In the course of those inquiries, I discovered that you had made similar inquiries about me. As a preliminary to getting to know each other, such investigations are doubtless necessary, but can only be the merest beginning.

Ysella nodded. *In short, what we've each discovered is far from what we need to know about each other.*

Because our present has been formed in part by our pasts, any beginning must also take into account some matters of the past. As you doubtless know, my marriage to Khael Wythcomb was considered a necessity by both families. As such, while we respected each other, our affection was tempered because we had very different views on many matters. I was three years older than Khael and raised in rather different circumstances by my grandparents. They were quite traditional, but my grandfather was always kind

> *and respectful of my grandmother, even as they did their best to deal with a land and a family that had been altered significantly over their lives . . .*

A slightly less direct way of saying that she expects to be respected, not dominated.

> *. . . the evening meal was always a time for conversation and speculation about events, political and otherwise, while remaining polite over disagreements. As a child, my views—although not always accepted, and often critiqued, when necessary—were listened to in the same manner as anyone else's. I was raised to learn and do everything necessary on a holding, even if I might never have that responsibility . . .*

As he continued to read Aelyn's letter, Ysella saw why she might not have been especially happy being wed to Khael Wythcomb.

> *. . . growing up as I did, I found there were times when there wasn't enough time to accomplish all that was expected and times where I had to entertain myself. In those times, I often read history and much older tomes, because those were what filled the library shelves. One of the most intriguing books was a series of essays entitled* Averra— The City of Truth. *When I asked my grandparents about Averra, they couldn't tell me anything except that it had been a small land somewhere—they thought—in Sudlynd or perhaps on the fringes of Teknold and it perished long ago. No other history mentioned Averra. Yet, I sensed from the essays that Averra had once existed. So I was intrigued to learn that your house in Machtarn stands on Averra Place. Do you know any more about Averra?*

Ysella shook his head, as if Aelyn had stood beside him and asked the question, and he, too, wondered about the odd connection. After several moments, he continued reading. When he finished, he reread the last paragraph.

> *Now that you know a bit more about me, I'd like more insight about you, especially about growing up as the third son of former royalty and why you chose the comparatively mundane profession of a water legalist, not that I don't appreciate and haven't benefitted from your expertise.*

I do look forward to hearing from you.

Aelyn Wythcomb

How do you write a reply that's as honest as what she wrote?
For a good third of a bell, Ysella tried to write a decent opening paragraph. Finally, he decided, in a fashion, to follow her example.

Ritten Wythcomb—
As you so aptly wrote, we are the result of what we have done, or not done, in the past. In lesser fashion, we're also a reflection of what our parents and grandparents did. In some ways, my brothers and I grew up as you did, although we were not thought mature enough to do more than listen at the dinner table until we were able to physically labor effectively on the holding.

The majority of the family lands were taken after the fall of Aloor. Those left would support, at most, two families, and my grandfather had two sons and no daughters. I have two older brothers, and I knew from an early age that I would not inherit land. I also knew it was not in my nature to be happy running a holding or of mind, or temperament, to marry for those lands. For whatever reason, as a boy, I wondered about the rules under which we live, both those set in law and those unspoken, and that led to my apprenticing as a legal clerk and eventually reading the law and becoming a legalist.

I was incredibly fortunate to learn the law and much more from Legrand Quaentyn. He taught me how to be a legalist, as well as the spirit of evenhandedness in which law should be interpreted and enforced. I can honestly say I visited with him every time I returned to Aloor and gained something from every conversation.

Ysella paused, then continued.

While you were essentially coerced into marriage, the requirements of being a good legalist, then a good councilor at a comparatively young age, effectively took enough of my time that, by the time I was partly established, I realized the eligible women I met were more interested in my position and title than the substance of what I found important. As you so accurately pointed out, what a councilor can do is indeed limited, and it can make a difference at times, but only if a councilor is willing to spend long bells finding a way to make that difference.

There's little true glamour to being a councilor, except possibly the title. You may read about the Imperador's Yearend Ball, but in the eight years I've been a councilor, I've spoken to the Imperador once—this past Yearend, when he asked me, for political purposes, to dance one dance with his daughter, who will now shortly wed Premier Detruro. The position of councilor embodies a great deal of routine: shaping or changing laws to make them fairer or more effective without offending the Imperador, holding hearings on a range of matters that may or may not require remedial legislation, and answering letters from writers in Aloor that address all manner of problems, some of which the Council can do little to change. For all that, I do believe that in the Council lies the hope for the future of Guldor. That is why I will remain a councilor so long as the people of Aloor will have me.

I have no doubt, even from our brief conversation and a few letters, that you understand far more than most people about the complexities and complications of life, and thus, of government. Your questions of me are well-written and perceptive. Such perception is far rarer than most people realize, and I find both intelligence and hope in your words.

As for Averra, your inquiry told me more than I've been able to discover anywhere else, and for that, I also thank you.

Every time I've written, I've looked forward to your reply, as I do now.

Ysella replaced the pen in its holder and waited for the ink to dry before finally rereading what he had written.

When he reread the letter, he set it down, wondering if he'd been too dry or not conveyed enough emotion.

But she clearly wants honesty. But the problem, as Ysella well realized, was that trying too hard to convey honesty risked dishonesty. *And too polished a letter also creates the impression of deceit.*

Finally, he signed and sealed it.

56

ON Unadi, Ysella saddled Jaster, with only a few twinges in his ribs, then led the gelding out, mounted, and rode to the Council Hall through a misty and hazy spring morning. He felt glad not to have to impose on Caastyn every time he had to go somewhere and equally pleased that the weather was warm enough that he didn't need a riding jacket.

When he neared the Council Hall, he saw no excessive number of carriages, suggesting nothing untoward had occurred. After reaching the Council stables, he dismounted and led the gelding inside, then unstrapped his leather case.

"Glad to see you back riding, Councilor," said the ostler who took Jaster.

"Thank you."

Ysella walked quickly to his office, but the moment he stepped inside, he saw Reimer Daarkyn waiting. Stifling a sigh, Ysella waved a hand. "Come on in, Reimer." Then he kept walking to his personal office, where he set his case on the desk.

Daarkyn followed, closing the door behind himself.

Ysella gestured to the chairs and sat down behind the desk. "What's on your mind this morning, Reimer?" *As if I didn't already know.*

"You represented the Council at the engagement dinner for the Lady Delehya and the Premier. Yet you said you knew nothing. You lied or at best misled me."

Ysella shook his head. "I never said I didn't know. I said that I couldn't tell you. That was true. I was ordered not to tell anyone."

Daarkyn snorted loudly. "You're like all legalists, twisting words so that people hear what they want."

"Like newshawks, you mean?" said Ysella.

The newshawk ignored the sarcasm and asked, "So when are they actually getting married?"

"I understand it won't be a long engagement."

"Have they set a date?"

"I believe so."

"But you can't tell me?"

"Exactly."

"Why do you say you believe so, if you know?"

"Because I don't know if the Imperador has confirmed it."

Surprisingly to Ysella, Daarkyn said, "That's fair. Now, what do you know about the usury-cap legislation?"

"I don't know any more than what I told you earlier. I suspect that the Commerce Committee chairman is considering reporting out a bill to lift the cap, but I have no idea to what level or when."

"Can you tell me anything else?"

"I've heard, indirectly, that the Treasury Administrator doesn't like the idea, but that's at least thirdhand, and I've heard nothing about why he might oppose it."

"Does that have anything to do with the new regional banque charters for Devult, Eshbruk, and Suvion?" asked Daarkyn.

"I have no idea. All I know about that is what appeared in the *Tribune*."

"Have you heard the latest about Commerce Administrator Laergaan?"

"I haven't heard anything about him lately. I saw him at the engagement dinner, but never talked to him."

"You didn't talk to him at all?" pressed Daarkyn.

"No. I talked with quite a few people, but not him."

"What about Treasury Administrator Salaazar?"

"I haven't spoken to him since we exchanged brief greetings at the Yearend Ball a year and a half ago. He's not inclined to meet with anyone besides the Premier or the chairman of the Commerce Committee, if absolutely necessary. Why? What is the latest about Laergaan?"

"He came home from the engagement dinner ill and got worse. Word is that he might not live."

Ysella didn't have to feign surprise. "That's . . ." He shook his head.

"When people get that ill after having been at the Palace . . ."

"There's always a question of whether it's just an illness—is that what you're insinuating?"

"You have to admit that there have been more than a few strange occurrences possibly involving the Palace," said Daarkyn, "such as Fleet Marshal Elias Haarwyk. Not to mention Councilor Daenyld."

"How does that involve Laergaan and Salaazar? While Salaazar may be against lifting the usury cap, I'm not aware that Laergaan has expressed any opinion at all."

"Did you know that Administrator Salaazar opposed any borrowing by the government when the Council debated the last appropriations measure?"

"I heard the Palace told the Premier that the banques wouldn't buy any government bonds."

"That had to be Salaazar," confirmed Daarkyn. "I've talked to several banques. None of them were aware of that possibility. Salaazar told *them* the Imperador opposed borrowing, even on a short-term basis. He also told the Premier that the banques wouldn't buy notes or bonds."

And Laergaan was talking to the presidente of the Banque of Machtarn at the dinner . . . if Laergaan found out that Salaazar was lying to the Imperador . . .

Daarkyn frowned. "You know something, don't you?"

"I don't know anything you don't, and you clearly know more than I do. I wonder why Salaazar didn't want anyone to know that banques near Machtarn would have been willing to lend to the Treasury."

"It can't be just that," Daarkyn pointed out.

"You're right," agreed Ysella, "but if it is a case of poison, would Salaazar risk it at a reception? Or is there someone who'd like to make Salaazar look guilty?" While Ysella could envision Lorya Kaechar using empathic abilities to conceal someone poisoning Salaazar for repeatedly lying to the Imperador, would she allow someone innocent, or comparatively innocent, to die so that Salaazar would take the blame? *Even given what Laureous and the Heir have likely already done, it's unlikely, but not impossible.*

"There are quite a few possibilities, when you put it that way," said Daarkyn. "Do you have any other ideas?"

"Not at the moment. I had no idea that Laergaan was ill . . . or poisoned, until you told me. So, I haven't had much chance to think about it."

Daarkyn stood. "Thank you." Then he turned and left, quietly closing the door.

For several moments, Ysella sat, thinking. He could see why Salaazar didn't want Laergaan to have the chance to tell Laureous that Salaazar had lied, but enough to poison Laergaan? Why hadn't anyone else told the Imperador? Then, too, Laureous didn't trust or believe the local bankers and wouldn't meet with them, and Poncetaryl hadn't been seated close to the Imperador. Normally, Laergaan wouldn't be dealing with financing or interest rates, but if he told Klempt or Detruro about Salaazar's duplicity . . .

But what was so important to Salaazar that he had to keep the interest rate cap so low?

Ysella had no idea, but Stefan Nortaak might know, since he represented Oersynt and Salaazar came from Oersynt. Because Ysella had to meet with the Waterways Committee legalist to look over the draft legislation dealing with waterway safety guidelines and liability, he could stop by Nortaak's office after that . . . and possibly Detruro's office later, depending on what he learned.

He stood and walked into the outer office. "Lyaard, I'm going to the Waterways Committee staff office. I'll be a bit."

Ysella only saw a staffer or two on his walk to the first level and to a door on one side of the main committee room. Ysella knocked, then entered. Although Arturo Palaan was the Waterways Committee legalist, his office was scarcely bigger than a small washroom.

Before the older legalist could react, Ysella motioned for him to keep his seat, then sat in the single chair. "We need to go over the waterway safety code draft."

"Yes, sir." Palaan turned and picked up a file, which he handed to Ysella. "This is the current draft, sir."

"With all the changes?"

Palaan nodded.

Ysella began to read, slowly and carefully. While the draft only consisted of five pages, close to a third of a bell passed before he finished reading and looked at Palaan.

"Sir?"

"I have a few questions and thoughts. First, the definition of 'inland waters.' Not all inland waters are navigable. Do you think we should clarify that the provisions of the bill only apply to those waters that are navigable? I understand that, in reality, the provisions are self-limiting because we won't have boats getting in each other's way on non-navigable waters. From a political point of view, however, we don't want to give the impression of trying to extend government to all waters, only those that are navigable and only as a guideline for action and determining liability."

Palaan nodded. "There shouldn't be any problem in addressing both points."

"Also, is there any reason to describe the recommended code as 'most widely used and accepted' in the text of the bill itself?" asked Ysella. "We know it is, but couldn't that open it up to nitpicking? We just want to establish that this is the recommended code . . ."

Palaan frowned. "I see what you mean."

The rest of Ysella's concerns took another third to address enough to guide Palaan.

When they finished, Ysella asked, "Can you have eight copies for the committee by Tridi?"

"That won't be a problem, sir."

Ysella stood and smiled. "Thank you, Arturo."

From Palaan's office, Ysella climbed the steps to the second level and walked almost to the end of the corridor, since Stefan Nortaak was one of the more junior councilors.

When he entered the office, one of the clerks said, "The councilor's not here, Councilor Ysella."

"If you'd tell him that I'd appreciate his dropping by sometime today."

"Yes, sir."

Ysella returned to his own office and read the latest batch of incoming letters. Several complained of flooding after heavy spring rains in the upper reaches of the Khulor River. The writers insisted that the flooding could have been avoided if more funds from the waterways bill had gone to Aloor. *Except that repairs couldn't have begun for another month, even if additional funds had been available.*

Then he read more letters, stopping and rereading a phrase here and again, before writing his notes on each.

About a third before midday, Khaard knocked on his slightly ajar door and said, "Councilor Nortaak, sir."

"Have him come in." Ysella stood to greet Nortaak, who was a good ten years older, then gestured to the chairs.

"You stopped by my office earlier, Dominic," said Nortaak as he seated himself.

"I did."

"Is this something about the committee?"

"No. It's about something involved with legislation concerning the cap on usury."

"That's a bit afield for you, isn't it?"

Ysella ignored the slightly patronizing tone. "Not completely. I introduced a bill to raise the cap and testified informally before the Commerce Committee, at the request of Chairman Klempt. He's asked me about things a few times. I understand that Treasury Administrator Salaazar is from Oersynt."

Nortaak frowned, then said, "He is, but I only met him once or twice before I became a councilor. His family owns, or at least controls, the Banque of Oersynt. He was assistant manager of the banque, in charge of lending, as I recall, and his older brother is the manager of all operations."

"Do you have any idea how he became Treasury Administrator?"

"Not for certain. Some said that his grandfather loaned marks to the Imperador during the Alooran occupation, when some of the other banques couldn't provide enough."

"Is there another banque in Oersynt?"

"There's the Commerce Banque. It's newer, but it's grown at lot in the past few years. They loan more to commercer types."

Ysella couldn't miss the slight scorn in Nortaak's reference to commercers, but simply said, "That would suggest that there are more manufactories in Oersynt these days."

"Unfortunately."

"Do you recall anything of interest about Administrator Salaazar?"

"Not particularly. The Salaazar family is one of the older landor families, very well established and well thought of. Why do you ask?"

"He's been rather vocal about government not borrowing from banques, but if his family was willing to lend to the Imperador, that would seem a little contradictory. So the Premier asked me if you might be able to shed some light on the apparent contradiction."

"The Premier?"

"He's asked me to work with him on a few matters besides waterways, and since you're on the Waterways Committee . . ."

Nortaak fingered his chin. "You were at the engagement dinner, weren't you?"

"At the request of the Premier and the Imperador," Ysella confirmed.

"Is the Premier considering a change in the floor leader?"

"Not that I know. He's felt the commercers need a spokesman."

"Don't you think they already have enough power?" asked Nortaak.

"That decision has to be the Premier's. Perhaps he feels that having Maatrak close keeps matters more under control."

"I'm more inclined to believe that it merely encourages the commercers."

"I appreciate that insight." *But not the way you're likely to think.* "I'll pass it on. Do you have any other thoughts about Administrator Salaazar?"

"I'd tend to believe that his heart is in the right place."

Ysella stood. "Thank you so much for returning my visit. You've been very helpful."

"You're welcome, Dominic. I'm always glad to be of assistance." The patronizing tone crept back into Nortaak's last words.

Ysella waited until Nortaak was well on his way before walking swiftly down to the Premier's office, hoping to find Detruro available.

The Premier was indeed present and saw Ysella immediately.

Ysella related what Daarkyn had said.

At Ysella's mention of Daarkyn, Detruro frowned and continued frowning. Once Ysella finished, he asked, "Why do you meet with the newshawk?"

"Because I occasionally learn something, like what I told you." Ysella paused. "Did you know about Laergaan?"

"I haven't heard anything yet, and, if Daarkyn is correct, it may be a while before anyone tells me . . . if they do at all."

"I imagine his illness or death will show up in the *Tribune* sooner or later. I doubt Daarkyn would blatantly lie." *Possibly exaggerate or slant, but not tell an outright falsehood.*

"We'll see." Detruro pulled on his earlobe, almost absently. "I get uneasy about your talking with Daarkyn, but better you than me."

Ysella smiled. "Exactly." Then he related what Nortaak had said about Salaazar and the Banque of Oersynt.

Detruro shook his head. "So Salaazar opposes the increase in the usury cap because it will put the Banque of Oersynt at more of a disadvantage compared to the Commerce Bank?"

"That's my guess. But his real problem is lying and hiding things from the Imperador."

"Laureous hates being deceived. But why would Salaazar persist? He could simply have told Laureous that none of the banques were in favor of increasing the interest cap last year, but some of them considered favoring it because times were changing." Detruro frowned again. "Unless the Banque of Oersynt is shakier than anyone knows. Or Salaazar's position within the family is precarious."

"Nortaak emphasized how well-respected the family is."

"Respect is often the last illusion to collapse before failure," said Detruro dryly.

"Bankers have to build respect, but you've already achieved that. Perhaps you should consider founding a banque at some point," said Ysella with a chuckle. "After you no longer want to be premier, that is. With your personal connections and those of your wife-to-be . . ."

"What a horrifying thought," declared Detruro, his lips twisting as if to a bad taste.

"I don't know," replied Ysella. "I've talked to bankers. Some of them have no imagination and no vision. That might be why the Banque of Oersynt is slowly failing."

"We don't know that. It's a learned guess right now. Besides, there's this very small problem about fixing government before the Heir becomes Imperador."

"There is that," admitted Ysella. "Have you considered any possible changes to the reform plan?"

"The plan doesn't need changes. We need to obtain more support first, especially among the senior marshals in the Navy and Army."

More support? That sounded like Detruro had already garnered some support, possibly with Delehya's assistance.

After a moment of silence, Detruro said, "You mentioned some committee legislation . . ."

"There are two bills that might affect the Navy. I could ask Fleet Marshal Dhaantyn for an appointment to talk about them, or one of them."

"That would be good. It certainly can't hurt."

"By the way, where will the wedding be held?"

"At the Palace. Where else?"

"And you two will be living . . . ?"

"My house, for now, that is, after I change a number of items and get a new bed. Even then, she'll be spending most of her day at the Palace, helping her father."

"Does Laureous trust her or merely allow her to be close?"

"Insofar as he trusts anyone," replied the Premier, asking after a brief hesitation, "Is there anything else I should know?"

"Not that I know of. I won't take any more of your time." Ysella stood and inclined his head.

"Unlike too many others." Detruro laughed softly, but harshly.

After leaving the Premier, Ysella returned to his office, where he immediately drafted and dispatched a message to Fleet Marshal Dhaantyn, requesting an appointment to discuss pending legislation that might be of interest to the Imperial Navy.

He spent the rest of the afternoon dealing with correspondence and making notes for his possible meeting with Dhaantyn, notes that he could and would turn into a detailed letter if Dhaantyn declined to meet in the near future.

57

As he rode through a light misting rain to the Council Hall on Duadi, Ysella wondered when or if he'd hear back from Aelyn Wythcomb, but pushed that thought away once he reached his office.

Before reading through the few incoming letters, Ysella checked the committee schedule, particularly for the Commerce Committee, but found no mention of action on measures dealing with either the usury cap or the Imperial regional banque charters. Then, after reading through the correspondence and signing or changing responses, he headed down to the Waterways Committee.

Once the committee members were all present, Ysella gaveled the committee to order and declared, "Today's meeting will deal with the port standards bill. First, I'd like each of you to go over the list of duplicative terms. Those are listed on the sheets before each of you, with the most widely used term for a service placed first."

While Ysella could have simply given the other members of the committee the lists and proceeded from there, he'd learned there was always someone who didn't bother reading such routine material—who then complained in the markup sessions of a bill, usually loudly and at length, that he hadn't been properly informed.

Ysella waited while the others scanned the sheets.

In less than a sixth, Astyn Coerl asked, "Sr. Chairman, why are shore handling and stevedoring separate categories?"

Ysella refrained from sighing. "Stevedoring is the same as cargo handling, you will note. Both terms refer to the loading or off-loading of cargo from a vessel. Shore handling is the movement of cargoes previously off-loaded or awaiting loading to different locales within the harbor or port. Depending on the harbor or port, stevedores may handle both duties, or shoreside cargo handlers may be the ones to do the shore handling."

"Isn't that a distinction without a difference?"

"Not to those paying the fees," replied Haans Maessyn.

"And why are wharfage charges different from cargo-handling charges?" asked Coerl.

"Because wharfage charges, or cargo dues, are based on the weight, volume, or number of the goods, and are split between the port and the government, while handling charges are for the labor involved in loading or unloading."

After a good third of explaining terms, mostly to Coerl, Ysella and the other councilors went on to discuss various possible provisions for setting standard terminology and procedures for all Imperial ports and Guldoran harbors, a tedious process Ysella could tell would require at least two or three more committee meetings, if not more. The process could have been shortened if Astyn Coerl didn't seem to require detailed explanations of everything.

Ysella had the feeling that either he'd hear from Haans Maessyn about Coerl, or Coerl would hear directly from Maessyn.

After Ysella gaveled the meeting to a close, he returned to his office, where he spent more time refining the material for presentation to Fleet Marshal Dhaantyn. After that, he studied the Waterways Committee schedule for the next few months to see what meetings could be changed.

As Ysella suspected, Haans Maessyn walked into Ysella's office just after first bell of the afternoon.

Once Maessyn closed the door to Ysella's private office and sat down, he said quietly, "How can you be so calm with Astyn's continued stupidity? The man doesn't think, and he makes no effort to learn anything."

"Because displaying the anger I feel would make matters worse." *Not to mention that it would also suggest I'm not all that competent.* "Also, revealing his shortcomings publicly would diminish the Council, and that's the last thing we need right now."

"What do we need right now, really?"

"A Council with more real power and an Imperador with less."

"Just how are we going to get that?" asked Maessyn acidly.

"That's a good question, and I don't have an answer at the moment, except that an armed uprising won't work."

"Why not?"

"Because the Army and the Navy have all the power, and they'll put down an insurrection. They probably wouldn't oppose some form of mostly peaceful change if it preserved their position and power." Ysella paused, then added, "That's my opinion. I've never talked to any senior officers or marshals about it."

"Maybe someone should, possibly our noble Premier," suggested Maessyn sardonically.

Ysella was about to respond when he realized that Detruro couldn't be the one to make overtures to the marshals, because, if the marshals didn't agree, the Council as an entity could be so discredited that the Imperador's power would increase—and that was the best of outcomes under those circumstances. By the same token, the marshals couldn't make overtures to the Council, not without immediately risking their lives. "It's not that simple. Somehow, both the Premier and the Imperador have to be put in a position where both have to agree."

"And how could that ever happen?"

Ysella managed a laugh. "If I knew that . . ."

Maessyn shook his head. "Maybe you'd better figure it out. No one else seems to be even trying."

"I'll keep that in mind, Haans."

"That's all I had. You're a good listener, Dominic."

Ysella stood. "You've made some good points. I'll do what I can."

Maessyn stood as well. "You always do . . . unlike some."

Once the other councilor had left, Ysella paced slowly around his office, thinking, and asking himself if he really wanted to do what he had in mind. *But if Dhaantyn won't see you, you'll have to come up with something else.*

He'd only gotten back to looking over responses drafted by the clerks for perhaps a third of a bell when Khaard rapped on the half-open door.

"A message from someone in the Navy for you, sir."

"How . . ." Then Ysella shook his head. The envelope likely bore a seal.

"Besides the seal and the fact that a Navy messenger delivered it, sir?" asked Khaard in an amused tone.

"That would do it," returned Ysella lightly, standing and taking the envelope.

Once Khaard left, Ysella opened the envelope. The message was simple.

Councilor Ysella—

I'd be happy to meet with you on Furdi, the twenty-second of Springfirst, at third afternoon bell, to discuss possible pending legislation that could have an impact on the Navy and naval operations.

Enter the Palace through the entrance to the north wing.

The signature was that of Raul Dhaantyn.

Dhaantyn's acceptance meant that Ysella would have to make another change to the Waterways Committee schedule. He set aside the reply and drafted a note to all committee members as well as one to Arturo Palaan notifying that consideration of the draft waterway safety code bill would be postponed until after the committee received comments from the Imperial Navy. He didn't explain why he deviated from the usual practice of providing a copy of the bill after initial markup.

He added an additional notation to Arturo Palaan asking for two copies of the latest version of the water safety code bill by the end of Tridi.

Then he wrote a message to Detruro, requesting the use of the Council's official coach on Furdi for a meeting with the Fleet Marshal to discuss legislative proposals that could affect the Imperial Navy.

All of that, he knew, was the easy—and safe—part.

58

On Furdi afternoon, Ysella stepped into the Council's official coach at a third past second bell. The coach arrived at the palace gates a third later, and as Ysella was prepared to present the letter from Dhaantyn, the duty guard said to the coach driver, "The councilor is expected. Straight to the north wing entrance. You can wait for him there."

The coach came to a halt opposite the north wing doors at a sixth before third bell.

The moment Ysella left the coach, carrying his leather case with copies of the water safety code legislative proposal, a uniformed ranker in crisp whites stepped forward. "Councilor Ysella, this way, sir."

Ysella nodded and followed the ranker through the polished bronze double doors, past two armed naval marines, rather than Palace guards, and down the wide marble-floored corridor for roughly thirty yards before turning left into a shorter corridor that ended at a single door.

The ranker opened the door for Ysella, and followed him in.

Ysella stepped into the anteroom, and another ranker at a desk immediately stood. "Just a moment, Councilor. I'll tell Marshal Dhaantyn you're here." Then he turned and walked to the door behind and to the right of the desk, knocked, opened the door slightly, and said, "Councilor Ysella, sir."

Ysella didn't catch the response, but the ranker returned to his desk, but did not seat himself.

In moments, Raul Dhaantyn appeared in the doorway of his office. "Please come in, Councilor."

After Dhaantyn stepped back and entered the office, Ysella followed, closing the door behind himself, and took the middle seat of the three before the wide desk, largely clear except for papers in one of the two document boxes.

"Thank you for seeing me on short notice," Ysella began as he opened his case and extracted one of the copies of the water safety bill. "I brought a copy of the current version of the proposed waterway safety act." He extended the document to Dhaantyn.

The Fleet Marshal took it and set it to one side. "Why do you think this legislation might be necessary?"

"We're setting forth or codifying the largely long-accepted right-of-way procedures for waterways and near offshore waters, so as to clarify the bases of damages and liability. There's no unified legal basis for it, and Alooran and Guldoran legal precedents have some conflicts. We're not setting hard and fast regulations, but what you might call a standard of reasonableness. Since Guldoran law does allow claims against naval vessels, albeit in limited circumstances, I only felt that bringing this to your attention early would be best."

Dhaantyn nodded and said pleasantly, "We certainly appreciate the advance notice. The Navy will be happy to comment on the water safety code bill, and the port standards bill, once we receive it. We should be able to suggest some improvements. We appreciate that opportunity . . . very much."

"We hoped that would make eventual passage much easier," replied Ysella, waiting for Dhaantyn's next words.

The Fleet Marshal leaned forward just slightly. "I couldn't help but notice that you were the Council representative at the Lady Delehya's engagement announcement dinner, although you're not the Council floor leader . . . and you were the only one she talked to besides the Premier and her father. You requested this meeting, something that no other committee chair, besides the chairmen of the Military Affairs Committee, has done in years, if ever."

"I did," replied Ysella. "Possibly, I'm reading too much into matters, but I've gotten the impression that the Navy and possibly the Army have certain military concerns that are shared by the Council, but not by the Imperador and the Heir."

"That's happened before," replied Dhaantyn evenly. "With a powerful Imperador, we're limited in how we can express our concerns, as is the Council."

"Theoretically—and I say this only in theory—the Imperium might have more effective and popularly supported government if both the Navy and the Army and the Council were freer to at least discuss the military and other challenges in a less . . . indirect fashion."

"Open discussion could be beneficial, provided it is really discussion and not merely each side stating unyielding points."

"I couldn't agree more," said Ysella. "Of course, the difficulty is always in the details of how to establish such constructive dialogue and discussion."

"Isn't it always?" asked Dhaantyn ironically.

"Part of the problem, currently, lies in the imbalance of power."

"That's required by the Establishment Act."

"True, but the Establishment Act can be changed," said Ysella. "In principle, anyway."

"In practice, that seems unlikely."

"It might be possible, though," suggested Ysella, "if the Imperador thought that not changing it might imperil his legacy and reputation."

Dhaantyn frowned. "That's a reasonable observation, but the Imperador . . ."

Ysella understood. Dhaantyn couldn't utter the obvious, not with the possibility that Lorya Kaechar might ask what he'd said to Ysella.

"You're right, of course, at present," said Ysella as if Dhaantyn had spoken the implication. "But if it were possible, if the changes to the Establishment Act shifted the balance of power slightly, so that the Imperador had a bit less and the Council a bit more, how might that be received?"

"How much less?" asked Dhaantyn.

"Theoretically, of course, if perhaps two-thirds of the Council could override an Imperial veto of legislation . . ."

"Since you're talking the impossible, why not make the Imperador a figurehead?" asked the marshal.

Ysella shook his head. "The Council ruling completely would be worse than the present situation, believe me."

Dhaantyn chuckled. "I believe you in that, but even if it were possible, what changes to the Establishment Act would that require?"

"Whatever changes that needed to be made," said Ysella, "would have to be carefully drafted . . . very carefully drafted."

The marshal nodded, then said, "You're one of the few legalists in the Council, and the only one not on the Justiciary Committee, as I recall."

Ysella wondered exactly how Dhaantyn knew that.

As if he'd read Ysella's face, Dhaantyn said, "The First Marshal asked me to dig up everything we could on you."

"Even I didn't know that," replied Ysella. "I suspected it, but you don't go around asking other councilors—unless you're the Premier, which I'm not." He paused, then said, "If you don't mind my asking, were you at all close to Fleet Marshal Haarwyk?"

"Close? I wouldn't say that, but there are so few senior officers that we certainly know each other. Elias was a good man. He had sound judgment about what was best for the Navy."

"From what I've heard, at times that can be a handicap."

"It can. That's why senior officers have to weigh every word spoken in public, and any word spoken to more than one person at a single time is effectively spoken in public."

Ysella understood both messages, and one of them meant that he wouldn't be speaking to Dhaantyn again for some time, if ever. "I can see that."

"That's because you're a councilor."

Ysella smiled. "Sometimes, it helps. Sometimes, not. You've been very kind to see me. Speaking for the Waterways Committee, we appreciate the Navy looking at the draft bill, and look forward to seeing the Navy's recommendations. When the standards bill is ready, can I have it sent to you? After that, if there's any need for further meetings, you can let me know. Is that acceptable?"

"Very acceptable, Councilor. It's been a pleasure and most useful talking to you." Dhaantyn stood, as did Ysella.

Then the Fleet Marshal extended a card. "In case you have need to reach me at less convenient times, here's my home address."

Ysella accepted the card. "I appreciate that courtesy. It's most thoughtful of you, and I'll not abuse that privilege."

Dhaantyn offered an amused smile. "I know. I wouldn't have offered otherwise." He hesitated, before adding, "I do expect the same care in anything you draft."

"How could it be otherwise?"

"Indeed," replied Dhaantyn. "Convey my regards to the Premier."

"I certainly will." Ysella picked up his case, then nodded politely before turning and leaving the office.

Outside, the same ranker who had escorted him in waited to escort him back to the waiting Council coach. The ranker remained at the north wing entrance at least until the coach pulled away.

Although it was past fourth bell when Ysella reached the Council Hall, he immediately went to Detruro's office. He had no doubts that the Premier would be there, wanting to know what had transpired at the meeting.

Even so, Ysella had to wait a sixth or so until Stefan Nortaak left Detruro's personal office. Nortaak avoided looking anywhere close to Ysella and strode out with a certain stiffness of carriage suggesting displeasure. After several moments, Detruro appeared in the doorway of his personal office and gestured for Ysella to come in.

After entering and closing the door, Ysella said, "I take it that Stefan was displeased that I'm also interested in the usury cap . . . and possibly that I'm not deferential to my elders?"

Detruro sat down and said, "He didn't mention the deference, but that's because I've told him that quite a few things are more important than age. He did ask, short of demanding, why you were exceeding your responsibilities as Waterways Committee chair. I told him that both Oskaar and I had requested your views and assistance."

Ysella took the chair closest to Detruro. "And he wanted to know why he wasn't consulted?"

"He didn't ask, not in words, but his whole demeanor did."

"He wouldn't look at me as he walked out."

"That's not why you're here, I hope."

"No. I thought you'd like to know how my meeting with the Fleet Marshal went." Ysella recounted the meeting, including Dhaantyn's not putting anything in words that could be construed as either disloyalty to the Imperador or an endorsement of change in government. He also mentioned the card Dhaantyn had handed him.

"That's about what Solatiem told me to expect."

"I'm assuming you want me to send the reform charter plans to Dhaantyn, but you've never given me anything beyond your additional comments."

"Anything else would be minor, and it's important to get the proposed charter to Dhaantyn as soon as you can."

"I don't have a spare copy, and it will take me a few days to write out another. I'm assuming that you don't want anyone else seeing it."

"For the moment. When you finish the copy, don't deliver it personally. Do you have someone trustworthy who can do that?"

"I do, but couldn't people track him as well?"

"They could, but it's unlikely anyone will notice. Retainers and messages going to the marshal's home are scarcely rare. A personal delivery of anything by a councilor is, especially with documents of some sort." Detruro fingered his chin, then added, "Dhaantyn and Solatiem may want changes. If either of us gets a reaction, we should talk."

Ysella merely nodded.

"Is there anything else?"

"I postponed the markup on the water safety code and associated liability until we get the Navy's comments on the bill."

"Understandable and necessary," replied Detruro. "If that's all . . . ?"

"For now," said Ysella, standing.

Having left Detruro's office, he made his way back to his own office, where he dismissed Khaard and Jaasn for the day, and began to read and sign the correspondence replies that they'd drafted, knowing his nights would be long until he finished copying the draft charter and had Caastyn deliver it to Dhaantyn's house.

59

YSELLA woke early on Quindi morning out of a nightmare where he kept trying to finish copying the draft charter and couldn't because Reimer Daarkyn kept showing up and asking what he was doing and Stefan Nortaak kept peering in Ysella's study windows.

As Gerdina served Ysella his breakfast—fried eggs, ham strips, and biscuits—she said, "You worked late last night."

"Something came up."

From across the table, Caastyn said, "There's another story in the *Tribune* about that crooked legalist. The newssheet says Faarn paid him."

"We knew that, and Reimer Daarkyn's known that for weeks." Ysella picked up the newssheet and began to read the front-page story.

> The *Tribune* has verified reports that the late Machtarn District Legalist Wyllum Smootn received at least a thousand marks from Sollem Faarn, the missing legalist who used a fraudulent trust in the name of a deceased criminal to conceal illegal acts. Faarn also ordered the attack that killed Smootn and severely wounded Imperial Councilor Dominic Ysella. Records from the Banque of Machtarn confirm Smootn's deposit of two hundred marks every month in addition to his pay as District Legalist . . .

How could Smootn be that stupid?

> That source also claimed that Laureous the younger, the Heir to the Imperador, received marks from Faarn for "services to the Heir."
>
> Another possible link lies in the crossbow bolts used by Faarn's hired armsmen to kill Legalist Smootn and wound Councilor Ysella. Those bolts were identical to those used in the attack on Councilor Symeon Daenyld, who died from his wounds after opposing the Imperador's demands for funding more first-rate ships of the line. All five crossbow bolts bear the mark of the Palace Guard, but the Palace insists that the bolts were either stolen or obtained fraudulently from the smithy that forged them . . .

Ysella lowered the newssheet. "The *Tribune* must have fairly strong evidence to print this."

"Do you think the Imperador will shut down the *Tribune*?" asked Caastyn.

"I doubt it," said Ysella. "That would tacitly confirm the linkage. Right now, the Palace can claim theft. Either way, it's likely that the Heir had ties, indirectly of course, to Faarn. The bolts could have been stolen, but if they were, Faarn probably had it done, then let the Heir know that Palace Guard bolts had been used. From what I've seen, that's very much the way he operated, although I doubt anyone will ever find out more than what's in the newssheet."

"Then the Heir ought to be very grateful to you both," interjected Gerdina in a quietly acidic tone.

"We certainly didn't plan it that way," replied Ysella.

With Faarn and his men dead, and Ysella having been one of Faarn's targets, the chances were good that the Heir didn't know why Faarn targeted Ysella, or how much Ysella knew. That could be useful in the future. *It could also make you one of the Heir's targets.*

Caastyn shook his head.

As Ysella cut and ate a ham strip, he wondered how soon he should resume wearing the leather-silk armor. He ate quickly, finishing his breakfast, and heading to the stable, where Caastyn had Jaster ready and waiting.

"Just be careful on the ride, sir."

"I will."

Although Ysella was especially watchful on his ride to the Council Hall, and there were more riders and wagons on Imperial Boulevard, no one showed the slightest interest in him, but then, he was just another rider.

As soon as Ysella entered his front office, carrying his leather case, Khaard stood and handed him an envelope. "The messenger said it was important. It's from the Premier."

"Thank you." Ysella set his case on the edge of the clerk's desk, opened the envelope, and read the few words on the note card. "He wants to see me now."

He picked up the case, walked into his personal office, where he left it on his desk, and headed back out to the Premier's office.

One of the clerks showed Ysella into Detruro's personal office and shut the door.

Detruro didn't stand, but gestured to the chairs in front of his desk, then said, "I assume you read the *Tribune* this morning."

"I did. Is the Imperador furious?" Ysella took a chair and sat.

"I imagine so, but more likely at the Heir than at the *Tribune*."

"Any insights from Lady Delehya?"

Detruro smiled pleasantly, although the expression didn't reach his eyes. "How are you coming on making a copy of the draft charter?"

"I should be able to complete that by Unadi, Duadi at the latest."

"Good. The sooner the better."

"Is the Imperador ailing again?"

"He had a bad day Tridi, but was better yesterday. He's unlikely to die soon, but I doubt he'll last the year. Delehya shares that view."

"And the Heir?"

"The Imperador refuses to see him."

"Was that the reason he wasn't at your engagement dinner?"

"Among others."

"Is that part of why the Heir tries to convince everyone that Laureous is out of his mind, in that he won't talk to his own son?"

"He's weak of body, but none of his administrators think he's weak of mind."

"How much of a private army has the Heir raised, do you think?" asked Ysella.

Detruro raised his eyebrows. "Isn't that a bit of an assumption?"

"Possibly, but when the entire harbor area knows about and fears the Heirs' snitches *and* the Heir is 'borrowing' marks from everyone he can, *and* no one is talking about personal extravagances, it would seem he must have a use for those marks. Those who are lending must either believe he'll repay them—or fear that not lending them is dangerous to their health." Ysella paused momentarily. "Of course, the most likely source of that private army might well be the Palace Guard, in which case, the First Marshal might find it useful to bring some forces of his own into or near Machtarn."

"What would be the purpose of that? Young Laureous is the Heir." Detruro's tone was bland and unconvincing to Ysella.

"The Heir might wish to abolish the Council and the Establishment Act and rule by decree. I'm certain you've thought about that possibility."

Detruro's smile turned sour. "It's more than a possibility. He's said repeatedly that his father babies the Council far too much and that the Establishment Act was a mistake."

Even though the act held Guldor together? "Does he want a civil war?"

"He thinks he can handle that, and that's one of the things worrying the First Marshal."

"So we not only have to get the Imperador to approve a new charter, but also keep the Heir in line?"

"Among other things," replied Detruro dryly.

Such as marrying Delehya and hoping she can help transition Guldor from a near-absolute monarchy to an Imperium with structural limits on the Imperador. Ysella refrained from asking if there was any real affection between Iustaan and Delehya, or merely a partnership based on mutual survival.

"If there's anything else you need . . . ?" asked Ysella.

"For now, the important thing is to get a copy of your charter to Dhaantyn."

"I'll take care of that."

"Good. Have a productive endday."

"You, too." Ysella stood, nodded, and closed the door as he left the inner office.

For the next several bells, Ysella handled various committee tasks and correspondence, then left the Council Hall before first afternoon bell, since the most pressing task he had was to finish copying the proposed new charter for Guldor.

As he rode up the drive from Averra Place to the stable, Ysella saw Caastyn hurry toward him.

"Sir! Is something the matter?"

"Quite a few things, but there's not much you can do about any of them. There's some pressing work I need to do, but it's better done here than at the Council Hall. Sometime late tomorrow, hopefully, I'll need you to deliver something. I know you usually get the day off, but I'll need you for about a bell, likely after fourth bell."

"You're sure, sir?"

"Absolutely," declared Ysella with a cheerful tone he didn't totally feel, "except it would help if you'd unsaddle and groom Jaster."

"I'll take care of him."

"You always do when necessary, and I appreciate it." Ysella dismounted, handed the reins to Caastyn, unstrapped his case, and headed toward the house.

"There's a letter on your desk," said Gerdina as Ysella entered the house through the rear door into the kitchen. "Looks to be from the Ritten in Aloor."

"Thank you. That would be good." *You hope.*

Once in the study, Ysella set down his case, removed his coat, and picked up the solitary envelope on the desk. He carefully slit it open, extracted the letter, and began to read Aelyn's elegant and precise script.

Councilor Ysella—

Your latest letter did indeed address the questions I posed, but answers often lead to more questions. For the moment, I will set those aside because you have asked very little of me, except for the privilege of writing. From your obvious kindness in offering help to someone you knew not at all and your politeness and discretion in contacting me, I feel you are reluctant to be as bluntly forthright as I have been. Although I have learned you made a number of quiet inquiries about me, those inquiries reassured me to some extent, in that they show you appear to consider me as more than an image or a caricature.

In the interests of honesty, I must make you aware of those aspects of my character and temperament some men might find distasteful, if not repugnant. I do my best to not lie or engage in falsehoods, whether by words outright or by omission, or by silence. I have difficulty in uttering polite lies. I believe quiet truths are sufficient, and that using facts as verbal battering rams is unnecessary and uncouth. I do forgive mistakes, but not unthinking repetition of the same mistake. I tend to withdraw rather than engage in heated arguments, but I will discuss matters of disagreement politely. I also recognize that harmony between individuals does not require absolute agreement on every aspect of life or thought, but does require mutual, and equal, respect of the other person . . .

Meaning no condescension or mere verbal profession of respect unsupported by actions and behavior.

You have doubtless discovered the outline of my familial background, but I never entered into my marriage to Khael expecting the everyday luxuries of a wealthy landor household, nor would I place that expectation on any man, should I choose to marry again. I would expect continuing affection and respect, for those are of far greater value to me, given that wealth can vanish in an instant . . .

As she well knows.
Ysella continued to read and to consider Aelyn's carefully chosen words.
A good bell later, after deciding not to reply immediately and to think more about what she had revealed, none of which did he find out of her character, as least as he'd observed from their one brief conversation and her letters, he put the letter in the top desk drawer, and resumed copying the charter.

60

YSELLA skipped services on Quindi evening, worked late copying, and rose early on Findi, spending almost two bells before breakfast copying. When Gerdina announced that breakfast was ready, he picked up the *Tribune* from the front porch basket and carried it to the breakfast table.

"You weren't jesting when you said you'd be working hard," said Caastyn as Ysella seated himself.

"Some days are like that." Ysella paused, then added, "As I told you yesterday, I'll have a delivery for you to make late this afternoon. It's not something I can do, and, no, it shouldn't be dangerous. If you could be back here by fourth bell . . . it shouldn't take more than a bell."

"This isn't like with that legalist Faarn, is it?" asked Caastyn warily.

"No, you'll be delivering to someone quite honest, but people might get ideas they shouldn't have if they saw me there." Ysella grinned. "And no woman is involved."

"We hadn't planned anything until evening," said Gerdina.

"Caastyn should be finished well before that," promised Ysella, then took a sip of café and scanned the newssheet's front page, his eyes going to a smaller article below the fold.

> **COMMERCE ADMINISTRATOR RESIGNS**
>
> Taeryl Laergaan, the Imperial Administrator of Commerce, announced his resignation for reasons of health late yesterday afternoon. Sr. Laergaan fell ill immediately after attending the Palace dinner announcing the engagement of the Imperador's daughter, Lady Delehya, to Imperial Council Premier Iustaan Detruro. The illness was severe enough that many feared Sr. Laergaan would not recover.
>
> The Imperador has not yet announced a replacement for the Commerce Administrator, but it appears likely that some of his functions will be temporarily assumed by Treasury Administrator Tybaalt Salaazar . . .

Ysella set the newssheet aside, and took a bite of the cheese-egg scramble.

"Anything interesting, sir?" asked Caastyn.

"The Commerce Administrator resigned for reasons of health after falling ill at the Lady Delehya's engagement dinner."

"You think someone poisoned him?" asked Gerdina. "Or was it the food?"

"I don't think it was the food, since no one else got sick. Poison is possible, but I doubt it was the Imperador. Laergaan might have gotten a flux, but since he resigned, I'd say poison. Beyond that, who knows?"

"I don't think I'd want to spend much time around the Imperador," said Gerdina, "not that he'd even look at us."

"The Heir's likely worse," commented Caastyn, pausing before he looked to Ysella and added, "You've never said much about Lady Delehya, except that you danced with her."

"I danced one dance with her and passed a few words at her engagement dinner, but from those moments, I'd trust her far more than her brother or her father. Given them, though, that's not saying much."

"Sight unseen," replied Caastyn, "you'd likely be better off with the Ritten in Aloor."

Ysella laughed softly. "You're doubtless right, but we'll have to see."

"Will we ever see her?" asked Gerdina.

"I'd like to think so, but I don't know. We scarcely know each other."

"Begging your pardon, sir," said Caastyn dryly, "but if it takes you as long as the Council to do things, you'll both be dead before we can meet her."

Ysella offered a rueful smile. "Right now, I don't have much choice, but you've made a good point."

"And you don't have to make it again," Gerdina said to her husband.

Caastyn looked down at the table for a moment, then grinned sheepishly.

After breakfast, Ysella returned to his study, where he returned to copying the draft charter. He finished that and proofing the copy before fourth afternoon bell. After sealing the pages into a large envelope, he was writing out the address Raul Dhaantyn had given him on a card when Caastyn knocked on his study door.

"Sir?"

"I have everything ready." Ysella stood and handed over the card.

"Cuipregilt Avenue," said Caastyn as he looked at the card. "That's not far at all. What should I say?"

"Just that it's from Councilor Ysella, as requested. Let me know when you return."

"Yes, sir."

After Caastyn headed out, Ysella turned his attention to Aelyn's letter, rereading it carefully and considering how to reply. He was still mulling over his response when Caastyn returned and knocked on the study door.

"Sir, you didn't tell me that that package was going to Marshal Dhaantyn."

"I knew it was going to him, but I didn't know who was going to accept it for him. Did he take it personally?"

"Had to be him. He was in his dress uniform, and there's only one fleet marshal so far as I know. Looked like he was headed somewhere or maybe had come from somewhere."

Ysella smiled wryly. "I guess that confirms his address. I'd appreciate your not mentioning you delivered something to him, except to Gerdina."

"I'm getting the feeling you're in dangerous waters again, sir."

"More like I'm trying to keep us out of those waters, Caastyn."

"The Heir or the Imperador? Or both?"

"Both . . . for different reasons." Ysella smiled sardonically. "There's nothing else you can do now. I apologize for keeping you. Now, you and Gerdina go and do whatever it was I postponed or interrupted."

"Neither, but you don't ask much."

"I'll see you in the morning. Thank Gerdina for understanding."

Once Caastyn left, Ysella turned back to rereading Aelyn's latest letter. After almost another bell, he began to write.

Ritten Wythcomb—

I enjoyed your last letter. More than that, I deeply appreciate the honesty contained in, and behind, your words, and the elegance with which you expressed your thoughts and revelations.

Although I dislike dishonesty intensely, I find myself in a position as councilor where some of my colleagues and those with whom I must deal are often less than honest and, even when technically honest, withhold information. While I have not been consciously dishonest in my position as a councilor, I have withheld information rather than lie outright on occasions where the truth could have conceivably led to my death in the current political situation.

And almost did in dealing with Faarn.

I can say truthfully that, as a legalist, I neither knowingly lied nor misled clients, opposing legalists, or justicers. Upon occasion, I have withheld facts when their revelation would have served no purpose other than to cause unnecessary pain to those already suffering. At the same time, I also know how we can deceive ourselves, and that is one of the reasons why I find myself wanting to know you better, because shared honesty, not used as a weapon but as a way to understanding, begets more honesty, whereas deception begets deception. And deception separates and alienates . . .

Ysella continued to write, adding a few paragraphs about his time as a legalist and how Legrand Quaentyn had influenced him, then began what he knew would be a long conclusion.

Inasmuch as you effectively asked me why I would be interested in you, my additional answer is that, even in our brief conversation in your parlor, I felt sensitivity, wit, and humor in what only could have been a concerning situation for you after all that had recently occurred in your life. Each of your letters has strengthened that impression. You asked why I remained unmarried. That answer is similar to what you implied in your letters. Until I met you, I did not encounter a woman whose demeanor and intelligence attracted me, although my family attempts matchmaking every time I return to Aloor. Unlike you, I have been able to avoid wedding someone who might well be unsuited to me, or me to her, while earning enough that I do not have to marry for marks or land. Whether we are well-suited to each other, we will have to discover, but I would appreciate the chance for us to explore that possibility.

After all my words, I worry that I present too much of the legalist and too little of the man, but the man and the legalist would indeed wish to know you better and for you to know me as well.

With warmest wishes

In the end, he signed and sealed the letter.

61

ON Tridi morning, Ysella woke to heavy clouds and a light rain that gave everything a winter-like appearance. At breakfast, he read through the *Tribune* and found an interesting article at the bottom of the next-to-last page.

> Late on Unadi afternoon, Machtarn District Justicer Deitre Lhuhan found Mallyk Torrenz and Jaahn Rysten, property legalists associated with Machtarn Harbor Properties, guilty of knowingly concealing the fraudulent nature of the Gustov Torryl Trust scheme used by the missing legalist Sollem Faarn ... both Torrenz and Rysten were fined one thousand marks, stripped of their registration as property legalists, and prohibited from engaging in property transactions for twenty years.

At least, Foerst followed through on that. Ysella doubted that the conviction would have much effect, except on the two who'd been convicted.

After breakfast, he set out for the Council Hall, wearing an oilskin over his jacket.

As Jaster carried him through the rain, Ysella continued to ponder the possible causes of Laergaan's "illness" and who might be behind it, as well as worry about how Fleet Marshal Dhaantyn would react to the proposed government reorganization. He also had concerns about his letter to Aelyn and hoped she wouldn't take anything he wrote in a manner he never intended.

By the time he dismounted at the stables, between the rain, the warmth, and the oilskin, Ysella was sweating slightly and relieved to remove the oilskin once he reached his office.

An envelope from the Palace rested on top of his small stack of correspondence. Ysella frowned, hoping that it was the invitation to Delehya and Detruro's wedding. *But these days one can't be sure of anything.*

The invitation was simple, like the one to the engagement dinner, and unlike everything else connected to Delehya.

> *The Imperador and the Imperadora*
> *are pleased to request your presence*
> *at*
> *the wedding of their daughter,*
> *the Lady Delehya,*
> *to Iustaan Detruro*
> *on the thirty-sixth of Springend*
> *at third bell*
> *and at the dinner following*
> *the ceremony.*

As before, there was no request for a reply.

Ysella immediately slipped the invitation into his personal case, and turned his attention to the next envelope, another letter from Gherard Brandt. Ysella skipped through the pleasantries and focused on the second paragraph.

> *Since I last wrote you in mid-Winterend, Professor Gastaan Ritchen has completed a larger steam device, which is now being tested in various applications, including pumping water and propelling a watercraft by powering a screw or paddle wheel . . .*

After Ysella wrote notes for the clerks, he realized Brandt still hadn't asked for Waterways Committee funds.

Is there even any device? All you have are his letters.

Then again, there were the industrial glaziers in Devult—he struggled to recall the name, then remembered—Duffay & Lybraan.

He worked on correspondence for the next bell or so, leaving his office at a sixth before fourth morning bell. He was still the first councilor in the committee room, where he took his seat behind the long, curved desk.

As soon as the last committee member—Astyn Coerl—arrived, Ysella tapped the gavel. "The committee will come to order. This morning, committee members each have a third to discuss any concerns with the legislative proposal to establish the legal meaning of terms used in harbor and port operations."

"Sr. Chairman," said Nortaak in a tone almost unctuously polite, "before we proceed to the matter at hand, might the committee know why the markup of the safety code and liability bill was postponed, so preemptively?"

"You may, indeed. The Fleet Marshal felt that it would be better if the Navy could review and make recommendations prior to markup. The committee does not have to accept any recommendations, but it would seem better to smooth out differences, if there are any, quietly rather than publicly, as happened with the matter of first-rate ships of the line."

"So the committee should always defer to the Navy as part of the remaining emasculation of the Council?" asked Nortaak, even more unctuously.

"That emasculation of the Council, as you term it," replied Ysella, "was created by the Establishment Act, you may recall. The Council will continue to have that difficulty unless and until the act is changed. Without changes to the act, or without an act granting greater power to the Council, there is the possibility that, in time, the Heir might attempt to rule by decree, in which case, there would be less of a role for the Council. Does that answer your question, Councilor?"

"The Navy is being even more unreasonable," pressed Nortaak.

"Considering that the Fleet Marshal's predecessor died under questionable circumstances, as did the committee chairman dealing with the information provided by that predecessor at the Council's request, I can certainly understand the present Fleet Marshal's caution in dealing with the Council. If you would like to lodge your complaint with the Fleet Marshal, you certainly may do so, but it will be disavowed by the committee to the extent that it is *your* complaint, and not that of the committee." As Ysella finished, he watched Nortaak's face redden and his jaw set.

"I thank you, Sr. Chairman, for that most cogent rationalization."

"You're welcome, Councilor. Each member has the right to express themselves, but only the Premier—or legislation passed by the Council—has the right to speak for the Council as a whole." Ysella managed a pleasant smile. "Now, to the business at hand." He turned to Haans Maessyn, as the next most senior committee member. "Your questions or concerns, Councilor?"

"Some ports or harbors have been using words that have different meanings entirely in other ports. They won't change easily or quickly."

"You're right. But we're not forcing them to change their language, only their accounting. Whatever they call wharfage has to include the same services and requirements in any port . . ."

A sixth before noon, Ysella gaveled the committee meeting to a close, and walked to the Council chamber, where he settled into his small desk to wait for the session to begin.

"Committee meeting?" asked Staeryt.

Ysella nodded.

"Not so good?"

"The meeting proper was fine. What Stefan Nortaak asked before the regular meeting wasn't." Ysella explained as briefly as he could.

"He got upset on the Navy wanting to comment before final markup?"

asked Staeryt. "Who else would know better? They've got more ships than anyone. Seems to me that would save time."

"He thinks, because he's older, that he should be running the committee."

Staeryt lowered his voice. "He's only a councilor because his family didn't want him in Oersynt, not that he's about to tell anyone that. His son runs the lands, and his daughters avoid him when he comes home during Council recesses. None of them care much for his second wife. He likely won't win the next election."

Ysella kept a smile to himself and said, "I suppose Treasury Administrator Salaazar could run. He's from Oersynt, and his family has lands and controls the Bank of Oersynt."

"If Salaazar lives that long."

"Do you think he's the one who poisoned Laergaan?"

Staeryt shook his head. "Too obvious. Salaazar was the only one who might have gained from that, and all of Machtarn knows it."

Sometimes, being too obvious is better than being considered being above it.

The chime rang. Maatrak stepped to the lectern, tapped the gavel once, and declared, "The business of the Council today is to vote on the supplemental appropriations requested by the Imperador to pay for the repair of damages to the port of Encora caused by Atacaman pirates. The bill is privileged, and the only vote will be on passage."

Another pro forma vote. Not that Ysella objected to paying for such damages, although they might not have occurred if the Navy had more frigates and cutters and fewer massive first-rate ships of the line.

Two-thirds of a bell later, Maatrak announced the vote—forty-three for, two against, and five not voting through absence—then recessed the Council until Duadi.

While most of the other councilors swiftly left the chamber, Ysella took his time standing up, to see if someone might be looking for him.

A few moments passed before Oskaar Klempt approached.

"Dominic?"

Ysella half turned. "Yes?"

"Have you heard the latest about Administrator Salaazar?"

"Besides the rumor that he might have been behind Laergaan's illness?"

"He stopped by my office this morning and offered a few pleasantries. He also mentioned in passing that the Heir worried I was working too hard for the good of my continued health."

Ysella chuckled sardonically. "Do you think he mentioned the Heir as a bluff? Would the Heir really care that much about the interest rate cap?"

"He should, at least if all the rumors about his 'borrowing' are accurate, except he'll never pay them back, except in cold iron, if they press him."

"Have you talked to Omar Poncetaryl recently? He might know something. He was at the engagement dinner for Lady Delehya and the Premier. If he were close to the Heir, I doubt he would have been invited, but that's a guess."

"I haven't talked to him lately," said Klempt. "He's declined publicly supporting an increase in the usury cap and an invitation to meet with the Commerce Committee, even informally."

"I thought most of the banques around Machtarn were in favor of some kind of increase."

"They are. But Poncetaryl's wary of saying anything that would upset either the Heir or the Imperador. Last fall, he said he personally thought the cap was too low. Now, he won't even talk about it or see me. And that was *before* Laergaan's sudden illness."

"Do you think Salaazar is close to the Heir?"

"Closer than he lets on, given that he got the position because his family loaned to the Imperador years back."

"So you think he's playing both of them?" asked Ysella. "Or is he only trying to stay on good terms with the Heir so he doesn't suffer when the Imperador dies?"

"I don't know, but I wouldn't put anything past him. He hasn't visited you, has he?"

"Not yet. Why would he? The Waterways Committee can't do anything for him."

"No, but you're seen as being close to the Premier, and Salaazar likes to be in contact with those who might have power . . . or who can influence power."

Until they're no longer useful . . . or become a threat. "So how long will the usury-cap bill remain in committee?"

Klempt shrugged. "Until it's no longer dangerous."

Which could be years, especially if Salaazar manages to survive the Imperador's death.

62

AT breakfast on Quindi morning, Ysella's eyes immediately focused on the lead story in the *Tribune*.

> **WARSHIP UNDER CONSTRUCTION DESTROYED**
> A week ago, a fire raged through the Neewyrk shipyard of Haamyt Brothers, totally destroying the first-rate ship of the line under construction. The cause of the fire is unknown, but Fleet Marshal Raul Dhaantyn said, "The Navy is investigating possible causes." The marshal also declared construction on the warship would resume as soon as possible . . .

"That won't set well with the Imperador," Ysella murmured, more to himself.

"The warship fire, you mean?" asked Caastyn from the side of the table. "Wouldn't think so, not with what a ship like that costs."

"Well . . . the Council will hear about it, loudly, and before long."

"Probably better you're not on the Military Affairs Committee, sir."

Ysella nodded, thinking about poor Alaan Escalante. Then he saw the smaller story at the bottom of the page stating that the frigate *Plaatz* had attacked and destroyed an Atacaman balinger engaging in supplying the pirates operating out of the Cataran Delta.

Balinger? Must be some sort of shallow-draft vessel.

"Might think about taking an oilskin with you, sir," said Caastyn. "Heavy clouds to the northeast heading our way."

"I appreciate the warning," replied Ysella, hoping he could strap the oilskin behind the saddle and not wear it until he left the Council Hall in the afternoon. *Maybe the rain will have passed by then.*

Ysella finished his breakfast, then rode to the Council Hall, reaching it before the clouds obscured the sun. By the time he entered his office, carrying the oilskin and his leather case, the rain had begun to fall. As he set down the case and hung up the oilskin, he wondered, as he had for almost a week, what Dhaantyn's reaction to the proposed charter might be. As for Aelyn, he tried not to think about her response.

After dealing with incoming letters and replies, Ysella updated the

Waterways Committee schedule, then thought about ways to persuade the Imperador to accept the proposed charter.

Except you won't be the one doing the persuading, not with Iustaan marrying Delehya.

Right before the first afternoon bell, Jaasn knocked on Ysella's door. "Sr. Reimer Daarkyn would like a few moments."

"Show him in," replied Ysella, in mild resignation.

"Good afternoon, Councilor." Daarkyn greeted him before he took a seat across the desk from Ysella. "Do you have anything you can share on Lady Delehya's wedding?"

"Not at the moment."

"So the wedding hasn't been canceled, and the Imperador still refuses to see or speak to the Heir?"

"Nothing's changed about the wedding. I know nothing about whether the Imperador and the Heir are currently on speaking terms."

"What about the usury-cap legislation? It's not on the Commerce Committee calendar."

"You'd have to ask Chairman Klempt or the Commerce Committee staff about that."

"He's decided not to talk to me, and the staff won't, either. Do you know why?"

"I don't know. After Laergaan's apparent poisoning, even if he's calling it an illness or a health problem, and Salaazar's opposition to raising the cap, I can see why most anyone dealing with the usury issue would be wary of speaking out."

"That brings up another question. Omar Poncetaryl—the presidente of the Banque of Machtarn—was at the engagement dinner. How well do you know him?"

"I met him there for the first time."

"In all the years that you've been in Machtarn?"

Ysella offered an amused smile. "I've been dealing with water issues all that time, and from what I recall, Poncetaryl's only been presidente of the banque for two years. I didn't even know what he looked like until I met him at the reception." *Most men of power and position in Machtarn deal as little as possible with the Council.* Daarkyn certainly knew that, which suggested he was ignoring it in hopes Ysella would reveal something.

"Did he say anything about the usury cap?"

"Nothing. In fact, his sole question was why wasn't I pursuing the Lady Delehya, since I was a descendant of royalty and single." Ysella went on quickly. "Why haven't you asked Poncetaryl about the usury cap?"

"Right now no one there will say anything. Do you have any idea why?" Daarkyn began tapping the floor with the toe of his boot.

"Someone powerful must have expressed opposition to raising the cap."

"Whoever it is has got Poncetaryl and the banque definitely worried." Daarkyn shook his head. "Do you have any idea who it might be?"

Ysella knew full well Daarkyn had to believe it was Salaazar, but he said, "I don't know enough to guess. You probably have a better idea than I do."

"You've got a good idea, don't you?" pressed Daarkyn.

Ysella chuckled. "So do you, and we both know it."

"You should have been a newsie."

"You're better at it." Ysella stood. "I do have a few things to take care of this afternoon."

Daarkyn was on his feet before Ysella finished speaking. "I have a few other matters I'd like to discuss with you, but those can wait."

Ysella also knew what those were. "You know where to find me."

Once the newshawk left, Ysella walked to the office window and looked out into the heavy rain, wondering why Daarkyn hadn't yet brought up the matter of his harbor properties, but suspected the newsie was trying to find a way to make the disclosure bigger than it was.

He also hoped that the rain would let up before he left the Council for the day, but doubted he'd be that fortunate, and he really should attend services, rain or no rain.

With a last glance out the window, he returned to the papers on his desk.

Two bells later, he sent Khaard and Jaasn home early and closed the office, then donned his oilskin and hurried through the near-empty Council halls to the stable outside, where he reclaimed Jaster.

The gelding tossed his head when Ysella rode out from the sheltered overhang of the stable doors into the pelting rain.

"I know. It's miserable, but it's not going to stop anytime soon."

Once he and Jaster reached the stable at the house, Ysella dismounted and led the gelding in, unsaddled him, and went to work toweling off the worst of the rain. When he finished dealing with Jaster, Ysella made his way to the house.

As he entered through the kitchen door, removing his oilskin and hanging it on one of the pegs beside the door, Gerdina looked up from the stove and said, "You got a letter, but it's not from Aloor."

"Thank you." Ysella made his way to the study.

On his desk was a single envelope, the size to contain a card or an invitation. He opened and read it, smiling as he did.

Ritter and Ritten Chaarls Aashen
Request the Honor of Your Presence
For Dinner
Findi, the Sixth of Springend,
Fourth Bell of the Afternoon.

Chaarls and Bhettina never forget that you're family, if distant. Even if they usually "remembered" when they could also take care of other obligations. But then, Ysella certainly couldn't complain, and he did have them for dinner at least twice a year.

He wished that the envelope had come from Aelyn, but there hadn't been enough time for that. He also wished that the rain would stop before he had to walk to services.

63

YSELLA woke to the sound of hail on the roof, followed by a steady, near-freezing rain. *Of course, just the thing for the last Unadi of Springfirst.* He forced himself out of bed and readied himself for the day ahead.

The rain continued through breakfast and pelted down steadily for the entire ride to the Council Hall, but by the time Ysella reached the Council stables, it had dwindled to a drizzle. When he entered his personal office and looked out, the rain appeared to have stopped entirely, although the day still looked gray and cold. He hung up the dripping oilskin and glanced at the incoming letters on the desk.

"Sir," said Khaard, appearing in the doorway and extending an envelope, "you have a message from the Premier."

"Thank you." Ysella walked over and took the envelope. "He's likely calling the Council into session."

"That's not good, is it?"

"We'll have to see." He opened the envelope, read the body of the message, and nodded. "A brief session at noon." He didn't mention the note added in Detruro's handwriting at the bottom.

> *I'd appreciate it if you'd stop by my office after first afternoon bell.*

That indicated that Detruro had more in mind for Ysella than what he'd announce to the entire Council. *Regarding either Solatiem or Dhaantyn or something else?*

Whatever it might be wasn't likely to be good.

Putting that thought aside, Ysella settled behind the desk and picked up the first letter, from Daffyd Shaeldn, asking if Ysella had given any more thought to having the Council set minimum standards for poorhouses. *You did promise to look into the matter.* With a small sigh, he wrote a note to Khaard, asking him to see if there were any bills introduced dealing with poorhouses.

By fourth bell, he'd dealt with the correspondence and turned his attention to the latest draft of the bill to standardize port service terms. That required word-by-word, line-by-line scrutiny, and he was glad to set it aside when he had to leave and make his way to the Council chamber.

As soon as Ysella took his seat, Staeryt asked, "Do you know what this session is about?"

"I have no idea, except it's likely to have something to do with the Imperador."

"As usual," replied Staeryt in a resigned tone.

After calling the Council to order, Maatrak turned the lectern over to Detruro.

The Premier let all the murmurs die down before speaking. "As many of you doubtless know, a fire swept through the Neewyrk shipyard of Haamyt Brothers over a week ago, destroying the first-rate ship of the line under construction. The Imperador has effectively ordered the Council to put an end to the carelessness which the Council and the Haamyt brothers have tolerated for all too long." Detruro paused, presumably to let the impact of the words sink in, then went on, "Therefore, I am instructing the Military Affairs Committee to work with the Navy in investigating the cause of the fire and to look into more stringent supervision of military shipbuilding, including additional legal requirements, if necessary."

The Premier paused once more, surveying the Council before proceeding. "The Imperador has made it clear that he will not tolerate any further carelessness. Very clear." Detruro stepped back, nodding to Maatrak.

Maatrak took the lectern, rapped the gavel, and declared, "The Council is hereby recessed until noon on Tridi."

"The Imperador must be really upset," said Staeryt quietly, "for Iustaan to call the Council into session for that sole statement."

"If he hadn't, the Imperador would be more upset," replied Ysella, "and he's getting upset more often, it seems."

"Not a good sign," said Staeryt.

"That's a bit of an understatement," declared Caanard from beside Staeryt.

"You think?" said Staeryt sarcastically.

As Caanard and Staeryt continued talking, Ysella stood and went looking for Staanus Wrystaan, whom he found in the corridor outside the Council chamber.

"Do you have a moment, Staanus?"

"I'm not headed anywhere, except back to my office."

"After what the Premier said, I wondered if you know something about the Haamyt brothers?"

"Some, but I'm no shipwright. They build ships, sturdy ships, from all I've heard. They've got a reputation for careful preparation and good crafting. If they're as careful as their reputation indicates, a fire that consumed an entire ship, even one half-built, would seem unlikely unless it had some . . . assistance."

"Atacaman saboteurs, you think?"

Wrystaan frowned. "That doesn't make sense. The frigates and smaller ships are the ones giving the Atacamans trouble. It's more like someone wanted to anger the Imperador, maybe get him riled up enough to stop his heart. Or maybe a rival shipbuilder, because the Haamyts don't get paid until the ship's finished and accepted by the Navy. Even if they have insurance, the most the insurers will cover is around four parts in ten of the loss."

"How do you know all that, if you've been in papermaking all your life?" asked Ysella, genuinely curious.

Wrystaan laughed. "Everyone needs paper. After a while, you pick up things."

"Which might be why you were picked to succeed Symeon."

"Also because no one expected Daenyld to be killed, because I'm not a stripling, and because I said I wouldn't stand for reelection. Part of a term is enough." He ticked off each point with a finger.

When the two reached the door to Ysella's office, Ysella said, "I appreciate the information. Thank you."

"You're welcome. I might be asking about port funds come appropriations time."

Ysella chuckled. "I'll keep that in mind." He watched Wrystaan for several moments, then turned and entered his office.

After signing or changing the responses prepared by his clerks, which took almost a bell, Ysella made his way down to the Premier's office on the lower level. He waited a sixth before Paolo Caanard left, a bemused smile on his lips, and Detruro motioned to Ysella.

Ysella barely closed the door before Detruro handed him a single sheet of paper. "Read it. Then we'll talk."

Ysella's eyes took in the letterhead of the Imperador before he began to read.

Premier Detruro—
The fire that destroyed the first-rate ship under construction is unforgivable. I fail to see how you, as Premier, could allow slipshod shipbuilding practices that not only weaken the Navy but waste thousands of marks. It is frustrating enough that I must contend with brainless councilors who seem totally unable to understand the necessity for strong ships, but for the Council to allow such brazen carelessness, or possibly encourage Atacaman saboteurs at a time when there appear to be traitors everywhere . . .

From there, the rhetoric got more strident.

When Ysella finished, he handed the letter back to Detruro.

"You can see why I didn't want the text made public. Not yet, anyway."

"There will be a time for that, but that time isn't now. You'd think the Heir would have kept something like this from being sent." Ysella had a good idea why that hadn't happened, but wanted to hear Detruro's thoughts.

The Premier smiled, if sadly. "You know why that didn't happen as well as I do, Dominic."

"The Heir has no contact with his father now because Laureous distrusts him, and Lady Delehya is limited in what she can prevent, possibly because she has to be wary of the Heir. Or am I missing something?"

"Very little," replied Detruro. "Do you have any suggestions?"

"Make sure that the First Marshal and the Fleet Marshal see that letter. Don't trust Salaazar, and make sure Lady Delehya knows about him, if she doesn't already."

"Salaazar avoids her."

That means Salaazar suspects that she has empathic abilities. It also meant Salaazar worried about what Delehya might discover or could do, at least until he could prove she was an empath and could benefit from revealing it.

Detruro lowered his voice. "I mentioned your banque suggestion to Delehya."

Ysella raised his eyebrows. "And?"

"She thought it was a horrible idea as well . . . but an acceptable alternative if matters don't go well for her in Machtarn."

"She could run the banque, particularly in Enke, and stay away from the Palace and politics, and the banque might gain depositors because you two controlled it."

"It's still a sordidly commercial fate," declared Detruro, "but better that for both of us than having titles and little else. I can't spend the rest of my life as premier, and being a councilor after being premier . . ." He shook his head.

Ysella understood what Detruro hadn't said—that neither he nor Delehya wanted to be lapdogs to the Imperador, especially not to the Heir, and remaining in Machtarn could be unnecessarily dangerous. "Salaazar might present a problem."

"Salaazar presents a problem for many people," replied Detruro, "but both the Imperador and Heir would likely not look favorably on any action by Salaazar prejudicial to her."

"Are you sure about the Heir?" asked Ysella.

"He doesn't care much for Delehya, but anything happening to her would reflect badly on him." Detruro paused, then added sardonically, "Except for rumors impugning her behavior."

"Have you heard anything from Solatiem or Dhaantyn?"

"Solatiem said the senior officers were interested in preserving a government that remained a stable Imperium with a balance of power."

"That sounds like they might be persuaded, but aren't about to commit to anything now."

"Would you in their position?" asked Detruro.

"Hardly, but I'd also be worrying about the Heir."

"I'm sure that they are."

"So . . . ?" asked Ysella.

"We keep being good and devoted councilors for now. You might think about a change to your plan that provides a bit more power and access to the First Marshal and the Fleet Marshal as well as gives the Imperador some influence over the First Marshal and the Fleet Marshal."

So the marshals have a stake in supporting the charter. Ysella nodded again.

"That's all for now. I wanted to make sure you saw the Imperador's actual words."

Ysella understood the reason for that as well. "Thank you. I'll have to give some thought as how best to accomplish what you requested. It might take a few days."

"I understand, but the sooner the better. You're also the best legalist for this."

Not necessarily the best, but possibly the only one skilled enough that you can trust. With that thought, Ysella inclined his head, then turned and left.

Once in the main hallway, Ysella wondered how long it would be before it was clear that the Imperador could not rule effectively much longer.

Then a thought struck him. While he had no doubt that Delehya influenced the Imperador, was she fostering or boosting his distrust of the Heir as part of her efforts to keep her half brother off-balance and to reduce his ability to gather and consolidate power?

Are white cougars predators? He smiled coolly.

64

When Ysella started to seat himself at the breakfast table on Furdi morning, even before he took his first sip of café, he glanced at the front page of the newssheet and stiffened. He sat down quickly and began to read.

BANQUE PRESIDENTE KILLED

Omar Poncetaryl collapsed moments after leaving the banque Tridi evening, as he was about to enter his carriage ... Machtarn Patrol Captain Khaasliew reported the cause of death appeared to be two frog-poison darts, although none of those near the carriage seemed to see the attacker ...

Poncetaryl had headed the banque for only two years, following the death of his father, and was known to be close to the Imperial family. He and his wife were among the few to attend the engagement dinner of Lady Delehya, the Imperador's daughter ...

Why didn't anyone see the attacker? Ysella read the entire article, but the only hint was that the article reported that no one *seemed* to notice. *Two people, possibly? The attacker and an empath suggesting everyone look at Poncetaryl?*

"Sir?" asked Caastyn.

"I was disconcerted to read about the banque presidente's murder."

"Did you know him?" asked Gerdina.

"I met him for the first time at Lady Delehya's engagement dinner. We only spoke briefly." As Ysella recalled, Poncetaryl had been enthusiastic, but seemed disconcerted when Delehya made a clear move to favor Ysella. Then, last week, both Klempt and Daarkyn had mentioned that Poncetaryl refused to talk to them ... about anything.

"Why would anyone kill a banque presidente?" asked Caastyn. "The banque's going to keep doing what it does, no matter who's in charge. That's the way banques are."

"Unless it was for personal or other reasons," Ysella pointed out. "There's been a quiet controversy about increasing the amount of interest permitted by law. Most bankers would prefer the cap be raised, but none of them have said so publicly."

"Did he have a mistress?" asked Gerdina cynically.

"I have no idea," replied Ysella, "but he and his wife seemed at ease with each other at the engagement dinner, and they were seated close to the Imperadora."

"Maybe the banque foreclosed on someone," suggested Caastyn. "They often do that, and people get angry when they lose everything."

"It could be." Personally, Ysella doubted that most who were foreclosed could have obtained frog poison and an empath to distract bystanders, suggesting that Poncetaryl's death was connected to the usury cap or yet another subterranean conflict.

Ysella sipped more café, then finished the newssheet and his breakfast before setting out for the Council Hall on a warm and pleasant morning.

At his office, he only had one message, atop a short stack of incoming letters, from Fleet Marshal Dhaantyn.

Chairman Ysella—

The Imperial Navy appreciates the advance notice that the Waterways Committee has supplied in the form of draft legislation to provide guidance for watercraft in all navigable waters.

While we do not anticipate requesting major changes in the proposal, given that it largely reflects standard naval ship-handling procedures, I have sent copies to fleet commands, and anticipate their comments in the next few weeks.

You have my thanks for your preparation and careful drafting.

The seal and signature were those of Raul Dhaantyn.

Ysella smiled faintly, suspecting that the last words had nothing to do with the watercraft bill. He slipped the message into his desk drawer and turned his attention to the incoming correspondence.

At fourth bell he left the office and walked to the Waterways Committee room.

Even before calling the committee to order, he saw that Stefan Nortaak wasn't present. It wasn't unusual for a councilor to occasionally miss a meeting, especially one as routine as another discussion of terminology for uniform port procedures throughout Guldor. Still, Ysella wondered if Nortaak's absence reflected anger at the committee chairman.

What could possibly make you think that?

After gaveling the committee to order, Ysella said, "Before we trudge through terminology, I'd like to know if any of you have gotten a reaction to this proposed legislation." He glanced from one side of the dais to the other, then said, "Councilor Ditaero?"

"Sr. Chairman, I wouldn't say it was a terrible reaction, but the portmaster at Endor wanted to know what benefit the bill would really have, since most of the cargoes leaving Endor are timber of some sort, and those shipping have known the terms and procedures currently used for decades, if not longer."

"It's a good question," replied Ysella. "The best answer I can give is that the bill will make it easier for ships and shippers who aren't familiar with those terms to understand them, which might entice other shippers and merchanters to consider trading into and out of Endor. It also requires all ports to provide a listing of overall services, what they entail, and the cost basis for assessment of service. This should reduce misunderstanding or complaints . . ."

When Ysella finished, Ditaero said, "Thank you. Pretty much what I thought. You say it better."

The only other reaction was from Astyn Coerl. "Some of the flatboat shippers want to know if all this is really necessary for inland waterways."

"Some of it isn't. If a river port doesn't supply certain services, they don't have to comply with standards for services they don't supply."

With that, Ysella began reviewing the remainder of the terminology. Thankfully, the committee finished well before the Council session, giving him enough time to return to his office to address correspondence replies before heading to the Council chamber.

Once back behind his desk, Ysella signed or changed the replies prepared by the two clerks and had some time to puzzle over Poncetaryl's death before he headed down to the Council chamber. He slid into his seat as Maatrak gaveled the Council to order.

"The matter before the Council is consideration of the Tariffs Act amendments, under a privileged rule, allowing no amendments," announced Maatrak. "Speaking to the proposal is Councilor Klempt." After his brief statement, Maatrak left the lectern to Klempt.

"Councilors," began the chairman of the Commerce Committee, "these amendments do not change any tariff levels. What they do accomplish is to increase the penalties for avoiding tariffs, including, in some cases, confiscating the vessel carrying contraband . . ."

While Ysella listened to Klempt, he doubted the amendments would do much, except to raise the price of certain goods without improving the revenues of competing Guldoran growers or manufactories.

When Klempt finished, Paolo Caanard rose in opposition, making the same argument Ysella would have voiced.

Then Maatrak called for a vote.

Two-thirds of a bell later, the floor leader announced, "With thirty-eight voting in favor and eleven opposing, the proposal is passed." Almost in the same breath, he added, "There being no other matters to consider, the Council is recessed until Duadi, the second of Springend at noon."

While Ysella didn't rush to leave the chamber, neither did he dawdle, only to find Oskaar Klempt outside in the corridor beckoning to him.

"What is it, Oskaar? You were successful with the tariff amendments." Ysella joined Klempt next to the corridor wall.

"I know how you feel, Dominic, but the Imperador wanted them. So did the Heir, according to Aksyl. I didn't feel like opposing either of them, not now." Klempt hesitated, then resumed, further lowering his voice. "I didn't tell you this before, but someone close to the Premier should know, especially after what happened to Omar Poncetaryl. One of the reasons Poncetaryl wouldn't speak to anyone about the usury-cap increase—or anything else recently—is likely because the Banque of Machtarn was lending marks to the Heir, even after the Imperador had forbidden him to accept marks. Laureous didn't want his son privately indebted to anyone."

"How do you know that?"

"Taeryl Laergaan told me months ago that the Imperador had forbidden anyone in the Imperial family to seek funds from anyone but the Imperador."

Ysella could see Laureous doing that. "How could Poncetaryl do that without others at the banque knowing?"

"Most likely he set it up as a legitimate loan."

"But why?"

"Would you want the Heir and his small personal force pressing you? I'm guessing Poncetaryl wouldn't or couldn't lend any more or told the Heir he'd go to Laureous if the Heir insisted on more marks." Klempt glanced in both directions along the corridor, although Ysella didn't see anyone nearby. "That's all I can say, but you should know. Just you, *please*."

"I'll do as you say." *Unless something happens to you.* But, then Klempt wouldn't be telling Ysella if he weren't worried. *Very worried.*

"One other thing. Don't trust Stefan Nortaak. He's too close to Salaazar and the Heir." Klempt glanced around, then said, in a normal tone of voice, "That's all I had, Dominic. We can talk later."

As Klempt walked away, Ysella wanted to shake his head, but didn't. He wondered what threats the Imperador might have made to the Heir about not accepting personal "loans" from banques or others.

65

ON Quindi morning, Ysella only found one article of interest in the *Tribune,* both for what it stated and what it did not.

SHIPYARD BLAZE SABOTAGE

Late yesterday afternoon, after a meeting with the Imperador, First Marshal Gunnar Solatiem announced the fire that destroyed the half-built hull of the unnamed first-rate ship of the line in Neewyrk was deliberately set. The Navy is continuing its investigation to determine the perpetrators and how the fire was set . . .

Good fortune in finding any evidence leading anywhere. And if Solatiem did find evidence revealing the perpetrators, would he survive the discovery?

Ysella quickly read through the rest of the newssheet, noting in passing that Aloor, Paelart, and Daal had been pummeled by heavy rains. *Most likely not to the family's advantage, especially not for Haarkyl.*

He set aside the newssheet and took a sip of café.

"Do you think they'll find out who fired the ship?" asked Caastyn.

"One way or another, I doubt we'll hear more about who was really behind it, and if someone announces it was Atacaman saboteurs, don't believe it." Ysella turned his attention to his breakfast.

By half past second morning bell he was in his office and had read through the Premier's message to all councilors about the shipyard blaze, a message that revealed nothing beyond the *Tribune* story.

With the Council not in session and no Waterways Committee meeting, Ysella finished dealing with official correspondence and replies just after midday, then turned his attention to adding to and modifying the Waterways Committee meeting schedule for the next month, occasionally wondering if and when he might hear from Aelyn Wythcomb.

At fourth bell he dismissed both clerks and closed the office, before walking to the Council stables and waiting for an ostler to unstall Jaster. Although he kept alert on the ride back to the house, he didn't see anyone suspicious.

No letters awaited him.

When the time came to leave for services, he set out on foot. A light breeze kept the eight-block walk to the Trinitarian chapel from being too hot, although Ysella strode quickly. He arrived a bit early and stood outside in the shade of a goldenwood flanking the stone-paved walk to the main entry. The towering tree had seen better days, and Ysella had often wondered whether Presider Haelsyn would have it cut before it toppled onto the roof of the chapel.

As Ysella turned to resume walking toward the chapel, he saw Alaan and Amaelya Escalante moving toward him and waited for them.

"Sometimes, I think I see you more here than at the Council Hall," said Alaan.

"I certainly do," added Amaelya. "I have to ask you what the Lady Delehya's engagement dinner was like."

"Very formal and very small, considering who she is. Less than fifty people, and the Heir and his wife weren't present."

"Unsurprising," replied Amaelya. "From what Alaan has told me, neither the Imperador nor Lady Delehya get along well with the Heir."

"Sr. Poncetaryl and his wife were there, though," said Ysella, "and five Imperial administrators."

"His death was a shock," said Alaan. "What's the point of killing a banker?"

"You're too charitable, dear," replied Amaelya. "Almost every family has a story about problems with bankers. They don't tell them outside the family."

"That's true," mused Alaan. "One of the problems we had with the last appropriations arose because the Imperador didn't want to deal with bankers."

Ysella refrained from correcting his colleague. "You're both right. There are problems with bankers, but let's hope that Presider Haelsyn doesn't talk about them in his homily."

"Better bankers than what he said last week," said Alaan.

Ysella nodded, an expression of recall, but not agreement, since Haelsyn had, rightly in Ysella's opinion, suggested that the district councils and the Imperial Council needed to recognize that not all the poor were undeserving, and even the Almighty recognized a difference between those who would not help themselves and those who could not. Then he said, "We probably should get to our pews."

Amaelya smiled. "I can't imagine that either one of you wants to be seen entering after the service begins."

"Better to be blamed for sins of commission, than one of mere tardiness in devotion of the divine," added Ysella.

Alaan shook his head, but he and Amaelya resumed walking toward the chapel doors, as did Ysella.

66

WHILE Ysella read *The Machtarn Tribune* thoroughly on both Findi and Unadi, there were no stories dealing with the Council, the Imperador, the Heir, or Lady Delehya. Nor was there any follow-up on Omar Poncetaryl's death. The only article dealing with the Navy was a brief story on Unadi, reporting a raid by Atacaman pirates on Paensantz, a small coastal village sixty milles northeast of Zeiryn.

Ysella made a mental note to ask Voltar Paastyn about the attack, since it had occurred in Paastyn's district.

On Unadi morning, Ysella left the house a trace earlier than usual. He stepped through the outer office door a third past second bell, and Khaard leapt up from his seat.

"Something urgent?" asked Ysella, his leather case still in his hand.

The senior clerk handed over an envelope. "Yes. From the Premier, sir."

Ysella opened the envelope and read the note. "I'll be back when I can be," replied Ysella, walking to his desk and leaving his case, then heading back to the corridor and the stairs to the lower level and Detruro's office.

The moment he entered, the nearest clerk stood and gestured toward the closed door of the inner office. "You're to go right in, Councilor."

"Thank you." Ysella walked to the door, entered, and closed it behind himself.

Detruro looked up from some papers, motioned to the chairs, and said, "Oskaar Klempt was killed late yesterday when he walked out of his house. Crossbow bolts smeared with frog poison. The bolts might not have been fatal. The poison was."

"The same kind of bolts used against Daenyld, me, and Smootn?"

"It appears so."

"Then the Heir's sending a message to us."

Detruro frowned.

"Last Furdi, Oskaar cornered me in the corridor after the Council recessed. Months ago, Taeryl Laergaan told Oskaar that the Imperador had forbidden anyone in the Imperial family to seek funds from anyone but the Imperador himself. Oskaar also said that Poncetaryl was killed because he'd been lending marks to the Heir. Oskaar believed that, for some reason, Poncetaryl couldn't or wouldn't lend more, and said that, if the Heir insisted, Poncetaryl would go to the Imperador."

Detruro fingered his earlobe. "I don't see Laergaan lying about that, and the Imperador's always wanted to be in control. But Poncetaryl should have known better."

"With all the Heir's snitches and what seems to be a covert armed force killing people?" asked Ysella.

"The Heir and his family live in their own apartments in the Palace. They're twice the size of both my houses combined, and it won't be that long before he becomes Imperador. It's hard to believe he needs that many marks, even if he's had a few women on the side. He might be bribing administrators—"

"Not all of them—Tyresis can't stand him. At your engagement dinner, he was the one who told me young Laureous was 'borrowing' wherever he could."

"I knew things were bad, but this . . ." Detruro shook his head. "What do you suggest?"

"Could Delehya let the Imperador know? Tell him that unless the Establishment Act is amended, the Heir will destroy Guldor in mere years, if not sooner?"

"I don't know if that's wise, but I will tell her." Detruro sighed softly. "For all I know, she knows about her brother's borrowing."

"She might suspect, but she likely doesn't know that it's the reason for the killings. If he's responsible for so many deaths *before* he becomes Imperador, no one will be safe if he has his father's power. Even if we can limit his powers, the transition will be dangerous," Ysella pointed out. "Most people outside of Machtarn have no real idea about the Heir. With only one possible successor, and the Heir's sons not really old enough to reign, neither the Imperador nor the Heir wanted the younger Laureous's intrigues known, and bringing them up now would make matters worse." As he said that, Ysella couldn't see how all the intrigues could stay hidden or how matters wouldn't get worse.

"I'll let you know once I find out anything more."

Understanding that Detruro wasn't about to say more, Ysella nodded, then turned and left, making his way back to his own office.

He'd barely been there for a third of a bell before Khaard appeared in his doorway and said, "Reimer Daarkyn, sir."

Of course. "Have him come in."

The newshawk was in Ysella's office almost before Khaard could get out of the way, but Daarkyn closed the door quietly, then spoke before he sat down.

"What can you tell me about Councilor Klempt's murder?"

"I only found out a little while ago, Reimer. You may know more than I do."

"I have some doubts about that. Klempt invited you to speak before the Commerce Committee about increasing the usury cap. I've heard that didn't set well with other councilors."

From Nortaak or Haarst, most likely. "If a councilor attempts anything that might be constructive, there's always another who doesn't like it. As I told you before, I thought that raising the cap is a good idea. So did Oskaar Klempt. Some of the others on the Commerce Committee have their concerns, but I doubt any of them were involved." *At least, not directly.*

"He was hit by poisoned crossbow bolts, like Presidente Poncetaryl, and you and several others. That's not exactly coincidence. Neither Poncetaryl nor Klempt would talk to me, and now they're both dead."

"And both were in favor of raising the interest cap," Ysella said.

"So were you, and you were also shot."

"That was well before I introduced my proposed legislation."

"Were you shot because you wouldn't sell any of your harbor properties to Sollem Faarn?" asked Daarkyn almost casually.

"More because his attempt to buy them led me to find all the illegalities he was involved in."

"Isn't it a conflict of interest for you to be chairman of the Waterways Committee and to own harbor properties?" pressed Daarkyn.

"I bought all but one of them before I became chairman, and they're all located outside the area affected by either legislation or government funding."

"There's still an appearance of conflict, wouldn't you say?"

Ysella smiled wryly. "Unfortunately. But, unlike a number of councilors, I inherited nothing. I bought the least expensive properties I could with funds I saved as a single legalist. I spent more marks improving them. Now, for the sake of appearances, I'm supposed to sell them?"

"It might not look that good."

Ysella said nothing.

"Did you borrow marks to buy any of the properties?"

"No. That's a very good way for a councilor to get into all sorts of difficulties."

Daarkyn smiled. "You're very traditional. In this instance, that's commendable. But why would anyone kill both Poncetaryl and Klempt over interest legislation that hasn't made it out of committee and doesn't seem likely to?"

"Maybe they discovered something," said Ysella. "There are rumors . . ."

"That the Heir has been borrowing funds wherever he can? That's scarcely new."

"The Imperador's never liked borrowing. He refused to let the Council borrow funds. That created quite a few difficulties."

Daarkyn frowned. "Your point?"

"If . . . and only if . . . the Heir owed a great deal . . . how might someone close to him react if he thought someone might tell the Imperador about those debts? Especially if they'd been trying to keep matters quiet?"

"That's so . . . obvious."

Ysella nodded, then asked, "Who would dare tell the Imperador? Who would have the easiest access to funds?"

"Do you have any proof?"

"Proof? Not in the slightest. Klempt and Poncetaryl might have, but that's a suspicion. Laergaan might have known something or might have started to look. Again, that's just a guess."

"I told you that you could have been a decent newshawk."

"You're much better at it." *Unfortunately for me.*

"Do you know anything else about this?"

"All I have are suspicions, hints, and rumors . . . well, except for the facts you already know, like the crossbow bolts. Oh . . . wait . . . there is one other thing, Treasury Administrator Salaazar is the younger son of the family that owns the Banque of Oersynt."

"I hadn't heard that." Abruptly, Daarkyn stood. "At some point, we may need to talk about your properties."

"I'm not going anywhere, Reimer."

Once Daarkyn was well out of the office, Ysella took a long deep breath, knowing sooner or later there would be a story about his "apparent" conflict of interest.

And selling the properties now would actually strengthen the charge.

He also wondered why Daarkyn hadn't brought up Salaazar's name.

Because he wanted you to? Ysella shook his head.

He heard nothing for the rest of the day, and, as he rode back to his house, he wondered what Delehya's reaction to the most recent events would be, and how she and Detruro would handle the slowly spreading situation—if they even could, given the Imperador's intractability.

Ysella's apprehensions weren't at all allayed when he saw the letter from Aelyn Wythcomb resting on his study desk, but he used his belt knife to slit it open carefully enough to preserve the seal.

The first lines of Aelyn's letter removed the worst of Ysella's fears.

Dear Dominic (if I may),
While I think we have much more to learn about each other, the care and thoughtfulness with which you attempted to address my questions says more than your choice of words...

Ysella smiled, if ruefully, at the words "with which you attempted," but knew her assessment was accurate.

With your background and formal personal presentation, I must admit I had concerns about your capability for depth of feeling, but all the people who know you remark well upon your loyalty and concern... and an almost hidden warmth. Even those who know you but slightly consider you honest and fair, if reserved. I couldn't help but discover the warmth and respect you showed over the years to Legrand Quaentyn, something that both his daughters remarked upon more than once.

I also appreciated your words about the dangers of self-deception and how being honest with another, provided she is equally honest— and gently so—can allow greater honesty for both...

As I mentioned previously, my marriage to Khael was one of mutual respect, but little more. He was as kind as he was able, and certainly honest. There was little we could initially talk about, although I did my best to learn everything I could about the mine and mining...

I may have mentioned my great-uncle, Maelcar Scalante, who was briefly councilor from Silverhills when I was a child. What I did not mention was that, after his early death and later, after the death of my grandmother, I occasionally wrote his widow, Aelyssa, asking her things I was never able to ask my grandfather, for fear of appearing ungrateful. She and I still exchange letters, semi-regularly, although she is quite elderly now. I wrote to her about you after your first letters, but heard nothing. Last week, she finally replied, saying that she regretted the delay, but that she had been "temporarily felled by a troublesome flux." She also replied to my inquiry that, according to the newssheets, it was a wonder you survived the attack. I had no idea from your letters how close to death you were...

At the time, I didn't either, and later it would have seemed boastful to say so.

Ysella kept reading, taking in every carefully penned word.

67

AFTER rereading Aelyn's letter and sleeping on what she had written, Ysella decided to put off penning a reply for a day or so, and he woke on Duadi morning more convinced that he shouldn't rush to reply.

As he half expected, the *Tribune* carried a front-page article on Klempt's murder. The article revealed little Ysella didn't know, but stated that the crossbow bolts involved appeared to be similar to those used against Daenyld, Smootn, and Ysella, and all were smeared with frog poison, as were the darts used to kill Poncetaryl. The article pointed out that three of the attacks were on councilors, unprecedented in the history of Guldor. There was no mention of the Heir or the usury-cap issue nor speculation on the hand behind the killings.

"They don't mention the Heir at all," said Caastyn as Ysella finished his breakfast. "Seems to me that everything points to him."

"If you owned the newssheet, would you print a question of the Heir being involved?" asked Ysella dryly.

"Not if I wanted to see the next morning," admitted Caastyn.

When Ysella rode to the Council Hall through a light misting rain, he did so wearing the silk and hardened leather armor, although he knew the armor was only partial protection. *But better than no protection.*

After he reached the Council stables and turned Jaster over to one of the stableboys, he hurried to his office, where he addressed his clerks: "Any messages?"

"No, sir."

"Then I'm headed to the Premier's office."

When Ysella walked into Detruro's outer office, the nearest clerk informed him, "He's not here, sir. He's at the Palace. He left word that he'd let you know when he returns."

Ysella returned to his office, thinking that Detruro's being at the Palace didn't bode well. Still, he could do little about it, except get on with the business of the day.

Arturo Palaan had left a note saying that everything was ready for Tridi's markup session for the port terminology legislation, which Ysella had half forgotten.

Then Ysella read through another letter from Cyraen Presswyrth. He frowned at one section and reread it carefully.

> ... I know you to be a most responsible councilor, but I worry greatly about the Council as a whole and its apparent tendency to provoke the Imperador at a time when a strong leader is more necessary than in recent years ...

Provoke the Imperador? What in the name of the Almighty has Cyraen been reading or who has he been talking to?

For the moment, Ysella set the letter aside and began to read through the other incoming mail, penning his notes for the clerks.

Khaard knocked on the half-open door. "A message from the Premier, sir."

Ysella replaced his pen in its holder and took the envelope from Khaard. The message inside was simple: "Come to my office now." He stood.

"I'll be with the Premier. It shouldn't take that long." Ysella felt comfortable saying that because no meeting with Detruro took long and never had.

Less than a sixth later, Ysella was in Detruro's private office with the door firmly closed. His first words were simple. "I take it that matters have gotten worse."

"In some ways, perhaps not in others. The Guard captain briefed me. Tybaalt Salaazar was killed by a Palace guard while trying to escape after the Guard captain discovered Salaazar had suborned three guards and ordered them to remove Poncetaryl and Klempt in order to hide the fact that he'd repeatedly lied to the Imperador." Detruro paused. "That won't be what the newssheets will say."

"Even so, from what we know, that's true ... as far as it goes," said Ysella. "It's also a cover-up for the Heir."

"Or a warning to the Heir and to the Palace Guard," said Detruro.

"If that's true, it suggests that the Guard captain is more aligned with the Imperador than the Heir ... or wants the Imperador to think so."

"I've already pointed out both possibilities to Delehya and asked her to have Lorya Kaechar get that message to Laureous."

"Is he in a state of mind to comprehend that?"

"He's always ready to look into disloyalty, but he may not act immediately."

"Because that would alert the Heir?"

"More that a known traitor might be less dangerous than a lesser-known replacement."

"What about Solatiem and Dhaantyn?"

"I wasn't in a position to let them know, but I will. They've had suspicions that a number of Palace guards have greater loyalty to the Heir than to his father."

"So what do we do now?"

"Nothing . . . for the moment." Detruro paused. "I've been thinking . . . about your charter. What if the charter required the Imperador to pick the First Marshal and Fleet Marshal from career senior officers, commodores and admirals, with a provision that they can't be removed for at least three months after appointment, either by the Imperador or by the Council? *And* that both can't be removed in the same three-month period? Think about it."

"That would allow more power than we provided in the draft . . ."

"Just think about something along that line."

Ysella nodded slowly.

"That's all I have for now."

"That's more than enough," replied Ysella as he stood.

"We share that thought," said Detruro dryly.

Ysella smiled wryly as he turned and left the office.

68

ON Tridi morning, the *Tribune* ran a brief story about Salaazar, stating that he'd been found dead in a courtyard in the Imperial Palace and three guards were missing. Palace Guard Captain Fhaeryn said that the Guard was looking into "certain irregularities." The rest of the article sketched Salaazar's background.

Ysella wasn't surprised that Salaazar was widowed, although he couldn't help but wonder if Salaazar's wife died of natural causes.

Ysella arrived in his office at a third past second bell and, with no messages waiting, immediately read through the incoming letters, and then signed or corrected the responses to previous correspondence prepared by Khaard and Jaasn. After that he studied the draft port standards legislation once more.

At a sixth before fourth bell, case in hand, he headed down to the Waterways Committee room. Besides Arturo Palaan, the committee legalist, the only other person in the chamber was Haans Maessyn.

Palaan turned to Ysella. "There are copies of the draft bill at each councilor's place."

"Thank you, Arturo."

Palaan nodded, then moved to the small staff desk to the side, but remained standing.

"Do you think we can finish the markup this morning?" asked Maessyn, his tone of voice dubious.

"If not, I'll recess the committee until immediately after the Council session," replied Ysella cheerfully, "and we'll continue until we are finished."

"Might help if you announced that before we begin," suggested Maessyn.

While Ysella already planned to, he simply said, "Excellent suggestion. I will."

"You'd already planned that, hadn't you?" Maessyn offered an amused smile.

"Planned what?" asked Dannyl Grieg as he entered the chamber.

"To expedite the markup," replied Ysella, walking toward the dais.

Maessyn and Grieg followed.

By the time fourth bell sounded, Voltar Paastyn, Gaastyn Ditaero, and Astyn Coerl were all in their places. Ysella gaveled the committee to order, suspecting that Nortaak would arrive late, if he even showed, and stated, "The committee will complete the markup of the standards legislation today, either before the Council session, or after it."

Only Astyn appeared surprised, but said nothing.

"We'll begin with the title," declared Ysella. "It now stands as 'A proposal to establish in law standard definitions for terms describing services rendered by ports and those entities functioning as ports and to require complete description of services rendered and the basis on which users of those services are charged.'" After reading the title, Ysella looked around.

"Is there any way to shorten that?" asked Coerl.

"Committee legalist?" asked Ysella.

Palaan stood and replied. "The bill title must accurately reflect the scope of the legislation. The committee could add a phrase, along the lines of 'hereafter referred to as,' and use a shorter phrase."

"Thank you, Sr. Palaan," said Ysella before looking to Coerl. "Do you have a shorter title in mind, Councilor Coerl?"

"What about 'Port Standards Act' or something like that?"

"The term Port Standards Act has been proposed as an addition to the bill title. Is anyone opposed?" Ysella paused, then went on, "Seeing no opposition, the term is added as a short title. We'll now turn to section one . . ."

The committee completed the markup of the renamed Port Standards Act at a third before the sixth bell that marked midday, the quickness due in part to Coerl asking few questions and to the absence of Nortaak and his long and patronizing comments and inquiries.

Ysella then declared, "The markup having been completed, is there a motion to refer the proposed legislation to the full Council?"

"So moved," said Maessyn.

"All those in favor?"

All six councilors said, "Aye."

"All councilors present being in favor, the proposed legislation is referred for Council action."

After adjourning the committee, Ysella motioned to Voltar Paastyn.

"What is it, Dominic?"

"Nothing about the committee. I wondered how your people are doing after the pirates' attack on Paensantz."

"It's more a village than a town, and from what I've heard it was more of a raid than an attack. Only a few people were injured, but the next month or so will be hard on many of them."

"I'm sorry to hear that, but from what you say it could have been much worse."

"What does anyone expect? Except for Zeiryn and Encora, there aren't any real cities along the five hundred milles of coast southwest of Port Reale. Just small towns and villages, easy pickings for desperate pirates. They have to be desperate with what the Navy's doing."

"You think the Navy should back off?"

"By the Almighty, no. Those Atacaman bastards don't want to work. They want poor local holders to do all the hard work of planting and harvesting and picking so they can grab it up. Haarwyk and Daenyld were right, and so is what Solatiem and Dhaantyn are doing. It'd be better if the Council could put more marks into smaller ships. You don't need first-raters to deal with those scum." Paastyn paused. "What do you think?"

"I agree with you, but there's no point in saying so publicly. Not right now."

"Will there ever be?" asked Paastyn, with barely concealed bitterness.

"Not unless we can change the Establishment Act."

"And how are you going to do that?"

"By getting the Imperador to agree to the changes," replied Ysella sardonically, then added more cheerfully, "And that might be the easy part. Still, that's where we need to start."

Paastyn cocked his head. "You almost sound serious."

"Good." After a slight hesitation, Ysella asked, "Do you know why Stefan Nortaak wasn't here today?"

"No. He can't be sick, though. I saw him before the committee met. He looked like he was heading to his office. Why?"

"He never mentioned not being able to be here."

"He doesn't like explaining to anyone. Haven't you noticed that?"

"I have. I just thought that he didn't like explaining to me."

"It's everyone. Maybe a bit more with you because he's older than you." Paastyn paused. "Thank you for asking about Paensantz." With a pleasant smile, he turned and left the committee room.

As Ysella walked toward the Council chamber, he considered Nortaak's absence. Like Paastyn, he'd doubted Nortaak was ill, and from what Detruro said earlier, Nortaak was angry with both of them.

No doubt because neither of us recognizes his nonexistent superior abilities and his experience and age.

Given everything currently happening, Ysella was also glad he'd resumed wearing the silk and leather armor, hot as it might be over the weeks ahead. He also needed to spar with Caastyn, something he'd put off too long because of the damage to his ribs.

69

WHEN Ysella returned to the house on Furdi afternoon, after an uneventful day, he went straight to his study, resolving to write Aelyn. After a time, he began.

Aelyn—
I must confess that I have put off replying to your last letter for several days after receiving it, not because I have no desire to write, and not because I have nothing to say, but because there is so much you should know that I fear both overwhelming you and not telling you enough, or being selective in a way that presents me and what I've done in a more favorable light than I merit.
For that reason, it might be best that I start at the beginning. I was born the third son of Cliven Dumaar Ysella and Kaelyn Escoln...

From there, Ysella sketched out his early life quickly and dispassionately before addressing more fully the earlier questions she had intimated that he'd only "attempted" to address.

... as my two older brothers became more and more capable in undertaking all the tasks involved in running a holding, I realized I had no desire to follow in my father's footsteps or theirs, although I did not understand why. What I finally realized is that the success in running a holding requires recognizing patterns—those of the land, the water, and the weather, and those of the crops and the livestock, and even those of the markets where a holder must buy and sell. Moreover, all too often a holder can be fenced in by those patterns. In my youthful arrogance, I did not wish to be so imprisoned, possibly because I was not good at understanding those patterns. I thought that the patterns of law were better suited to my abilities. Also, while a holder can learn the patterns of nature, he cannot change them, only react and adapt, and I hoped that I could, in time, learn to change or affect the patterns of people. The problem, I discovered, is that while one can change the laws, it takes a long time for the laws to change the people, if ever.

> *I also discovered that it takes a long time, possibly a lifetime, to truly learn and understand the law ...*

He briefly described his years clerking for and practicing with Legrand Quaentyn and how that led into his desire to become a councilor, allowing him to become financially secure. Knowing that faith, or limits on faith, affected everyone, he took a deep breath and continued writing.

> *I must confess that, for better or worse, I do not know if there is an Almighty, but because faith offers hope and tends to instill better values, if they are not pressed to the extreme, I do attend services. Both Presider Haelsyn in Machtarn and Presider Maabak in Aloor have doubtless made some impression, enough that I have pondered at least some of their homilies, which I fear sometimes make more sense than a councilor or two ...*

Then he addressed his interest in her.

> *... over the past years, and to this day, my parents and well-meaning friends and acquaintances attempt matchmaking. I had a more meaningful conversation with you in that fraction of a bell when I first met you than I've had in an entire dinner with any of the women others have arranged for me to meet. One might claim that I simply haven't found the right woman. Such women are rare, but they do exist. Unfortunately, the few I have met, excepting you, are older and happily married, but they gave me hope that I would discover someone. Where our correspondence will lead, I cannot honestly say, but my heart says that we have at least the opportunity to learn more about each other and to see how well we fit.*

Ysella thought about writing more, being open, but Legrand had always said that there was a balance between too little information and too much.

You hope you're somewhere close.

70

YSELLA rode down the drive to Averra Place at a third before fourth bell on Findi afternoon, heading for the home—at least the Machtarn house—of Chaarls and Bhettina Aashen. He'd thought about wearing the silk and hardened leather armor, but decided against it, since few people would know he was leaving his house on Findi, let alone where he might head.

Yet, when Ysella reached Cuipregilt Avenue, not far from Alaan and Amaelya Escalante's house, he saw two men on horseback a block away. Instantly, he wished he were wearing the armor, even after the pair headed away. A half block later, he turned onto Alden Place and three houses later rode up the drive.

Chaarls stepped out onto the wraparound porch and said, "The first stall is open, as always."

After stalling Jaster, Ysella walked back to the house, not much larger than his own, except for the capacious porch. There he took the side steps and walked to the front door, where Cassyda, the serving maid, let him in.

"How are you doing this afternoon, Cassyda?"

"Well, thank you, sir. We haven't seen you in a while."

"Councilor Aashen and I have been, I fear, somewhat occupied, if differently."

"So Chaarls tells me," declared Bhettina as she walked toward Ysella, her not entirely natural black hair set in a firm bob. "And you're in the good graces of both the Premier and Lady Delehya."

"Only slightly," demurred Ysella, "but that's better than the alternatives."

Rather than leading Ysella to the parlor immediately, Bhettina halted and asked, "Red or white wine?"

"Red, please."

Bhettina nodded to Cassyda. "If you would."

"Yes, Ritten."

Once Cassyda moved away, Bhettina said, "We should have had you over again sooner. It'd been too long, especially since you're family."

"Extended family, but you've been kind for years," replied Ysella with a smile. "What should I know before I reach the parlor?"

Bhettina smiled in return. "We have friends from Sudaen—Fraedryk and Gloris Challys—and their daughter. Fraedryk is quite traditional . . . and Caarlya is far too young for you, but . . ."

"You'd like me to treat her as if she weren't?"

"That would be lovely."

"Consider it done. Is there anything else I should know about Ritter and Ritten Challys besides their being traditional?"

"He's recently ascended to his familial holding, under trying circumstances with his younger twin brother. There was a duel involved."

Traditional. Indeed. Ysella nodded, then walked beside Bhettina from the foyer into the center hall and from there into the parlor.

Fraedryk Challys stood, followed by Chaarls Aashen. Both Fraedryk and Gloris looked to be about fifteen years older than Ysella. Fraedryk was wiry, with a narrow face and brown hair and eyes, while Gloris had a rounder face, black hair, and gray eyes. Their daughter had her father's face and her mother's eyes and hair.

"Dominic," said Chaarls, "Fraedryk and Gloris Challys, and their daughter Caarlya."

"I'm pleased to meet you." Ysella took the vacant armchair next to the end of the davenport occupied by Caarlya.

Cassyda discreetly brought Ysella his wine. He took the smallest sip before setting it on the end table between his chair and the davenport.

"I saw that you rode here, rather than took a carriage," said Fraedryk.

"I don't live that far away, and in good weather it's more convenient," replied Ysella.

"You're one of the younger councilors, aren't you?" asked Fraedryk.

"Not so much anymore," replied Ysella. "I was the youngest when I was first elected, but that was eight years ago."

"That's a bit unusual, isn't it?" asked Gloris.

"There's something unusual about every councilor," returned Ysella. "The fact that I'm a registered water legalist is probably more unusual than my age."

"Is it true that you're the grandson of the last king of Aloor?" asked Caarlya, with a hint of a glint in her eye as she turned more to face Ysella.

"Absolutely—but I'm also the third son of his heir, and that's about as useful as spoiled milk or melted ice."

"I read in the newssheets that you danced with the Lady Delehya." Caarlya fixed her gray eyes on Ysella. "Is she really promiscuous?"

"I only danced once with her. She dances and converses well. I doubt that she's at all promiscuous. It's unlikely she could be, even if she were so inclined, since she's never allowed to be alone with any man."

"That's not what the Sudaen *Record* printed," said Gloris. "The *Record* suggested she might have been . . . intimate with the former Fleet Marshal."

"I asked her about him," replied Ysella. "She said he was a good man, and that being a good man was dangerous."

"Good in the bedroom, she likely meant," said Fraedryk snidely.

"I very much doubt it. The Imperador is rather protective."

"I'm sure he is. That's why the late Fleet Marshal is no longer with us," replied Fraedryk.

"That's more to do with Fleet Marshal Haarwyk being honest about what kind of ships the Navy needed," replied Ysella.

"Most likely it was both," said Gloris. "That's why he has to marry her off quickly."

"I suspect he's marrying her off quickly to protect her, and it's the only match that made sense for her or for the Imperador. Iustaan Detruro is not only premier, but a Ritter by landholding. He's intelligent and a rather physically imposing figure."

Gloris's expression was one of disbelief.

"People are saying that the Imperador isn't well," interjected Fraedryk. "What do you know about that?"

"He's gotten old, but he still knows his own mind. Crossing him remains unwise."

"What do you think about the Heir?" asked Fraedryk.

"I've never met the Heir. I also haven't talked at length to anyone who knows him well. I've heard from others that he shares his father's belief in building large warships and that he maintains a significant armed personal guard."

"What of it?" countered Fraedryk. "Guldor needs to be strong and have a strong Imperador to hold it together. The Council is . . . limited . . . in what it can do."

"You're right," replied Ysella in an amiable tone he scarcely felt. "The Council is indeed limited. By the terms of the Establishment Act, it can never override a decision by the Imperador, while the Imperador can override any decision by the Council. That kind of government works well only so long as an intelligent, perceptive, and necessarily cautious man is Imperador."

"Why necessarily cautious?"

"Laureous created the Imperium through a combination of audacity, military prowess, and calculated caution, knowing when each was necessary."

"Behind that careful wording," declared Fraedryk, "you sound dubious about the Heir."

"History supports what I said about the Imperador, but there are no public indications about how the Heir will act. That's why I'm cautious in coming to publicly judge a man I've never met and who has not revealed his capabilities or lack of such."

"Would that some other councilors were so perceptive or—"

"As I told you earlier," interjected Chaarls Aashen firmly, "Dominic is very thorough and fair. He's likely the best chairman of the Waterways Committee in years, if not ever. In time, he'd make a good premier, but I think we've said all that needs to be said this evening on the subject. We will find out what the Heir is made of when the time comes. And I do believe dinner is about to be served."

At dinner, after a brief blessing from Chaarls, Ysella sat between Gloris and Caarlya and across from Fraedryk and Bhettina.

After Chaarls lifted a fork, Ysella sampled the spring salad, then asked Caarlya, "How are you finding Machtarn?"

"I thought it would be larger. It's not that much larger than Sudaen. Of course, Sudaen doesn't have an Imperial Palace or the Council Hall, but the harbors are about the same size, and there are more shops in Sudaen. The weather is more temperate as well . . ."

For the remainder of dinner, Ysella kept his side of the conversation pleasantly prosaic, but that wasn't terribly difficult, given that both Chaarls and Bhettina had the same objective.

After dessert and a round of cordials that followed, Chaarls Aashen was the one to accompany Ysella to the door, where he paused. "Thank you again for coming, and for your comments. I fear that Fraedryk represents quite a few landors in his outlook regarding the Imperador and the Heir. He has no idea what you're capable of."

"I'd rather he didn't. I'm not exactly proud of it."

"I think I can intimate that challenging you would have been unwise." Aashen paused. "On another matter, I was thinking about whether I should stand down when the next election is called, but Fraedryk has hinted that, in time, his younger and only surviving brother would like to be a councilor."

"If you're up to it, it might be best for Guldor for you not to step down quite yet."

"These days, Dominic, you're closer to the Premier than I am. Do you know if the Imperador is likely to call for an election soon?"

"I have no idea, but if anything should happen to the Imperador, the Heir would likely call one as soon as the Council showed any sign of disagreeing on anything."

"I thought as much." Aashen sighed. "Thank you again."

"You're welcome. Now, I have a question for you, not related to either the Imperador or your guests. Does the name Aelyssa Scalante mean anything to you?"

Aashen smiled, and laughed. "Feisty old lady. She lives three doors down. Same house for years after her husband died. He was the councilor from Silverhills before he died. We pass a few words now and again. Why?"

"I met her grandniece when I was last in Aloor."

"I didn't know she had a grandniece."

"You do now. Her name is Aelyn Wythcomb. I just wondered. Best of fortune with your guests."

"Thank you. They're leaving on Duadi." Chaarls smiled ruefully.

Ysella inclined his head, then departed.

Riding back to his house, he worried about the weeks and months ahead, given that too many landors outside Machtarn supported the Imperador and the Heir unthinkingly and either distrusted the Council or thought it weak, while those in Machtarn and in the military weren't that thrilled with either the Imperador or the Council.

He couldn't say he was surprised that Chaarls Aashen knew Aelyssa Scalante, since several councilors lived or had lived in the area. But then, Aashen had been a councilor longer than most.

71

UNADI was uneventful, except perhaps for a short evening sparring session with Caastyn that showed Ysella's lack of recent practice. Ysella arrived in his office just after second morning bell on Duadi to find a letter with a councilor's seal on the top of the incoming correspondence—a seal he did not immediately recognize, although it seemed familiar.

He opened the envelope, saving the seal, and began to read.

Ritter Dominic Mikail Ysella—
  Any Ritter of Guldor deserves courtesy, and one of my station and standing certainly so. Yet you have repeatedly refused to honor or even accept my standing. I must insist on an apology for your lack of courtesy. Failing that, I insist on satisfaction through blades, or I will announce to all Guldor your cowardice in refusing that satisfaction.

The signature was that of Stefan Nortaak.

Ysella shook his head. *Who put him up to this? It had to be the Heir or someone close to him.*

He slipped the short letter into his inside coat pocket and stepped into the outer office. Since Khaard wasn't in sight, he said, "Paatyr, I'm headed to the Premier's office. I don't how long I'll be gone."

"Yes, sir."

After Ysella reached Detruro's office, he had to wait a good third before Luaro Maatrak departed and the Premier was free.

"You have a worried expression, Dominic," said Detruro, gesturing to the chairs.

"This worry concerns both of us." Ysella removed Nortaak's challenge letter and handed it to Detruro before sitting down.

The Premier read the letter, then handed it back. "And?"

"I'll be happy to offer an apology for any inadvertent lack of courtesy and to say that I had no intention of offending him or impugning his honor," said Ysella, "but I worry that, no matter what, he'll insist on an idiotic duel. He doesn't even understand what that would do."

"What do you think it would do?" asked Detruro.

"Make the Council less respected. The way this is set up, he'll reject any apology as insufficient and insist on blood, if not more. That way, the Council could easily have a dead or badly wounded councilor and one disgraced for being involved in such a mess. That's despite the fact that I've never said a dishonorable thing to him, no matter what he claims." Ysella paused. "Frig! He was fine until he found out I was pressing for an increase in the usury cap. Oskaar told me not to trust Nortaak, but he didn't say why, but I'd wager the Heir's behind this."

Detruro offered a sour smile. "I wouldn't wager against you."

"Dueling over so-called honor is barbaric. Perhaps it was necessary a hundred years ago, although I'm not certain about that." *Not after Sudaen.*

"You may be right, but not all landors would agree. Stefan is one of those. What do you plan to do?"

"Write him a polite and courteous apology, insisting that I had no intention to slight or malign him in any way, either as a Ritter or as a councilor, and that I hold him in the same esteem as all other councilors."

Detruro nodded. "Excellent . . . you should respond quickly, but send me a copy first so that I get it well before Stefan does. Then I'll see what I can do." He paused. "You are right about a duel serving no one well, except for the Heir."

"I can do that." Ysella stood, knowing that there was little else to be said, then inclined his head and left.

As Ysella walked back to his office, he hoped Detruro could persuade Nortaak to accept the apology. Although duels were uncommon, they still were fought, usually among outraged or hotheaded landors, or upon occasion, junior navy officers. *As you well know, even if it was over fifteen years ago.*

Once back in his office, Ysella wrote out the necessary apology to Nortaak, then had Jaasn carry a copy to the Premier. After busying himself for almost half a bell, he sent Jaasn out again, this time with the apology to Nortaak.

Just after midday, he received a message from Arturo Palaan that the floor leader's office had scheduled the Port Standards Act for floor debate and final vote on Tridi, the fifteenth of Springend. Ysella noted it on the committee calendar and had his clerks send notifications to all Waterways Committee members.

Just after second afternoon bell, Khaard appeared in the inner office doorway, a surprised look on his face. "The Premier, sir."

"Show him in and make sure the door is closed."

"Yes, sir."

Moments later, Detruro entered but remained standing. "This won't take long, but I thought you'd like to know. I told Stefan he should accept your apology, and that it would be best for him and the Council."

"And he accepted?" asked Ysella, coming to his feet in respect.

"Well . . ." Detruro offered a crooked smile. "I pointed out that if he accepted, he'd have both the apology and his life, and the Council wouldn't lose one or possibly two councilors. I did have to make an allusion, because, as we both know, he's not as intelligent as he thinks he is."

"Allusion?"

"Sudaen and a duel that led to the death of three landor midshipmen. He turned a little pale then."

"You knew all along? I was only eighteen."

"Of course." Detruro offered a broader smile. "I mentioned that he could take great satisfaction in your apology, although it might be best if he didn't flaunt it. He agreed."

"Do you think he realized that he was being used as a sacrifice?"

"Why do you think he paled?" After a moment, Detruro added, "I do hope he won't be quite so supportive of the Heir."

Ysella nodded, although he had doubts that Nortaak would change much, then asked, "Is there anything new about the ship fire in Neewyrk?"

"Dhaantyn didn't have anything to say." Before Ysella could ask more, Detruro added, "Delehya hasn't had much useful time with her father. He's still weak. How are you coming on some language about the First Marshal and the Fleet Marshal?"

"I've got some ideas."

"Draft something. We may not have as much time as I thought."

"I'll have something in the next few days."

"Good. I'll let you know if things change." Detruro turned and let himself out of the office.

After Detruro left, Ysella took out pen and paper, thinking about how he could word what Detruro had suggested, especially in a way that didn't block Council action over time, but didn't give the Imperador too much control over the selection process.

A bell later, he'd written out several possibilities, but wasn't pleased with any of them.

Just before fourth bell, Khaard stood at Ysella's door. "A message from Councilor Nortaak."

Ysella took the envelope. "Thank you."

After Khaard returned to his desk, Ysella opened it and read the few words there.

Dominic—
I appreciate and accept your apology.
                                                            Stefan

Ysella nodded. *That's the best you'll get, and you'll need to be very courteous with Nortaak for a good while.* But it was far better than any of the alternatives, and the result would certainly disappoint the Heir and lead to something else, especially given Nortaak.

72

AT a third past second bell on Tridi morning, the fifteenth of Spring-end, Ysella walked into his office, worried because there had been no newssheet stories about the Imperador for days. That suggested that Laureous was still ill, but not getting worse. The Palace hadn't mentioned who would replace Laergaan or Salaazar, or who was acting in their steads. There also wasn't any new information about pirates, about the Navy's response to pirates, or about the Fleet Marshal's investigation of the Neewyrk shipyard fire. The Commerce Committee's new chairman—Aksyl Haarst—had issued an updated committee hearing schedule, one containing no mention of any bills dealing with the usury interest cap.

Of more immediate concern was the fact that Stefan Nortaak had been quietly polite at the Waterways Committee meeting the previous Furdi dealing with assessing reports of damage to levees and channels from the spring runoff.

At least Ysella hadn't been invited to any dinners—matchmaking or otherwise.

That left his worries about Aelyn Wythcomb, particularly about the length of his letter, which was far, far longer than he'd ever written to anyone, primarily because he'd had the sense she felt he had withheld too much or was too reserved. Now, he wondered if he'd written too much.

You'll find out sooner or later, possibly later if indeed you wrote too much.

"You've got a letter from Argental, it looks like," said Khaard.

"Argental?" For a moment, Ysella couldn't imagine who from there could be writing him, then realized it had to be either Ramon or Leona Hekkaad. "I suspect it's from the recalled Argenti envoy. If it's not, I have no idea, because he and his wife are the only Argenti I know."

Waiting on the top of the pile was a still-sealed letter with an address in Cimaguile. Ysella slit the envelope, not wanting to disturb the seal and the various stamps around it, and began to read.

Councilor Ysella—

In view of your past kindness, and my sudden departure from Machtarn, I wanted to let you know of our safe return to Cimaguile . . .

Ysella frowned at the stilted language so unlike Ramon, then picked up the envelope and examined it, especially the seal, and nodded. *Ramon knew anything he wrote would be read by someone.*

... the trip was arduous, especially in the southern part of the mountains, but we encountered no delays north of the border ...

Suggesting that Guldor still hasn't really dealt with the brigands on its side of the border.

... although the weather in Argental was unseasonably cold, even by Argenti standards, particularly once we reached Cimaguile, but returned to its usual winter chill after several days ...

Ysella suspected that meant Ramon had gotten a chilly reception and some intensive questioning, but had survived it.

... Unless the weather changes markedly in the weeks ahead, it's likely to remain cold in Argental. From what we experienced in the southernmost mountains, they are likely to heat up considerably, far more than usual, by summer.

I have been given a new post, reporting directly to the Assembly for the next several months, and updating the members on developments in Guldor. Any information that you feel free to share would be most welcome.

I remain,
Ramon Hekkaad

"Another worry," murmured Ysella, if only to himself. He got the feeling from the letter that the Assembly was less than satisfied, but whether they blamed Hekkaad or were pressing him for information and recommendations Ysella couldn't tell.

The way he read the letter was that the Assembly wasn't at all pleased with Guldor's failure to rein in the brigands on Guldor's side of the border and Argental was likely to pursue those brigands into Guldoran territory. That was something that both Detruro and Alaan Escalante needed to know. But it wouldn't matter much if he talked to Detruro after the Council session.

He slipped the letter into his inside jacket pocket and picked up the next letter, which, unsurprisingly given the recent heavy rains around Aloor and Daal, was another plea for funding to improve the stream banks along the upper reaches of the Khulor River. Ysella jotted down a few phrases for the clerks and moved on to the next letter.

A bell later, he picked up the last letter in the pile, and it was the last because it was from Ondeliew. Yet another letter from Gherard Brandt. Ysella quickly skimmed to find what Brandt wanted, because he doubted Brandt was merely informing him.

> ... since last I last wrote you, Professor Ritchen has completed testing his larger steam device. The results have been most promising, especially in pumping water and propelling a small boat. The device is now being tested at a flooded coal mine, and we expect results before long.
>
> Neither shipbuilders, merchants, nor the Navy are interested in any device that cannot produce results for a larger vessel. Unhappily, neither the professor nor the college have the funds or contacts to obtain such a vessel, even one in poor repair ...

Ysella shook his head. The Waterways Committee didn't have any extra funds. He instructed Khaard to draft a response suggesting Brandt contact the chairman of either the Military Affairs Committee or the Commerce Committee and keep Ysella informed of the test results.

By then, it was time for Ysella to head to the Council chamber.

He took his seat, and when Ahslem Staeryt seated himself as well, Ysella asked, "Is it me, or have things been comparatively quiet for the last week?"

"I'd have to agree with you, but it might be that people are holding their breath while the Imperador decides whether to fight back or die."

"If it's in his power, he'll fight back," declared Ysella. "I also think he wants to see his daughter married and somewhat settled."

"If anyone can settle her, it'd be Iustaan."

"More like he's the only one she'd allow to settle her."

Luaro Maatrak gaveled the Council to order, then declared, "The business before the Council is the Port Standards Act. Chairman Ysella will speak to the bill."

Ysella took the steps to the dais and stood beside the lectern. "Often cargo vessels have a tendency to frequent only a handful of Guldoran ports and harbors. At times, that's simply because they can obtain certain goods nowhere else, or they know there are purchasers of their cargoes in those ports. Inquiries by the Waterways Committee revealed another reason, especially for less frequent traders. The array of terms, practices, and services provided by harbors and ports can differ widely from port to port ..."

When Ysella finished and relinquished the lectern, Maatrak said, "Speaking against the bill is Chairman Haarst of the Commerce Committee."

Haarst smiled warmly before speaking. "I deeply respect the chairman of the Waterways Committee and his legal expertise particularly. I also respect his integrity, but the success of commerce is a product of what happens in each part of a land, and the practices that develop in each area are those best suited to that area. Even minor changes can disrupt trade and commerce, and when those changes are enshrined in law, and do not reflect the values and practices of that area, they raise costs and disrupt the smooth flow of trade . . ."

As he listened, Ysella wanted to shake his head. The bill was a straightforward attempt to clarify what charges were levied for what service. It wouldn't do in the slightest what Haarst suggested. The details misrepresented by Haarst could only have come from Nortaak. But then, Nortaak definitely had an interest in making Ysella look incompetent, and Haarst's questioning of Ysella when he'd talked to the Commerce Committee had been more than casual.

A partnership of convenience . . . and poor Oskaar did warn you not to trust Nortaak.

When Haarst finished, Maatrak called for the vote.

Two-thirds of a bell later, he announced, "With twenty-two voting in favor, twenty-five voting against, and two not voting, the bill is defeated and returned to committee."

Ysella took his time leaving the Council chamber and then walked the short distance to Detruro's office, where he waited until the Premier finished talking with Maatrak.

"What is it this time?" asked Detruro almost before Ysella closed the door. "Besides Nortaak getting Haarst and the Commerce Committee to oppose your bill on spurious grounds?"

Rather than say a word, Ysella handed Hekkaad's letter to him, then waited.

Detruro read the letter and looked up. "And?"

"The thing is," said Ysella, "when he wrote this, he knew it would be read, but he made the letter as formal and indirect as he could, hoping it wouldn't be confiscated."

"He apparently succeeded," mused Detruro, "unless the Assembly wanted you to get the message."

"That's a definite possibility," agreed Ysella, "especially knowing I'd share it with you."

"There's not much I can do with this, you know?"

"I understand. The Imperador would be angry to learn about a councilor having correspondence with an envoy from Argental, just as the Assembly is likely angry with Hekkaad. But I thought you should know as soon as I received the letter. It suggests the border conflicts may get worse."

"That they could, and I appreciate the information, Dominic."

"Have you heard more on the Imperador's health?"

"I understand he's better, and considerably stronger. The Heir's trying to see him, but Laureous's personal guards, the Imperadora, and Delehya have so far forestalled that. How long they can keep that up is another question."

"Has Dhaantyn any more information about the shipbuilding fire?"

"If he has, he's said nothing to anyone."

Ysella nodded. "That's all I had."

"Your standards bill is still a good idea, but let Nortaak savor his little victory for now. You could press the matter and change the outcome in weeks. I'd hope you'd wait."

"I trust your judgment." *I may not like it, but I trust it.*

As Ysella walked back to his office, he couldn't help wondering what, specifically, Detruro had in mind for Nortaak and Haarst . . . if anything.

73

JUST before midmorning on Furdi, Jaasn announced that Haans Maessyn was hoping to see Ysella for a few moments.

"Of course," declared Ysella.

In moments, Maessyn sat in one of the straight-backed chairs facing Ysella across the desk. "What did you do to piss off Nortaak so much that he got so many high-and-mighty landors to vote down a nothing bill?" Maessyn paused. "Pardon me, but you know what I mean. It shouldn't have been controversial. All it did was translate all the different port terms into a form so anyone could understand them and require ports to be honest in what they charge."

"So far as I can tell, the only thing I did to offend him was not worship at his feet because he's an older landor who deserves respect." Ysella paused. "And there's the small matter that I apologized for inadvertently offending him so that I didn't have to fight a duel with him."

"Do landors still do that shit?"

"Apparently, dear Stefan does, or would like to. A duel would have been a losing proposition either way. He was out for blood. First blood wouldn't satisfy him. So I would have had to kill or wound him badly, which would destroy my political career, because most of Guldor agrees with you, and so do I. Or I'd get killed."

"You didn't accommodate him conveniently. So he tries to make you look incompetent."

"He did a decent job of it," replied Ysella, "and I doubt he's done. But he'll get others to do it, especially Haarst."

"Do you mind if I share some of that with a few others?"

"If you do it quietly, I'd appreciate it."

"Too bad you couldn't have killed the arrogant bastard," replied Maessyn.

"That, unhappily, would have made matters worse. We'll have to deal with Stefan the hard way and make sure we have the votes for even the most uncontroversial measures."

"That means it will take longer before we report any bills to the full Council," Maessyn pointed out.

"Probably, but that's better than getting them rejected by the full

Council because Nortaak has a grudge." Ysella hesitated. "Even if I left the Council, the Premier wouldn't appoint Nortaak as chair, and he'd still be subordinate to someone younger." Then he grinned. "Likely you, and you're certainly no landor."

"I'm in no hurry," replied Maessyn dryly.

"If you hear of anything that reeks of Nortaak, I'd appreciate knowing."

"We can do that, sir."

After Maessyn left, Ysella considered some other aspects of the vote. Even before Klempt's murder, most of the Commerce Committee members had been very traditional landors or commercers, opposed to both transparency and government oversight, and the Natural Resources Committee wasn't much different. According to Klempt, Aksyl Haarst had ties of some sort to the Heir. The Agriculture Committee was heavily landor, but Georg Raathan was fair-minded, and not unthinkingly traditionalist.

All that pointed out that, once he got back the Navy's comments on the water safety code, he'd need to spend time he hadn't planned in making sure the votes were there, and positioning the issues so that anyone opposing the measure increased the costs and liability exposure to the Navy, something that would not please the Imperador . . . *or,* if the matter dragged on, the Heir.

Maybe you should have accepted the duel, and crushed Nortaak's throat enough so he couldn't talk. Except you're likely too rusty to be sure of that.

Ysella shook his head and returned to his correspondence.

74

THE days following the defeat of the Port Standards Act were busy, but routine, although Ysella worked in two short sparring sessions with Caastyn. Nortaak even offered constructive questions at the Waterways Committee hearing about progress on the Machtarn port improvements, though Ysella had no doubt that Nortaak was biding his time and looking for another opportunity to undermine Ysella.

Over endday, Ysella finished the provisions for appointing and dismissing the First Marshal and the Fleet Marshal in the draft government-reform charter. Then he rewrote that section of the charter on Unadi afternoon and evening.

He worried, again, about how Aelyn had taken his letter. Before, she'd replied almost immediately, and almost three weeks had passed since he'd written her. *Maybe the weather slowed the posts ... or she had family obligations elsewhere ... or ...* He shook his head and tried to think about other concerns.

On Duadi morning, the twentieth of Springend, Ysella rode Jaster through scattered light rain to the Council stables, and was making his way to his office when Paolo Caanard, headed in the direction of the Council chamber, suddenly turned and approached Ysella.

"Good morning, Paolo," said Ysella. "You're looking worried." He shifted his leather case from his right to his left hand.

"I am. Alaan Escalante and I just got word from the Army Marshal that there's been trouble on the northern border."

"That's hardly new. The Argenti have complained for months that we aren't stopping Guldoran brigands from attacking hamlets in Argental."

"This time is different."

"How? Did the Argenti forces follow brigands based in Guldor back across the border and attack them?"

Caanard frowned. "Why would you think that?"

"Before he was recalled, the former envoy told me that the Argental Assembly was getting tired of brigands from Guldor attacking hamlets in Argental and then fleeing back to Guldor. Especially since Guldor wasn't doing anything about them."

"What they did two weeks ago was worse. The mountains got hit with a heavy spring snow, and the Argenti border forces started an avalanche that buried an entire town."

"A town or a brigand encampment posing as a town?"

"It doesn't matter, Dominic. The avalanche killed more than a hundred people, some of them women and children."

"What do the Argenti say?" asked Ysella.

"The Argenti are claiming that Guldoran brigands started the avalanche by launching an attack across unstable snow in an attempt to attack an Argenti border force."

"Do we have solid evidence to the contrary?"

"Only a handful of people escaped," said Caanard.

That isn't proof of anything but the avalanche. "One way or another, that's not good," said Ysella. "We don't need to be fighting border skirmishes with Argental while we're occupied with the Atacaman navy and so-called pirates."

"The Argenti are trying to cause trouble when we can't easily respond."

"Why would they do that?" asked Ysella. "It's scarcely to their benefit."

"Well, they did it. The proof is in the avalanche."

"Avalanches happen every year. Right now, all we have is one side saying it was an accident caused by brigands' stupidity and on the other side survivors are claiming that the Argenti caused the avalanche. If I were you, until you have more evidence, it might be best to wait before placing blame. Just say it's a bad situation either way, and jumping to conclusions could only make matters worse."

"I don't think you understand, Dominic," said Caanard coolly. "The Army Marshal has called it an attack."

"I see. That makes it an attack, whether it was or not."

"I'm not interested in following the path taken by Symeon and Oskaar, and I would have thought you'd be a little averse as well."

"I understand," replied Ysella. "In that case, I suggest that you and Alaan say that, according to the Army Marshal, Argenti forces started an avalanche that killed more than a hundred people. That's truthful, and it's in accord with what you know."

Caanard frowned, then said, "That's a better way of putting it."

"I appreciate your letting me know, Paolo. That could make matters for the Council even more complicated." *Especially if the Army Marshal is close to the Heir.*

"As if they're not complicated enough already. I'll see you later." Caanard smiled briefly before turning and continuing toward the Council chamber—or possibly the Premier's office.

Three steps into his outer office Khaard stopped Ysella. "You have two messages. One's from the Premier. The other one doesn't have an outside address." He extended both.

"Thank you." Ysella took them with his free hand and walked to his office, where he set aside the case and opened the message from the Premier—a request to come to Detruro's office before the Council convened.

The second message simply said on the envelope in block letters, "COUNCILOR YSELLA." The message inside, also in block letters, read, "DON'T TRUST NORTAAK."

With the use of block letters and the shortness of the message, Ysella had no way of recognizing the writer, and if a clerk had handed it to a messenger, there was a good chance that none of the Council messengers would remember where the envelope had originated.

For that matter, it could have come from a staffer.

Ysella definitely didn't trust Nortaak, but he wondered what Nortaak had done to alert whoever sent the message.

Since there's no urgent legislation before the Waterways Committee, it might be a good idea not to complete any markup or send anything to the floor in the next few weeks.

After going through the incoming correspondence and making his notes, Ysella left his office, his case in hand, and headed for the Premier's office. If Paolo Caanard had gone to see Detruro he should have finished and departed, given that Detruro never held long meetings.

The Premier saw Ysella immediately.

"I'm glad you came early, Dominic. I met with Fleet Marshal Dhaantyn at the Palace late yesterday afternoon. The fire at the Neewyrk shipyard is more concerning than I feared. The Heir met with the Haamyt brothers last year and suggested a procurement of more first-rate ships would go more smoothly with the Imperador if he were involved. The Haamyt brothers told him they appreciated his support. At the beginning of this year, they got a letter from the Heir implying they were not honoring their agreement to reimburse him for his efforts. They wrote back, thanking him for his support, and saying that they were continuing to construct the ship under the terms of the contract with the Navy."

"Shortly after they sent that letter, the fire occurred, and two weeks later they got another letter from the Heir telling them that they should have included him in the shipbuilding process, and that without his involvement, the brothers might continue to encounter difficulties."

"Young Laureous put that *in writing*?" asked Ysella, wondering if the Heir was really that stupid . . . or massively arrogant. *Likely both.*

"He did. Dhaantyn compared writing and signatures. He briefed the Imperador on Findi, and made sure that the First Marshal, the Imperadora, and Sra. Kaechar were all there. He also told the Imperador that copies of all the documents would go to the newssheets and the Council if anything happened to him or the First Marshal, including disappearing."

"Since you're telling me, the Fleet Marshal is still alive."

"So far. The Imperador was furious, but after the first sixth, that anger was mostly at the Heir and his stupidity. He exiled the Heir and the Princesa to the summer palace indefinitely with an army guard."

"I'd trust naval marines more," said Ysella.

"So would I, especially since the Imperador was so angry that he had a bit of a relapse."

"Frig..."

"My thoughts precisely. We can hope, though. He's still tough."

"Along those lines..." Ysella opened his case, took out the large envelope holding the revised charter, and set it on Detruro's desk. "Here's the revised charter with the new section about the First Marshal and Fleet Marshal."

"Excellent. When I saw your case, I hoped you might have it." Detruro glanced toward the door.

"There is one other matter. I take it you heard about the avalanche wiping out a small town on the northern border."

"Both Alaan and Paolo were in here earlier. They were... emphatic." Detruro offered a bemused smile.

"I imagine. Paolo was quite that way this morning." Ysella summarized his conversation with Caanard, adding, "I'm a little concerned about his reference to the Army Marshal, particularly after what you told me. That could be a problem if councilors think the marshal is linked to the Heir and he's not... or, worse, if he is."

"Right now, there's no indication that Army Marshal Lekett is close to the Heir. He has been close, at times, to the Imperador, but, when I get the chance, I'll mention it to Delehya, Dhaantyn, and Solatiem."

Sensing Detruro's impatience, Ysella stood. "I won't take any more of your time."

Detruro smiled with a hint of warmth, and said, "I appreciate your efforts not to waste my time, and your abilities to get the necessary tasks done."

Ysella returned the smile. "Until later."

Then he made his way back to his own office.

Once there, he dealt with correspondence, then began to make minor changes to the Waterways Committee schedule, with the effect to assure there wouldn't be any legislative bills coming out of the committee in the next month.

By then, it was time to leave for the Council chamber, and Ysella walked down the steps to the main level quickly. He was one of the last to enter the Council chamber, barely in his seat when Luaro Maatrak took the lectern.

Moments later, Maatrak gaveled the Council to order, declaring, "The business before the Council is consideration of a supplemental appropriation for the Navy. Chairman Escalante will speak to the measure, followed by Chairman Caanard of the Foreign Affairs Committee."

Ysella frowned. Maatrak hadn't referenced Caanard as opposing the supplemental, not that a councilor was likely to publicly oppose any military spending at the moment.

Alaan Escalante stepped up to the dais, took the lectern, and cleared his throat. "As we all know, the Navy has been required to deal with the greatly increased activities of Atacaman pirates in the Gulf of Nordum, particularly in the Cataran Delta. In addition, the pirates were successful in using a fireship to destroy the *Obaanax*, a first-rate ship of the line. These continuing operations have also resulted in the loss of two cutters and one sloop. The operations have required the transfer of more ships to Port Reale and to the Southern Fleet . . . There will also be additional training and manpower required to deal with difficulties with Argenti brigands along the northern borders . . ."

Argenti brigands? Ysella kept from shaking his head and continued to listen as Escalante listed all the items that required funding, and then concluded, "For this reason, First Marshal Solatiem requests additional funding." Almost immediately, he surrendered the lectern to Paolo Caanard.

Caanard surveyed the chamber briefly before beginning. "I'm not speaking in opposition to the supplemental, for reasons we all know and understand. I am speaking to remind all councilors that passage of this measure will exhaust the reserve funds, and unless the Treasury receives unexpected revenues, by the end of summer, the Treasury will not have the funds necessary for all government activities." Caanard paused. "That's all that needs to be said." He left the lectern and returned to his seat.

Maatrak stepped to the lectern. "The vote is on passage of the supplemental naval appropriations. Councilors have one third to cast their vote."

Staeryt looked to Ysella. "By saying that, Caanard could be making himself a target."

"He didn't say a word against the Imperador," Ysella pointed out. "He just pointed out that funding will be reduced."

"And who decides where those funds will be reduced?" asked Staeryt. "Not the Council, but the Palace or the Treasury."

"Or perhaps administrators picked by the Imperador," suggested Ysella.

Staeryt shook his head, then reached for his voting card, as did Ysella.

Slightly less than two-thirds of a bell later, Maatrak announced, "Twenty-eight voting in favor, and twenty voting present, the supplemental appropriation is passed." Almost without a pause he added, "The Council is recessed until noon on Quindi." He rapped the gavel as he said "Quindi."

The Council chamber emptied quickly, but when Ysella stepped into the main corridor he found Georg Raathan waiting.

"What's really going on, Dominic?"

"Going on?" asked Ysella, not wanting to answer without knowing a bit more.

"In the last three months we've had three councilors killed or almost killed, one administrator killed and another poisoned, a banque presidente killed, and a fleet marshal most likely poisoned. Envoys from other lands are leaving without replacements. The Premier suddenly gets engaged to the eighteen-year-old daughter of the Imperador. A warship under construction was torched. Last week, Stefan Nortaak got too many landors riled up, and they voted down an unremarkable and perfectly decent piece of legislation. Now Paolo and Alaan are worrying about brigands in the north, as if they're anything other than what they've always been—an annoyance. We'll run out of funds well before the year is over, and all Paolo will say is that we'll run out of funds."

"The Imperador is slowly dying," replied Ysella, "and the only successor is spoiled, arrogant, and largely incompetent, but quite capable of extorting funds and orchestrating violence against anyone he thinks is a threat. The Imperador is losing his strength, but so far, not his mind."

"What are you doing about it?"

"Working with the Premier to find a way to restrict the powers of the Imperador, to make the Council relevant, and to get enough support so that Guldor doesn't fragment."

Raathan looked straight at Ysella. "If it were anyone but you . . ." He shook his head, then asked, "What can I do?"

"For the moment, insinuate the idea that, if Guldor is to hold together, the Imperador needs less power and the Council more, and that any government where the power rests in one person—or the Council alone—will fail."

"What are you doing?"

Ysella smiled wryly. "I drafted a charter that does that. Some influential people are considering it. If we're fortunate, the Imperador might sign it." *Most likely, almost on his deathbed.* "And then the hard work will begin."

"Fifty councilors are too few."

"How about sixty-six, split into three parties, with maximum and minimum representation, no party having less than sixteen seats and none more than thirty."

Raathan frowned. "I don't know that I'd care for that."

"I can't see any other way, Georg. Every election there are fewer landors."

"Even put that way, it'll be a hard sell."

"If we don't do it that way, in a generation or two, maybe a bit longer, we'll be the next Teknold with the commercers in control."

"Isn't it a little strange that you're the one proposing this?"

"You mean because I come from a line of rulers?" Ysella laughed softly. "My family proved rather effectively the faults of complete Imperial rule. I'd rather not see Guldor prove them again. The Imperador already removed his eldest son, the youngest died mysteriously, and the remaining scion will likely destroy Guldor unless restrained by law." *And possibly other means.* "We let him be Imperador, but give him a veto, which a two-thirds vote of the Council can override."

"I wouldn't trust most of the current councilors," pointed out Raathan.

"That's why, under certain circumstances, the Imperador would be able to dissolve the Council and call for new elections. He just wouldn't be able to do it often."

"I'll need to think about some of that."

"If you have better ideas, let me know."

"Knowing you, I probably won't."

"I would appreciate you not mentioning it to Stefan Nortaak."

"He's not talking to me. He might dislike me as much as he dislikes you." Raathan grinned. "After what he did to your standards act, I told him he made sowshit seem tasty."

For a moment, Ysella didn't know quite what to say.

"I figured that might give him pause." Raathan hesitated, then added, "I appreciate your being frank. We can talk later." Then he turned and walked toward his office.

Ysella could only hope he'd judged Raathan correctly, but he should have been talking to a few others earlier. *Not only much earlier, but with more specifics.*

Except he hadn't had the specifics.

75

THE first article to catch Ysella's eye in the *Tribune* on Quindi morning was the report of another Atacaman pirate attack, this time on the small town of Taectyn, some thirty milles north of Zeiryn. A warehouse caught fire and exploded, killing twenty-three people—men, women, and two children. Six pirates were also killed.

"Do you think the Navy will ever get rid of the pirates?" asked Caastyn.

"Not until we have better government in Machtarn," replied Ysella sardonically. "The Council can't look into corruption or bad decisions, and the Palace and its administrators won't."

"Would a stronger Council be any better?" asked Gerdina.

"Not without significant changes. The Premier and I and a few others are working on it."

"The Imperador won't accept it," said Caastyn.

"Not now, but he might accept something that changes matters after his death," replied Ysella.

"The Heir would reject those changes."

"He would," agreed Ysella, "unless he had no choice."

"Good fortune with that," said Caastyn sarcastically.

"It'll be difficult," affirmed Ysella.

Caastyn looked quizzically at Ysella, who merely smiled pleasantly.

Later, when Ysella reached his office, he found, atop a short stack of incoming mail, a large envelope with a cover letter from Raul Dhaantyn explaining that the Navy's comments on the draft water safety code were attached or added to the draft. Ysella skimmed the draft, and from what he could tell, none of the comments would be a problem, and several definitely improved the legislation.

He found himself smiling at the last line of the cover letter.

> *The First Marshal and I appreciate your legislative efforts and look forward to working with you on future legislative improvements.*

He drafted a reply to Dhaantyn, thanking him for expediting the Navy comments and expressing his hopes that future joint efforts would be equally productive.

Ysella then wrote a cover letter to accompany a copy of the rejected Port Standards Act to Dhaantyn. In that cover letter, the key paragraph read:

> *The majority of the committee felt this bill was not particularly controversial, but apparently a number of councilors expressed concerns we did not foresee. For that reason, among others, the committee would request knowing if the Navy has their own concerns with the legislation as presently drafted.*

The two letters to the Fleet Marshal would support Ysella's acts to avoid sending committee legislation to the full Council for at least several weeks in a way that Nortaak could scarcely gainsay, not that the older landor would likely say anything to Ysella.

After that, Ysella wrote a message to Arturo Palaan, asking him to incorporate the Navy's comments and changes to the water safety proposal, then had Jaasn carry both the Navy's comments and his note down to the committee legalist.

Ysella turned his attention to the incoming correspondence, but only finished reading and writing his notes to the clerks on three when Khaard showed the Premier in, then withdrew, closing the door.

"You're always busy, aren't you?" asked Detruro, immediately seating himself.

"This session, anyway," replied Ysella. "It must be important, if you're here."

"I just got word on the Imperador. He's much better, but still weak. He's looking forward to the wedding."

"What about the Heir?"

"He's sent several insistent letters to the First Marshal, demanding that he be allowed to act in place of the Imperador until his father fully recovers. Solatiem replied that he'll follow the Imperador's past policies and orders until he hears otherwise directly from the Imperador. What he didn't tell young Laureous was that one of those orders is to disregard any orders or decrees from the Heir—and the First Marshal has that in writing."

"I take it that the Heir and the Princesa won't be at the wedding."

"Hardly, but *you* will be." Detruro's words were commands.

"I'm not about to miss it."

"Excellent!" The rare warmth behind Detruro's exclamation surprised Ysella. Detruro stood. "Until later . . . whenever that is," he added, whimsically waving a hand in the air, before he turned and left the office.

For the first time, Ysella had the feeling the often-dour Detruro actually looked forward to marrying Delehya, and he couldn't help feeling happy for him.

The remainder of the day was routine, and Ysella let the clerks go and closed the office at a third before fourth afternoon bell.

He didn't even mind the scattered showers that intermittently splattered him on the ride back to the house.

He was unsaddling Jaster when Caastyn entered the stable.

"How was your day, sir?"

"Not bad. And yours?"

Caastyn grinned in return. "Raf and Krynn brought us some fresh doves. Gerdina is waiting for you to start roasting them. You're home early. So, we can eat before services, if you're going."

"I should. But doves, they're a real treat. How are Krynn and Raf doing?"

"Well. They're really settled now." Caastyn paused, then smiled. "You got another letter from the Ritten."

"That's good."

"You don't sound so sure."

"She wanted to know more about me. I told her. It took her longer to answer."

"If she's not right for you, better to find out sooner than later."

Ysella smiled wryly. "I know that, but I worry."

"Go read the letter, then you can enjoy the roasted doves . . . or console yourself with them." Caastyn grinned again.

Ysella shook his head, then returned to dealing with Jaster.

After that, he made his way to the study. He stared at the sealed envelope. Finally slitting it open, he took out the letter, refusing to look at it until he sat behind the desk.

Dear Dominic—

I have to apologize for being so long in replying, but I've been occupied in dealing with the wills and the mine, and finally settling matters legally. I followed your earlier advice and didn't sell. Your friend Bruuk Fettryk has been so helpful in dealing with all the legalities. He and Gineen are such good people, but you already know that. I can't thank you and them enough for your advice and support in handling the mine.

I did so enjoy and appreciate your letter. You made quite an effort to be open and objective. It's clear that you're far better suited to be a legalist and a councilor than to be a landholder, although you'd do better at that than you think you would, because you're nothing if not diligent. Both Bruuk and Gineen are emphatic about that.

Yet, from your admission about why you're interested in me, and your decision to warn me about not selling the mine without first having more information, and your reactions to Mylls (I found out about that also, and he doubtless deserved it) you have to have an impulsive side. I'm glad of that, because I do as well, although I work to keep it under rein. I initially feared that you might turn out to be only diligent and methodical, but I have the feeling you're far more than that, perhaps more than you realize.

I'm also writing because I have some family obligations to attend to, and as you know my family situation is anything but simple. I won't be able to receive or reply to any letters for several weeks. I want you to know this, because I don't want you thinking I'm disregarding you. Anything but!

These obligations are necessary, but I'll be in touch as soon as I can be.

Affectionately,
Aelyn

The letter was short, but not curt, and too many phrases indicated that she was anything but displeased.

Still . . . necessary family obligations?

Ysella puzzled that over until he reached the dining room table, but as Caastyn had predicted, the succulent aroma of roasted dove brought a smile to his face.

After the very tasty doves and the cheesed potatoes, Ysella walked quickly to the Trinitarian chapel off Camelia Avenue east of Imperial University.

Once there, he took his seat in his small section of the pew and waited, half listening to the harpsichord as he watched others in the congregation enter. Before that long, Presider Haelsyn, in his plain green cassock, stepped to the center of the sanctuary, before the three golden orbs set in an arc on the stone wall behind him. The harpsichord died away, and everyone rose.

The presider began with the familiar words, "Let us offer thanks to the Almighty for the days that have been . . ."

Following the invocation, the anthem, and the Acknowledgment, the presider moved to the lectern on the right and began his homily. "As we near summer, and the new life in the fields and the trees moves from determined but vulnerable beginnings into what, the Almighty willing, will lead to a bountiful harvest in the months to come, each of us should consider the patterns of the seasons and the fact that life is built upon patterns, not upon random impulses or the feelings of a moment. Yes, we should appreciate and enjoy the feelings of the moment, for they are part of what we are, but we should understand which feelings increase our understanding and joy in life and which are transitory and vanish before the light of the next morning..."

But don't our actions also determine which feelings increase that understanding?

As the service came to a close, Ysella waited for those more in a hurry to leave the chapel, then stood, still thinking almost absently, about the interaction of acts and feelings, only to find Presider Haelsyn approaching. Resigning himself to a polite reminder of his not entirely regular attendance, Ysella smiled pleasantly.

"Councilor," said Haelsyn, "might I prevail upon you for a few minutes, in private? I would appreciate it greatly if you'd share some of your expertise as a councilor with me."

"Of course." Ysella wondered what his expertise had to do with the presider, but followed Haelsyn to his study, closing the door as he entered.

Haelsyn did not sit or motion to the chairs before his desk, but turned and said, "Last week, I offered a prayer for the Imperador, asking the Almighty to help and console him, given how ill he was reported to be, and to pray for his daughter in her efforts to assist him. After the services, several parishioners asked how I could possibly offer prayers for such a debauched woman. I pointed out that the Almighty offered consolation to even the wicked, although I certainly had no knowledge of debauchery on her part. I asked how they knew she was debauched. They were most adamant, however, but just kept saying that she was, that the Palace guards knew all about it. That concerned me. I read earlier that you had at least some knowledge of her." Haelsyn looked inquiringly at Ysella.

"She's not debauched in the slightest. Although I've only spoken with her twice, I know others closer to her. She is attractive, even beautiful, intelligent, and very devoted to her father. Her brother is trying to become Imperador before his time, and she supports her father. She's agreed to marry the Premier, I suspect, for her own safety and to get out of the Palace and away from her half brother. There are rumors about her and the late Fleet Marshal Haarwyk. They're false. Haarwyk was a mentor, nothing more. She called him a good man, and people deliberately twisted her words. Those rumors were likely spread by those close to the Heir who wish to discredit her. There will doubtless be more and worse rumors in the weeks ahead. Too many people want to believe the worst, even when they suspect it may not be true." Ysella looked directly at the presider. "That's what I know."

"How ill is the Imperador?"

"I doubt he'll last the year, from what I've seen and know, but . . . who knows?"

Haelsyn sighed softly. "I feared something of the sort. I thought about speaking to other councilors . . . but . . ."

Ysella wasn't about to address that. "I only met the Lady Delehya because the Imperador insisted I dance with her—once. She and the Premier are well-suited, despite the difference in their ages."

"And you?"

"I'm courting a lady from Aloor. It's slow and quiet, given the distance, but I'm hopeful."

Haelsyn smiled, if faintly. "I wish you well, and thank you for your information. I will discourage rumormongering, although I fear that will only slow the flow of scandalous speculation."

"We do what we can, Presider."

As Ysella walked home, he had no doubt the rumors about Delehya would get worse, and some might speculate that Detruro was only marrying damaged goods for political gain and the off chance of becoming Imperador.

76

FINDI passed in quiet, and so did the next few days, although, quiet or not, Ysella continued wearing the silk and hardened-leather armor under his jacket, hoping the days would remain springlike for a time.

On Tridi morning, a light breeze made the air cool enough that he didn't feel in the slightest overheated on his ride to the Council Hall. After turning Jaster over to one of the stableboys, he walked quickly to his office.

The only councilor he saw in the upper-level corridor was Astyn Coerl, who offered a pleasant "Good day" before continuing toward the steps down to the first floor.

Once in his own office, Ysella looked to Khaard. "No urgent messages, I take it?"

"No, sir. Only a few letters as well." Khaard paused. "Might I ask, sir, why Councilor Nortaak's clerks will no longer speak to us?"

"Probably because I refused to accept an invitation to duel him and offered an apology for any inadvertent offense I might have given."

"What offense . . . begging your pardon, sir?"

"I spoke before the Commerce Committee in favor of increasing the usury cap, without consulting with him, and then asked what he knew about the background of former Administrator Salaazar. He felt it was improper that I should make such inquiries. He accepted my apology, but it's clear he wasn't happy about it."

Ysella could see Khaard's puzzlement and added, "If I'd agreed to the duel, he would have insisted at least on first blood, possibly to the death. Quite aside from killing or severely injuring him, *if I even fought a duel,* I'd have disgraced my position as a councilor . . . or I'd likely have been killed, given his anger. Either way, I'd be removed from the Council."

"Someone wants you off the Council that badly?"

"So it would seem." Ysella managed a shrug. "I have suspicions as to whom, but without conclusive proof, I'm not about to voice names. You can tell Paatyr, but I'd appreciate not spreading what I said widely."

"Thank you, sir." Khaard half turned, then paused.

"I once was very good with a blade, Lyaard. That's why I don't carry one."

"Yes, sir."

Ysella walked to his office and looked at the few letters on his desk, then sat down and began to read.

> Councilor Ysella—
> It is with some concern that I find myself writing you, hoping that you can use your good office to persuade the Premier not to marry the Imperador's daughter. Doing so would tarnish his reputation beyond any possible repair, at least in my estimation . . .

The remainder of the letter contained more allusions to Delehya's purported wickednesses. The signature was that of "A concerned citizen of Aloor."

Two more in different handwriting, paper, and ink, while not conclusive, suggested someone was stirring up trouble in Aloor. Ostensibly, the letters were aimed at her, but if Detruro went ahead with the wedding, the focus would turn to discrediting him.

At that moment, Jaasn eased the door open. "Reimer Daarkyn, sir."

Ysella smiled sardonically. Daarkyn's absence for over a week had been too good to last. "I'll see him."

As usual, the newshawk shut the door. "Good morning, Councilor."

"The same to you, Reimer. I was a little surprised not to see you after the death of Tybaalt Salaazar."

"What was there to ask?" Daarkyn settled into the chair facing Ysella. "I already suspected Salaazar's involvement in covering up the Heir's extorting funds—or borrowing, as he would likely put it. You had all the other information, and Salaazar's death confirmed it."

"And what might be the question today?" Ysella inquired cheerily.

"I've been hearing . . . assailed more like, by rumors about the Imperador's daughter. Suggestions of impropriety, sexual liaisons with high officials when she was only fifteen . . ." Daarkyn looked to Ysella.

"Likely all false. I've heard the sexual-impropriety rumor from the most unlikely source, who at least had the decency to ask what I knew."

"What kind of source?"

"A Trinitarian presider."

"You actually attend services?"

"Moderately regularly, both here and in Aloor."

"Interesting. And what did he say?"

"He asked if I knew whether there was any truth to them. So far as I know, there's not, and I told him so. She was friendly with Haarwyk, but more like he was an uncle, and she got him to teach her about military matters. Behind the attractive façade, I think there's a very sharp mind. She said Haarwyk was too good a man to be Fleet Marshal."

"That's hardly what I heard."

"You heard what the Heir wants you to hear. That's one reason why he and the Princesa were exiled to the summer palace last week."

Daarkyn's momentary silence suggested that was new to him, but he asked, "How do you know?"

"The Premier told me, but he'll deny telling me. So I'd appreciate making no mention of either of us. You could say that the Heir and Princesa are unlikely to attend the wedding, since they also weren't at the engagement dinner."

"So the Imperador finally knows that the Heir has been gathering funds?"

"I would assume so from his removal from the Palace, but that's something I don't know."

"And you think he's behind the rumors about Lady Delehya?"

"I don't *know* that," replied Ysella. "I *suspect* that they at least come from someone close to the Heir. No one else would have any reason to discredit her, and by association, the Premier."

"Definitely a side-door attack on him," mused Daarkyn. "What about Councilor Nortaak?"

"What about him?" asked Ysella evenly.

"He's the councilor from Oersynt. Salaazar was from there as well. Word is that Nortaak has something against you."

"He does. He got a number of landor councilors to defeat an uncontroversial, almost housekeeping bill to embarrass me. But you'll need to ask him why. He certainly wouldn't talk to me about it."

"I tried. He won't see me."

Ysella laughed, quietly sardonic. "You must be on to something, Reimer. The last people who wouldn't see you ended up dead."

"Anything else you'd like to tell me?"

"By now, you likely know more than I do."

Daarkyn stood. "I appreciate your seeing me." He didn't quite hurry from Ysella's office.

After going through the last of the incoming letters, Ysella again made his way to Detruro's office, where he waited until Graandeyl Raendyr left. Raendyr avoided looking anywhere close to Ysella.

As Ysella entered Detruro's office, he said, mock-cheerfully, "You've got an unhealthy threesome?"

Detruro gestured to the chairs. "In addition to everything else . . . if you'd care to be less cryptic."

Ysella summarized his meeting with Daarkyn, then said, "What I meant by a threesome was that first of three rumors was brought to my attention after services on Findi . . ." Ysella then quickly listed the three separate incidents of the clearly planted rumors about Delehya. "While it's not pleasant, I thought you should know."

"Some of it I already know. I've gotten several letters, and Staeryt and Georg Raathan told me about letters they've received."

"I'm sorry for both you and Delehya. It shouldn't be this way."

"It is what it is, but, unlike some, you really mean it."

"Is there anything I can do?" asked Ysella.

"Actually, there is. I've been thinking. We might have a chance to get the Imperador to sign your charter. Then what? How do we convey the impression of power and support? Who manages changing administrations subject to the Imperador into departments or ministries?"

"You're saying we need a transition strategy and an implementation plan."

Detruro bent to the side and opened a desk drawer, then extracted a large envelope that he handed to Ysella. "I've been making notes, but right now . . ."

"You've got too much to do. I can start on those immediately, if you like."

"Please, but put the two together. We need to be prepared to act immediately if we get him to sign the charter. I thought I'd have more time . . . but . . ."

"I can handle it." *At least, I've got more time.*

"It's another thankless task. You seem to get those."

"I did mention the need for reform to Georg Raathan."

"I know. He saw me late yesterday. He was worried, then almost supportive when I said we'd been working on it together."

"I should have asked you, but I didn't know if I'd have a better chance."

"What do you think Daarkyn will do?"

"Write a story, but he would have anyway."

"Let's hope you tempered the worst of his newshawk tendencies."

Ysella nodded, then stood.

After leaving Detruro, he returned to his office, where he signed or corrected responses, then turned his attention to reading Detruro's notes. He barely finished before it was time to head for the Council chamber.

He slipped behind his small desk as Maatrak gaveled the Council to order.

The floor leader glanced around, then announced, "In addition to the regular schedule, the Council will first vote on a measure approving regional banques in Devult, Eshbruk, Suvion, and Enke . . ."

Ysella stiffened slightly at the mention of Enke.

"This measure should have been considered earlier," Maatrak continued, "but was delayed by the illness of Taeryl Laergaan, the Imperial Administrator of Commerce, and the untimely death of Tybaalt Salaazar, the Imperial Administrator of the Treasury, and by the need to revise the application and approval of the Enke District Banque."

Revision and approval? Ysella sensed that Detruro had something to do with that, but he momentarily wondered how Detruro had gotten Haarst to agree to the addition of Enke, until he remembered the obvious—that Haarst was the councilor from Suvion.

Slightly less than a bell later, Maatrak announced that the approval of the four regional banques had passed by a vote of thirty-five to thirteen, since Klempt's seat had not been filled, and since Detruro would have refrained from voting if Ysella's suspicions were accurate.

Then the Council began debate on the Post Roads Improvement Act, which would increase the costs of sending letters by post in order to fund improving and extending post roads throughout Guldor. Because both the Army and the Navy considered the post roads a necessity, the measure had been marked up and reported from the Military Affairs Committee.

As Alaan Escalante began to speak in favor of the proposal, Ysella couldn't help thinking that there really should be a transportation administration or ministry. *Perhaps in the future, if . . . if we ever get a new charter for Guldor.*

In the end, however, the proposal was rejected and returned to committee, largely because, Ysella suspected, most of the landors and the crafters didn't want to pay more for letters, given that postage was already expensive.

After Maatrak recessed the Council, Ysella surveyed the Council chamber, looking for Nortaak, in order to avoid him. He didn't want to give the older landor another chance to claim insult or disrespect. Nortaak was nowhere to be seen, probably having left after voting.

That was fine with Ysella, and he kept an eye out as he left the chamber. The only councilor who turned to him in the main corridor was Aldyn Kraagyn.

"Dominic? Might I have a moment?"

Ysella smiled, partly in relief. "Of course."

"You seem to have some contact with the Palace. Can you tell me what's going on with the Imperador and the Heir?"

"Not in any depth. I've heard, indirectly, that the Imperador wasn't pleased when he discovered how much the Heir had borrowed from various people and possibly banques."

"Do you think that's why Omar Poncetaryl was killed?"

"I don't know, but it's likely."

"Why would the Imperador take it out on Poncetaryl?"

"I doubt it was the Imperador, Aldyn," said Ysella quietly. "Laureous forbade his family to borrow or coerce funds from anyone. I suspect someone didn't want Poncetaryl revealing how much the Heir had borrowed."

"I can't see the Heir doing that," declared Kraagyn.

"Neither can I, not directly. No one has explained the death of the Treasury Administrator or three Palace guards."

Kraagyn frowned.

"It is a bit disturbing," said Ysella, "to consider the current power of the Imperador in the hands of the Heir."

Kraagyn stiffened, and his voice hardened as he looked directly at Ysella. "You're not suggesting revolt?"

"Almighty, no. That would be a disaster. Within years, Guldor would fragment. It might be better if we could find a way to lessen the power of the Imperador and increase that of the Council. Some landors have felt that their concerns are always being overlooked."

"They often are," said Kraagyn, not quite grudgingly.

"Absolute rule by either the Imperador or the Council will destroy Guldor, and we have to find a way to balance their power." Ysella smiled politely. "I'm sorry. I digressed from your initial question."

"An interesting, possibly impractical digression, but I appreciate your information about the Heir's . . . borrowing. Most distressing . . . most distressing."

Clearly distracted, the older councilor turned toward his office, murmuring to himself.

Ysella headed toward the stairs to the second level and to the fragments of an implementation plan that had become more urgent.

77

O N Furdi, the *Tribune* didn't carry any stories about either the Heir or Lady Delehya, and Ysella wondered why—until he picked up the newssheet at breakfast on Quindi.

HEIR AND PRINCESA TO MISS WEDDING?
Reliable sources have confirmed that the Heir and the Princesa are currently residing at the summer palace and will not be attending the wedding of the Lady Delehya and Premier Iustaan Detruro at the Imperial Palace a week from tomorrow. Neither attended the engagement dinner.

With a recent flurry of rumors less than favorable to Lady Delehya, some have questioned the propriety of her planned marriage to Premier Iustaan Detruro, Ritter in his own right, as well as Councilor from Enke. The Palace has refused to comment on the rumors except to say that the Imperador's health has improved greatly and that he is looking forward to the wedding. The number of those attending the ceremony will be small, as with Lady Delehya's engagement dinner and in keeping with the long-standing wishes of the Imperador that personal family events not be public spectacles. A list of invitees has not been made public, but it is likely that certain notables will be present, possibly First Marshal Gunnar Solatiem; Engar Tyresis, Imperial Administrator of Waterways; Carsius Zaenn, Imperial Administrator of Natural Resources; and, of course, Councilor Dominic Ysella, who appears to be extremely close to both Lady Delehya and Premier Iustaan Detruro . . .

When he read the last paragraph, Ysella didn't know whether to grimace, shake his head, or laugh. *But there's another nasty implication there.*

"I saw that story," said Caastyn, smiling. "That one dance with the Lady Delehya's made you more well-known."

"That and a one-sentence thank-you at the engagement dinner."

"Most councilors would kill for that kind of notice," said Caastyn.

One actually tried to, if not just for that. "I didn't ask for any of it."

"Maybe that's why you got it," said Gerdina, with a glint in her eye.

"Some of my old friends have been asking about you. They never did before."

Ysella took refuge in his café, cheesed eggs, and oatmeal muffin.

After breakfast, he packed up the incomplete charter implementation plan he'd worked on late the night before, and the night before that, then left for the ride to the Council Hall. His thoughts alternated between the plan and the *Tribune* article.

When he reached his office in the Council Hall, Ahslem Staeryt stood waiting.

Ysella sensed the older councilor's concern. "My office?"

"If you would."

Once the two were seated behind closed doors, Ysella said quietly, "I hope I haven't inadvertently done something to offend you."

"Not me, Dominic. Stefan Nortaak is furious. He claims you caused Tybaalt Salaazar's death and you think getting the eye of the Imperador's daughter will cover everything."

"As I told everyone, the Imperador ordered me to dance with her, and Salaazar was responsible for his own death, and for the deaths of Omar Poncetaryl and Oskaar Klempt."

"For Oskaar's death? How?"

Ysella explained, in more detail than he preferred, but he knew Staeryt was a legalist, with a legalist's mind.

Staeryt's frown deepened, and when Ysella finished, the older councilor said, "That all follows, but I got the feeling that Nortaak's family is close to Salaazar's, and none of them see much wrong with 'lending' to the future Imperador. Laureous broke that pattern, but too many landors recall the old days and ways favorably."

"That's another problem," agreed Ysella.

"It won't change for years, if ever," said Staeryt.

"Probably not."

"If the Heir was behind all this," continued Staeryt slowly, "or ordered others to do his bidding, why is he safe in the summer palace?"

"What else can the Imperador do? He's slowly dying, and there's no other acceptable successor."

"Is that why Detruro is marrying Lady Delehya? Possibly to become Imperador?"

"Some people might think that, but the Heir already has two sons. Given them, especially, I think that would be inconceivable and unacceptable to the Imperador."

"What about to Detruro?"

"I don't think he'd have me drafting a new government charter reducing the power of the Imperador if he were trying to succeed Laureous."

"He might, if that's the only way possible for him."

Ysella smiled. "I'm fairly certain that's not what he has in mind, but if he wants to be Imperador with limited powers and with a stronger Council, wouldn't we still be better off?"

"Even if he doesn't want it, what if Lady Delehya wants to be Imperadora?"

Then the Heir would already be dead. But Ysella only said, "I've gotten the impression she wants out of the Palace, not to be trapped in it for the rest of her life."

"You never know, Dominic."

"You're right, Ahslem, but I'd wager against an Imperador Detruro." *Because I doubt he'd want that life either, but if there's no real other choice* . . . Ysella repressed a shudder.

Staeryt smiled wryly. "I haven't done well wagering against you, but I still worry."

"So do I, but my biggest worry is having a Laureous II without any restrictions on his powers. It should worry the entire Council." Ysella paused. "Even Stefan Nortaak and the Salaazar family."

"They won't see it that way, especially Stefan. You need to be careful around him."

"I will." *But I'll likely need to be more careful when he's not around.* "I appreciate your letting me know."

"My pleasure . . . and duty. The Council needs you far more than Stefan." Staeryt smiled sadly. "I won't keep you."

Once Staeryt left, Khaard appeared. "The Premier would like to see you now."

"He needs my skills." *Or thinks he does.*

Leaving his case on the desk, Ysella hurried down to Detruro's office, but he didn't have to wait.

"I assume you saw the *Tribune* story," said Detruro, leaning back slightly in his desk chair.

"I did. So did my man and his wife. All of her friends are likely gossiping about it, and you and Delehya didn't need that nasty insinuation about me."

"It could have been worse," mused Detruro.

"If it had been," replied Ysella, "the *Tribune* and its editor would likely no longer be in existence."

"Including your friend Daarkyn."

"I hope you mean 'friend' very loosely." Ysella hesitated, leaned forward a touch, then said, "Ahslem Staeryt was waiting for me this morning. He told me that Nortaak blamed me for Tybaalt Salaazar's death. I explained about the Heir's borrowing. I think he understands, but he's convinced it won't change anything with Nortaak. He cautioned me to be careful."

"I'd agree with Ahslem."

"Have you had a chance to talk with Solatiem or Dhaantyn?"

"Dhaantyn. He was already quietly moving in several companies of naval marines, and has scouts watching the summer palace. Solatiem wasn't in the Palace yesterday, or at his quarters in the palace grounds."

"And Delehya?"

"She's spending a great deal of time with her father. So is Lorya Kaechar."

"Are there other empaths around?"

"The only other is at the summer palace at present."

"On Kaechar's recommendation? Too close to the Heir?"

Detruro nodded.

"I thought the Imperador had more."

"He did. He didn't trust them. More important, neither did Sra. Kaechar and Delehya."

"Your bride has traces of that," said Ysella.

"More than that," said Detruro. "Just like you're more than merely empath-resistant. Both Kaechar and Delehya told me."

"I've tried to be discreet."

"I doubt anyone in the Council knows, but there's no restriction on isolates."

"Isolates?"

"I've been told that's the term for those who can't be sensed by empaths."

Isolate . . . that fits, in a way. "Does that concern you?"

"It did at first, before I realized that you can't be emotionally forced or enticed to do anything against your will. Right now, that characteristic is important."

"I take it you're resistant, but not a full . . . isolate?"

"That's what Delehya tells me. That's also why she was only interested in the two of us." Detruro smiled wryly. "You made it easy for everyone."

"It might not be so easy for you."

"Experience in politics helps." Detruro paused. "How are you coming on the latest?"

"I've worked late every night, and will tonight and on Findi. I'm working on how to turn the various administrations into ministries reporting to the Premier. We can work out expanding the Council and setting an election system later, if necessary."

Detruro nodded. "But . . . reporting to the Premier?"

"Only as the head of the Council. I'm thinking that the heads of ministries have to come from that ministry, or possibly from another ministry, and that the Premier can only dismiss a minister for cause, and not often."

"You're trying to balance power at several levels."

"The charter won't work otherwise." *It might not, anyway.*

"Keep at it. We may not have much time. When you finish, it would be helpful to have several copies, if possible."

"Do you want to see it first?"

Detruro shook his head. "I'd just get in the way and slow things down. If matters proceed more slowly, then I'll have time to look."

Because Ysella could tell Detruro had finished, he stood. "I'll get back to work on the plan, then."

"Good."

As he walked to his office, Ysella kept thinking about Detruro's concern about time. Was the Imperador closer to dying, or was the Heir preparing to oust his father before nature took its inevitable course?

It doesn't matter. If he's wrong and matters remain as they are for longer, that gives you time to refine what you've drafted.

The rest of the day at the Council Hall remained uneventful, particularly since the Council wasn't in session, and Ysella spent his time drafting part of the ministries section. Then he closed the office at third bell and headed home, where he spent the time before services working on the implementation plan.

He thought about skipping services, but he really wanted to hear Haelsyn's homily and whether the presider mentioned rumors.

He kept drafting as long as possible before walking quickly to the Trinitarian chapel, arriving as the harpsichord began the prelude. As he headed for his pew, he noticed a much older white-haired woman in one of the forward pews talking to a gray-haired woman, but both turned and looked at him a bit longer than seemed casual.

Because of the newssheet story, no doubt.

He wondered how long before his notoriety faded, but it would fade. It always did. He doubted that even a few score of people recalled the death of District Legalist Smootn only months before.

He settled into his pew and watched as Haelsyn moved to the center of the sanctuary. While Ysella's responses weren't quite rote, after years, they didn't take much effort, and his thoughts were more concerned with structuring the implementation plan.

When Haelsyn walked to the lectern to begin his sermon, Ysella shifted his attention to the presider.

"One of the greatest tools we as people have is language. Language allows us to share experiences, to convey thoughts and feelings, to teach, to praise the Almighty, especially in the combination of words and music that become hymns. In its written form, language literally holds society together. Language is one of the greatest of tools bestowed on us by the Almighty. Yet, like all tools, language can be misused. It can wound. Language misused has destroyed lives and families. It has brought down the highest and it has undeservedly degraded people today and throughout history. We take language so for granted that we often fail to see its destructive powers. Oh, we know about the great instances, but what about the little destructions created by thoughtless gossip, whether about the boy on the next street or the young woman around the corner. Were they really involved in something illicit when they smiled at each other? Was the young woman about to be married who spoke to the friend of the man she will marry doing something wrong? Gossip is so like forbidden fruit . . . such a guilty pleasure, and so often those who are the subject of gossip never know. Yet, at times they do, or worse, everyone else knows—even when the subjects of gossip don't know what is said behind their backs and have done nothing wrong . . ."

Ysella kept his grim amusement to himself, as Haelsyn hammered home the evils of gossip.

After the service, Ysella was one of those who waited to speak to Haelsyn, who greeted Ysella warmly. "It's so good to see you, Councilor."

"I especially appreciated your homily, Presider," said Ysella in a slightly louder tone than usual. "I see this too often in politics, especially when most people have no real idea of what occurred, yet they repeat what they hear blindly, with no thought of questioning the accuracy of what they were told."

"I'm most certain you do," returned Haelsyn, a slight twinkle in his watery green eyes. "I'm glad you found it relevant."

"I did indeed, and thank you. I so often find gems in your homilies." *Not always, but enough.*

Once he was away from the chapel, he smiled. The homily might only have reached a few people, but that was better than none, and it might keep a few of the rumors muted.

And now you have to get back to drafting the next part of the implementation plan.

78

AFTER a long day of drafting and some redrafting, by the time Ysella went to bed late on Findi evening, he had a rough version of the method and procedures for expanding the Council and transforming Imperial administrations into ministries under the expanded Council. He also had a headache, likely from listing the details of every step necessary in order to minimize confusion and give an impression of a long-thought-out and well-considered plan.

He woke on Unadi morning clearheaded. Wearing his silk and leather armor, he left the house before second bell. Once he reached the Council Hall, he dropped off his case in his office and hurried to meet with the Premier, although he didn't have an appointment.

As Ysella neared Detruro's doorway, he saw a man step out, moving toward the main entrance. Ysella thought it might be Carsius Zaenn, but couldn't be absolutely sure.

Why would Zaenn be here so early in the day? Whatever the reason, Ysella doubted that it was good.

Even so, the older clerk gestured for Ysella to enter the Premier's personal office.

Detruro looked up in mild surprise as Ysella entered his personal office. "Don't tell me you're finished."

"I've got a very rough draft. The framework's all there, but it needs more of the small details, and some smoothing and polish."

"You're telling me this for what reason?"

"So you know I have it all put together, but that it needs more work to give those who read it and have to use it the impression of a plan carefully thought out over time."

"How long will that take?"

"The more time I have, the better, but the plan is usable now."

"Can you have something more polished by Furdi?" asked Detruro. "You can keep improving it after that, but I'd like to be familiar with what you've written."

"I can do that." Ysella paused, then said, "Along those lines, I'd like to meet with Luaro Maatrak and Haans Maessyn and tell them about the idea of the charter and the proposed party structure."

Detruro frowned.

"Maatrak is already the de facto leader of the commercers, and from what I can tell, Maessyn is in a similar position with the crafters. I learned recently"—*if not all that recently*—"that Maatrak was going to push councilors to declare their affiliations. Given that, if we have to implement something, it might work better if we didn't just drop this on them. And since the split is already occurring . . ."

"I have my own ideas, but why should you be the one discussing it, and not me?"

"Because I'm not the Premier or the floor leader. If you meet with them and talk about parties and a charter, it could be construed as rebellion or revolt. I'm not in the leadership. I'm just exploring possibilities. You know about my explorations, but that's all they are so far."

"You're getting very close to deep water, Dominic."

"Perhaps, but I come from a monarchist background, and I can plausibly claim that I'm trying to find a way to save the Imperium in a way that will preserve the position of the Imperador as a vital part of government and not as a mere figurehead."

"I can see that. Whether others will is another question." After a brief pause, Detruro said, "You just missed Carsius Zaenn."

"Might I ask what the illustrious Administrator of Natural Resources wanted?"

"Ostensibly to tell the Council that various mining interests found it financially difficult to mine coal and other minerals under the Council's amendments to the Coal Act."

"And indirectly to suggest that with such impediments the Imperador might seek to call for new elections or do away with the Council entirely?"

"He didn't go that far, even by implication. He strongly suggested that 'excessive oversight' would not be appreciated."

"Particularly by the Waterways Committee, since what the Natural Resources Committee reported to the floor was what Zaenn's administration proposed. I'd be surprised if he and Stron Thaalyr weren't as close as adjoining fingers in drafting the original version of the Coal Act."

"He did mention he found the Waterways Committee amendments 'challenging.' He also offered condolences on the latest nasty rumors circulating."

"Something about you this time?"

"Of course not, I'm the noble premier who caved in to the Imperador's insistence that I marry Delehya to cover up her debauched character, now that she had the administrator who tried to reveal the truth about her killed . . . and has the Imperador under her thumb."

Ysella winced.

"My thoughts exactly," said Detruro. "Even dead, Salaazar's helping the Heir."

"And Zaenn's definitely the Heir's agent. I can't believe the Imperador doesn't know." Ysella frowned. "This may sound stupid, but if he knows, why doesn't he do something?"

"You don't think he hasn't?"

"Salaazar?"

"That makes more sense than the Heir being the one who had him removed, especially since Salaazar still had value to the Heir. The Imperador can't do much more. That's one of the problems with rumors. They spread faster than they can be squelched, and killing those who spread them tends to perpetuate and give credence to the rumors."

"Unfortunately," sighed Ysella.

"Do you have anything else?" asked Detruro, glancing toward the door.

Ysella stood. "Not for now."

As he left Detruro's personal office, he saw Ahslem Staeryt waiting, nodded politely, and said, "Good morning, Ahslem."

"The same to you, Dominic." Staeryt raised his eyebrows.

"I didn't give him any bad news, if that's what you're asking."

"That's a small favor, and I'm grateful." Staeryt offered an amused smile, then walked to the doorway where Detruro stood.

Ysella walked into the main corridor, then up to his office, passing several staffers, but no other councilors.

Back at his desk, Ysella wrote messages to both Maatrak and Maessyn inviting them to meet with him at third bell of the afternoon. Then he turned his attention to the Waterways Committee schedule, making sure all his changes had been included, before beginning to read the incoming mail. When he finished with that, and the responses drafted by Khaard and Jaasn, he began the tedious work of redrafting the plan for implementing the charter.

Less than a bell later, he received a reply from Maessyn, and a third later, one from Maatrak. Both said they'd meet him at third bell.

Just before third bell, he put all his drafting papers in his leather case, as well as notes for changes in the parts he hadn't yet reviewed and redrafted. Then he waited.

Less than a sixth later, Maatrak and Maessyn stepped into his personal office. Maessyn closed the door before seating himself.

"You're up to something, aren't you, Dominic?" asked Maatrak.

"I am. You know that the Imperador likely won't last the year . . ."

"More like he won't last till fall," interjected Maessyn.

"... and the Heir will destroy Guldor if he's not reined in. I've been working on a draft charter to replace the Establishment Act. There's a possibility the Imperador might sign it into law as a decree."

"Why would he do that?" asked Maatrak.

"Because the younger Laureous will destroy Guldor in years, if not months, and the Imperador knows it. He wants his legacy to continue. A better balance of power—"

"What kind of balance?" asked Maatrak. "One with all the old landors firmly in control?"

"No. One where no one group can control absolutely..." Ysella went on to explain, including the reasons why he wanted to talk to them.

"You're out of your mind," declared Maatrak. "How are you going to do that?"

"That's my problem. My other problem is that, if I do get this done, I need both of you to work as party leaders with Detruro to expand the Council with sixteen new districts that make sense. More of the new districts will have to be commercer or crafter."

"I don't understand why you want to do it this way now," said Maatrak, "not that I'm going to object to changes that make the Council more balanced."

"I want to do it this way so we don't have a bloody revolution. I want to do it this way because I don't want Guldor collapsing the way Aloor did. So that councilors have to consider needs beyond their own party, and it has to be done in the near future, or it won't ever happen." *And I don't want the landors to get absolute power now, only to have the commercers get absolute power in a generation.*

"Does the Premier know what's in this charter?" asked Maessyn.

"He does, but I drafted every word of it, and I told him what I believe—that this is the one time in hundreds of years that something like this might... *might* be able to be done."

"This could be treason," said Maatrak. "It is treason."

Ysella shook his head. "If the Imperador signs it, it becomes law. If he doesn't, we can't force this on the Heir. We might get him to sign it later, when things start to fall apart, but without force, we've merely drafted a reform plan. The Imperador could reject it. Or he could sign it."

"Why isn't Detruro doing this?" asked Maatrak. "Or does he plan to be premier and Imperador?"

"He definitely doesn't want to be Imperador, and one of the reasons the Lady Delehya agreed to marry him was to escape the Imperial Palace."

"What if he becomes Imperador anyway?"

"He doesn't want it, but if unexpected circumstances lead that way, he'll be bound by the charter as well."

"Are you sure?" asked Maatrak.

"I'm the one wagering my life," said Ysella. "If things go wrong, who drafted all this?"

"Why you?" Maatrak looked hard at Ysella.

"So far as I know, I'm the only legalist not on the Justiciary Committee."

"He also has the best grip on administrative law," added Maessyn, somewhat to Ysella's surprise.

"If the charter is signed," Ysella went on, "either by the Imperador or the Heir, we'll need to implement the provisions quickly. I'm assuming that you two are effectively the de facto leaders of the commercers and the crafters."

"Aksyl Haarst might like to claim that," said Maatrak, "but I'd have more votes."

"What do you want from us, right now?" asked Maessyn.

"Almost nothing. I'd appreciate it if you don't say much about the charter. You might mention that we'd be better off if the Council could find a way to have a bit more power and the Imperador a bit less. If we don't get the charter signed, we'll proceed as if nothing happened. If we do, then we'll have a lot to do in a very short time."

"How will we know what exactly we're supposed to do?" pressed Maessyn.

"There's a plan for that as well. You'll each get a copy when the time comes."

"You wrote that, too?" asked Maatrak sardonically.

"Who else? That way, if it doesn't work out, no one else gets blamed." *And I'll likely be executed for treason.*

"You're risking a lot," said Maessyn.

"I know what happened in Aloor when no one really risked anything."

Maatrak and Maessyn exchanged glances.

"All that is why I wanted to meet with you."

"You think you can keep this secret?" asked Maatrak.

"That's up to you, isn't it?" returned Ysella quietly.

"We'll do our part," said Maessyn, looking hard at Maatrak. "As Dominic says, we won't get this good a chance in years, if ever."

"I just . . . never thought . . ." said Maatrak.

"Exactly," replied Maessyn, his voice quiet, his tone firm.

Ysella stood. "I appreciate your coming. If you have further thoughts or questions, you know where to find me."

Ysella sat at his desk for a time after the two left. He had the feeling

Maessyn had some sort of influence over Maatrak. He hoped that would be enough.

Then he stood and picked up his case. There wasn't anything urgent happening at the Council Hall, and he could get more redrafting done at the house.

79

EVEN after working late, Ysella woke early on Duadi. At breakfast he had a few sips of café before picking up the *Tribune*. The lead story was about fires set in the Southtown area of Machtarn where an empath amplified interest in the blaze, enough to distract shopkeepers and others and to enable thieves to use smash-and-grab tactics to grab valuables and marks.

Ysella hadn't heard of that, and it made sense. Unfortunately, so did the second article.

> **NEEWYRK SHIPBUILDER KILLED**
>
> Sammis Haamyt, the younger brother of Kierkyn Haamyt, was found dead in a storeroom at the Haamyt Brothers shipyard in Neewyrk. From his wounds, the younger Haamyt was apparently attacked by several men with clubs and blades . . .
>
> Several blocks from the shipyard patrollers found another body, that of a local man suspected of earlier assaults, with a crushed skull. The second man had been dragged a distance and then left in an alley.

So young Laureous didn't like the shipbuilders telling Dhaantyn about his extortion attempts. That was Ysella's conclusion, and it was all too likely the older brother would suffer a similar fate before too long, unless matters changed drastically for the better in Machtarn.

He finished breakfast, gathered his case with the draft implementation plan, and made his way to the stable, where Caastyn had Jaster waiting for him.

"I'll likely be back earlier today."

"So you can work later," said Caastyn dryly.

"That's about right."

"Maybe, if Ritten Wythcomb lived closer, you wouldn't be working so late."

"Right now, it wouldn't change much. After the next few weeks, it might." *And then it might not.* Ysella strapped the case behind the saddle and mounted.

The day definitely felt warmer, but in less than a week, it would be summer, and wearing the silk and leather armor would be far less comfortable. He was warm, but not sweating by the time he turned Jaster over to the ostler at the Council stables.

Leather case in hand, he didn't rush, nor did he dawdle, to his office, but still arrived less than a sixth past second bell.

He finished reading through the incoming mail, which included several more letters opposing the marriage of the Premier on the grounds of Delehya's scandalous past, when Khaard announced Gaastyn Ditaero.

The crafter councilor closed the door quietly, sat down, and said, "I looked at the latest committee calendar. Why don't we have any committee bills scheduled for floor action?"

"What happened," said Ysella in a cheerful tone he didn't feel, "to the Port Standards Act when it came up for a vote?"

"A bunch of landors voted it down because Nortaak was pissed that you wouldn't duel with him."

"I assume most of the committee now knows that."

"You're not just a Ritter by office but by birth. Why didn't you accept the duel?"

"Because any result of such a duel would cheapen the Council and effectively remove my effectiveness as a councilor."

"So we're blocked right now?"

"For a bit. We'll have to work around it for any legislation to pass the full Council. To have enough support on the water safety measure, we needed to have the Navy's comments. We received those last week, and once they're incorporated, the committee will discuss the changes."

"You're not exactly in a hurry to report out anything right now, are you?"

"No, I'm not. Most of the landors on the Commerce Committee and on the Natural Resources Committee will blindly oppose anything the Waterways Committee brings to the floor. That means we have to persuade everyone else to support any bill. That was why I wanted the Navy's support for the water safety measure. I also sent the Port Standards Act to the Navy for comment for exactly the same reason."

Ditaero frowned.

"The Premier and the committee need the Navy's support on several matters, especially while the Imperador isn't fully recovered."

"Haans said you'd agreed to support a crafter party. That so?"

"I've agreed that the Council should have a crafter party. I didn't say that I'd agree with everything such a party might advocate."

"You really would?"

"Gaastyn, if we don't work out a government with separate parties for landors, commercers, and crafters, all I see is Guldor fragmenting like the Grand Democracy of Teknold."

"How does the Premier feel about that?"

"After I explained what could happen, and how, he agreed."

"Talk is cheap."

"I know that, but talking to get an agreement is a lot less bloody."

"How long will all this take?"

"I can't say, but I would guess that you'll have an answer before the end of the year, possibly a lot sooner. First, we have to get through the wedding this endday."

"What does the wedding have to do with anything?"

"It doesn't. It's that we can't deal with the Imperador until after the wedding's over. He's concentrating on that. So are a lot of people in the Palace."

Ditaero shook his head. "I can see that. Weddings . . . they take over, especially for important people."

"If you have any other questions, I'm here."

"Not now."

Only then did Ysella stand.

Once Ditaero left, Ysella finished his notes on the mail, then returned to drafting. He kept drafting until half before fourth bell, with the exception of a third of a bell in midafternoon where he signed and corrected responses.

After putting all the draft pages into his case, he told Khaard to close the office and headed out to the Council stables, where he reclaimed Jaster and rode back to the house.

There, once he unsaddled and groomed Jaster, he carried his case to the study and set it on the corner of the desk, taking in the two envelopes on the desk. Neither was from Aelyn.

Are you hoping for her to be more than anyone could? Ysella wondered, but how could he know until they knew each other better? *And, long distance, that's going to take some time.*

After several moments, he picked up the letter addressed in his mother's handwriting, opened it, and began to read.

Dominic—

Not all that much new has occurred here. As I wrote earlier, we were spared the worst of the heavy spring rains, but Haarkyl and Saera had barely reseeded when a heavy storm south of Aloor washed out more crops. That holding's always had problems. It might be why it was marked for the second son.

> *We still don't have a replacement for Kyranna, and I wonder if we'll ever find one. It seems like more and more of the empaths have gone to the cities and larger towns, and there never have been that many. I have to say that I worry about Caethya. Haarkyl has no lands for a dowry, and I don't see her working as an empath for another landor family, at least not around Aloor. While it wouldn't happen to Caethya, too many empath girls end up walking the streets and persuading extra marks from their momentary conquests . . .*
>
> *The* Chronicle *has printed some stories implying an improperly close relationship between you and the Lady Delehya. Anyone who knows you in the slightest knows you wouldn't do anything like that. Sometimes, the newssheets go too far . . .*
>
> *Jaeralyn has seen that nice Ritten Wythcomb several times and talked to her once or twice. Jaeralyn says she's kind and charming, although a bit reserved. There's nothing wrong with a bit of reserve . . .*

Ysella smiled as he thought about the way Jaeralyn quietly influenced the family, then read through the rest of the letter. At least his family seemed to be in decent shape, despite the loss of Kyranna, unlike Haarkyl and Saera.

He picked up the second letter, written in a hand he did not immediately recognize, and without a return address.

> *Dishonor will be avenged!*

That was all.

The handwriting might have been that of Nortaak, but without comparing it directly to the note he'd received at the office, he couldn't tell. He hoped it was from Nortaak, if only because he didn't want two people trying to get him into a duel—or something worse.

With a little bit of effort and good fortune, he thought he could finish the revised draft of the implementation plan in another bell.

Then you'll need to start making copies.

He took a deep breath.

80

WHEN Ysella entered his Council office on Furdi morning, he had two copies of the implementation plan completed, in addition to the one he'd delivered to Detruro, and was working on a fourth, although he had taken a short break to spar with Caastyn on Tridi after dinner. With all that, he was short on sleep, but three plans besides Detruro's would have to do.

The *Tribune* hadn't printed any more information about the Haamyt brothers, or anything or anyone else of concern to Ysella, and the comparative newssheet silence worried him.

Even at the Tridi Council session, the only business was a measure to allow any funds not needed for the port repairs at Endor to be made available for rebuilding wharves or docks at Paensantz and Taectyn, if indeed such excess funds would be available.

Ysella had compared the writing from the four-word note and the envelope that held it to the two letters he'd received from Nortaak. While there were similarities, the script certainly wasn't identical. Ysella still thought Nortaak was the most likely writer.

Contained in the incoming mail on Furdi were several more letters protesting the Premier's forthcoming wedding to the "scarlet lady Delehya." One demanded the Premier's removal if he went through with the wedding. None were signed, of course, but all likely came from those at least moderately well-off, given that sending letters was not inexpensive.

Ysella still heard nothing from Aelyn Wythcomb. Despite her affectionate words he felt concerned, partly because she'd mentioned "family obligations," and, from what he'd learned from her and from his own parents, family matters had tended to be lethal among her relations.

Ysella pushed those thoughts away as he turned to reading and signing the responses that Khaard and Jaasn had prepared for either his signature or revision.

Roughly a bell and a half later, after Ysella finished the correspondence and returned to copying the implementation plan, Khaard announced the unexpected arrival of Sammal Haafel.

"What brings you here?" asked Ysella as Haafel entered the office and quietly closed the door.

"I just wanted to see to your health," said Haafel. "Both Haanara and

I have been concerned, especially with that idiot Nortaak trying to get himself killed at your expense."

"Does everyone in the Council know?" asked Ysella, a touch of bitter amusement in his voice. "Or only the more traditional landors?"

"One way or another, most do. Many of the more traditional landors wished you'd accepted the challenge and killed him."

"Oh?"

"You were wise, Dominic. That way, they'd have been rid of him and likely you. Not all of us traditionalists feel that way. Certainly, your cousin Chaarls doesn't. Georg doesn't, although his family has the oldest lands in Gaarlak. Nor Alaan, whom you've saved from himself at least twice, even if Amaelya had to point it out to him. He does listen to her, you know. That's why he can get in trouble when she's not around. The same's true of Alaaxi, as you well know. Paolo isn't sure about you, but Patrice is, and I have to admit that Haanara is also fond of you."

"I'm fond of her as well." Ysella managed a warm smile, because in his rambling way, Sammal had told him who his more traditional landor supporters were and, by omission, those who weren't. "And Alaan and Amaelya have always been welcoming."

"I noticed that the Waterways Committee hasn't reported or scheduled any bills lately."

"I decided the Navy might prefer to comment on the next two before we send them to the floor. I had a very productive talk with Fleet Marshal Dhaantyn a month or so ago. Both bills could make certain aspects of naval operations somewhat easier, and I don't see much point in making it harder for the Fleet Marshal."

"That certainly can't hurt."

Meaning that it might not be enough. "You're right about that, but we'll have to be persuasive in other ways as well." Ysella leaned back slightly.

"Aksyl Haarst remarked the other day that you've been much closer to the Premier lately."

"He asked me to research an obscure aspect of administrative law. That's what water legalists do all the time. I gave him the report he asked for yesterday." Ysella shrugged. "Now, we'll see what he does with it . . . if anything."

Haafel chuckled. "In all the years you've been in the Council, I've never heard a lie or a deliberate misstatement from you. I have heard the absolute truth stated in a way that people didn't understand fully. You're sounding like that now."

Ysella laughed softly. "Doubtless I am. It's far safer than lying. I don't lie well."

"Most people, even councilors, don't. They just think they do, and then get angry if anyone questions their veracity. All you can be faulted for, if that, is for rhetorical obscurity."

"You know me too well, Sammal."

The older councilor shook his head. "I doubt anyone knows you well, possibly not even you. If you ever find and marry the right woman, in time she might." He chuckled again. "Haanara understands me better than I do, the Almighty knows." Then he stood. "A pleasure talking with you, Dominic. If I don't see you tomorrow, enjoy the wedding." He paused. "I assume you're invited."

Ysella stood and said, "I was, thanks to the Premier."

"But the Lady Delehya had to agree, I'm certain."

"I suspect so, but I never asked." *Some questions are better left unasked.*

"Also wise of you."

With a parting smile, Haafel turned and left the office, leaving the door ajar.

Ysella closed the door and returned to his desk, and his copying.

81

WHEN Ysella reached his Council office on Quindi, Khaard handed him a message.

"It just came from the Premier."

"Thank you, Lyaard. I imagine you'll both be glad once this is all over and the Premier's finally married to Lady Delehya."

"Lots of people aren't happy about it, are they?"

"Mostly supporters of the Heir, I think."

"Why does it matter to the Heir, sir?"

"I'm guessing, but part of it might be that once she's out of the Palace, he can't try to tell her what to do."

"But once he's Imperador . . ."

"That could be a problem, but less of one if she's not in the Palace or too close to him."

"The Imperador can't live that much longer, can he?"

"I doubt it, but I don't know. It seems clear he wants his daughter married to someone strong enough to have a chance of protecting her." *And that might be another point to encourage him to sign the charter . . . if it doesn't infuriate him, which it could.* Ysella wanted to shake his head because there was likely no way he'd be anywhere close enough to the Imperador to make suggestions, although Detruro would be.

Ysella looked at the envelope, wondering about what Detruro had in mind, since the Council was in recess until the following Duadi, then looked back to Khaard. "I'd better see about this."

He carried his case into his office, set it on the desk beside the incoming letters, and opened the envelope, which held a note requesting his presence at his earliest convenience.

He was in Detruro's office in less than a sixth, the door closed behind him.

"Is it something urgent?"

Detruro shook his head. "I thought we should talk while we have a chance. I also thought you should know how various matters stand at the moment."

"Are you doing anything special . . . before?"

Detruro shook his head. "Tomorrow will be quite enough."

Ysella nodded and waited.

"Laureous is stronger now. He's doubled the guards in his part of the Palace. Lorya Kaechar senses everyone, and no one except her, the Imperadora, and Delehya is allowed close to him. He'll be semi-isolated at the Palace chapel for the ceremony and at a separate table with the Imperadora at the wedding dinner. You'll be driven to the Palace?"

"I will."

"Can you safely leave a copy of the charter with your man? He's obviously good with arms or you wouldn't be alive."

"You have a copy."

"Yours is just in case. We'd planned to see if we could get him to consider signing it Unadi morning before we're scheduled to depart the Palace, but anything could still happen."

Ysella had the feeling that Detruro was more than merely considering, but only asked, "What about the Palace Guard captain? Is he reliable?"

"Kaechar vouches for Fhaeryn."

"Does that mean those more loyal to the Heir are spread among the guards or that they're concentrated among the guards with the Heir at the summer palace?"

"There's no way to tell without having Sra. Kaechar spend time with each one, and there are too many to do that now."

"Why wasn't it done before?" asked Ysella.

"The Imperador doesn't like having many empaths around, and Kaechar is one of the few, and the only one at all close to the Imperador. If she's checking the guards for loyalty, she's not protecting him."

"Is there anything else you need from me right now?"

"For the moment, not that I can think of, except I'd appreciate your arriving two thirds before the ceremony."

That meant Detruro either worried or had something in mind he didn't want to share. *Possibly both.* "Are you two going anywhere after the ceremony?" asked Ysella.

"Originally, we were going to the summer palace but that option's been foreclosed. So we'll spend the night at the most opulent guest suite in the Palace and then leave sometime in the next few days for the hunting lodge northwest of Machtarn. That's the plan . . . *if* nothing disruptive occurs." Detruro's smile was both sour and sardonic.

"Which may be more likely than not," suggested Ysella.

"We both agree with you on that," replied Detruro. "Delehya thinks it's almost certain some disruption will occur."

"I trust you two have contingency plans."

"Several," said Detruro. "If I were you, Dominic, you might be as prepared as when you went to meet that corrupt district legalist."

Ysella stiffened slightly. "Will I need additional documentation?"

"Besides a copy of the charter, not that I can think of. If something comes up, I'll let you know. Otherwise, I'll see you tomorrow around second bell. Someone will escort you."

Ysella stood. "Then . . . until tomorrow."

As he walked back to his office, he knew, even if he couldn't prove it, that once Detruro and Delehya were married, Detruro had definite, if flexible, plans to get the charter signed and implemented, most likely against the wishes of others, most likely to be armed.

Except, if Laureous does sign it, you're going to be very involved in that implementation.

If it all failed, one way or another, Ysella wouldn't be a councilor and possibly wouldn't even be alive.

He swallowed hard with the thought.

For the remainder of his day at the Council Hall, Ysella busied himself with correspondence and other routine matters. He closed the office at third bell and rode home, where he immediately went to his study, hoping for a letter from Aelyn, but there wasn't one.

Gerdina fixed a light early dinner, since Ysella decided that attending services couldn't hurt, might help, and in either case, should keep his thoughts from being excessively worrisome.

He walked the eight blocks to the chapel, trying not to hurry, then paused outside when he saw Alaan and Amaelya Escalante approaching.

"Good afternoon," offered Ysella.

Alaan nodded in return, saying, "We weren't sure you'd be at services, what with the Premier's wedding tomorrow."

"So far as I know, there aren't any prenuptial festivities, not involving me or the Premier at least."

"But you'll be at the wedding tomorrow?" asked Amaelya, readjusting her headscarf.

"I'm attending as the Council representative."

"But you'll be there," declared Amaelya. "Isn't that going to be exciting!"

In some ways, I hope not. "I'll be there, and I hope it's cheerful and everyone's pleased."

"Just pleased?"

"I'll take pleased, given that the half-brother of the bride has made himself scarce and that the father of the bride is ailing."

"You're not excited?" asked Amaelya. "Is anyone?"

"I suspect that the bride will be excited when she can finally leave the literal confines of the Imperial Palace, and when her husband can whisk her some distance from her relations."

"That, I can understand," declared Amaelya. "Alaan definitely unconfined me, and it must be far worse for Delehya."

As the faint sounds of the harpsichord drifted toward the three, Ysella said, "The music suggests . . ."

"Yes, we should," agreed Amaelya. "Enjoy the wedding if you can, Dominic."

Alaan looked to Ysella and offered the faintest of headshakes, then walked with Amaelya into the chapel.

Ysella entered and glanced to the front, wondering if he could see the white-haired woman who'd looked at him so intently the week before, but he couldn't tell if she was present as he eased into his place, thinking in part how men and women could have very different opinions about weddings and marriages.

Ysella tried to keep his thoughts focused on the service, but he worried about Findi . . . if the wedding would occur as planned . . . or at all.

As Presider Haelsyn began his homily, Ysella concentrated on the words.

". . . as we stand on the edge of summer, at a time that is neither too hot nor too cold, we often forget that such times can often be few and should be treasured, not only as a blessing from the Almighty, but also shared with those we love, not hoarded like golds in a locked strongbox . . ."

It's a bit hard to share and treasure a time when there's no one here to share with and when all Guldor could fragment into squabbling principalities . . .

Still, Presider Haelsyn had a point.

At the end of the service, Ysella waited a few moments, then turned and headed for the door on the east side.

"Councilor Ysella," declared a commanding but feminine voice.

Ysella turned to see the white-haired woman who had studied him. She wore a trim, well-cut, but dark green dress and a matching headscarf, and behind her stood a taller woman in light gray with a similar headscarf.

"Yes, Ritten?" He was guessing, but she *sounded* like a Ritten.

"I'm Ritten Aelyssa Scalante, and I'd like to formally introduce you to my grandniece, the Ritten Aelyn Wythcomb."

For a long moment, Ysella stood there, stunned, then glanced past Ritten Scalante to Aelyn, who tried not to laugh, and failed. Even her gray eyes held warm humor.

After another long moment, Ysella replied, "Ritten Scalante, I cannot tell you how much I appreciate that introduction, and more, how much I appreciate the presence of your grandniece." His eyes returned to Aelyn, fully taking in her eyes, her lips, and her shimmering short-cut black hair. Then he grinned. "Family obligations?"

"Of course," she said warmly. "This way, Dominic, we're officially and properly introduced by someone from my family with unimpeachable character . . ."

"And you can have a late supper with us," said Aelyssa Scalante. "That is, if you're available and so inclined."

"I'm available and could not be more inclined." Ysella meant every word. "But I can offer no carriage. I walked here. My house is only eight blocks away."

"I know," replied Aelyn. "We drove by on the way to the chapel."

"My carriage will easily handle three," added Ritten Scalante. "Naercyl can drive you back after supper. This way. He's doubtless waiting." She turned toward the door, adjusting her headscarf.

As Aelyn and Ysella followed, he caught sight of Presider Haelsyn, who appeared deeply amused.

When the three reached the carriage, older, but well-kept with oiled wood and green trim, harnessed to a matched pair of chestnuts, Ysella asked, "Could we stop by my house? I should let my man and housekeeper know. With all that's going on . . ."

"You mean," said Aelyn, "with your penchant for getting yourself attacked, you'd like to reassure them that you haven't been assaulted or kidnapped?"

"I would. They'll also be pleased, after seeing me waiting for your letters over the past months." Ysella added humorously, "What if I hadn't come to services this evening?"

"Then you would have received a formal invitation from me for refreshments," said Ritten Scalante.

"And I wouldn't have been able to see the astonishment on your face," added Aelyn.

"I've been worrying about you. When you wrote about family obligations and with what you've said and I've heard . . ."

"Good!" declared Ritten Scalante. "You listened and remembered."

Ysella opened the carriage door and offered a hand first to the gloved older Ritten, then to Aelyn, whose gray gloves and headscarf matched her dress.

Her fingers tightened just slightly around his hand before she released it and said, "Thank you."

Ysella followed them into the carriage, closed the door, and sat in the rear-facing seat across from the two women.

As the carriage began to move, Ritten Scalante said, "You're moderately good-looking. Aelyn said you were handsome—and she's not given to overstatement—but the brightest of women aren't always as accurate about men in whom they're interested."

"I see that a certain conversational discernment runs in the Scalante bloodline," replied Ysella cheerfully, noting Aelyn's attempt to conceal a smile.

Ritten Scalante gave a rich, deep laugh. "You've noticed that already?"

"I did my best to reply to one of her questions, and her response said that she gratefully appreciated my attempt."

"But he did respond in much greater depth," said Aelyn. "Much greater. That's another reason why I'm here."

"I'm very glad you are."

"The way you look at her, directly into her eyes, says more than words," said Ritten Scalante dryly. "Maelcar always said that where a man first looks at a woman, unguardedly, shows what about her most attracts him."

"He must have been very observant," offered Ysella.

"He was, and I still miss him. But that's *my* past, and you two might have a future if you don't waste it." Her eyes went to Ysella. "You look rather young to be a councilor."

"I am. I'm thirty-four. I was twenty-six when I was first elected."

"That will do, a year older then than Aelyn is now."

"You're giving away all my secrets, Auntie A."

"He likely knew, close enough, anyway."

The coach came to a stop, and Ysella glanced out, realizing they were already in front of his house. "I'll be just a few moments."

"We're not going anywhere," said Aelyn.

Ysella made it to the front porch before Caastyn opened the door, his eyes going from Ysella to the carriage and back to Ysella.

"Ritten Wythcomb and her great-aunt have invited me to a late supper at her house, Ritten Scalante's house, that is." Ysella gestured. "That's Ritten Scalante's carriage."

"Handsome outfitting. Matched pair, too," declared Caastyn. "Ritten Wythcomb came to Machtarn?"

"She did. She and her great-aunt surprised me after services."

"Then you'd better get on with the surprise." Caastyn grinned. "Do I need to pick you up?"

"Ritten Scalante has offered her carriage and driver to return me. I accepted."

"Don't let me keep you. You've waited long enough." Caastyn shooed him emphatically toward the carriage. "Go!"

Once Ysella hurried back and reentered the carriage, he looked across at Aelyn, still marveling at her presence. "What made you decide to come to Machtarn?"

"Nothing *made* me come," she replied in a gently amused tone. "I wrote you that I had an impulsive side. Then, our meeting felt so improbable. When I found out that you'd almost died from that attack, I decided not to leave matters to time and chance, and I wrote Aunt Aelyssa and proposed my plans. She agreed, and here I am."

Ysella doubted it was anywhere near that simple. He looked to Ritten Scalante.

She gazed back with a pleasant smile . . . and said nothing.

"You both knew I'd be at services and that I'd accept, didn't you?"

"I knew you'd be at services," said Ritten Scalante. "Presider Haelsyn said you seldom missed, unless you were in Aloor or seriously ill. He told me you came when you could barely walk."

"From your letters, I thought it unlikely you'd decline," added Aelyn. "Unless it had something to do with the Council."

"I'm glad it was today. Tomorrow and possibly Unadi, I won't be free."

"I do hope it's doesn't involve another woman," said Ritten Scalante sweetly.

"Unfortunately, it does. The Lady Delehya, in fact. I'm the Council representative at her wedding to the Premier tomorrow, and at the wedding dinner."

"Why you?" asked Ritten Scalante. "You're not that senior a councilor."

"Because I suggested to Lady Delehya that the Premier was a good match for her. She agreed and requested that I attend the engagement reception and dinner. Once the Imperador agreed and indicated there would only be one councilor beside the Premier . . ." While Detruro hadn't said as much, he'd certainly implied it, as had the arrangements.

"How long have you known Delehya?" asked Ritten Scalante even more sweetly.

"Properly speaking, I don't know her at all. The Imperador requested, tantamount to an order, that I dance a single dance with her at the Year-end Ball. That was when I suggested the Premier was a good match for her. At the engagement dinner, I was not seated near her, but as she and the Premier left, she broke protocol and thanked me for suggesting the Premier. Those are the only two times we've met or spoken."

"Then why . . ." Aelyn stopped.

"I suspect, but do not know, that she is an empath or has some abilities and could sense the honesty of my suggestion. That's also only a guess on my part."

"Why do you think that?" asked Ritten Scalante, with a tone of honest curiosity.

"When I danced with her there was this . . . pressure . . . of warm strength, and from what I've been able to discover, everyone likes her except her half-brother."

"The Heir, you mean?" said Aelyn.

"Delehya is his daughter by his second wife," said Ritten Scalante. "The first died bearing his youngest son, while he was occupied with one of his mistresses."

"Those nagging details seldom show up the *Chronicle*," said Aelyn. "I was surprised that it printed that you danced with Lady Delehya."

"I've made an effort to be accessible to one of the newshawks. In turn, when I'm in Aloor, I visit him and learn what I can. At times, he harasses me, but it's mutually beneficial."

"Gineen Fettryk said that you visit every shop and business in Aloor at least twice a year."

"I stop in each. People do not always wish to talk. Most are polite, some complain. The town proper is small enough that I can do so."

"In Maelcar's time, most of the landors would have been scandalized," said Ritten Scalante.

"Some still are, either because someone with my name shouldn't stoop to that or because it's undignified. But I've learned more by listening than by talking."

Ysella caught something between the two women, but said nothing as the carriage slowed. He glanced out to see that the carriage was turning in to the drive of a house on the corner of Cuipregilt Avenue and Alden Place.

Aelyssa Scalante's gray stone dwelling looked to be slightly larger than those on either side, with an outbuilding off the side drive holding a moderately large stable and servants' quarters, all reinforcing the impression that Ritten Scalante did not lack in resources. The carriage stopped on the drive where a walk led to the covered side porch.

Ysella helped both women from the carriage, then followed them to the porch and from there to a door into a side hall. They continued into an untraditional-looking small dining room with a circular table set for three places on one half. The goldenwood table and matching sideboards displayed a style Ysella had never seen, with simple, if slightly curved lines, and the chairs were upholstered in a rich blue velvet that, while not new, showed no traces of wear.

"This was Maelcar's gaming room," explained Ritten Scalante, "but I've found it most useful as an intimate dining room. Most men prefer not to game with a woman, especially after they discover she might be good at it." Her smile was almost predatory as she added, "That was how I bought the flour mills. Dhaarl runs them now."

A middle-aged serving woman in deep blue livery appeared, and Ritten Scalante half turned, telling her, "We're having a light supper. Wine, lager, or ale?" She nodded to Aelyn.

"Red wine, please."

"I'll have the same," said Ysella.

As the serving woman left, Ritten Scalante moved to stand behind the middle place at the table.

Ysella gallantly seated her, glanced at Aelyn, then watched as the senior Ritten gestured to her left, where Ysella seated Aelyn, before taking the chair to Ritten Scalante's right.

Within moments, the serving woman returned with three wineglasses, each holding red. Once all three were served, Ritten Scalante raised her glass. "To Presider Haelsyn, without whose assistance arranging this supper would have been far more complicated."

Each took a sip.

Then Ysella raised his glass. "And to you, Ritten Scalante, for making this possible."

"I only enabled what it appears you both want, a chance to know each other well enough to decide whether you're suited."

After Aelyn and Ysella sipped their wine, the serving woman returned with two large platters.

Ysella spotted baked prawn slices topped with cheese on toast rounds, likely with a hint of lemon, sliced spring apples with sweet soft cheese, miniature puff pastries, although he couldn't discern the filling, and braised fowl slivers in nut sauce. He didn't recognize some of the other dainties. "If this is light fare . . ." He was about to say he'd need to fast for a day or two if Ritten Scalante served heavier fare, but realized that would sound too presumptuous.

"These days, almost everyone my age is either dead or doesn't enjoy or can't eat good food. It's a treat to have young people with appetites."

"It's a treat to be here," said Ysella. *And not just for the food.*

"Your social life is somewhat constrained, isn't it?" asked Ritten Scalante.

"It is. I'm younger than most councilors, and I'm not married. More than half of the limited dinner invitations I get are to fill out a table or to introduce me to some young woman whose parents—or relatives—are seeking to find her a husband."

"Even on first meeting," said the older Ritten, "you strike me as not interested in a woman trained to be a typical Ritten."

"I'm afraid I never was." Ysella paused and took a sip of the wine, so good that it was likely a Silverhills reserve. "That's why, after I first met Aelyn, I bent the rules of propriety to write her."

"You might tell Dominic your reaction to his letter," suggested Ritten Scalante in an amused tone. Then she picked up one of the puff pastries and ate it in one bite.

"I'm sure I came off as a too-proper legalist for a time," Ysella said quickly.

Aelyn offered a smile that held a trace of chagrin. "Somewhat, but I knew you were more than that."

"I was concerned you wouldn't see me the first time." Ysella tried one of the fowl slivers, finding it slightly peppery, yet piquant.

"I almost didn't, but I wondered why a councilor wanted to see me, especially one I knew only by name and infrequent newssheet stories." She glanced down. "In a way, I was almost disappointed that you'd come on a legal matter, but I was also touched that you cared enough to offer help and advice to someone you'd never met."

"You were very proper, except for one question."

Ysella was surprised that Aelyn actually blushed.

"I couldn't help wondering how a councilor as young as you, and as good-looking, wasn't married. My impulsiveness got the best of me."

"I'm glad it did. That question gave me a bit of hope."

"Might I ask why you were so interested in Aelyn so quickly?" asked Ritten Scalante.

"I don't know. I saw her, and . . . well . . . just everything. I didn't want to leave, but I also didn't want to intrude when she'd been so recently widowed."

"Best thing that ever happened to her," declared Ritten Scalante. "I was against that marriage from the beginning, but Rhycard insisted. Probably because he knew he was dying."

"He wanted me taken care of," said Aelyn evenly.

"And you didn't want to be cared for that way?" asked Ysella gently.

"Did you?" returned Aelyn in a sardonically amused tone, lifting her wineglass but barely sipping.

"Of course not. That's a tendency we share."

"You used the words 'cared for that way,' Dominic," said the older Ritten. "What precisely do you mean?"

"When I made it clear to my parents that I didn't want to marry for land or follow the family patterns, they weren't pleased, but after a year or so, they saw what I was doing was for the best, and stopped pressing. They cared and wanted the best for me, but on family terms. So, I suspect, did your grandfather, Aelyn. A marriage to someone who would have property was his way of caring for you, whether . . ." Ysella didn't quite know how to finish the phrase, so he didn't.

"It's not the same for a woman, most times," said Ritten Scalante. "I was fortunate in that regard. Aelyn wasn't." She paused, then quickly stood. "Enjoy yourselves. I'll be back in a while. I'm having trouble with these shoes."

Ysella immediately went to his feet.

"Enough propriety, Dominic," said Ritten Scalante. "I will be back. You can stand then."

Ysella understood—make the most of the time you have—but he didn't reseat himself until the older woman left the room, and then, before he sat down, he turned his chair enough that he could look directly at Aelyn.

"You do have a certain regality of manners," she said with an amused smile as she shifted position enough to face him.

"It tends to rub off when your father was raised to be king, even of a land already falling apart." Ysella paused. "Now that you've seen me in more than a passing instance . . ."

"I could ask the same of you."

"I'm so glad you were impulsive . . . and that your great-aunt helped you."

"She was quite concerned at first. She had some of her trusted acquaintances look into your finances. Despite her skepticism, she was pleasantly surprised, both by your holdings and by your reputation."

"I'm not especially well-off," demurred Ysella.

"Dominic . . . according to Auntie, you're better off than half the Council, and that doesn't count whatever you have in Aloor."

That surprised Ysella. After a moment, he said, "She must care a great deal for you."

"I've come to realize that. One of her conditions was that she be present when we met."

"Given how she felt about your first marriage—"

Aelyn laughed softly. "I think that phrase alone answers my question."

Ysella found himself flushing, but managed to say, "I hope your observation answers mine."

"It does." After a moment, she added, "I think the letters were for the best . . . for us, anyway."

"I do need to caution you . . ."

Aelyn stiffened.

"No . . . not about us, not in the slightest. Tonight, even if your great-aunt insists I leave the moment she returns, has been the happiest evening in years, if not in my life."

She frowned. "Then . . ."

"Guldor . . . I fear . . . may be on the brink of falling apart. I've been working with the Premier to try to make some changes with the Imperador . . . but the Imperador's slowly dying. He's utterly reasonable compared to the Heir. Matters could get . . . very uncertain over the next few days or weeks. If you have something planned . . . and I'm not there with no explanation . . . please don't think the worst. Not until you see me." Ysella swallowed. "I know I'm making excuses for something that may not happen, but in the last few months, two other councilors and two high administrators have been killed, and I've been threatened with a duel—"

"Threatened with a duel?"

Ysella explained as quickly as he could, not wanting to go into details.

"You're leaving out quite a bit, especially since, with your background, you can't be unfamiliar with duels."

"What I said about the business with Nortaak is exactly what happened."

"I have the feeling . . ."

Ysella realized that Aelyn deserved to know why and held up his hand. She frowned, then said, "Yes?"

"Like every heir in the Ysella family I trained and drilled in blades from the time I could hold one, although the first ones were wooden. Later, they were blunted and the point flattened. My father insisted on expertise, fearing we'd be challenged because of my grandsire's surrender to avoid having Aloor leveled. That didn't happen until I was eighteen and visiting relatives in Sudaen.

"As was the custom back then—and still is in many places—I wore my gladius and felt rather proud of it. Several older Imperial midshipmen made improper advances to a cousin, although she was five years older than me and married. She inadvertently revealed my name. One of the midshipmen instantly challenged me. Anyone close by left, except for a patroller who simply watched. I tried to demur. The other three made threats and unsheathed blades. I didn't see any way out. So I accepted the challenge.

"I pinked him straight off, and he went mad, and refused to accept first blood. I was good enough to kill him, but not good enough to disable him. The second one charged me. He was enough ahead of the third one that I could strike first. The third one took longer. He kept trying to kill me, and in the end I killed him." Ysella paused. "The patroller and my cousin verified what happened. It was in the newssheets how three midshipmen attacked an eighteen-year-old stripling Ritter who killed all three. If I hadn't been wearing the gladius, it would have been unpleasant, but not fatal. Or if I'd known more. After that I decided against wearing a gladius whenever possible. Since councilors are forbidden to wear blades on Council property, and I've seldom been anywhere but Aloor and near the Council, I've avoided duels."

"Mylls said you attacked him."

"Mylls attacked me, and I used a truncheon to stop him. He admitted that to the patrol. After that first duel, I learned as much as I could over the years in various forms of defense to have a better chance of prevailing without killing anyone. Nortaak is so arrogant that first blood wouldn't satisfy him, and when he found out about Sudaen, that made him more determined to destroy me politically."

Aelyn shook her head a touch, with an expression of amusement and sadness. "You don't always take the easiest course, do you?"

Ysella wondered if his honesty had ruined everything. "Easy is often wrong, I've found. Not always, but enough that I have to question when something feels easy."

"I never let you finish explaining why you might be . . . suddenly unavailable." Aelyn's tone of voice was uneven, but not unpleasant.

"There's not much more. The Heir is being confined to the summer palace by order of his father, and the marriage of the Premier and Lady Delehya may be the only way to get all the conflicting parties together . . ."

"I've had that impression from what you've written and from the newssheets, but what exactly does that all have to do with you?"

"I've drafted a charter to increase the power of the Council and restrict the powers of the Imperador. The charter would also make the Council more representative of the people, but it requires the signature of the Imperador not to be a revolt or revolution. It's possible that, right now, if the Heir or the Imperador found out, I could be imprisoned, or worse, although merely writing a proposed charter isn't against the law. You're one of the very few outside of three other councilors who knows what I've done."

"Why are you telling me?"

"Because I trust you, and because I don't ever want to lie or conceal things from you."

"We're not even engaged, and we've only known each other a few months."

Ysella managed not to swallow. "It seems much longer. What else would you have me do?"

"Only what you just did." Her eyes met his, and Ysella saw the brightness of tears in her eyes. "For that alone . . ." Then she smiled. "We need more talks like this. I won't ask you more about the Council. You can tell me what you can when you can. What you've said here is enough."

Ysella felt relieved, but he also wondered what Aelyn had almost said and that made him unsure of what to say next. She spoke again.

"I have a question for you. I ran into your oldest brother's wife, Jaeralyn, over a month ago. She asked, hesitantly, if I'd heard anything from you. When I said that I had, that we'd exchanged a few letters, she gave me the warmest smile, and said, 'Thank you. I hoped he'd write you.' Might I ask . . . ?"

Ysella smiled sheepishly. "I told the family about our meeting over the mine and the water-rights issues. No one said much except about the mine. Later, Jaeralyn caught me alone and hinted that I should write you."

"Hinted?"

"She thought we'd be good for each other and mentioned formal mourning only lasted a month." Ysella paused. "She also said she wouldn't tell anyone."

"I've only seen her a few times since then and passed a pleasantry or two, but nothing more. Why would she say that?"

Ysella had a feeling that Aelyn already knew, but just said, "She wants me to find someone who's right, and she's hoping you're that someone."

Aelyn raised her eyebrows.

"Every time I come back to Aloor, there's a dinner to which acquaintances of my parents are asked, always with a marriageable daughter. Those daughters are invariably landed to some degree, attractive, stylish—and insipid. You're not only beautiful and stylish, but most important, also intelligent and anything but insipid."

"I think you're overstating my attributes," replied Aelyn. "I'm not conventionally landed, not with a currently near-worthless tin mine. While I'm not unattractive, I tend to dress more conservatively than is stylish. My intelligence is more than adequate, but likely inferior to yours, and I'm not insipid only because I refuse to defer to stupidity, if as quietly as possible."

"You couldn't be insipid, if you tried." Ysella grinned. "But you're so tactful in that refusal to defer, which I appreciate greatly. With every letter, I've admired how you've gently corrected any error or misapprehension on my part. Those gentle corrections reveal more intelligence than you profess."

Aelyn smiled warmly, then replied, "And I've admired your responses."

Ysella was about to speak when he heard a cough from the doorway as Ritten Scalante reentered the intimate dining room.

Ysella stifled a smile as he observed that the Ritten wore the same shoes as before.

"I took a bit longer than I thought." She gestured to the serving woman, who had followed her in, then took her seat. "We won't be keeping you much longer, Dominic, but I thought we should have a round of cordials before you go." Once the serving woman cleared away the plates and platters, Ritten Scalante went on, "Would you possibly be free for an early-afternoon dinner a week from tomorrow? At third bell?"

"I'd be delighted," replied Ysella, "with the proviso that only a command from the Imperador or the Premier could keep me from coming."

"Are matters that serious?" The older Ritten's tone was even and not amused.

"The Imperador is slowly dying, Ritten. When that occurs, schedules will doubtless be affected. Although I doubt it will be as soon as next week, predicting death accurately isn't one of my talents."

"I'd heard he was ill, but not to that point." She smiled. "That proviso is acceptable. I think you'll enjoy the cordial I've chosen. Maelcar and I always did."

In moments, the serving woman returned and presented each diner with a cordial glass half-filled with a light amber liquid.

Ritten Scalante lifted her glass, saying, "It's been a pleasure, Dominic. I do wish Maelcar could have met you, but that wave broke over the reef long ago."

"It's been my pleasure as well, and I cannot tell you how much I appreciate this entirely unexpected"—he grinned—"but perfectly proper introduction and supper." He sipped the liqueur, finding it smooth, with a warm, but not burning aftertaste holding a hint of pear and apple with enough sweetness that it was neither cloying nor bitter. "This is the best liqueur I've ever tasted."

"You've never had it?" asked Ritten Scalante. "From your background, I would have thought you might have."

"My experience with strong spirits is limited. My immediate family frowns on anything stronger than wine or ale."

"That's not the greatest of virtues," said the older Ritten dryly.

"If caution with spirits is a vice," replied Aelyn, "I'm perfectly happy with it."

"As you should be, dear." Ritten Scalante looked to Aelyn. "If you'd escort Dominic to the porch, Naercyl should have the carriage ready."

Ysella had hoped the supper would last longer, but he rose, and inclined his head to Ritten Scalante. "As I said earlier, I cannot thank you enough . . . for everything."

"You owe me no thanks, Dominic, but I appreciate the courtesy."

Ysella understood. Ritten Aelyssa Scalante would do anything *for* her grandniece and anything *to* one Dominic Ysella if he hurt Aelyn in any way. He inclined his head a second time.

Aelyssa Scalante offered a brief, almost amused, sardonic smile.

Once Ysella and Aelyn were in the side corridor, he offered his arm, which she accepted as they walked slowly toward the door. He said quietly, "Your great-aunt will do anything to protect you, and she has the resources to do just that."

"You don't miss much."

Ysella laughed softly. "I miss a great deal. She made certain I wouldn't miss that. You also are good at calling my attention to what I've missed, if less obviously."

"Does that trouble you?"

"Not in the slightest. With your letters—and tonight—you've given me the greatest gift I've ever received."

"You've done the same for me." Her fingers tightened around his wrist as they stopped before the door to the porch.

"Until a week from tomorrow," he said gently, "and it will be a long week."

"But far less time than a letter takes," she answered.

"Such bittersweet consolation," he replied with a smile.

Aelyn released his arm, took both his hands, and turned to face him, saying impishly, "I've always wondered how it would be to say, 'Until then, sweet prince,' and now I can, honestly."

Ysella didn't know whether to shake his head or laugh, so he did both.

82

FINDI morning, Ysella woke later than usual, feeling slightly disoriented from half-recalled dreams where he tried to save either Aelyn or Delehya, or perhaps both, from some lurking menace.

As if either one needs saving. You're far more likely to need saving in the days ahead.

He stretched, yawned, and half rolled, half climbed out of bed, thinking about the evening before, shaking his head at Aelyn's well-planned, perfectly formal, socially acceptable—and amazing—effrontery.

You could love her just for that, and there's so much more there.

He also understood why she'd contacted her great-aunt. Even at her clearly advanced age, Ritten Aelyssa Scalante was more than simply formidable. What Ysella couldn't understand was Aelyn's late husband going out to Paddock, or especially Corners, when he had her at home.

Still half thinking about the previous evening, Ysella washed up, shaved, and dressed in old trousers and a shirt for breakfast, since he'd be in formalwear for the wedding, then made his way downstairs.

When he reached the breakfast table, Caastyn looked at him. "Dare we ask about last evening?"

"I had an excellent late supper at Ritten Aelyssa Scalante's capacious and stylish dwelling on the corner of Cuipregilt Avenue and Alden Place. Ritten Wythcomb and I both enjoyed it, and I have an invitation for a late-afternoon supper a week from today."

"The big place right on the corner?" asked Caastyn.

Ysella nodded and took a sip of café.

"I take it that you're still interested in her, then?"

"More than ever, but matters could get complicated, between the Premier's wedding, the Imperador's illness, and the Heir's unhappiness. Not to mention Councilor Nortaak's desire to remove me from the Council—or worse."

"Does she speak as well as you found her to write?" asked Gerdina.

Ysella took a sip of café, then said, "She does. So does her great-aunt, and Ritten Scalante thoroughly investigated me before she agreed that Aelyn could come to Machtarn and stay with her."

"It sounds as though the great-aunt is at least willing for you to court Ritten Wythcomb," said Gerdina.

"That's an accurate summary," replied Ysella. "Ritten Scalante opined that I was at least moderately good-looking, financially capable, and demonstrated a certain degree of integrity. We'll see how matters progress, but I'm hopeful." Ysella drank more café. "The Premier wants me at the Palace slightly after second bell."

"You mentioned that," said Caastyn dryly.

"He also suggested that you and the chaise contain arms and that I wear armor under the formalwear."

"Are you two going to a wedding or a war?" Gerdina interjected.

"I'm fairly certain about the wedding," replied Ysella. "The rest depends on the Imperador and the Heir. I'd prefer not to end up fighting at or after a wedding." *Especially since I'm not in the greatest shape.* "That's in the hands of others, for better or worse, but it's best to be prepared for the worst."

"And I thought things couldn't get worse after that thieving legalist," said Gerdina.

"That's because you cheered up," replied Caastyn.

"Better than glooming around and spoiling a perfectly good breakfast," countered Gerdina.

Ysella busied himself with the scrambled eggs and ham.

When he finished breakfast, he went to the study and wrote two thank-you notes, one to Aelyn and the other to her great-aunt, sealed them both, and gave them to Caastyn to post immediately.

Slightly before the first afternoon bell, he finished dressing in his gray-trimmed deep blue formalwear, with the silk and leather armor barely visible, and a small truncheon under the full formal coat.

Better that than nothing.

Then he headed downstairs.

Carrying his scabbarded gladius and the envelope holding the spare charter, Ysella walked from the house to the drive, hoping the slight breeze out of the north continued. If it didn't, with the white sun shining brightly in the clear pale green sky, he would be uncomfortably warm by the time they reached the Palace.

He studied Caastyn, noting that the older man looked stockier, then smiled.

"You said armed, sir. I just followed your example, especially since you ordered me to." Caastyn grinned.

Ysella shook his head, thinking of the apparent absurdity of being armed at a wedding, then slipped the envelope under the chaise's thin seat cushion.

"What's that for?" asked Caastyn.

"It's a copy of a legal document. The Premier has the original. This is in case something happens to it."

Caastyn frowned. "Spare legal documents at a wedding? Is the Premier going to try to get recognized as the Imperador's successor?"

"Nothing at all like that," declared Ysella. "We're hoping we can get a bit more power for the Council."

"The way things are going, you'll need more than a bit, and quite a number of men with crossbows and blades."

"It's up to the First Marshal and the Fleet Marshal to keep that aspect of matters settled." Ysella climbed into the chaise, glancing at the space below the dashboard, then put the gladius against the base of the seat, behind his boots.

Caastyn climbed into the driver's seat. "The small crossbows are behind the panel, along with the short spear, additional quarrels, and a cranequin, just in case."

Ysella raised an eyebrow to Caastyn.

"You said to be prepared."

Ysella nodded. "I hope they're not necessary."

"That makes two of us." With that Caastyn flicked the reins.

While they saw several carriages on Camelia Avenue, once Caastyn turned onto Imperial Boulevard, Ysella only saw two and neither was within a hundred yards. Both turned off Imperial Boulevard before they reached the Way of Gold.

When Caastyn reined up at the gates to the Palace grounds, Ysella tendered his invitation, then studied the gate guards, noting how attentive all four were.

"Thank you, Councilor," said the guard who'd taken the invitation, and compared it to a list. "You're to go to the south entrance. You'll be escorted from there."

As Caastyn eased the chaise through the gates, he glanced at Ysella. "That guard acted more like a naval marine or army special."

"He might be, but I hope he's a naval marine."

Caastyn grinned. "The specials are tougher."

"Let's hope they're not needed, or that their presence keeps them from being needed."

Ysella studied the grounds as the chaise climbed the gentle slope up to the Palace, but discerned nothing that seemed out of place. That alone suggested that someone had everything under tight control. Ysella hoped it was either Solatiem or Dhaantyn.

As Caastyn guided the chaise past the north entrance and the east entrance, Ysella noted the east entrance already had Palace guards and footmen in place. When Caastyn eased the chaise to a halt at the south entrance, there were no guards or footmen, but two naval marines in dress uniforms stepped out quickly.

"If you'd come with me, Councilor," said the first.

The second slipped into the chaise and said to Caastyn, "I'll direct you."

Caastyn looked to Ysella.

"Just take care of everything."

"Yes, sir."

Once Ysella was inside, another ranker appeared. "The Premier is expecting you, sir."

"Where?" asked Ysella.

"Next to the Palace chapel, sir. This way, sir."

Ysella followed the ranker for what seemed like a hundred yards before turning left along a narrower side corridor ending in two closed bronze doors. Two naval marines flanked a closed door on the left some four yards back from the double doors.

One of the marines knocked on the door and announced, "Councilor Ysella is here, sir."

While Ysella didn't hear a response, the marine opened the door and said, "Sir."

Ysella stepped into the small chamber that contained a settee, two armchairs with a side table between them, and a sideboard holding two decanters and half a dozen wineglasses. One decanter held red wine, the other white. The settee and armchairs were upholstered in a deep red. The chamber smelled faintly musty, as if it were seldom used.

Detruro rose from one of the armchairs. He wore formal whites, trimmed in thin green lines.

"You certainly look imposing," said Ysella cheerfully. "Has the Fleet Marshal replaced all the Palace guards?"

"Not all." Detruro gestured to the decanters and glasses. "Help yourself." Then he reseated himself.

"I'll pass for now." Ysella took the other armchair, noting that Detruro's wineglass looked close to untouched. "What should I know?"

"Most likely nothing, but a number of Palace guards from the summer palace and close to a company of men in army uniforms have mustered in an orchard a mille north of the Palace. There are likely others."

"You don't sound or look that worried," replied Ysella.

"Good."

That one word told Ysella that Detruro was concerned.

"Before I forget," said Detruro, "your place is in the front pew on the right side of the chapel at the far right beside Fleet Marshal Dhaantyn and his wife."

Front pew, if on the side? Ysella had mixed feelings about that. "Is there anything else I should know?"

"I hope not."

"I'm assuming that Lady Delehya is well-guarded."

"Naval marines and Lorya Kaechar."

And the Imperador? Ysella decided not to ask that question, partly because there wasn't anything he or Detruro could do about those arrangements.

In time, the door opened, and a graying but round-faced figure in the green cassock of a Trinitarian presider entered the chamber.

Detruro stood, as did Ysella.

"Dominic," said Detruro, "this is Presider Chaelmyn. He's the Palace chaplain. Presider, Councilor Dominic Ysella."

Chaelmyn inclined his head. "I'm pleased to meet you, Councilor."

"And I, you," replied Ysella.

Chaelmyn looked to Detruro. "We should take our places before the processional."

"Dominic," said Detruro, "come with us. You can enter the nave from where we'll be waiting. You'll also be less obvious, which might be for the best."

Ysella nodded, following the two from the chamber, then through the now-open double bronze doors and down a narrow corridor separated from the right aisle by a gray stone wall. The corridor ended at a featureless stone wall, with a single closed door on the left, where a Palace guard stood, attired in whites and armed with a scabbarded sabre.

"Through there?" asked Ysella.

Detruro nodded, as did the presider.

Only the guard's eyes moved as Ysella opened the door, and entered the transept, closing the door behind himself quietly. Even so, the door clunked faintly.

Ysella stopped and quickly surveyed the Palace chapel. It wasn't as large as the chapel in Aloor, despite the lofts set above the side aisles. Behind the transept there was a loft on the right for the harpsichord and other musicians and one on the left with two pews for the Imperador and his very immediate family. Only the Imperador and Imperadora were present.

Above and to Ysella's right, the harpsichord and violins played softly as he took his place in the first row of the chapel near the side aisle. To his left sat Luciala Dhaantyn, with Fleet Marshal Dhaantyn to her left, followed by Myra Solatiem and First Marshal Solatiem. Surprisingly, to the marshal's left, flanking the center aisle, were Waterways Administrator Engar Tyresis and his wife Heraana. In the row behind them sat Carsius Zaenn with his wife, as well as an older naval officer and several others that Ysella did not recognize.

Ysella seated himself beside Luciala Dhaantyn, who quietly said, "It's good to see you here, Councilor. Raul speaks highly of you."

"I speak highly of him," Ysella murmured in return.

Then, Chaplain Chaelmyn and Detruro entered the chapel, past Ysella and the others in the first row of pews, and walked to the center of the transept. There, Detruro turned and looked down the center aisle, while Chaelmyn took the low step up to the sanctuary and also turned to face the rear of the chapel.

Behind them a golden-edged tapestry hung from a shimmering gold rod that nearly extended the width of the sanctuary. Against a pale green background three golden orbs formed an arc. Within the orb on the left was a silver-edged leaf, while the middle and highest orb held a green-edged ray of golden sunlight, and the orb on the right portrayed the outline of a ship haloed with reddish-gold light.

The harpsichordist and the violins began playing the bridal processional, a procession consisting only of Delehya, escorted by the older man Ysella had seen at the engagement dinner, presumably her maternal grandfather. She wore the traditional flowing gown of pale green, with gloves, shoes, and veil in matching green, and carried the usual bridal bouquet of white and green gardenias.

She looked straight ahead toward Detruro and Chaplain Chaelmyn, both positioned to see her as she approached the sanctuary.

When Delehya neared Detruro, she handed the bridal bouquet to her grandfather, who stepped to the side, his eyes following his granddaughter.

Detruro and Delehya turned to face the presider.

Chaelmyn waited several moments before speaking. "Today, we are gathered here to witness and acknowledge the marriage of Iustaan Emyll Detruro and Delehya Daarya D'Laureous and to grant their union the blessing of the Three."

The presider turned to Delehya. "Is this indeed your wish and intent, freely given?"

"It is."

Then he turned to Detruro and repeated the question.

"It is."

Chaelmyn lifted his eyes and addressed those in the pews. Interestingly, at least to Ysella, he did not turn his head or eyes toward the Imperador and Imperadora. "As we acknowledge to the Three, our days are but moments in endless time, yet in this fleeting existence, one buffeted by the storms of fate and chance, the ties we make and hold enable us to weather the storms of life. Among the strongest of these ties is the commitment of a man and a woman to each other. So powerful and meaningful is this tie that it is specially blessed by the Three."

The presider turned his eyes back to Detruro and Delehya. "Marriage is a commitment not to be taken lightly. While it can afford the greatest of rewards, it is not a commitment to abandon in times of trouble or temptation. For, like threads that are stronger when woven together, remaining bound together in times both of triumph and tribulation leads to the greatest of rewards." Chaelmyn turned to Delehya and nodded.

She turned to face Detruro.

Chaelmyn lifted two rings and said, "These rings symbolize your decision and commitment to each other. In the sight of the Three and those gathered here, you pledge that commitment." He handed one ring to Delehya.

She accepted the ring and slipped it onto Detruro's ring finger, saying as she did, "With this ring, I pledge my faith and love to you and to us both."

As the presider handed the second ring to Detruro, Delehya removed both gloves and slipped them into Detruro's left-side slit pocket.

Detruro took the second ring and placed it on her finger, saying, "With this ring, I pledge my faith and love to you and to us both."

They both turned back to face the presider.

"In the sight of the Three, you have affirmed your love and commitment. May it always be so."

At that moment, Ysella heard the slightest hint of creaking and swiftly turned to his right, glimpsing a red and gold uniform behind the opening door. He yanked out the small truncheon with his left hand, vaulted over the low frontal, and took three quick steps before knocking the small crossbow up with his right forearm and slamming the truncheon into the midsection of the Palace guard who'd been aiming at the Imperador. His right knee went into the guard's groin, followed by his right elbow ramming into the guard's throat.

Two naval marines appeared, one of them shoving Ysella to the side before looking at the thrashing figure on the aisle floor.

Ysella glanced across the chapel, but the Imperador's pew was empty.

Two marines pinned Ysella against the wall, but a strong voice ordered, "Unhand the councilor! Hold the door!"

Both marines looked past Ysella, and released him. Ysella bent and recovered his truncheon, replacing it at his belt. By then, Dhaantyn stood beside Ysella, and every door was filled with armed Imperial marines.

"I'm sorry about that, Councilor," said Dhaantyn. "It appears something went awry. I'm very glad you were that quick. How did you know?"

"I didn't. I did think, if there was an attack, it would be exactly when everyone would be looking at the newlyweds, and the moment the door moved and I saw a red uniform, I knew."

"Thank you," Dhaantyn said to Ysella. "Now, if you'll excuse me." The Fleet Marshal turned and walked to the side door, leaving the chapel.

Ysella moved back to the pew and stood before the frontal, looking to the center of the transept where four naval marines surrounded Detruro and Delehya, then toward the back of the chapel where most people stood looking around, since they couldn't go anywhere, given that every door was blocked by marines.

A piercing whistle filled the chapel, and Solatiem stood at the edge of the sanctuary, while Presider Chaelmyn had stepped back, clearly disconcerted.

"QUIET! QUIET!"

When the voices lowered, the First Marshal began to speak. "Please remain in the chapel for the moment. You're perfectly safe here, and we need to capture and dispose of a few loose attackers. It shouldn't take that long."

Solatiem remained standing, and everyone slowly seemed to calm down. Ysella realized that Delehya had to be the one projecting the calmness. The various voices in the chapel dropped into quiet tones and murmurs.

"You were quite effective, Councilor."

Ysella turned to see Myra Solatiem. "I did what I could."

"Indeed you did." She offered an amused smile.

Then a marine moved toward Ysella. "The Lady and the Premier would like to see you, sir."

"Thank you." Ysella inclined his head to Myra, then followed the marine to where Detruro and Delehya stood. Delehya had pushed back the headscarf and veil so they rested around her shoulders.

"Thank you, again," said Detruro, smiling wryly. "I'd hoped something like this wouldn't happen." He turned to Delehya. "You were right about the likelihood of some kind of disturbance, but you settled people down."

"I've had a great deal of practice in calming situations," replied Delehya.

Ysella suspected that was an understatement, but only said, "What next?"

"The wedding reception and dinner, of course," declared Delehya. "My father won't attend, not after this, but my mother and my grandparents *will* be there."

Of that, Ysella had no doubt.

Less than a third of a bell passed before Dhaantyn returned and drew Detruro and the First Marshal aside. The three talked briefly before Detruro motioned to Ysella and Delehya, who both joined the other three.

"The naval marines are finishing up dealing with the Heir's men," Dhaantyn explained. "There looked to be almost two companies' worth. So far as we can tell right now, he wasn't with them, but he might have left when he saw we were prepared. There are also newsies at the Palace gates wanting to know what the fighting north of the Palace was about. Your thoughts?"

Since no one immediately spoke, Ysella did. "Tell them that the Imperador is considering making changes to the Establishment Act, and that partisans of the Heir apparently found out. The Heir didn't appear to be with them, but you haven't determined that definitively yet. Either way, his supporters attacked the Palace. One infiltrated the Palace in a guard's uniform and tried to assassinate the Imperador at the end of the wedding ceremony. The would-be assassin was killed in the chapel before he could get to the Imperador."

"The Imperador hasn't said he'll do any such thing," declared Dhaantyn.

"That doesn't mean he isn't considering changes," replied Ysella. "If he doesn't like the changes, he can say that he considered and rejected them. Either way, that puts the Heir in the position of attacking before the Imperador ever decides. You can say you don't know what changes, if any, he might be considering."

"That also makes it harder for the Imperador if he doesn't accept your charter," said Solatiem.

"If he doesn't," replied Ysella, "that's the least of Guldor's problems. If he does, then there's a news story indicating that he was at least thinking about it."

Detruro looked to Solatiem. "What do you think?"

"That's your decision, Premier, but I shouldn't be the one talking to the newsies. That implies it's more serious than we'd like them to think."

Detruro turned to Delehya. "Can you get the guests into the salon for an overlong reception, then see to your father?"

Solatiem said, "I'll help with that." He turned to Dhaantyn. "Tell the newshawks that Commodore Raeklyn and the naval marines are dealing with the interlopers, and that you are only here because of the wedding." He offered a slightly twisted smile. "That's actually true."

"I'll have Jhevaan get a coach to take you three down to the gates," said Delehya.

"Jhevaan?" asked Ysella.

"The Palace seneschal," said Detruro quietly.

"Maybe it should be just you and the Fleet Marshal," suggested Ysella.

Detruro shook his head. "The way things are going you need to be seen more."

The firmness in the Premier's tone suggested that Ysella not argue, so he didn't.

In less than a third Dhaantyn, Detruro, and Ysella stepped into a small coach outside the east entrance to the Palace.

Four newsies stood outside the closed gate when the carriage came to a stop and the three got out. Ysella saw that Daarkyn wasn't among the newshawks, most likely because he was assigned to the Council and not the Palace.

Dhaantyn led the way, but stopped a yard short of the bronze-railed gate and addressed them. "I understand you have some questions about the wedding."

"The wedding? What about the fighting north of the Palace?" shouted one of the newshawks. Before he could say more, the other three tried to speak at once.

Dhaantyn held up his hand. "Just a moment. I'll tell you what we know. About the time the wedding ceremony began, a group of interlopers climbed the wall around the grounds and rushed the Palace. We'd heard rumors that something like that might happen, and Commodore Raeklyn had prepared for the possibility. At this point, all the intruders have been taken care of."

"Taken care of? What does that mean?"

"Why are you here, Fleet Marshal, if it's only a bunch of intruders?"

"It's a large bunch, possibly two hundred, but Commodore Raeklyn has the matter well in hand. I happened to be here because I was invited to Lady Delehya and Premier Detruro's wedding."

"Where's the First Marshal?" demanded another.

"He's with Lady Delehya and the rest of the wedding guests at the reception following the ceremony."

"It looked like a pitched battle, not casual interlopers," shouted another newsie.

"They appear to be fervent supporters of the Heir. They wanted to disrupt the wedding. Apparently, they heard a rumor that the Imperador was reviewing the Establishment Act and considering whether he should make changes. As that's a rumor, I can't speak to it, but I can say they definitely attempted to storm the Palace."

"Was the Heir with them?"

"He did not appear to be among the casualties."

"Casualties?"

"All the interlopers were armed and attempted to use those weapons. One of them got as far as the chapel, but was stopped before he could attack the Imperador. That isn't acceptable."

"Was the Heir behind this?"

"You'd have to ask the Heir."

"Where is the Heir?"

"He was supposed to be at the summer palace. He isn't presently on the Palace grounds. At the moment, I can't say where he might be."

"Is the Imperador alive?"

"He was alive and in his usual health when I saw him about a third ago. I have no reason to believe anything has happened since we left the Palace."

"How do you know these interlopers were connected to the Heir?"

"They came from the direction of the summer palace and some of them were observed gathering outside the Palace grounds late yesterday afternoon."

Which means that Dhaantyn brought in the naval marines from the south.

"Is that why there are three navy ships tied up in Machtarn?" asked one of the newsies. "And why the Premier is here?"

"You can draw your own conclusions," replied Dhaantyn. "That's all I have to say for now. We'll know more in the morning."

"What about the Premier?" shouted one.

"Who's that with you?"

"That's all," declared Dhaantyn, turning and walking back to the coach, followed by Detruro and Ysella.

83

TWO bells later, Ysella stood beside Detruro and Delehya in a small chamber near the same Palace dining room that had held the engagement dinner and that would shortly hold the wedding dinner. They waited with First Marshal Solatiem for Fleet Marshal Dhaantyn, while the majority of wedding guests either enjoyed or suffered through a reception in the salon.

Dhaantyn entered the room and said quietly, "It's over. There were almost two companies of Palace guards and mercenaries in the force attacking the Palace, but none of them got that close. Over the past few weeks, Delehya and Sra. Kaechar managed to finish weeding out most of the Palace guards loyal to the Heir, but the handful remaining . . . that could have been a disaster, except for the councilor."

"How did they get a crossbow that close to the chapel?" asked Solatiem.

"We'll likely never know," replied Dhaantyn. "Everyone involved with that is dead." He glanced to Ysella.

"I was more interested in stopping him than in how I did it," said Ysella.

"You did, and that's what counts," said Solatiem.

"Any survivors?" asked Detruro.

"Only a few, but they . . . succumbed to their wounds," replied Dhaantyn. "Before they did, we learned that the Heir was never with them."

"I'm certain," said Detruro, "that he'll insist they took matters into their own hands."

"He'll claim that they restrained him at the summer palace and he could do nothing," said Delehya.

"We have two companies moving to invest the summer palace," added Dhaantyn.

"He'll likely be tied up or locked up by the time they get there, and any other Palace guards or armsmen will have fled," said Delehya.

Ysella noted no one disputed or looked mildly surprised at Delehya's prediction.

"Your recommendation, Premier?" asked Solatiem.

"If Lady Delehya is correct, you should report to the Imperador what happened in the attack on the Palace and anything Commodore Raeklyn discovers at the summer palace later. Offer no speculation, just the facts. They should be sufficient."

The two officers exchanged glances. Then Solatiem said, "We'll do that now. Otherwise . . ."

"I understand completely," said Detruro.

"Warn Lorya first," added Delehya.

As the two marshals left the small room, Ysella looked to Detruro. "This was planned to wipe out all the armsmen that the Heir had, wasn't it? You never had any naval marines in the Palace area until last night or this morning, when it was too late for anyone to get word to the Heir?"

"Whatever happens, the Heir is likely to be more . . . tractable in the future," said Detruro.

"What did the newshawks say?" asked Delehya.

Detruro smiled wryly. "There were four newsies at the Palace gates. Dhaantyn told them the Imperador was considering making changes to the Establishment Act, and partisans of the Heir found out. They didn't want any changes and attacked the Palace and tried to assassinate the Imperador at the wedding ceremony."

"You really don't want to be Imperador, do you?" asked Ysella.

Detruro shuddered. "I don't."

"And I don't want him to be, either. Ever!" added Delehya.

"But . . . your brother?"

"Under your new great charter, he'll be greatly limited, especially since the Council will be able to remove any future First Marshal who wants to return power to the Imperador."

"I worry more about the Council," said Ysella sardonically.

"The First Marshal and the Fleet Marshal will back you," said Detruro.

"Back me? You're the Premier."

"They'll back both of us, but when we get the charter signed, you'll be the one directing the reorganization of the various administrations into ministries and I'll be the one reorganizing the Council."

Ysella wondered what had changed enough for Detruro to say "when" rather than "if." Or had Detruro calculated that failure of the Heir's attack and assassination attempt left the Imperador with limited choices?

"It will take *both* of you," added Delehya.

And you. Ysella didn't need to voice that. He understood that Detruro had far more knowledge about the political currents and structures throughout Guldor, while Ysella had previously worked with administrators and designed the new organization.

"We should make an appearance at the reception." Delehya looked to

Ysella. "I'd appreciate it if you'd stay close." She smiled. "Especially after your efforts in the chapel."

"Dominic," added Detruro, "we'd very much appreciate it if you'd remain here after the dinner, at least for a little while. We have to meet with the Imperador, and I'd like you to be nearby."

"Whatever you require."

"We can talk about that later. For now . . ." Detruro gestured toward the door.

Almost everyone in the salon turned as Delehya entered, flanked by Detruro and Ysella.

Myra Solatiem was the first to greet the three, looking directly at Delehya, and saying, "We wish you both the best. Listen carefully, especially to what you truly feel."

Luciala Dhaantyn smiled warmly and murmured something that Ysella couldn't make out, but which caused Delehya to blush momentarily.

Then came Engar and Heraana Tyresis. While the Waterways administrator smiled pleasantly, Heraana said, "Our best wishes to you both. Just keep avoiding the human snakes and you'll be happier."

After that, Ysella couldn't keep track of everyone, especially since almost half of those who greeted the couple were people he'd never met or only knew by name. He noticed that neither Carsius Zaenn nor his wife personally greeted either Detruro or Delehya. Zaenn avoided looking at Ysella.

Almost two-thirds of a bell passed before Solatiem and Dhaantyn returned and made their way to Detruro, who said, "How did it go?"

"As expected," replied Solatiem dryly. "He likely would have ordered a few executions, but since there were no survivors, he had to be content. He wants a report on the Heir and the summer palace when we get word from Commodore Raeklyn."

Shortly after the two marshals returned, the doors to the dining room opened and the guests were ushered from the salon to the dinner.

Detruro and Delehya sat at the head of the table, with the Imperadora to Delehya's left and First Marshal Solatiem to Detruro's right. Beside the Imperadora sat her father, flanked by her mother. Ysella sat between Myra Solatiem and Fleet Marshal Dhaantyn, an arrangement definitely odd, although there was semblance of protocol, given that Ysella represented the entire Council, and First Marshal was certainly the most powerful position in the Imperial government outside of that of the Imperador and the Premier.

Once everyone was seated, Detruro stood and lifted his wineglass. "There won't be any speeches or anecdotes, embarrassing or otherwise, just a toast to the Lady Delehya, who is also now my wife, and the very reason for this event, and to the Imperador and the Imperadora, for allowing me the privilege of wedding this lovely lady."

After everyone except Delehya and the Imperadora drank, Delehya stood, surprisingly, because Ysella had never seen a bride offer a toast, and lifted her glass. "To my parents, and to First Marshal Solatiem, Fleet Marshal Dhaantyn, and Councilor Ysella. Without all of them, this happy event would not have been possible."

When Delehya proposed the toast, Ysella surveyed the table, noting barely veiled disapproval on the faces of several men, including Carsius Zaenn and High Justicer Kaahl.

As the servers appeared and provided each diner with a grape and greens salad, garnished with crushed nuts, Myra Solatiem leaned toward Ysella and said quietly, "You smiled following Lady Delehya's toast. Might I ask why?"

"I enjoyed the not-quite-concealed distaste on the faces of several men who don't have the ability to lick her shoes." Ysella took a small bite of the greens, then a grape.

"Quite a few aren't that pleased with her. I'm sure you've heard the rumors."

"I have. Yet they'd all be outraged if the same sort of salacious gossip circulated about them."

"Were you in love with her?"

"No. I'm attracted to someone else."

"Why isn't she with you?"

"She arrived in Machtarn yesterday, earlier than I expected, and it was a bit late to include her."

"Perhaps it was better that way, at least for the Imperador."

"And for the people of Guldor," replied Ysella.

"Do you think that many of them care?" asked Myra.

"About the Imperador? Most probably don't, but they'd care a great deal if the Imperador were killed, especially now. Uncertainty in government never bodes well."

"Even change for the better?"

"If change designed for the better isn't managed well, it can be worse than a bad ruler."

"Isn't that why even a significant change should be described as merely a slight improvement?" asked Dhaantyn blandly.

"Of course," replied Ysella, understanding Dhaantyn's caution. "It also helps if the overall structure appears largely unchanged, and the government continues to function." He paused as a server removed what was left of his salad.

In moments, another server presented a gold-edged plate containing baby asparagus with a white sauce, cheese-laced potato strips garnished with basil, and a petite fillet with a wine reduction.

"With all the delays, it's amazing that it's all warm," said Dhaantyn.

"Not really," replied Myra. "All of this can be cooked in a short time."

Ysella hadn't thought of the dinner in those terms, but it made sense.

The remaining conversations were light and largely inconsequential, and shortly after the dessert course, an apple tart drizzled with a hint of apple brandy, the bride and groom slipped away, as a matter of custom.

That left Ysella wondering where he was supposed to go, but when he left the dining room, a page appeared. "Councilor Ysella?"

"Yes?"

"Lady Delehya and the Premier wish to see you." With that, the page led Ysella to a study with an attached sitting room, where Detruro and Delehya were seated in chairs separated by a side table. Delehya had changed out of the bridal gown into dark green trousers, tunic, and black boots. Detruro was still in his formalwear.

"I see the page found you," said the Premier.

"It wasn't that hard. I was doubtless the only one looking around slightly bewildered."

"You never look bewildered," said Delehya.

Detruro said, "I sent word to your man—Caastyn Cruart, is it?—that you'd be tied up for at least several bells if not longer. We also sent him some dinner."

"I appreciate that, and I'm sure he did." Rather than ask what the two wanted, Ysella said, "Any strange wedding gifts?"

Detruro and Delehya exchanged glances; then both laughed.

"Only two." Detruro offered an amused smile. "We each got a ten-thousand-mark Imperial Treasury warrant, handed to us by Laureous personally. In time, if necessary, as you suggested, we might be relocating to Enke, one way or another."

"You're not thinking of resigning as premier?"

Detruro shook his head. "As I told you before, Dominic, I can't be premier forever." He stood. "We three need to go see the Imperador."

Ysella looked to Delehya as she stood. "Is he expecting me?"

"I told him you killed the traitorous Palace guard who would have assassinated him," she replied, "and that you might have something useful to say."

Detruro walked to the desk and picked up an envelope that looked familiar.

"The charter?"

"Exactly."

As he followed Detruro and Delehya, Ysella doubted the Imperador would be receptive to signing the charter in the slightest. *But it is a possibility after all that the Heir has done, if a slight one.*

Delehya led the way to the Imperador's extensive quarters on the third level of the northeast wing of the Palace, through an interior gate guarded by naval marines, and then past two more marines guarding the personal quarters.

"He'll be here in his personal study," said Delehya, opening a door, stepping inside, and then closing it after Ysella entered.

While the chamber might be called personal, it was still capacious, with two desks, and a settee and several chairs set well back from the larger and more ornate desk. The Imperadora sat on the settee, while Lorya Kaechar stood beside a chair set against the wall between the desk and the other chairs.

Ysella looked to the Imperador, seated behind the larger desk, his face far gaunter than two months before, his skin blotchy in places, wearing a sleeveless gold tunic over a black shirt. Ysella wondered if the black shirt was to conceal blood or other traces of age and illness.

"Father, Councilor Dominic Mikail Ysella."

Laureous looked at Ysella. "So you might have saved my life. Am I supposed to be grateful?"

"No," replied Ysella, "but the people of Guldor should be."

Laureous offered a rattling laugh. "Why? They're never grateful."

"No, but they should be," Ysella repeated.

"Why?" asked Laureous peevishly.

"Because it will give you time to ensure your legacy."

"I've already done that."

"No, sir. You've built an empire, but you haven't done what needs to be done to assure that it continues."

"Who are you . . . to tell me that?"

"I'm the grandson of a king whose father thought he'd live forever and neglected too many things. He had to surrender to you because he had no other choices."

Laureous started to open his mouth, then burst into a coughing fit, finally blotting his mouth after the coughing subsided.

Ysella saw traces of blood on the cloth Laureous used to cover his mouth, and waited.

"Are you trying to tell me to step down, and turn everything over to the Heir . . . or worse to that infantile Council?"

"No, sir. The Imperium needs both an Imperador and a Council, but if the Imperium is to last, there have to be some restraints on your successor."

"Why not restrain me now? Isn't that what you all want?"

"I don't agree with all your decisions, but you earned the right to them. The Heir didn't, and he's already made more mistakes while not being Imperador than you did in your entire life."

Abruptly, Laureous looked to Lorya Kaechar, then to Delehya, who moved to stand by his shoulder.

They both nodded.

"So . . . do you have any real idea of what would be involved?" asked Laureous. "Any idea at all?"

"I'll let you decide, piece by piece. Premier Detruro has an envelope. It contains a plan. If you're willing to go through it, I'll explain—"

"Who drafted it?" Laureous looked to Detruro. "You?"

"No, sir," replied Detruro. "I asked Councilor Ysella to draft the best plan he could. I believe he also asked for recommendations from the First Marshal and the Fleet Marshal."

Laureous turned and glared at Delehya. "Was all this your idea? To soften me up on your wedding day?"

"No, Father. I wouldn't have thought of it, even today . . . not until my half brother sent two companies of armsmen to attack the Palace."

Despite his barriers, Ysella could almost see a wave of calmness and reassurance emanating from Delehya.

"If she hasn't thought of it," snapped Laureous, looking straight at Detruro, "why do you have this plan so conveniently handy?"

Before Detruro could speak, Ysella said, "Premier Detruro asked me to draft a plan that could be applied to the Heir. Most of the Council and even the First Marshal and Fleet Marshal have been worried about what the Heir could do if he had all your power with none of your judgment. We wanted to be prepared."

"He certainly hasn't behaved well in the last year, dear," said the Imperadora quietly. "Particularly lately."

"While I haven't always been myself, you mean? Is that what you mean?"

"Yes, dear."

Laureous turned back to Ysella. "Why did he pick you?"

"You'd have to ask him, sir. It wasn't a task I sought."

Laureous looked to Kaechar, who nodded. That stunned Ysella, because he knew she couldn't sense his emotions.

"Why him?" Laureous demanded of Detruro.

"Because he's the best legalist in the Council for this kind of law. He also survived what happens when a ruler fails to prepare for the future."

"What are the major provisions in this ... plan?" Laureous asked Ysella.

"First, the plan is just a plan. It could be signed and made effective today or signed today and not become effective until your successor becomes Imperador."

"When I die, you mean?"

"Yes, sir."

"Go on."

For the next sixth, Ysella explained.

When he stopped, Laureous remained silent. Then he asked, in a hoarse and strained tone of voice, "Why should I consider signing something like this ... charter?"

"Because—" began Detruro, his voice even.

"Not you!" interrupted the Imperador, jabbing a shaking finger at Ysella. "You. You're the only one who might understand. Tell me."

"To save everything you've built, sir," replied Ysella. "Most rulers aren't as capable as you are. My grandfather wasn't. Your son isn't."

Laureous looked to Kaechar.

She nodded slowly.

"And you are?" demanded Laureous.

"No, sir. There's no one person who could do what you did." *If not for the reasons I'm implying.* "The new charter allocates power so that neither the Council nor the Imperador has enough power to destroy Guldor. It also establishes an independent justiciary to rule on conflicts of this power."

"Why would you, of all people, want to preserve my legacy?"

"Because you have the chance to do what my great-grandsire failed to do." Ysella saw the momentary surprise in Kaechar's eyes before she again nodded.

"And the pusillanimous Council can hold Guldor together?"

"No, sir. The restrictions of the charter prohibit one group from ever holding complete power. The Imperador retains the power to appoint the First Marshal, who controls the Army and Navy. They have to work together, and the Imperador can still dissolve the Council and call new elections."

"You're talking about three parties. There aren't any parties now, and they don't get anything done."

"I beg to differ, sir. There are already three parties. They just pretend they're one."

"Why three?"

"So no one party can dominate. Right now, either the landors or the commercers would dominate. Would you like either group in total control?"

For a moment, Laureous said nothing. Then he laughed. "You have a point." Abruptly, he asked, "Why didn't you pursue Delehya?"

That question caught Ysella momentarily off guard, but after a brief hesitation, he replied, "Because it wouldn't have been right or fair to her. I couldn't give her what she needs, and I'm in love with someone else." *For better or worse.*

"Hmmmph..."

"If you would, sir," said Ysella. "I'll tell you what's on each page. Lady Delehya can tell you whether it's so..." He held his breath, waiting.

Laureous glanced around the study. "Lorya, Delehya, you stay. Premier, you leave and keep everyone out while Councilor Ysella explains this wondrous plan in detail. He at least deserves the opportunity. He was the only committee chairman who listened to me and who didn't favor his own district."

The Imperador's words reminded Ysella that, physically weak as Laureous was, he retained a fair amount of his faculties.

Once Detruro handed the envelope to Ysella and left the study, Laureous turned to Ysella. "I may want some changes. You can do that, can you not?"

"I can, but it might be best if you tell me what you don't like, step-by-step, and let me explain why I worded things in a given way."

Laureous frowned, then gestured. "Go over to the writing desk. There's paper and ink there. Start at the beginning. Tell me about each section."

Ysella moved to the writing desk, hoping that Laureous could last and wouldn't become as intractable as he was said to be upon occasion.

Some parts, such as changing administrations to ministries, and administrators to ministers, Laureous almost skipped over. Expanding the Council to sixty-six members didn't concern him much, either. Getting him to understand and agree to allow two-thirds of the Council to override the Imperador's veto took more time and effort, and likely some gentle emotional pressure from Delehya, and possibly Kaechar.

At one point, he paused and glanced at Delehya, seeing the tightness in her body, and understanding how hard she was working. *Trying to keep him open to what you're saying or even persuading him... or just keeping him calm?*

Ysella had to clarify the time period between dissolutions and added a provision that any change to the charter had to be approved by two-thirds of two successive Councils, as well as the provision that the charter became immediately effective upon his death and could not be revoked by any successor and could be changed only by two succeeding Councils two years apart.

Interestingly enough, Laureous didn't balk at the limits on how often the Imperador could call new elections or dismiss the premier. *But then, they're not that onerous.*

Almost two bells later, well into evening, Ysella finally finished amending and rewriting a fair draft of the revisions, and Delehya surreptitiously blotted her forehead before calling back Detruro.

Ysella wasn't totally surprised to see the First Marshal accompanying the Premier.

Then Detruro and Laureous initialed every page, and Laureous signed the Charter, as well as a decree that Ysella had drafted establishing the Charter as a replacement for the Establishment Act.

Ysella tried not to exhale as Laureous signed the last pages of each document and dated them.

After that, Ysella had everyone in the room sign as witnesses.

After everyone signed, Laureous looked to Kaechar, who nodded, and back to Ysella. "You didn't lie once. That's something around here." Then he looked to Delehya. "Was this the right thing?"

"Yes, Father."

The Imperadora did not speak but nodded, offering a quiet sigh of relief, then said, "It's been a long day. You need some rest, dear."

For an instant, Ysella wondered about her approval, then belatedly realized that anything that restricted the Heir was to her benefit.

Kaechar and two naval marines accompanied the Imperador and Imperadora, presumably to his bedchamber or private salon.

Ysella turned to the others. "We need to have the Imperial scriveners make copies of these documents, as many as we can."

"I can take care of that," said Delehya.

"Then what?" asked Solatiem.

"That depends on the Imperador," replied Detruro.

"If he'll agree to address the Council committee chairmen and a newshawk or two, that would quiet rumors that someone is trying to get rid of the position of Imperador entirely," said Ysella. "It won't stop them."

"He won't agree to anything like that," declared Delehya.

"What about a statement saying that he has no intent to change his rule, but that he's taken steps to preserve the Imperium for generations to come, and he's put changes to the Establishment Act in place to codify those changes?"

"That might be possible," said Delehya.

Detruro looked to Ysella.

Ysella refrained from sighing and began to write, working to keep the statement brief but clear.

Detruro read the statement over and suggested some changes. Delehya suggested a few wording changes to reflect the way her father spoke.

Ysella made the changes.

Shortly after he finished, Kaechar returned. "He's already asleep." She paused, then asked, "What are you going to do with the Heir?"

"Is there some way you could influence him?" asked Ysella. "Permanently?"

"Not without severe damage to his mind," said Kaechar. "It would also be obvious that an empath had done it."

And since there are only two empaths in the Palace, and one other, likely beholden to the Heir, those responsible would be obvious.

When neither Detruro nor Solatiem spoke, Ysella did. "Then we'll have to compile a listing of what he cannot do, and make sure that all ministers and marshals understand those limits, and give them a simple reply along the lines of: 'The Charter forbids me to do that, sir.'"

"And who will enforce that?" asked Solatiem.

"If you're agreeable, we all will," said Detruro. He looked to Ysella. "Dominic, you've had a long day, and we'll both have to be at the Council Hall early tomorrow morning. You need to head home." Then he turned to Delehya. "I'm afraid our little getaway will have to wait."

"I can't imagine why, husband dear," replied Delehya in a sweetly amused tone.

"If you're willing to stay here until I return, Lady Delehya," said Kaechar, "it might be best if one of the marines and I escort Councilor Ysella out of the Palace."

"We're in no hurry, not at the moment." Delehya turned to Ysella. "I sent a messenger to your man. He'll be waiting at the north entrance. That's the closest."

"Thank you." Ysella turned to Kaechar. "Shall we go? The sooner we leave, the sooner you can return."

"You have a great deal farther to travel than I do," she replied lightly.

"There is that."

"Quite a day for you, Councilor," Kaechar commented after she and Ysella, along with the marine, walked through the interior gate and headed down the steps toward the first level.

"It was harder for you and Delehya, I imagine," replied Ysella.

"Harder for Delehya, but you noticed that. You don't miss much."

Still more than I should.

Kaechar was silent for a time, then asked, "Do you really have someone you're interested in?"

"I do. I had a late supper with her and her great-aunt last night."

"You're effective enough with the truth that you don't have to lie. You'll make a good premier. Just be careful."

Ysella almost missed the next step.

"It will take both of you to make it work," Kaechar went on, "even with Lady Delehya's power of persuasion."

"If I might ask . . . how long do you think the Imperador can last?"

"That would be a guess, Councilor. His physician's surprised he's still alive."

"What will you do, then?"

"I'll leave the Palace. I'll decide where I go when that time comes."

"How do you think the Heir will take matters?" Although Ysella hadn't ever met the Heir, from what he'd read and seen, the younger Laureous would be furious.

Kaechar's smile was catlike. "He won't like it, but he'll accept it, then do his best to undermine it."

"That might be difficult, given that most of his armsmen didn't survive."

"He'll try to recruit more."

"We'll have to oversee his spending carefully then, and the Charter will allow us to limit the number of armsmen he can have."

"I imagine you'll quickly become his third-least-favorite person."

"After Delehya and Premier Detruro?"

"Of course."

"Do you have any advice for me?"

Kaechar laughed quietly but harshly. "Watch everyone and trust no one."

"Except you, Detruro, and Delehya."

"Why do you trust me?"

"You've proved trustworthy . . . and loyal, and you're as invested in the Imperador's legacy as he is . . . if not more."

"Why are you?"

"Because anything else would be a disaster, and so few can see that."

As they neared the double doors of the north entrance, Kaechar stopped and said, "Just be careful. Very careful."

"I will . . . and thank you."

"Thank you."

Ysella inclined his head, then turned and walked out through a door opened by a footman. In the entry area beyond were Caastyn and the chaise—as well as four mounted marines, two in front of the chaise and two behind.

"The First Marshal ordered us to escort you home, Councilor."

"I appreciate that," replied Ysella before climbing into the chaise.

Caastyn glanced at Ysella, then shook his head. Only after he guided the chaise away from the Palace and down the drive toward the main gates did he say anything. "I saw all the naval marines coming back to the Palace, and there were wagons heaped with bodies. What exactly happened?"

"The Lady Delehya and the Premier got married. I stopped an assassin. The Heir dispatched two hundred armed men to attack the Palace. The Fleet Marshal had five companies of naval marines waiting. They slaughtered the attackers. Then there was the wedding dinner, after which the Premier, Lady Delehya, the First Marshal, and I met with the Imperador. After that, Lady Delehya watched while the Imperador read—and amended—the charter I drafted to improve and change the structure of the Imperium's government. Then he signed it and so did everyone else. Outside of that, not much happened."

Caastyn sat in silence for several moments. "All that? Just today?"

"I drafted the first version of the charter weeks ago. You took that to the Fleet Marshal. The rest happened today."

"Won't the Imperador change his mind tomorrow?"

"He could, but I doubt it. The Charter's the only way to rein in the Heir and protect the rest of his family as well as the only way to hold Guldor together. It takes effect when he dies, and it has a provision saying that only two different and successive councils can change it. Both the First Marshal and Fleet Marshal stand behind it. I imagine the naval marines will remain in Machtarn for a while."

Caastyn glanced at the naval marines leading the way toward the gates. "Someone thinks you might be a target."

"Just to avoid brigands tonight, I suspect. It wouldn't look good for anyone involved if something happened to me. Tomorrow, it might be a different story. You'll have to take me to the Council Hall."

"The last two days have been something for you, sir."

"Quindi was much more enjoyable," said Ysella dryly. *Much more.*

84

TIRED as he was, Ysella woke early Unadi morning, yawning several times before he got to his feet. He didn't look forward to what was likely to happen at the Council Hall. He'd been part of the small elite group that had potentially changed the entire governing structure of Guldor and effectively enlisted the military to support that change. Some wouldn't take that well.

But elites are usually the only ones with the power and position to effect change without a bloody revolution . . . and sometimes that makes matters worse.

Ysella hoped that wouldn't be the case as he washed, shaved, and dressed quickly. He wore the silk and leather armor again, then made his way downstairs.

"Quite a spread in the *Tribune*," remarked Caastyn as Ysella entered the breakfast room, "but they don't mention your charter."

"The newssheets doubtless didn't get that information until this morning, or they might not have gotten it yet. There was a lot to copy." Ysella sat down and took a slow swallow of café before picking up the newssheet and beginning to read.

PALACE BATTLE AT LADY'S WEDDING

Lady Delehya's wedding to Premier Iustaan Detruro occurred as hundreds of heavily armed partisans swarmed across the Palace grounds toward the chapel. One reached the chapel and attempted to fire a crossbow at the Imperador before he was stopped and killed by an unnamed guest. Imperial naval marines quickly put down the attack, purportedly made by supporters of the Heir, who feared that the Imperador might change the government or the succession once Premier Detruro wed the Imperador's only daughter . . .

Casualty figures were not available, but marine sources said that very few of the attackers survived. The Heir apparently did not take part in the attack, and did not attend the wedding, but remained at the summer palace.

Palace Seneschal Jhevaan stated that the wedding, the reception, and dinner following the ceremony, while delayed, took place as planned, although the Imperador did not take part in all activities after the ceremony...

Seneschal Jhevaan did not name either the assassin or the guest who stopped him...

At least that's not in the newssheet.

Neither Caastyn nor Gerdina spoke while Ysella read, but when Ysella lowered the newssheet, Caastyn asked, "How accurate is it?"

"Mostly, as far as it goes. The Premier definitely doesn't want to be Imperador, and Delehya doesn't want him to be, either." Ysella took a sip of café and a bite of his muffin.

"Very few attackers survived?" Caastyn raised his eyebrows.

"Commodore Raeklyn wanted to make certain there wasn't another attack. From what I've overheard in the past few weeks, at least half had to be thugs who carried out killings for the Heir. The others weren't likely any better. I don't think the Imperador had any idea just how corrupt his son is."

"Isn't the Imperador just as bad?" asked Gerdina.

"Laureous is arrogant, easy to anger, sometimes misguided, stubborn, and self-centered, but he's not corrupt. He doesn't think that way. I think that's why he found it hard to believe his son was. It also may be why he signed the Charter." Ysella chuckled ironically. "But other than a short conversation at the Yearend Ball, I never really talked to him before last night, and that was two bells of just the two of us."

"Did that change your mind?" asked Caastyn.

"Not really. He seemed the kind of man I'd already surmised."

"Not very nice, possibly not even good, but not corrupt?" said Gerdina sarcastically.

"That's a fair summation. The Heir is much worse."

"And you're going to let him succeed his father?" asked Gerdina.

"He does have two sons," returned Ysella blandly.

Caastyn and Gerdina exchanged glances before he said, "And you're not going to do away with the Imperador?"

"I've served in the Council long enough to know that the Council without some checks would be worse than the Heir."

"I hope you're right, sir."

"So do I," replied Ysella. After a moment, he ate the last of the egg scramble.

When he finished, he thought about riding to the Council Hall, since his name hadn't appeared in the newssheets. Word was bound to get out, though, possibly sooner rather than later. He turned to Caastyn. "It might be best if we both rode to the Council Hall—armed."

"Yes, sir. I was wondering about that."

"And you might have said something if I didn't?" Ysella smiled.

"I didn't have to, sir." Caastyn smiled.

In less than a third of a bell, the two rode west on Camelia Avenue, both with crossbows. Ysella didn't notice much difference in the number of people, not until they were headed north on Imperial Boulevard, where there were definitely fewer people out, especially when they neared the Council Hall, but he didn't see any armsmen or naval marines.

When they reined up outside the Council stables, a good third before second bell, Caastyn asked, "Fourth bell?"

"Unless I send a messenger."

"Let's hope not," returned Caastyn, who watched as Ysella entered the stables before turning back west on Council Avenue.

Before turning Jaster over to the stableboy, Ysella uncocked the crossbow, removed the bolt, and replaced the bolt and crossbow in its case. Then he headed toward his office.

The moment he stepped through the door, Khaard was on his feet, a message in hand. "The Premier sent word to all offices, sir. The Council will convene at fourth bell. There's also a separate message from him."

The message was short—for Ysella to see Detruro immediately.

When Ysella arrived at Detruro's office, the Premier beckoned him in and began to speak before either of them sat down.

"I had copies of the Charter delivered to the newssheets, along with a signed statement from the Imperador close to the one you drafted last night."

"About not changing his rule, but limiting his successor? What did he change?"

"He specifically said the Charter was binding on any future successors."

"What about the Heir?"

"He's confined at the summer palace, and will be at least until the Imperador dies. Commodore Raeklyn reported the younger Laureous was apparently relieved to be alive. He was less happy to learn that his powers as Imperador had been significantly reduced."

"What about Solatiem and Dhaantyn?"

"Both worried and relieved. The five companies of naval marines will remain in Machtarn for a time."

"We owe a great deal of this to Delehya and Lorya Kaechar," said Ysella.

"And to you as well," replied Detruro. "Lorya and Delehya wouldn't have trusted anyone else to work out the final details of the Charter with Laureous. Neither would Laureous." After a pause, he added, "Earlier this morning, Laureous told Delehya he wasn't sure what he was thinking when he agreed to the Charter, but after learning what the Heir had attempted, he said that whatever he'd been thinking was for the best. He also remembered what you said—that he'd earned the right to his mistakes and that neither the Heir nor your grandsire had."

"That wasn't quite what I said, but I'm glad he recalled it."

"Now comes the hard part—presenting it to the Council and implementing it. Just so you understand, I'm going to tell the Council that several months ago I ordered you to draft a reform package, which went through several versions, and when we presented it to the Imperador, he insisted that you draft the final version based on what you had worked out and upon the recommendations of the First Marshal, the Fleet Marshal, and several administrators . . ."

Detruro finished by asking, "Have I left out anything?"

"Not that I can think of."

"How would you suggest we approach planning for new Council districts?"

"Start by picking the sixteen largest cities and towns that don't have a councilor, and then work with Maatrak and Maessyn to figure out which are best for possible new crafter or commercer seats, and firm procedures for readjusting after the first election of the sixty-six."

"Readjusting?"

"What happens if the crafters only win fourteen seats? They get a minimum of sixteen. You'll need an absolutely firm way of deciding, most likely by disallowing the landor or commercer who had the lowest proportion of votes in winning. It has to be numerical, and not judgmental."

"You didn't make it easy, did you?"

"Nothing really workable and even halfway fair in politics is easy," countered Ysella.

Another third of a bell passed before Ysella returned to his office, where he quickly went through the mail before beginning to think about which administrators to work with to prepare for the transition to ministries.

He left his office a third before fourth bell and walked quickly to the Council chamber.

"Do you know why this meeting is so urgent?" asked Staeryt when he settled behind his desk beside Ysella. "We all already know about the details of the attack on the Palace by the Heir's armsmen."

"Well, it might be about the government Charter the Imperador signed last night as a result of the Heir's attempt to have the Imperador assassinated, or something along those lines," replied Ysella evenly.

Staeryt froze. "Is he disbanding the Council?"

Ysella wanted to shake his head, given what he'd previously said to Staeryt. "It's probably not that bad, but he should be the one announcing it." *Which is the way it should be, since he's the one that made it all possible.*

"What's not that bad?" asked Paolo Caanard as he took his seat.

"The Premier's announcement," replied Ysella.

As soon as the fourth bell rang, Detruro took the lectern, rather than Maatrak. "As some of you know, I've been a little preoccupied the last day or so . . ." From there he stated almost exactly what he'd told Ysella earlier, outlined the basic provisions of the Charter, and concluded by saying that by early afternoon all councilors would receive a copy.

"Are there any questions?"

"Why wasn't the Council consulted on this?" demanded Nortaak brusquely.

"For several reasons," replied Detruro. "First, there was the likelihood that Councilor Ysella might not have survived had it become known, because the Heir certainly would have opposed the reduction in the power of the Imperador. This was a real threat, since the Heir or those around him likely killed two administrators, poisoned another, as well as killing two councilors and a banque presidente, not to mention trying to overrun the Palace during my wedding ceremony. Second, under the Establishment Act, the Imperador—and the Imperador alone—had the power to change the structure of government. The Charter was the best we could get from him. Under the Charter, however, after two years, the Council will be able to make further changes under the procedures outlined in the Charter."

"The Council should have been consulted!" insisted Nortaak.

"We didn't have that choice," returned Detruro. "After the Heir's attempted attack on the Palace, the Imperador was willing to talk about changes. His health is tenuous at best, and we might not ever have had another chance."

"You've engineered what amounts to a revolution," snapped Nortaak.

"Really?" asked Detruro. "You all wanted the Council to have more power. Under the Charter we get that. You wanted a way to override the Imperador's veto. We get that. You wanted the Council to control the appropriations process. All the administrations will report to the Council, not to the Imperador. Has anyone else been able to get any of that, especially with limited bloodshed, with most of the blood coming from the Heir's thugs?"

"What will guarantee the Heir won't try again?" asked Maatrak.

"The First Marshal and the Fleet Marshal, and five companies of naval marines, among other things." Detruro held up a hand. "Those are the immediate questions. The Council will meet tomorrow at noon, after you all have had a chance to read the Charter. Remember—for now, nothing changes." He rapped the gavel once. "The Council is recessed until noon tomorrow."

Ysella watched as Maatrak followed Nortaak from the chamber into the hall, certain that the commercer had more than a few things to say to Nortaak.

"How close is the Charter to what you drafted?" demanded Staeryt.

"Reasonably close," replied Ysella.

"Did you have to give the crafters a party?" asked Staeryt.

"The Imperador didn't want either the commercers or the landors to have an absolute majority—ever. He said he didn't trust either." While the Imperador had only agreed to that, Ysella didn't feel that deceptive, since Laureous felt that way.

"Two parties would have been better," declared Staeryt.

"If you want to create a never-ending fight and no practical way to compromise," replied Ysella mildly.

Staeryt stiffened.

"Just think about it, Ahslem," said Ysella.

Staeryt's short laugh was bitter. "I will... only because wagering against you is costly."

After Staeryt walked away, the only other councilor to approach Ysella in the corridor was Georg Raathan, who smiled as he joined Ysella. "I don't know how you two did that, but congratulations." The smile vanished. "Will the Imperador keep his word and his decree?"

"The odds are very good he will. He knows he'll die before too long. He wants the Imperium to last, and he knows that his son, without restraints, will destroy it. Everyone else close to him is praising him for his foresight, and the last thing Lady Delehya wants is to be imprisoned in the Palace for the rest of her life."

"Your last answers my other question."

"In more ways than one," replied Ysella. "The Premier also doesn't wish to be imprisoned, either, and short-term expediency would likely cause long-term instability."

"I see." Raathan smiled again. "I'll help as I can, but you'll have to watch out for Stefan."

"I appreciate it. Thank you."

"Just let me know."

"I will."

No one else approached Ysella on the walk to his office, and he received his copy of the final version of the Charter at just after first bell of the afternoon. He read it carefully, but so far as he could remember, what he read was what he and Laureous had worked out.

Then he went back to working on correspondence before turning his attention to what administrative procedures needed to be changed for the various Imperial administrations to report to the Council, effectively the Premier.

Just before second bell, Maatrak appeared. Once in Ysella's office, he said bluntly, "You and Detruro delivered more than you promised. That could be a problem."

"Some councilors who are really commercers don't want to choose because they're afraid they'll lose landor backing in the next election?"

Maatrak nodded.

"With the expansion of the Council, no one will lose his seat, but they'll have to choose."

"Without saying so, you're going to make the Council more accountable."

"With more power, there has to be more accountability."

"What about you, Dominic?"

"For better or worse, I'm a landor, if unlike most landors."

Maatrak laughed softly. "You can go against other landors and survive. No one can challenge your background, and every commercer and crafter in Aloor knows what you've done for them."

"A number of landors in Aloor aren't that happy with me."

"From what I've heard, they're in the minority."

"What about you?" asked Ysella.

"I don't see a problem. Commerce comes first in Ondeliew."

"Have you ever heard of a Professor Gastaan Ritchen at Ondeliew College?"

"Of course, but I'm surprised you have."

"I'm interested in his efforts to build a steam device that could power a boat or pump water from mines."

"He's formed a business to manufacture those engines. Looks very promising."

"If those engines aren't too costly, I might know some who would buy them." Ysella smiled. "Is there anything else?"

"Not at the moment, Dominic. As I said before, you're one of the few who can be trusted to deliver what you promise. Don't let that change." Maatrak smiled. "That's all I had."

Even a third after Maatrak had departed, Ysella continued to puzzle over what the de facto commercer leader had said and implied. The only way anything would change for Ysella was if he gained more power, but he was the most junior of the committee chairmen. While he'd designed and drafted the Charter, only Maatrak, Maessyn, and Georg Raathan had any idea how involved he'd been, at least until Detruro had announced it to the entire Council.

He decided to go back to working on the reporting and accountability structure for the renamed ministries.

85

"You're in the *Tribune* again this morning," declared Caastyn when Ysella walked into the breakfast room on Duadi morning.

"How bad is it?"

"It could be a lot worse," replied Caastyn, grinning.

Ysella decided to take several sips of café before lifting the newssheet and beginning to read the front-page story.

AILING IMPERADOR GRANTS COUNCIL INCREASED POWERS

Immediately after his daughter Delehya's wedding to Council Premier Iustaan Detruro, Imperador Laureous signed a sweeping decree granting expanded powers to the Imperial Council and limiting the powers of his successor, a decree that takes effect immediately. This does not restrict Laureous's powers, however, but does those of any and all successors . . .

After the attack on the Palace on Findi by supporters of the Heir, the Imperador apparently decided the younger Laureous was not capable of wielding all the powers granted the current Imperador under the Establishment Act and took immediate steps, with the assistance of Councilor Dominic Ysella, who is also an accomplished legalist . . .

The document was signed by Laureous and witnessed by the Premier, the Imperadora, the Lady Delehya, First Marshal Solatiem, Councilor Dominic Ysella, as a representative of the Imperial Council, and by Sra. Lorya Kaechar, the Imperador's longtime and trusted personal empath . . .

The remainder of the story listed the major provisions of the Charter.

Ysella set down the newssheet and looked to Caastyn. "You're right. It could have been much, much worse." *And it still might.*

"You need me to ride with you again today?"

"I'd appreciate it very much, likely for the next week or so." Ysella suspected that most people were more surprised than angry at the moment, but the anger would surface later, particularly among landors who, upon reflection, would blame Detruro and Ysella for causing the loss of political and economic power that had largely already occurred. Some, like Nortaak, would take the political reflection of that change personally.

A third of a bell after breakfast, Ysella and Caastyn rode down the drive. They arrived at the Council Hall just before second bell, and Ysella was in his office a sixth later.

He had barely seated himself behind his desk when Jaasn announced, "Reimer Daarkyn, sir."

"I'll see him."

As usual, Daarkyn shut the office door, then said, "Certain sources insist you were the unidentified wedding guest who stopped the would-be-assassin who was after the Imperador."

"I'm glad there was someone who stopped him," replied Ysella.

"Were you or weren't you?" asked Daarkyn.

"Does it really matter, Reimer? The important thing was that the Imperador wasn't hurt or killed."

"Are you defending him? After all the trouble he's caused the Council?"

"I'm not attacking or defending him. I'm glad he realized that Guldor needed a government with some limits on future Imperadors."

"Were you the one who persuaded him to that realization?"

"I doubt it. I suspect that the attack on the Palace by something like two hundred armsmen gathered by the Heir was the deciding factor."

"You were among the group that signed the Charter. Why were you included?"

"Because I was there at the wedding, and because I have the most experience in administrative law of any councilor. The Premier wanted the Charter to be as legally correct as possible."

"So you were the one who drafted it?"

"The Imperador said what he wanted, and I did my best to turn those wishes into workable law."

"One of the legalists at the *Tribune* studied the Charter. He said there was no way that even the best legalist in Guldor could have written something that good in less than days, if not weeks."

"Your legalist is right except for one thing. The Premier ordered me to draft legislation that included the various possibilities for reforming government. He sent for that work when it appeared that the Imperador wanted to create such a charter. I assembled those sections which the Imperador approved as well as I could."

"So the Premier dictated what the Imperador would see?"

Ysella shook his head. "The Imperador ordered the Premier to leave the study. Then he told me what sections he wanted. The Lady Delehya, the Imperadora, and Sra. Kaechar remained to assure that the Imperador's wishes were carried out. The Imperador and Imperadora wanted a strong empath present to make sure of that. The Premier never saw the final document until it was ready to sign. Neither did the First Marshal."

Daarkyn's intent expression didn't change. "Interesting. That was what the Imperador's empath and the Palace seneschal both said as well. I wasn't aware that the Imperador had such a legalistic background."

"He doesn't. He just knew what he wanted in the Charter. He might not be able to write legislation, but he can certainly read and understand it."

"You're a landor. Why would you agree to draft a document that reduces the power of landor councilors?"

"What I drafted didn't reduce the power of the landor councilors. It recognized what has already occurred. It also made it difficult, if not impossible, for any party to dominate completely the other two parties."

"Those parties don't exist . . . or didn't."

"They do exist, if quietly, because the Establishment Act never recognized political differences." *And because the Imperador could just override those differences.*

"Do you think this . . . Charter will really work?"

"It should, but that depends on the Council, the High Justicer, and the people of Guldor. It certainly reduces the power of the Imperador."

"Why are you always involved in everything important this past year?"

"Other councilors have been involved as well. Some of them didn't survive. I was more fortunate."

"Some have suggested you're bolder and more heroic."

Ysella burst out laughing. "I'm anything but heroic. Trying to stop a thieving and corrupt legalist by revealing an illegal trust is scarcely heroic. I was successful in managing the Waterways appropriations because I didn't oppose the Imperador's recommendations and worked out compromises with the other committee members. I certainly don't believe that duels over honor solve anything, unlike some landors."

"Then why do such duels persist?" asked Daarkyn.

"Because landors generally have more training with blades, but all a duel proves is who happens to be better with a blade. That just builds anger and resentment over time."

"I heard you apologized rather than fight a duel."

"I did. I said I hadn't meant anything dishonorable and that I was sorry my words were taken that way."

"How did that work out with Councilor Nortaak?"

"I suspect he's still angry. He didn't want an apology. He wanted blood, and didn't seem to understand that no matter what happened we'd both lose. Sometimes, people are so fixated that they lose sight of what's important."

"Which is?"

"As far as I'm concerned, what's important is the continuation of the Imperium so that differences can be worked out in a way that respects all parties. I think the Charter offers the best possibility so far."

"What do you think Nortaak's view is?"

"I doubt he's thought it out, but what he's said suggests he wants a return to a landor-dominated Guldor. You might ask him."

Daarkyn shook his head. "He still won't talk to me. Newshawks are beneath him."

"That should tell you something."

"It does, but it's not printable," replied Daarkyn, smiling, standing as he did. "Thank you."

After Daarkyn left, Ysella realized the newshawk had never even alluded to Ysella's harbor properties, and he wondered when Daarkyn would write about those.

Then Khaard handed Ysella a message from the Premier, requesting Ysella meet him half a bell before noon. That gave Ysella some time to deal with correspondence before going back to trying to work out the finer details of the administrative transformations.

Ysella arrived at the Premier's office at half a bell before noon, and one of the clerks showed him in.

"There are a few questions that are bound to come up," said Detruro. "One that the First Marshal and I have anticipated by getting High Justicer Kaahl to rule that the decree implementing the Charter was rightfully and lawfully made."

"So anyone opposing it could be charged with revolt or rebellion or acts against lawful order?"

"One of those, but only if they used force," said Detruro. "I can handle most of the questions, but I think you'd better stand next to me at the lectern." The Premier grinned. "After all, you and the Imperador drafted it while I wasn't present."

Ysella shook his head. "You're not going to let me forget that, are you?"

"That's better than saying you drafted the entire Charter and only made the changes that the Imperador demanded, and not all of those."

Much better. Ysella offered a rueful smile.

"Speaking of that," said Detruro, "what do you think of a meeting with all the Imperial administrators and acting administrators, and the three marshals, to brief them on what will be required after the Imperador dies?"

"It will make the transition easier," replied Ysella, "but it could send some of them scrambling to meet with the Imperador."

"They won't get meetings. I can assure you of that. The Imperador is sleeping most of the time now."

"Then it sounds like we should have that briefing soon."

"I'll see if I can set it up for Furdi afternoon. The Council session shouldn't be long. You should be the one conducting the briefing. You're the legalist and the one who drafted the Charter to meet the Imperador's requirements." Detruro smiled wryly. "I'll have the Council clerks make copies of the section of your implementation plan dealing with the ministries so that they won't come up with excuses and unnecessary delays when the time comes."

"I trust you won't mind if I point out that the power to appoint and remove ministers will shift from the Imperador to the Council—except for the First Marshal and Fleet Marshal."

"That would be helpful," replied Detruro dryly.

"Anything else?" asked Ysella.

Detruro chuckled sardonically. "I think that's quite enough."

So did Ysella.

He made his way to the Council chamber, where Alaaxi Baertyl cornered him.

"Dominic, is this Charter you drafted real? I mean, Stefan Nortaak thinks it's just legal chicanery."

"Nortaak's not a legalist. High Justicer Kaahl has ruled that the Charter meets the legal requirements, and he's not known for tolerating legal chicanery. Since he's ruled against Laureous once or twice, I don't think Nortaak would find much support there."

"Aksyl Haarst says the Charter's designed to remove landor control of the Council."

"That makes no sense, unless he's trying to stir up trouble. Haarst opposes almost everything landors support, even as he uses them to his own ends. You saw what he did to the Port Standards Act."

"Haarst was behind that?"

Ysella managed not to sigh. "Unfortunately."

"But why? It was a good bill."

"Because Stefan Nortaak asked him to."

"I don't understand why some people go around making trouble."

"Often, because it hides what they're really up to. Now . . . we'd better be getting to our desks."

"Oh . . . yes. Thank you, Dominic."

"You're welcome."

As Ysella took his seat, Staeryt asked, "What did Alaaxi want, if you don't mind?"

"He wanted to know why Nortaak and Aksyl Haarst didn't like the Charter."

"Nortaak doesn't like anything he doesn't understand, and that's most things, and Haarst loves to stir things up."

"That's about what I said."

When the six bells of noon finished ringing, Detruro gaveled the Council into session. "I promised you all time for questions about the Charter. To begin with, each councilor will get a sixth of a bell. If there's a need for a second round, and it's past fifth bell, we'll resume tomorrow. We'll proceed in order of seniority." Then he gestured for Ysella to join him before he said, "Councilor Maatrak?"

Maatrak stood. "Is there any likelihood of a legal challenge to the Charter?"

"I've discussed the matter with High Justicer Kaahl. Under the Establishment Act, there are no legal grounds to contest a decree rightfully made by the Imperador. The High Justicer has already ruled that the decree was rightfully made."

Ysella smiled faintly as he saw the surprise on the faces of several councilors, one of whom was Nortaak.

"Does the Charter allow the formation of parties before it takes full effect?" asked Maatrak.

"There isn't a prohibition of parties under the Establishment Act," replied Detruro, "but under the act, parties had no role. So parties can be declared now, but will have no official role until the Charter takes full effect."

"When would councilors have to declare a party?"

"Anytime they wish to, but no later than the day after the Imperador dies."

"Can they change parties?"

"Only when the next election is called," replied Detruro.

After Maatrak, the next most senior councilor was Georg Raathan, who only asked, "How will the Charter affect election procedures?"

Detruro nodded to Ysella, who answered, "The Charter mandates that each party must offer a candidate in each district. How that party determines its candidate is up to that district, in accord with existing law, with the exception that the district may not adopt practices that advantage or disadvantage any party or candidate."

Stron Thaalyr was next, asking, "Who or what sets the standards for whether someone is a landor or a commercer?"

"That's up to the party and the district to determine," replied Ysella.

Paolo Caanard asked, "Who will choose the heads of the ministries?"

Detruro answered, "The authority rests with the Council. The Premier will propose from candidates recommended by the ministry, and the Council will hold hearings, and then vote."

Many of the following questions were essentially variations on previous inquiries, but Stefan Nortaak asked, "How soon can this bastard Charter be changed or amended?"

Again, Detruro nodded to Ysella.

"The Imperador could issue another decree, since he retains those powers. If he does not, it would take a two-thirds vote of the first new Council and a two-thirds vote of the Council after the next election, as well as a period of at least two years between those votes. If the second council doesn't pass the exact same measure, then the process starts all over again."

"That's absurd!"

"Do you have further questions, Councilor?" asked Detruro.

"What's the point? You and the Imperador have turned the Council over to marks and the mob."

"As opposed to allowing landholders to determine everything without challenge or question?" asked Detruro.

"You're a traitor to your heritage. I have no further questions."

The questions ended at a third before fifth afternoon bell, when Detruro recessed the Council until noon on Furdi.

By then, Ysella was slightly hoarse, and all he wanted was to get out of the Council chamber and leave the Council Hall. He could tell that a number of the older landor councilors were either worried or possibly displeased, although none of them would lose their seats, except possibly in future elections, and likely only to another landor. Rather than deal with more questions, he waited until the chamber was nearly empty before stepping off the dais and leaving.

Maessyn had clearly been waiting in the main corridor and joined Ysella as he walked back to his office. After several moments, the crafter councilor glanced around, and then said, "I couldn't believe what Stefan Nortaak said to the Premier. I mean, if there ever was a landor premier, it's Iustaan Detruro."

"But he's not a stupid landor premier," returned Ysella. "He can see that the commercers will take over before long, and he doesn't want marks to destroy the land. Splitting power up permanently reduces the effect of marks."

"And what are the crafters, the wedge between the two that gets ground down?"

"That's why the Charter specifies a minimum party size," Ysella pointed out. "In years to come, lots of years, probably, the minority party will be the landors."

"You really think that?"

"Even in Aloor, there are fewer landors every year. It gets harder and harder to maintain a large holding. There are more prosperous commercers all the time, and they'll need more crafters."

"You make it sound easy."

"No. It won't be easy on anyone, and as long as the Charter lasts, people will complain about its provisions and wonder why anyone dreamed up such a patently idiotic system, at least until they've served as a councilor or possibly a clerk to a councilor."

"What about you, Dominic?"

"I imagine I'll face opposition in the next election."

"You'll win. You ever consider being premier? After Detruro, of course."

"Not really. There are four or five more senior councilors."

"Give it a thought." Maessyn smiled. "I won't keep you any longer."

Ysella laughed to himself.

After all your explanations on the dais, and the fact that it's clear you had a lot to do with crafting the Charter, who will ever vote for you as premier?

86

TRIDI went by uneventfully, with only one political newssheet story—one about the Heir remaining at the summer palace, which included a mention that the Imperador had been seen in a Palace garden with the Imperadora. While Ysella had thought there might be unrest or at least some councilors stopping by to talk with him, that didn't occur, and the only message was from Detruro, confirming the meeting with the Imperial administrators.

On Furdi morning, there was a *Tribune* story speculating about what the Heir might do to contest the Charter, which quoted High Justicer Kaahl's opinion that the Charter was legally valid.

Ysella was still thinking about the almost-eerie calm when he left the house, wearing his leather and silk armor. Caastyn accompanied him on the ride to the Council Hall, but no one approached him either on the ride or during the walk to his office.

He'd barely finished reading through the incoming letters, although it was far too soon for any of those from Aloor to comment on the events of the previous endday, when Khaard announced Ahslem Staeryt.

Even before Staeryt was fully inside the inner office, he asked, "Do you have a little time, Dominic?"

Ysella gestured to the chairs. "Of course."

"I don't know if you've heard, but these days I don't know what anyone's heard, and it's hard to believe most of it . . . anyway, the Premier has put me and the Justiciary Committee in charge of planning the expansion of the Council . . . and since you had more to do with the Charter than anyone, except maybe the Imperador and the Premier . . ."

"You'd like my thoughts?"

"If you would."

"In principle, it's simple. You and the committee need to set up sixteen new districts for councilors, and those districts need to be from the largest towns or cities that don't have a councilor. You'll also need to establish procedures for appointing temporary councilors—in accord with the Charter—until the next election—"

"Dominic, right now we don't even know how many current councilors will choose what party."

"I imagine you've got a pretty good idea—can you think of any councilor from a landor background who'd want to be anything else? Or any from a crafter or commercer background who'd want to change?"

"I can't think of any, offhand."

"You know the limits for parties, and to be fair as possible, and to avoid charges of favoritism, the additional councilors should be added by party in the same proportion as those parties now have. The next election will tell how accurate you were . . ." Ysella continued to offer suggestions for a sixth, then asked, "Does that help?"

"It does. You've obviously thought this out."

I had to. "I certainly tried."

"I suspect more than tried, but I won't press you. I appreciate the advice." Staeryt rose, nodded, and hurried out.

He really doesn't want to know. But then, he's been like that for months.

Ysella turned back to reading and signing, or changing, the few responses prepared by Khaard and Jaasn. When he finished with those, he turned his attention to going over his notes for the afternoon meeting with the Imperial administrators who would likely become ministers reporting to the Council before that long.

A third before noon, he left his office and walked down to the first level and the Council chamber.

As he entered, Staanus Wrystaan stepped forward. "If you wouldn't mind?"

"Not at all, Staanus."

The two walked to the far side of the chamber, where Wrystaan said, "I'd like your thoughts on this problem of declaring a party."

"At this point, no councilor has to declare anything—"

"I understand that, but my problem is a little different. I'm a crafter who became successful enough to be appointed by what amounts to a commercer district, but barely, with a vocal and powerful landor faction."

"And you could certainly declare for either crafter or commercer." Ysella frowned. "You told me you didn't intend to stand in the next election."

"I don't, but declaring crafter would certainly hurt my sons, who sell mainly to commercers. At the same time, I'd like to see a strong crafter presence in the Council."

"I suspect both Haans Maessyn and Gaastyn Ditaero will represent the crafters well. Also remember that the Charter mandates a minimum number of councilors for each party. I suspect that crafters will need that guarantee. But if you declare crafter, that's one less, effectively, and since no one knows how any councilor votes . . ." Ysella hesitated, then added, "And that would also effectively create another commercer seat."

"You're being very open, Dominic."

"More senior councilors have doubtless already made similar calculations. I'm pointing out your options and the implications."

"I appreciate your clarifying those options. Thank you."

"You're welcome."

Wrystaan smiled, then inclined his head before turning toward his own seat.

Ysella was about to take his seat when Paolo Caanard eased up to him. "Just be careful around Stefan Nortaak. He's angrier than ever."

While Ysella wasn't certain that was possible, he said, "Thank you. I appreciate the warning."

Caanard shook his head ruefully, then stepped back to his desk and sat down.

Staeryt appeared just before the Premier gaveled the Council to order, but didn't speak to either Ysella or Caanard.

"There is no legislative business today," announced Detruro, "but I thought the Council should be aware that, according to the Imperador's standing order, the Heir will be restricted to the summer palace indefinitely. That order will remain in force until the Imperador revokes it or in the event of his death.

"Also, given the finding by the High Justicer that the Charter signed by the Imperador is legally valid, unless he, and only he, should revoke it, the Council will proceed to prepare for its implementation. That said, I must emphasize that the Council can only plan and prepare until the Charter becomes effective.

"There being no other business, the Council is recessed until noon on Duadi, unless earlier recalled into session." Detruro tapped the gavel once, then left the lectern.

Ysella stood and glanced around, but every councilor seemed to be headed out of the chamber, as if no one wanted to hear any more. Then Alaaxi Baertyl walked toward Ysella, glancing around nervously.

"What is it, Alaaxi?" asked Ysella cheerfully.

"I've been talking to Alaan, and he says that the marshals all support the Charter. But Eduardo Maalkyn and Graandeyl say they really don't. So does Aksyl Haarst."

"Eduardo's close to Aksyl Haarst, I take it."

"They knew each other before they were councilors."

"None of the three have served on the Military Affairs Committee, have they?" Ysella knew that would have been a rhetorical question for anyone but Baertyl.

"I don't believe so."

"Alaaxi, do you remember former Fleet Marshal Haarwyk?"

"Of course, he died."

"He died, rather suspiciously, after the Imperador found out that he provided accurate information on what ships were necessary to fight the pirates. And do you recall what happened recently to the first-rate ship of the line under construction in Neewyrk?"

"It burned."

"It burned, and one of the brothers building it was killed, because they wouldn't pay off the Heir."

"I know that."

"Well, if you were the First Marshal or the Fleet Marshal, would you feel safer dealing with the Council or with the Heir?"

Baertyl frowned. "When you put it that way, Dominic . . ." Then he asked, "So why do Eduardo and Graandeyl say that the marshals won't support the Charter?"

"Because Aksyl doesn't like the Charter and has been closer to the Heir than most councilors. It could be he wants the Heir to have more power than the Charter provides, so that he'll benefit personally."

Baertyl nodded slowly. "Aksyl has always been out for Aksyl, but I didn't know he was involved with the Heir."

"I wouldn't say much about it. Oskaar Klempt was the one who told me."

"Do you think . . . ?" Baertyl's eyes widened.

"I have no idea, but it's something to consider."

Baertyl nodded. "Junae said I should ask you. She was right. Thank you." With a quick nod Baertyl turned and headed in the direction of his office.

Ysella kept walking to his own office.

Once there, he dealt with correspondence and went over his notes for the afternoon meeting.

Two bells later, Ysella walked into the Waterways Committee room at just before third afternoon bell and took the seat he occupied as chairman, then surveyed those seated facing the dais—all the Imperial administrators or acting administrators, the High Legalist, and the First Marshal, Fleet Marshal, and Army Marshal.

After several moments, he said, "You all have a copy of the Charter signed by the Imperador, and witnessed by the Premier, the Imperadora, the Lady Delehya Detruro, and others. The staff legalist has provided each of you an envelope containing the changes necessary to comply with the provisions of the Charter. To make matters clear, when the Imperador dies, whenever that may be, all Imperial administrators will immediately become ministers reporting to the Imperial Council, and their administrations will become ministries. Any replacement ministers will be chosen by the Imperial Council from senior officials at each ministry. The Council cannot order you to do anything at the moment, but I would urge you to look over those steps. Let me know if you have any recommendations for improvements." Ysella paused, then asked, "Are there any questions?"

Carsius Zaenn asked, almost arrogantly, "Even if the Imperador dies without revoking this . . . Charter, why would we accept this?"

"For several reasons. First, it's an Imperial decree, signed and sealed by the Imperador. Second, the High Justicer has ruled that it is the law of the land. Third, the Premier, the First Marshal, the Fleet Marshal, and the Army Marshal all support it, and have moved forces into Machtarn to assure that the transition to a Chartered Imperium goes smoothly when the time comes."

"It's still nothing more than a takeover by the Council," Zaenn declared.

"Well," said Ysella, "by the same token, the creation of the Imperium was a takeover of Aloor and Endor by Laureous. This way, there's no more bloodshed; the laws and bureaucracy essentially stay the same; the Council becomes more representative; and the Imperador's powers are limited. Oh, and the High Justiciary has the power to rule on whether future laws are against the provisions of existing laws or the Charter."

"If I might point out to the others, Councilor Ysella," interjected First Marshal Solatiem, "the efforts of the Heir to assassinate his father, and they were his efforts, illustrated all too clearly the dangers of the position of an Imperador with unrestricted powers. The Navy and the Army both prefer and will support the Charter."

"That's even worse!" snapped Zaenn.

"Administrator Zaenn," said Ysella firmly, "the Imperador agreed to every provision in the Charter. A number were his idea. By serving as administrator, you accepted the provisions of the Establishment Act, which the Imperador created. He is still Imperador, and his directives still apply to you and all other administrators. He chose to restructure future government. For you to accept his authority in one instance and to reject it in another suggests that you only wish to obey the laws when you agree with them. This meeting, however, is not to argue about the Charter, but to help administrators implement it."

"What happens if I don't?"

"Nothing . . . until the Imperador dies. At that moment, all power over all Imperial functionaries shifts to the Council, and the Council will determine whether you remain as Minister of Natural Resources. In the meantime, here, I'll answer questions relating to implementation."

Zaenn glanced at Solatiem, then glowered at Ysella, but said nothing further.

"How does this affect the Heir?" asked Hektyr Teilmyn, the acting Administrator of Commerce.

"The Heir is currently restricted to the summer palace, by the order of the Imperador," replied Ysella. "He remains the rightful successor to the Imperador, although his powers, and those of every future Imperador, have been reduced by the Charter."

"What about existing laws and regulations?" asked Prudhyr Fraenk, the Agriculture Administrator.

"The Charter doesn't change any laws or regulations applied to individuals, structures, or legal entities, other than changing to whom the government entities regulating them report." Before Fraenk could say more, Ysella added, "I could give the longer legalistic phrasing, but what it all means is that the final authority will be the Council and not the Imperador, although the High Justiciary will have the authority to review acts, laws, or procedures as to whether they comport with existing law or the Charter."

The questions went on for almost another bell, after which most of the administrators departed, leaving Solatiem and Engar Tyresis.

Solatiem walked to the dais, waited for Ysella to step down, then said, "You were succinct and clear, but the Council may have some problems."

"Mostly with landors, I fear," said Ysella dryly. "Are you having any problems with the Heir?"

"I understand he and a legalist are studying the Charter."

"He's doubtless considering what he can do the moment he becomes Imperador."

"If I read the Charter correctly, he can dismiss the Premier, call new elections, dismiss me or Fleet Marshal Dhaantyn."

"He can still veto legislation, but not at the moment, because nothing's before him."

"I will affirm," said Solatiem, "that all the marshals, as well as all the senior officers, approve the changes created by the Charter." He smiled wryly. "I also appreciated your briefing and explanations. Let us know if there's anything else we can do."

"I hope there won't be a need for that, but, if there is, the Council will. Thank you."

"Thank you, Councilor."

After Solatiem left the committee room, Engar Tyresis joined Ysella.

"You know Carsius Zaenn will try to find any way possible to invalidate the Charter."

"That's hardly surprising. A number of landor councilors don't care much for him. What do you think his chances are?"

"Slender and not at all. The Charter was signed by the Imperador with enough witnesses that it would be hard to sustain claims of coercion, and the fact that the Imperador released a subsequent statement strengthens that." Tyresis smiled. "And with the High Justicer and all the marshals behind the Charter, who's going to support Carsius? Especially since no one but the Heir loses anything, and almost no one trusts him."

"There also might be a certain relief to see an Imperador with less power," suggested Ysella.

"Except for those with ties to the Heir."

Like Haarst. "We'll have to deal with them when the time comes."

"You likely will," replied Tyresis. "So far you've done well."

As Ysella walked back to his office, he could only hope that he and Detruro could keep the Charter in place and effective for however long it took for Council, administrative, and popular acceptance.

87

Quindi was yet another quiet day. Although Ysella had the feeling that something momentous, somewhere, was bound to occur, nothing out of the ordinary happened. Nor did he encounter Reimer Daarkyn or Stefan Nortaak, or see either anywhere.

Findi morning's *Tribune* had a brief story noting that naval marines remained in Machtarn, both on the Palace grounds and elsewhere, but that Commodore Raeklyn had reported no signs of unrest or insurrection. The commodore also declined comment on the casualties incurred by the mob that had attempted to storm the Palace.

In Ysella's mind, that confirmed the fact that few indeed survived or escaped—and that the marshals had no intent of allowing young Laureous the powers held by his father or to amass or maintain enough force to render the Charter toothless.

After breakfast, Ysella realized, with everything that had happened, it had been some time since he'd written his parents, and he went to the study. A bell later, he set aside his pen momentarily. While he'd filled in some of the details about Detruro and Lady Delehya's wedding, including the attack by the Heir's thugs, he did not mention his thwarting the traitorous Palace guard. He also withheld the details about how the Imperador came to sign the Charter and all that he had to do with it. He decided against mentioning his surprise meeting with Aelyn Wythcomb and her great-aunt. He didn't want anyone in Aloor to know, given a definite possibility of unpleasant gossip if it got out that he was seeing her in Machtarn.

Then he wrote a short letter to Bruuk Fettryk, with a few details about the Imperador signing the Charter and what he hoped might come of it. He mentioned only that he and Aelyn were exchanging letters and that he enjoyed getting to know more about her.

Because Ysella wasn't about to disrupt Caastyn's day off, and because it was rather warm, he decided to ride to Ritten Scalante's small mansion for the afternoon supper with the Ritten and Aelyn. He left the house at half before third bell and took his time, but was watchful for the entire ride.

When he reached the Scalante dwelling, Ysella tied Jaster to the second hitching rail, which was partly shaded, then walked back to the side steps up to the porch. He'd barely reached the porch when Aelyn appeared, wearing a forest-green dress with a lighter green short jacket.

Ysella looked into her gray eyes and smiled. "I still can't quite believe you're here."

"Neither can I."

He offered his arm.

She took it. "I see you rode."

"Findi is Caastyn's day off, and I'd rather not take that away from him, if it's not necessary."

"That's kind of you."

"More like thoughtful," replied Ysella.

"You don't like being called kind?" Aelyn's voice held a hint of teasing.

Ysella smiled ruefully. "Certain words hold connotations for me. 'Kind' is one of them. Possibly because of the way I was brought up, 'kind' embodies a certain condescension, that someone is less just because of where they were brought up or their backgrounds and that you need to be kind to them for that reason. 'Nice' is another one, implying, at least in my family, 'nice try, but you could do better.'"

Aelyn cringed.

"That's my reaction; it's not you." Ysella grinned and added, "You did tell me when I really didn't answer your questions."

"Fair's fair." She squeezed his wrist gently. "Growing up in your family wasn't as easy as people might think, was it?"

"It was much better than most people, and I didn't have to go through what you did. But, at times, conversations could be cutting in a way most outsiders wouldn't catch or understand." He laughed softly. "But I suspect that's true in many landor families."

"You're right, and it was in mine. That was something neither Thenyt nor Khael ever understood." She paused, then added, "Auntie's waiting for us on the rear porch. It's cooler there, and there's enough of a breeze that it keeps off most of the flying bugs."

"I'm very glad to be here with you." *Especially after the past week.*

"And I'm glad you're here."

When the two reached the rear porch, Ysella saw that Ritten Scalante was seated in the middle armchair of three arranged in an arc around a low table under the roofed porch, looking out over a walled formal garden.

She turned her head. "Good afternoon, Dominic." She gestured to the chairs.

"And the same to you, Ritten." Ysella escorted Aelyn to the chair on Ritten Scalante's right, then waited a moment for Aelyn to seat herself before he took the one to her left.

"According to the newssheets, you've been rather busy," said the older Ritten in an amused tone. "You were at Lady Delehya's wedding. Were you, perchance, the unidentified guest who stopped a possible assassination?"

"It looked like a possible assassination, but it didn't get that far," replied Ysella.

"I don't believe you answered the question, but that's sufficient for me."

"I appreciate that, Ritten."

"Beyond that . . . copying out the new Charter at the behest of the Imperador, no less. How much of it did you draft?"

"The Premier and I worked on a draft that he then put before the Imperador. I made some changes the Imperador insisted on, persuaded him out of others, and reworded a few others."

"How accurate was the *Tribune* rendition of the Charter?"

"The newssheet summary of the major points was quite accurate. And no, there wasn't deceptive or contradictory wording elsewhere in the Charter."

"Why in the world did he sign it?"

"Because he didn't want the Imperium destroyed." Ysella went on to explain all about the Heir.

When he finished, Ritten Scalante offered a sardonic smile. "Would it be fair to say that it's likely you were shot by some of the Heir's toughs?"

"I think whoever shot me was paid, indirectly, by the Heir, but I couldn't prove it."

"What will happen next?"

"Nothing until the Imperador dies. Possibly not much even after that."

"In which case, you and the Premier will have changed the entire future of Guldor."

"No, Ritten, if that happens, it will be due to scores of others as well."

"You two guided them. The Premier won't stay premier that long. Then what?"

"I'll do whatever I can to make sure the Charter remains the basis of government."

Abruptly, Ritten Scalante turned to Aelyn. "You've scarcely seen a fraction of what could happen. Do you still want that future?"

"More than ever, if that's what it takes." Aelyn paused. "Didn't you?"

The older Ritten laughed, a sound somehow softer than its harshness. "I did, but there's a cost to it, dear. Politics is a far more jealous god than the Three in One. And definitely crueler than the gods of the marketplace."

As the serving woman appeared, Ritten Scalante asked, "We'll be having fowl later. Your preference for beverages?"

"White wine," said Aelyn.

Ysella looked to the elder Ritten.

"Shaelda knows my preferences."

"White wine," said Ysella.

"One of your traits I find worthwhile, Dominic," said Ritten Scalante, "is your practicality, and the fact that you seem to be able to retain a certain amount of idealism without becoming impractical. In that, you and Aelyn are well-matched." She turned to her grandniece. "How would you feel about splitting time between Aloor and Machtarn?"

"As you know, Auntie, it's not as though I've ever had a firmly established home. I'd rather have, as you might put it, an established and practical husband who cares for me."

Ritten Scalante looked to Ysella. "I expect I know the answer, but I want it to be clear. Have you entertained other women in either of your dwellings?"

Ysella could see a hint of discomfort in Aelyn's eyes at the question.

"Only the wives of councilors who accompanied them to dinner at my house here. The only woman who's ever been in the Aloor house is an elderly family retainer, a woman, and both houses were significantly rebuilt after I acquired them. The Aloor house is slightly smaller than the one here."

"I know," said Aelyn. "I drove by it several times."

"Excellent!" declared Ritten Scalante. "Too many young women marrying older men, although you're not that much older than Aelyn, have to contend with various past . . . reminders. If you two do decide to wed, those won't exist."

"You're being quite practical, Auntie," said Aelyn dryly.

"You don't have anyone else to be practical for you, dear."

What Ritten Scalante didn't say, and didn't have to, Ysella knew, was that family "practicality" had forced Aelyn into an awkward and loveless marriage.

At that moment, Shaelda returned with three wineglasses, one red and two white, serving the red to Ritten Scalante first, then white to Ysella and Aelyn.

Ritten Scalante lifted her wineglass and took a small sip.

Once Shaelda left, Aelyn looked to her great-aunt and sweetly asked, "Do you have any more personally practical questions for Dominic?"

"Not at the moment, but I reserve the right to ask any if they come to mind." Ritten Scalante turned to Ysella. "What are your thoughts about Aelyn's mine?"

"For now, she should keep it. From what I've heard, there's still tin there . . ." Ysella explained about the steam engines and the possibilities of making the mine productive again, then finished, "Whether she eventually sells or keeps it, it will have greater value if the steam engines work out." Ysella sampled the wine, finding it an excellent white Silverhills.

"Not that Mylls will ever thank you for that," said Aelyn.

"That kind of man never does." Ritten Scalante turned to Ysella. "How long have your man and his wife been with you?"

"Not quite five years. He'd spent twenty years in the Army and took a stipend. That was about the time when I could afford him and Gerdina."

For the next third, Ysella largely answered questions, most of them from the older Ritten, at which point the three repaired to the smaller dining room, where the late-afternoon supper consisted of early summer greens, poached whitefish covered in lemon cream sauce accompanied by summer squash and new potatoes, with cherry tarts.

Dinner conversation was varied, but mainly dealt with family history, including how Aelyssa and Maelcar met.

Following dessert, Shaelda served the three Herraeth, an excellent cherry liqueur that Ysella hadn't ever tasted, but Ritten Aelyssa only had a few sips before she stood, gesturing to Ysella not to stand.

"I'm not so young as I used to be. Aelyn, when you two call it an evening, please make sure that the doors are secure. Don't keep Dominic too long. I expect he has a long week ahead." Ritten Scalante smiled warmly and looked to Ysella. "Would you join us for services on Quindi and for a late dinner afterward?"

"I'd be delighted, but . . . the next invitation after that, for both of you, must be at my house, possibly the following Quindi?"

Before Aelyn could reply, Ritten Scalante replied quickly, but warmly, "That would be perfectly lovely. Enjoy your time together."

Once the older Ritten had left, Aelyn smiled at Ysella. "You didn't have to, but Auntie was pleased that you did."

"I'm glad of that." Ysella stood and slipped into the chair Ritten Scalante had vacated, wanting to be closer.

Aelyn looked at Ysella, with a hint of worry. "What will happen when the Imperador dies? Really. You said possibly little would change. That suggests other possibilities."

Ysella took a small sip of the cherry cordial, then said, "I think the chance of an armed revolution is slight. Most of the Heir's armsmen were killed or severely wounded, and the Fleet Marshal has five companies of naval marines posted here in Machtarn. While some individual commercers and landors won't be happy, the Charter doesn't change their rights and privileges in the slightest. The Council will have more power, but since no one party can have an absolute majority, that should temper any extremes..."

When he finished, Aelyn said quietly, "So you could be very influential?"

"It's possible, but not certain. I've told you about Stefan Nortaak. He'd certainly like me removed, one way or another. There might be others. The one in the most tenuous position is the Premier. The Heir could dismiss him immediately. I wouldn't, if I were the Heir. I'd wait to see how things turn out, possibly use the threat of dismissal as leverage."

"Is the Heir that reasonable?"

"At times, but not always."

Aelyn laughed, softly. "You're saying that we'll have to see."

"I am."

"What do you think about us?"

"The more I see you, the more I talk to you, the more I want you close. We've both been impetuous. Had I been able, I would have liked to have done what you did, but if I had, it would have jeopardized our future happiness. People remember councilors who abandon their duties long after they're no longer councilors." Ysella swallowed. "You took a great chance and risk coming here, even with your great-aunt's support. I want you to know that I understand that... and... that I love you for that. Not just for that, but... for everything." He reached out and took her hand.

Both her hands firmly grasped his and drew him closer.

88

YSELLA woke on Unadi morning out of mixed dreams, some of being even closer to Aelyn, and others far more disturbing, including one where the two of them were sheltering behind the heavy doors of the tin mine while the Heir's thugs were using axes to cut through the timbers, and all through that dream he kept wondering what a water legalist and his wife were doing in a mine. *But at least you two were together.*

As soon as he walked into the breakfast room, Caastyn looked up and said, "You're smiling. I take it you had a good supper."

"Excellent fare, and good conversation," replied Ysella, "except for a third or so when Ritten Scalante interrogated me on whether I had intimate relations with other women in either of my houses."

Caastyn chuckled.

"That's sensible," declared Gerdina. "She's looking out for her grandniece. She doesn't want her surprised."

"Aelyn's the one who was married before," said Ysella.

"And you haven't. That's *exactly* what she should be worried about."

The only women in my houses have been in my dreams, and, until now, none of them were exactly fulfilling. But Ysella only said, "She doesn't have anything to worry about."

"We know that," declared Gerdina, "but she didn't."

"How did Ritten Wythcomb take that question?" asked Caastyn.

"I think she was a little embarrassed, but pleased with the facts."

"When are you going to ask her?" Caastyn grinned.

"Not until I've at least come close to getting her great-aunt's approval."

"The aunt's an idiot if she doesn't approve," said Caastyn.

"She'd be more of one if she didn't look into the background of someone her niece had barely met," countered Gerdina.

Ysella smiled cheerfully. "You're both right." He paused, then added, "I'm going to dinner there after services next Quindi, and I invited them both here for dinner the following Quindi after services."

"Good," declared Gerdina. "That gives me time to come up with the right menu."

"Whatever it is will be good," replied Ysella.

"That's easy enough for you to say, Ritter." But Gerdina smiled.

Ysella took a long swallow of café before he picked up the *Tribune* and began to read through it. The only article about the Imperador reported that he hadn't left his personal apartments in several days, which was unusual.

There was a short story about the Southern Fleet's success in intercepting four pirate craft about to attack Suuthyn, a town Ysella had never heard of north of Encora. Two frigates and a pair of sloops destroyed all four craft. On the next-to-back page was an announcement that Gharlyn Poncetaryl had become presidente of the Banque of Machtarn, succeeding the late Omar Poncetaryl, whose murder remained unsolved.

And will likely remain unsolved.

When Ysella finished eating and stood, Caastyn said, "Good. Keep wearing that armor until you're sure things are really settled."

"That could be months."

"Could be. Could be tomorrow . . . or Yearend. Just keep wearing it, and I'll keep riding with you."

Ysella couldn't gainsay Caastyn's experience and judgment. "That's for the best, but I wish I didn't have to inconvenience you so much."

"Someone putting an arrow or a quarrel through you'd be a lot bigger inconvenience for everyone, especially Ritten Wythcomb, after she traveled all that way to see you."

Ysella offered a wry smile. "A much bigger inconvenience for both of us."

A third of a bell later, Ysella and Caastyn rode east on Camelia Avenue. For all of their concerns, neither saw anything remotely threatening for the entire ride to the Council Hall.

When Caastyn reined up beside Ysella, he said, "Fourth bell?"

"Unless I messenger you."

"Try not to get into too much trouble, sir."

Ysella grinned. "I'll try." Then he rode to the stables, where he turned Jaster over to one of the ostlers, unstrapped his case, and walked toward the Council Hall.

Although Ysella stepped inside his office a good third before second bell, he saw Khaard pacing back and forth.

The senior clerk turned and said, "Sir, the Premier wants to see you immediately. The messenger didn't say why."

Ysella handed his case to Khaard. "I'm on my way. If you'd put this on my desk?"

"Yes, sir."

Ysella walked swiftly down to the main level and to the Premier's office.

One of the clerks said, "Don't leave, sir. He's talking to Councilor Maatrak, but he needs to see you now."

Less than a sixth passed before Luaro Maatrak walked out of the Premier's office, then turned to Ysella. "Dominic, I'd really appreciate it if you'd stop by after you see the Premier."

Given Maatrak's serious demeanor, Ysella replied, "I'll be there as soon as I can."

"Good."

The Imperador is dead or dying. It can't be anything else. Ysella turned to see Detruro gesturing and hurried into the office, closing the door, and asking, "The Imperador?"

"He died before dawn this morning. I knew it was likely. Delehya spent the night at the Palace with him and the Imperadora." Detruro's lips curled into a twisted smile. "You were right to suggest banking. The Heir just sent a message. He's already back in the Palace. He's dismissed me as premier, which he can do under the Charter. That means I'm also no longer a councilor, not that anyone will throw me out of the Council Hall in the next day or so."

"He didn't call for new elections?"

"He was smart enough to realize new elections, especially under the Charter, might cost him support in the Council."

But not smart enough to realize dismissing the Premier without calling for new elections precludes dismissing the next premier or calling for elections for three months. "What about the First Marshal? Did the new Imperador dismiss him, too?"

"He decided against replacing Solatiem, because he'd be stuck with Dhaantyn, and he likes him far less than Solatiem. He might try something in three months. The immediate problem is that the Council has to select a new premier. I hope you're ready to take that on."

"What about Luaro? He's the acting Premier."

"He doesn't have the votes, and he knows it. There's no one better suited than you. No one else knows the Charter in any depth, and you've got some support from all three groups. Luaro's already sending messages to all councilors to tell them that tomorrow's session will be to elect a new premier. It'll likely take several votes for you to obtain an absolute majority."

"Even with Haarst and Nortaak opposing me?"

"Luaro can hold half the commercers, but you'll need to talk to Maessyn, and persuade a few landors as well."

"What can I do for you?"

"Just hold the Council together. That'll take all you have. Now . . . go talk to Luaro."

"You're headed to the Palace?"

"Where else? I can support Delehya, and my being here will only make things more difficult for you. Go talk to Luaro."

"Thank you."

Detruro snorted. "I should be thanking you. You're the one who'll have to reorganize the entire government and clean up whatever we overlooked and forgot."

"Take care and give Delehya my condolences."

"She'll appreciate that."

From the Premier's office, Ysella walked swiftly to Maatrak's office, where one of the clerks ushered him into the floor leader's personal office.

"You weren't that long, Dominic."

"There wasn't much I could say or do for Iustaan, and he wanted to go to the Palace. I imagine Delehya's had a hard time, even with Solatiem being there."

"Oh, that's right. Will he support the Charter?"

"He said he would, and he's not the type to go back on his word. I doubt any of the senior officers want the new Imperador able to have the power his father did, and the Charter gives them the legal authority to disobey his orders."

"You worked with them, didn't you . . . in drafting the Charter?"

"I did."

"Detruro said you ought to be premier. How do you feel about it?"

"I never really thought about it, but . . . I don't see anyone else who knows the Charter as well and who's worked with as many senior administrators."

"Neither do I, and, landor or not, you've been fairer than anyone else might be." Maatrak grinned and added, "Except maybe me, and only a few landors would support me. Haarst and his friends would vote for a landor rather than me. So you're the one."

"After we're done," said Ysella, "I thought I'd go talk to Haans."

"You don't need to, but he'll appreciate it."

"I need to." After a pause, Ysella asked, "Is there anyone or anything else you can think of?"

"Besides avoiding Nortaak, not at the moment. According to the Council rules, anyone nominated for Premier gets to speak for a sixth of a bell. I thought I'd second you, but you need a landor to nominate you."

"Who would be better—Sammal Haafel or Alaan Escalante? Or someone else?"

"Haafel," Maatrak said firmly. "Even people who don't like his views respect him and, well . . . Alaan looks to you often and might be seen as too beholden."

"I appreciate the honesty."

Maatrak smiled. "Unlike some, you mean that."

"The Council session will start at noon tomorrow?"

"It will. Just in case some haven't gotten the word."

"I'll be there early. And thank you."

From Maatrak's office, Ysella walked to Maessyn's, but the single clerk there said that Maessyn hadn't come in yet.

"Just tell him that I stopped by."

"Yes, sir."

Ysella then made his way to Haafel's office and was shown in to see the older councilor.

"Sammel, I take it that you've heard about the Imperador's death and that the Heir—the new Imperador—immediately dismissed Iustaan as premier. I'd thought that he would have given Iustaan a little time. Dismissing Iustaan just limits the Imperador's options."

"You see that. Young Laureous doesn't. There's a lot he doesn't see and never will." The older councilor leaned back slightly. "You're thinking about being premier?"

"I hadn't, but I am now."

"Good."

"I'd like to ask if you'd nominate me."

"I can and will do that, but, if you think there's anyone better . . ."

"I don't think there's anyone better." Ysella smiled. "That's why I'm asking you first."

"I appreciate the compliment, Dominic. You do know Stefan Nortaak will be furious, don't you?"

"Anything I do or say will infuriate him."

"I've gotten that impression. Who will second you?"

"Luaro's offered."

"That's also good."

"Is there anyone else I should see?"

"It's generally not received well if a councilor personally seeks support, but I'd suggest telling Ahslem Staeryt that you're running, but make it clear that you just didn't want to surprise him."

"In that instance, I should also tell Chaarls in the same vein, since he is a cousin."

"Good idea, and acceptable." Haafel grinned. "I'll take care of the others. Might even enjoy it."

"I appreciate it."

"Not as much as I will. I'll see you in the Council chamber."

Since Aashen's office was only two doors away, Ysella walked there.

Aashen stood outside his personal office, talking to one of his clerks, but beckoned for Ysella to join him.

Ysella closed the inner door after following Aashen, who turned.

"I have a suspicion why you're here, Dominic." The older councilor's tone was one of warm amusement.

"You're likely right. The new Imperador has dismissed the Premier."

"I hadn't heard that, but I thought it likely, and your presence confirmed it."

"I'll be running for premier. I'm not asking anything, but since we are related, I thought you shouldn't be taken by surprise."

"Very thoughtful of you. Aksyl Haarst had mentioned running if Iustaan were dismissed."

"I can't say I'm surprised," replied Ysella, "but even if I'd known that, it wouldn't change my mind."

Aashen chuckled. "I told Aksyl I'd only support him if you weren't interested. He said he understood."

"I appreciate that, Chaarls. I really do."

"My pleasure. Be good to have some power back in the family."

As Ysella walked to Staeryt's office, he understood exactly what Aashen had implied: that Haarst might do anything—rather get someone else to do anything—to keep Ysella from seeking the premiership.

Ahslem Staeryt was in his office and saw Ysella immediately. The conversation was similar to the one Ysella had with Aashen, except that Staeryt didn't mention Aksyl Haarst.

Then Ysella headed back to his own office, keeping an eye out for any strange figures—or Stefan Nortaak. He saw neither.

As soon as he stepped into his office, he asked, "Lyaard, any visitors or messages?"

"No, sir. Not since you left." Khaard looked inquiringly at Ysella.

"The new Imperador dismissed the Premier, but didn't dissolve the Council. We'll start voting for a new premier tomorrow. I'm running, but I'd appreciate you and Paatyr not saying a word about it until the session tomorrow."

"Yes, sir!" chorused both clerks enthusiastically.

"Too bad you can't vote for me," said Ysella cheerfully. "Now, I might as well see to the incoming mail and replies while I can."

Ysella finished reading and writing his notes on the incoming mail and was about to leave to see if Maessyn was in his office when the crafter councilor appeared and closed the personal office door.

"Good morning, Dominic. I didn't realize that the Imperador would decide to die on a morning when I slept late because I figured nothing would happen."

"I don't think any of us thought it would happen this soon . . . except maybe Laureous himself. It might be why he signed the Charter."

"I take it you're going for premier?"

"I am. So might Aksyl Haarst."

Maessyn grimaced. "That figures. The only councilor who makes the Heir look reasonable."

"I'd have to agree, especially after the Port Standards vote."

"I'm pretty sure I can get some of the crafters to vote for you on the first vote, and most by the second card."

"I'll likely need them, because Haarst has the most conservative landors and a handful of commercers who vote the same way."

"Is it still a simple majority under the Charter?"

"It is. The most important aspects of the Council that the Charter changed are making the premier the head of government and limiting how and when the Imperador can dismiss the premier or call for elections." Ysella went on to add a few more details.

"It's going to be different. Should be better, at least with you as premier. Haarst'd just frig it up. I'll do what I can. The crafters all know you're the only one who played fair with us. Just be careful. You can replace Detruro. Right now, there's no one to replace you."

"I appreciate that thought, but there's always someone." *They might be a disaster, but that's another question.*

Maessyn smiled. "I'd better get busy." Then he turned and hurried out.

Ysella took a deep breath, then started signing or correcting the responses prepared by the clerks.

He finally left his office at fourth bell, leaving his case in the office, since he wouldn't need it until Duadi. The only other councilor he saw was Astyn Coerl, who stepped outside while Ysella came down the stairs from the upper level.

Once outside, he walked swiftly toward the Council stables, surveying the area carefully. He was almost to the stables when Nortaak stepped out of the afternoon shadows and deftly tossed a scabbarded gladius on the walk almost at Ysella's feet.

"Detruro's gone, and you're next, one way or another."

Ysella barely looked at the gladius, instead saying, "So now you're doing Haarst's dirty work for him."

"Leave Haarst out of it. You're a poor excuse for a landor with that prissy Alooran background. Your cowardly grandfather wouldn't fight, just like you."

"Sometimes, Stefan, it takes more courage not to fight."

"Pick up that gladius. You will fight. And if you run, I'll have no compunction about stabbing you in the back." Nortaak smiled cruelly. "And if you outrun me, it'll prove to all the landors that you're a coward."

"You don't want to do this, Stefan."

"You're not ever going to tell me what to do or not do. Never again."

Ysella didn't see anyone nearby. Although the Council guards flanking the nearest Council Hall doors could certainly see the two of them, if they were even looking, they certainly couldn't hear the conversation or discern what was happening. While his silk and leather armor would reduce the effect of thrusts to his chest, the rest of his body was definitely vulnerable. "Very well. I trust you won't try to run me through before I pick up the blade. The Council guards would see that."

"I'm honorable, unlike you."

Ysella scooped up the scabbard and immediately stepped back, smoothly drawing the blade, which felt serviceable, if little more.

Nortaak thrust-feinted, then followed with a slash at Ysella's right leg, which Ysella slid off his blade and circled away.

"You won't stand and fight!" snapped Nortaak, thrusting low.

Ysella circled to his left, parrying a wild cut, knowing that he could have come back and sliced Nortaak's throat, but Nortaak's death would accomplish much the same result as Ysella's death would.

Ysella kept moving, sliding, blocking, but avoiding ever attacking Nortaak himself.

"Stop frigging dancing!" shouted the older councilor, loud enough that Ysella thought the Council guards certainly should have heard, but he certainly wasn't about to look. He kept moving, keeping Nortaak off-balance, working at wearing the other councilor down.

Nortaak's thrusts and lunges became wilder, and Ysella couldn't help but admire Nortaak's puffing endurance.

At the same time, Ysella wasn't about to attack until he had a clear opening for a particular move that Caastyn had taught him, one never taught to honorable and serious landor duelists.

Then as he circled right, forcing Nortaak to turn, he said, "Too bad you haven't any real honor, just a desire to bully and bluster."

Nortaak lunged, and Ysella twisted, turned his blade, and slammed the flat down on Nortaak's wrist with full force, enough that he could feel the bones break.

Nortaak yelled, even as Ysella stepped on the fallen blade.

"That's enough," snapped Ysella.

"It certainly is," said another voice, one that turned out to be that of Maatrak, flanked by two Council guards.

Holding his wrist, Nortaak said, "He challenged me."

"I don't think so," said a third voice, that of Caastyn, who had not dismounted and had a crossbow leveled at Nortaak.

"I also saw," Maatrak continued, "that Councilor Ysella never attacked. He only defended until he could disarm you. You not only violated Council rules by carrying a gladius on Council property, but by threatening another councilor. On top of that, you lied. Councilor Ysella doesn't even have a sword belt or a scabbard. You will face the discipline committee, and you will be incarcerated in the Council Hall until that time." Maatrak gestured to the guards. "Lock him up. Then summon a physician for his wrist."

Ysella picked up the scabbard to the blade he'd used, sheathed the blade, and handed both to Maatrak. "For evidence, if you need it."

"I doubt it will be necessary, but we'll keep it, just in case."

"How did you know what he had in mind?" asked Ysella.

"Detruro told me, one way or another, Nortaak would force you to fight. I had a few people keep an eye on him, and when one of them reported him carrying two blades we went looking, but he circled around the stables and doubled back." Maatrak grinned. "I have to admit I was skeptical about the way Iustaan reported your skills, but after seeing you, I think anyone would be a fool to think they could prevail."

"I was good as a young man, and I've kept working at it," replied Ysella, "hoping I'd never have to use them for real, but knowing I couldn't afford not to be prepared."

"That's another reason you'll make a good premier," said Maatrak. "Now . . . you need to ride home, Dominic. Tomorrow will be a long day for all of us."

"Thank you for anticipating this."

"Thank Iustaan. He was the one who saw it coming. We'll miss that."

Ysella nodded. "We will, indeed." *Especially I will, I fear.*

After walking the few yards to the stable and reclaiming Jaster, he mounted and rode over to where Caastyn waited. "I'm sorry for the delay, but I didn't exactly have much choice in the matter."

Caastyn turned his mount and rode beside Ysella along Council Avenue. "That was Councilor Nortaak, wasn't it?"

"It was."

"I thought so, but I've never seen him before. I would have liked to put a quarrel through him."

"I wouldn't have been displeased if you had," replied Ysella, "but this way is much better."

"You never thought you'd need that flat-blade move, did you?" Caastyn grinned.

Ysella smiled back. "I've learned not to object, and he'll have trouble using a gladius effectively for some time."

"Too bad your lady couldn't see that."

"She's not my lady, not yet."

"She will be," Caastyn predicted, "if you have anything to say about it."

"That has to be her decision."

"Just don't be so deferential that she doesn't know how much you care."

Ysella chuckled, thinking about the moments before they parted the night before. "I think I've made that very clear."

89

YSELLA spent a fair part of the evening after dinner on Unadi working on what he'd say after Haafel nominated him for premier. While he went to bed at his usual time, he didn't sleep that well, still thinking about Nortaak and hoping that duel would be the very last he had to fight. When he finally got to sleep, he didn't have nightmares, at least not any that he remembered.

When he walked into the breakfast room, Caastyn said, "Quite a bit in the *Tribune* this morning. The death of the Imperador, the dismissal of the Premier, the upcoming vote for premier, and the newssheet thinks you might be one of the possible candidates, despite your trouble with Nortaak."

"Any councilor could be elected, except Nortaak and Detruro. I'm more likely than some, but I'm still among the younger councilors." Ysella sat down, forced himself to take a modest swallow of café, then picked up the *Tribune,* where he read a largely accurate account of his encounter with Nortaak. One section troubled him slightly.

> . . . Councilor Ysella's obvious skill in disarming Councilor Nortaak without Nortaak's blade ever touching Ysella suggests that there's far more behind Councilor Ysella's pleasant appearance, modest height, and considerable legal skills, as evidenced by his success in unveiling a long-standing criminal conspiracy in Machtarn, by managing appropriations that thwarted his predecessor as Waterways Committee chairman, and by his selection to represent the Council at the engagement, wedding, and wedding dinner of the Lady Delehya and former Premier Detruro, despite being the youngest committee chairman . . .

It's almost as if the Tribune *is setting you up.*

Ysella knew all too well he had vulnerabilities, especially his harbor-area properties and his being unmarried, but some time, and Aelyn, might remove that liability.

The last article of interest was in the back with miscellaneous financial news, a short piece about the Banque of Oersynt being bought by Oersynt's Commerce Banque following the abrupt resignation of Jhosef Salaazar as presidente of the Banque of Oersynt.

From that story and from what had happened to Treasury Administrator Tybaalt Salaazar, Ysella suspected the various Salaazars had likely been involved in some shady banking matters. *Especially since Nortaak thought their hearts were in the right place.*

With that thought, Ysella took another small sip of café and turned to the fried eggs and ham—and the oatmeal muffin.

After a time, Caastyn said, "I'm riding with you today, and if you become premier you might think about getting a sturdy carriage. You'll need it anyway once you finally marry Ritten Wythcomb."

"One step at a time," said Ysella after he swallowed what he was chewing.

"Sir, you take very large steps," replied Caastyn dryly.

Ysella managed not to choke on the café.

After he finished breakfast and before heading out to the stable, Ysella went to the study and folded the papers he'd worked on the night before and slipped them into an inside jacket pocket, since he'd left his case at the office.

The ride to the Council Hall was uneventful, and when Ysella and Caastyn reined up outside the Council stables, Caastyn simply said, "Fourth bell?"

"I shouldn't be any later. Even three rounds of voting shouldn't take four bells . . . but I could be wrong, like yesterday."

"Sir?"

"I knew Nortaak was furious with me, and I kept a lookout for him, but I really didn't think he'd actually force me into a duel."

"You were prepared. That's all that counts in the end."

"True enough, but don't hesitate to remind me, if you see the need, not that you've ever hesitated before."

Caastyn laughed, and Ysella went to turn Jaster over to one of the stableboys before heading to the Council Hall.

Khaard immediately rose from his desk when Ysella entered the office.

"The acting Premier?" asked Ysella. "In his own office, not the Premier's office?"

"Yes, sir. At your earliest convenience."

"What now?"

"The messenger didn't say, sir."

Ysella hurried down to Maatrak's office, where one of the clerks ushered him in to see the acting Premier, closing the door behind Ysella.

Ysella seated himself and asked, "What is it?"

"I thought you should know. Nortaak hanged himself in his cell sometime in the middle of the night."

"How did he do that?"

"He unwound the cloth strips holding his splint in place. Neither of the guards had anything to do with it, according to the Council empath, and no one else entered the cell area."

"One-handed?"

"He managed. Is there anything else?"

Ysella shook his head. "You likely know most of the story, but the newssheet article on the takeover of the Bank of Oersynt suggested to me that the Nortaak family might have been more involved with the Salaazars than anyone knew. When I asked Stefan about Tybaalt Salaazar's connection to banking he got quiet in committee meetings, if snide sometimes. You know what he did on the vote to pass the Port Standards Act. I even got an anonymous note to the effect that dishonor had to be paid for. It had to be from him."

"Keep that safe for a while, just in case." Maatrak frowned and leaned forward slightly in his chair. "I just wanted you to know."

Ysella had the feeling Maatrak didn't want to say more or to actually dismiss him. So he said, "You have a lot to do today. I won't take up any more of your time. Thank you for letting me know." Then he stood and smiled. "I'll obviously see you later."

Ysella walked back to his office, wondering if Nortaak had taken his own life at least partly because he'd failed to remove Ysella from the Council. He also realized that he'd never told Khaard and Jaasn about Nortaak's forcing a duel.

The moment he entered the office, he summoned both clerks into his personal office and briefed them on what had happened with Nortaak.

"Sounds like he had other problems," observed Khaard.

"I'm thinking so, but we may never know."

Khaard nodded. "He wasn't arrogant just with you, sir. More than a few clerks had bad encounters with him. His clerks weren't much better."

"Scaellyt, especially," added Jaasn.

"Is there anything else that's happened this morning?" asked Ysella.

"No, sir. There aren't many letters, and we're caught up on responses."

"Good. I'll be busy getting ready for the vote."

"Can you tell us how it looks, sir?" Khaard glanced back over his shoulder, although no one was there.

"I'm hopeful, but with matters so chaotic, especially with the Imperador's death and then Nortaak's, there's nothing certain."

"A few of the clerks I know are hoping it's you," said Jaasn.

"I appreciate knowing that. We'll see if they're right."

With a brief smile, Ysella settled behind his desk and went through the incoming letters, writing his notes on each. Then he pulled out the papers holding his thoughts on what he'd do as premier and why those tasks were important.

He'd finished those when Khaard appeared and handed him a sealed message. "From the acting Premier."

"It's likely about Nortaak's death, but we'll see. Stay until I find out." Ysella opened the envelope and began to read, then nodded. "It's about Nortaak. It says that he was incarcerated for a severe breach of Council regulations and, while incarcerated, took his own life, rather than face his peers in judgment. The Council will be briefed prior to the day's proceedings."

"Sounds like the acting Premier wasn't too fond of Councilor Nortaak, sir."

"More than a few councilors weren't. You can tell Paatyr." Ysella handed the message to Khaard. "Just file this."

"Yes, sir."

For the next three bells, Ysella struggled to refine his talking points into greater clarity, then made his way to the Council chamber, where he took his usual seat.

Within moments, as the Council chamber filled, Staeryt eased into his desk beside Ysella. "What did Nortaak do?"

In a few brief sentences, Ysella explained.

"He never understood you were a better legalist and a better blade."

"Oh, he understood. He was willing to lose his life if it meant ousting me from the Council. That's why I could never draw blood."

Staeryt gave a low whistle. "For how you handled that alone, you should be premier."

"Haarst will use that against me, possibly imply that I maneuvered Nortaak into acting unwisely out of honor that some councilors apparently no longer respect . . . or words to that effect."

"You think so?"

"I could be wrong. We'll see." Ysella turned to the dais, where Maatrak stood behind the lectern, rapping the gavel until the murmurs died away.

"The first matter before the Council is the death of Stefan Nortaak. Councilor Nortaak carried two gladiuses into the Council Hall, then trailed Councilor Dominic Ysella and confronted him beside the Council stables . . ." Maatrak went on to give a detailed description of the events, including the anonymous threat Ysella had received, and the results. "Councilor Ysella made every conceivable effort to avoid a physical confrontation, short of actually running away, which he deemed unacceptable, and events forced him to pick up a gladius. Even so, he managed to hold off Councilor Nortaak without touching him except to disarm Councilor Nortaak with the flat of his blade. Under the rules of the Council, permitting self-defense, and with the only blow being struck to disarm an attacker, the matter is closed."

Maatrak struck the gavel several times to quiet the murmurs. "The Council will be in order. The matter at hand is the nomination and vote on candidates to be Council premier. According to Council rules, after the nominations are closed, each nominee and his nominator have a sixth in which to speak. Those statements will be in the order in which the candidates are nominated. The floor is now open for nominations."

Graandeyl Raendyr immediately rose. "I nominate Aksyl Haarst of Suvion for Premier."

"Is there a second?"

"I offer a second," declared Haamlyn Commodus.

"Councilor Aksyl Haarst has been nominated and seconded," declared Maatrak. "Are there other nominations?"

Sammal Haafel stood. "I nominate Dominic Ysella, of Aloor."

"I will second that nomination," stated Maatrak. "Are there other nominations?"

"I nominate Haans Maessyn, of Uldwyrk," stated Gaastyn Ditaero.

"Second!" declared Astyn Coerl.

"Are there any other nominations?" asked Maatrak, scanning the councilors. After several long moments, he declared, "Seeing none, the nominations are closed. Councilor Haarst, you have the floor."

Smiling broadly, Haarst almost sauntered to the dais. The smile vanished when he began to speak. "We're here to elect a successor to Iustaan Detruro. He was a good premier, if not outstanding, but through his efforts, the Council now has powers it previously lacked. Those powers must be used judiciously, especially where the expansion of the Council is concerned and in the appointment of ministers. We should not blindly disregard years of tradition just because the Council has been empowered. Recently, younger councilors have proposed more aggressive and untried measures, as well as laws that will reduce the productivity of Guldoran manufactories. But that is not all. One of the greatest strengths of the Council has been an underlying belief in respect for age, experience, and honor, regardless of the cost, not relying on mere legality or the blind expansion of power to those who never had it or those who lost it through the lack of wisdom of their forebearers . . ."

Ysella listened intently as Haarst continued in the same vein for most of his allotted time, and then as Graandeyl Raendyr reiterated the same themes.

Ysella walked in measured firm steps to the dais and the lectern. He surveyed the Council chamber for several long moments, then began. "As the esteemed councilor from Suvion said, Iustaan Detruro was a good and effective premier who fought successfully to curb the excessive and often unwise use of power by the Imperador. He also understood that unchecked power by either the Imperador or the Council would be the downfall of Guldor, and that is why he had the Charter drafted as it was, with legally binding and balanced language . . .

"As others have indirectly alluded, I am not just a councilor, but a legalist, and one of my forebearers lost power—precisely because he ignored laws and blindly relied on tradition. He demanded respect for those in power from those who had none, regardless of their intelligence and skill. Without respect for law, tradition and power become tyranny, and they weaken a land."

Ysella paused, then added, "I should know. I saw the results as a boy. Without good and effective laws, government becomes the tool of the powerful, who then oppress both their peers with less power and the powerless.

"So . . . although I come from a long landor background, I'm also proud to be a legalist, and one who's always striven for laws fair to all, laws that penalize neither those with power nor those without power. Power must be used wisely. The more astute members of the Council protested—both quietly, and sometimes loudly, and to their detriment—when the previous Imperador insisted on building massive and mighty warships that were unsuited to dealing with the pirates of Atacama. As a result, Guldor had towns fired, and at least one councilor was killed.

"What makes a land or an Imperium strong and enduring is not blind respect or tradition designed to protect power and little else, but good laws—laws that are fair, effective, and enduring. That is what we should strive for, not just because it is right or ethical, but also because, in the long run, all of us will benefit from such an approach. Laws are the fundamental tools for governing and shaping a land . . ."

When Ysella finished, he inclined his head slightly and returned to his desk.

"Not bad," murmured Staeryt, almost reluctantly, thought Ysella.

When Haafel took the lectern, he was brief. "I nominated Dominic Ysella because he's always been effective and fair as committee chairman. He also uses facts and logic and doesn't stoop to unbased innuendo, unlike some, and you always know where you stand. That's something I also admire about Iustaan Detruro. We need to continue that trait in our premiers."

There was a definite silent surprise as Haafel left the lectern and returned to his seat.

"Councilor Maessyn," prompted Maatrak.

Maessyn, also surprised by the brevity of Haafel's statement, hurried to the dais, where he stood beside the lectern, offering an amused smile to the councilors, and then clearing his throat before speaking. "I have no illusions. The Council will not elect a crafter premier today. It will not elect one in my lifetime. In time, if Guldor endures that long, it may. Whether Guldor does endure will depend largely on who we elect premier today. One of the other candidates trumpeted tradition and respect, wielding the terms like a hammer. I know. I'm familiar with hammers. But even hammers need to be handled with skill.

"The other councilor talked about legality and the need to use laws as tools to strengthen the legal foundation of Guldor. He's right. The Imperium was founded by force and conquest, but Guldor needs a stronger foundation and framework.

"Like I said, I'm just a crafter, but every crafter knows that without a solid framework, and the skilled use of tools, what you build won't last. So the question before us is which councilor will become the premier to give Guldor a lasting foundation and framework. I'll say that again, as a question." Maessyn spaced out the words, emphasizing each one. "Which councilor will become the premier to give Guldor a lasting foundation and framework?"

He let silence follow the repetition, then finished with "Thank you," before turning to Maatrak. "No need for my nominator to speak. I've said what was necessary."

Maatrak took the lectern. "Councilor Ditaero, you have the right to speak."

"I waive the right to speak. I affirm the words of Councilor Maessyn."

Maatrak moved to the lectern. "Each of you has several voting cards, each one with one name upon it. Pick the card with the name you wish to become premier and place it in the blank envelope. If you do not wish to vote for any of the three, place a blank card in the envelope. Then present the envelope to the tally clerk. Councilors have one third in which to vote."

Ysella made sure he picked the card with his name, put it in the envelope, then waited for the more senior committee chairmen to vote before he carried his envelope to the tally clerk.

When he returned to his seat, he turned to Staeryt. "What do you think?"

"Did you tell Maessyn what to say?"

"No. He came up with that on his own. I liked it, but I can't claim credit for those words."

While Ysella waited for the other councilors to vote, he considered the possibilities. He had no doubt that not quite half the commercers would vote for Haarst, as would about half the landors on the Commerce and Natural Resources Committees, as well as one or two other landors. That totaled between seventeen and twenty votes for Haarst, and with all crafters voting for Maessyn, that would leave between nineteen and twenty-one voting for Ysella.

If your assumptions and calculations are correct.

Slightly less than a third of a bell passed before Maatrak returned to the lectern and rapped the gavel. "The Council will come to order." He waited until the chamber was quiet. "Those councilors voting for Councilor Haarst numbering eighteen, those for Councilor Ysella numbering twenty-one, those for Councilor Maessyn numbering seven, with one vote abstaining, there is no councilor with enough votes to be elected premier. Councilor Maessyn is removed from the second vote, having received insufficient votes to continue. Councilors have a third in which to vote."

From where Ysella sat, he couldn't see Haarst's face, but he noticed that Stron Thaalyr looked worried.

Ysella again waited for the more senior—and older—councilors to vote, then took his envelope to the tally clerk, and returned to his desk. If . . . if his calculations were correct and if just four crafters voted for him, he should have enough votes, but it would be best if he had more of a margin. He simply sat, keeping a pleasant expression on his face, waiting.

A third of a bell later, Maatrak returned to the lectern, his face impassive as he gaveled the Council to order, then announced, "Those councilors voting for Councilor Haarst numbering eighteen, those for Councilor Ysella numbering twenty-eight, with one vote abstaining, Councilor Dominic Ysella is hereby elected Premier of the Imperial Council of Guldor." Then, Maatrak smiled. "Congratulations, Premier Ysella." He held out the gavel.

Ysella stood, then took the steps to the dais, accepted the gavel, and turned to face the assembled councilors.

"In this time of change, even with a certain amount of unforeseen chaos, you all have done your duties and assured Guldor of continued stability and the beginning of a time of shared power between the Council and the Imperador. We still have a great deal to accomplish in the immediate weeks and months ahead, but I will work with each and every one of you in the spirit of cooperation and fairness, and I thank you for your faith in me. I would like to thank Acting Premier Maatrak for his steadiness and Councilor Haarst and Councilor Maessyn for their honorable efforts in seeking to be premier. Over the next few days, I will meet individually with each of you.

"The Council is hereby recessed until noon on Furdi."

Maatrak stepped up beside Ysella. "Nicely done, sir. All of Premier Detruro's personal effects have been removed, and the materials pertaining to Enke are in temporary storage and will be moved to your former office once you vacate it. The office of the Premier is open to you. All the clerks remaining work for the Council, but you have an allowance for three clerks of your choice, to maintain services to your district."

"I appreciate the quick briefing, Luaro. It may take us a day or so to make that move."

Maatrak smiled. "Very understandable, sir."

"I'll also need to visit the new Imperador, but that can wait until tomorrow."

"I'm sure it can, late as it is in the day."

"For the moment, I need to thank a few others." Ysella immediately headed for Sammal Haafel, who was smiling broadly as Ysella approached. "Sammal, thank you for your support and a very effective nomination."

"You did most of it. I did enjoy your quiet rebuttal to Haarst. Nothing he could complain about, but effective . . ."

Ysella moved next to Haans Maessyn, and praised him for his short and most effective support, and then Chaarls Aashen, Ahslem Staeryt, Georg Raathan, Gaastyn Ditaero, Staanus Wrystaan, and others. He would have liked to have spoken to Haarst as well, but he'd left the Council chamber moments after Maatrak announced the final vote.

Close to a bell later, he headed back to his office, an office that soon would belong to whoever was selected to be Detruro's successor as councilor for Enke.

"Congratulations, sir!" chorused Khaard and Jaasn, not quite simultaneously.

"You two both had a part in it . . . and, unfortunately, it'll also mean more work, because we have to move to the Premier's office."

"For that, I'll work extra," said Jaasn with a grin.

"In the meantime, I need to dash off some thank-you cards . . ."

Ysella wrote four cards before Khaard peered into his office. "Reimer Daarkyn wants to see you, sir."

"I'll see him."

When Daarkyn entered and closed the door, he said, "Now that you're premier, will you still see me?"

"Of course, but at times, you might have to wait longer."

"Did you ever think you'd be premier?"

"I didn't even consider it until I was deep in drafting the Charter and Premier Detruro suggested I should think about the possibility. He knew if he pushed the Charter through somehow, it might cost him the premier's office. You want a political hero, he's the one. The Charter was his idea. I just drafted it, and I think I improved on his ideas, but he was the one behind it." *He and Delehya.*

"What will he and Lady Delehya do? Do you know?"

"They've said they have no intention of remaining in Machtarn. They're both very intelligent, and I suspect they'll succeed in accomplishing noteworthy achievements in Enke."

"You sound like you have some idea what those achievements might be."

"Premier Detruro said that he couldn't be premier forever and, when that time came, he would look into other pursuits." Before Daarkyn could press that question, Ysella added, "On that, he'll have to speak for himself. He did indicate that he and Lady Delehya would be returning to Enke."

"Nothing more?"

"He's always been very private, Reimer. You should know that."

"Did Nortaak really hang himself?" asked Daarkyn.

"Yes. No one else could have done it. Acting Premier Maatrak took special care to make sure he didn't have any way to harm himself. I don't think anyone would have thought he'd unwind the cloth binding his broken wrist and use it to hang himself."

"But why would he do that?"

"Let's see... he carried dueling blades into the Council Hall and grounds. He threatened me—"

"But you disarmed him."

"That wasn't the threat. He threatened to attack me if I refused to fight, to stab me in the back if I refused. Given that, if I ran away, and I could have, that would have branded me as a coward, and made it impossible for me to be reelected or to be effective in future. If I agreed to a duel, that's against Council rules, and that also would have cost me dearly, especially if I got killed or wounded or killed him. I had to disarm him without ever drawing blood, and I had to make that clear with every movement. Do you want to try that against a madman who will die to destroy you?"

"There's more to it than that, isn't there?"

"There always is, Reimer. There always is. You know that, because you're a good newshawk. I don't know, but I suspect there's some involvement between the Nortaak family and the Salaazar family, given what looks to be the collapse of the Banque of Machtarn."

Daarkyn nodded, then said, "We never did finish talking about your harbor-area properties, Premier."

"I don't know that there's much to talk about, Reimer. As Premier, I'm no longer a member of any committee. And that's a relief, because the Council has to add sixteen councilors, restructure the existing committees, and adjust or modify which of the ministries report to which committee. We'll also have to create a few more committees, since the Council now has oversight of all the old Imperial administrations."

Daarkyn looked stunned, if only for an instant. "But you still own them—"

"I do, but none of the already-funded harbor improvements directly affect them."

The newshawk nodded. "Pursuing that might not be worthwhile."

Not with potentially more newsworthy opportunities being revealed within the old administrations, particularly the Treasury.

"Do you have any other suggestions?"

"Not at the moment, but you're welcome to stop by occasionally. I would appreciate your giving me a few days to get resettled, though."

"Resettled . . . oh, to the premier's office. Of course. But I will be in touch."

Ysella smiled wryly. "Of that, I have no doubt."

Even before Daarkyn was out the door, Ysella was back writing cards, knowing that they had to be in his hand.

More than two bells passed before Ysella felt able to leave the Council Hall, but Caastyn was waiting outside the Council stables when Ysella rode out.

"Congratulations, Premier." Caastyn smiled, then added, "You think being premier will entice Ritten Wythcomb?"

"Not if she's got any sense," replied Ysella. "I hope she'll accept me in spite of my being elected premier."

"If she has any sense, she will. I get the feeling she's quite sensible."

"So is her great-aunt." Not wanting to speculate further on Aelyn's feelings, Ysella said, "I don't know if you heard, but Nortaak hanged himself." He turned Jaster west on Council Avenue.

Caastyn rode beside him, his eyes scanning the way ahead. "I didn't hear about that. It doesn't surprise me, though. Didn't even have the guts to face judgment."

"Nortaak's from an old family, and old families too often believe they're above judgment. Until they're judged and everything changes. My family discovered that the hard way. They ended up with a tiny fraction of what they once held."

Caastyn laughed. "That's why you became a legalist and ended up premier. How will they take that?"

"My mother will write and tell me to be careful. My father and my brothers will be happy that I found something almost as good as being a truly landed landor, and that they no longer have to explain why I left

Aloor. Jaeralyn will be happier that I'm courting Aelyn, since she thought we'd be a good match. The rest of the family will be relieved that I'm interested in a landor, but they'll never mention her first marriage."

"Families are a mixture of blessing and trial." Caastyn laughed softly. "At times more trial than blessing, but in the long run the blessings mean more."

Ysella nodded, then asked, "Have you been looking for a suitable carriage and more horses?"

"Have been for a few weeks. I had a feeling you'd become premier sooner or later. I'm glad you took care of that arrogant bastard Nortaak in a way that didn't keep you from becoming premier."

"Do you have any ideas for a driver? I'll need you for more important work."

"I figured as much, especially after you marry. I've been asking around. Wouldn't want to leave that for the last moment."

"You never do."

"Neither do you, sir," replied Caastyn amusedly, "not if you have a choice. Might be best if you didn't leave the Ritten to the last moment, either."

Ysella laughed, if wryly.

90

ON the ride to the Council Hall on Tridi morning, accompanied by Caastyn, Ysella could see that Camelia Avenue, Imperial Boulevard, and Council Avenue looked no different from any other morning, suggesting that most people didn't care all that much if the power balance between the Council and the Imperador had shifted.

At least for now, they're not protesting in the streets.

After entering the Council Hall, he immediately arranged for the official Council coach to be readied and the Palace informed, then spent almost a bell with Khaard and Jaasn going over moving arrangements.

Once those were taken care of, he walked out of the Council Hall to the waiting coach, with two Council guards in place of footmen, still slightly amazed that he was the Premier heading to pay his first official visit to the Imperador.

And not as a subordinate to receive orders.

When the coach passed through the gates to the Palace grounds, Ysella noted that two of the four guards were naval marines. The grounds and gardens flanking the drive up to the Palace looked unchanged.

When the coach came to a stop outside the north entrance to the Palace, as Ysella stepped out, he was surprised that Fleet Marshal Dhaantyn stood waiting to greet him.

"Welcome to the Palace, Premier Ysella," said Dhaantyn, smiling widely. "And congratulations."

"Without your assistance, none of it would have been possible."

"Without your Charter and planning, no one would have wanted to help."

"I take it that Premier Detruro and Lady Delehya have left the Palace."

"Yes, sir. Yesterday. They went to his dwelling here in Machtarn, and they'll be departing for Enke later today. We're supplying a small escort."

"Thank you. They deserve it."

Dhaantyn turned and gestured toward the bronze double doors. "The Imperador is in the official main-floor study." He chuckled. "There's a great deal of rearranging taking place on the upper levels. The former Imperadora has already departed for the summer palace, temporarily, I imagine."

Ysella walked through the doors with Dhaantyn, then asked, "And the First Marshal?"

"He's looking at property."

For a moment, Ysella wondered why, then nodded. "You're keeping most of the naval facilities where they are in Veerlyn, but building a modest military ministry in the general vicinity of the Council Hall?"

"There was a certain transition plan . . ."

Ysella smiled wryly.

"It made sense then," said Dhaantyn, "and it still does."

Ysella was glad that most of the other ministries already had buildings separate from the Palace, but the elder Laureous had wanted the senior officers close at hand. "I imagine you're ready to leave the Palace."

"You had to ask?" Dhaantyn's words conveyed wry amusement. He gestured to the side corridor ahead. "This way."

"Is there any recent news about pirates and the Gulf?"

"Not since we took out that last group of pirates. We've eliminated most of the enclaves around the Cataran Delta. We'll have to keep patrolling, and there will always be the possibility of occasional attacks."

"I can see that." Ysella paused. "Now's not the time, but the First Marshal, you, and I need to spend some time talking about the future of the Navy. The Council won't dictate, but funds aren't unlimited, and we need to know your concerns, and you need to know ours."

"I'm sure the First Marshal would be pleased with that approach." Dhaantyn stopped short of the end of the corridor, where two guards flanked a single door. "I'll wait here for you, sir."

Being addressed as "sir" stunned Ysella for a moment, as did the fact that the Fleet Marshal would be waiting for him. "Thank you. I doubt I'll be very long."

One of the guards opened the door and held it for Ysella.

Ysella entered the study, smiling ruefully, thinking how strange it was that he and the former Heir, now Imperador Laureous II, had never met, let alone been in the same chamber before.

The Imperador sat behind a wide goldenwood desk in a high-backed goldenwood chair that hinted at a throne. He had wider cheekbones than his father. The brown hair touched with streaks of gray reminded Ysella that he was at least ten years older than Ysella. His brown eyes and warm smile conveyed an impression of warmth and trustworthiness at odds with his past actions, but also explained in part why so many had followed him.

Ysella stopped short of the desk, inclined his head slightly, and remained standing. "Imperador."

"You don't look all that prepossessing, Premier Ysella," said Laureous II, in a resonant and mellow voice, "but I imagine that's one of your many strengths. From what I've heard, despite your regal lineage, you're always underestimated. I understand you're the one who conccived and wrote this Great Charter that has made me largely a figurehead and may well destroy Guldor."

"No, Your Highness. Former Premier Detruro came up with the concept. I merely drafted it into law. And I must disabuse you. You're not just a figurehead. You retain a certain amount of power, just not unlimited power, as you must understand from your study of the Charter."

"Ah, yes, your Great Charter. I can't believe you gave me any real powers, but you did. Why didn't you make me a figurehead?"

"Because not giving you those powers would destroy Guldor. A Council with unlimited powers would be far worse than your sire at his most irrational." *Or you, for that matter.*

"You believe that, don't you?"

"So do most in Guldor, especially the very rich and the very poor."

"According to this, I can remove you. Why shouldn't I?"

"You can, if you wish, but not for another three months, since you've already dismissed Premier Detruro, and you'd have to dissolve the Council and call elections. I suspect the next Council would not be markedly different from the present Council, and even if you did call for another election, it wouldn't change matters much, and would likely weaken what support you retain."

"What's to keep me from calling for an election in the future?"

"You don't have to. In less than two years, the Council will have to. Those provisions of the Establishment Act were incorporated by reference."

"Besides which," declared the Imperador sourly, "the First Marshal, the Fleet Marshal, and the Army Marshal have strongly recommended against it. Why did you do it? To become a great popular hero?"

Ysella laughed, if softly. "I didn't do it alone. We all did it because it needed to be done. The ones remembered in history, if anyone at all is remembered, will be your father, Premier Detruro, and your sister." *All likely remembered for the wrong reasons.* "You and I just have the largely anonymous duty of making sure that the Imperium continues."

Laureous II offered a sardonic smile. "There are worse fates."

EPILOGUE

PREMIER WEDS WIDOWED RITTEN

On the last day of Fallfirst, Premier Dominic Mikail Ysella wed Ritten Aelyn Scalante Wythcomb in a simple ceremony at the Camelia Avenue Trinitarian Chapel. Premier Ysella is the grandson of Cliven Mikail Ysella, the last ruler of Aloor, and was first elected to the Imperial Council in 812, where he rose to being chairman of the Waterways Committee, before being directed by then Premier Iustaan Detruro to draft the Great Charter that reformed the governmental structure of the Imperium. After Imperador Laureous II dismissed Premier Detruro, the Imperial Council elected Ysella as Premier.

Ritten Scalante Wythcomb Ysella, born of a landor background from Silverhills and Aloor, was suddenly widowed shortly after her first marriage. She is also the grandniece of Ritten Aelyssa Scalante and the late Councilor Maelcar Scalante . . .

The Machtarn Tribune
1 Fallend 820

ABOUT THE AUTHOR

L. E. MODESITT, JR. is the author of more than eighty books—primarily science fiction and fantasy—including the long-running, bestselling series the Saga of Recluce and the Imager Portfolio, as well as a number of short stories. *Legalist* is the fourth book in his Grand Illusion series *(Isolate, Councilor,* and *Contrarian).*